C000055797

BOX SET

DEATH'S
KISS
SERIES

USA TODAY BESTSELLING AUTHOR

C.J. PINARD

This book is an original publication of Pinard House Publishing.

This is a work of fiction. The names, characters, places, and incidents are products of the writer's imagination or have been used fictitiously and are not to be construed as real. Any resemblance to persons, living or dead, actual events, locales, or organizations is entirely coincidental.

Copyright © 2014-2022 Pinard House Publishing, LLC

Cover Art and Design by Kellie Dennis at Book Cover By Design

This is licensed for your personal enjoyment only. No part of this book may be reproduced, scanned, or distributed in any printed or electronic format without permission. Please do not participate in, or encourage, piracy of copyrighted materials in violation of the author's rights. Purchase only authorized editions.

All rights reserved.

PRINTED IN THE UNITED STATES OF AMERICA

ISBN 9798359302272

PINARD HOUSE
PUBLISHING

TABLE OF CONTENTS

DEATH'S KISS SERIES

SOUL REBEL

Book 1 in the Death's Kiss Series

BY

C.J. PINARD

SOUL REBEL

"THE MOST POWERFUL WEAPON ON EARTH IS THE HUMAN SOUL ON FIRE." FERDINAND FOCH

Chapter 1

PROPOSALS & PERFIDY

The last time I could remember sweating this much was when I played football in high school. The motorcycle I had been restoring just didn't want to start. Who the hell bought a 1999 P.O.S. Kawasaki crotch-rocket and expected it to run, anyway?

I used a red oil rag to wipe my forehead and tossed it into a nearby bin. I had my coveralls stripped off before I reached the men's room. Those too went into a bin, and I scrubbed my hands as best I could. After drying them off, I looked at my grimy fingernails, the dirt and grease smeared under them. I could vaguely remember my older sister's warning when I told her I wasn't going to college, but was going to restore old motorcycles instead.

"Your hands will never be clean," she had scolded as she made a face. "No girl wants to be touched by hands that look filthy all the time."

But I had proven her wrong. I'd been told many times that my hands looked strong and protective, despite the permanent half-moon of black under each nail.

I grabbed my backpack from out of my locker in the grungy men's room and fished out my keys. My red and white Ducati Monster was parked right out front. I looped my arm through the other strap of the backpack and mounted my bike. It started with what passersby probably thought was an obnoxious rumble, but sounded more like a purr to me. I was about to shove the matching helmet on my head when I heard my name.

"Nolan!"

I slid the helmet back up and whipped around to face the direction of the voice. "Yeah, boss?"

The shop's owner, Archie Ross, a man in his late fifties who lived hard and fast like he was still in his twenties, came lumbering out, waving an envelope. "Got the pay done early due to the holiday weekend 'n all." He gimped up to my motorcycle, a wad of dip in his bottom lip.

I took the envelope and smiled at him. "Thanks, boss. This'll come in handy this weekend."

Archie reached up and scratched his head, the gray in his hair shining under the setting sun, a diamond stud glinting in his left ear. Archie was still in his coveralls, but I knew he would be in his leather vest and pants later tonight when he met with his motorcycle club. Archie walked with a limp from a stab wound to the thigh he'd received in the 1980s during a bar fight—or so I'd been told.

He spat a wad of chew in a brown stream out onto the sidewalk and looked at me, raising his voice over the rumble of the bike. "No problem, kid. You gonna go show off the new bike this weekend?" He pointed at it.

I shook my head. "Nah, gonna take the car. My girl doesn't like the bike so much."

Archie laughed and shook his head as he limped away. "Women."

I smiled again, folding the envelope and put it in my front pants pocket. I slid on my helmet. With a twist of the handlebar and a pulse of my foot, I was off, zooming down the street and weaving in and out of traffic with horns blaring at me.

It didn't take much time to reach home. The large apartment complex was only five miles from the shop. It was one of those fancy ones with the immaculate landscaping, gym, tennis courts, and swimming pool.

Because a swimming pool wasn't a luxury in Louisiana, it was a necessity.

Shreveport, a city with a small-town feel, was large enough to be the home to several big-name businesses, but was also known to be very family-oriented and slow-paced. There wasn't much to do, but I had lived here all my life and I knew where the all hot spots were.

I parked my bike under the covered carport in spot 272 and dismounted the bike, my helmet under my arm. I sprinted up the stone steps to my apartment and slid the key in the lock. The place was clean and tidy, just the way I'd left it.

I always laughed when people would act shocked at my clean apartment. Just because I was a grease monkey and stayed dirty all day didn't mean I liked my home that way, too. Refusing to get a roommate for that very reason, I was happy to live alone. I was twenty-one years old and enjoyed my solitude.

I closed and locked the door behind me. Dropping my backpack on the sofa, I then tossed my keys onto the kitchen counter. After snatching a bottle of water from the fridge, I cracked it open, practically downing its entire contents in one gulp. The humidity always made me thirsty, and since it was the start of the Fourth of July weekend, the heat was relentless. I pitched the empty bottle into the recycle bin and had most of my clothes peeled off my sweaty body before I reached the bedroom. I left them in a pile on the floor and went into the adjoining bathroom and started the shower. As it heated up, I looked at my reflection. I had a smudge of dirt — or was it grease? — on my forehead and I wiped it away. Lime-green eyes stared back at me, and I lifted a sleeved-up tattooed arm, flexing my bicep, admiring my newly developing biceps. I sucked in my stomach, which really wasn't necessary since there was no fat there anyway, and ran my fingers over the bumps of an evolving six-pack. Scrubbing a hand along my short light-brown hair, I huffed at the light five o'clock shadow on my face. I grabbed the razor and shaving cream and decided to shave in the shower today.

As soon as I was as clean as I was going to get, I wrapped a white towel around my waist and padded into my bedroom. I was a bundle of nerves and excitement thinking about the upcoming weekend. I felt myself being pulled as if by an invisible rope to my sock drawer. I slid it open and plucked out the small black velvet box. I turned it around in my hand and carefully opened its lid with a squeak. Staring at the one-carat princess-cut solitaire diamond, I sighed.

I remembered going to Sarah's house while she had been at school and speaking to her father, asking for his permission to marry his daughter. Her father was a friendly man, but was overly concerned with education, and hadn't been at all thrilled that I didn't want to go to college. But with my natural charms and strong argument about how most good mechanics could make as much, if not more, than a lot of businessmen, her father had eventually relented and gave his blessing. I smiled at the memory.

I closed the lid, placed the box in my pocket, and wandered over to my closet, removing a large duffel bag to begin packing. I couldn't wait to take Sarah to New Orleans this weekend and ask her to be my wife.

I parked the bike in my usual spot in front of her condo and trotted up the slatted stone steps, excited to pick her up for our special weekend. I tried the doorknob before inserting the key she'd given me — one of my quirky habits — and was surprised to find the door unlocked. I eased the door open slowly with a furrow of my brow.

"Hello?" I called.

"Oh, shit!" said a male voice.

My eyes went wide as time seemed to stand still, and then slowly propel forward as if in slow motion. I saw a tall man wearing absolutely nothing, holding one of the couch cushions in front of his family jewels, his brown eyes wide. Sarah, also wearing absolutely nothing, jumped up from the couch, her hair a nest of a mess. With smeared makeup, her lips looked swollen, and her hazel eyes were huge. Her cheeks were bright red, not only from embarrassment, but whisker rash, I was sure. The two were frozen as I stared at them.

Sarah threw an arm across her breasts and yelled in shock. "Nolan!"

Then time seemed to speed up and stun me like a lightning bolt, and I flew into action. I threw my keys and phone to the floor and launched myself at the man, pushing him back down to the couch. Sarah moved away just in time, running into the bedroom as we went rounds. The guy was throwing punches in defense, but I had my hands wrapped around his throat, and I was squeezing. He managed to kick me in the chest and I went flying to the ground. The man jumped on me, but I pushed him off and pinned him to the ground. I had my right hand around his throat, and I was throwing left hooks at his face in quick succession. Blood flew out from the guy's nose and splashed the light-colored carpet. I didn't give a fuck.

Sarah came out and was now dressed, screaming at me to stop. I barely registered her demands, thinking she was going to be next if she didn't shut up. I felt fingernails digging into my neck and shoulders as Sarah began to pull. Then, she slapped at my head.

"I'm gonna call the police if you don't stop, Nolan! You're gonna kill him!" she screamed.

That was enough for me to let up, and when the guy got a leg free, he gasped in air and immediately kicked me in the stomach. I bent over, coughing and sputtering. The asshole grabbed a pile of clothing from the floor and scurried out the door, covering himself with them as he raced down the stone steps.

I stood, panting from the kick to the gut with a hand wrapped around my middle. With eyes burning with unshed tears, I turned to Sarah and glared at her, half in disbelief and half in rage.

"Nolan, please," she whimpered, trying to touch me. "You weren't supposed to be here until six. I'm sor—"

I coughed once more. "Save it. I don't ever want to see you again. Your shit will be on my porch, come get it by midnight or I'm burning it."

With my arm still wrapped around my stomach, I grabbed my keys and phone from the floor, stalked to the door, and slammed it behind me. Sarah was screaming for me to wait, but I barely heard her. I wouldn't hear her. I got on my bike and drove off with no destination at all.

Chapter 2

THE BLUE ROOM

Reds and golds painted the heavens of the horizon. The lake was calm as the sun began to set where the gently rippling water met the sky. A few broken clouds were scattered throughout the sunset, but the scene was otherwise breathtaking. There was only a slight warm wind, and the air was as thick and as heavy as my heart.

I sat on the pier's wooden dock next to a boat slip on Cross Lake. The dock jutted out into the lake and I had my bare feet in the water. A small cane fishing pole was set next to a bucket of lures and worms, its line lying lazily in the water, but I wasn't getting any bites. *Just my luck,* I thought as I stared at the sad pole.

I gazed back up at the beautiful sunset and wondered what I'd done; where I'd gone wrong. Hadn't I given her everything? What else could she have possibly wanted?

I hadn't seen or spoken to Sarah in over a month. She'd tried calling my cell, the motorcycle shop, even my parents' house, but I wouldn't take her calls. What could she have to say? She was sorry? There was no coming back from that. There was no Hallmark card for "I'm sorry I fucked some dude on the couch you bought for me." No amount of talking, apologizing, or justification could make me forgive her. She'd never bothered to come get her stuff, so I threw it in a box and wrote "FREE" on it before setting it on the curb outside the apartments. It had been gone by the next day.

Apparently, during the scuffle, the damn ring had fallen out of my pocket in Sarah's apartment. After she'd finally given up on the phone calls, she'd had the decency to return it to my parents. I had yet to go pick it up, because that would mean facing my parents, too. Not to mention the embarrassing and arduous task of either trying to return it or, or worse, taking it to a pawn shop and getting a third of what I paid for it.

Now that I thought about it, I should have just let her keep the defiled hunk of metal and stone.

And that jerkoff who so carelessly violated her on her couch, no thoughts about anyone other than himself and his needs. I vowed if I ever saw that guy again, I was going to fold his teeth back with my fist.

My stomach roiled and my heart clenched painfully in my chest at the thought of her face. Despite the pain, I was angry at myself for missing her. I tried to keep thinking about that day, the gravity of her betrayal and disgusting behavior, but all I kept remembering were the happy times. The beginning of our relationship to the end, and what was once the happiest day of my life when I'd bought that ring and booked that trip. Her shiny blonde hair and playful hazel eyes floated through my brain and I closed my eyes, wishing the visions away.

My stomach grumbled, this time in hunger, but I ignored it. I'd just have to poke another hole in my belt because the thought of food was still revolting to me.

I glanced at my cell phone sitting to me. I gasped a little when I realized I'd been here for three hours. I collected the pole and lures, shoved my phone into my pocket, and stood up, wincing at the pins and needles zipping down my legs from too much time sitting. I normally never sat this long, but lately, I'd not had much energy for anything else, and fishing helped clear my mind.

As I drove back to my apartment in town, I gazed at the lake once more as I rushed by it, grateful for its beauty and solitude to help ease my aching soul. I felt as if Sarah had ripped a piece of it out when she'd left, and I resolved that no other woman would ever do that to me again.

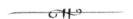

I trudged up the stairs to my apartment and had just opened the door when my phone chirped with an incoming text. I set my things down and clicked on it. My friend Parker was urging me, once again, to go out to a club with them. I let out a breath, and with my thumb hovering uncertainly over the screen, I debated on how to respond.

I had to admit that I was getting tired of sitting home on the weekends, watching TV and drinking beer alone. My friends, Parker Mathis and Brennan Diaz, had been sympathetic to my plight, and felt a night of partying would cure my heartsick condition.

In a moment of weakness, I responded I'd be there and asked for details. I plugged my phone into its charger on the dining room table and went into the bathroom to shower.

After washing away my melancholy under the hot water, I got out and swiped a hand over the mirror to clear the fog. I began brushing my teeth as I studied my face and rubbed at the dark smudges under my eyes. It was clear the fitful sleep was catching up to me, along with not eating properly. I no longer had to suck in my stomach, as it was concave on its own, all the hard work of the six-pack I'd been developing at the gym before the breakup now gone. I could even see a few ribs poking through. I shook my head and became angry that I'd allowed that *whore* to do that to me.

No, Nolan, you allowed it, a little voice told me. *You should have been a better boyfriend.* I shook my head again and realized the little voice could suck it. "You can't help how you feel, but you can control your actions." I parroted the words of my big sister, who loved to dish out advice and clichés like ice cream.

But had I allowed it? Hadn't I given her all she ever wanted? Maybe that was the problem. Women these days… they wanted men who were assholes to them. The bad boys. Maybe I should turn into a raging jerk player like my friend Parker; maybe I'd get a woman who was faithful to me. I shook my head. No matter how hard I tried, there was no way I'd be able to treat women like Parker did.

I went back out to my kitchen, wrapped in nothing but a towel, and checked my phone again. Turned out Parker had invited me to a new club that had recently opened up in the industrial section of town. *Strange place for a club,* I thought, but then Parker explained that abandoned warehouses not only have great space and acoustics, they also don't get complaints from neighbors about noise.

Padding back to my bedroom and over to my closet, I chose a red button-down shirt and some fitted jeans. I slid them over my lithe body, tightening the brown leather belt to the very last notch to keep them up, and sprayed my newest cologne across my body. I gave myself the once-over in the mirror. I thought I looked pretty damn good, considering I'd been tinkering with motorcycle parts for a few hours before my fishing trip, and had just had my heart ripped out over a month ago.

I scrubbed a hand through my too-long hair. Gone was the buzz cut, replaced by something longer that would require some sort of hair product. I searched the bathroom drawers until I found some and rubbed it onto my head, leaving it messy-looking. I'd get a haircut during the week sometime. I had forgotten to shave, too, but didn't care about that, either. I thought the stubble matched my purposely-messy hairstyle.

Content that I wasn't getting any younger staring at my reflection, I wandered into my kitchen and pulled two slices of cold pizza from the fridge. I munched on them as I scrolled through the text messages on my phone. I had received four while getting ready.

One from a girl I met last week at a coffee shop, whom I gave my number to in a fleeting pass of bad judgment, and now regretted.

Delete.

Two more from Parker with directions and a demand of assurance, asking if I was still going. I responded with the affirmative.

The last was from my mother, saying hi. I supposed I should be grateful my mother actually texted and didn't call all the time like most mothers did. She only lived across town, and I always tried to visit my parents on weekends, so I shot a quick text back saying I was fine and would be by tomorrow for a long-overdue visit.

With two pieces of cold pizza forced down the hatch, I checked my wallet to ensure I had some cash, to which I realized I only had a five-dollar bill, and remembered my paycheck. I sprinted over to my hamper and searched the pockets of my jeans until I located the folded paycheck. I ripped open the envelope, tore off the stub, and placed it in my wallet for deposit at the ATM on my way to the club to meet the guys for a night of who knew what.

I walked out of the comfortable air conditioning of my apartment and into the heat and humidity, inhaling a deep breath, feeling as if I was breathing in pea soup.

My Ducati thundered to a stop in front of flashing blue lights. I got out and parked it on the side of the building, away from the flashy sports cars and jacked-up trucks.

Until I'd reached the club, the warehouse district in Shreveport had been eerily quiet. The club had a strange feel to it, being in such a deserted area. I let out a breath when I saw Parker and Brennan standing at the front of the line. A large bouncer stood at the door, checking IDs under a large blue sign that read *The Blue Room* in fancy script writing. It was the only fancy thing about the place.

Parker, with his short, dark hair, tanned skin, and blue eyes, always

got whatever woman he wanted. In fact, he appeared to be talking to one right now. My other friend, Brennan, wasn't so lucky. Dark, but neat hair, brown eyes, and barely clearing five-foot-seven, he always had on boots and a hat to try to make himself taller, but still never got much play from the ladies.

I made my way over to the boys and bumped fists. They were dressed similarly to me, in nice club wear and smelling manly.

"Have you ever been here before?" I asked Parker, pointing to the large blue sign.

Parker shook his head. "Nope, it just opened last weekend, man." He smirked at me, giving me the once-over. "I'm glad you could make it. Although you look like you could use a sandwich or two."

I nodded. "Yeah, don't get me started…"

Brennan adjusted his baseball cap. "What kinda music they play here?"

"Hip-hop and Top-40, I think," Parker said, looking into the sky as if the answer was there.

I laughed. "Yeah, can't you hear Kanye's voice pumping out through the door?"

Parker pulled a piece of lint off his black shirt. "Yeah, well, I don't care what kind of music they playin' in here. I came here for the hot girls. I heard it was off the chain last weekend."

I looked around. "Looks like it might be the same this weekend, too." I motioned to the line.

We finally reached the door, showed IDs, paid our covers, and wandered inside. We made our way to the bar and each ordered beer. Strolling back into the shadowy recesses of the club, we stood around the dark establishment, watching people on the dance floor as they bumped and grinded to the booming bass blasting out of the massive speakers mounted to the ceiling and walls. A DJ booth was displayed at the helm of the dance floor, and an Asian guy with a large set of headphones was running the show, sweat already dribbling out of his spiky haircut. He was mixing music as if it was the only thing in the world he was meant to do.

As I lifted the beer to take a sip, the bottle paused at my lips when I spotted her. A gorgeous redhead with a short, straight haircut swaggered into the club on a set of white stilettos, a beautiful pair of creamy legs poured into them. Her white shorts and sky-blue tank top made her red hair stand out. She had a vixen look about her; harsh slices of eyeliner smeared around her pale-blue eyes, pink lip gloss popping off her mouth like a set of strobe lights.

She briefly made eye contact with me and smiled, chomping on gum and giving me a wink as she sauntered up to the bar. She was flanked by three girls, a blonde, a brunette, both with long wavy hair, and a beautiful Black girl with sleek raven-colored hair. All girls were dressed similarly in high heels and shorts or skirts.

I went to nudge Parker—or Brennan, whoever was closest—but realized I didn't need to. They were already staring at the quad of girls, along with every other person in the club, male and female. They looked like the Southern version of the Pussycat Dolls—and we could tell that they knew it, too.

"Holy shit," Brennan breathed. "That blonde is way hot."

Parker took a sip of his beer and nodded his head. "They all are."

I whistled through my teeth. "That redhead is awakening parts of my anatomy I thought were out of commission."

The three of us laughed at my joke and watched the girls until they all had colorful drinks held in their well-manicured fingers. They made their way to a VIP seating area in the corner of the club marked *RESERVED*.

"Should we go talk to them?" Brennan asked, downing the rest of his beer.

I laughed and used my bottle to point toward the girls. "Yeah, dude. Take a number."

The four girls already had a line of male admirers trying to get into the VIP area of the club. A large, tattooed Black man, with a small strip of hair in a mohawk at the top, was picking them off one by one. And one by one, each dejected male would leave the area with their heads down, the promise of talking to the pretty girls a lost hope of the night.

I stared at the girls again. The club was dark, and I strained to see them sitting under the harsh red lights of the VIP area, but I could definitely see the redhead. Her hair made flaming by the club's lights, she seemed to look at me again, and I swore I saw her wink at me once.

"I think we should go talk to them," I suddenly said, the liquid courage of my third beer setting into motion what was the first in a series of bad decisions.

Parker and Brennan looked at me like I had a tree growing out of my forehead.

"Are you blind, dude?" Brennan asked, pointing with his second beer. "Those other guys just got bounced by the bouncer." He then laughed at his own pun.

"Seriously. But you should go try. In fact, next round is on me if you can get through Mr. T over there," Parker mused.

With my confidence rising by the second, I displayed a cocky grin and said, "You're on, asswipe!"

We bumped fists.

I began walking—no, swaggering—over to the VIP area. I kept my gaze locked on the redhead, and she glanced back occasionally, offering me a lippy smile. I stopped at the bar once more and ordered something a little stiffer—a Jack and Coke. After tipping the bartender, I flicked the little black straw into a nearby trashcan. I downed most of it in one gulp, trying not to wince at the burn, wandered over to the VIP area, and spoke directly to the bouncer.

"Hi, I think Red over there wants to invite me in." I looked at her, and without breaking eye contact, said, "Don't you, sweetheart?"

Holy crap, where did that come from?

Her friends broke out in a laugh as they watched the interaction. I turned my attention back to the very large and scary-looking bouncer, who was clearly not amused. He had his massive arms folded over his chest, and after staring him down for a few intimidating moments, I turned my attention to the redhead, seemingly for permission. She bit her lip ever so slightly, as if trying to make a decision she knew she had already made, and then nodded to the bouncer.

Before entering the VIP, I finished the rest of my cocktail, and said, "I'm happy to join you, but my friends are gonna need some company, too." I hooked a thumb toward Parker and Brennan, who practically had their mouths open, and then looked back at Red. She grinned as if amused, then nodded to the bouncer again. I slowly turned back around and beckoned my friends over. They practically tripped over themselves on their way over to the lounge.

Before entering the VIP area, the bouncer pat-searched us one by one, running his large hands over our chests, waistbands, and pantlegs to ensure we had no weapons. I had my arms spread out on either side of me, keeping eye contact with the redhead as I got searched.

Once the bouncer was done, I walked up the two steps and took a seat right next to her. Parker and Brennan took seats randomly on the black leather couches amongst the other beautiful ladies.

I went to take another sip of my drink, not breaking eye contact with the redhead, when I realized it was now empty. My head was starting to spin from the booze, so I set the glass on a round table in front of me. "Hi, I'm Nolan. Thanks for the invite."

She laughed. "I'm Eva, and I didn't invite you. But you're persistent, and I like that."

Chapter 3

SUCCUBUS

arker and Brennan seemed to be having the time of their lives. Brennan fingered a curl of the blonde's hair, and Parker was sandwiched between the brunette and the dark-skinned beauty. He looked to be in pure heaven.

Eva ran a shiny black fingernail down the buttons of my shirt while looking at me. "So, Nolan, what do you want to talk about now that you've wormed your way into the VIP area?" she asked with a smirk.

I thought her voice sounded like a melody, purring from her mouth in breathy tones that made me want to do wicked things to her.

I scrutinized her shiny pink lips and looked back into her light eyes. "First, you tell me how you got into this VIP area. You pay for a couple hours or somethin'?" I asked.

She threw her head back and laughed again, her straight red hair swishing along her shoulders. "No, silly. My uncle owns the club. I get first dibs on whatever lounge I want."

I raised an eyebrow at her. "Seriously? Your uncle owns this place? Since when?"

She ignored my question and said, "So, what do you do, Nolan?"

With my hands resting on my knees, I replied, "I restore old bikes."

She wrinkled her nose. "Bikes? Oh, like motorcycles?"

"Yeah." I laughed. "It's kinda like getting paid for doing a hobby."

She looked down at my hands and said, "You do have strong hands. I bet you can do a lot with them."

I just laughed again and said, "Oh, yeah. So, you didn't answer my question, Eva. When did your uncle buy this place?"

She licked her lips as her blue eyes shifted around before coming back to mine. "Okay." She moved in very close to me. "My daddy actually owns it too, but don't tell anyone, okay?"

Now, she was an inch from my face. I could smell the alcohol on her breath and the strawberry scent of her lip gloss. I sucked in a breath, nervous, but excited. Not since Sarah had I been in this close of proximity to a woman. I had to admit — it had been a while. Eva was awakening parts of me I thought were closed for business. With the alcohol still running through my system, and my inhibitions tossed away, I made up my mind that if this extremely hot woman wanted to come home with me tonight, I was game.

I inhaled her scent and felt my entire body relax more. "I won't tell anyone. I can keep lots of secrets, Eva." I fixed her with an intense stare as I licked my lips.

Her mouth twisted into a half-grin. Then she opened those pillowy pink lips and moved in closer to me. Her mouth softly brushed mine as she whispered, "That's good, Nolan, because I have a lot of secrets."

With no more control left, I leaned forward and captured her mouth, hungrily accepting all she returned. Her tongue playfully mingled with mine, causing goosebumps to pepper my entire body. I lightly placed my hand on her jaw. Her hand that was resting on my thigh slid up into dangerous territory, and I gasped when she boldly went where no woman had gone in a very long time.

Or, at least it sure felt that way.

She pulled her mouth back slightly, and suddenly, the room seemed to go still. As I gazed into her eyes, no more music could be heard. No lights were flashing. My friends were gone. The room went black and the only thing in my vision was her piercing blue eyes framed in violent black, and a blunt line of red bangs curtaining them as if they were going to shut down the show at any minute.

As she sucked in a breath right out my mouth, I lost all my air. I lost my sight. I lost my sense of smell. I lost my mind. The only sense I had left was touch, and every nerve-ending felt as if it were being doused with ice water. She tipped her head back and made a brief but odd screeching-sucking noise that jerked me back into reality. I blinked, unseeing, at her beautiful face.

Life resumed again, the thudding bass from a hip-hop song played in my ears with fierce intensity. The smell of alcohol and sweat floated into my nostrils, and I jerked my head forward and looked right into Eva's eyes. Eyes that were now blue again where I could have sworn had been jet-black with no pupils at all just seconds ago. My jeans felt like they'd shrunk two sizes, and as I looked into her smiling face, I noticed her cheeks were red and flushed.

I ran the tip of my finger down her pallid, freckled arm. Then, leaning in close, I breathed in her ear, "Wanna get out of here, sweetheart?"

She sucked in her cheeks and gave a condescending smile. "No, Nolan. I think I'm good."

Shock rippled through me and I couldn't compose myself as my mouth opened slightly. I was going to say something, but then closed it again, unsure what was left.

My chest felt heavy. My mind fuzzy, but my thoughts were disturbed. My emotions seemed nonexistent. I flipped my head around to look at my buddies and noticed they were smiling at their female companions. They seemed to be having a good time, oblivious to my moment of confusion and the bizarre kiss I'd just had with the redhead.

I stood and looked down at Eva, who had a large cocktail glass to her lips, the pink liquid inside it sliding into her mouth with ease. A cocky grin formed around the glass as satisfaction and flirtation danced in her eyes.

I grew angry—no, anger wasn't the right word—I felt indifferent. I suddenly couldn't care less about this woman. I felt dead inside. Nothing about me cared for her any longer. She didn't even seem that attractive to me anymore. My head spun. I needed to get home.

"Hey, guys, I'm gonna take off," I shouted over the music, my eyes flicking between Brennan and Parker and their dates.

Neither of them hardly took notice of me. The blonde's hand was slithering up under Brennan's shirt. Parker's hand was on the brunette's bare thigh, his eyes closed, and her palm glided over his hair as she kissed his neck.

I stumbled out of the club, dizzy, confused, and trying to catch my breath. When I reached my bike, I bent with my hands on my thighs and sucked in gulps of hot, Louisiana night air. I felt as if I had run a marathon and was suddenly very sober.

I tried to internally digest what had just happened. Sure, I'd kissed plenty of girls before. All right, that was kind of a lie. I'd kissed five. One in middle school, a few in high school, then Sarah. But none had felt like that. None had had the intensity of the one I'd shared with Eva. None had taken my breath away and made the world disappear temporarily. So why didn't she want to continue the passion back at my place—or hers? I couldn't figure it out, but I suddenly realized that I didn't care. Shouldn't I be feeling something? Disappointment? Anger? Frustration? I felt nothing. All I felt was hungover and tired.

Shaking my head, I fished my keys from the pocket of my jeans. I flung my leg over the leather seat of the Ducati, started it up, and thundered off down the street. I didn't bother with the helmet or the law as I headed toward my apartment to sleep off whatever this was.

The shrill of the ringtone bolted me out of sleep. Without opening my eyes, I patted my nightstand until I located the offensive device and hit a button, dragging it to my ear.

"Yeah," I mumbled.

My eyes opened halfway and I closed them again. Yellow light streamed in through the blinds I forgot to close the previous night and assaulted my sensitive pupils. I rolled over and sat up, placing my feet on the floor. I ran a hand through my hair with the phone still to my ear.

"What time is it?" I asked my sister on the other end.

My eyes flew fully open. "What! Damn. I musta been more tired than I thought. I'll be over in a bit. Give me thirty."

I ended the call and stared at the screen incredulously. How did I sleep in until two in the afternoon? I slogged out of bed and tossed the phone onto it. Stripping off the clothes I was still wearing from the night before, I started a hot shower and waited for it to heat up. I looked in the quickly-fogging mirror like I always did and realized I didn't look as bad as I thought I would for being as hungover as I felt. My eyes were a bit bloodshot, but the dark circles were gone and I looked rather pale.

I opened the glass shower door, and after closing it behind me, I watched how it quickly fogged back up. Dipping my head under the shower, I groaned as the hot water rained over my body, massaging my very taut muscles. I scrubbed hands over my face and grabbed for the shampoo bottle, then squirted some into my hand and massaged it into my hair. After a good head-to-toe scrubbing, I emerged from the shower feeling somewhat better. I still couldn't believe I had slept in until two! I completely missed brunch at my folks' house, but was headed there now to see them.

After throwing on a pair of shiny black athletic shorts and an LSU T-shirt, I snatched up my motorcycle keys and phone and darted outside.

I rounded the corner to my parents' house. They still lived in the home I'd grown up in, a large ranch-style house on two acres of property. My parents raised and boarded horses as their retirement income, but I had always had a horse growing up. As I rumbled to a stop outside the home, I turned off the ignition. I looked out to see my brown and white horse, Juniper, grazing in the field. My parents had since erected a large set of stables that could house up to twenty horses, and I was happy Juniper had such nice accommodations.

Without knocking, I walked straight in, making my way to the living room where I knew everyone would be. A pitcher of sweet tea sat on an antique tea-cart in the corner, and next to it was a blue tin of cookies.

My sister, Natalie, popped up off the couch, ran over, and threw her arms around me. "Hey, sleepyhead!"

I wrapped my arms around my much shorter sister and kissed the top of her head. "Late night," I mumbled into her dark hair.

She looked up at me. "I'm just glad you got out. Who were you with?" she asked, leading me to the sofa to sit.

"Where are Mom and Dad?" I asked, snatching a cookie from the cart before sitting on an adjoining loveseat.

"Dad's out back, and Mom's in the bathroom."

Just then my mother, Abby, came out. Her face lit up when she saw her only son. "Come here, boy. Where you been?"

I hugged my mom. "Sorry, Ma, I've been away. Just haven't felt like I'd be very good company lately."

"Oh, nonsense. I know you're still upset about Sarah, but we's family, boy. You don't let some dumb girl keep you from seeing your mama."

"Mom. He knows that. He just needed some time to himself," Natalie said, defending me.

Our mother nodded and sat on the sofa after pouring herself a glass of sweet tea. She set the sweating glass on a coaster.

"So, you didn't answer my question. Who did you go out with, Nonie?"

I cringed; I hated that nickname. "Just Parker and Brennan." I looked down at my fingernails subconsciously. My sister always commented on how dirty they were so I was checking to be sure they weren't.

"Those boys are trouble, but at least you got out. Where did you go?"

Geez, what is this, an inquisition? I sighed. "To that Blue Room place in the warehouse district."

Natalie wrinkled her nose. "I haven't heard good things. Lots of fights and stuff."

I lifted a shoulder in a shrug and swallowed the bite of cookie I'd been munching on. "I didn't have any problems."

Mom beamed. "So did you meet anyone special?"

I laughed and shook my head. "At a bar? No. I was talking to some redhead, but she was just a big tease is all she was."

"Nolan Andrew Bishop!" my mother snapped.

I heard the back screen door slam and we all turned to see my father come in. He was in his overalls and rubber wading boots. He yanked off his canvas gloves and set them on the counter. Smiling as he spotted me, he hurried over and hugged me.

"Hey, son! Where ya been, boy? I was beginnin' to worry about ya!"

"Hey, Dad. I've been around. I've missed you. You been cleaning out the lake again?"

My father laughed. "It's more like a pond, but yeah. Horses like to mosey over there and drink from it. I was skimming it for algae and such."

My father, Mark, was a big guy, well over six foot, with receding wavy blond hair and a permanent reddish-brown sunburn on his skin. He had the same lime-green colored eyes, while my sister shared brown hair and light-brown eyes like our mother.

Dad went to the breadbox on the kitchen counter and slid the door up by its small knob. He pulled something out of it and walked over to me. "Here." He plunked the object in my hand.

I looked down to see the small black ring box and frowned.

"Sarah dropped that by some months ago. We kept it safe for ya in case you wanted to try to return it or somethin'," my dad said with a sympathetic look. He then walked away and began scrubbing his hands in the sink.

My eyes were still on the black box. I swallowed the lump in my throat and cursed myself for still being upset about the breakup. I couldn't believe how much emotion the box itself stirred up in me, and I didn't have the heart to crack the lid open and look at the sullied ring. I felt an arm around me.

"Come on, come sit back down," my sister said, patting the sofa.

I sat, the box still burning a hole in my hand, and I didn't look up from it.

Natalie reached over and gently pried it from my fingers. "If you have the receipt, I can go return this for you."

I shook my head. "I do, but they won't let you. I have to do it, they want to see the credit card I used, ID, and all that. I already called."

"I'll go with you," she said, squeezing my hand.

I stood up, shoved the box into my pocket, and said, "I think I'm gonna go."

"No! You just got here. Please stay for dinner? I'll fix your favorite," my mother pled, standing.

I looked into my mom's sweet brown eyes, then snatched a glance at Natalie, who had the same look on her face. Not feeling like eating, but knowing I needed to stop being a big, sulking baby, I sighed. "All right."

The four-hour visit turned out to be good for me. I always felt better being around my family and I vowed I wouldn't stay away so long next time. My dad walked me out to the driveway and whistled through his teeth.

He eyed the Ducati and said, "What happened to the Honda?"

I pointed at the bike. "A rich dude came in with three older Ducatis and said if I fixed the other two for free, I could keep the older one. This one's almost six years old, but of course I've fixed it up a little."

"Well, that was a good deal."

I snorted. "Took me almost a month to restore the other two, but yeah, totally worth it."

I gave my father a manly one-armed hug, and with the offensive ring box still in my pocket, I got on my bike and drove away into the night, suddenly feeling very tired and drained again. On my way home, I remembered I needed a few things at the store. Cursing myself for bringing my bike instead of the car, I told myself I'd only grab the bare necessities and go back tomorrow for more with the car.

Chapter 4

B.S.I.

I pulled into the lot of the Stop-N-Shop and parked my bike on the side of the small building. After entering the store, I snatched a green shopping basket and made my way to the coffee aisle. I stared at the not-so-large selection of coffee and decided on a generic brand. As I plopped the orange bag into the basket hanging over my arm, I looked up and saw *her*. I froze as my eyes fixed on the redhead at the end of the aisle, who was loading items into a wall freezer from a small cart. Something looked different about her, but I couldn't figure it out, as my eyes were fixed on her icy blue ones.

She, too, was frozen on the spot, staring at me, but her face was a mask of confusion mixed with intrigue.

I made my way slowly toward her, and the corners of my mouth twisted into a slight grin. "Hi, Eva. I didn't expect to see you here. Or, ever…"

She placed the items back in her cart and removed her gloves. She frowned, plunking her pale hands on her slender hips. "I'm not Eva."

My eyebrows bunched together in confusion, and I looked at her closely again, realizing her red hair was very long and curly, but her face was the same. I kept a polite expression, but was confused. "What do you mean? We met last night, or do you not remember me fighting every man in the place for a spot next to you on the VIP couch?"

Her face grew even more grave. "Eva's my twin sister. You met her last night? Where?"

A look of surprise was quickly replaced with chagrin. "Uh, yes, I suppose I did. At The Blue Room. You two must be identical…" I replied.

"You didn't kiss her, did you?" she asked.

I was taken aback. "Um, that's kind of a personal question. Why do you want to know?"

"Tell me!" she demanded.

I was very put off by her and shook my head, walking away from the deranged girl. I concluded both twins were crazy and hoped I never saw neither one ever again. After I paid for my items, I couldn't leave the store fast enough.

As my motorcycle rumbled up to the apartment complex, I pulled into my parking spot under the carport, but noticed a plain white sedan parked in the spot next to my Charger. A man sat in the sedan but quickly got out when he spotted me.

I ignored the guy and made my way to the stone staircase that would take me to my apartment.

"Nolan Bishop?"

I closed my eyes. *Great, what did I do now?* Only cops drove those not-so-inconspicuous plain white Fords. I turned around, holding my backpack in one hand and my keys in the other. "Yeah?"

The clean-shaven man who approached me smiled slightly, trying to look nonthreatening. He looked to be in his early forties and wore a plain, dark three-piece suit with a navy-blue tie. His hair was thinning, but not gone, and his light eyes regarded me. He slid a small, black ID holder from his breast pocket and flipped it open. "Special Agent Roger Nelson, U.S. Department of Justice. Do you have a minute?"

I felt a rush of adrenaline zip through my body and flush my face. I was alarmed, wondering what on earth the Justice Department could want with me. "Uh, sure. What's this about?"

Agent Nelson smiled. "I just need to ask you a couple of questions about your whereabouts last night. Is there someplace private we could speak?"

I swallowed hard. *What the hell could he want with me?* "My apartment's just up there." I pointed.

"That would be great," said Agent Nelson with a friendly expression.

We reached the top, and as I nervously unlocked the door, Agent Nelson said, "It's a nice night, isn't it?"

"Uh, yeah. Hot, but nice, I guess."

I flipped on lights as I went in and pointed to the couch. "You can sit there. I need to put these away." Out of my backpack, I pulled out the grocery bag that contained three items: Milk, creamer, and coffee. I had been too flustered by seeing Eva, or whoever she was, at the Stop-N-Shop to remember what else I needed. I carefully put the items away and turned and looked at the agent.

"Uh, do you want something to drink? I have beer, water, and uh, coffee."

Agent Nelson replied, "No, thanks. I'm good."

I went to the living room, sat on the recliner next to the sofa, and said, "What is this about?"

"You went to The Blue Room last night?"

I nodded. "Yes."

The agent cleared his throat. "Had you ever been there before?"

"No. First time."

"I see," Agent Nelson said. He was writing on a small notepad. "And did you meet anyone new while you were there?"

I was already annoyed by the questions, and this stranger wasn't helping my already sour mood. I lifted an eyebrow and folded my arms. "Judging by your questions, I'm thinking that you already know I did."

"I see," he said again. "So, the woman you met... what was her name?"

"She said her name was Eva. I didn't get a last name." I took a deep breath and continued before the agent could fire off questions I already knew he would ask. "She had short, straight red hair, a lot of makeup, long legs, and a great rack."

Agent Nelson chuckled a little and continued writing. "Okay, fair enough. Great... rack. Got it. So, what did you and this Eva talk about?"

I shook my head. "You know, not much. I just asked how she got into the VIP area, she said her uncle owned the club. But wait... that's what was weird. Then she said she lied and her daddy really owned it. Or something. It was really strange, but I was pretty buzzed and didn't really care. I just wanted one thing."

The agent lifted his gaze from the notepad and smirked, then looked back at his pen. "Well, I can certainly appreciate your honesty."

"Hey, just keepin' it real, Officer."

"I'm a special agent, not an officer," he replied dryly.

"Okay, whatever. But why does the Justice Department care that little ol' me went to a club and tried to pick up a girl?"

Special Agent Roger Nelson slapped his notebook closed, placing it back in his breast pocket. He looked right at me and set his hands on his thighs. "Because that was no girl you kissed last night. That was a succubus, and I believe she took something that belongs to you."

I tilted my head to the side. "A *what*? And what did she take? I had my wallet when I left."

The agent shook his head. "Not your wallet, son, your *soul*. I don't just work for the Justice Department. I work for a special branch called the Bureau of Supernatural Investigation—the BSI—and I'm afraid you're going to be in a lot of trouble if you don't listen very carefully to me."

"Okay..." I said, feeling weirded out. "I think you need to leave." I stood.

"Sit down."

I glared at him, but slowly sat.

"I hate to tell you this, but you have seven days to kill this Eva creature, or you will become a vampire."

I barked out a laugh and stood back up. "You're shitting me. Did you just tell me to *kill* someone?" I shook my head. "I think you need to go. I don't know where you got that very authentic-looking badge, but I'm gonna call the police if you don't get the fuck outta my apartment." I folded my arms over my chest. My heart beat double time underneath it.

Agent Nelson grinned and stood up. "I get that a lot. It's okay if you don't believe me. You will in seven days when you try to go outside and get the worst sunburn of your life. Your throat will turn dust-dry, but no amount of water will quench it, and then you'll puke your guts out if you try to eat any sort of regular food. But hey, I guess you can learn the hard way."

I had absolutely no response to that. "Have a nice night, *Agent* Nelson," I replied.

As I went to close the door, he turned around and said, "Oh, and Nolan... *you* have to kill her, nobody else. You understand?"

I shook my head without a reply as I closed and locked the door. I reeled in shock as I sat on the couch and stared at the wall. I only had one thought: I had to go find Eva's twin sister—and fast.

After Googling "secret division of the Justice Department" and coming up with absolutely nothing but weird books, websites, and a bunch of *X-Files* results, I left my apartment. Of course, the first place I looked for that chick's twin was the Stop-N-Shop. The conversation with that agent — if he really was one — had taken way too long, and by the time I got to the store, it was closed. In that part of town, nothing stayed open twenty-four hours. It just wasn't good for business. I briefly wondered if I should visit The Blue Room again. Maybe I could find that red-haired bitch and ask her myself.

As I sat on my bike and stared at the quiet, dark Stop-N-Shop, I wondered if I had truly just lost my mind. How does someone get their soul taken? It wasn't as if I actually believed this. Did I?

I replayed the previous night's events in my mind over and over. The whole club had been enamored by the group of girls. Were they all succubuses...? What was the plural to succubus? I'd have to look that up. Yeah… in my spare time.

I'd admit that kiss she gave me was something else, and not in a breathless, erotic, toe-curling way. It was eerie, if I could even remember. If I were honest with myself, I'd admit that I didn't remember the actual kiss. I remembered vying for her attention in the VIP section, then leaning in to kiss her. Then stumbling out of the club, my alcohol buzz gone, replaced by a different kind of fog. It was like someone had removed my brain and wrung it out like a wet rag, then replaced it, dry and useless. Even as I had slept it off, I had still awoken the next day tired and groggy.

As I drove home, the warm August night wind blowing my too-long hair and caressing my bare arms, I racked my brain as to how I was going to try to find Eva's twin sister. I didn't even know her name. I concluded I'd just have to keep coming by the Stop-N-Shop until I found her.

Chapter 5

WHICH REDHEAD IS A WITCH?

The next day I went to work and barely got anything done. I put the wrong part on the wrong motorcycle and installed a set of wires completely backward.

"What's the matter with you, kid?" Archie asked as he found me cursing at the undercarriage of a Harley. A cigarette bounced out of the corner of his mouth as he spoke.

I slid out and wiped the grease from my hands with a rag. Standing up, I replied, "Nothing, boss. Just tired, that's all."

Archie, still dressed his coveralls, a blue bandana around his head, eyed me speculatively. "You sure? You seem… off today."

"Nah, just girl trouble, Arch. I'll be all right."

Archie let out a fatherly chuckle and flicked the cigarette to the concrete, grinding it out with his worn, steel-tipped boot. "Yeah, women. Who needs 'em?"

I nodded and went into the back room to change out of my coveralls and go home. It had been a long, unproductive day and I was in no mood to talk about my troubles.

My exhaustion wasn't just from stress. I'd been plagued with nightmares the night before—nightmares of *her*. Her icy eyes boring into me right before I kissed her. Whispers of temptation flitting through my dreams, her breath and voice soft and alluring.

I stopped by the Stop-N-Shop on the way home, but she again was not there. After I got home, and after eating some leftovers, I fell asleep on the couch watching some reality TV show I didn't know the name of. When I woke, I checked the clock and saw it was one a.m. I dragged myself to my bedroom and fell back to sleep the minute my head hit the pillow.

When my alarm went off at seven that morning, I felt like I'd slept for about six seconds total the entire night. After a shower, I stopped at the Stop-N-Shop to pick up a premade sandwich and a Coke for lunch later and to see Eva's sister. I placed my things on the belt and froze as I spotted the redhead behind the check-stand staring at me with the same piercing blue eyes that had been haunting my dreams.

Early morning light filtered in through the store windows and cast a bit of an orange halo around her head. I blinked in shock at how identical they were, as her crystal eyes met mine.

The only thing I could think to say was, "I need to talk to you."

Her look turned smug. "I bet you do."

Since the store was virtually empty, I felt like there was no time like the present. "I need to find your sister."

She sighed, placed my sandwich and Coke in a grocery sack, and handed me my change. "I thought you'd say that."

I tapped my booted foot. "Well?"

"Well, what?" she shot back.

"Where the hell is Eva? She and I need to have a little chat."

She measured me with a long stare. Placing both hands on the cash register in front of her, she snapped, "My name is Charity, by the way, thanks for asking."

My expression softened. "I'm sorry, Charity, my manners have gone out the window lately. I'm Nolan."

She smirked a little and slid some of her unruly ginger hair behind her ear. "To answer your question, I don't know where Eva is. I heard she hangs out at that club you said you met her at, but other than that, she's been pretty elusive."

I raised an eyebrow. "Really? You and your sister not very close then? You sure as hell look alike."

She huffed. "No, we're not. I mean, we used to be, since we're twins 'n all, but over the past few years, we've drifted apart."

I folded my arms over my chest. "I see."

"So, I take it you kissed her?" she asked in amusement.

I sighed. "Obviously. Where can I find her?"

She lifted her hands off the cash register and folded her arms over her chest, which was hidden under a plain white shirt covered by a blue apron. "Seriously, Nolan, I don't know. She hangs out in clubs, but we really don't speak."

I blew out a breath and raked a hand through my light-brown hair. "What do you suggest?"

Her blue eyes shifted around the nearly empty store. "Meet me back here at sundown."

I lifted an eyebrow. "Sundown? Are you serious? What is this, Cloak and Dagger?"

A small smile lifted on a corner of her pink lips. "Of course. Eva can't go out before sundown."

I looked at her, my eyebrows dipping in confusion.

"She's a vampire." She rolled her eyes as if it had been completely ludicrous that she'd had to explain that to me.

A gasp escaped my lips. Either I was dreaming, or had slipped into the *Twilight Zone* or an episode of *Supernatural*.

"What the hell?"

After a long day at work, I zipped down the street on my bike, the word *vampire* flitting through my head, taunting my brain.

An ironic grin found me when I thought about the ridiculousness of it. I would find Eva, shake the truth out of her, and be on my way. I had to admit I was a little disturbed that both Charity and that agent from the Justice Department had mentioned the word *vampire* regarding to Eva, but maybe it was a coincidence. Maybe the agent had gotten to Charity, too. Maybe Eva was a wanted felon and they were using me and her sister to find her.

A thought suddenly came to me. As I went inside my apartment and closed the door behind me, I pulled my phone from my pocket and hit the contact icon for Parker.

"What's up, man?" he answered.

"Hey. I have a question. Did you hook up with any of those chicks from The Blue Room when we were there?"

There was a slight pause and Parker sighed. "No. I was about to kiss that hot brunette when the music stopped and the damn fire alarm began to blast. Apparently, some dumb girl had lit her lighter against the sprinkler in the ladies' bathroom and made the alarms and sprinklers go off. We all had to evacuate. It was chaos."

My eyebrows bunched together. "Why would she do that?"

Parker laughed. "Word was, she was there on a date, and he ditched her for another chick. She got pissed and brought the rain down on him — and all of us for it."

I shook my head. "Well, that's stupid."

"Tell me about it."

"So did Brennan hook up?" I asked.

Parker replied, "Nope, he didn't even get to first base, man. He was still flirting with the blonde when the fire alarm went off. We all kinda scattered. Haven't seen those chicks since."

I sighed. "I see. You or Brennan didn't happen to get their numbers, did you?"

Parker laughed. "Not even close. What's with the twenty questions, dude?"

"It's nothing. But I have one more."

"Okay…"

I closed my eyes and slumped down to the couch, my left hand massaging the back of my neck. "No cops or strange government officials have been by to see you, have they?"

Parker laughed again. "Uh, no, they have not. What's going on, Bishop? You rob a bank or something?"

"No, nothing like that. I think I need to get more sleep or something."

"Yes, yes, you do. Gotta go, time for work. Later, dude."

Parker hung up and I was back at square one. I just hoped Charity could help me locate Eva. As absurd as the vampire notion was, I had a strong feeling both she and Agent Nelson were telling the truth.

And that scared the living shit out of me.

As promised, I met Charity at the Stop-N-Shop around sundown, which really wasn't until around seven-thirty in late August. I sat straddling my bike and wiped a bead of sweat that dripped down through my new haircut I had gotten earlier today.

I smiled when I saw a shimmer of unruly auburn hair bouncing out of the store. She untied her apron and balled it up, shoving it into her big green handbag. I could see she was pretty fit, a nice, slim hourglass figure with a decent sized chest and slender legs. She had on white cutoff shorts under a fitted black tank top. I shook my head, thinking I already knew her physique; it had to be the same as Eva's, which I had studied extensively a couple nights prior in The Blue Room.

Charity walked over to my bike, grabbed a handful of red curls, and twisted them up to the back of her head, securing them with a small clip.

"Hi," she said, smiling at me.

I watched as the fading sun cast orange and pink beams onto her freckled face, and her lips glowing pink. I looked down at her mouth, then into her brilliant blue eyes.

I cleared my throat. "Hi, Charity. Where to first?"

She shrugged a freckled shoulder. "I don't know. All I know is Eva hangs out in clubs."

I huffed out a breath. "Seriously? That's all you got?"

Her orange eyebrows lifted her hairline. "What else do you think I have? I already told you I don't talk to her."

"Fine, get on. We'll find her."

"You want me to get on that *donorcycle*?" she asked incredulously, eyeballing the Ducati.

I chuckled. "Scared of a little rumble and muscle?"

She lifted her chin. "No."

"Then get on, sweetie. We have a vampire to find."

"Do you at least have a helmet?" she asked.

"There are no helmet laws in Louisiana."

She stomped her foot. "I couldn't give a crap about the law. I don't want brain damage when you crash this death machine."

I laughed again. "I ain't gonna crash." I had left my helmet in my apartment, but didn't want to tell her that.

"Yeah, well, I must already be brain damaged to get on this thing with you." And with that, she huffed, slung one long leg over the seat of my Ducati, and put her arms around my abdomen. I pumped my leg, starting the *donorcycle*, and sped down the street.

I watched as the sun sank behind the horizon. Colors illuminated my face as the wind whipped through my newly shorn hair. The feel of a soft pair of arms around my waist was oddly comforting.

I pulled off the back country road, steering my bike to the side of the dirt road. I killed the engine and dismounted, leaving Charity standing there, looking dumbfounded. Dust and dirt billowed up around her bare legs.

"I can't keep driving around. I need to know where we're going," I simply stated.

Charity turned her head in curiosity. "I told you, I don't know where she hangs out."

I studied her for a long minute. "How are y'all twins and you don't speak? I mean, I thought twins had some kind of psychic link or somethin'?"

She shook her head. "We never had a psychic link. We did have a bond, but that was broken when she was turned."

I turned my head to the side. "Turned?"

"Yes, into a vampire. She was messing with a really weird crowd about three years ago. Then one night, she disappeared. I didn't see or hear from her for three months. It was awful."

"Then what happened?" I asked, totally intrigued.

She sighed, fingering a stray red curl that had escaped from the clip. "Well, she literally just showed up one night at my job. I was stocking pickle jars and dropped one when she walked in. It shattered, but barely made a sound as far as I was concerned. I looked into her face and couldn't believe it. I screamed and ran to her. I had truly thought she was dead."

I was quiet, waiting for her to continue, hanging on every word.

"I hugged her so tight I thought I was gonna hurt her. But she barely hugged me back. I looked into her face, and through my tears, I saw a void, empty expression. I wiped the tears from my vision and looked into her eyes. They were dead and emotionless. I no longer saw the fire and curiosity in them I had seen when we were growing up. I grabbed her shoulders and asked her what was wrong. She just shook her head and told me, 'Nothing.' It was so weird. I knew something was wrong, but I didn't know what.

"I walked with her out of the store and into the dark parking lot. She really didn't say much, just that she didn't want me to be worried and that she wanted me to know that she was all right. And that was it."

My brows pinched together and I looked at the ground, then back up at her. "That is quite strange. She didn't say where she'd been?"

Charity shook her head. "No, not really. When I asked, she said she had been staying with some friends and had gotten into some bad stuff, but was okay now. I thought it was drugs."

"And it wasn't?" I asked.

She let out a humorless laugh. "No, it so wasn't drugs."

"The vampire thing?"

"Yes."

I turned my head to the side "How did you figure that out?"

She put her hand on her hip. "Why, I followed her, of course."

My motorcycle zoomed down the Louisiana back country roads, scattering dirt and waking the neighbors in the quiet neighborhoods we flashed past. I slowed the bike as I approached the large, wrought-iron gates of a huge estate.

I killed the engine and placed both feet on the ground to steady the bike. Craning my neck around, I glanced at Charity. "What now?"

"Well, this is where I had followed her to a few months ago. I don't know if she lives here, or what."

I looked at her incredulously. "You could have told me this from the get-go."

She snorted. "Maybe I just wanted a ride on your death machine."

I couldn't help but grin. "Oh, yeah, I'm sure that's why you kept this info from me."

"Seriously, though, I didn't think of it 'til you said something. I wouldn't have been able to tell you where it was, anyway. I had to drive here to see. I never pay attention to street signs," she said with a blush.

"Well, what kind of car did she leave in when she showed up at your work that one time?"

She sniffed. "That's what was weird. She just kinda left on foot, disappearing into the night. I got into my car and saw her walking, but then, after a mile or so, she got into a big fancy black car that had pulled up next to her."

"And the vampire part?"

She jutted her chin toward the mansion looming behind the large, black gates. "Do normal people live in homes like this?"

I laughed. "Uh, yeah, they actually do, Red."

"Don't call me Red," she replied narrowing her eyes.

It was the *in* I'd been looking for. "Oh, you don't like that?"

"No."

"Okay." I chuckled. "So, you just assumed she was a vampire because she came to this big, scary-looking mansion next to a swamp? You watch too much TV."

She snorted and stomped her foot. "No, you jerk. I followed her for weeks, wearing disguises. I saw what she did to guys at different clubs around town. One night, some bikers were in the parking lot of the Beach Club downtown and I heard them say her name, and then they called her a succubus. I couldn't believe it. I went home and Googled that shit."

"And you believed it?"

She nodded, pulling a piece of gum from her mouth, and flicked it to the dirt ground below. "Yep, and it all made sense then. Plus, I saw her feed on a guy in the back of a club once. It was totally gross and it freaked me out bad. I cried for like two days. I never thought vampires were real."

I raised my eyebrows, as I was sure disbelief swam in my eyes.

"So, we just gonna go knock on the door, or what?" she asked, staring at the large, brooding house.

I dismounted the bike. I shoved the keys in my pocket and helped her off. "No, not *we*. You are. They'll let you in. I'll stay here, and once you're inside, I'm gonna sneak round back."

She stared at me for a minute, then nodded. Surprisingly, the large gate wasn't locked and opened with a wail when she pulled on it. She began the slow trek up the walkway, which was lined with pristinely manicured shrubs that set a barrier against lush, trimmed green grass. Light from an almost-full moon lit up her path as I watched her black Converse take slow, measured steps up the concrete path.

She pulled a gray knit beanie from her pocket, shoved it on her head, and took a deep breath. As I ran toward the back of the house, I hoped she'd be okay.

Chapter 6

SISTER SUCCUBUS

Charity

I knew what I was getting into. This wasn't the first time I'd dealt with Eva's friends. I knew exactly what Eva was and what her friends were, and knew I had to play the game in order to stay alive while trying to get information. Truth was, I had thought of doing this before, but knew doing it alone wouldn't be the smartest idea. But who could I have asked to come? Nobody. I would have sounded insane.

My heart clenched at the reason I was out here tonight looking for Eva. I knew she had stolen Nolan's soul, and he had to be confused about what he was feeling—or not feeling—and just wanted answers. Eva could give him answers. However, the other reason I'd never come here before was that I just didn't know what I would say to my twin. She knew where I lived and worked, and had made no effort to see me. She obviously didn't care about me, so I had sort of taken the same attitude about her. I missed my only sister, but I wasn't going to be rejected. That being said, I knew this day would come. I knew one day I'd have to find her when she had truly hurt someone. And now that I was standing on her doorstep, my emotions were raging a battle inside my heart.

With a deep breath, I raised a pale hand to the large, round iron knocker on the door and gave it three raps. It wasn't long until a good-looking dark-haired man in his early twenties answered the door. He narrowed his light eyes at me, then his features softened.

Before I could speak, the man said, "Eva, what are you doing? I thought you'd be halfway to New Orleans by now."

That surprised me, but I managed to rein in my astonishment. Thinking fast, I shrugged a shoulder and decided to roll with it, since obviously Eva wasn't here. I confidently pushed past the man. "I was, but I forgot something… uh, including my key." I jutted a thumb at the door.

The man snorted. "You're such a ding-dong. You sure you ain't a natural blonde?"

Screw off, was what I was thinking. Instead, I muttered, "Very funny."

I quickly climbed the stairs, not sure where the hell I was going, but I knew I had to keep up the ruse. Thankfully, the man didn't say anything else or follow me, and I was left alone to wander down the long upstairs hallway of the dark and creepy house.

I felt as if I were in some reality show episode. Any minute now, a film crew would pop out of one of the rooms with a light in my face and tell me I'd been *Punk'd.* The hallway had wood floors lined with a long, red paisley throw-rug complete with gold tassels on the ends; there were paintings on the walls of people dressed in old world clothing whose eyes seemed to follow me. Dark wood paneling was halfway up the white walls, and all the doors were very dark and ornate — and closed. No, forget *Punk'd;* I was in a frickin' *Scooby-Doo* episode.

I stopped in the long hallway and wondered which door to choose. One of them had to be Eva's room. I decided on the first door. Taking a deep breath, I turned the squeaky oval antiquated doorknob slowly and cracked the door open. What I saw as I peered in was a large bedroom was a nineteenth century-style canopy bed that looked like it had vomited lace and ruffles. The room was cloaked in darkness, save for the moonlight streaming in through the open window. A heavy, black velvet drapery flanked the one large window on either side, but it was otherwise quiet. I had no idea if this was Eva's room or not, so I wandered inside, shutting the door behind me.

There weren't many personal effects in the room. A sitting area with a large, ornate vanity mirror and table complete with a padded chair sat in the corner, and I strolled over to it. I sat down and slowly pulled open the delicate top drawer. Reaching in, I plucked out an assortment of photos and papers. As I began to flick through the pictures, my heart fluttered as I came across one of Eva and me as children. We wore identical yellow dresses and had short pixie haircuts. We had our arms around each other and appeared to be laughing. I grinned at the realization I had reached Eva's room on the first try.

I slowly flipped to the next picture and saw the two of us on the day of our high school graduation, dressed in blue caps and gowns, with our arms around each other. I smiled sadly at the memory. Eva's face was caked with tons of makeup while I had barely worn any. I knew it would be god-awful hot and it would melt off anyway. With a sigh, I gently set the photos down and unfolded a piece of paper with my own handwriting. It was a letter I remembered penning to my twin one time after Eva had tried to move in on my middle school crush. I grinned as I read the letter and the young teen angst that was scrawled into emotion-filled words, with lots of exclamation points and underlining.

As I put the photos and papers back into the drawer and closed it, I looked at the surface of the dressing table. Picking up an old-fashioned pink glass perfume bottle, my eyebrows scrunched together as I studied the small, thin hose coming from the top of it. At the end of the hose was a large bulb with a white tassel attached. I gingerly picked it up and ran my fingers along the bottle. Lifting it to my nose, I sniffed it and was surprised at the familiar scent. It was Eva's favorite. I pondered at how Eva got the popular, modern perfume into the old-fashioned bottle. I squirted a couple of sprays on my neck.

I stood and looked around the room again with my hands on my slender hips. I put my hand on my head, making sure the beanie cap was still in place and no stray curls had escaped. Eva had short, straight hair and my long, wavy locks would definitely raise suspicion. Although the guy who'd answered the door didn't seem like the brightest bulb in the box.

The bed had nightstands on either side, and I saw a laptop on one of them. It appeared to be charging with a cord plugged into the wall, and when I wandered over to it, I could see it was a newer model. I lifted the lid and watched as the screen flickered to life. Sitting softly on the large bed, I pulled the machine into my lap and clicked on the Internet icon. While I waited for it to load, I snuck a glance behind my shoulder to make sure nobody was coming into the room. I wondered if I should lock the door.

As the homepage came up, I quickly found the browsing history and my eyes went wide at Eva's last Internet search: A huge ball in New Orleans celebrating, witches, vampires, and everything freaky. It was happening in two days, and I rejoiced at my discovery. At least I now knew why the creep at the front door had commented on her being in New Orleans.

A floorboard creak caused me to almost drop the laptop. I smacked it closed and left it on the bed, then bolted to the closet door. I opened it, throwing myself into darkness as I shut it quietly.

I could hear the door to the room being opened with the same creak I'd caused as I'd entered. The door to the closet was slightly ajar and I peered through it with one eye to the gap, a slice of light illuminating my eye. I saw the same guy — vampire? — who had answered the door wander into the room. Knowing he thought I was Eva, I figured I didn't need to hide.

As I was about to emerge from the closet, I turned around and saw all of Eva's clothes hanging neatly inside. I recognized the flirty blue summer dress I had let Eva borrow and had never seen again. My eyes slid down to the shoe rack at the bottom of the closet and I scanned the massive shoe collection until I spied the matching white sandal-type heels she said would look "to die for" with the dress. I frowned at the memory. Angry, I reached down and plucked the shoes from the rack.

Shaking myself out of my reverie, I backed out the closet holding the dress and shoes.

"Oh, here it is!" I exclaimed.

The dark-haired vampire whipped his head around and stared at me in shock.

I, in turn, looked at him with mock surprise. "What are you doing in my room?"

He stammered, "I... I was just wondering where you'd gotten off to."

Damn, I wish I knew his name.

"Well, get outta here! I just came for this dress, and, uh, my perfume." My eyes shifted to the dressing table.

The vampire rushed over, picked up the perfume bottle, and sniffed it. "Who you trying to impress with this chemical crap? Your natural smell is much sweeter." He lifted his eyebrows as if daring me to refute his claim.

"Fuck off. Give that to me," I said, internally cringing as I hated to cuss, but knew Eva didn't.

He handed it to me, letting his fingers linger on mine a bit longer than necessary. When I looked down at his hand, I could see the letters B-R-A-D tattooed on each finger of his right hand.

Bingo.

"Brad, go away," I said with more confidence than I felt, *so* hoping his name wasn't really Darb or Darby.

He smirked at me, his light-blue eyes playing at mine. "How about a quick roll on that big bed of yours for old time's sake?" He jutted his chin at the ridiculously large canopy bed.

I scrunched up my nose. "No. Go away."

"All right. Then how about a taste? I'll let you have one in return." He swiped a finger down my neck and was practically drooling at my neck.

I shuddered, and a spike of panic shot through me at the thought of being bitten, so I gasped. "Absolutely not. I need to go, gonna be late for the ball and all that."

Brad made a face and stepped back. "You smell funny. You just eat?"

I was confused by this, and then remembered reading that vampires had an acute sense of smell. I was glad I had sprayed the perfume. "Uh, yeah, just ate. Had me some blood from a nice, fresh human, and sucked me down a really good soul, I did."

He looked at me again, biting back a smile, but then his brows furrowed. "What's wrong with you? You drunk or somethin'?"

"Maybe. Leave me alone." I brushed past him for the second time that night, flying down the hall and toward the back of the house, hoping I would find Nolan and the back door.

I heard Brad yelling "Eva" after me, but I ignored him. I had to find Nolan and get the hell out of there. I looked down at the blue dress in my hand and wondered where I was going to store it and the shoes while on the back of Nolan's bike.

Because I was *so* not giving them back.

I saw Nolan peering into the windows at the back of the house as I scurried out the back door. His eyes went wide as he spotted me. He glanced at the dress in my hands and then slid his gaze back into my eyes, and I felt a bit chagrinned as I lifted the arm with the garment draped over it. "My sister borrowed this three years ago. I never thought I'd see it again."

His gaze slipped down to the white shoes in my hand and he grinned. "Gonna wear those on the bike? 'Cause that would be hot."

I snorted. "Absolutely not."

He put his hand out and I grabbed it. He dragged me around the house and through the gates. We both let out the breaths we had been holding as we reached his bike. I made to get on it, but he held up a hand. "No, let me walk it a bit before I start it up, it's loud."

I nodded. "Good idea."

"Did you find anything?" he asked.

"Yes. Eva's on her way to, or already in, New Orleans."

His eyebrows went up. "Really? Did you find out why?"

"Well, at first I wasn't in a position to ask because the creep in there thought I was her."

He lifted a brow. "And then?"

"Well, after telling him to get lost, and then some good sleuth work, I found out she was doin' Internet searches of some big masquerade ball in Nawlins."

"...and?"

"And, it's tomorrow night." I looked at Nolan for a response.

He shook his head. "Okay, Cinderella. Guess we're gonna go to a ball."

I shook my head at him with a small laugh, then looked one last time over my shoulder at the big, creepy old house. I couldn't believe *that* had been my sister's home for the past few years.

I let out a sad sigh.

I missed my sister. We had grown up as close as sisters could. We shared everything; clothes, shoes, food, and most of all, secrets. Being identical, we had fun tricking friends, boyfriends, and teachers. We had even tricked our dad once, but were caught when he realized the ruse. While Eva had been good at math, I excelled in English and grammar. So we would often swap places in high school classes and do each other's homework. We were true mirror-image twins.

I shook my head at the memories and cursed myself for not taking the photos and letters from Eva's room. I also found myself fighting back a tear. I still loved my twin sister, and as I slid a glance at Nolan, I bit my lip. I knew Nolan had been told to kill my sister. *Kill her*. It made my chest ache and my breath hitch in the back of my throat. Yes, Eva had become a monster, a vampire—a *succubus*, but that didn't mean I wanted to witness her murder. I suddenly wondered what I was doing on this mission with Nolan. Could I truly sit back and watch as he plunged a knife or a stake through my only sibling's heart? Shoot her with a gun? Or worse, decapitate her with God knows what?

"What?" Nolan asked as he looked over at my stressed expression.

I shook my head and plastered on a smile. "Nothing."

"Oh, come on," he said, "I can tell you were deep in thought. I lost you there for a second."

I nodded slightly. "Can I ask you something?"

"Of course," he said, his hands still on the handlebars as he steered the heavy bike down the dirt path lined with swampland on either side of us. He risked a glance behind us at the fast-disappearing path to the house, and then looked back at me.

I eyed the muscles bunching in his arms as he gripped the bike, then back into his eyes. "What are you going to do when you find my sister?"

He sucked in a breath. "Charity, I don't know. I just don't. I mostly have questions."

My eyebrows knit together. "You're not gonna kill her?"

He smirked. "I don't think I'd do well in prison."

"Yeah, you'd definitely be somebody's bitch," I said, nudging him with my elbow, feeling relieved.

"Hardly!" he retorted.

He looked back one last time and hopped on the bike, patting the seat behind him. "Get on, I think it's safe."

I awkwardly climbed on, holding the shoes. I had already stuffed the dress into my crowded backpack.

"Sure you don't want to wear the shoes?" he asked with a mischievous glint in his lime-colored eyes.

"No."

"All right. Let's get the hell out of here then." Nolan pressed on the gas with his foot and pumped the handlebar, leaving a wake of dirt from his tires as we left the creepy mansion in the dust.

Chapter 7

PUTTING THE 'A' IN AWKWARD

Nolan

ot, humid wind whipped us both in the face as the motorcycle zipped along the Louisiana highway. The sun had set, but that didn't mean the temperature would cool off. It just meant that the sun wouldn't add to the already miserable climate.

I steered the bike back to my apartment complex. As I parked in my designated spot, I killed the engine and dismounted.

Charity looked at the tall apartments. "Why are we here?"

"I need to grab some things if we're going to be in Nawlins for a while."

She raised a ginger eyebrow. "A while?"

I shoved the keys in my pocket and crossed my arms over my chest. "Unless you know exactly where your sister is, I doubt what needs to be done can be accomplished in a day."

"And what exactly does that mean?"

I shook my head and turned on my heel, heading toward the stone staircase that led to my second-story apartment.

She trailed behind me into my apartment and stood in the living room as I went into my room and filled a duffel bag with clothes and toiletry items. She followed me to my room and watched me, eyeing my queen-sized bed. The look on her face was indecipherable and then she slid her gaze to me. She couldn't seem to take her eyes off my tattooed arms as I packed my bag, and I wondered if she was having the same thoughts about me as I'd had about her.

But I had to push that from my mind. I had some serious things to deal with once we reached New Orleans, and the unknowing of it all was stressing me out the most. I wasn't even sure I believed what was going on.

I yanked my phone charger from the wall in the kitchen and shoved that into the duffel bag, too. After plucking a purple and yellow LSU baseball hat from the counter, I shoved it on my head and said, "Let's go."

She nodded and followed me out. As I locked the door, I led her down the steps and to my Charger.

"Is this your car?" she asked as I disarmed the muscle car.

"No, I just decided to steal it," I replied, biting back a smile.

Her blue eyes went wide.

I laughed and shook my head. "Of course it's mine. Get in. Unless you'd like to take the trip on the bike? Because I really don't mind —"

"No, this will be fine." She cut me off.

I grinned and started up the car with a loud, obnoxious rumble that made my teeth rattle.

As I drove down the street, she looked at me and said, "I need to stop at the shop real quick."

I glanced at the dash clock and then back at her. "They close in ten, I doubt we'll make it."

She cleared her throat. "I don't need to shop. I need to grab a few things."

I lifted an eyebrow at her, waiting for her to elaborate, then put my eyes back on the road.

She sighed. Looking straight at the dark street ahead of her, she said, "I live there. In a small apartment above the shop."

I nodded and pressed on the gas with a loud grumble.

When we reached the convenience store, I parked in the small lot and watched as she quickly got out of the car and went around to the back of the building. I followed her inside a small back door, which led to a dark staircase.

"I'll only be a minute," she said as she unlocked the door with a key she'd pulled from her backpack.

Once inside, she hung the key on a hook and set the backpack and shoes down. She wandered over to a dresser, opened the top drawer, and began rifling through it.

I watched her and then looked around the small studio apartment. It had no decorations at all, and the small kitchen was nothing more than a fridge, a microwave, and a very small oven. There was a double bed in the corner of the room and the dresser she currently had open. A small laptop was on top of an overturned gray milk crate she used as a makeshift nightstand.

After she had removed some things and then stuffed different clothing into her backpack, she picked up the white shoes and tossed them into a plastic bin full of shoes that was set next to the dresser. Then she made her way to the kitchen and pulled the lid off a red Folgers coffee can. I watched in curiosity as she dug a wad of cash from it. She shoved the cash into her backpack, along with her beanie cap. She looked sheepishly at me as she smoothed down her unruly copper hair. I grinned at her. She was cute when she was embarrassed. A blush creeped up her neck and into her freckled cheeks.

She looked away from me and peered around the apartment. "I think I got what I need."

I pointed at her bag. "Got your toothbrush and stuff?"

She put her hair up into a clip and nodded. "Yes, I always carry that stuff in my backpack."

"Okaaayy. Well, let's get going then. We're going to be driving most of the night. Do you have any idea where we're gonna stay?"

She knit her eyebrows together. "No, but we'll find someplace. If you have a smartphone, I can make a reservation as we drive."

I chuckled. "Yeah, I have a smartphone. You don't?"

She shook her head as we both left the apartment. As she locked the door, I watched her long, slender fingers work the key into the lock. Then I signaled for her to walk ahead of me. I enjoyed the view of her long legs and tight shorts.

The drive was quiet. I had given her my phone, and she quickly made us a reservation at a chain hotel near the Quarter. We didn't speak much, but I did glance over at her a few times. I didn't want to stare at her, because then I would want to touch her. I had had the sudden urge to run my fingers over her smooth leg, but of course I didn't. Instead, I said, "Tell me about Eva."

She glanced over at me, and with a shake of her head she said, "Well, the most important thing you need to know about Eva, is that she always gets what she wants."

I nodded. "She seems the type."

"I was thinking earlier, when I saw you, that she probably knew exactly what she wanted the minute you'd entered our father's club."

My brow furrowed. "Why's that?"

She cleared her throat and seemed nervous. "Well, look at you. You're tall, good-looking, and are a nice guy. A perfect victim. The purer the soul, the better the feed."

I laughed. "There's nothing pure about me, trust me."

"Well, I don't know how a succubus knows, but they do."

I changed the subject. This conversation was too weird and was making me uncomfortable, even though I was secretly happy she thought I was good-looking. "So, your dad does own that club? Eva had told me that. Does he live around here?"

"Yes. Our parents still live in a nicer part of Shreveport. My dad and his brother bought the warehouse a few months back and turned it into The Blue Room. Then he was stupid and let Eva pretty much take it over. He still doesn't know what she is, and I have no idea how I could even tell our parents about Eva's... transformation."

"They don't question as to why they only see her at night?"

Charity shook her head. "Eva has always been a free spirit and did what she wanted, when she wanted. So, when she showed up late or not at all on holidays or whatever, our parents didn't seem to question it. Just my mom would briefly complain. That was when she was human, though. Now, she doesn't come around at all."

"She sounds like a real peach," I said dryly.

She laughed, but there wasn't much humor in it. "Eva always made me mad when it came to stuff like that. I'd always been the good girl, the one to take care of everyone else, the one to protect my sister. And sometimes it felt like I lived in her shadow. Now, even after all the selfish moves and neglect, I still give a crap about her wellbeing. I don't know why I bother."

Her wellbeing? What did that mean? I wanted to ask her, but decided not to. She almost seemed to be talking to herself instead of me. I guessed she has issues.

After a couple of hours, I cut over three lanes of traffic to get off the interstate as I spotted a familiar exit in Lafayette I always used when I went to New Orleans. Then I thought about Sarah and now we were supposed to go there so I could propose before she ruined it. The memory of the day I discovered her betrayal tugged at my brain and then smacked my heart like a broken guitar string, reminding me that times were simpler and happier then. Now they just seemed to be getting complicated and ugly.

I shooed the memory of Sarah out of my brain and stopped at the gas station. As I got out of the car, I watched as Charity wandered into the station's store. I eyed her legs and butt, marveling at how much better they'd look if she'd worn the white high-heels she left at the apartment. The Converse sneakers didn't do them justice.

As soon as the gas pump clicked indicating my tank was full, I saw her emerge from the shop with a small plastic bag in her hand. She pulled out an energy drink and handed it to me, along with a bag of beef jerky. I was kind of impressed.

I popped open the energy drink and took a large swallow. "How'd you know I like beef jerky and caffeine?"

She grinned. "You're a guy, it wasn't difficult."

I chuckled. I couldn't argue with that, so I replaced my gas cap and helped Charity into the car.

I chugged the last of the drink, then crushed the can and tossed it into a nearby trashcan. I then threw the bag of jerky into the backseat. We were soon back on the interstate, only a couple more hours away from reaching New Orleans.

Big city buildings and factories with smoke billowing out of their stacks were now in clear view of the night sky. Big bridges stretching over the Mississippi River loomed in the distance, illuminated against the dark sky. It was nearly two a.m., and both Charity and I were exhausted.

I pulled up a map on my phone that instructed me where to go. When we finally reached the hotel, we parked in a nearby parking garage. After grabbing our backpacks, we exited the car and headed to the front desk.

Charity slid a stray curl behind her ear. "Hi, checking in," she said.

A dark-skinned girl in a smart blue suit working behind the counter grinned at us with perfectly white teeth. "Sure, Name?"

"Charity Sheridan."

She nodded and typed into her computer. "Ah, here you are. Two keys?" she asked, her brown eyes flicking between us.

Charity nodded. "Yes, please."

The hotel worker fumbled with some card keys then asked for a credit card. She bit her lip and looked at me. "Do you have one? I don't use credit cards."

"Can I pay with cash?" I asked.

The hotel attendant's eyebrows dipped into each other. "Well, no, sir. We need a card to hold the room. For incidentals."

"I only have a debit card," I responded.

She nodded. "That should work."

I handed her the card and waited with my breath held as she ran it.

With a smile, she handed it back to me. "Okay, that worked. Here are your card keys, room two-zero-one on the second floor. Y'all have a pleasant stay."

We silently took the elevator to the second floor. Finding room 201, I slid the card key into the room's door. When the light turned green, I turned the knob and then groaned when I saw a single king-sized bed in the room. I'd forgotten to ask for two beds. I swore under my breath and set my duffel on it.

She did the same and looked around the room.

"I'll sleep on the floor," I said quickly.

Charity huffed out a breath. "This is stupid, I requested two beds online. Or, at least I thought I did. I'm so sorry."

I shook my head, and as I wandered into the bathroom, I said, "It's not a big deal. It's just a place to sleep. We'll find Eva at that event tomorrow, get our answers, then leave. No worries." I closed the bathroom door before she could respond.

Chapter 8

NOTHING EASY ABOUT THE BIG EASY

fter a long, hot shower, I emerged from the bathroom to find Charity lying in bed. She was tucked neatly under the covers with her long, curly hair splayed out on the pillow, her breathing even and steady. I watched her for a few minutes. It was so tempting to slither into those cool, white sheets and sidle up to her soft body. I could wrap my hand around her hip and nuzzle my face into her neck.

I shook my head clear of the fantasy and slid the mirrored closet doors open, searching for an extra blanket and pillow. Relieved to find them both, I lay down on the floor and hoped I could get some sleep on the hard hotel carpeting of the cheap room. I tried not to think about what may or may not be trapped in it, and told myself to just let it go. I punched the lumpy pillow a few times and covered myself in the thin blanket as the day's exhaustion overtook me.

"Nolan, I need you."

I pant, my lips just millimeters from hers. "No, Eva, I can't."

"I know you want me." Her crystal-blue eyes drill into mine. Mine are locked onto their diamond depths, unable to break the gaze.

"Your blood, it calls to me. I know you desire me, Nolan. Don't fight it. Your soul belongs to me. I can feel its light inside my dark heart. I can feel its purity shining into the very core of my being."

My eyes drift down to the mouth emitting the enchanting and frightening words. "My soul was never pure," I breathe.

A tiny laugh floats from her mouth, and like bubbles in a champagne glass, they seem to penetrate my brain. "Oh, my sweet, hot lover, yes, it is. More than you know."

I look back into her eyes. Her fingernails rake through my short hair and my own eyes roll back in my head as her scratches soothe me.

"Kiss me." Her voice seems to come from far away as I slowly re-open my eyes to meet her gaze. Instead now, where there was once brilliant blue, is solid black with no whites at all. An evil grin lights up her frighteningly pretty face.

I yell in terror.

Morning light flooded the room, and I jumped as Charity bolted upright in bed and looked down at me. I was sitting up, my hands on either side of my head as I looked down at my bent knees.

Charity jumped off the bed and laid a gentle hand on my knee, which was still under the blanket. "You okay?"

I nodded my head and blew out a breath. "I think so."

"Was it a nightmare?"

I slowly lifted my head and met the stare of eyes that had just obliterated my sleep. I gazed into their blue depths for a moment longer, curiosity and concern reflecting back at me, and nodded. "Yes, nightmare."

"Care to talk about it?" she asked, her eyes flicking between mine. Her hand was still on my knee.

I looked down at her soft, pale hand and she jerked it off with a flush of her cheeks. I looked back into her eyes. "I was dreaming about your sister."

She blinked several times, letting it sink in, before she groaned. "Eva... ugh. Figures."

I scrubbed a hand over my tired face. "Yes, and she's close by. I can feel it."

Charity's eyebrows went up. "You can *feel* her? That's odd, but it doesn't surprise me." She regarded my tired face for a moment, then said, "Tell me more about the dream."

"Well, her eyes were black. It was scary as shit."

She cocked her head to the side. "You've never seen her eyes like that before?"

Confusion colored my features. "What do you mean? I only met her the one time, so of course not."

"I bet she wiped your memory," Charity murmured.

"What?" I got up and sat back down on the bed.

"Her eyes would have turned black as she kissed you that first night, if she did, in fact, take your soul. It's what they do."

"*They?* There's more than one of her?" I asked in horror.

"Yes, succubi. They are female vampires, *femme fatales.*"

I stood and put a shirt on. I could tell she was trying not to stare at the muscular plane of my chest and stomach. I saw her gaze land on the small tattoo of script writing on my right hip as the shirt slid lithely over my torso.

I ran a hand through my hair again and said, "How do we even know she took my soul, or whatever? I mean, I know that cop, or whoever he was, told me. But how the hell does he know?"

She stretched and looked at me. "Honestly, I'm surprised to hear you say a cop visited you, because I can assure you none of the locals around Shreveport know anything about the succubus problem."

I shook my head. "It wasn't Shreveport PD. It was a fed."

Charity's eyebrows shot up. "Did he say what branch of the feds he was from?"

"Yes, but I don't remember. I do remember the Justice Department, but nothing beyond that. I thought he was bullshitting me and I asked him to leave."

She gasped. "You did?"

I put my hands low on my hips. "Yes, I thought it was a joke. I mean, come on. Didn't you flip out a little when you found out this stuff?"

"Yes, but only because it involved my sister. I wouldn't have believed these creatures existed otherwise."

I grinned and folded my arms over my chest. "So, do you see why I asked the fed to leave? It was too silly to comprehend."

Charity paused in thought for a minute. Then she looked up at me. "But you knew from the moment she kissed you that it was wrong—that she was different. Right?"

I ran my palm along the back of my neck. "I just don't know. I did feel strange, but of course I didn't attribute it to anything like that. I thought I was just hungover or something."

"And now the nightmares." She stared up at me.

I slowly nodded, knowing I'd be unable to deny it since this one had woken us both. "Yes, I admit it's pretty disturbing."

"I bet. I think it's part of the process."

I turned my head to the side. "What process?"

She sighed and looked down at her delicate hands in her lap. "The transformation to vampire."

I opened my mouth to speak, then closed it again.

She looked up at me, then stood. "I'm gonna use the facilities." She pointed at the bathroom before she disappeared behind its door.

I watched her bare legs under her short silky shorts as she walked away. Shaking my head, I slipped on a pair of jeans and began folding up the blanket I'd used. I made the bed, then piled the blanket and pillow I'd used on it when she came out.

"I'm gonna brush my teeth and whenever you're ready, we can go get something to eat, then go see what we can find in this city on succubuses and vampires. Maybe even an exorcist and a witch-doctor, if we're lucky." I smirked.

She punched me in my bicep. "Very funny. You better start taking this seriously or you're gonna regret it."

I snorted. "Okay, Red."

I heard her huff as I closed the bathroom door behind me, a grin etching my features.

Since we were staying downtown, we decided to just walk to wherever we needed to go. The city was tourist-friendly and easy to navigate, and after walking a few blocks, we found a small café to eat breakfast.

We both ordered coffee and omelets and I stared at Charity as she gazed out the large plate-glass window. The morning sun cast a glow on one side of her pretty face, her freckles looking orange in the sunbeam. Her nose was small and a little upturned, and her blue eyes glistened and seemed as if they might water. She had pinned her wild hair up, but a few curls had escaped, wrapping themselves around her neck and ears. She had her cherry-red lips pursed in thought, when she seemed to feel my gaze on her.

She brought her hand down from her mouth and fixed her eyes on mine. "What?"

I grinned. "Nothing. You okay?"

She opened her mouth to speak, but the young server brought over two steaming plates. He set them down and looked at us. "Y'all need anything else? More coffee or anythin'?"

I looked at Charity, who shook her head. I looked back up at the server. "No, we're good. Thanks."

He walked off and we ate our breakfast silently.

When we couldn't eat any more, Charity set her napkin on her plate and looked at me. "So, where are we gonna go?"

I wiped my mouth with my napkin. "I was thinking we should start with some historical places, like museums or libraries. I bet there is some serious supernatural history in this town—it is famed to be the most haunted in the country, right? So there has to be some documentation somewhere, I would think?"

She nodded and her lips twitched. "I'm sure. Did you want to take a ghost tour?"

I rolled my eyes. "No way. I want to find some real stuff."

"That's my boy."

I bit back a smile as the server returned to retrieve our plates and set the bill on our table.

After paying and leaving, we strolled down the streets until we found a place giving away free tourist maps of the city. I grabbed one and stopped walking. After spreading it out on top of a metal trash can, I scanned it quickly. Charity leaned in close and looked over my shoulder.

I tapped on a drawing of a small building. "Looks like there's a historical library only a few blocks from here. I say we start there."

Charity nodded. "I agree."

I folded the map and shoved it into the back pocket of my cargo shorts. Charity watched the action with curiosity and I could tell she was trying not to stare at how good my ass looked in these pants.

Heh…

"See something you like?" I asked, biting back a grin.

She rolled her eyes and started walking. As we strolled, I stared at all the old, historic buildings and Gothic structures which sat quietly along the street. To our right was the Mississippi River, and a warm morning breeze blew onto the street. I toyed with the idea of grabbing her hand as we strolled, then quickly dismissed it. *She probably doesn't even think of me in that way,* I mused.

We stopped short when a policeman on horseback clambered off his horse and put handcuffs on a man who had been urinating into the grass in front of St. Peter's Cathedral. The guy was clearly drunk and I watched the entire episode with raised eyebrows. The smell of booze and piss saturated the air.

I turned to Charity and shrugged. "It's five o'clock somewhere."

She giggled at the joke. We walked around the cop's horse and kept strolling until we reached the street sign indicating we needed to go north to reach the library.

The eloquent building was not hard to miss. Almost resembling a church, the old structure had chipped black and white paint, and regal steps leading up to its antique-looking front double doors. We walked up the steps. I pulled on the right-side door as it wailed on its hinges, and with a wave of my hand, I indicated for Charity to go inside.

The library was something one would see in an old movie. Cool air conditioning blasted us as we walked in and I sighed in relief. The smell of old books filled my nose. I looked up to see the ceiling was ornate and intricate; its height reaching well over twenty feet above us. It was so silent, we could hear each other's breathing. I walked past the librarian's desk when I heard a quiet voice.

"May I help you?"

I turned to see a woman, maybe mid-forties, wearing a green dress and a white sweater sitting behind a desk. She brushed a strand of black hair behind her ears and adjusted her glasses.

I contemplated asking the question, staring at the woman a few seconds longer than I should have. Deciding I had nothing to lose. I could feel Charity's stare on me, waiting for me to take the lead.

I cleared my throat. "Uh, yeah, my friend and I"—I pointed at Charity—"we're doing research on succubuses and that sorta thing."

The librarian looked at us both, then pushed up her glasses again. "I believe the plural is succubi." She grinned. "But let me look."

My eyes wandered down to her nametag, which read *Wendy*. As her attention was focused on her computer, her face lit up by its light. "Oh yes, section twelve, aisle three."

I smiled politely. "Thank you, Wendy."

She dipped her head. "I'll be here if you need anything else."

We wandered over to aisle three and began scanning the large, old books which sat neatly on the shelves.

A large, red, leather-bound book titled *Vampyre Mythology* caught Charity's eye and she used both hands to pull the book from its comfortable spot on the shelf.

"What'cha got there?" I asked.

I followed her to a reading counter where she set the book down and opened it to the table of contents. I stood behind her, easily able to read over her shoulder with my height. Her finger scanned the table of contents and stopped on one of the last sections: *Vampyre Variations*.

She turned to the appropriate page and she and I were greeted with intricate, hand-drawn illustrations of all sorts of creatures. Some resembled devils and demons with human bodies, but horns, tails, and fangs; some were beautiful, voluptuous women with fangs and red eyes. There were animals resembling gargoyles tearing humans apart with their teeth. The beautiful topless women, of course, caught my eye.

I tapped the photo of one woman with fiery red hair and huge boobs. "There's your sister."

Charity jabbed me in the stomach with her elbow. "Stop it."

I snorted at my own joke, but remained otherwise quiet.

She looked down and read the caption aloud: "A succubus is a beautiful vampyre with the power to enchant and control in order to feed off the blood and essence of unsuspecting but willing males." She frowned and looked up at me. "Well, that's not useful."

"I know," I agreed. "That doesn't tell us anything we don't already know. Except she didn't take my blood." I scratched at my right elbow with my left hand and stared at the bookcase. "I don't think."

Silently, we both scanned the rest of the book, skimming through chapters, looking for keywords like "soul" and "seven days" and "black eyes" but did not find any.

Back to the bookshelf we went. We each chose books that specifically had the word "succubus" in the title or contents, and skimmed over those. The information in the books was vague and did not cover in-depth what exactly a succubus was or how she could steal souls and turn humans into vampires. Frustrated after two hours, we both met back at the reading table.

"I got nothin'," I said with a shrug.

She sighed. "Me either."

"Guess we should go look elsewhere."

She grinned. "You sure you don't want to take a ghost tour?"

I narrowed my eyes at her and suppressed a smirk. "You know, they offer vampire tours here too. At night, of course."

She snorted and rolled her eyes. "Yeah, no thanks."

As we made our way toward the front of the library, we thanked Wendy. But before we could reach the front door, Wendy called out to us. "Didn't find what you were looking for?"

We both turned around. I put on my most disarming smile. "Not really. We were looking for something extremely specific."

Wendy adjusted her glasses, folded her hands together on her desk, and eyed us both, her brown gaze searching me curiously. "Such as?"

I cleared my throat. "Well, we had heard that a female succubus can steal a man's soul with a kiss, and within seven days, he becomes a vampire."

I did not get the laugh or the look of mockery I was expecting, so I continued cautiously. "I mean, this is all for a research paper on Mythology, you see," I lied. "I just wanted to report what true history says on the matter."

Wendy regarded us carefully, and then removed her glasses, setting them on her desk. "I don't think you're gonna find anything with that sort of detail in it... in these books, unfortunately." She inclined her head toward the book stacks. "However," she said, sliding open her desk drawer and pulled out a small card, "I know a person who could help you get more detailed information." She handed me the card.

I looked at it and my eyebrows dipped together. "Li Grand Zombi?" I looked at the librarian. "Ma'am, with all due respect, I don't understand."

She replaced her glasses and her eyes drifted back to her computer screen. "Just visit him at the address at the bottom. He will have some more information on the answers you seek."

I looked at Charity, then back at Wendy. "Well, okay. Thanks."

We left the library, making our way to the address on the card. Which wasn't difficult, since it was on the next street over.

Chapter 9

SOUTHERN VOODOO

Charity and I stood on a hot, cracked sidewalk in front of a small building with peeling pink paint. It quite easily could have been a house, but was now converted into a small business. A sign swaying on a white post on the lawn read: *Tarot readings and more.*

I looked down at her. "Are we gonna go in?"

She lifted a pale shoulder in a shrug. "I guess we kinda have to if we want answers."

"Do you think this person is gonna want money for answers?"

She laughed. "I'm quite positive of that."

I put my hand out for her to take. She looked at it, then back up into my face, and smiled. My palm was sweaty, but then again, so was hers. Aside from the humidity and heat, we were both nervous.

I rang the doorbell and squeezed her hand.

Almost a full minute passed before the door creaked open and a large Black woman wearing a long, colorful dress and an even more colorful headwrap opened the door. She narrowed her eyes at us.

"Yeah, may I help you?" she asked in a heavy accent.

I cleared my throat again and clutched the card in my hand. "Yes, ma'am, we'd like to see Li Grand Zombi."

She stared at me for a minute before bursting out laughing. "Boy, da snake diety has not been alive fo' many years. Li Grand Zombi is da name a' our shop."

Me, a bit chagrinned, but already growing annoyed, forced a polite smile and said, "Well, we were looking for some information. May we come in?"

The woman again regarded us carefully, then dipped her head in a nod. With a flourish, she ushered us inside.

I tried not to stare at the multiple figurines and religious artifacts that were littered around the small house. A strong, smelly incense that burned my nose and eyes wafted throughout the small area. It was dark inside, and a single large sunbeam dancing with dust motes was our only light. A curtain of pookah shells rattled as the woman walked through them to the kitchen area. There was a bald man with dark skin and bright green eyes sitting at a polished oak table. With precision and practice, he was shuffling a deck of what looked like oversized playing cards. Two tall, tapered candles encased in glass flanked him on either side, and more incense burned in a small bowl next to the sink.

"Who is this, Babet?" the man asked in a deep voice, looking at the woman.

"They be lookin' for some help," she replied.

The man nodded and set his cards down carefully into a neat pile. He indicated for us to sit. "What can I do for ya?"

I looked at Charity, and she nodded. I pulled a wooden chair out for her and then sat myself in the one next to it.

"Well, sir… should I call you sir?"

He nodded. "Mathieu is what I am called."

"Okay, Mathieu, we were told you might be able to give us some information on the history of the succubus."

He stared at me hard, then flicked his eyes to Charity. He seemed to stare a little bit longer than necessary at her hair, making her squirm. Looking back at me, he said, "Yet, it is more than history you seek. You seek information on a particular succubus, isn't dat right?"

"Yes, sir," I replied.

Mathieu picked up his cards and began spreading them out on the table. I recognized them as tarot cards.

"I am going to do a reading on you both. But it is twenty dollars each."

I shook my head. "Oh no, we don't want a reading, we just want —"

"It's non-negotiable, young man. I cannot help you find this demon you seek until I know who you are first," he replied, cutting me off. His voice was calm, but firm.

Charity flinched a little at the demon comment, but kept her mouth clamped shut.

I pulled two twenties from my wallet and laid them on the table. "Okay, proceed."

I was annoyed. I didn't believe in any of this fortunetelling voodoo bullshit. I sat and wondered what the hell I was even doing in this strange shop, in this strange city, with a girl I barely knew. How had my life become so complicated in such a short time? It felt like a dream I might wake from at any moment. I went from barely believing in God to having to believe in every aspect of the supernatural in one day. But I knew it wasn't a dream. I was having plenty of those, and they were just about as unpleasant as they came. The dreams about Eva were constant; every time I closed my eyes, she haunted me with a fierce aggression that disturbed me to my very core. She always taunted me, and sometimes they were so erotic, I'd wake up embarrassed. I had left that part out to Charity. I didn't see a reason to divulge that—although something told me she already knew.

"I am not liking these cards," Mathieu said. He stared at me, his deep voice breaking me out of my thoughts.

I narrowed my eyes at the cards, then back at the strange man. "And why's that?"

He held up a card depicting a hooded skeleton on a horse. "This is the card of death."

I was slightly amused. "Are you saying I'm gonna die soon?"

"Boy, this is no game. This succubus you seek, she took your very soul, didn't she?"

I sighed. "So I'm told. It's my understanding I need to find her and kill her. But honestly, I don't think I could kill her—or anyone, for that matter."

Mathieu's eyes once again drifted to Charity. He quickly shuffled them again and pulled out a card with what looked like a child sitting on a horse with a sun behind it. "This card represents the sun. You are the light to your other half, which is the dark night."

She frowned a little. "That is right. My twin sister is the succubus we need to find."

The man grunted and put the cards down. "That is very unfortunate. Because your friend is correct. If he wishes to not become a night-dwelling demon, he must kill your twin, and do it soon. I can already see your aura turnin' black, where it was once very bright yellow."

"Yellow? What does that mean? Uh… sir?" I asked.

Mathieu chuckled softly. "A yellow aura is someone who is always struggling to maintain control in their life. These people don't like to not have control of their surroundings, but are also very compassionate, generous people. Your yellow aura is fading into black, much like when the day turns into night along the horizon." Mathieu moved his gaze from mine to look over my head. "You must not squander this opportunity to get your soul back, boy. This is life or death. You will not be human any longer in three days' time."

Charity gasped as tears sprang to her eyes. "He really has to kill my sister?" She whimpered.

"Yes, girl. He must. I'm sorry. The world will be better off if he rids it of this demon who used to be your sister. She is your twin no longer. I'm sorry, child."

"Excuse me." She got up and left the room.

I sucked in a breath and looked right at the fortuneteller. "You're sure? There's no alternative?"

"Not dat I know of, son. I'm sorry."

"Any particular way? Stake through the heart? What?" I couldn't believe those words just came out of my mouth.

"It matters not," Mathieu answered. "Three days at the most, but the sooner, the better. The effects will be more permanent, the longer you wait." He looked back down at the cards, and the last one he flipped over was a card depicting a naked man and woman looking up at something in the sky. He smiled a little to himself and looked back up at me. "Card of lovers."

"What?" I asked.

He shook his head. "You have more pressing matters in which you need to tend to." He put the card of lovers back into the stack. "Now, go handle ya business, boy."

With my shoulders slumped in defeat, I thanked the man, gathered up Charity, and left the house.

I could never kill someone. Even if she wasn't human any longer.

"For whatever it's worth, I'm sorry," I murmured as Charity and I walked back in the direction of our hotel.

She sniffed and just nodded.

"Say something," I pled.

She looked up at me with bloodshot eyes. "What do you want me to say? Please don't kill my twin sister?"

"Yes."

Shock registered on her pretty face and then her copper eyebrows dipped into her forehead. "What?"

I stopped walking and took her hand. "You don't actually think I want to kill someone, do you? I don't particularly like Eva, but I don't have it in me to murder her."

"But to save yourself… anyone in your shoes would. And nobody would blame you. Like he said, she's a demon now."

I continued walking but kept hold of Charity's hand. While looking straight ahead, I said, "I don't know. I need more proof or something. This whole thing is straight outta Hollywood. It's too unreal for me."

Trying not to choke up, she swallowed hard. "Let's just find Eva. Maybe she can tell you what happened. Maybe succubi are a myth and she just took some of your blood."

I could tell she knew she was grasping at straws. She knew exactly what her sister was, but was trying to comfort me somehow.

I nodded. "She's going to that fancy ball tomorrow night, right?"

"Yes, and I think we should go. I was doing some Internet research and it seems that people wear masks and such, so she might not even recognize us. We're gonna have to find some clothes, though, it's pretty dressy."

My mouth twisted into a grin. "I know just the place."

Twenty minutes later, we found ourselves inside an eclectic costume shop I had noticed on our walk earlier. The store was small and crowded with costumes of all types, complete with props, costume jewelry, and accessories. Mannequins adorned the small front window and a counter with a cash register sat on the far right wall.

A tall, thin man wearing eye makeup, pale skin, and shiny black windswept hair smiled at us between chomps of gum. "Hey, folks. Lookin' for something specific, or just browsin'?"

Charity nodded. "We were wondering what people wear to that

vampire ball. We want to fit in and look nice, but not stand out."

The man came out from behind the counter and placed a hand on Charity's arm. "Oh, honey, I have a dress that I know will look to-die-for on your tiny little frame!" he drawled.

She followed him to the back wall. There were poles littered with poufy, gawdy gowns hanging off them, and the shop clerk began maniacally rifling through them. He pulled out a strapless dress boasting a black bodice and black-and-white checkered skirt. It reminded me of the floor of a barbershop or an old diner.

She wrinkled her nose. "Seriously? It looks like a checkerboard."

The shop clerk threw his head back and laughed. "Darlin' this is mild compared to what people are going to be wearing there — or should I say, not wearing."

I gasped at his comment and turned around holding a plain black tuxedo I'd found on a rack. "You're jokin'."

The man grinned. "Absolutely not. Some people show up in just body paint. Sometimes you have to look real close, but I can assure you, it's a trip."

Charity's eyebrows rose. "You're sure I won't look like the bride of the Mad Hatter in this thing?" She pointed at the dress.

The clerk again grinned. "Sweetheart, you absolutely *will* look like the bride of the Mad Hatter in this thing, but that's the point."

She pawed at the dangling price tag and shrugged a pale shoulder. "Well, it's only thirty bucks. Can I try it on?"

"Of course," he said, ushering her toward the back of the store with a flourish.

I shook my head and went back to the racks. There wasn't much of a selection for men, and an even smaller selection for tall men, but I was still clutching the black and white tuxedo. It looked a bit dated, like maybe some prom date had worn it in the late nineties, but I really couldn't care less. I just wanted to get into this ridiculous party and find Eva and get some answers. I held the garment up to me and then wandered to the back of the store where the fitting rooms were. Yanking open a curtain, I went inside and stripped off my cargo shorts and T-shirt. I pulled the pants on first. They fit, mostly, and then I shrugged on the white button-up shirt. It barely buttoned across my chest, but I huffed in satisfaction as I got the last button secured. Lastly, I pulled on the jacket and stretched my arms back and forth to ensure it wouldn't tear. Since there was no mirror in the crude little dressing room, I pushed back the curtain in search of one. As my eyes scanned the shop, they fell on Charity, who was also just exiting her fitting room.

The gown fit her like a glove. Her pale chest and shoulders were an elegant contrast to the black bodice of the dress, and made the black and white checks of the dress look like it was made for her. I noticed her gaze scan me from head to toe.

"That looks smokin' on you," I blurted out.

I looked over at the shop clerk, who was grinning in satisfaction.

She sucked in a breath. "Tuxedo, huh? I never pictured you to clean up that nice, but I have to say, it suits you. No pun intended, of course."

I shook my head and laughed, then wandered back into the fitting room and put my T-shirt and shorts back on. Carefully hanging the tuxedo back on its hanger, I wondered where I was supposed to get tickets to get into this big ball. What if they were sold out?

Fifty dollars poorer, we exited the vintage clothing store when we heard someone shout. "Kids!"

Charity and I turned around and saw the clerk walking quickly out of his store.

"You're gonna need these." He held two black feathered masks with sticks attached. "On the house."

Charity and I looked at each other and laughed.

"Thank you," I said with a bow of my head.

"Have fun!" he called out with a wave.

We headed back to our hotel to put our new garments up. On our way in, I stopped at the front desk.

"Hi, folks. Can I help you?" asked the clerk.

"I need to pay for another night," I said.

She smiled. "Sure, room number?"

"Uh, two-oh-one," I said.

The woman punched keys on her keyboard and gave me my total. She ran my debit card and re-swiped our card keys. As we went into the room, we carefully hung up the garments. I pulled out my phone, doing a search of New Orleans balls. One came up, a vampire ball being held downtown.

I laughed and turned the screen so she could see. "Is this the one?"

She squinted at the screen and said, "Yeah, it is."

"So stupid," I muttered. "This thing looks like a bunch of Gothic freaks obsessed with vampires and playing dress-up. I just wonder why your sister is interested in going." I looked back down at the phone and began clicking links to see how to buy tickets.

Charity gasped. "Oh, my God."

I looked up, alarmed. "What's wrong?"

"My sister has been to this ball before. In fact, she goes every year. I can't believe I'm just remembering this now."

"Huh?"

Charity had her thumbnail in her mouth, gnawing on what was left of it. "Every August she comes here. She always used to ask if I wanted to go, and I said no. I thought she was partying here. I am not into the party scene, really. She always was, though. Always dragged me to wild pool parties in high school and stuff. I refused to come here with her every year, though."

A thought hit me. "Do you think this is where she met someone who made her a succubus?"

She nodded slowly. "Yes, I'm positive of it. When she disappeared three years ago, it was right after one of her trips here. I'm thinkin' this ball is more than a bunch of posers." She looked up at me. "We're gonna have to be careful."

I looked back down at my phone and punched in my debit card numbers as I bought two tickets to the vampire ball. "Well," I said, "I won't leave your side, and once we find Eva, we're outta there. I mean it."

She seemed happy with my sincerity and need to protect, and said, "Thanks."

"I guess we'll need to formulate a plan. What are we gonna do once we find Eva?"

Chapter 10

VAMPIRE BALL

Charity fidgeted with her dress, pulling up the strapless number to ensure everything was covered. She continually smoothed down the black and white checkered skirt and toddled awkwardly on high heels. Partygoers stood in front and behind us, waiting in line to enter the large hotel that was very dark inside, from what we could see.

I curiously studied her. She had put on some extra makeup, which included smoky eyes and bright red lips, and I couldn't stop staring at her. I normally did not care for a heavily made-up face, but since I'd seen her without much on before, I found it intriguing and a little disturbing that she looked so much more like her twin now.

The thought of Eva made me shudder and my stomach to turn. I fought back nausea and tried not to think that I'd be seeing her here tonight, stealing souls and sucking blood.

But did succubi really suck blood? That was a question I never got answered. From my research in the library, I learned that a succubus did indeed need blood to survive; however, they did not need as much as a regular vampire (whatever the hell that meant), and also needed the soul of a good person to feed their life force.

I never thought of myself as a good person. I had done some things in my life I wasn't proud of, but then I remembered my dream, where Eva had told me I was a good person and how much she really liked my ju-ju… or whatever she'd said. It was almost erotic and satisfying for her to tell me I was good. I racked my brain, trying to remember the night we met. Had she produced fangs? Had she sunk them into my neck and caused me to be so tired that I had slept in until two in the afternoon the following day? And what of the nightmares? Night after night, they were relentless. Why was the crazy bitch plaguing my dreams?

Because that was how it worked, apparently.

I shook my head. I again wondered how this shit was real. Vampire, succubi, voodoo… *maybe zombies and werewolves were real, too,* I thought.

My eyes again flitted to Charity and I sucked in a breath at how pretty she looked. I wondered if I should admit my feelings about her. She was beautiful and simple and just what I'd been missing from my life. I didn't need or want complicated. But wasn't that just what I'd got? My soul stolen, my impending vampire status, and no love life to speak of. Weren't vampires immortal and allergic to sunlight? That would seriously cramp my lifestyle. I wanted no part of the life of the undead.

A shudder racked my body and I again looked at Charity, who smiled up at me with swimming blue eyes masked by black satin and feathers.

"You okay?" I asked, my hand clasped in hers.

She looked down at our linked hands and back up to me. "Nervous, but okay."

I stared down at her, my eyes scanning what I could see of her face. My gaze landed on her plump red lips and I had a sudden urge to lean down and kiss her.

This is highly inappropriate, I told myself. We were in the Big Easy to find Eva, get some answers, and go home. The thought of actually killing her was niggling at the edge of my brain, too, though, the government agent's words plagued me with every thought: *You have seven days to kill her, or else become a vampire.*

What in the holy hell did that mean, anyway? Vampires didn't exist. Well, they didn't until I'd met one. A beautiful one with sleek red hair and a luscious, jiggling ass in a tight mini-skirt.

"Tickets, please."

A voice bolted me out of my daydreams. I fished my phone from my pocket, pulled up the tickets, and handed it to a doorman, who resembled Beetlejuice. The man narrowed eyeliner-clad eyes at the screen and then up at me. Raking my body from head to toe in an uncomfortable stare, the man's gaze landed back onto me and he said, "Go inside, and have fun."

More goosebumps peppered my skin as I dragged Charity by the hand into the lobby area. We followed the signs that indicated the location of the vampire ball.

I had to suppress an eye roll as we entered the massive room. The Gothic theme was laid on extra thick, with red paint resembling blood spatters all over the walls, along with curtains in the shape of fangs flanking each doorway. The room was annoyingly dark, with a huge disco ball flickering as it twirled slowly above us. Red and white lights shone harshly onto the empty stage at the far end of the room. Eclectically dressed people milled about, some talking, most with drinks in their hands, and some of them were in the corners with their faces at each other's necks. Had I not just been through what I had in the past few days, I would have laughed at it. But now, I knew they probably were doing just what I knew vampires did best.

Resisting the urge to shudder once again, I led Charity over to the bar.

"What do you want?" I asked her.

She frowned. "I don't drink."

I raised an eyebrow and told the bartender, "Whatever you have on draft, and a Coke."

I looked back at Charity as the bartender obeyed. She was staring wide-eyed at the partygoers, but she was also scanning the crowd. I knew why.

"That's five dollars."

I turned and handed the bartender seven dollars in cash and passed Charity a plain soda in a plastic cup with a little red straw in it.

She smiled up at me. "Thanks."

I pressed the beer to my lips and winced as the bottle clanked against my mask. I'd tied the black masquerade masks behind our heads, then torn free the stick that came with them. I didn't care if it was uncool or unacceptable; no way was I holding up some stick to my face all night long. I had a feeling I'd need both hands free.

But… it turned out, I wasn't alone. A lot of the partygoers had straps around their masks.

As we stood near the bar, I asked, "Do you see her yet? Or anyone else you recognize?"

Her mouth paused at the small straw. "Not yet. And I'm only looking for Eva. I don't know any of her creepy friends. Well, now I guess I do, a guy named Brad lives at the house in Shreveport with her, and apparently, they have or have had a thing in the past."

My eyebrows shot up. "A thing?" I practically yelled over the Muse song blasting through the speakers placed strategically around the ballroom.

She nodded with the straw at her lips. I again wished I could touch them, even if just with my finger. I stared at them she spoke. "Yes, he made a disgusting proposition to me as I was in Eva's room earlier."

I chuckled. "Disgusting how?"

She wrinkled her nose and let her plastic cup dangle at her side. "Uh, do you really need details?"

"Yes, yes I do."

She waved her free hand. "Men. Do you think of anything other than sex?"

I shook my head. "I don't think so, no."

She snorted again. "Well, apparently he lives in the ridiculous mansion with her and God knows who else, and he indicated that they may have had a previous sexual relationship."

My beer paused at my lips and I looked down at her. "Why do you need to make it sound so clinical? So they were friends with benefits. So what?"

She shrugged. "You asked, I was just telling you."

I shook my head, wondering what kind of woman Charity was. While her twin oozed sexuality and inhibition, she seemed a lot more closed off and conservative. I wasn't sure if I liked it or not.

Still standing at the bar, I set my empty bottle on the bar top and signaled for another. The bartender complied and I was soon sucking down a second frosty beer. I looked at Charity and pondered her. Had she ever been in a relationship? Was she jealous of her sister? What did she plan to do with her life? Was she a virgin?

The last thought made me kick myself mentally. *None of your business, dude.*

"Do you want to dance?" I blurted out, pointing the tip of my beer bottle at the quickly crowding dance floor.

She nodded, setting her almost empty soda cup on the bar. "I would love to," she answered close to my ear.

I chugged the last of my beer and set the empty bottle on the bar.

I grabbed Charity's soft hand and she went pliantly with me. A slow Paramore song crooned through the speakers and I pressed Charity's body up close to mine. She seemed to melt into me and I closed my eyes. It had been way too long since I held a beautiful woman in my arms. She smelled amazing and I inhaled her hair. She linked her arms around my neck and craned hers to look up at my masked face.

We began the slow dance circle, and after the third turn, I leaned down and whispered in her ear, "The mask is really hot."

She bit back a smile and replied, "Hot as in, cool and sexy, or hot as in, sweating your ass off?"

I threw back my head and laughed, my body shaking as I held her. "I meant sweaty, but on you? Cool and sexy for sure."

She gave a faux gasp and drawled, "Are you flirting with me, Nolan?"

I nodded with a grin. "Yeah, it looks that way."

"What's your last name?" she blurted.

"Bishop."

She nodded. "Mine's Sheridan. Not that you asked or anything…"

I laughed. "Well, I didn't need to, I heard you tell the hotel clerk earlier. I'm not gonna lie, that's quite a mouthful."

She giggled. "I know. I still can't get our parents to tell us why we gave us such odd names."

"I don't think Charity and Eva are odd names," I said seriously.

"We were born premature, about two months early. I think when we survived, our parents were very… charitable. To God or whoever."

I nodded. "I see."

"I still don't know why they chose Eva, though…"

"Well, Eva sounds like Eve, the first female who cursed y'all. Sounds appropriate to me."

"You do have a point there, I never thought of that…" Her rambling was cut short.

I felt a tingle crawl up my spine and looked in the direction she was staring. An entourage of beautiful women entered the club. She stopped dancing and jutted her chin toward the ballroom's entrance. "I think my sister has just arrived."

The same group of smokin' hot women I'd seen at The Blue Room entered the ballroom. Except this time, they had traded in their miniskirts and midriff-baring tops for ball gowns. Each of the beautiful entourage had on ones in red, black, and white. Eva's gown was, amusingly, black and white, just like her twin's. Except this one had a white bodice with spaghetti straps and a black skirt overlaid in lace. The huge difference, however, was that Eva had no shame in showing off plenty of cleavage, her tits practically spilling out the top. Her blonde friend, along with the dark-skinned one, flanked her. She and her friends again caused all the patrons to stop and stare. Except now they all wore party masks over their faces. But I could spot Eva a mile away. She still had the sharp, blunt red haircut and shiny lips. After all, there wasn't much she could do with hair that short, and as I looked down at Charity, I went to say something, but she was already frowning.

"It *is* Eva," she breathed.

"I know," I whispered in her ear.

She blew out a breath. "I haven't seen her in… forever."

"I have an idea," I said, letting go of her hand. "Let me approach her. Tell her about the vampire stuff. Maybe she'll talk to me."

"She'll want to do more than talk," Charity said with narrowed eyes.

I huffed out a breath. "Isn't this what we came here for? To find your sister and get answers?"

She reluctantly nodded, letting go of my hand.

"So we meet again," were my first words to Eva, spoken with more confidence than I felt.

Eva's head swiveled in the direction of my seductive suggestion, and her three friends' heads followed suit.

An evil smirk twisted up on her pale, powdered face and she breathed, "Oh, I didn't think I'd see you again, Nolan."

Surprised she'd remembered my name, or could even recognize me with the mask, I retorted with arms folded, "What's a vampire doing at a vampire ball? That's a bit cliché, don't you think?"

Her confident and flirty grin turned into a frown. She eyed me from head to toe. "A grease monkey in a monkey suit. That's rich." Her friends cackled with laughter, but Eva kept a straight face. "What the hell do you want?" she asked me.

Thankfully, the beer had relaxed me enough where the intended insult didn't get under my skin. Instead, I plastered on my most disarming smirk and replied, "What do I want? I want my soul back, *succubus.*"

More shock registered on her face, then she put on a face of impassivity. "Good luck with that, asshole."

I wanted to gasp in surprise. I wanted to wrap a hand around her throat and squeeze until she cried and begged for forgiveness and bargained for her life. But I knew something like that would not only get me kicked out of the party faster than a vampire on LSD, it would also be done very painfully by what I assumed were very strong vampire bouncers positioned around the room.

I stared down at her, my hands balling into fists at my sides as I stretched them open and closed in order to maintain control. I decided on another angle. "So, I guess you won't mind that when I turn into a night-crawling demon, if I just go ahead and eat your sister then? Because I have to tell you, Eva, that I'm already feelin' kinda twitchy and craving blood, and hers calls out to me the more time we spend together," I lied.

It was Eva's turn to register shock. Her blue gaze slid behind me to see her sister standing about ten feet away wearing the black and white checkered ballgown. The mask did nothing to hide her identity from her twin, and the mass of red curls piled on her head was unmistakable.

She shifted her angry gaze back to me, her blue eyes turning black, causing me to flinch. "You wouldn't dare."

I reined in the fear I felt at her frightening appearance, knowing I'd hit a nerve. "I have no idea what I would do or not do, Eva. From what I understand, I'll be something close to an animal. Charity has sure taken a liking to me, and I imagine with her sweet and caring nature, she's gonna want to help me through this difficult time. Who's to say I won't snap and bite her—even kill her once I change over?"

Her eyes went back to blue and the war inside her head was reflected through her angry gaze. Seeming like she was trying to hold onto her pride and tough exterior, the depths of her own soul, if she had one, reflected back fear and uncertainty. It was the desired response I had hoped for.

"Follow me." She turned on her high heel and stormed toward the exit.

I obeyed, prepared for the worst.

As we exited, I glanced at Charity, putting up a finger to indicate for her to stay put. I could see her face grow stormy as she shook her head. She set her soda cup on a nearby empty table and weaved her way through the ever-expanding crowd. I sighed. I knew she wasn't going to stay put.

After exiting through the back door, we found ourselves in an alley.

There were two dumpsters pushed up against the wall, and a tall streetlight above us lit them all in a hazy orange glow.

I opened my mouth to speak, but Eva started first.

"Listen here and listen good, you bastard. If you so much as harm one hair on Charity's head, I will rip you apart slowly, and I will enjoy every second of it—"

"Don't you dare threaten me, you crazy bitch," I cut Eva off, pointing a finger in her face. "You did this to me! You had no right to steal from me!"

Eva lifted a shoulder in a shrug and looked at her fingernails. "A girl's gotta eat."

I lost it. "You're gonna stand there and tell me you had a *right* to do what you did? Why don't you do everyone a favor and kill yourself."

She gasped. "You're an asshole. Go to hell!"

"That's where you're headed if you don't give me back what's mine. Do that weird eye thing you did and give it back."

She folded her arms over her chest and narrowed her eyes. "No. You came out here to kill me, didn't you? I don't see any weapons on you."

I took a deep breath and ran a hand across the back of my neck. "Eva, why do you think I approached you civilly tonight? I'm asking you to give me another way out of this. I could have waited for you to leave tonight, followed you, then shoved a stake in your heart, but I didn't. I am trying to be reasonable about this before it gets ugly. There has got to be another way. There just has to be. Tell me, Eva. Tell me now. I'm only gonna ask once before I stalk you to the ends of the Earth. And if you think I'll stop once I turn into this freak of nature, you have another thing coming, sweetheart. I will never, ever stop."

She clamped her mouth shut and licked her teeth, regarding me. She again seemed to be warring with herself. Her eyes flicked around and she spotted her sister. "Charity, what are you doing out here? Go back inside the party."

I turned around. As I did, I felt something hard hit the back of my head. I went down with a thud to the pavement and Charity let out a blood-curdling scream, rushing over to me.

I groaned and turned over, trying to get up, but stars floated in my vision. I could see two of Eva standing over me, grinning and shaking out her hand. "That fucking hurt. But it was worth it. Go to hell, Nolan."

Damn. *She hits hard for a girl!*

Charity looked up to her sister with tears forming along her lashes. "Why did you do that? He was trying to be civil!"

"He threatened me. You tell him when he wakes up that if he ever threatens me again, I'll kill him. I mean it. And, Charity? Stay away from him. I'm not kidding."

"You're a monster, Eva," her twin choked out. "I hate you."

Eva laughed and signaled for her friends to follow her back into the party.

Charity looked down at me, and right before everything went black, she screamed, "Somebody help me!"

Chapter 11

UNEXPECTED HELP

I awoke in a strange, dark room and blinked several times, trying to get my bearings. The air reeked of something heavy and perfumy, and there were low voices mumbling something off in the distance. My head pounded along with the beat of a far-off bass drum. My mouth felt as if I'd been sucking on cotton. I groaned and sat up slowly on my elbows.

I rubbed my eyes then put a hand to the back of my head. The base of my skull was tender to the touch and swollen, and I racked my brain to try to remember what happened.

Eva! I had been talking to Eva and Charity showed up. I remembered nothing after that. I sat up further and squeezed my temples with my palms, trying to get the pounding to stop. I opened my eyes to slits and looked around. The room I was in seemed to be some kind of office storeroom. There was a faint red glow illuminating the room as its only light, and as my eyes drifted past the neatly stacked piles of janitorial supplies, alcohol bottles, and glasses, I saw a desk and a chair, a large window to its right. I eyed the crude cot I had been lying on and shook my head. Where the hell was I, and where was everyone else?

I got up, slowly walked to the window, and peered out. The glass was tinted dark, and as I looked out over the ballroom I had just been in, I could see the party was in full swing. I lazily brought my watch up to my face and squinted at it. It had just gone past midnight, and I sighed. I found a case of bottled water and used what little strength I had to punch a hole in the plastic overwrap and snatch out a bottle. Cracking off the lid, I downed the contents and wished I had some aspirin. I sat back on the cot.

I again wondered how I'd gotten up here. Surely Charity couldn't have dragged me up, even if there was an elevator. There was just no way, I was too heavy. But where was Charity? Did her sister hurt her or take her, and some stranger brought me here? I began to panic.

I then remembered the reason I'd awoken. I had been dreaming, again, of that evil bitch. I shook my head to rid my brain of the disturbing and erotic images and groaned, again grabbing my head to try and stay the dizziness.

I got up again slowly, sliding my phone from my pocket. As I made my way to the door to leave, it swung open. Charity and a tall, older man in a suit walked in. They were followed by a shorter plain-looking man, also in a suit. When the older man smiled at me, wrinkles creased around his light-brown eyes. His salt-and-pepper hair was mostly covered by a derby hat.

"Finally awake, I see," he said in a deep voice that sounded threatening, but belied the friendly look on his face. The other man went to stand in the corner of the room with his hands folded in front of him. Like a guard.

"Oh, thank God!" Charity cried, rushing over to me. She was still in her party dress, her mask long since discarded. I realized mine was also gone.

"How do you feel?" the stranger asked.

I looked up at him, and said with irritation coloring my tone, "Who are you?"

The man dipped his head and smiled again. "My apologies. My name is Joel Reichert, and this is Ansel. I own this hotel."

I sighed. "How did I get up here in this room? Why am I here?"

"I carried you. Ansel and I heard your girlfriend scream." He inclined my head at Charity, then to the silent stranger.

"Oh, I'm not his—" she started.

I cut her off. "Did you see who hit me?" I got up and went to the window, looking down at the crowd.

"She's not there," Charity said, as if reading my thoughts.

I turned a little too quickly to look at her and moaned again, holding the back of my head. I then looked at Joel. "Do you have an ice pack or something?"

Joel nodded. "Of course." He went to a small fridge I hadn't noticed before and opened it up. As the door was open, the interior light revealed several stacks of bagged blood. I bit back a gasp. The man pulled a small ice tray out from the fridge's upper freezer and popped them out into a washrag, balling it up and handing it to me. He shut the fridge.

"Here ya go," he said.

I didn't take my eyes off the man. "You're a vampire."

Joel again nodded. "Yes, young man, I am. And from what your girlfriend told me, it seems you will be one soon, too."

My eyes drifted to the silent stranger standing in the corner, then back to Joel.

"Can you help us stop it?" Charity asked, helping me adjust the ice pack onto the back of my head.

"I don't know, but I'm gonna lean towards no."

I studied him again. "You're not what I expected from a vampire. I haven't met any yet. Well, except a succubus."

Joel nodded. "Yes, that's why I don't think I can help you. Vampires made from a succubus are different from ones made through a blood exchange."

"What's that even mean?" I asked on a sigh, exhaustion suddenly seeping into my body.

"Well," Joel said, going to stand in front of the large, one-way window and peering down at the party. "Normal vampires are made when a vampire feeds a human being his blood. He, in turn, has to drink a little of the human's blood. Not a lot, just enough. In three days, he or she fully matures into a vampire, ending their human existence and becoming a creature of the night, never to age, never to go in the sun again."

I wrinkled my nose. "Why would anyone even want that?"

The man snorted, his whole body jerking at the gesture. "I have asked myself that every single day for the last one hundred and seven years."

Charity and I gasped in unison.

Joel turned around and looked at us. "But a vampire made by a succubus stealing a soul is different. It doesn't require a blood exchange, or any blood at all. Becoming a vampire is just a nasty side effect of the soul-stealing. Since we are, as we have come to find out, soulless creatures. But please don't mistake that for not having a heart, so to speak. We can still feel physical and emotional pain and have compassion and empathy. It's just a bit more limited and clipped the older we get. However, the vampire made from a succubus really cannot. They are feral creatures, only bent on satisfying their own physical needs, both hunger and sexual."

"You're joking," I said, narrowing my eyes at the man.

"I am not. You better pray to whatever god you have, boy, because by the looks of you, I bet you've got about three to four days tops to find your succubus and kill her, or your fate will be just that."

"Can you help me kill her?" I asked suddenly.

Joel shook his head. "I can help you find her, but you ultimately have to end her life, nobody else. It cannot work any other way. If I kill her, you will still turn into a monster."

I frowned and said, "Oh." Then I turned to Charity. "What happened in the alley?"

She cast her eyes down at her wringing hands. "I came out to see what was going on and Eva spotted me. As she called my name, you turned around, and she hit you very hard, knocking you unconscious."

A growl emitted from me and surprised everyone in the room.

"Eva Sheridan?" Joel asked as I inclined my head to the side.

Charity nodded, surprised. "Yes, she's my sister."

Joel's face lit up in a smile and he snapped his fingers. "That's why you look so damn familiar. I know Eva. She makes a large donation every year to the vampire ball."

"Yeah, she's quite charitable," Charity snapped under her breath.

Joel turned and looked at me. "Why were you talking to Eva Sheridan in the alley, young man? Don't you think you have enough succubus problems? I know they're beautiful and all, but you really should stay away from them."

I stood, ignoring the pain in my head. My hands balled into tight fists, I roared, "That *is* my succubus!"

Joel's eyes went wide, then lit with amusement. "And you didn't kill her because...?"

I sighed. "I was trying to reason with her. Trying to get her to tell me if there was another way to get my 'soul' back without resorting to murder." I made air quotes with my fingers.

"How did you even know you had to kill her?" Joel asked out of curiosity.

"I read a lot," I replied flatly.

"Well, kid, you shouldn't believe everything you read. Especially these days. Everyone loves themselves a vampire book, and most of them aren't even close to reality. But lucky for you, whatever you read was correct. If you kill Eva within seven days, you will get your life back."

"It wasn't a fiction book I read, I found some old literature at the library here in New Orleans," I replied through gritted teeth.

Joel nodded and went to look out the window again. "Smart young man you are, such a waste…" he trailed off quietly.

"Tell me, Mr. Reichert, what happens if you go in the sunlight?" I asked suddenly.

Without turning around to look at us, his hands still behind his back, he replied, "We die."

I nodded and looked at Charity, then asked, "Can you be more specific?"

Joel turned around this time, half sitting on the windowsill. With his arms folded across his chest, he said, "All right. We begin to smoke, then our skin catches on fire. We then erupt into a searing ball of flames, and we turn to ash and die forever."

"Thank you, that was very specific. This goes for all vampires, right? A succubus included?"

Joel narrowed his eyes at me. "Yes. But I suggest stabbing, shooting, or decapitating. It's quieter and quicker. Well, maybe not the shooting, but you get my drift. Unless you use a bow and arrow…"

Charity whimpered and her eyes got misty. "The thought of you doing any of those things to my sister makes me sick. Let's go, Nolan."

I nodded. "Thank you for the water and the ice pack." I set the soppy washcloth on a nearby desk.

"Anytime, Nolan. I wish I could have been more help. I really do. Best to you."

I nodded at Joel, then shot a glance again at the other man in the corner of the room. Charity and I left, softly closing the door behind us. However, something told me to listen at the door before we left. I indicated to Charity to be quiet as I pressed my ear to the door.

"Ansel, what do you think?" Joel asked.

In a deep drawl, he replied, "Like always, Joel, feral animals need to be put down so they don't expose us all."

Joel sighed. "You keep a tight tail on him, and if he doesn't kill his succubus, he's all yours."

Chapter 12

DEFEAT WITHOUT DESPAIR

I loosened my tie with my finger, slid it off in a loop from around my head, and threw it on the floor. I sank down on the bed in our hotel room and put my head in my hands.

"What in the hell am I supposed to do now?"

Charity came to sit next to me and swallowed hard, replying quietly, "It seems you only have one option if you want to live."

I lifted my head and stared into her eyes. "Murder? Really?"

She shrugged, sighed in sorrow, and then shook her head. I watched as she went into the bathroom and closed the door.

I hated Eva. She had assaulted me, and had raped me of my soul, and she needed to be stopped. But did I hate her enough to kill her? The more I thought about it, the more I decided yes, I did. I was getting to the point where I was starting not to care about her life anymore. It was clear she was not going to stop. After all, didn't she need to continue to steal souls in order to live? Continue to hurt and kill men to live? She had to be stopped. Her attitude at my confrontation, combined by her physical assault and the growing rage I felt bubbling up in me growing stronger every hour, I decided I no longer cared.

I heard Charity softly sobbing in the bathroom through the thin, wood door, and swore under my breath. I suddenly realized I did care. I knew I'd hurt her if I did it. I'd lose her. But did I really have her? There was something blossoming between us, that was for sure. I was feeling things I hadn't felt in a very long time, and it was all soft and happy feelings when it came to Charity. It was in direct contrast to the feelings I had toward her twin, which were angry, violent, and homicidal.

I again grabbed my head, but this time to calm the war raging there. It was as though the feelings were in my head—in my brain—not in my heart. The organ in my chest felt empty. It was conflicting, scary, and extremely unpleasant. I stood up and began pacing on the cheap carpet of the hotel room. It was down to me versus her. I could save myself and lose Charity, or lose myself and she'd inevitably lose me, too. How was that even a choice? I'd have to swallow back the sadness I saw Charity's eyes when the subject came up and deal with the aftermath. The fallout would be ugly and she'd hate me forever, but at least my forever would only be about fifty more years, not five hundred.

Besides, I reasoned, what did I owe her, anyway? Nothing, really. She was trying to help me, sure, but why did she come along with me to New Orleans? She was trying to help her sister, and help me. Perhaps she didn't know what she really wanted. She had to know deep down that whatever her sister used to be was long gone. I had heard that twins could have opposite personalities, but there was just no way Eva was this much of an evil bitch before becoming a succubus.

My pacing increased and a knuckle went to my mouth as I wondered something. How did Eva even become a succubus? It couldn't have been through a "blood exchange" like Joel had explained. There was something else, and I was going to find out. There had to be more to this. I also wondered why my friends Parker and Brennan hadn't been affected — hadn't had their souls stolen. Weren't Eva and her beautiful friends all succubi? Too many questions rolling around in my brain caused my already pounding head to hurt even worse. I remembered Parker saying they hadn't even got to first base with them. Maybe the kiss was the key?

Charity emerged from the bathroom wearing shorts and a tank top. Her gaudy ball gown was slung over her arm and she hung it up in the closet. She held a tissue to her nose and sat on the bed. "I'm very tired, Nolan, I'm gonna go to bed now."

I looked at her freshly scrubbed face with her red-rimmed eyes and her mouth pulled down into a frown. I could practically feel the sorrow oozing off her. I sucked in a breath as my stomach did a flip-flop.

I sat on the bed next to her and grabbed her hand. It felt warm and soft and I stroked it with my thumb. "Tomorrow I'm gonna drive you back to Shreveport. This is something I need to handle alone, and I was wrong to ask you to come with me."

She sniffled. "You didn't ask me, I wanted to come. I guess I just wanted to say goodbye to Eva." The last word caused her voice to hitch, a sob jerking up out of her throat.

"Fuck." I pulled her into a hug. She melted easily into my broad chest and cried until there were no more tears. I smoothed her hair and closed my eyes as guilt washed over me and my anger from earlier ebbed. She, with just a look, had doused the fires of rage and caused my resolve to waver once again. I laid her down on the bed and then lay down too, curling my body around her small frame. I held onto her like I never wanted to let her go. Pushing her wild hair away from her face, I kissed her cheek, then lay back on the pillow.

She seemed to have trouble falling asleep. I had no doubt she was overcome with exhaustion like me, but her mind was probably reeling like a movie on fast-forward like mine was.

"Nolan?" she whispered.

"Yes, beautiful?"

She exhaled a sigh. "I couldn't stop crying over the sight of seeing you fall to the ground unconscious. That scared me more than anything." More tears of anger spilled from her eyes. "My sister caused that. She is nothing but an evil shell of the person she used to be… and… and I keep telling myself I need to let her go. It's just so… hard." She squeaked, and more sobs jerked her small body.

I held her tighter and waited for her calm down. I stroked her arm with my thumb and shushed into her ear. Eventually, her breathing became even and slow. When I was sure she was asleep, I finally let go of everything and fell asleep too, exhaustion blanketing me.

The room is a mixture of Gothic and Victorian. A large bed with a lacy canopy, an antique sitting table in the corner, two nightstands, one with a laptop on it, and a closet, its door closed. Moonlight shines through an open window, its lacy black curtains blowing in the breeze. The colors of the room are all blacks and reds.

"She may look like me, but she doesn't have my skills," Eva says, breaking me out of my evaluation of the room. Her red fingernail traces up my bare chest.

"That may be true, but you have yet to show me any real skills," I reply flirtatiously, licking my lips and staring at her plump pink ones.

Eva leans down slowly and runs her tongue and mouth over my neck, and I moan in appreciation. I begin to slowly unbutton her sheer white top, and once I reached the last button, I throw it off her shoulders. I groan at her perfect breasts pushed up by a lacy white bra.

"See? You want me, you have always wanted me, Nolan," she says, taking in my satisfied expression.

My eyes rake once more over her smooth, pale body and I lean down, unzip the side zipper of her short, black skirt, and slide it off her creamy thighs. The matching white lace panties are pretty, but in the way.

"That's right, take me. You will never have anything so perfect in your life."

I run kisses up her thigh, stomach, and the valley between her breasts. My mouth reaches her neck and I inhale sharply. I'm consumed with an overcoming and surprising desire to bite her. Giving in without a second thought, I feel my mouth water and my eyeteeth sharpen, and then I bite into her soft, pallid flesh. Blood squirts out and splashes her white bra and she laughs. "That's right, baby, that feels so good."

I lift my head and look into her now-black eyes. With my head tilted up, I catch a glimpse of myself in the mirror attached to Eva's headboard. I see my own eyes, black as crude oil with no whites at all. Blood drips down my chin and my fangs peek out over my bottom lip. I scream.

Charity jerked up as my holler assaulted her ears.

I was already out of bed. I had rolled out and onto the floor in shock from my dream. I stood up and looked at Charity, who stared at me in horror. She reached over and flipped on a bedside lamp.

"Do I even need to ask?" she drawled in a raspy voice.

I shook my head and began to pace. "They're getting worse. God, I wish it would stop. I was the vampire in this one. I swear that crazy bitch is slithering into my dreams. She's probably laughing right now as we speak."

She worried her lip and looked down in thought. "I don't think you dream the same dream as her. I think you guys are just connected somehow after she did what she did to you." I thought she looked a little jealous.

I fixed her with a stare and turned my head to the side. "How do you know so much?"

She smirked. "I read a lot."

I huffed out an ironic noise and continued to pace.

"Come back to bed," she said quietly. "I haven't slept that well in months."

I looked at her and licked my lips. "Until I screamed in your ear."

She grinned. "Right. But before that, it was totally awesome sleep."

I looked at the bedside clock, which read 5:03 a.m. I yawned and crawled in, spooning her once again, trying not to think of my dream about Eva. I might embarrass myself if I didn't put my thoughts elsewhere. I heard her sigh contentedly as I slung a tattooed arm around her and smoothed her hair back with my hand. I was tired, but afraid to go to sleep.

The drive back to Shreveport was done mostly in silence. I spent it looking at the lush, green Louisiana landscape as it passed by in a blur. My thoughts were scattered. Still with no firm strategy in mind, I did plan on waiting in Shreveport until Eva came back, then I would strike. I had an advantage over her: I knew where she lived, and she had no idea I was privy to this information. I was going to do this alone and leave Charity out of it.

The Charger slowly rumbled to a stop in front of the Stop-N-Shop, and I killed the engine. Night blanketed the city, and the only lights were from the store as they reflected off Charity's copper hair.

I looked at her, then at the store. "I can't believe you live here."

"Thanks," she replied dryly.

I shook my head. "No, I meant, you don't seem like the type. You could do so much more."

She sighed. "You sound like my parents. After Eva went missing, I sort of felt like my life was on hold. I just didn't feel like moving forward. I'd dropped out of college and worked at the Stop-N-Shop stocking shelves." She looked down and fidgeted with the hem of her shirt. "Living in the small loft above the store was one step up from living with my parents, I guess. I certainly didn't want to be twenty-one and still living at home."

"Nothing wrong with it, though," I said quietly.

She chuckled softly. "Trust me when I say that stocking shelves isn't a career, but instead something to bide my time until I could figure out how to get Eva back. Yes, I've been wasting the last three years of my life hoping Eva would come back to me. To us."

I felt so bad for her, but nodded at her to continue.

"But after this weekend, I realized that just wasn't happening." With a sigh, she looked over at me. My eyes searched hers questioningly and I saw her gaze rake over my arms and chest. I was wearing only a snug blue T-shirt and the harsh lines and swirls of my arm tattoo were peeking out from beneath the sleeve. She reached up and traced her fingers over the intricate design.

She licked her lips and looked back up into my eyes. "I do what I gotta do. I don't rely on anyone but myself. I work hard to keep a roof over my head and food on my small table." She let out a little grin.

I nodded at her. "And that's all we can do."

She put her hand on the door handle, and then said, "What's next for you, Nolan?"

I broke her intense stare and looked straight ahead. "I don't know. I will find Eva again, and when I do, it will be then that I decide if I want to live or if I want to die... or be undead, as I'm hearin'."

Charity frowned. "I wish I could help you with that, but as you have probably guessed, I'm at... what do we say?" She looked off into the black night. "Oh, an impasse."

I stared at her. "Is that so? I haven't won you over with my charms? Do you think I'll be more charming and sexy as a vampire? Hey, maybe I'll sparkle in the moonlight."

She laughed. "I'll admit, after meeting Mr. Reichert, I was surprised that vampires could seem so normal. Although, he seemed a bit emo, don't you think?"

I turned my head to the side. "Emo?"

She snorted. "Depressed, down, melancholy."

"No, he seemed like a normal guy to me."

She sighed. "Maybe I was just reading into it then."

"May I walk to you to the door?" I asked, gesturing toward the store.

With that, she smiled. "I'd like that."

As I got out, I noticed she waited in the car. This made me grin. She'd been raised right. Wished I could say the same for her witch of a sister.

I opened the passenger door and helped her out. I glanced around the dark parking lot as I relieved her of her backpack and held it loosely in my hand.

"Lead the way," I said with a flourish.

We went around to the back of the store, which was nothing more than an alley. A heavy gray metal door was set to the back of the building, and as soon as we reached it, I pushed her up against its cold surface and dropped her purple backpack to the ground.

Moonlight danced off her pale skin before I brushed a stray red curl from her face and pressed my lips down onto hers. She only had a second to gasp before my lips sealed over hers.

Slowly snaking in my tongue, I grinned around her mouth when I felt her tongue slide onto mine. Her short fingernails were soon raking through my hair, and I felt her press her soft body into mine. My unmistakable arousal was pushed against her, and I wrapped a hand around her slim waist.

Coming up for air, I looked down at her and said, "No matter what happens, I will never be sorry I met you. I just wish it had been under other circumstances."

Panting and out of breath, Charity wiped her puffy bottom lip with her finger and then traced it down my temple, slithering it around my cheekbone, then down to my jaw. "Nolan, I think you should do what you gotta do. I will be here when you're done. No hard feelings, either."

She leaned up and pressed her lips once more to mine. Then she broke contact, shoved a key into the lock of the ugly gray door, and disappeared behind it. I was left standing speechless. Although the smile that crept up my face was impossible to erase.

I got into my car, started it with a rumble, and headed back toward my apartment. I was unable to wipe that grin from my face until my mind eventually drifted to my current predicament. That had me pounding my steering wheel in frustration and cussing under my breath.

WEAPON OF VAMP DESTRUCTION

I slammed the door to the apartment a little too hard. Half relieved and half disappointed there were no federal agents waiting for me in the parking lot when I got home, I threw my keys on the dining room table and grabbed a beer from my fridge.

I slumped down onto the sofa and didn't even bother picking up the remote. I sipped the cool, bitter liquid, languishing at the feel of it sliding down my throat. With my other hand, I tapped out an imaginary rhythm on my left thigh, wondering what was next for me. Truth be told, I was almost afraid to go to sleep. The dreams about Eva were relentless, and something told me they were on purpose. That Eva had some way of worming herself into my dreams and causing me to think of her.

Well, I was sick of it already.

I downed the rest of my beer and tossed the bottle into the trash. I pushed the button to boot up my laptop. I barely used the damn thing. I was usually too tired or too busy at the end of the day to get on it. After a few agonizing minutes, I went to Google and typed in *Succubus*.

The results were frightening. Foolishly, I clicked on the Wikipedia link and gasped. "Demon? Just like Mathieu had said."

Although, that did not stop me from continuing to read. My eyes skimmed hungrily over the webpage, feeling horrified at what I saw. Yet, like a train wreck, I couldn't look away.

Did I dare click on "images"? Of course I did. More frightening photos of female demons, some of the photos very X-rated—much like my dreams about Eva.

I searched and read for almost an hour. I couldn't find much about a succubus turning a human into a vampire. It was all very vague and folktale-ish and with a sigh, I shut down the device and slammed the lid shut.

I wandered into the kitchen and pulled open a drawer. At the top was the card for the federal agent who had come to see me. I studied it again. It looked pretty legit to me. "Roger Nelson, Agent, Department of Justice." Nothing about the supernatural. But as I studied the card more, I looked closely at the yellow logo and could see something about a supernatural bureau on it, which featured an eagle with an olive branch in its mouth set in the center of an official-looking seal.

There was a phone number on it that I contemplated calling. I felt like I was losing my mind. I had kicked Agent Nelson out, and now, here I was, contemplating calling him for help. But what could this agent do for me? The only thing he was going to do was tell me to kill Eva. Another shudder racked my body and I threw the card back in the drawer, slamming it shut.

I made my way into my bedroom and found myself being pulled to my walk-in closet. I flipped the light on and a dim beige glow lit the small space. Neatly hung clothes lined the racks, all the hangers one finger width apart, just how I liked them. Neatly stacked shoeboxes of letters and other treasures were piled on top of the shelves.

Then, I saw it.

Tipping my head to the side, a small grin twisted my lips. Standing on tiptoe, I reached up and grabbed the large buck knife my father had given me on my eighteenth birthday. My dad had always been a big outdoors person. Hunting, fishing, camping, Mark Bishop had dragged his wife and kids out camping and fishing every year whenever the weather was nice. I also loved it. My sister, Natalie? Not so much. She went along with us, but she was a typical girl. No showers or electrical outlets and she whined.

I carefully pulled the large weapon from the top shelf and unsheathed it. The shiny, unused blade glinted off the soft light from the overhead bulb. I stared down at it and ran my finger gingerly over the metal.

Could I plunge this through Eva's chest? *A very nice chest, I might add.* Feeling a bit twitchy and uneasy, I continued to run my finger over its shiny surface and envisioned it splattered with blood. I then imagined running my tongue along the blade and licking the blood clean off its smooth exterior.

I lightly smacked my own face. "Get a grip," I groaned to myself.

I re-sheathed the blade into its leather casing and took it to the living room, setting it on the coffee table.

Going to the fridge, I opened the door and grabbed a beer. As I popped the top off, I wondered how many I had to drink in order to stop me from dreaming about her once my eyelids slid shut. I also had a headache and rubbed a hand along the back of my head. A large lump had formed and was tender to the touch. I shook my head and sat on the couch once again, staring at the buck knife. It was so large, it almost resembled a sword. The weapon reminded me of my father, and I briefly wondered if I should go to my dad for advice. I always did when I was having any sort of problem. My father had always been my rock, my mainstay, my friend. But when it came to this, I knew I couldn't. Dad had a big heart and would do anything for his family, but he was simple; as simple as they came. A family man. A Louisiana native who had only left the state once in his life to travel to Mississippi in high school to play a state football championship, I knew my dad wouldn't get this. He would probably laugh at me and ask me if I was doing drugs or something.

My thoughts drifted to my sister. I wondered if she could help. Natalie had just graduated from LSU with a degree in Education. She had just interviewed for a job teaching American History at a local high school. I wondered if she would believe me, or be of any help. Either way, I believed that in three or four days' time, I was going to turn into something sinister and inhuman, and the last thing I wanted was to harm my own family. I would have to disappear, and my family would have to know why. I wouldn't leave them wondering if I was dead, lying in a ditch somewhere. Maybe my sister was the one person I could talk to. Maybe she could help. Perhaps she had some words of wisdom for me, like always.

With the beer bottle paused at my lips, my gaze coasted back to the knife. I wished I could bring it into my dreams with me, just like in the old *A Nightmare on Elm Street* movie, and kill my stalker while I slept, just so the dreams would stop and the nightmare could end.

Candlelight bounces off the blue silk sheets, casting a glow like the choppy sea onto the white walls of the small bedroom. Black lace curtains billow in the breeze from a partially open window, and moonlight streams in. I look up and see the now-familiar lace canopy of her bed and know right where I am. A tickling sensation on my torso causes me to suck in my stomach and look down. Sleek, red hair is dragging up my belly and heading toward my face. Blue eyes matching the sheets are looking at me, and a beautiful plump mouth is parted and panting. I'm lying on my back and my hands feel frozen at my sides. Eva's very beautiful and very naked body is slithering up mine, and all I want is to capture her mouth with

my lips. Eva grins in satisfaction, as if she can read my thoughts; as if she knows she's got me right where she wants me.

Her mouth crashes down onto mine, and I hungrily accept. There's nothing I've wanted more and I buck my hips slightly, pressing my arousal into her creamy, pale thigh. Her warm, soft breasts press against my chest and I want nothing other than to be inside of her. My hands find a way to move and I run them up her sides, then her back, and then slide one into her slick hair. Gripping at the scalp, I wrench her head to the side and lick her neck from her collarbone to her ear. She groans in pleasure and lets out a small giggle. Without any preamble, I bite into her neck with my new fangs and begin sucking on her neck. Her blood is sweet, like the red wine made from a muscadine grape, and as I swallow it down, she slams her body down onto mine, joining us together. I moan my pleasure as I continue to swallow.

A gasp from the entryway of the bedroom causes me to lift my head. We simultaneously look over and see Charity standing in the doorway of Eva's bedroom. Her red curls are wild and cascading over her shoulders, and she's in shorts and a T-shirt, a tattered backpack slung over her shoulder.

Charity's face is contorted into a mask of confusion, and then terror as she sees what she's walked in on. She then lets out a shuddering, blood-curdling scream that rattles the windows and makes me gasp in horror.

I jerked awake, knocking over the half-empty beer bottle with my hand. The foamy liquid spilled over onto the carpeted floor and I jumped up from the couch with a start to pick it up.

Letting out a string of curses, I ran a hand through my hair and went to the kitchen to dump the rest of the beer out. I pitched the bottle into the trash then fetched a towel and some carpet cleaner from under the kitchen sink.

On my hands and knees in the living room, I scrubbed the smelly liquid from my carpet and shook my head in anger. I hated those dreams, and now my subconscious was apparently injecting Charity into them. I wished it was just me and Charity in the bed without Eva anywhere in the picture. How could I hate someone who looked so much like the person I was sure I was falling in love with?

Throwing the towel into the bathroom hamper, I wandered back into the kitchen. Picking up my phone, I saw I had three text messages.

Charity: *I hope you're okay. I worry about you.*

I smiled at that one. She'd been thinking of me as much as I'd been thinking—dreaming—about her.

Then I read the other two:

Parker: *Hey bro, Blue Room again this weekend, you in?*

Parker: *Don't you bail on us. Maybe those hot chicks will be there again.*

I frowned at the last text. Oh yes, I hoped the "hot chicks" would be there again, too. I had a nice present for one of them. My eyes slid to the buck knife and I wondered briefly if it would fit inside my boot.

Chapter 14

MYTHOLOGY

Mid-morning sunlight streamed in through the curtains of my parents' living room as I watched my sister pace a hole into the floor.

"What in the hell are you talking about?" snapped Natalie.

I winced at my sister's reaction. "I'm not joking, Nat. Calm down."

She blew out a breath and combed her long fingers through her thick, dark hair. She continued pacing, and I watched her carefully, wondering if I'd just made a huge mistake.

Natalie lived at home in the house we grew up in. She was helping take care of the horses and stables until she got a teaching job. She was currently walking back and forth over the already-worn beige living room carpeting. Thankfully, my parents were in town getting groceries and running errands.

"Have you lost your freaking mind, Nonie? Vampires? A succubus? Are you doing drugs?"

I sighed in frustration. That was the reaction I expected from my father, not my sister.

"Would you please just help me? I'm gonna turn into a damn vampire in about two days. I'm already feeling the symptoms. I am having dreams about her. We have wild, raunchy sex in them. Then I bite her and drink her blood. I've had other dreams about roaming the streets and biting people. It's disturbing and I can't take much more of it. I'm not sleeping."

Natalie stopped pacing and folded her arms across her small chest. "Nolan, a twenty-one-year-old guy having sex dreams isn't exactly something I need to call CNN about. You been playing Warcraft or something? They have vampires and zombies and crap in those games. It's probably creeping into your subconscious."

I stood, went to the wall, and pounded my fist into it. I turned back around with my fists balled. "Nat, I'm not making this shit up. I have all the signs. The nightmares, the sunlight sensitivity, and most of all…" I lowered my voice and said, "the craving of blood."

Natalie let out a gasp and stared at me, probably wondering if her baby brother had lost his mind.

I met her stare head-on and a long, heavy silence blanketed the air between us until I felt like I needed to open a window. I reached down into my boot and pulled out the buck knife.

Natalie stared at it in horror. "Why in the hell do you have that?"

I unsheathed it and twirled it around, running a finger along its pristine blade. "I'm going to kill Eva with this."

She walked slowly over to me while keeping eye contact. She easily pried it from my fingers. Continuing to look me in the eye, she said, "You're not going to be killing anyone. Just sit down and let's talk about this."

I nodded and sat on the blue and white flowered sofa. She grabbed the sheath from the wooden coffee table and put the blade back into its leather protection before setting it down.

"Nonie, look at me."

I swiveled my head up and stared into her light-brown eyes.

"Listen. I just graduated from college. I have a degree in American History. Do you know what my minor was in?"

I shook my head, embarrassed.

"First of all, you suck for not knowing this, but Mythology was my minor."

I narrowed my eyes. "So?"

She sighed. "I studied a lot of stuff on myths and legends. I even took a class on vampires and Gothic literature that lasted a whole semester. Most of it was just fun folklore and tales, but I found the origins of the stories interesting. Most are rooted in the church and the paranoia of the religious folks back then. For instance, do you know that people with the blood disease porphyria were thought to be vampires in the seventeenth century? It causes sunlight sensitivity and their vomit and urine to be blood-tinged, suggesting they'd drunk blood. Also, their hair and gums would recede, giving the appearance of fangs. When they died, they would have their heads chopped off and then the coroner would place the head at the feet of the corpse, so it could not re-animate and come back and feed off them or kill them after death."

I made a face. "Ew."

She laughed. "The idea of a succubus, as you call Eva, is a female demon who descends from an evil goddess named Lilith who seduced human men to produce offspring. These legends and myths have been going on since the beginning of time, practically, but it's believed these were made up by horny men who got caught having sex with beautiful women outside their marriages and blamed the devil." She ended on a snort-laugh.

I blew out a breath. "Maybe I am going crazy." Then I thought of something. "But Nat, someone from the government came to see me. He told me Eva had taken my 'soul' and she had to be destroyed. It was freaky."

Her eyes widened. "What? Someone from the government told to you kill her? This is just too weird…"

"And another thing," I said, taking a deep breath. "When Charity and I were in Nawlins, she and I met a real vampire."

Natalie shook her head and held up a finger. "Wait. First off, who is Charity? And second, I… don't even have words for your vampire comment."

I couldn't stop the small smile. "Charity is Eva's twin sister."

She looked at me incredulously. "And you just took off and went to New Orleans with her?"

I sat back and told her the whole story, starting from what happened at The Blue Room to when I got back yesterday. Natalie listened with keen interest, and once I was done, she was almost speechless. Almost.

"So, you truly believe this Eva is a succubus. Why didn't her 'superhot' friends do this to Brennan and Parker, too?"

I laughed humorlessly. "You know, I asked that of the vampire in Nawlins, and he said that they were just regular vampires and only Eva was a succubus."

Natalie turned her head and regarded me. Then she asked, "Did you say Eva was a redhead?"

I nodded and swallowed hard, the dream about her running her silky red hair over my naked body flashing through my brain without permission.

"I'll be right back." And with that, she disappeared into one of the back bedrooms.

My fingers twisted together with stress. I felt like I was losing my mind. I felt a little better for unloading on my sister, happy that if something did happen to me in a few days, that she would be prepared and be able to tell my parents something… not that they would believe it for a second. I racked my brain for a way out of this. I could sneak up on Eva at her house and kill her. And then I wouldn't become a vampire. If she wasn't a demon or succubus or whatever, then there would be a dead body and an open police investigation. I'd be caught in a New York second.

Natalie returned with a tattered hardback textbook. She set the book down onto the wooden coffee table with a thud and opened it. She licked her index finger, flicking through pages until she found what she was looking for. I could see photos of demons and demigods drawn in intricate detail, most were naked or half-nude with horns, wings, and some with tails. All were females, and all were beautiful. They looked like the images I had Googled earlier.

Natalie pressed her finger to the page and began to read: "According to myth, if a human female is turned into a vampire by the sharing of blood by ingestion or injection, then the human will become a full vampire in three days' time. However, if that female has the combination of red or auburn hair and blue eyes, she will become a succubus, feeding off both blood and the essence or soul of human males. These succubi can also steal the essence or soul of human females, but they derive much more satisfaction from the stealing of a male soul. It is also said the succubus uses sexual contact and desires of the flesh to distract males in order to get what it wants and needs easily.

"These succubi cannot continue to live without stealing souls. They cannot survive on blood alone. The only way to kill one is to destroy its heart or remove its head. One should approach a succubus with extreme caution, as it can possess extreme physical strength and an ability to hypnotize a human by gazing into their eyes.

"When a regular vampire feeds from a human, this does not turn him or her into a vampire. That requires the blood exchange; however, some tales reveal that the victim of a succubus will turn into a vampire just by having his or her soul or essence taken."

I rubbed the back of my head. She definitely had extreme physical strength. Anyone else would have broken a finger or two punching the back of my hard head like that.

"This is unbelievable," Natalie breathed. "Let me guess, Eva has blue eyes?"

I nodded. "Oh, yes, beautiful eyes the color of the sky. Same with Charity, they are identical."

She snapped the textbook closed and placed it on the table. "You falling for the sister?"

I shook my head. "I don't know. No. Yes. Sorta. I... I don't have time for romantic entanglements right now."

Her mouth edged into a grin. "There's always time for romance."

I sighed again. "Natalie, what in the hell am I gonna do? Should I kill her? I don't want to. I hate the bitch, but there has to be another way. I can't murder another person — succubus — vampire... whatever she is. I just can't..."

She came to sit next to me and put her hand on mine. "Nonie, we're gonna figure this out. It's unbelievable, yes, but in all my life I have only known you to be level-headed and sane. This is the weirdest thing you have ever come to me with, and I want to help." She thought for a minute. "What if we go see a priest? Maybe he can give you some holy water or something?"

I laughed. "Would that burn her skin like in that movie *Fright Night*? That would be kinda funny. She has perfectly pure, white skin, I'd love to see that."

"What if you drink it? Maybe you won't turn into a vampire?"

I lifted a shoulder in a shrug. "It can't hurt, I guess."

"I find it odd the book didn't mention you having to kill her. It just didn't say anything, like becoming a vampire was inevitable." Natalie stared off in thought, her finger to her mouth.

"I noticed that. I wonder where that came from?"

She looked at me. "Where did you hear that, anyway?"

"The federal cop told me, and then a voodoo guy in New Orleans said the same thing. So did the vampire guy, Joel."

She lifted a dark eyebrow at me. "You saw a voodoo guy?"

I nodded. "Yes, the librarian at the old library we visited gave us his card and said we should go see him."

"Well, you left that part out of your story."

I scoffed. "Sorry, didn't remember until now."

"That's weird the librarian would be referring normal people to a voodoo priest."

I shrugged again. "It's a weird city, and honestly, she was a little creepy herself."

Natalie laughed, and then we heard the tires of our parents' car crunching over the gravel of the driveway.

"I'm gonna go," I said, standing.

My sister hugged me. "We're gonna figure this out."

I patted her back and fished my bike keys from my pocket. I eyed the knife on the table, reached over, and slipped it back into my boot.

"Thanks, Nat," I said as I pushed open the screen door and stepped onto the rickety front porch. It squealed under my weight as I bounded down the two steps and headed toward my bike.

My parents got out of the car. "Nolan Bishop! Where do you think you're going?" my mother said.

I winced. "Hi, Mom." I kissed her cheek. "I gotta run, I was just talking to Nat."

"Hey, Dad," I said to my father, who was carrying a few bags into the house. My dad grunted a hello and disappeared into the house.

"I wish you could stay for dinner. I bought a pot roast."

I nodded. "I know, Mom, but I have some things to take care of. I'll be over on Sunday for dinner, or brunch, whatever you want."

That made my mother happy. She kissed my cheek once more before I pulled my helmet from my bike and slid it on. With a frown, I started the loud bike.

By Sunday, I'll be a monster.

Chapter 15

SHAKE THE TAIL

My bike zipped into the parking lot of my apartment complex. It was near dark, the sky a deep-blue with the faintest pink and orange sunset painting the edge of the city's horizon. The wind was warm against my skin as I parked in my designated spot and killed the engine to the bike. I pulled the helmet from my head and wiped the sweat that always seemed to accumulate underneath it. As I climbed the steps to my apartment, I felt as if someone was watching me. A shiver slithered up my spine and I held my breath.

I had my keys in my hand and debated reaching for the knife in my boot. I first unlocked my front door, and then turned around and stared down into the darkening parking lot from the small landing at the top of the stairs. A very plain-looking man was sitting in a car that was backed into one of the guest parking spots. He made no move to hide himself or the fact that he was watching me. The man's face looked vaguely familiar. It wasn't the agent from the Justice Department, because he surely wouldn't be driving a Mercedes Benz.

I stared the man down for a minute, and then he started the car and drove off. As I went inside my apartment, I closed and locked the door, including the deadbolt and chain. I was a bit disturbed that someone seemed to be watching me, but with what I was going through, nothing should seem weird to me anymore.

I pulled my phone from my pants pocket and remembered I had forgotten to text Parker back, so I replied: *Yes, I'll be there tomorrow night. See you then.*

I was definitely going back to The Blue Room. If Eva was there, it was my last chance to confront her and try one last time to get back my soul, or my "essence", or whatever it was she'd taken from me.

I wearily walked to my bedroom, scrubbed a hand over my stubbly chin, and sat on my bed. My head was in a fog, like it had been over the past few days. I constantly felt like I couldn't clear my head or think straight. My emotions were almost nonexistent. The only thing I ever really felt was an attraction to Charity, and even then, I wondered if it was because she was identical to the woman who had been sexually assaulting my dreams for the past four days, or if I really felt something for her. I did know I felt bad for her when she would cry. Yet, I never had the courage to ask her why she was crying. Was it because she knew I had to kill Eva to survive? Was she lonely? Where were her parents? Did they have any other siblings? I suddenly felt like a total ass for not bothering to find out anything personal about her. I could blame my foggy mind and the preoccupation with finding Eva and trying to save my own life, but it was still deeply out of character for me.

I thought about how I had to go to work the next day. I'd called in sick for the past two days, but I knew Archie wasn't going to buy it for a third day. I at least needed to keep my job if on the off chance I was actually going to survive this.

<hr />

Charity

I sat in the poky rented room above the Stop-N-Shop and stared at my small laptop screen. I'd spent the past two hours on the Internet researching vampires, demons, and succubi. I'd found a lot of information, most of it myth or legend. Slamming the laptop lid shut, I realized I was now more confused and upset than I had been when I'd first started the search.

I pulled myself down on the bed, sitting cross-legged on it. I used a hair clip to get my unruly hair out of my face. With my thumbnail in my mouth, I stared at the wall.

I loved my sister, she was my twin, after all, and I didn't want to see her destroyed. Even though our relationship was nothing like it was growing up, or even like it was a couple of years ago, the thought of her being wiped off the planet caused my stomach to twist into knots and my heart to clench in my chest. I wrapped my arms around my stomach. My twin, she was a part of me—my other half—and I couldn't bear the thought of her dying. Regardless of how cruel and truly soulless Eva had become.

A couple of months ago, I had briefly thought about approaching Eva and asking to become what she was, just so I could feel that connection with her again. But I knew Eva's ego would never agree to it. I knew my twin would want to be the only succubus in the family. And being that we were identical, she couldn't have two of us running around. Besides, was that what I really wanted? After all the research I had done earlier, it really wasn't. Eva had always been the one with the mean streak, the confident one. I didn't think that becoming a succubus had caused those traits in her, only enhanced them. So, I thought maybe if I became one too, my good traits would be enhanced. But I quickly dismissed it. I wouldn't want to have to exist at night, drink blood, steal souls… I shuddered. I had only entertained the thought so my sister and I could be close again.

My mind drifted to Nolan. His sea-green eyes, his chiseled jawline, and of course his sculpted body. My brain kept replaying how he'd looked without a shirt on. The truth was, I hadn't been with a lot of guys. I thought about the one in high school and then the one who had worked at the Stop-N-Shop for a brief time before quitting to join the Air Force. In my short twenty-one years, I didn't have much experience with men at all, but I did know one thing; my attraction to Nolan was nothing like I'd ever felt. I just lacked the confidence to act on it. Still, that did not stop my brain from floating to his face and body every two seconds, it seemed.

I thought about Eva kissing Nolan, her pale hands on his perfect jaw, her body pressed up against his. I thought about her eyes boring into his as she stole from him. I thought about how Nolan had admitted to dreaming about Eva constantly. I knew what that meant, I wasn't stupid. Especially after I'd spent hours of Googling. I had to push those images out of my mind. It was making my blood begin to boil. Maybe my sister really should get a stake through the heart.

I couldn't take it anymore. I pushed the laptop to one side and then slipped my feet into some flip-flops. After snatching my keys and purse, I got into my small, beat-up old Corolla. I remembered seeing his address on his driver's license as he'd handed me his wallet to book a hotel room on the drive to Nawlins, and knew where the apartment complex was.

I knew Nolan wouldn't be expecting me, and I grinned at the thought of surprising him. I parked in the guest parking and walked toward apartment 272. As I slowly climbed the stone staircase, I wondered if I had made a mistake. What if he wasn't home? Or worse, what if he wasn't alone? I lifted my hand to knock, hesitating. I instead put it to my mouth and thought about what I was doing. What *was* I doing?

Taking a deep breath, I regained my confidence and raised a hand to knock, but the door swung open. The only thing I saw was a gigantic blade, its metal glinting off the light from the apartment's lot lighting.

I screamed and stepped back, then looked beyond the blade. Nolan's face was a mask of rage and shock.

His features immediately softened and he lowered the knife. "Charity! Oh, my God! I'm so sorry! What are you doing here?"

I was frozen in fear and couldn't move.

He stepped closer to me on the stone landing outside the apartment door. He grabbed my hand. "Come on inside. Let me explain."

I snapped out of my shock and nodded, following him, but with my eyes drifting to the weapon. "Uh, could you put that away?"

"I'm so sorry. Here." Nolan walked to the kitchen counter and grabbed its sheath, securing the blade inside of it. He walked to the doorway of a bedroom and tossed it onto a bed. Coming back into the living room, he said, "Better?"

I nodded and let out a shaky breath. "Yes, thank you."

He grabbed my hand once more and led me to the sofa. "What are you doing here?"

"Why do you have a knife, Nolan?"

He blew out a breath and rubbed the back of his neck with his large hand. "I heard a noise outside my door. I seem to be able to hear things really, really well the past couple days. Anyway, I looked through the peephole and thought you were Eva. But then I realized your hair was up, not short. I'm sorry I scared you."

I licked my lips. "Were you gonna stab me... her?"

He shook his head. "No. Well, I was going to defend myself if need be, but that's it."

I searched his face and eyes for any dishonesty, but didn't find any.

I just simply nodded.

"So, you gonna answer my question now?" His eyes searched mine.

"Oh." I wrung my hands together in my lap. "Well, no real reason, really. I just had this feeling you didn't want to be alone. I want to spend some time with you before, well, you know." I swallowed a lump in my throat.

This made him grin. "Is that so? What did you have in mind, Charity?"

I shrugged one shoulder. "Dunno."

"Are you hungry?" he asked.

I nodded. "Maybe a little. Do you cook?"

He got up and went to the small kitchen. "Yes, mostly for myself, but I do have some leftover pizza if you want. Sorry, I need to go to the store. Just been a little busy."

"Do you want to get out of here?" I asked, getting up.

He nodded. "You're right, let's go out to eat. There's that huge Mexican place with all the colorful tables near the interstate. Their food is so good. That okay with you?"

"Of course," I said. I felt kind of excited, like it was a date. It was odd that he had kissed me the night before as he'd dropped me off from our New Orleans trip. It had felt spontaneous and exciting, but this was, too. Like starting over. My excitement was short-lived when I realized he'd soon be a monster, something I wouldn't be able to be around.

Just like my sister.

"I need to grab something real quick," he said as he was about to lock the door with his key from the outside landing.

I nodded but said nothing, looking down into the apartment complex's parking lot.

Chapter 16

STAY

Nolan

While Charity waited by the door, I quickly grabbed the knife from my bed and shoved it into my Justin cowboy boot.

As we drove a short distance to the restaurant, I reached over and grabbed Charity's hand as we drove. This seemed to surprise her, and she smiled at me.

We parked, and once inside, there was no wait and we were shown a table. I kept hold of her hand as the hostess led us to a yellow table. After we were seated and chips and water were delivered, I looked over to the entrance and saw a familiar face. I furrowed my brow as I tried to figure out how I knew the guy. My stomach did a flip, and I almost lost my breath when I realized it was the same guy who had been watching me at my apartment complex a couple nights ago.

Am I being followed?

Charity followed my line of sight and then looked back at me. "What's he doing here?"

My eyes slid back to Charity's. "You know him?"

"No, but," she said, a chip paused at her mouth, "that's the guy who was with Joel Reichert in New Orleans. The bodyguard or whatever."

I gasped. She was right. "He's a vampire, then?"

"Oh, I'm sure of it." She shoveled the chip in her mouth.

"I wonder what he's doing here," I murmured.

She shook her head. "We're nowhere near New Orleans. That's totally weird."

I risked a glance in his direction again, and the man was sitting at a table alone, nursing a bottle of beer. He was looking at his phone and didn't seem to have a care in the world. He wasn't eating anything and did not look up at us even once.

"I have enough problems." I sighed. "I don't need this shit."

Charity set her water down after taking a gulp. "What are you gonna do?"

"If I see that dude one more time after today, I'm gonna confront him."

She shook her head. "Not a good idea. Do you know how strong vampires are?"

I rubbed the back of my head and said, "Yeah, I do. I have a goose egg to prove it."

She frowned. "It still hurts?"

"It's getting better by the day."

The server came and interrupted us, a pretty brunette with a friendly face and a nice figure. She prattled off the specials and Charity and I gave her our orders.

We continued with an easy conversation that didn't involve vampires, succubi, assaults, or even New Orleans. Once our food was served and the waitress walked off, I looked over and saw an empty table where once my vampire follower had been. Smiling to myself, I finished my enchiladas and asked for the check.

The warm, humid night air hit us as we made our way out the front door to my Charger. As I slid the keys from my jeans pocket, I noticed the same man—vampire—sitting in a luxury car parked close to mine. My hackles went up and rage began to bubble over into my brain and then leak down into my fists.

I stalked with purpose toward the man's car, but before I reached it, the vampire was out of it and standing against the driver's side door with his arms folded. The motion of him getting out of the car and closing the door seemed to happen in a blur.

I didn't care.

I went up to him, and in one fluid motion, pulled the knife from my boot and put it to the vampire's throat. "Why in the fuck are you following me?"

The man laughed and wrenched the knife with ease from my hand, tossing it over his shoulder. I fought the urge to cry out as my wrist exploded in pain, feeling like it might break.

"Calm down," the vampire drawled in a heavy Southern accent. "I'm just keepin' an eye on you, boy. Word on the street is you're about to become a vamp. I just gotta make sure you ain't gonna go tearin' through an orphanage or somethin' once your turn is complete."

Charity gasped. "He would never do that!"

"Who sent you to follow me?" I asked, rubbing my wrist.

"Don't worry about it," the stranger said, making a motion to get back his car.

I ran over and grabbed my knife. I put it up against the tire of his car. "I'm gonna slash your tire if you don't give me some damned answers!"

Charity gasped again.

The man's hand was paused on the door handle and I turned around. "My name is Ansel and I work with Joel Reichert. I'm not sure what else you want me to say."

I turned my head to the side. "Ansel? What the hell kinda name is that?"

Ansel snorted. "A very old one."

"Why did Mr. Reichert have you following me?"

Ansel shook his head and I studied his face. He looked to be in his thirties and his stature was shorter than mine. He had short brown hair and dark eyes.

"I already told you why I'm following you," he replied dryly.

I let out a humorless laugh and said, "You seriously think I'm gonna become a vampire?"

Ansel nodded. "Yes. And not just any vampire, an out-of-control feral vampire with no restraint. Mr. Reichert and I want to make sure you don't wander into a Wal-Mart and eat everyone in the store. They have security cameras in there, you know, and we have a secret to protect."

I tried not to laugh. This guy was beyond serious and seemed to believe every word coming out of his mouth. "So, you're gonna kill me once I turn?"

"No, we will tame you and teach you how to behave as a vampire."

Charity looked at us both incredulously and shook her head. "Two very large, grown men having a conversation about vampires."

I ignored her and looked at Ansel. "Stop following me." I folded my arms, still holding the knife, and then fixed Ansel with a stare as I began to walk backward toward my car, keeping my eye on him. I grabbed Charity by the hand and opened the car door for her. I then shoved the knife back into my boot and got into the car.

I left Ansel standing against his black Mercedes in the parking lot of the Mexican restaurant, staring at us. I peeled out of the parking lot.

Once we reached the apartment complex, I killed the engine and looked into my rearview mirror. I sighed in exasperation, knowing the vampire already knew where I lived and wondered why I was even bothering to look around. I got out of the Charger and went around to open Charity's car door.

She got out and shot a glance at her Toyota. "I should go."

I grabbed her arm, gently yanking her back to me. "Please don't?"

The pleading of my stare must have worked. She swallowed hard and nodded, letting me lead her up to my apartment. Once inside, I closed and locked the door, and then threw my keys onto the kitchen counter. I walked over to her as she stood by the front door, and placed both hands on either side of her face. "Please stay the night. I need you."

She swallowed hard, and looking up at me with big blue eyes, she whispered, "You need me?"

I rubbed a thumb over her bottom lip and stared down at it as if it were the most interesting thing in the world. My gaze drifted back to hers. "You have the most beautiful eyes. They're like the color of the sky."

She simply nodded and breathed, "Wow... Thank you."

I leaned down and sealed my mouth over hers gently, rubbing my thumb along her smooth cheek. My other hand snaked around her waist and I drew her in closer to my body.

She swooned under my kiss. Every part of my body tingled with excitement. She put both arms around my waist and seemed to try to pull me closer to her. She was by far the best kisser I'd ever had the pleasure of locking lips with.

Charity groaned in the back of her throat when I broke the kiss. I began running gentle nips down her throat and neck. I placed small kisses on her collarbone as I gently slid the strap of her tank top down so I could kiss her shoulder. She tilted her head back to give me access.

I slowly eased my hand from her back, sliding it across her hip and it came to rest on her flat stomach under her top. I could feel her body erupt in goosebumps and she moaned again. I lifted my head and grabbed her hand, leading her to my room. She followed pliantly.

I was relieved to see that my bed was made and there was no shit on the floor. Bright blue moonlight streamed in from the large window, the blinds open, striping the remaining walls.

"Thank you for staying with me," I said, grabbing both her hands.

"Of course. I don't think you should be alone right now, anyway." She smiled warmly at me. "I don't think I should either, for that matter."

She swallowed hard when I looked down into her eyes once more. I wondered if my gaze matched the stare of desire she looked at me with. It was then I knew she'd be putty in my hands. I leaned down once more and kissed her passionately, and I had to hold on to her tight, as she seemed to be able to barely stand on wobbling knees. I broke the kiss, eased her tank top off, and threw it to the floor. Then I removed my shirt. My eyes trailed down to her white push-up bra and then up to her mouth. Pressing my mouth to hers again, I gently pushed her toward the bed until she fell onto her back. She giggled in surprise and then slid back so her head was on the pillow. I climbed up the bed like a jungle cat on the prowl and stopped when my face was right over hers.

Running a finger over her cheek, I pushed a stray red curl from it and tucked it behind her ear. "You're so beautiful, Charity."

I looked down to see her eyes welling up.

I was confused. "Are you okay?"

She nodded quickly. "Yes, I'm great. Wonderful. Perfect... just kiss me again. Please," she finished on a whisper.

I smiled and obeyed, causing another groan from Charity. I ran a finger down her neck and traced it to her chest, over her bra, then to the valley between her breasts. She shuddered at the motion and clawed at my hair with her short fingernails.

My brain and body were on overload. I'd never been this turned on by a woman before. Every nerve ending was on fire and my head was spinning. For days, it had felt like my emotions and brain had been in a daze, like I couldn't feel anything but anger. Now that I was here, it was like feelings of desire, infatuation, and definitely lust were breaking through the dense fog. I didn't want to be alone tonight, even if meant just holding her and nothing else, but the promise of what was to come was better than I could have hoped for.

I slid my rough hand down her soft, warm body and tugged at the drawstring holding her pants on. With a swift yank, the laces untied and I slid a hand under the material to rest on her hipbone. I heard her pant into my mouth as I was still kissing her. The feel of her hands and nails on my scalp and neck was electrifying and turning me on. I barely noticed the bump on the back of my head anymore.

"Charity, I want you," I whispered into her mouth.

She nodded slightly and breathed, "I want you, too, Nolan. Please."

I closed my eyes and continued to stroke my hand up her body between her hip and chest. As I was fumbling for the clasp of her bra between her breasts, an ear-splitting scream broke us both out of the hazy lust cloud.

My hand froze and my head jerked up. I shot a glance at the window. I looked at Charity, who had a look of horror and fear on her face, jumped up, and went to the window and looked out. She was right behind me as we both peered down into the parking lot of the apartment complex.

I couldn't see anybody, or even where the scream had come from. But then I saw something. A shiny black Mercedes with two people inside parked next to my motorcycle.

"Son-of-a-bitch!" I growled.

I looked down to the floor and my gaze roamed until I found the knife where it has slid out of my boot. I picked it up and stalked toward the door.

"Where are you going?" Charity cried out. "Nolan! Don't!" she screamed.

I was down the steps to my car faster than any human could move. Filled with rage, I ignored how weird that was. I reached the Mercedes and yanked open the driver's door when I saw him biting the woman in the passenger seat.

I pulled the monster out by his jacket, completely surprising him. I threw him to the ground, but he did not stay down long. The vampire was on his feet, fangs out and eyes as black as coal, a frightening sight I was unfortunately all too familiar with.

This time, I put the knife behind my back as the vampire spun me around and slammed me up against the car.

"What the hell do you think you're doin', boy?" the vampire growled in his thick accent.

"I told you to stop following me, asshole," I said through gritted teeth.

I watched in horror as Charity went around to the passenger side of the car. I followed her movements and saw a blonde woman who looked to be passed out or asleep on the seat.

Charity opened the car door just as I heard Ansel say, "I wouldn't be doing that, little girl. Just leave her be, ya hear?"

She ignored him, and as she went to check for a pulse, I used the distraction to push Ansel. "Get your hands off me!"

I pulled the knife out from behind my back and plunged it into the vampire's chest with both hands and a yell. Ansel gasped in surprise, then began to turn an ashy color. His body crumbled into a pile of ashes, leaving nothing but his clothes and a pair of shoes covering the ashes.

Unfortunately, Charity had seen the whole thing. She let out a blood-curdling scream that had lights popping on all over the apartment complex.

I panicked. "Oh, fuck! Oh shit! Oh fuck, fuck, fuck! I killed him!"

Charity seemed to shake off the shock faster than me. She grabbed my arm. "Come on, we have to get inside before someone comes out and see us!"

I couldn't take my eyes off the pile of clothing and ash. Then my gaze drifted to the inside of the Mercedes. "Oh, my God, that's my neighbor, Holly."

Charity dragged me by my arm. "She's alive, just passed out. Leave her. Let's go."

I reached down, picked up the knife, and we ran back up the stone steps to my apartment.

Closing and locking the door behind us, I gasped for air. With my eyes still wide with shock, I asked, "What the hell just happened?"

Charity's eyes were also big. "You just staked a vampire! Did that just really happen? Am I dreaming?"

She went to the window and looked out. Ansel's driver's side door was still open, the dome light illuminating the pile of ash next to the car.

I followed her over. My hands were trembling so hard, I could barely move the curtain. "We should clean that up. We... we have to do something!"

Charity put a hand to her mouth. "Yes, we should. Let's wait 'til everyone in the complex calms down and turns their lights off, though. I don't hear police sirens, so that's good."

I looked at her excited but frightened face, and wrapped her in a hug. "Thank you for dragging me away from there. I… I can't believe that just happened." I licked my dry lips and shook my head, as if that would clear it somehow.

She buried her face into my bare chest. "I was so scared when he pushed you up against the car," she murmured. "Thank God you had that knife."

I closed my eyes and shook my head. "That's what sucks. I don't think that guy would have hurt me. I just panicked and reacted." I pulled away from her slightly so I could look down at her. "Do you think I should call that Joel guy and tell him what happened? What if he puts a hit out on me or something?"

Charity looked frightened. "I don't know. How's he gonna know you killed Ansel?"

I sighed and pulled her back into my body. Resting my chin on her head, I said, "I don't know. But we need to clean up that mess."

CHAPTER 17

CONFESSION

 linding yellow light made me throw an arm over my eyes. I was quickly aware that I wasn't alone in my queen-sized bed. I looked down and saw a mass of red hair splayed out on the pillow next to me. Her warm body was spooned up against mine, the strawberry smell of her hair filling my nose.

I immediately recalled the night before and frowned. The night hadn't quite concluded with the happy ending I thought it was going to, but after our little run-in with Ansel, we had both collapsed in exhaustion onto my bed, hoping that if we both went to sleep, we'd wake up and it would have all been a dream. I rubbed my fingers over the freckles on her arms as the sunlight blanketed us in my room.

I felt her stir, then she slowly opened her eyes, blinking her baby blues up at me. "Good morning."

She yawned, her hand over her mouth. "What happened last night? Did you stake a vampire?"

I laughed. "I don't know. Did I? I was wondering if I had dreamed it."

She sat up and stretched. "No, you didn't. But at least we cleaned it up."

I vaguely recalled sprinting down the steps to pick up Ansel's clothes and shoes, and closing his car door. I had deposited the clothes into the apartment complex's dumpster and left the ash there, hoping it would be blown away in the wind. We also left Holly to sleep it off inside his car. I figured she was smart enough to find her way back to her apartment. I just hoped she didn't remember getting bit. Charity had filled me in on the multiple bite marks Holly had.

I watched Charity walk to the bathroom. She was still in her inside-out tank top and drawstring pants, and I smiled as I watched her very nice backside jiggle.

With my hands behind my head, I again wondered if I should call Joel Reichert and tell him that his friend—or colleague—or bodyguard, or whatever he was, was dead, or gone, or whatever. Joel had given me a business card so I had a way to get ahold of him. I also knew that it was Saturday, exactly one week since I had met Eva and my life had turned into a chaotic roller coaster. I figured since I was currently basking in sunlight, that meant tomorrow would be the seventh day: Doomsday. My phone chirped on the nightstand and I yanked it up. It was 8:30 a.m. and Parker was already texting me: *Blue Room @10 tonight – you better be there*

I sighed. Yes, I most definitely was going to be there. It would be my last-ditch effort to talk Eva into sparing me. I thought I might even grovel or beg if I had to… nah, I wouldn't take it that far. I'd resort to violence instead. I just hoped she was there tonight, otherwise, I'd be on a wild succubus chase around town all night.

Charity exited the bathroom and came to sit on the side of the bed where I was lying. I looked up at her and partially sat up, propping my head on my hand.

"Thank you for staying with me," I said.

Her cheeks flushed pink and she looked down. "I'm sorry the night didn't go as you… well, as we both probably wanted it to."

I pulled myself into a full sitting position, the morning sun exposing my naked chest, and I looked at Charity. "I didn't ask you to stay because I wanted to have sex. I just wanted someone to stay with me. If that makes me weak, well, then so be it."

She shook her head and visibly swallowed, then looked up to meet my gaze. "Weak… no, Nolan, you are the most non-weak person I have ever met. I wanted to stay, I wanted to be with you. I knew you didn't want to be alone, and honestly?" She paused a beat, meeting my stare. "I didn't want to be alone, either."

I smiled. "Thank you."

The room went silent for a few minutes as she crawled up next to me and laid her head against my chest. I lay back down and she sidled up against me so that we were once again lying side by side. I kissed the top of her head.

"Is today the seventh day?" she asked quietly.

I nodded. "I think tomorrow is, since I'm not frying in the sunbeams. By the way, I'm going to The Blue Room tonight."

She gasped quietly. "Why?"

"I'm gonna approach Eva one last time. Maybe she'll have mercy on my soul."

She snorted. "Yeah, and maybe Hell will freeze over."

I let out an ironic grunt. "A guy's gotta try. Do you think I can win her over with my good looks and charm?"

"I'm pretty sure your good looks and charm are what got you into this mess to begin with."

I chuckled. "Well, I have to do something. I don't think you want a vampire for a boyfriend, do you?"

She lifted her head from my hard chest and looked at me. "So, you're my boyfriend?"

"Maybe for today. Tomorrow I'll be a monster who wants to eat you."

She raised a quizzical eyebrow at me.

"Okay, that came out wrong."

She giggled and laid her head back on my chest. "I've been thinking, and… I think maybe you should call Joel Reichert."

I actually agreed with this. I knew I owed it to the man to tell him his vampire friend Ansel was no longer in existence. I also had it in the back of my mind that if Mr. Reichert was angry enough at me for killing another vampire, maybe he'd just kill me too — and I would let him. That way, I'd avoid turning into something evil and inhuman and risk killing those I loved.

It had not gone unnoticed by me that once I did, in fact, turn into a vampire, that I put the very people I loved at risk. My parents, Natalie, my boss Archie, hell, even Charity. *Especially* Charity. And while my emotions and had been in a fog since Eva had stolen my soul, or my essence, or whatever, I still knew there was something deep and serious brewing with Charity. I had questioned as to whether it was just a sexual infatuation with her since I was having very erotic dreams about her identical twin, or if something more in-depth was going to develop with her. The one thing I did know, though, was that if I didn't find a way out of my current predicament, there would be no future with her. There would be no future for me, either, because I refused to live as a vampire, to live as a monster.

I would rather die.

I got out of bed and put on shoes while Charity looked around the apartment for hers. Once they were located, she put them on. I walked her to her small Toyota in the parking lot. She opened the driver's door and then rested her chin on it with her keyring dangling off her finger.

"Thank you for staying," I said, staring at her.

She smiled. "You already said that."

"Well, I meant it," I replied sincerely.

"I know, Nolan..." she breathed.

I leaned down and kissed her, rubbing my thumb along her jaw.

As I broke the kiss, she asked, "Are you really gonna confront my sister tonight?"

The stars in my eyes were quickly replaced with storm clouds. "Yes. I can't give up, Charity. I have to try."

"Do you want me to come?"

I shook my head. "Absolutely not. But I'll be by your place after, if that's okay?"

That seemed to make her happy. "Yes. It's okay."

I was surprised. "You're not scared?"

Her ginger eyebrows furrowed together. "Of what?"

"Me turning into a vampire tonight?"

She laughed a little. "No, I'm not. I know you won't hurt me."

I looked down. "I'm going to call Joel Reichert today. I have to let him know what I did."

She nodded. "Be careful. Okay?"

I gazed into her sparkling blue eyes. "What do I have to lose, Charity? Besides, I've been wanting to talk with him some more, anyway."

"You're not going to New Orleans, are you?"

I shook my head. "No, absolutely not. I'm staying here in Shreveport. He can come here if he wants, but I'm not going anywhere."

She smiled in relief. She got into the car, closed the door, and started it up with a rumble. I watched as she drove off in her beat-up little car. Turning, I looked over to where the black Mercedes was still parked. I walked over to it, and with my hands cupped on the windows, I peered inside and didn't see anyone. I hoped Holly had gotten home okay. I made a wide berth around the remaining ashes that were scattered by the driver's side door and went upstairs to my apartment. After making the bed, I stripped my clothes off and put them in a nearby hamper. I flicked on the shower to start it up, and when the water was good and hot, I stepped in and let it pound over my body.

My mind replayed my murderous actions over and over in my head as I saw Ansel disappear in a puff of ash, the look of surprise and horror on the vampire's face repeating in a loop like a broken movie reel. I leaned my head against the slippery beige tiles of the shower and closed my eyes. I wanted to cry or get upset. I wanted to feel a gut-wrenching remorse for what I'd done. I longed to start grieving that the end of my life as I knew it would be here tomorrow. But I couldn't. Nothing would come out. I wasn't sad, angry, happy, or depressed. I felt… nothing.

I opened my eyes with a gasp as I realized Eva *really* had taken my soul. It had to be why I couldn't feel much anymore except fleeting moments of want or need. Things that really did not involve much emotion. All those love songs, movies, and books about how love and feelings come from the heart… no. I shook my head. I still had my heart, and I knew this because of how I felt about Charity. It was my soul I was missing. Eva had taken it… and I wanted it back. I was normally an even-keeled kind of guy. Didn't dwell too much on things. Never sweated the small stuff. But to be unable to cry over my own impending death was not fair. It made me angry. Anger was an emotion, wasn't it? Great. It was all I had left.

I rinsed off and shut off the shower. After drying off, I brushed my teeth and shaved. I threw on my work pants and a plain white T-shirt. With a sigh, I went to sit on my bed. I had left Joel's business card on my nightstand and picked it up. I stared down at it, flipping it over and over between my fingers.

The shrilly ringtone of my phone made me jump. I looked at the caller ID. Archie.

"Hey, boss," I answered.

"How you feelin', boy? You gon' be at work today? I got three bikes in that need complete engine rebuilds."

I blew out a breath and ran a hand along the back of my neck. I had called in sick three times in the past week to take care of all the crazy business I had been dealing with, and I absolutely hated lying to Archie about anything, but there was no way the truth would be okay.

"Yes, I'm feeling better today. I'll be in. Give me about an hour."

"All right, kid. See you in a bit." And with that, he hung up.

I wondered why I was even bothering to go in on a Saturday. Then I realized I had to at least say goodbye to Archie somehow. And, if there was a very small chance I could change this curse I'd been dealt and somehow survive, I would still need a job. Plus, it sounded like there would be lots to keep me busy with at the shop today, which was just what I needed; a distraction.

I slipped on my button-up work shirt with the name patch on it and pulled on some socks and my greasy boots. Grabbing my phone, wallet, and keys, I went down the steps and mounted my motorcycle. I glanced in the direction of the Mercedes and was alarmed to see it was gone. I hadn't bothered to remove the keys and thought maybe it had been stolen.

Oops.

Before starting the Ducati, I pulled my phone and Joel's business card from my pocket. Taking a deep breath, I dialed the New Orleans number and my hand shook as I heard it begin to ring on the other end. After six rings, it went to voicemail, an automatic message with just the phone number, telling me to leave a message.

"Mr. Reichert, this is Nolan Bishop. I need to speak to you about Ansel. Please call me back at this number."

I hung up after rattling off my cell number and started the motorcycle with a rumble. I didn't bother with a helmet. I no longer cared about my own safety.

It was two p.m. I had the engine to a 1985 Harley in a thousand pieces on the garage floor. Archie and I were currently sorting out the pieces when my cell rang from my pants pocket. I wiped my hands on my coveralls and unzipped them to get to my pants pocket. The caller ID read *blocked*, and I frowned.

"Hello?"

"Nolan Bishop?"

"Yes."

"This is Joel Reichert. I'm returning your call." The vampire sounded as calm as could be.

I put a finger up to my boss and then used it to point outside, where I wandered to get out of earshot.

Then, I sighed. "Mr. Reichert—"

"Call me Joel, please," the old Southern vampire drawled.

"Joel, there's no easy way to tell you this, but Ansel is dead."

There was silence on the other end of the line. I expected to hear shouting or cursing, maybe a heavy sigh, or perhaps even crying. I heard nothing. I pulled the phone away from my ear and looked at the screen to see if we were still connected. "Hello? Mister... uh, Joel, are you still there?"

"Yes, I'm still here. I figured Ansel was dead when my guy went to check on him at your place earlier and found his car unlocked and some ash by the car. I just didn't want to believe it. Ansel never, ever leaves his car unlocked, let alone the keys in it."

"I'm sorry, Joel."

"You wanna tell me how he died, Nolan?"

My brow furrowed. "You wanna tell me why you were having me followed?"

"That, Nolan, I already explained to you when you were here. Your soul was taken by a succubus. You will soon be one of us. You cannot be allowed to run around Shreveport like a wild animal unsupervised. Ansel was in charge of bringing you to Nawlins once you turned."

"I'm sorry, Joel, but he attacked me. He was biting my neighbor and I panicked. Ansel pulled me from the car and he threatened me. I had a knife. I was only defending myself." I said the words, only to save my own ass, but knew they were weak and feeble, at best. Problem was, I lacked the capacity to feel any remorse about it.

As if reading my thoughts, Joel replied quietly, "Nolan, Ansel would have never hurt you, except in self-defense." A long pause ensued, and I waited. "I've known Ansel for over fifty years. This is a huge loss. He will be greatly missed."

With that comment, I thought maybe I should feel guilt—or something—but I still felt nothing.

"You gonna kill me now? 'Cause I'm at work and I'd like for my boss and coworkers not to be caught in the crossfire, if ya know what I'm sayin', Joel."

Joel sighed. "Of course I'm not gonna kill you, but I would appreciate it if you would please come to New Orleans after you get off work. We need to protect you—and the general public—if at all possible."

I shook my head. "Not gonna happen. I'm going to the club tonight to confront Eva Sheridan one last time. Maybe I can talk some sense into her. I just… I can't turn into a vampire." I rubbed a greasy hand along the back of my neck. "Ya know what? This is a ridiculous conversation. Sorry about your friend, Joel, but I gotta get back to work." I pulled the phone away from my ear, hit the end button. I wiped sweat from my forehead, leaving a greasy print there.

After pocketing the phone, I zipped my coveralls back up. Plastering on a fake smile, I walked back into the garage and eyed Archie, who was watching me carefully. He had a worrisome look on his face that suggested he had heard the whole conversation. But I knew that was absurd; I had been speaking in hushed tones to Joel, even during the heated part of the conversation.

I ignored my paranoia and said, "Where were we?"

Archie raised a bushy silver eyebrow at me. "Everything okay, kid?"

I waved carelessly. "Sure, boss. Just woman trouble."

Archie said nothing else. We continued putting the old motorcycle back together and enjoyed a day of chatting that was just… normal.

When five p.m. rolled around, I changed out of my coveralls and scrubbed my hands and face in the staff restroom's sink. I looked up into the mirror at my reflection, and my dripping face was pale. There were deep, dark circles under my eyes. I frowned.

With a shake of my head, I left the bathroom as I pulled my keys from my pocket. As I went toward my motorcycle, I noticed Archie, along with five other middle-aged men, standing around my Ducati. All were sporting leather vests, chains, and ponytails, and had their arms either folded across their chests or their fists balled at their sides. My hackles went up and I looked to Archie, my head tilted to the side.

"Everything okay, boss?"

Archie approached me, then laid a fatherly hand on my shoulder. "Kid, I think you need our help."

My brows furrowed together. "I don't understand."

"I know about the succubus. I don't want to lose you, neither as an employee or a friend."

I blinked in shock and dropped my keys to the ground where they landed with a loud clink.

"How did you...?"

He spit a wad of chew out onto the sidewalk and pierced me with a serious look. "Eva Sheridan is a nasty succubus. She's been stealin' souls and creatin' vampers for a couple a years now. We've been trying to take her down for a while, but it seems we now have the perfect bait."

My eyebrows went up. "Wait. How did you...? I mean. Fuck." I scrubbed a hand along the back of my head. "Who's we?"

Archie laughed and gestured to his friends. "The Rebel Riders. It's the name of our club. Why do you think we're called that?"

I folded my arms over my chest. "Well, Archie, it isn't exactly an original, ground-breaking name for a motorcycle club. I didn't even think twice about it."

"Listen, Nolan, there's a rumor that if you drink or inject the blood of the succubus who stole your soul, you won't turn into a vampire. If you're going to The Blue Room tonight, we're gonna back you up. If we have to cut the bitch ourselves and force feed you her blood, we'll do it. It's how strongly we believe in you."

I blinked in shock. "How did you even know what happened to me?"

Archie sighed and dropped his hands to his side. "I went to your apartment a few nights ago to have you sign some forms. Before I could reach the steps to your place, I saw you and the redhead coming down the steps. I was stunned. I thought you were with Eva until I realized it wasn't her.

"I tailed you guys for a few miles and then it hit me: it can't be Eva, she would never casually hang out with a guy whose soul she stole."

I made a face. "How in the hell do you even know about this stuff? You guys some sorta vigilante vampire hunters, or something?"

A slow, sly grin crept up Archie's rough face. He shot a look at his comrades, then back at me. "Ya know what, kid? I like that term. Vigilante hunters. That pretty much describes what we do."

My eyebrows hit my hairline. "You're vampire hunters? Seriously?"

Archie pointed to his leg. "You wonder why I walk with a limp?"

I snorted. "No, I don't wonder. You told me you were stabbed in a bar fight in the eighties."

Archie replied, "I was. I was trying to stake a vamp but it grabbed the stake and shoved it into my leg. We were rasslin' around on the floor of the bar. Thank the heavens it stabbed my leg and not my chest."

"You're jokin'." I deadpanned.

"No, kid. I'm not." He laughed. "No way." His club brothers nodded their heads.

I shook mine and smirked. "Okay then. Meet me at The Blue Room at ten, and let's do this."

Archie's comrades let out a whoop. I hopped on the bike, started it up, and screeched out of the parking lot with a grin on my face.

Chapter 18

SUCCUBUS, PART II

A loud, obnoxious hip-hop song blasted out of the club's front doors and open windows as Parker, and Brennan, and I once again found ourselves standing in line to get into The Blue Room. Since its opening a couple of weeks prior, everyone in Shreveport who was in a party mood had flocked to the club, ready to dance and have fun.

Especially the succubi.

I was freshly shaved and had chosen a navy-blue button-up shirt and jeans, along with my black Durango harness cowboy boots. Of course my buck knife was shoved inside the left one.

As I was getting ready earlier, my mind had drifted back a week prior when I was at The Blue Room and *Mr. T* had patted me down to see if I had any weapons. The large, musclebound bouncer had run his hands around my chest, waist, and pantlegs. He hadn't checked the inside of my boots. I knew I could easily get to Eva with the knife on me, even after a good pat-down. I also knew the club had no metal detector in case I wanted to bring a gun as well.

Being a plotting murderer has caused some severe changes in my thought process, I mused.

My mind immediately drifted to Charity's sad face — the one she made every time we had a discussion about what had to happen to her sister.

I dismissed the thought and the image. I had to.

I eyed Parker dressed in a sharp, black fitted T-shirt, baggy jeans, and black boots. His hair was gelled up all shiny and spiky, and I was eye-to-eye with him, as he matched my six-foot-two height. There were girls further back in the line giggling and waving at us. I rolled my eyes.

Brennan had on a ten-gallon Stetson cowboy hat and Justin boots with a heel. His deep brown eyes almost seemed to search for approval with Parker and me as we looked at him.

As we paid our cover charge and pushed through the turnstile, we all immediately wandered up to the bar and ordered beers. My eyes involuntarily wandered over to the VIP section. It was void of anyone, just a few couches scattered around with nobody occupying them.

"Holy shit, check her out," Parker said, nudging me in the ribs.

I resisted the urge to massage my ribs and my gaze drifted to a redhead with long, curly hair. The short blue dress made her red hair pop and made her skin look creamy. Her high-heeled white sandals caused her calf muscles to glint under the harsh fluorescent lights.

Parker's mouth dropped open when I walked with purpose toward the woman. She lifted a hand and put it on my face, placing the other hand around my waist.

I was still in shock as I peered down at her. "What are you doing here, Charity?" I breathed. "I told you to stay home."

Her hand slid down my face, neck, and chest, and came to rest on my stomach, while her other was still on my lower back. "You're joking, right? You think I'm gonna sit at home while this all goes down?"

"That's what I was hoping," I replied on a sigh, my arms still at my sides.

She frowned. "You think I'm scared of Eva? I'm not. I want to help."

"Aren't you going to introduce us to your very hot friend, Bishop?" Parker said, suddenly appearing beside us. My eyes remained on Charity.

I hid my annoyance. "Parker, Brennan, this is Charity."

"And what kind of charity is she offering?" asked Parker, chuckling at his own joke.

I flicked a sideways glance at him and growled, "If you want to keep all your teeth, I suggest you shut the fuck up."

Parker lifted his hands in surrender. "I was just joking. Geez."

Charity narrowed her eyes at Parker. "You think that's the first time I've heard that stupid line?"

I grabbed her by the arm and led her away from the horny boys.

"Nice friends you have," she said dryly, pulling away from me and folding her arms across her chest.

I sighed. "I don't want Eva to see you here. We're gonna try to get into the VIP section again when she gets here, then you can talk to her."

She jutted her chin toward the lounge. "I can get you into the VIP area without you having to grovel to Eva for access."

"That's right, your dad owns this place." I shook my head. "They're loaded and you live in a tiny room above a Stop N Shop?"

"I told you before. I take care of myself. I don't need nobody else." She finished on a shrug.

I sighed. "I know, and I'm sorry. Please just stay in the corner of the club and don't let her see you. I need this to go down my way. Plus, Parker and Brennan have no idea what's going on. I want it to stay that way."

She stared up at me for a minute, and then nodded in resignation. She walked away with her hand still attached to mine, and I let go of it as she walked toward the bar.

I went back to my friends and put a beer bottle to my lips so I wouldn't have to explain.

"Now I know why she looks familiar." Parker stared at her retreating figure, and I had to resist the urge to punch him. "Ya know, she looks just like the redhead you were supposed to hook up with last week here. They sisters?"

I nodded. "Yes, twins."

Brennan grinned and nodded, the shadow from the brim of his hat covering half my face. "Twins. Hot."

"So you gonna try to hook up with her sister tonight? Is that why you told her to bounce?" Parker asked, pointing in Charity's direction. "Or hey, maybe you could get them both. Nice!"

I rolled my eyes. "It's not like that, dude. Just let it go. I need to talk to Eva, but I have no interest in her."

Before I'd even finished my sentence, Eva and her entourage of vampires entered the club. Just like last week, they were dressed in skirts and high heels, made up like dolls, and attracting the attention of everyone in the club. We all stared at the girls as they slunk into the VIP lounge. Seemingly out of nowhere, the bouncer from last week appeared and posted up at his spot by the girls. He let someone come in and deliver them drinks, and I knew nobody had even asked them what they wanted to order. Eva sat sipping what looked like a martini and was talking with her friends. I stood and watched, my eyes never leaving her. I waited a minute or two, and after finishing the last of my beer, I began walking toward the VIP. Brennan and Parker noticed this and were right on my heels.

The bouncer put out a dark, muscled arm and looked at me. "I don't think so."

I dipped my head toward Eva and locked eyes with her, who was now watching me. "I need to speak to her."

She shook her red head, her shiny bob haircut swishing with the sharp movement. "Hell no. Get lost, stalker."

Bouncer looked back at me and hooked a thumb over his shoulder. "You heard the lady. Beat it."

I faced Eva and said loudly, "Fine, I'm sure the people in this club would like to know that it's more than money we give up when we come in here. How many more of your special friends are sleazing around this place, huh, Eva?"

"Keep your damn voice down, Nolan!" Eva snapped, pointing at me.

I folded my arms. "Let me in. I'm not gonna be here all night. Your presence makes me sick, not to mention," I gritted out, "I'm a bit sleep-deprived."

She regarded me with an annoyed expression, a war seeming to rage behind her crystal-blue stare like she was trying to think of a way to get rid of me. She finally nodded at the bouncer and he moved out of the way so I could climb the steps. I sat in a chair opposite of Eva and leaned my elbows on my knees.

"Dude!"

I turned and saw my friends were being blocked by the bouncer. Parker had his arms up in question.

"I don't think my friends need to donate any blood tonight. Find yourselves new victims," I said, looking at Eva's three friends. I ignored Parker for now and turned my attention back to Eva.

She sighed and looked at her fingernails as if she were bored. "What do you want, Nolan? You're ruining my buzz."

"Well, you're ruining my *life*. By the way, thanks for the sucker punch to the back of my head. If I turn into a vampire tomorrow, I'm gonna kick your ass, and I don't care if you're a girl."

She narrowed her eyes at me. "You still didn't answer my question."

"You know what I want. Tell me how to reverse this. Look into my eyes again and undo what you did a week ago. I have a life to live and you had no right to take it from me. Why don't you go visit a prisoner doing life, or a mental hospital, and go steal from someone who has nothing to lose?"

She threw her head back and laughed. "You have no idea why I do what I do. I need your essence to survive; the vampire transformation is just a nasty side effect. It's not my fault."

He stared at her in shock. "Not your... Oh, my God." I was scarcely holding onto my control. "Give it back, Eva. I mean it. I'm a desperate guy barely hanging onto the edge here. And you know what they say about desperate men."

She smirked, and I wanted to slap her. "What's that?"

"We have nothing left to lose." I thought about the knife in my boot. Could I pull it out and commit murder in this club in front of everyone? Was I that *desperate*?

"Come outside so we can talk, I can't hear myself think in here," I said.

She laughed. "No."

I took a deep breath. "Then give me some of your blood."

She laughed again. "Not yet. We'll be doing plenty of blood sharing in my bed once you turn, honey. I can't wait to see you naked." She raked me from head to toe with her gaze.

There was no hiding the shock on my face and I gritted my teeth. "I would never willingly sleep with you. You disgust me."

She frowned, and her countenance quickly turned angry. She pounded her fist on the chair's arm and shot forward, getting in my face, her jaw grinding. "Oh, but you will, Nolan. When you have nowhere left to turn and you can't go in the sun, and you're hungry and even more desperate than you are now. You'll be crawling on your hands and knees, begging for our help." She gestured to herself, then her friends.

I reached down and under my pant leg, pulling the knife from my boot. All four girls gasped, and one screamed. I tried to be quick, but the vampire bouncer was much quicker. He wrenched my arms behind my back and forcefully removed the buck knife from my hand. He escorted me by the arm through the club with everyone watching. He opened the back door and threw me out, chucking the knife at me. The handle hitting me in the forehead.

"Fuck," I groaned.

"If I ever see you in here again, boy," he said in a deep voice, "you won't live to see the next day."

I got up, rubbed my head, and picked up my knife. I turned around without a word to head back to the parking lot. I was greeted by a group of half a dozen Harleys with men sitting on them.

The Rebel Riders had shown up.

"Nolan!" I turned around to see Charity running out of the back door toward me. She reached me, breathless and desperate. She gripped my biceps. "Are you okay?"

I looked down at her and hugged her. "Yes. I'm just even more pissed off than I was."

She pulled away slightly and looked down at the knife dangling from my fist. "Were you gonna use that?"

I blew out a breath. "I don't know, Charity. Eva said some pretty cruel and disgusting things in there. My rage got the better of me."

"Well, doing it in a public place like that isn't a good idea." She swallowed hard. "I wish there were an alternative."

"Did you get any of her blood, kid?"

We both turned around to see Archie gimping toward us.

I shook my head. "Are you kidding me? I'm no match for their vampire speed. I was thrown out the minute I pulled the knife out, boss."

Charity had a confused expression coloring her pretty features. "Boss?"

"I'm sorry." I sighed. "Charity, this is my boss, Archie. He's also, apparently"—I cleared my throat—"a vampire hunter… or something."

She looked at the middle-aged man and smiled politely. "Nice to meet ya, sir."

"Sweetheart, don't call me sir. That's for old folks, and I ain't old. Archie or Arch is just fine."

She grinned. "Okay, Archie." She eyed his biker friends, then looked at me. "Care to fill me in?"

I laughed humorlessly. "I have no idea. I just found out my boss goes to New Orleans in his spare time and hunts vampires. I thought he was just a biker dude who loved repairing old bikes."

Archie tipped his head back, silver ponytail sliding down his back, and laughed. "Boy, we been doin' this for twenty years. Vampire killin' is our specialty."

Charity looked at him wide-eyed. "Are you gonna kill my sister?"

Archie leaned back on his Harley, his arms folded across his leather vest. "See, that's the thing, sweetheart. I can't kill her. Nolan here has to do it if he wants his life back. I will, however, try my best to get him some of her blood."

Her eyebrows dipped into her forehead. "What do you need her blood for?"

Archie spit a wad of chew in a brown stream onto the chipped concrete of the parking lot. "Well, word is that if Nolan drinks or injects the blood of the succubus who took his soul, he may not turn into a vampire. Other rumors say he will still become one, but not a crazy, animalistic one."

Charity gasped, then looked at me. "Did you get some of her blood?"

I laughed. "Are you serious right now? Did you miss the part of the story where I was kicked out of the club faster than you can say 'succubus'?"

She wrinkled her nose. "Geez, Nolan, you don't have to be such a smartass. I was just askin'."

"Listen, little girl," Archie said, getting up from his semi-seated position and pointing at me, "this is the new Nolan if we don't either get me some of her blood, or have him stake that bitch. So ya better get used to it."

She narrowed her eyes at him and folded her arms over her chest. "Never."

Archie grinned at her and spit again. "I like your spunk, kid. You really like our boy, don't ya?" He inclined his head at me.

"I do. But I love my sister, too. It's been a rough week." She ended on a whisper.

The back door to the club opened and Parker and Brennan came out. They eyed me and Charity, and then the bikers.

"Dude, you joinin' a gang?" Parker asked with a laugh, then hiccupped.

I rolled my eyes. "You're drunk, asshole. Go back inside or call a cab."

Parker laughed.

Brennan looked at me, and his eyes were pleading.

"Can you get his keys and drive him home?" I asked my shorter friend.

Brennan shook his head. "Nah, I'm pretty buzzed myself." He glanced at Parker. "But this dude's totally plastered. I don't know how much longer I can hold him up."

I nodded and pulled out my phone and dialed the local cab company. I knew the number by heart because the phone number was all fours.

I clicked the end button and told Parker, "Your cab will be here soon. Go wait around the front of the club." I looked at Brennan. "I'm dealing with a situation here, so can ya help me out and get him home?" I shifted my eyes to Parker, who was barely standing. "I'll text you tomorrow."

Brennan nodded and led Parker around a set of dumpsters and then disappeared on the other side of the building.

"Nice friends ya got there," Archie said, amusement dancing in his eyes.

"That's not the first time I've heard that tonight," I murmured, shaking my head.

Charity ignored my comment and looked at Archie and his friends. "So what's the plan here, people? You gonna try to kill my sister when her and her friends come out later?"

Archie wasn't amused by the sarcasm in her voice. "Listen, girl, there's something you need to get through that red head of yours." He pointed toward the building. "That succubus bitch in there is no longer your sister. She's a soul-stealing, inhuman demon who only looks after herself and her needs. The quicker you grasp that, the better off you'll be. Ya hear?"

Charity's bottom lip quivered and tears glistened in her eyes. She bit her lip to keep it from wobbling and said, "I do know that. But you don't have to be so mean about it."

I wrapped an arm around her. "Shh. It's okay."

Archie said, "She needs the truth, boy. Not hugs."

"I know, boss, but this is her twin sister. Why do you think I haven't killed her yet?"

One of Archie's friends piped up, "Because she's a vampire and too fast for you." All his friends erupted in laughter.

"I'll handle this, Archie," I said through gritted teeth. "And if I fail, I won't be at work Monday."

I led Charity over to my car, where we stood and I grabbed her hand. Archie and his club members were still standing near the side of the building next to their bikes. I expected them to start them up and drive off, but they remained there, their asses propping up their motorcycles, as if waiting for something.

"I want you to stay in the car."

Her voice jerked on a sob. "Are you going to kill Eva?" A single tear cascaded down her face.

"Charity, just stay in the car." I was tired of that question. I was tired of looking out for everyone but myself.

I was just tired.

I closed the door to the Charger and walked back toward Archie and his friends. "So what's the plan?"

Archie's eyes slid to the back door of the club, then back to me. "When the succubus and her she-devils come out, we're gonna attack. Any way you can get back into the club? Warn us when they're leaving so we have the element of surprise?"

I shook my head. "The bouncer threatened me with violence if I step foot back in there."

Archie's mouth twisted in thought. "What about Red? Can she go back in and then call or text when the demons are leaving?"

I put a hand low on my hip, and then rubbed my forehead where the knife had hit me. "I don't know, Arch. If Eva sees her…"

"Kid, this isn't funny anymore. I don't care if the succubus recognizes her twin or not. Unless she's gonna be suspicious that her twin is there?"

I snorted. "Probably. She's more of a stay at home and chill type."

Archie regarded me with a confused look on my wise face. "Well, regardless, boy, this succubus needs to go down. You gonna man-up and do it?"

Chapter 19

SHOWTIME

I couldn't do it. I couldn't use Charity as bait. The one thing I hadn't told Archie—or anyone, really—was that I kind of always knew where Eva was. I could feel her, or sense her. One annoying side effect of this was that I was also inexplicably aroused, which irritated the shit out of me.

"I'm gonna just wait on the side of the building until they come out. I'll know when she gets close to coming out, and then I'll try to grab her and drag her around the back."

Archie regarded me for a moment, trying to decide if I was going to say what I was thinking.

"What?" I asked.

"What if you use the sister as a hostage? Would that get her to do what you want?"

"No. No way. Not to mention, I don't think she cares about Charity. Not really, anyway. She's a soulless bitch. She looks out for number one. No way would she risk herself over Charity."

Archie nodded. "I figured. Okay, you go round front and signal when they're coming out—"

One of Archie's friends let out a low whistle. I turned and looked at his fellow biker and the guy extended his long, bearded chin toward the club. "Here come the bitches."

"Shit, it's showtime!" Archie barked out.

Thankfully, it was just the four girls, no bouncer. They were laughing and chatting. Two of the girls had their arms linked together and were talking amongst themselves. Popping out from around the corner, I ran up to Eva, snatched her by the arm, and began dragging her toward the back of the building. Archie and his friends grabbed the other vampires and did the same.

Eva hissed and her eyes turned black. She produced a set of fangs, and with a sharp stiletto heel, kicked me in the thigh, which caused me to lose my grip on her. She screeched like an angry cat and stalked toward me. I was limping backward at her fierce, frightening look, and when she reached me, she raised her arm to slap me. I caught her arm and reached for my knife again. She twisted out of my grip and kicked me again.

I fell on my back, but before I could reach the knife, a biker grabbed her from behind. She reared her head back with supernatural speed and broke his nose with her head.

The biker roared in pain as blood gushed like a fountain down his goatee and lips. "Bitch!"

I had the knife out now and decided I had to get over the fact that this was a woman. I dismissed my father's voice ringing in my ears. *Never, ever hit a woman, son.* I shook my head and ran full force toward her, tackling her legs like the football player I used to be, and she fell on her back with a thud.

A screech caught my attention as I watched Archie plunge a wooden stake through the chest of the pretty Black vampire with the shiny hair. Her look of shock was replaced by dust and ash as her clothes and shoes landed on a pile of ash.

The other two vampires were fighting with two bikers. The vampires were vicious; trying to bite them, and hissing like deranged cats. I wanted to help, but I had bigger fish to fry. Then I heard police sirens. The split-second moment of distraction was all Eva needed. She kneed me in the stomach and I bent over and coughed. She walked over and kicked the knife out of my hand, probably breaking a couple of bones in my hand. I screamed in pain. Eva ran at an unnatural speed and snatched her two remaining friends. They ran off in a blur around the side of the building.

I walked hunched over to Archie and panted, "Get the hell out of here. Cops are on the way. We'll have to get them another time."

Archie was out of breath. "Kid, you don't have any more time. It's all but up. I hope you enjoy your new life. Don't come to my house when you're hungry, because I won't hesitate to kill you."

I reeled in shock. "Are you serious?"

Archie's eyes were sad. "I loved you like a son, boy. I still do. But I can't love a vampire. Vampires cannot be trusted. You will see. You will have no more feelings or emotions, just primal needs like an animal to eat and stay alive. It's no way to live. There is no joy, there is only survival."

He looked at me hard, but the orange overhead lights caught a glistening in Archie's eyes as he said with a hand on my shoulder, "May God have mercy on your soul."

He turned around and got on his bike, and his three comrades followed him out of the parking lot with a rumble.

I pulled up whatever resolve I had left and got into the driver's seat of the Charger. Charity was still in the passenger seat, sobs heaving out from her. I didn't even look at her. Cradling my left hand in my lap, I used my right to shove the key in and start up the car. We drove off before the police arrived.

We pulled into my parking spot of my apartment complex. I killed the engine and finally looked at Charity. She had dried her tears and now had a blank expression on her face. She was stared out of the window, but slowly turned her head to look at me.

"Do you want me to take you home?"

She shook her head. "I don't want to go home."

I looked straight ahead and said, "I don't know why I even asked you. It's not safe for you to be around me right now." I glanced at the dash clock. "It's two a.m. and who knows when this supposed transformation is gonna take place? I need to take you home."

She put her hand on mine and gasped. "You're burning up."

I nodded. "Yes, I feel a bit feverish. Plus, my hand is throbbing like a bitch." I looked down at it and it was purple and swollen, but no longer felt like it was broken.

"Please don't take me home. I'm with you until the end. I owe it to you. I know you could have killed Eva, but you didn't."

I shook my head. "Did you watch that whole thing? I couldn't even get my knife out. I had no chance against her strength and speed."

"Would you have done it?"

I blew out a breath. "Honestly, I don't think so. I was just going to slice her good and then try to get some of her blood in my mouth." I shuddered. "Disgusting."

She nodded. "Do you still have the knife?"

"Yes, why?"

"Let me see it." She held out her hand.

I raised an eyebrow. "Why, you gonna kill me?" I reached down and pulled it out, handing to her. I truly didn't care if she did kill me at this point.

She held the knife up and slowly unsheathed it. The lights from the parking lot glinted off of it as she stared at it. Then she looked around the car and spotted a white Starbucks cup. She popped the lid off and dumped the remaining coffee out onto the street through her open window. She placed the empty cup between her legs and gripped the knife firmly. She took a big breath, then began slowly slicing the palm of her left hand. She cried out in pain, but didn't stop.

"Oh, my God, what the hell are you doing?" I yelled. "Stop it!" I yanked the knife out of her hand... but it was too late.

She made a fist and squeezed the blood from her hand into the cup. She kept squeezing until she couldn't get any more drops out.

"Do you have a first-aid kit or something?" she whimpered, cradling her hand, palm-side up.

I reached into the backseat, grabbed a T-shirt, and wrapped her hand up. "Want to tell me what you think you're doing?"

I tied the shirt in a knot around her hand, and when I was done, she picked up the cup and said, "Drink it."

I made a face and said, "Why?"

"Because you're desperate. I'm desperate. That Archie guy said drinking Eva's blood might reverse your curse. We're identical twins with identical DNA. I think we should try anything we can."

The use of the word 'we' resonated. It did not go unnoticed by me that she was risking her very safety just being in the car with me, when it was well past midnight on the seventh day. As I stared at her pleading blue eyes, I could see love and compassion shining out of them. I had never had anyone but my family care for me like this before. I was standing on the edge of a deadly cliff that could end my very life, and here she was, staying right by my side, like she was reaching down into a desperate place in her very soul to help me out, when she got nothing out of it. Her life could be in at risk, her heart could get torn into a million pieces if I turned into a monster, and instead of caring about herself, she cared about me more. If that wasn't the definition of love, I didn't know what was.

Without one more thought, I picked up the Starbucks cup and gulped down the entire contents. I thought I might gag or choke, but what scared me was that the blood did not taste that bad.

That was a bad sign. A very, very bad sign.

"I'm concerned you did not choke, gag, or even make a face as you drank that," she said, her fingers to her mouth as her thoughts mirrored mine.

I wiped away some blood from my lip with my thumb, then wiped it on my jeans. "Yeah, it's a bit strange."

"Now what?" she asked.

I looked at her for a long minute and said, "I don't think I should be around people right now. I'm gonna go sit at Cross Lake and wait for the sun to come up."

She gasped. "If you turn into a vampire, that will kill you."

I smiled sadly, my heart aching. I started up the engine. "I know."

Chapter 20

SITTIN' ON THE DOCK OF THE BAY

Arriving at Cross Lake, I parked the Charger in the same exact spot I had on the day after my breakup with Sarah. The night was still dark, a star-shot sky overhead with not a cloud in the sky. A slight, cool breeze was blowing, indicating the cruel summer was almost coming to an end. As Charity and I got out of the car, I led her by the hand down the long, wooden dock. We didn't have anything us except the clothes on our backs, and of course, the knife in my boot.

We reached the end of the dock, and I pointed at her feet. "Take your shoes off."

She nodded and did as she was told. I also removed my boots and socks and rolled up my pantlegs. We both sat down at the edge of the dock and put our feet in the water.

"Feels nice. I thought it would be cold."

I laughed. "It's summertime. It's always kinda warm this time of year. This isn't the Pacific Ocean."

She looked at me curiously. "You ever been to the Pacific Ocean?"

"No, but I wanna visit one day."

She grabbed my hand and said, "I really hope you get to."

"Will you come with me?"

She smiled and slid some hair behind her ear. "Yes, of course. I've always wanted to visit San Francisco."

"Me too," I replied quietly.

We said nothing else. She rested her weary head on my muscled shoulder and we sat there, holding hands and not speaking for a long time. After about thirty minutes, I said, "Promise me something?"

She didn't hesitate. "Anything."

"When the sun comes up, and I catch on fire, just run. Run fast. The keys are still in the car. Just drive off and don't ever think of me again."

She snorted. "I was thinking of pushing you in the water, actually. You're crazy if you think I'm just gonna watch you burn."

I pulled out of our soft embrace and put both hands on her face. "This isn't funny, Charity. I want you to get as far away from me as possible. If I turn into a monster, I might hurt you. I can't believe I even brought you here. What was I thinking?"

"I'm with you to the end, baby," she drawled, and laid her head back on my shoulder.

We chit-chatted for hours about random things, the sadness in our voices drifting off into the choppy black waves of the lake, being carried out into the abyss.

A pink tinge to the horizon began to creep up the edge of the water where it met the sky. My stomach turned with nerves as I stared at it. I looked over at Charity. The pink caused her red hair to glow bright, and her pale face was lit up in the colors of the impending sunrise.

After only a minute or two, it seemed as though the sun was beginning to come up fast. Truth be told, I had never watched a sunrise before. I was ashamed to admit it, but in my twenty-one years, I'd just never taken the time to appreciate a gorgeous sunrise.

Charity's eyes glistened with tears and she swallowed down a sob. A single drop of despair leaked down her face as she broke the embrace from me. "I care for you, Nolan. But... what I don't care for is catching on fire."

She looked at me like she was getting dizzy. Then she began to burst out in crazed laughter. She looked like she was losing her mind.

"My boyfriend is going to turn into a vampire and then catch fire, like something out of a movie. Do I really believe this?" She laughed again.

She looked at me, half crying, half laughing. "This is insane, Nolan. I just watched you drink my blood earlier without wincing. I have spoken to a real, true-to-life vampire in New Orleans. I have visited with a voodoo priest who had told us with an expression on his face that meant business, that your days were numbered." Her expression just turned plain sad. "I endured the months of my sister being missing. I watched, with my very own eyes, as my boyfriend stabbed a vampire and it turned to ash and dust. Just a few hours ago, I had screamed at the top of my lungs from the passenger seat of your car as I had to watch another one of them die and crumble ash."

I wished I could say I was confused by her words and behavior, but I wasn't. Nothing would ever be normal again. I looked down into her eyes. "Yes, Charity, this is real. It's all real as hell."

Saying nothing, she looked at the pinking horizon of Cross Lake and began scooting away from me. "Will your eyes turn black like Eva's?" she asked.

She seemed to be looking around the dock in a panic. When she located what she was looking for, she gripped the buck knife in her pale, slender fingers and continued scooting away.

I didn't move or flinch. I just simply looked out at the glistening water and said, "You're smart to move away. You shouldn't have come."

I felt uneasy. I felt as though I should get up and walk away. I didn't want to hurt Charity. I began to shake and feel twitchy. I actually felt like I wanted to cry — that I should cry — but I couldn't.

I pulled my now wrinkled and pruny feet from the water and made to stand up when the first bit of sun began to peak over the horizon of the water. Sunbeams assaulted my face and I sucked in a breath, closing my eyes and waiting for the sun to set me on fire.

But then… like breaking the surface of the water after being submerged for too long, feeling like I might die of drowning, I sucked in a breath and gasped hard. I gulped in air harder than I ever had in my whole life. I felt like I was finally getting oxygen after being trapped in an airless coffin for a week. My lungs filled with glorious air and I let the yellow sunlight bask my face in its glow.

I glanced at Charity when she stood up. She watched dumbfounded as I tilted my face toward the heavens and laughed. With the knife still gripped in her bandaged hand, the other flew to her mouth as rivulets of tears began to stream down her freckled face.

"Why aren't you catching on fire?" she breathed.

I shrugged and closed my eyes again. "Who cares? I'm alive! And I feel!"

Now the tears came. They streamed down my face, but I didn't give a shit.

Charity sounded bewildered. "I don't understand."

I tilted my head down and looked at her. "Neither do I. But I feel different. I feel free. I just… feel."

I looked at her sitting there, despair, shock, and amazement, all one single emotion coloring her face. I walked over to her and helped her to stand. After placing one hand on her face, with the other, I gently pried the knife from her hands and tossed it onto the dock. It landed with a clank and the blossoming sunrise caused it to shimmer.

"God, I love you. I've loved you from the moment I laid eyes on you. You proved to me today that you deserve every bit of happiness and love." I leaned down and placed my lips gently on hers. She wrapped her arms around my waist and closed her glossy blue eyes, swooning.

We stood embraced in the early morning light for what seemed like hours, the orange ball sitting lazily over the horizon of the water, silhouetting us. There was nobody around and I was thinking how happy I was that we were alone.

"Dammit, Jimmy, how many times I gotta tell you? You can't put Hayabusa parts on a Yamaha!"

I grinned and shook my head as I listened to Archie yell at one of the new employees. I came around the side of the garage and stood in the open bay with one hand in my pocket and the other was holding Charity's hand.

"Give the kid a break, boss," I said with a smirk.

It was now four in the afternoon, and after Charity and I had slept most of the day away, we decided to visit Archie and thank him for my help the night before.

Archie stood there with his mouth slightly open and his eyes wide. He looked at Jimmy, who was hardly paying attention, and said, "I'll be right back, kid. Get those parts off."

Once he reached me, Archie gripped me in a manly, fatherly hug. He pulled me out of earshot of the people in the shop. "Holy shit, boy! I thought for sure you'd be either a pile of ash or sleepin' in a coffin by now."

I laughed. "Nah, no vampire here. And I plan to stay far away from that club and them, trust me."

Archie folded his arms over his chest and said, "What happened?"

I shook my head. "I don't really know. Charity gave me some of her blood and I drank it out of desperation. Then we went to Cross Lake and waited for the sun to come up."

"But that would have killed you if you had turned into a vamper," Archie gasped.

"I know, that was kind of the point. You think I wanted to live like that? I'd rather die."

Archie nodded and spit chew onto the sidewalk. "I get it, kid. Trust me. I would have done the same thing."

"Thanks, Arch. I'll be at work Tuesday. I just need a couple days off to relax and get back to normal."

"Of course, take all the time you need."

I grinned. "Thanks, boss."

Charity and I turned to walk off, my arm slung over her slender shoulders.

"Oh, Nolan," Archie called out.

I stopped walking and turned only my head around. "Yeah?"

"We have a spot for you in the Rebel Riders if you're interested. We'd be happy to have you as an honorary member."

I smiled. "I'll keep that in mind, Arch."

Epilogue

A quiet breeze blew through Eva's partially opened window. The vertical blinds were completely drawn and the curtains pulled shut, but the window itself was still cracked to allow some air in. The wind made the black lace curtains rustle.

The sky outside the mansion was still dark, with just a hint of blue in the east. The house was quiet and there was a floor fan to block out any distracting noises. The Victorian-era canopy above her bed was the first thing she saw as her blue eyes slammed open from a dead sleep.

She let out a blood-curdling scream that would wake the dead and bolted upright in her bed. Clutching her chest, Eva began to pant and tears streamed down her face. She was suddenly starving—famished.

After arriving home, she had licked her wounds from the fight with Nolan and the bikers, and thanks to her rapid healing ability, by the time she fell into bed, she wasn't in any more pain. Yet, now, just one hour later, her chest felt like it might rip open. The soul she'd stolen—the pure, sweet soul of Nolan Bishop—was no longer hers to keep. He had somehow taken it back, and the pain of it being ripped from her was excruciating.

Brad came bolting through her bedroom door, his hair sticking up from being violently jarred from sleep thanks to her screams. He blitzed over to the bed. "You okay?"

Eva was violently trembling. "I... don't know. I... I don't feel right."

He grabbed her soft hand and stroked it. "Anything I can do?"

She narrowed blue eyes at him and said, "Yes, as a matter of fact, there is…"

In an unnaturally fast move, she had Brad pinned on his back. Her eyes turned black and her fangs descended. She bit into his neck as she ripped his pajama bottoms off.

Brad didn't seem to mind at all. He tore her blue tank top off in one fell swoop and threw the shreds to the floor. He tilted his head back with a smile, and let her feed. Brad knew what he had to offer wouldn't satisfy the succubus. But he could at least let her satisfy him for a while.

When they were done, Eva told Brad to scram. He happily went back to his room and fell into a deep sleep, but hers did not come as easily. She lay in her bed and rage began to seethe under her pale skin. How in the hell did he take it back?

She gasped in realization and screamed, "Charity!"

Joel Reichert sat at his desk with his hand to his mouth. His face was basked in a red glow from the lights of the hotel's ballroom shining into his top floor office. He was lost in his thoughts and memories of his friend Ansel. They'd been friends for fifty years. Joel and Ansel had met at Woodstock in New York in 1969 and became instant friends. They met through a group of mutual friends who had traveled via caravan to the now-famous concert. They'd shared a couple of joints and a few hits of LSD while enjoying the psychedelic music and atmosphere of the concert. They became fast friends when they both realized we were from the South, Joel from Louisiana, and Ansel from Kentucky. Since that day at Woodstock, they had spoken often, and then in 1975, Ansel moved to Louisiana and they went into the hotel business together.

After a brief knock, the door to the office opened and Joel's newly-turned assistant walked in.

He set a small, silver urn on the desk and then stood up straight with his hands behind his back. His black suit and tie were pressed and neat, his young face stern and ready for his next order. "I collected all I could, sir. I'm sorry there's not more."

Joel nodded. "Thank you, Tommy. I'd like to be alone if, you don't mind."

Tommy nodded and left as quietly as he'd come.

Joel leaned forward and rested his elbows on his large desk. He stared at the fancy silver urn and, taking a deep breath, he lifted the small lid and peered inside. He frowned when he saw the ashes barely covered the bottom of the container.

He replaced the lid, sat back, and rubbed his forehead. Rage began to bubble up inside of him. That kid, Nolan Bishop, had had as much sympathy and sorrow telling Joel he'd killed Ansel as if he'd been delivering news of running over his cat by accident. But this was no accident. Self-defense or not, Ansel was dead, and Nolan was probably a vampire somewhere. A feral vampire who needed to be trained and contained. Except this time, there would be no training. That feral vampire would have to be put down, and Joel vowed to do it himself.

THE END

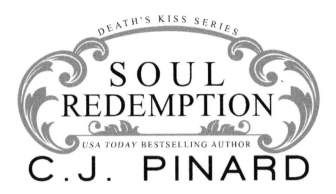

Book 2 in the Death's Kiss Series

SOUL REDEMPTION

"IN YOUR SOUL ARE INFINITELY PRECIOUS THINGS THAT CANNOT BE TAKEN FROM YOU." OSCAR WILDE

Chapter 1

SUNLIGHT, BLOODY SUNLIGHT

Nolan

I slipped on my aviator sunglasses, then slid my red and white helmet over my head. After slinging my right leg over the seat of my Ducati Monster, I pumped my foot and pushed the start button, revving up the obnoxiously loud machine and peeling out of the parking lot of my apartment complex in Shreveport, Louisiana.

I drove faster than I should have, just wanting to get to work and into the shelter of Archie's Garage, where I restored motorcycles for a living. Since it was September, the sun was shining down hard, and quite frankly, irritating the shit out of me.

During the short drive to the shop, I again racked my brain as to why the sun was suddenly bothering me. I used to love it. I would lie out on the small deck attached to my apartment and let it bronze my skin. Now, I just wanted to avoid it. To be inside and away from the hot, annoying ball of fire in the sky.

I parked in my regular spot and didn't remove my helmet until I was inside the garage. I went to the back room and put my belongings into my locker. Then, sliding my coveralls on, I strolled into the hot garage. Archie was on his back under an old Harley, grease covering his hands.

"Hey, boss."

Archie didn't look up. "Happy Monday, kid. There's a Honda with your name on it in the corner."

I looked up and saw a sad yellow Honda Supersport at the far end of the garage that Jimmy was tinkering with. I strolled up to him. "What's goin' on, Jim?"

Jimmy, the new kid, who had his hands wrist-deep in the engine of the

Honda, looked up at me. "Hey."

I bit back a smile and pointed at a Mitsubishi part lying next to the bike. "You're not putting that fuel pump on this Honda, are you?"

He stood up and wiped his hands on his coveralls. "Yeah, why?"

I stared into his anxious brown eyes and grinned. "You can't do that. That's not a Honda part."

The newbie looked stressed, picking up the part and walking toward the parts room.

I pulled my phone from the pocket of my jeans and saw I had three missed texts. They were all from Charity. I grinned at the simple messages, telling me to have a good day and informing me of which new restaurant she'd like me to take her to this upcoming weekend.

I thought about Charity and a smile lit up my face. If there was one bright spot in my otherwise dark world, it was her. I remembered how her ginger hair had reflected the early morning sunrays when we sat at Cross Lake. She hadn't run away, afraid of the monster I might become, but had stayed, telling me she was with me until the end. Charity was just what I needed in my life, and I was glad she felt the same way. I sometimes felt like things were moving a bit fast for us, but then I realized that because of the intense week we'd spent together, that maybe it had sealed our friendship-turned-infatuation into something more. I had to admit we'd cooled things off a bit in the last week. I still hadn't slept with her yet. Oh, I wanted to. I thought I'd get lucky the day I had realized the sun wasn't going to fry me. We'd gone back to my place to sleep it off, but no such luck. We were both too physically and mentally exhausted to have engaged in anything. We'd both passed out and slept the day away.

"You gonna stand there all day with your thumb up your ass, or are you gonna train the rookie?"

I looked up to see Archie standing next to the Honda, his arms folded over his coveralls, a wad of chew in his bottom lip.

I grinned. "Oh no, Arch, no screwing off here. I'm happy to train Jimmy."

Archie's eyes scrutinized me carefully, the earring in his left ear catching the light from the headlamp of a nearby Harley. "It's good to have you back, kid. I thought I'd lost you."

I smiled big. "Well, you didn't."

Archie's gaze cautiously scanned our surroundings, then fixed back on mine. "Have you given any thought to joinin' the Rebel Riders?"

"Not a whole lot, but you'll be the first to know if I do."

Archie seemed satisfied with that, and after nodding, limped off back to the old Harley he'd been tinkering with. I suspected it was going to be another one to add to his personal collection.

Truth was, the appeal of joining the Rebel Riders was calling to me. I also knew there was something terribly wrong with me physically and was determined to get to the bottom of it. I unzipped my coveralls and pulled Joel Reichert's card from the pocket of my jeans. I flipped it around in my fingers. I wondered if I should call the old vampire and beg him for answers to all the unanswered questions swirling around in my brain. Then I remembered killing Ansel, Joel's oldest vampire friend in the world, and realized that wasn't such a good idea after all.

My mind eventually drifted to the succubus, Eva. I wondered if she somehow knew that I'd survived the change. That I hadn't turned into a vampire after all. I contemplated whether that myth was even true. Maybe a succubus taking the soul of a human man didn't result in him turning into a vicious, soulless vampire. Maybe it was just folklore.

I thought back to all I'd endured during that week from hell and shuddered.

Maybe it wasn't.

The workday was long over. I had worked until almost eight p.m., losing myself in helping Jimmy restore the old bike. I'd worked far longer than any of the employees and had closed down the shop by myself. Taking off on my bike, I decided to head to the warehouse district in Shreveport. I was glad the sun had set, as the night made me feel alive.

Lifting my weary head, I stared at the huge cobalt sign illuminating the Blue Room. I could hear country music pumping out of the doors, and the distant sounds of laughing partygoers as they entered the club for country night. My bike was parked at the very back of the lot, hidden in the shadow behind a jacked-up Chevy 4x4 on oversized tires. I leaned on the handlebars, staring intently at the club and its patrons, hoping maybe I'd see her go in. Then I remembered what Charity had told me — that their parents owned the club, and that Eva had sort of taken it over. I quickly realized she'd never enter through the front door like a regular patron. She was too good for that.

I slid a hand over my shorn hair and blew out a breath. The night wind was warm and muggy, but I could feel a slight cooling in the air, as if fall may just come early. Something about that made me smile a little; I realized fall meant shorter days leading to winter. *Less sun.* Why this pleased me, I would never know, but I did know I should probably go see a doctor soon. I wasn't even twenty-two yet, but I felt sick during the day. The sun and its rays weren't friends of mine anymore.

I leaned up on my bike and prepared to start the Ducati's engine when my phone vibrated in my pocket. I pulled it out and looked at the text.

Charity: *Are you still at work? I miss you. Come see me.*

I smiled a little, really wanting to see her. And knowing her evil twin probably wouldn't hang out at her own club on country night, I turned on the bike and peeled out of the parking lot, heading straight for Charity's little flat that was set above the small Stop-N-Shop where she worked.

The night was fully dark and quiet now. The sun had set, and one small streetlight illuminated the dank parking lot. The dull red lights to the Stop-N-Shop's sign were on, and just a few random paper signs hung in the windows of the little store. It was otherwise dark inside.

I went around back, found the large, gray back door ajar, and pushed it open. I went inside, and as I closed the heavy door, I peered at the set of concrete steps that led up to Charity's small apartment. I took a deep breath and began climbing them.

As I reached the top, I knocked once, but the door was yanked open before I could lift my hand. She grabbed me by the front of my T-shirt, and before I could speak or take a breath, I was pulled inside with my lips being crushed to hers.

I smiled against her warm mouth and began kissing her back, my tongue snaking into her waiting, willing mouth. I dragged her into the kitchen and pushed her against the refrigerator as I continued to deliciously assault her mouth. After a few minutes, I broke away and inquired, "Why are we in your kitchen?"

She gave me a coy grin and said, "Are you hungry?"

I lifted an eyebrow at her. "Are you serious?"

She giggled. "Yes. But I really do mean food."

I looked down at my pants, which seemed to have shrunk two sizes, and said, "You expect me to think about food?"

Charity pulled away from me and scooted me back from the door of the fridge. Pulling it open, she lifted a package of sausage from the top shelf. "I'll make you some red beans and rice with sausage."

I backed myself up onto the counter of the tiny kitchen. "I'd rather be eating something else."

Her freckly cheeks flushed pink she and turned back around, the sausage in her hand. Leaning down, she plucked a pan from the cabinet and placed it on the gas burner without turning around. "I bet."

I sighed and made my way to her small living room, planting myself on her couch, hoping to distract away my arousal. After picking up the remote control, I began to channel surf. "There's nothing good on."

Charity opened a drawer in the small kitchen and pulled out some tongs. "I only have ten channels. You're lucky I even own a TV."

Sighing, I flicked the television off, rose from the couch, and strolled back into the kitchen. "You're right. I can think of other ways to occupy our time."

With her back to me at the stove, I came up behind her and moved some red curls to the side. I slid both hands around her slim waist and reached under her shirt, rubbing her taut stomach with my thumbs. I began to run soft kisses up her neck, and once I reached her ear, I murmured, "We can skip dinner. I'm really not hungry."

She turned around, her blue eyes blazing up at me. "B.S. You've been working all day. I know you're hungry."

My gaze flicked to the stove where the sausage was frying and the water was boiling for the rice. Then I licked my lips. "Not for red beans and rice."

She smacked my hard bicep. "Nolan Bishop! You really want our first time to be in this stupid apartment?"

I grinned a little and then ran my hand along the back of my neck. "I don't care, Charity. I just want you. All of you."

Chapter 2

REBEL RIDERS

va was lying in bed, her pale arms folded behind her head as she stared unseeing at the white ceiling. She felt weak, but the anger ebbing away at the hole in her chest was giving her strength. She had felt differently since a few nights ago, the one-week mark of when Nolan would have become a vampire.

Hadn't she taken his soul like every other chump she'd been with? Why was she feeling so empty and restless inside? Her mind twirled and her rage began to bubble. Eva disliked not being in control. She knew how things should be and didn't appreciate the change. The big, gaping hollow in her chest was a constant reminder that whatever she'd done to Nolan hadn't worked. She'd taken his soul—his *essence*—and had felt satisfied. It had filled her up to elation and completeness, sating the gap inside her where her own soul should be, the one she'd given up in exchange for beauty, bloodlust, and immortality. She remembered devouring it that night, and then she'd found a to feed on for blood. But a week later, she began to feel the hunger again. The hunger that normally took weeks to months to come back was gnawing at her again. This time, she felt utterly starved—famished—as if she hadn't fed in years. Her chest ached and burned, and her mind felt foggy.

There was nothing like the flush of a fresh soul seeping into her body. The burn was like a shot of whiskey traveling down into her very center; it was incomparable to any other rush of pleasure she could possibly experience. Stealing a soul refreshed her and made her feel vibrant, glowing, and beautiful. She felt powerful and invincible after consuming one. And Eva had felt like that after meeting Nolan at the Blue Room over a week ago. As she had bored her gaze into Nolan's, she'd known the soul she was sucking down and feeding on was pure and good. The cleaner the soul, the longer she could go without having to feed. She felt like she had won the supernatural lottery when she had spotted Nolan in the club that night.

But now, there was nothing. Yesterday, she had awoken with a scream as the pain from the shot to her chest had bolted her out of her daytime sleep. She should have been resting comfortably at that stage after feeding. Not now. She was restless and agitated, unable to sleep, unable to function. Eva couldn't figure out why she was feeling this way, but she knew there was only one way to find out. She'd track down Nolan Bishop and find out if he'd turned into a vampire.

Normally, the victims would come to her for help — if they had survived the change and had had the brains to stay out of the sunlight. And once they did, she either killed them, or made them into a sex slave or just a personal servant. Like Brad. He'd been a victim, a nearly pure soul she'd taken a few years back. He'd been tamer than most of the feral vampires she'd turned, and Eva had decided she could tame him further and had kept him at her beck and call.

Eva knew exactly where to find Nolan. He'd been hanging out with her annoying twin sister. With a pained smile, she decided that was an excellent place to start.

Nolan

Archie, along with myself and five other men were sitting around a table, playing cards. A large, tacky lamp with a beer logo was set above us, illuminating our game in an orange glow.

"Your turn, Bishop," Archie said, looking at me.

I nodded, gazing around Archie's small house — his bachelor pad — before surveying my cards once again, trying to decide on a move — which hand to play.

Truthfully, I knew only the bare minimum about poker. After Googling the rules, of course. Archie had invited me to hang out with his outlaw friends, and I wasn't going to turn down my boss. I was just grateful the game was at night, as the sun was still bothering me and not getting any better. If anything, the sun was annoying me more and more.

I spied the pile of plastic chips on the center of the table then looked back at my cards. My brow furrowed as I saw nothing but high numbers and no kings, queens, or aces. "Pass," I said.

Archie snorted and I looked up. Blue smoke swirled through the air, as if attracted by the lamp. I tried not to cough. It seemed as if my sense of smell had kicked into high gear in the past few days, along with all the other weird shit happening to me.

"Your poker face sucks, kid." Archie chuckled, wrapping his tanned and scarred fingers around a glass tumbler containing something honey-colored. He slammed the liquid back then set the glass down, studying his cards. "Flush, assholes," he said with a smile, fanning his impressive hand of cards on the table with a proud flourish.

I was glad the game was over, and tossed my cards onto the table. My true intention of going to Archie's was to get a feel for the other members of the Rebel Riders. As I looked at the other five men, I thought they seemed like a normal group of worn and ragged bikers, but I knew what they really were—a bunch of rebels who rode around at night, looking for vampires to kill. A month ago, the thought of such a thing would have been ludicrous and comical. I still couldn't believe it myself. How had my world been turned on its head in such a short time?

"Wanna ride with us?" Archie asked cautiously as I plucked my keys from my pocket, getting ready to leave.

I raised an eyebrow with a frown. "Where to?"

"To where the bloodsuckers are," Archie replied with seriousness lacing his tone.

Reeling with shock at the invitation, I reluctantly decided I had nothing else to do. Charity had to close the shop tonight, and I had to admit the curiosity of what this band of bikers did to rid the world of vampires had piqued my curiosity to epic levels.

With a lift of my shoulder, I replied, "Sure, boss."

Archie smiled, a big wad of dip in his bottom lip looking out of place against his happy face. "I knew you'd join us."

I snorted and kept my hands on my hips. "I'm not 'joining you'," I replied, using my fingers as air quotes. "I'm just tagging along."

Archie laughed and limped off toward his garage. I went out through the front door and started the Ducati, getting ready to follow the old rebels to God knew where to hunt for vampires.

How has my life become this?

It shouldn't have seemed awkward, sitting there with a group of bikers, watching an old house, but it was. Awkward, creepy, too quiet... what other words could I use to describe the surreal scene I now found myself in?

I flicked my eyes at the mansion. It was beyond enormous. Its old, white structure was probably built in the early 1800s but looked to be restored recently as far as I could see — with a precise eyesight I couldn't remember ever having before. The windowpanes looked fairly new, and the paint was so fresh, it looked almost still wet. Each window was framed in jet-black paint, and the slate roof tiles were definitely of the modern persuasion. It was flanked by a sprawling set of lawns that seemed to go on forever and was protected by a fortification of black wrought-iron gates that boasted sharp points on the end. They reminded me of the *Vlad the Impaler* photos I'd seen on the internet during my vampire research, and I shuddered just a little.

Kovah, the youngest member of Archie's little band of vampire hunters, looked at his watch, then up at the sky. "It's eight-thirty, and the moon is damn near full," he said, looking at Archie, the other bikers, then at me. "I imagine the bloodsuckers will be out any minute."

I studied Kovah, his youthful appearance seeming out of place amongst the other half a dozen older bikers, and I wondered what had caused him to join the rebel gang. Kovah's dark hair was shorn almost to the scalp, and he wore sunglasses, even at night. This intrigued me.

Archie nodded. "It's Friday night, they'll be heading into the city to feed."

And the vampires did not disappoint. As if on cue, two males and one female walked out the front door, laughing amongst themselves, but all I could think was how beautiful they were.

Both of the males, a blond and a dark brunette, were tall, dressed in stylish clothes, and boasted modern hairstyles. They looked as if they could grace the cover of any magazine. The female had long, black hair, a perfect figure, and her fresh marble-like skin glowed under the full moon. I thought she was beautiful and was inexplicably drawn to her, wanting to get to know more about her for some reason. I even felt my pants tighten a little at the sight of her. I couldn't take my eyes off her.

"Close your mouth, kid," Archie said, chuckling as the rest of the band

and I positioned ourselves on our bikes, getting ready to follow after the black Mercedes the vampires had piled into while I had been gawking.

I just nodded, my hand hovering nervously over the key to the handlebar, anxious to follow them for more reasons than one.

Once the vampires' luxury car was out sight, Archie twirled his finger in the air in a rally sign and all the bikes started up in a glorious roar of fierceness and power. I waited for them all to take off, and then took up the rear of the group, wondering what the night held for us.

"What the hell are we doing here?" I yelled into Kovah's ear over the heavy metal blasting through the speakers of the dark bar.

Kovah threw back a shot of something clear, but I knew it definitely wasn't water. "We're gonna watch the bloodsuckers. Once they feed on humans, we're gonna pull them out back and end their existence."

My eyebrows rose to my forehead. "You're going to kill them, just like that?"

Kovah set his shot glass down and turned his face toward me, but the sunglasses were still on, which made it hard to get a read on the guy. "First off, you can't kill something that's already dead." He pulled a pack of Marlboro Lights from his pocket and slammed the pack over and over against his palm as he spoke. "Second, vampires need to die. They only cause death and destruction. You should know this, man."

I watched as Kovah pulled a lighter from his pocket and lit the cigarette he'd just shaken from the pack. Smoke wafted up toward the black-painted ceiling of the bar.

"I'm not sure you can smoke that in here—" I started.

"Fuck off, Bishop. Nobody cares, and nobody's gonna say shit to me."

I stared at him, realizing he stood eye to eye with me, matching my six-foot-three height. Kovah looked like a badass with attitude, and for the first time, I noticed his arms were strewn with multiple tattoos. One on his inner forearm of a voluptuous redhead baring vampire teeth caught my eye.

"That's a cool tat," I said, pointing at it.

Kovah looked down and laughed without humor. "Reminds me to stay away from beautiful women. They'll suck the life out of you."

"Don't I know it," I murmured under my breath.

"Seriously, man. Chicks will suck you dry. Stay single, it's easier."

I folded my arms over the black T-shirt spanning my chest. "Jaded much?"

Kovah chuckled and nodded. "Maybe. But no more than you. Those redheaded succubus bitches ain't no joke."

My eyes grew wide. "What do you know about them? The succbuses?"

"More than one succubus—succubi. Yes, I've done my homework. Anyway, one tried to feed off me, but was interrupted. I was left like this." Kovah snapped off his sunglasses.

I gasped as I stared at Kovah's eyes—ones almost devoid of color. What little pigment left in the irises was such a light blue, it almost blended in with the white.

Stepping back involuntarily, I pointed and asked incredulously, "A succubus did that to you? How?"

Kovah slammed his glasses back on his face and threw me a grin shrouded in arrogance. But to me, he didn't seem like an asshole. He seemed like he was hiding something. I got the feeling we had more in common than we wanted to admit. The feeling was strong; it tugged at my gut like nothing I'd ever experienced.

"Yes, she did. I was about to get my soul taken, but my beeper went off, bolting me out of whatever trance she'd had me in."

I studied him for a minute. "Who is *she*?"

"Some redhead succubus I met in a bar. I had half my clothes off back at her place, but my sister began blowing up my pager, as she was at the hospital having her baby."

I stared at him, confused. "Pager? Who carries those anymore?"

Kovah chuckled. "Yeah, it was a long time ago."

"I was almost a victim, too," I admitted.

"So I've heard," Kovah said, setting his drink on a nearby table and resting his hands on the hips of his low-riding dark-blue jeans.

I raised an eyebrow. "What exactly have you heard?"

He scrubbed a hand over his dark shorn hair, taking a long drag from his cigarette. "Just that some succubus got to you. What I don't get is how you didn't turn into a bloodsucking freak that we love to hunt and kill." He pointed at the bikers, then back at himself.

I looked around, then back to him. "Long story short, I met the succubus's twin and drank her blood."

He ripped his glasses off again and looked at me with his creepy albino blue eyes. "You're shitting me."

I laughed. "Not in the least. And I may or may not be dating her."

Kovah set the smoldering cigarette on the bar and stood square in front of me. He gripped both my shoulders with very strong hands. "You're fucking the sister of the succubus who almost stole your soul?" His breathing seemed heavy.

"Something like that." I wanted to laugh, but kept my cool. "She's her twin, actually. We'd heard if you drink the blood the succubus, it can stop the vampire transition. She wasn't her, but we thought since their DNA was identical, and I was a desperate guy..."

Kovah's mouth hung unhinged as he stared at me.

"Before you ask, no her twin isn't a succubus. She's human, but she's just as hot."

Kovah smiled, a dimple on his left cheek exposing itself. "Got it, man. I've never heard that theory, but I'm glad you survived the soul-sucking bitch."

Yes, yes, I had, and I'd never felt so lucky. I felt like I should go buy a Louisiana state lottery ticket.

"If they're twins, the succubus will probably try to turn her sister to keep her from aging and dying, and if her twin is also a true redhead, you need to be careful. Those are the vampires who suck a guy's soul."

"Yes, I know," I replied, "but Charity isn't going to let Eva turn her. She doesn't want her sister to die, but I think she had sort of accepted it last week when she knew I had to kill her in order to remain human."

Kovah set his drink down and signaled a nearby waitress for another. He picked up the cigarette. "But you couldn't go through with it, so you searched for an alternative," he said matter-of-factly.

I nodded. "Yes, that's what I did. I was so close to killing her, too. I just couldn't. Guess I pussed out."

Kovah paid the waitress. He pulled the cap to his beer off with his bare hand and tossed it over his shoulder. "I killed my succubus."

"Really... you just said you were interrupted during the feeding. So why did you?"

Kovah chuckled. "Didn't want to take any chances. I pretended I had turned into a vampire, came to her at night where I'd met her, and she happily invited me to her bed. After I got what I wanted from her, I reached into my jeans that were on the floor and pulled out a knife. Drove it into her heart as I straddled her. She shriveled up right after she screamed. It was fuckin' awesome." He threw the cigarette to the floor and crushed it out with the heel of his boot.

My eyes grew wide. I wished I could see Kovah's eyes, but I knew I probably didn't need to. I knew they were filled with amusement and pride. Then something struck me. "When was this, exactly?"

He finished swigging his beer, then set it on a nearby table and put his hands in his pockets. He was facing me with his dark sunglasses hiding his eyes, but I knew he was staring right into mine. After a long, dramatic pause, he replied, "Nineteen years ago."

TRANSITION GONE WILD

Nolan

My mouth gaped open. I'd guessed Kovah to be between the ages of 20 and 25. "So you were, like, five years old when this succubus took your soul?" I knew it was a ludicrous inquisition since he had just mentioned sleeping with the woman before he'd killed her, but I was confused.

Maybe he was a lot older than he looked?

Kovah chuckled. "No, I was twenty-one."

"You expect me to believe you're…" I did some quick math. "Forty years old?"

"I am forty, technically. But I noticed about ten years ago that I wasn't aging. I don't understand it, but I wish I could bottle it and sell it. I'd be a billionaire."

"That explains why you had a pager." I laughed.

Kovah nodded with a smirk.

I had another question. "Do you heal quickly from injuries?"

"Yep. Check it out." Kovah pulled a Swiss Army Knife from his pocket, looked around briefly, and then sliced a small cut into his forearm.

I gasped in horror as it beaded blood for a few seconds, then started to close up rapidly. I looked into Kovah's dark glasses. "So you did become a vampire, and now you hunt them?"

"I'm not a fuckin' bloodsucker!" he snapped a little too loudly, his countenance growing dark.

I threw my hands up in surrender. "Hey! Calm down. You have all the symptoms of a vampire. I was just curious."

"No, I don't," Kovah quickly answered. "I don't need to drink blood, and don't want to."

"Okay, that's comforting. Bet you can't go in the sun though, can you?" I pointed at his sunglasses.

"Yeah, I can, but it's just uncomfortable, and of course it kills my eyes."

I scrubbed a hand over the back of my neck. "Me too."

Kovah raised an eyebrow. "You too? But you're so tan."

I laughed. "Not for long. I used to worship the sun. Now it's almost painful and depressing to be in it. I don't know why."

"Transition gone wrong, brother." Kovah clapped me on the shoulder. "You drink blood?"

"Hell no!" I quickly answered, thinking back to when I drank Charity's blood from the Starbucks cup and how it hadn't really been disgusting. "I don't crave it, anyway," I lied. "Still eating pizza and steak."

Kovah laughed. "Not rare steak, right?"

"What's all the commotion over here, boys? You two hitting it off?" Archie asked, unscrewing the cap to his chew can and snatching a big pinch.

I replied, "Yeah, boss."

Archie shoved the dip into his bottom lip and waved a finger at the both of us. "You two should. You have a lot in common."

"Such as...?" Kovah asked.

"Well," Archie mumbled. "You both like redheads, so there's that."

I gasped. "That was a low-blow, Arch."

Archie and Kovah both started laughing, Kovah's arm still on my shoulder. "You'll find it funny, eventually."

"Vampires at ten o'clock, boss," said one of the Rebel Riders, jutting his salt-and-pepper goatee toward the back of the bar.

We snapped to attention and followed his gaze. The vamps we'd trailed from the mansion were huddled in the corner of the bar talking to two young, attractive blonde females.

Humans.

Kovah swore as the dark-haired vampire placed his hand on the human's neck. He brushed her long, pale hair over her shoulder, then eyeballed her neck, eventually flicking his gaze back up to hers.

"He's gonna bite her," one of the Riders said.

I nodded. "I agree."

"Let's move," Archie said, his pack following him.

After rushing to the back of the bar, Archie grabbed one of the males, and two of his comrades snatched up the other two. The vampires hissed like frightened cats, their fangs out as the nearby humans gave us a wide berth, backing up then eventually running toward the exit.

The bikers escorted the three monsters out the back door of the bar and into a dank, putrid alley, with grates in the cement to drain excess rainwater, and a large dumpster practically steaming with nasty-smelling garbage.

One of the taller male vampires twisted his undead face in a grimace and punched Archie so hard, it sent him flying backward onto his ass. I watched as poor Archie tried to shake off the assault. A small trickle of blood dribbled from the corner of his lip, and I found myself staring at it, trying to decipher why this fascinated me. Except there was more than fascination in the air; it was almost a lust-filled reaction to blood that was anything but sexual.

I shook my head and watched as the vampire moved to try to run, but Kovah moved at unnatural speed and pinned him the wall. Without thinking, Kovah pulled a knife from his jacket and plunged it into the vampire's chest, where he collapsed into a heap, his clothes covering the ash he'd become. He hadn't even had time to scream.

But the female vampire did. Seeming to come out of nowhere, as she had run off earlier, her shrilly shriek ripped open the night, and it was grief-filled, feral, and... angry.

Livid.

She had black tears streaming down her face, slashing at one of Archie's rebels with her long fingernails, two of us trying to subdue her, while two more Rebels fought with the tall, blond male vampire.

I looked at Kovah and he nodded. We both held the female in place as Archie plunged a good old-fashioned wooden stake into her chest, and with one last scream of protest, she was nothing but a pile of slutty clothing and ash.

The last vampire wasn't hard to take care of. Even with his superhuman strength, seven on one was no match for him. He too joined his friends to wherever vampires went after they died.

Kovah chuckled and smacked his hands together as if he was getting rid of the filth. "Three more frickin' bloodsuckers gone. It's a good night, boys!"

I frowned with a sick, sinking feeling in the pit of my stomach as Kovah high-fived and fist-bumped the rest of the gang.

Who were we to go take lives like this without justification? It wasn't as though the vamps were killing anyone. Sure, they were probably going to feed on those girls, but who said they were going to kill them? Did they deserve to be destroyed? Was this what this biker gang did every weekend? I wasn't sure I wanted to be part of this world. This whole vampire-killing business seemed to almost be like us playing God—judge, jury, and executioner—with no accountability to anyone but ourselves. Why weren't there some sort of cops of the supernatural world, since obviously these vampires and succubi had been around for centuries?

Then I suddenly remembered the agent who'd visited me in my apartment last month. Where did he say he worked? The Justice Department? Oh yeah, the Bureau of Supernatural Investigation.

So there were vampire cops after all.

Pens, receipts, and various papers were flying out of the drawer in my kitchen, hitting the floor behind my flailing arms.

"Ah ha!" I said, holding up the business card to BSI Agent Roger Nelson. I pulled out my cell phone, noting it was 11 p.m., but I didn't care. I punched the numbers into my cell with shaking hands, and with a racing heart, waited to hear the inevitable voicemail, ready to leave a message before I lost my nerve.

"Agent Nelson," a groggy voice slurred.

Caught off guard by him actually answering, I drawled, "Uh... Mr. Nelson, sir, this is Nolan Bishop. Do you remember me?"

I could hear him shifting around before he finally spoke. "Of course I remember you, Nolan. What can I do for you?"

"I watched three vampires die tonight."

"I'm listening, Nolan."

"It freaked me out. A lot."

Agent Nelson sighed. "Was that the first vampire you'd seen killed?"

What an odd question, I thought. Then I remembered Ansel. "No, sir. I sort of… killed one a couple days ago myself."

"Don't go anywhere, Nolan. I'll be right over."

The line went dead.

While I waited for the agent to show, I paced my apartment, amped up on adrenaline and a buzz of nerves that zipped through my body. I felt twitchy. I practically wore a hole in the cheap apartment carpeting until a soft knock caused my head to jerk up.

I opened the door cautiously to see Agent Nelson standing there in his signature dress shirt and beige trench coat. Missing the boring striped tie, I thought maybe he'd just crawled out of bed at this ungodly hour for my benefit. Turned out, I was right.

"Hello, Nolan," the agent said, his blue, bloodshot eyes meeting mine.

"Hi," I said, indicating for him sit on my small loveseat.

As the agent sat, he pulled out a small notepad from his pocket, the same one he'd used as he'd interrogated me the first time he had shown up at my apartment a few weeks prior. A time when I lived in ignorance and bliss of the supernatural.

"Start at the beginning," the agent said.

I scrubbed a hand along the back of my neck and blew out a breath. "Well, I guess I'll give you the short version. You were right, Agent. The succubus, she took my soul. But I didn't turn into a vampire like you said I would."

The agent nodded, his pen poised over his notepad. "I'll admit, I… I was a bit skeptical about coming over here. I thought you were gonna drain me from the jugular. But from my experience, the vampires resulting from a succubus attack aren't that smart. They aren't cognitive enough to pick up the phone and invite a human over to be their meal."

I shuddered in understanding. "That's what I was getting to. The succubus's twin, Charity, see, she's my" —I paused, wondering which word to use, then decided to keep it simple —"girlfriend. I drank some of her blood out of desperation, hoping her identical DNA would be close enough to Eva's to keep me from turning into one of those… things."

That bolted Agent Nelson out of his fatigue as his eyebrows hit his hairline. His mouth was open big enough to catch flies, and I tried not to smirk. When his brain seemed to finally catch up to his mouth, he said, "And this worked? I mean, obviously it did, because you are sitting here with me and not attacking me, but that's it? You didn't do anything else —"

I held up a hand and cut him off. "Don't get too excited... I didn't say I was completely unfazed by what Eva did to me."

The agent was furiously jotting in his notepad. "Go on."

I licked my lips and raked a hand across my scalp. "You see, now there's this dislike to sunlight. I used to worship the sun. I used to dream about skipping work to head to the lake. But now, I just want to sleep all day. I come alive at night. That's weird, right?"

"Well, some people aren't morning people..." was the agent's only response.

"And the blood Charity gave me?"

The agent's eyes were fixed on mine, wide and curious. "What about it?"

"It tasted good. Real good — delicious. Not disgusting like it should," I whispered.

Roger nodded impassively, continuing to write on his pad, but I could tell he was putting on an act. I knew the agent wanted nothing more than to go back to his headquarters and tell his boss about the human kid who'd beat the succubus's curse and had lived to tell about it. And that was okay with me. I wanted the word out. I wanted to kill every last succubus living in Louisiana — heck, on the Earth. My anger made an irrational appearance all of the sudden. It was a red-hot poker, ready to burn the next person who even mentioned the curse.

"Is that all?" the agent asked me, breaking me out of my ire.

I slowly shook my head then took a deep breath to calm down. "No, it's not. I don't feel any more pain. I feel emotional pain and happiness, but there are no physical ailments. A couple of years ago, I'd hurt my back in a bike wreck right after high school. I'd learned to live with the pain, but the other day as I'd opened my medicine cabinet, I saw the pain pills and it dawned on me that I hadn't taken any in a couple weeks. There's no pain anymore. My headaches are gone, too. I don't know what to make of it, and while I'm grateful I'm not hurting anymore, it's kinda freaking me out. I ain't gonna lie."

The agent again looked dumbfounded, shaking his head and still writing. "This is the most interesting thing I've heard in years."

Well. Not only was that *not* the answer I wanted, it was vague and began to piss me off. I gritted my teeth. "What the fuck does it mean?"

Roger's pen paused at his pad, then he looked up into my irate face. He slapped the notepad closed and shoved it into the front pocket of his wrinkled dress shirt. "Irrational anger another side effect?" he asked.

I blew out a breath. "I guess so. There are just so many damn questions with no answers."

"Tell me more about this vampire you allegedly killed."

I looked at him incredulously. "Ain't no 'allegedly' about it, man. The dude was a pile of ash at my feet after I plunged my father's buck knife into his chest."

Roger nodded. "Where did this happen?"

Pointing to the front window, I said, "In the parking lot. He was biting my neighbor. I heard a scream, ran out there, and he flew out of his fancy black car. I don't know what came over me, but I was angry. So pissed off. I just stabbed him through the chest. One minute he was looking at me, scared shitless, the next he was no more. Just a big pile of ash next to his car. It was the weirdest thing I'd ever seen..."

"Did you know this vampire? I mean, I'm wondering what he was doing in the parking lot of your complex." The agent gestured around the apartment.

I shrugged casually. "He didn't know me, really. He's friends with another vampire I met in New Orleans."

The agent looked surprised again. "It seems you've been busy since I visited you last."

I finally sat down on the couch, rested my forearms on my knees, and started at the beginning. From when I'd finally believed the agent's words about my soul being taken, to my trip to New Orleans to visit the voodoo priest, to my journey of defeat back to Shreveport with my girlfriend, sitting on the dock at Cross Lake, waiting to die from a sunburn nobody could ever survive. What I left out was the information from my boss Archie and his band of bikers who called themselves the Rebel Riders. I didn't think the Justice Department would appreciate the competition.

Even if they were doing a better job at policing the vampires than the DOJ was.

"So, what's your plan of action, Nolan?" the agent asked.

I shook my head and put my face in my hands, which were resting on my elbows. "I have no clue. That's why I called you. I don't know what to do next."

The agent nodded. "Well, I do. Come with me to my regional headquarters in New Orleans and we'll help you."

Somehow, I didn't believe this for one second.

Chapter 4

REVELATIONS

Nolan

"Y ou are not going to Nawlins!" Charity screeched reaching an octave I was sure only dogs could hear, her small foot pounding into the floor.

I sighed. "First off, don't tell me what I am and am not going to do."

Her face remained red. "But—"

"Stop. Listen, you can come, but I'd prefer if you didn't. This is dangerous shit, but I need to do it."

Her face was just inches from mine in the dinky kitchen of her apartment. I stared into pleading, crystal-blue eyes I had become way too familiar with.

"No. No, you don't. You beat the curse. You're fine. Can't we just forget it all happened? Can't we just go on with our lives? I know you hate my sister, but I really do think she'll leave us alone."

I rested my hand against the back of my neck and stared at her. I had so much I needed to tell her. She knew nothing of my recent physical changes. She knew nothing of the true nature of the Rebel Riders. Her obliviousness to all of it was my only peace. Did I really want to bring her into this world? Did I really want her to know of the pain and chaos my mind had been warring inside my head the past week? No, I didn't. She should stay innocent and free. She should be happy and unaware of the dark chaos that had been ruling my heart and mind.

I thought back to Eva. The evil look in her eye as she'd done the unthinkable that night. She was Charity's twin. The other half of the DNA that made up the woman I loved. They had shared a womb, a childhood, secrets, clothes, and everything children could share. Yet now, the only thing they shared were piercing blue eyes and fiery red hair. But they were as different as night and day. One was an immortal bent on stealing souls, draining blood, and ruining lives. The other was purely human, only wanting to help people, and so kind and pure of heart, she couldn't even keep herself from feeding stray cats.

"Are you still having the dreams?" she asked, her bottom lip caught between her teeth as a look of innocence cloaked her face.

I shook my head. "No, not anymore. Not since... Cross Lake. In fact, I don't dream anymore at all. I used to have some crazy ones, too, especially since my motorcycle accident."

Charity looked confused. "What accident?"

"A long time ago, after high school. Messed up my back real bad."

"I had no idea, I'm sorry. Does it hurt you still?"

Conflicted on how I should answer, I just replied, "No."

She nodded and went back to finishing a sandwich she was making. I watched as she stuffed the sandwich into a paper bag and then threw a cold soda can from her fridge into the bag, too. Then she walked to her front door, plucked the Stop-N-Shop's blue apron from a hook hanging next to it, and slid it over her head. She then began fumbling with the back tie.

I quickly went to her. "Let me help you." I grasped both apron strings, slowly tying them around her waist. Once I was done, I let my hand linger on the small of her back. I leaned down from my position behind her, whispering close to her ear, "I won't be long, Charity. I promise. I'll come back to you and we can move on with our lives. A life I very much want you to be a part of."

She closed her eyes and nodded, a single tear skating down her pale cheek. Swiping it away, she turned around and looked up at me with an intense stare. "I'm scared, Nolan."

I was going to ask her what she was scared of, but I was afraid myself of the answer. I already knew, anyway. Scared I would be hurt while I was there. Scared Eva would come looking for me. Scared Joel Reichert would kill me while in New Orleans.

Truth was, I planned on seeking out Joel while I was there. I'd let the BSI do what they needed to do with me, but if I could sneak away, I was going to find him and try to get answers. And maybe throw a sincere apology or two his way for killing the guy's friend. Although something told me the old vampire wouldn't be so forgiving. Still, I knew I had to do it—and I had to do it bravely.

"What kind of music do you like to listen to?" Agent Nelson asked, looking sideways at me. He was flipping stations with his thumb using the steering wheel controls.

I threw him a glance and lifted a shoulder in a shrug. "I don't really care. You pick."

Agent Nelson nodded and settled on a station playing 80s pop music, and I grinned. I recalled my mother bopping around the house, cleaning as she listened to these songs. I smiled inside at the familiarity of the tunes.

I cleared my throat over the sound of George Michael crooning through the speakers. "Uh, so, what are we gonna do once we get to the city?"

"Check into the hotel," Roger answered, biting back a smile.

"Very funny, smartass."

"But seriously, I'm taking you to the regional headquarters of the BSI and you're gonna tell my boss everything you've told me. Your story is incredible. Rare, even. Nobody's ever survived a succubus attack and lived to tell about it—unless they'd killed her."

I nodded. "So, do y'all just kill these crazy vampires once their change is, uh, done or whatever?"

Agent Nelson hooked a finger into the tie at his throat and loosened it. He shifted his head from side to side as if he was giving it a good stretch. "Truthfully, yes. I wouldn't normally tell a civilian that, but I feel after what you've been through, that you deserve to know."

"Well, I appreciate the honesty, I suppose."

"It's not that we want to. I've known agents who've had to go spend weeks with the Bureau's psych after killing one. It can be quite traumatic, if I'm being honest here."

"I had the opportunity to kill Eva, but I just couldn't do it. I guess that makes me some kind of pussy."

Agent Nelson adjusted the air conditioning, turning it up two notches. "Well, you did take out that vamp in the parking lot, so you get it."

I just nodded.

"Look, you're just a kid. You should be out partying or going to college and having fun, not saddled with the burden of losing your life just because a pretty girl kissed you in a nightclub."

I choked down an unexpected jolt of sadness that leapt into my throat at the agent's words. He was right. He was so absolutely right. I'd been so drawn into the darkness and stress of my situation the past few weeks, that I didn't have time to grieve for what my life should be right now. The mundane and the fun. The struggles to pay rent. Falling in love and the angst of fights and quarrels with that person. The lovemaking that came after the fights, the lessons of life while loving and cursing them at all at once.

"I guess you're right," I drawled.

He chuckled. "I know I'm right. My kids are teens, I watch their carefree attitudes and the petty crap that's so damn important to them, and I just shake my head. They have no idea what the hell is in this world, and if I have any say, they never will. They will live in ignorant bliss for as long as I can protect them from it." He glanced sideways at me. I had my entire body and face craned in his direction. He then put his eyes back on the road. "As soon as I can retire, we're outta here. Going back to Arizona where I'm from. This part of the South is way too full of the supernatural. I don't know why, but it's damn creepy."

My eyebrows hit my hairline. "Really? I've lived here my whole life, and this is my first encounter with anything even remotely... supernatural, as you say." I couldn't believe the words coming out of my mouth. How had my life become this? I thought about my parents, and how my father would probably point and rack his shotgun at me if he'd heard his only son talking like this.

Roger made a scoffing noise in his throat. "You're, what, like twenty-one years old? You have no idea what's been around you your whole life. In fact, you've probably been exposed to it more than you realize. You were just raised here. The strange and unusual don't stand out to you. They pass right by you as you walk by with blinders on, unaware of their existence since you're so used to it. But someone like me, someone who's only been around it for this job, and with some years under my belt, it makes the hairs on the back of my neck stand up."

I screwed the lid of my Pepsi bottle back on after taking a big swig. "What are you saying, that you can spot vampires and succubuses and stuff anywhere?"

"Succubi, kid, succubi. And if you think a succubus or a vampire is the only supernatural thing out there, then you truly do live in a sheltered world that I'm beginning to envy."

"Are you for real right now?" I gasped. "Oh, hell. Tell me everything."

Laughing, Roger teased, "Shapeshifters, fairies—or sylphs as they want to be called—and even some human-type Immortals."

My head was spinning. "You're shitting me. Fairies?"

"Yep. And no, I'm not shitting you. A lot of these people, and creatures, they work together with the BSI. You can imagine that they have been around a lot longer than we have, even longer than the BSI."

Raking a hand through my hair, I said, "Damn, this is a lot to take in. Why are you even telling me this?"

Pulling into the parking lot of a popular hotel chain, the agent said, "Because you asked, kid."

Truth was, I did ask. I was just unprepared for the gravitational magnitude of the answer, which registered about 9.0 on the Richter Scale.

Chapter 5

TOO DEEP FOR THE DEEP SOUTH

Nolan

ervously, I set my backpack down on the single queen bed of the hotel room the agent had reserved for me. After giving the clerk his government credit card information for the room, Agent Nelson had driven off, telling me he'd call me tomorrow.

I looked around, remembering the last time I'd been in a hotel room. It was the last time I'd come to this very creepy and magical city with Charity, seeking the answers I never quite got. The whole trip had seemed like one big dream. Voodoo priests, strange librarians, books about vampires and succubi, images in my mind that would probably always be there. Then there was the vampire masquerade ball that almost ended my life. But through that, I had met Joel Reichert, a vampire I really wanted to seek out, but probably shouldn't. But I felt some sort of pull to the old vampire. I felt Joel could help me out. But why would he? I had killed his best and oldest friend—defending the life of a human, I justified—but I had killed him just the same, and my last conversation with Joel hadn't been the most pleasant.

"I was under just a little bit of stress," I mumbled to myself, plopping down on the bed in the room.

The phone buzzing in my pocket jerked me out of my memories. I saw Charity's face on the screen and cursed under my breath, realizing I'd forgotten to call her.

"Hi, beautiful," I answered.

"Hi."

"You okay?" I asked.

"Yes. I'm sorry for yelling at you before you left. I really am. I just… I'm… I don't know."

I nodded. "I know. You don't have to explain it to me. I'm worried, too. And confused. And need answers."

"But didn't we get the answers we needed when we were in Nawlins last time?"

"No, we didn't. Not by a longshot. The agent, he told me some things on the drive here—"

"What things?" she cut me off, sounding alarmed.

I sighed. "Incredible things. Crazy things." I knew I couldn't go tell her everything—hell, not anything the agent had told me.

"About vampires?" I asked.

"Yes," I replied vaguely.

"What are you going to be doing there with the government?"

"Honestly? I have no idea. I know some big wigs want to ask me some questions, and at this point, I don't feel I have anything to lose by answering them. But they'll be answering some of mine once I'm through." A grin stretched my lips at the thought.

"Oh, yes they will. I'd love to be a fly on the wall durin' that conversation," she replied.

"I gotta go now, beautiful. I'll call you tomorrow and let you know how it went, okay?"

"Okay. Bye, Nolan."

"Bye." I hit the end button.

Twirling the smartphone between my long fingers like a playing card, I stared at it as my thoughts spun once again in my brain, making me edgy and confused, but mostly nervous. Anxious as to what they were going to do to me tomorrow. What kind of questions they'd ask. I set the phone on the nightstand, clicked off the bedside lamp, and lay back on the bed, letting my thoughts pull me under into the blackness of sleep.

Stars twinkled in a clear Louisiana night sky. Eva sat in the passenger seat of Brad's shiny black Porsche while he played with the radio controls, finally settling on some angry rock music. Parked in the lot across from the Stop-N-Shop, Eva watched as Charity exited the store and pulled keys from the quilted messenger bag slung like a sash around her small frame. After she'd locked the door, she briefly looked around and yanked her long, red curls from where they'd been caught in the strap of the bag. She picked up the full white trash bag she had brought with her from the store and made her way around the back of the building, disappearing behind the gray brick structure.

Eva waited impatiently for her to come back out after dumping the trash so they could follow her home. Eva knew where Charity worked, but she didn't know exactly where she lived — she just knew it wasn't with their parents. Until now, she hadn't really cared.

"And what do you plan to do with the bitch once you do find out where she lives? Kill her?"

Eva sighed and looked at the vampire she'd made, his dark-brown hair slicked back, his light-brown eyes questioning but mostly vacant. Brad was one of the only ones she had been able to tame, and sometimes she wished he had flipped out so she could have killed him. "No, dick. She's my sister, why would I kill her?"

Brad snorted and lit a marijuana joint, popping it between his lips. "Well, she is going out with that guy you hate."

Eva shook her head and looked at the joint, wrinkling her nose. "You *do* know you can't get high, right?"

He blew a plume of smoke into her face and smiled. "I can't get high, but I can sure try." He laughed at his own joke.

She rolled her eyes and looked back toward the building, wondering why it was taking her so long to empty the trash. She opened the car door quietly.

"Where you going, hottie?" Brad asked.

"Stop calling me that. I'm going to see where my sister is."

"I'm comin' too," he drawled, opening his door and flicking away the rest of the joint.

She put her finger to her lips then indicated for him to follow her. He watched as her pale, muscular legs moved with stealth under her skin-tight black leather skirt. He laughed as she tried to tiptoe in shiny red heels. "Hey, babe, maybe you should take those off." His attempt at a whisper was a complete fail.

She turned around and with wide eyes, mouthed, "Shut up!"

Reaching the back of the store, a single orange streetlamp illuminated the alley, but the bulb was weak. There was a large dumpster, which only contained a single white trash bag, as Eva had made Brad check inside. He peered through the fence and saw a residential home, with all its lights off. Then, he scanned both ways down the alley. Charity was nowhere.

Brad pulled his right hand out of his pocket and pointed at a drab gray metal door set into the back of the store. "Eva, maybe she went back inside."

Shrugging, Eva nodded and tried the handle. "Locked tight. Dammit."

"Here, baby, let me." Brad chuckled, yanking so hard on the turn-handle that the tumbler exploded out of the mechanism and lock parts went flying, landing with loud clinks on the cement. "After you." He ushered her into the dark space with a flourish as he pulled the door open.

She bit back a grin at the gesture and then eased off her shoes. Surely they would make a lot of noise going up the staircase she saw in front of her. There were no other passageways. Just the stairs.

"I guess this isn't the store's backdoor," Brad murmured, looking around.

"Thanks for that, captain obvious."

He snorted, then placed a hand over his face to stifle the sound. Eva rolled her eyes again.

At the top of the stairs, they reached a single gray door. This was secured with an even flimsier lock, and to Eva's surprise, it wasn't even locked. She was about to turn the knob, but then noticed light pooling out from under the crack, so she looked at Brad.

"Want me to bust it?" he asked, puffing out his chest.

"No." Eva knocked on the door.

Brad's eyebrows went up. "Seriously?"

"Shut up."

"Who is it?" came Charity's voice.

"It's family. I've brought a pie," Eva said, winking at Brad.

Charity

The voice was unmistakable. After all, it was my own. It just came from a much more evil mouth.

Sliding the chain back, I yanked open the door with an annoyed sigh. As much as I had been expecting Eva, it was still a shock to see her standing there. Her bright red hair was still in that short, sharp, blunt bob and her eyes were fierce and cruel-looking with the black eyeliner smudged into cat eyes. Her lips were painted blood red, and I resisted commenting at the irony.

"What do you want, vampire?" I asked. There were no pleasantries needed here.

Eva gasped, placing a hand with long red fingernails over her chest and spit out in an exaggerated Southern drawl, "Well, I do declare. Has my sister finally grown a backbone?"

"What the hell do you want?" I repeated, annoyed.

Eva appraised me from head to toe and smirked.

I looked down at myself, curls lying lazily over my shoulder, my long-sleeved white flannel shirt hugging my curves, the pink polka-dotted sleep shorts showing off my pale legs. "What?"

Eva snorted. "Going to a party, are you?"

I rolled my eyes at my twin's rudeness and went to slam the door closed, but Eva's hand quickly stopped me. "We'd like to come in."

"Why, do you need an invitation to cross the threshold?" I smirked.

"No," Eva snapped. "But I do have manners."

I folded my arms across my chest. "Oh really? Did you ask Nolan's permission before you sucked his soul from him? Because honestly, Eva, that was pretty damn rude. Manners went right out the fuckin' window that night, didn't they?"

Eva gasped. "When did you develop such a potty mouth?"

I just stared at her. "I'll ask you again. What do you want?"

"I just want to come in."

"Why?"

"We need to talk," Eva said, seeming like she was trying to keep her temper under control.

"No, we don't. I have nothing to say to you." I lifted my chin. "Demon."

Eva sighed. "Fine. I'll cut to the chase. Where's Nolan?"

"None of your effing bee's wax, that's where."

"What are you, nine? Seriously. Where is he, Charity? I need to know."

"Why?"

With irritation on her face, she looked at Brad, jerked her head toward me, and waited for him to react. He didn't. He was staring at my braless chest and my legs with my mouth agape. "Brad! Today!"

I was confused. What were they doing? *What a couple of idiots*, I thought.

"Oh, sorry, babe." Brad rushed forward and grabbed me, tackling me to the floor. I screamed, and Eva laughed.

As he straddled me, he pinned my arms down and looked into my eyes. I screamed again and Brad clamped a cold hand over my mouth. "Shut it, bitch. We just want to ask you a few questions."

With my hand free, I began slapping Brad to try to get him off me, but Eva stepped on my arm.

I whipped my head side to side as a tear dripped out of my right eye and into my hair. As Brad's eyes bored into mine, my stiff body relaxed. "That's it, girl. Keep looking at me. Now, where is Nolan Bishop? Where is your boyfriend?"

As terrified as I had been, I now felt relaxed — at ease. As much as I knew what was happening was wrong, my brain refused to let me care. Deep down, I knew I shouldn't be answering, but something about Brad's gaze was making me feel helpless. He lifted his hand from my mouth, almost relieved when I didn't holler.

"He's not here," I finally answered.

"I know, Charity. Tell me where Nolan is."

"I can't."

Brad smoothed my hair back and ran his knuckles down the side of my cheek. Smiling at me, he said, "Sure you can, pretty girl. Just tell me where he is. I won't hurt him."

I suddenly felt tired, and my brains felt scrambled. Somewhere in the deep recesses of my brain, I knew I needed to keep my mouth shut. Not tell them about Nolan. But I just couldn't not talk. It was as if it was physically impossible. "He went to Nawlins with that cop."

Eva flew across the room at supernatural speed and looked into my eyes. "What fucking cop?"

I recoiled at the dead, black eyes my sister was glaring at me with. Eyes with no whites at all, the crystal blue gone and replaced with something dark and monstrous. Tears began to well and my bottom lip quivered. "I don't know, Eva. Some FBI guy. I really don't know who he is." Another tear dripped out.

"When's Nolan coming back, Charity?" my twin asked.

I shook my head. "I wasn't given a date. A… a couple of days, maybe…?"

Eva reached up and slapped me across the cheek, a stinging, burning pain left in its wake.

"Tell me when he'll be back!" she roared at me.

That hurt. I screamed at the assault and tears flowed like rain from my eyes. Through my sobs, I shook my head and said, "I don't know!"

Brad still had me pinned down and when he looked at me, his eyes were also black.

I whimpered. "Please just go. Please? Get out of my apartment. I'm tired. So, so very tired."

Eva's eyes went back to clear blue, and staring straight into my identical ones, she whispered, "Then sleep, sister."

Chapter 6

Q & NO A

Nolan

My eyes darted around the hallways of the office building I'd been led into. The building was just so normal; an older one in the heart of the Quarter. The metal detector I'd had to walk through in the lobby sort of defied the rustic look of the outside of the building. While I'd only visited New Orleans two or three times before, the familiar Louisiana structures in the Quarter all looked the same to me.

Dressed in athletic shorts and a Saints T-shirt, the only sound I could hear was the boring beige carpeting swishing under my Nikes as I walked. I'd asked Agent Nelson if I should wear something nice, but had never received a definitive answer. So in the end, I decided I'd rather be comfortable while being interrogated than having to loosen a tie or feel my feet swell in dress shoes I wasn't even sure I owned anymore.

"Right this way," Agent Nelson said, ushering me through a door to a large conference room. There were three men and one woman already in the room, all dressed in very professional business attire. I smiled politely at each one with a nod, and then sat in the chair I was instructed to.

The three seemed to be staring at me almost curiously. I tried not to show the visible lump in my throat I was forced to swallow, but figured I'd probably failed miserably. The men, one Black and two White, probably in their late twenties or early thirties, all wearing dress shirts and simple ties. The woman was tall and thin, probably early thirties. I thought she was beautiful with her dark hair pulled tightly away from her clear, pale complexion. Her hazel eyes held a tough scrutinizing gaze, though.

She spoke first. "Hi, Mr. Bishop. Please don't be nervous. We just have a few questions for you."

I nodded. "You can ask me anything."

She smiled in earnest. "Thank you. My name is Special Agent Mara Shields, and these are my colleagues, Agents Elliott, Orion, and Davis."

I smiled at them, but they did not smile back. I wondered if they even had souls, let alone brains. I focused my attention back on the pretty Agent Shields.

"It's our understanding you came in contact with a vampire in a nightclub a few weeks ago. Is that correct?"

I nodded. "Yes, a succubus."

"And what did this succubus look like?" she asked, jotting in her notebook.

I cleared my throat. "Uh, she had short red hair, very pretty, dressed kinda slutty, I guess."

All eyes popped to me, pens stopped in mid-scrawl.

"Did I say something wrong?"

Agent Shields chuckled, as did Roger Nelson, who was seated next to me with his hands folded on the large oak table we were occupying. "No, not at all."

I visibly relaxed. "Well. good. Because she and her friends were all dressed like club chicks. But they were all exceptionally beautiful, I'm not gonna lie."

She nodded and continued to write. "That is not unusual. Vampires are physically attractive in order to lure in victims. Please tell me what happened next, if you can."

"Well, I saw her enter the club, and something about her called to me. I can't explain it. It was like I had to talk to her. I couldn't take my eyes off her."

"Go on," one of the other agents instructed.

I looked at the agent who'd spoken and nodded. "Well, she and her hot girlfriends went and sat in the VIP section of the club. My buddies and I went to try to talk to them, but we were cock-blocked by some big ol' bouncer."

Again, all eyes swung to me and their jotting stopped. Agent Nelson coughed, but I knew he was trying not to laugh.

"Cock-blocked?" she asked.

I cleared my throat. "Sorry. The redhead's bouncer wouldn't let us into the area until I stared into his eyes and sorta begged his permission. Now that I think about it, it was a bit pathetic. But I had no idea what an evil bitch she was at the time."

"I see." Agent Shields laughed, still writing in her notebook.

"So anyway, she finally told the bouncer to let us through."

Agent Shields asked, "So you feel the bouncer was her own personal security and not just a club employee?"

I nodded. "Oh, yeah, he was only there for those girls. I could tell."

"Was this bouncer a vamp?" asked the Black agent.

I looked at him, my head bobbing up and down. "Yes, and I only know this now because later on, I went to the club to confront her, and I watched as he singlehandedly tossed like three dudes out of the club with his bare hands. It was freaky and unnatural."

Their jotting became more furious and I stayed quiet, waiting for the next question.

"We'll come back to your subsequent visit to the club later on. Tell me what happened once you got into" — she looked at her notepad — "the VIP section of the club."

"Well, we flirted a little, and then she kissed me. Except it ain't like no kiss I've ever had before. The sparks weren't there. You know what I mean?"

They all stared blankly at me, waiting for me to finish. I glanced at Agent Nelson, who was failing miserably at keeping a straight face.

I cleared my throat again and wiped my sweaty palms on my shorts. "Well, as I kissed her, I opened my eyes—and you have to know I don't ever do that—but what I saw scared the shit out of me. Her eyes were black. Like, her entire eye, not just the colored part. Which was blue before, by the way."

Agent Shields nodded. "Go on."

"That's kind of it. After I pulled away, I high-tailed it outta there. I felt sorta scared and weirded out. My friends stayed, but that was it. I asked them later what happened after I left, but they said the fire alarm went off and they weren't able to score with her friends."

"And did this vampire give you her name?" Agent Shields asked.

"Eva. That's all she told me. But I know her last name is Sheridan. Well, it was when she was human."

The agents shot off more questions in rapid-fire succession until I was mentally exhausted, but I told them everything, from the time I'd left the club, until I met Charity, and the drinking of her blood — which had elicited a collective gasp from the group. The only thing I'd left out was the Rebel Riders group. Something deep in my soul I wasn't sure I even still had told me that Archie's band of rebel vampire hunters needed to be kept secret from the government.

"Agent Nelson tells us you are having strange physical symptoms. Tell us about those?" Agent Shields asked.

I cleared my throat. "Well, as far as I've noticed, I don't care for the sun much. It makes me uncomfortable."

"Uncomfortable how?" one of the male agents asked.

"I don't know. I just don't like it… like, I try to avoid it, where before, I loved it."

"Continue," Mara said.

I nodded. "I also seem to not have any more pain. I haven't injured myself so I don't know if I heal quickly, but I might. I used to have back pain from an accident, but it's gone now."

At their silence, I continued. "I can hear and see better, too. I think, anyway."

"Do you still like drinking blood, Nolan?" Agent Shields asked.

That irritated me. "I don't *like* drinking blood, nor do I do it at all. I just said that when I had some of Charity's, it wasn't gross or anything like I thought it would be. That's the only time I had it."

She just nodded and kept jotting.

"Are those all the questions you have?" I asked.

Scanning her scribbles, Agent Shields looked me straight in the eye and said, "I think so, Mr. Bishop. Do you have any questions for us?"

I laughed without humor. "You can bet your ass I do. Let's start with this little government agency of yours. You guys the real, live *X-Files* or what?"

I thought I was funny — I thought I was being charming, but as I scanned their faces, all I could see was annoyance. My smile faded as I asked nervously, "I bet y'all get that a lot, don't you?"

The younger agent spoke up and smiled with perfectly white teeth. "Dude, you don't even know."

Dude?

I rolled with it. "How badass are you guys for doing this, though? I've heard there are more than vampires out there. That everything is real. Zombies, fairies, werewolves—"

I was cut off by Agent Shields. "There is no such thing as zombies, and the CDC has confirmed this."

"What the hell does the CDC have to do with zombies?" I asked, my perplexed expression not lost on the agents.

Agent Nelson cleared his throat. "Nothing, kid. Nothing at all." His eyes scanned his colleagues, then swung back to me. "You got any more questions?"

"Hell yes, I do! Tell me why I didn't turn into a vampire, yet, I still feel like I have symptoms."

The room went silent. I could hear ragged breaths coming from one of the older agents as they stared at me, looking perplexed.

"So you think those things you just listed are symptoms of vampirism?" Mara Shields asked.

"Well, aren't they?" I asked, wondering what kind of game they were playing.

More silence blanketed the room until Mara said, "I really cannot tell you. That's why we called you here. Do you mind if we get our lab to draw some blood?"

I lifted a shoulder. "I guess. Whatever."

"Great, thank you. What about an MRI, would you be okay with that?"

My eyebrows knit together as I stared at the intricate swirls of wood in the conference table. "That's like a brain scan, right?"

The agent smiled sweetly, but it didn't quite reach her eyes. "Yes. It's a large machine that takes pictures inside your body. You don't have to do anything but lie there. It's quite relaxing," she said, leaving out the part about me having to lie perfectly still inside a large, closed-in tunnel. My mom had one last year and had told me about it.

I nodded. "Okay, that's cool. I got nothing else going on, I suppose."

I thought of Charity and how I wished I was at her place in Shreveport having dinner with her. I thought about her big, innocent, sweet blue eyes as they looked up into mine, and the way her wild red curls always fell into her face. I imagined brushing them out of her curious eyes. I thought about how I wished I could be lying behind her in her little pull-out bed, my arm slung over her petite body as peace overtook my mind into sleep. But that wasn't on the agenda today. I had to help these agents figure out why and how I had beat the succubus curse and lived to tell about it. How I could still go in the sun without bursting into flames.

Because I really had no other options left, except killing Eva to see what would happen. And that, I reasoned, was still not off of the agenda.

"Lead the way," I said to the agents as we all stood up from the table and headed for the door.

With another hard swallow, I followed them down another carpeted hallway in the hopes I was doing the right thing. I was nervous about these tests. Fear ruled the front of my mind, but what other choice did I have? I needed to get answers. I wasn't sure the Justice Department had all of them, but I was willing to give them a shot. Because in reality, my only other option was seeking out Joel Reichert, and while risking my life for answers wasn't my first choice, it was worth considering. I just wished I could be a lot braver than I felt. Because at the moment, I felt as if I was going to be sick.

What kind of secret government testing was I going to endure? Was it going to be like the TV shows I'd watched on alien probing and hours of interrogation? I didn't know, but somewhere deep in my gut, I trusted Agent Nelson, who was walking alongside me. It was this trust that had prompted me to call him with my current predicament. I contemplated telling him about the old vampire who lived right there in New Orleans and ran the biggest, most lucrative hotel in the city, but something stopped me. I didn't know what. All I knew was that the looks of disdain on the faces of the agents earlier told me that vampires weren't to be trusted. I knew, if the opportunity arose, that each and every agent would kill one in cold blood if they had to, and would be able to justify it in their minds and in their government memos.

The thought caused shudders to rack my body as I turned the corner and walked into a sterile white lab.

Chapter 7

DECISIONS, DECISIONS

Nolan

The street was dark. Heavy rainclouds threatened overhead, which kept the streets quiet. The humid air was as thick as the angst that was surrounding my heart. I stood with my arms folded, my back pressed against an old-fashioned streetlamp on the concrete corner. I stared up at the top floor of the old hotel. A single orange light illuminated a small office. I blew out a breath, wondering what I should do. I knew the old vampire was up there, sitting at his desk, probably brooding over whatever the hell was ailing him today.

It was my second day in New Orleans. The tests I'd had the day before hadn't been too bad, just some pokes of a needle and about thirty minutes inside a white tube that made weird pounding sounds. I was thankful they had given me some headphones to listen to music while the big, intimidating machine took photos of every inch of my body. Once I'd left the building, Agent Nelson drove me back to the hotel as if the day had gone no differently than me just having some regular medical tests. While this should have comforted me, it just disturbed me even more. I briefly wondered where Agent Nelson went at night since it didn't seem he stayed at the hotel, but figured the government probably had some state-of-the-art accommodations for our agents. I knew he was stationed in Shreveport and that was where his home probably was.

I remembered reading in some of the big, old library books the last time I'd visited here that most vampires held a slight paranoia. It was part of their personality. I didn't know how the author of the book had known that, but I had thought at the time that it had been written with a bit of a personal edge, as if someone who'd studied — and possibly hunted — vampires had written that particular section. I remembered reading that vampires were constantly on edge; it was as if the author himself had interviewed one, just like in the famous book-turned-movie... set, ironically, in the very city in which I now stood.

I shuddered.

Pulling in a breath of confidence, I pushed myself off the dark-green lamppost and noticed that it flickered as I walked away. I turned my head in slight confusion and looked back at the lamppost, wondering if it was somehow warning me not to go do what I was about to do. But it was too late for that. My mind was made up. Agent Nelson was driving me back to Shreveport tomorrow.

It was now or never.

Slinking through the old revolving glass door of the hotel, I easily slipped into the lobby unnoticed. The modern décor of the old hotel belied its outside's classic look. Swirly green and beige carpet lined the lobby, and ornate glass chandeliers hung elegantly above me. A large welcome desk with a uniformed attendant manned it. I hadn't noticed this when I was there the month before for the vampire ball. It had been decorated so differently. Without saying anything to the attendant, I went to the shiny brass elevator and hit the button for the third floor. I hoped that was where I needed to be, as there were no other floors to choose from. As the elevator doors slid shut, I wondered why I hadn't taken the damn stairs.

My cell phone buzzed in my pocket and I pulled it out, smiling at the text from my little ball of fire: *I miss you. I think I'm ready.*

The seemingly cryptic message didn't need deciphering. I knew what she meant.

My relationship with Charity had been pretty tumultuous so far. As much as I'd wanted a simple girlfriend, sort of like I had with my ex, Sarah, I knew my relationship with Charity was anything but. The odds were stacked against us, but the weight of my feelings for her ruled my heart. They weren't light and fun like with Sarah. These were deep. So deep they'd buried themselves into my heart, and the fact that we hadn't expressed them physically both bothered me and consoled me. I wanted it to be right with her. I wanted her to want it.

After the blood consumption and emotional morning at Cross Lake, we'd both been too exhausted to move and had slept for a couple of days straight. After that, there'd been endless discussions about my beating the curse without resorting to murder, and us both being relieved that I hadn't had to kill her identical twin. The war inside Charity had been battling just as fierce as the one inside of me. We were both fighting a war that pitted loyalty against survival. To say it was a stressful one was the understatement of the year.

These problems were the reason I now found myself standing frozen in front of a fancy oak door with a gold plate reading *Joel Reichart, Owner.* My hand paused mid-knock, confidence wavering on whether I wanted to get myself into this trick bag.

I took a deep breath and knocked.

It seemed like an eternity before I heard movement inside the office. I could hear the squeak of leather, presumably the chair that sat behind a large desk. I heard the squelch of wheels from the chair as they rolled away from the desk. Then finally, I heard the swish of shoes on plush carpeting.

The locks clicking out of place were deafening in my ears. With my most brave face forward, I prepared for who would answer the door. As the large door slid open almost painfully slow, my eyes went big as a hurricane of expressions passed Joel's face in quick succession: curiosity, surprise, and then anger.

At the irate look on his face, my adrenaline spiked to the nth degree as my fight-or-flight response was activated. Fists balled at my sides, I prepared for the worst.

Which was exactly what greeted me.

Joel's normally light-brown eyes turned completely black, their whites totally gone. With a movement too quick for the human eye to see, Joel grabbed me by my lapels and yanked me into the office. Before I knew what had happened, I found myself flat on my back in front of the vampire's large and ridiculously ornate desk.

"What are you doing here, boy? You got a death wish? Because I'm feeling pretty homicidal tonight," Joel hissed in my face.

Disturbed by why I wasn't feeling fear, I snapped back, "How is that different from any other night, vampire?"

My smug smirk disappeared at the sound of bone cracking reverberating in my ears as incredible pain blossomed along my jawline. I grunted in pain, attempting to buck the old vampire off me. With rage unlike I had felt in a long time, I managed to get one hand free and pulled at the blue silk necktie that was hanging in my face. I wrapped it around my fist and yanked hard to the right. Joel went flying off me, and in a movement much faster than I thought possible, I was now face-to-face with him. My hand still tangled in the tie and Joel's back was flat against the wall of his office, where I saw a large crack in the old sheetrock and plaster begin to creep up the wall behind him. I grimaced through the fading pain my jaw.

"Don't ever hit me again," I spat in his face.

Joel lifted his knee and incapacitated me, causing me to let go of the tie. Once I was on my knees, the vampire reared his arm back and slammed me in my right temple with his fist. "That is for Ansel, you sonofabitch."

As hard as I fought to stay conscious, blackness began to creep in, and my body slumped to the floor in a heap.

I groaned and blinked my eyes open. I was lying on a sofa.

I saw Joel straightening his tie and then rubbing his neck where I could see bruises were healing. Seeing me awake, he stood at a safe but intimidating distance from the sofa with his arms folded over his chest.

"Holy shit," I groaned, my hand going to my head.

"Got a headache, do ya, boy?"

I narrowed groggy eyes at Joel. I sat up a bit too fast and grimaced, my hands cradling each side of my head. "Why didn't you just kill me?"

Joel stared at me for a long, uncomfortable minute, then said, "Because I have questions."

"Everyone's got freakin' questions," I murmured.

An uncontrollable chuckle burst out of Joel's mouth. "I bet. Who else you been talkin' to?"

I lifted my sore head to look at Joel. "The Justice Department."

Joel's eyebrows hit his hairline. "You're not serious."

I stood when I realized Joel was probably not a threat any longer and straightened my shirt. "I am. Did you know the government has an entire agency dedicated to y'all? Vampires, werewolves, and all kinds of other shit. Do you know fairies exist?"

Joel didn't look surprised in the least. "Yes, but I think they prefer to be called sylphs. Tell me more about this agency."

"You know about the fairies?" I questioned with disbelief coloring my tone.

"Yes, I've been alive a very long time, as I've told you before. Continue about the Justice Department. This intrigues me."

"You throw a mean right hook." I massaged my temple and flexed my jaw from side to side.

Joel sighed. "You killed Ansel. I wanted to do a lot more than that. You've got some balls coming here."

I hung my head. "I'm really and truly sorry. I am. I was freaked out when I saw him in the car with my neighbor. His mouth was on her neck and there was blood everywhere, and she was screaming. He didn't even care."

Joel, who'd been calm and cool the minute before, slammed his fist on his desk and yelled, "He was feeding! He wasn't killing her! She would have been fine once he was done, he would have stripped her memories of the feeding from her. But now she's probably traumatized and going crazy and unable to function. You did more harm than good!"

I shook my head. I wanted to tell Joel to go to hell, but I knew I couldn't. I'd come to his office for answers, and pissing him off wasn't in my best interest. "I'm new to this shit, dude! I had no idea." My teeth ground together, the stress of the last few weeks taking its toll on my teeth. I was frustrated and confused, and tired of feeling that way. "I came here tonight for help. I need help. I can't do this anymore."

Joel's features softened and his balled fists relaxed. Cocking his head to the side, he asked, "Can't do what? Be a vampire? It's really unpleasant at first, but after a few years—"

"What?" I cried. "I am not a vampire! What the hell are you talking about?"

Joel couldn't hide his surprise. "I... I don't know what to say. Your scent, while faint, is most definitely vampire. Why else have you risked your very existence to come here and confront me?" His haughty tone was undeniable.

Rage burned in my gut, traveling to my heart and expelling itself from my mouth. "I'm not a fucking vampire, Joel. I can't be. I beat the curse."

Joel chuckled. He actually *laughed*. "Oh no, kid. You are most certainly not human anymore."

Raising an eyebrow, I lifted my chin and said, "Oh yeah? Then why is it that I can walk around in the sun? I've been told vampires can't."

Joel's face went even paler. He opened his mouth and then snapped it shut with a click.

A small smile crept up my mouth. "That's what I thought, man. I'm some sort of half-breed or hybrid or some kind of *X-Men* superhero, right?"

His eyebrows knit together in confusion. "*X-Men*?"

I rolled my eyes. "Like an alien mutant. I do feel different, I won't lie, but I also don't feel like a vampire. Shouldn't I be tearing open carotid arteries and stuff?"

"In all my years, I've never heard of this," was all he could say.

I began to pace. "Now, I'm concerned."

Joel sat down at his desk and folded his hands together. He seemed to be deep in thought. He blew out a breath and said, "Look, Nolan. Throughout my hundred-plus years, I'd never seen the victim of a succubus turn out to be a normal vampire. Either they went apeshit and killed everything in sight, or they died in the sun because they had no idea what they were.

"Truth be told, I hated the succubi. They are ginger beasts, and if I had no heart or conscience, I'd spend my days killing every red-haired, blue-eyed human female just to prevent the possibility of their existence. And most are made in complete ignorance. Young, stupid vampires turning females, having no idea that the redheads were extra dangerous once turned."

"I never thought of that before," I breathed. "It actually makes me more pissed off."

"Look, you're not the first succubus victim I've known, and I know you won't be the last. The succubus is the vilest form of vampire, and quite frankly, I'm sick of the crazy bitches giving my race a bad name."

"I won't argue with you there," I replied.

Joel went to a cabinet, poured himself something out of a glass bottle, and then looked at me. "Bourbon?"

I shook my head. "No, but I could use some aspirin."

"The pain will subside shortly. Just wait it out."

"Okay."

Joel slammed back the bourbon and then put the lid back on. "Tell me about your symptoms."

I sat and explained, for the millionth time, it seemed, about what I had been through and what was going on with me physically and emotionally. Joel soaked it all in, curiosity coloring his expression at every word from my mouth. He was especially interested in the BSI, but I dared not tell him about the Rebel Riders.

"Interesting," he said. "Very strange and intriguing. I'll ask around, see if anyone else has encountered this. But I can tell you one thing; if I was a betting man, I would say that you killing Eva would probably get rid of every last symptom. Let's just hope it's not permanent."

I thought of Kovah, and his non-aging and freaky eyes, and looked up at Joel. "If I was a betting man myself, I'd take you up on that. Because I think you'd lose."

THE BLUE ROOM, TAKE II

Nolan

After exchanging cell phone numbers, I left Joel's office with more questions than answers. Why was the BSI so interested in me? Was it because I'd been the only survivor of a succubus attack? I'd been so confident that Joel could give me answers, but I'd come away empty. More frustrated than ever, but slightly relieved I didn't have a hit out on my life by Joel, I stared silently out the window of Agent Nelson's car as we made the drive back to Shreveport. My thoughts were a hurricane inside my muddled brain.

"You okay, Nolan?" Nelson asked.

I simply nodded, my hand at my mouth, my eyes still fixed on the blurred Louisiana landscape.

"You know we aren't going to harm you, right?" the agent asked.

I nodded again. "I would hope not."

"You're just a mystery to us, you see. Our agency has been around since the 1940s, and as I understand it, we've had to adapt, too. The world of the supernatural was something we had to accept and learn about. Just when we thought we knew it all—had seen it all—another creature or anomaly would show up. We've had to adjust, just as you will have to, too."

I whipped my head to the left and glared at Roger, venom dripping with my words. "Yes, you have. But when have you had to actually *live* it? Huh? That's a whole different story, so don't pretend you can 'relate' to me. Because you can't. And pray to God you never have to."

Agent Nelson's hands tightened on the steering wheel of his plain white government sedan. "While I will agree to that, I'm not the one who was thinking with my dick when I walked into a nightclub and fell victim to a succubus."

Chuckling without humor at the agent's crudeness, I replied, "What guy doesn't think with it when he goes to a club? And how was I supposed to know she was a monster? I was just trying to get laid. Ever done that before, huh, *Roger*? Or are you too old to remember being young and a little hard-up?"

Roger's gaze scanned me from head to toe. "Hard-up? You? I doubt that. And yes, I went to a few parties in college, until I met my wife."

I resisted rolling my eyes and went back to looking out the window. I was done with this conversation. I was done with helping the government. They'd gotten their blood tests and body scans and God knew what else they had done to me. I knew I was on my own with this, and nobody was going to help me. I had to help myself, adapt to this life.

I thought about Archie. As of now, he had no clue that my DNA had changed and I was part vampire. That was, if Joel was to be believed. I was so confused, and once I figured it all out, I knew I was going to be a force to be reckoned with. I had learned I really was a rarity amongst the supernatural community. A plot formulated in my head, and I knew soon I wasn't going to feel like a threat to Archie. I was going to come clean to my boss, the biker. I was going to join his merry band of vampire hunters. But first, I needed to find Kovah, the guy who was so much like me. Oh yes, Kovah and I were gonna have a little chat about this vampire-hybrid thing.

"The hell you need his number for, kid?" Archie asked as he used his finger to wipe the last bit of brown dribble from the hairs of his silver goatee. I looked at the pool of saliva dip in the small Styrofoam cup Archie held, and then back at my boss.

Plastering on a mask of impassivity, I shrugged. "Nothing too serious. Just wanted to hang out. He seems to be around my age and I need to drop the friends I have. Find some new ones, ya know?"

I was lying through my teeth. I was still friends with Brennan and Parker and they had nothing to do with this. I needed to talk to Kovah in the worst way.

Nodding, Archie limped back to the garage's filthy office and plopped down into a squeaky old office chair. He flipped a plastic lid back on his outdated Rolodex and began rifling through it. Yanking out an index card with multiple greasy fingerprints on it, he said, "Ah, here it is." He plunked it down on the desk.

I glanced at him, then at the card. After pulling my smartphone from my pocket, I clicked on the "contacts" and quickly added Kovah's number into it.

"Thanks, boss," I said with a forced smile.

Archie replaced the card and smacked the clear plastic lid closed. "No problem. Just be careful."

I tilted my head to the side, curiosity eating at me. "Be careful of what?"

Archie scratched at his head. "Ah, well, Kovah's kinda got a temper."

"Yeah? Well, so do I." I snorted.

Eying me speculatively, the old biker responded, "Kid, you've changed."

"Having your soul stolen by an evil, red-haired bitch will do that to ya, Archie."

He laughed. "I guess you're right. Well, just don't change too much. I kinda liked the nice, simple Nolan I used to know."

I was at the door of Archie's office, my hand resting on the doorframe, anxious to tackle the broken engine of an older Ducati. "Yes, well, sorry to say that nice and simple Nolan is gone."

Sadness colored Archie's face as he nodded. "Those evil monsters will do that to a person. I'm just glad you're not a crazed vampire I'd be forced to put down."

With a smile twitching on my lips, I replied, "So am I, boss. So am I."

If you only knew.

The day had been as long as it was hard, and I soon found myself frozen at the front door to the Blue Room. Was Kovah freaking kidding when he'd asked me to meet him there? I hadn't even been able to see Charity since I got back, and all I wanted was to go hang out with her and relax.

Earlier in the day, after I had slain the old Ducati's engine, I'd gotten the chance to call Kovah, who'd pretty much refused to talk to me over the phone and had suggested we chat over beers. Did the weirdo have to suggest we meet at the Blue Room? I was going to have to school him on my past and on the succubi and vampires who hung out there.

With a deep breath, I walked in through the front door of the club, after being patted down by a very large bouncer with cold hands. Eyeing me speculatively, the bouncer had sniffed the air around me, to which a regular human probably wouldn't have noticed, and then frowned in confusion at me. This amused me, and I threw the muscle-head vampire bouncer a cocky grin. I made my way to the ticket window and slid a five-dollar bill to the pretty but bored-looking girl for my cover charge.

It didn't take me long to spot Kovah sitting at the bar, nursing a beer from a dark-brown glass bottle. Dressed similarly to me in low-riding designer jeans and a tight-fitting black T-shirt with a popular fitness logo on the chest, I made my way there. Without having to say anything, Kovah turned in my direction and gazed at me with eyes encased in sunglasses. He used his bottle to point at the empty barstool next to him.

I nodded and folded my arms on top of the bar. "Any reason in particular you picked this dive?"

He chuckled around the mouth of the bottle and snorted. "You got a problem with this place?"

I craned my head toward the VIP section of the bar where I saw the evil red-haired bitch and her entourage, minus the one Archie's buddy had killed a few weeks back. I turned my attention back to my new friend. "You mean aside from all the vampires?"

Kovah followed my line of sight to the VIP, then back at me. "That your succubus?"

I raised a pale eyebrow at him. "Yes."

"What can I get you?" asked a pretty bartender who was rocking a low-cut V-neck tank top, her cleavage begging for my attention. Proud of myself for keeping my eyes on her brown ones, I smiled and replied by pointing at my new friend. "Whatever he's having."

"You got it, hottie."

My cheeks flushed at her flirtation. She popped the top off the beer and set the sweating glass bottle in front of me. I slid her a five-dollar bill and turned my attention back to Kovah.

"That's too bad," he said.

"Why's that?" I asked, my lips paused at the bottle.

He turned his head to look at the VIP section, then back at me. I knew he was eyeing her, even through his glasses. "Because she's hot."

I snorted. "Really? Well, apparently she really is. A hot piece of ass in bed, according to my dreams. Too bad I'll never find out."

"Your dreams?" he asked incredulously.

I nodded and set my beer on the cocktail napkin the bartender had slid under it. "Yes. For a week straight, I had the sickest sex dreams about that bitch. It drove me half crazy."

Chuckling, Kovah said, "Sounds awesome to me."

My face darkened and I glared at him. "Not at all. Knowing what I know now about a succubus, it was hell waking up after one of my dreams. Yeah, they were all sexy and erotic and shit, but they had a seriously frightening and dark side to them, too. I couldn't even begin to explain it."

Kovah's head swiveled to the VIP section, then back at me. "It looks like the beast has found herself a new victim."

I whipped my head around and watched as three guys made their way to the sofas with glee slathered all over our faces. I groaned internally and looked back at Kovah. "We can't let her do it again."

He nodded. "I agree. You got a plan, Stan?"

The way Kovah spoke sort of reminded me of the way my dad talked sometimes. I bit back a smile, realizing that Kovah should have been pushing forty, had it not been for what he'd been through that kept him looking like he was in his mid-twenties.

"No, I don't have a plan. If I had it my way, I'd run my dad's buck knife through her cold, dead heart and happily watch as she turned to ash."

He pulled his sunglasses off and stared at me with his freaky whitish-blue eyes. "See, that's where you have it wrong, brother. The succubus doesn't turn to ash. It shrivels into a disgusting corpse, the kind you have to dispose of."

After the shudders left my body, my eyebrows hit my hairline. "Are you screwing with me?"

Kovah slammed his glasses back on his face. "Not in the least. Wanna see?"

Chapter 9

REDHEADS & SUCCUBI

Nolan

What in the fu—" the young guy barked upon being yanked by the back of his designer shirt.

"Take a hike, asshole. The redhead is mine," Kovah said, jerking his thumb toward the front door.

I had pushed the guy's two friends out of the VIP area already.

Glancing at the very large vampire bouncer staring into space, his mouth agape, his bald head gleaming under the multi-colored fluorescent lights, Eva's face turned dark. "What did you do to T?"

Kovah chuckled, planting himself right next to Eva. Close enough to touch. The jealousy that unexpectedly pulsed through me took me by surprise. I hoped it was because she looked so much like Charity, and not because I still wanted to bang the seductive succubus.

Eva stared at Kovah's face in disgust. "Answer me, you prick."

Kovah slowly pulled his sunglasses off, which elicited a gasp from Eva.

"Get off me!" one of Eva's friends said to me, her light hair curled into ringlets around her shoulders, her eyes completely black.

As if that scared me anymore.

Chuckling, I gripped her wrists tighter and said, "No, I don't think so, blondie. Sit still."

Shock registered on her face, her eyes still black as she stared at me. I turned my attention back to Kovah and Eva.

"You need to get the fuck out of town, you succubus bitch. Nobody wants you here. And Nolan here has a headful of vengeance. I've been trying to keep a lid on his ass"—he made a tsking sound—"but I'm afraid one day he may drive something sharp through your heart while you sleep. And you wouldn't want that, would you, sweetheart?" He ran his finger down her pale cheek.

She flinched back and slapped his hand away. "Don't touch me, freak."

Kovah's gaze traveled down to her chest, then back into her angry blue eyes. "What happens to silicone when it's punctured with a knife? Does it weep all over your cold skin, or just pop and explode, like a water balloon?"

She raised a pale hand to slap Kovah's face, but he stopped her by grabbing her wrist, a sound of disapproval floating from his mouth.

Before he could speak, Eva said, "My boobs are real, dickhead, not that it's any of your business. Isn't that right, Nonie-boy?" Her eyes were fierce and serious as she stared at me.

With my eyes, I shot daggers in her direction, my hand still wrapped around the blonde's two bony wrists. I ground out, "I wouldn't know. Never touched your shit. Not that I'd want to."

Eva laughed, keeping her gaze locked on mine. "Well, when you've got your hands all up in Charity's white cotton bra, finally getting to first base, just know that they're real. We were blessed with incredible genes."

I let go of the blonde and lunged at Eva at preternatural speed. "Witch, do not mention Charity! You don't get to have her name come out of your filthy mouth!" I reared my fist back, ready to punch her.

Kovah's strong grip on me brought me back to reality. "Uh-uh. We don't hit chicks, bro." He narrowed his eyes at Eva. "Not even if they're evil vampires who steal souls and suck human blood."

Smiling in triumph, Eva jutted her chin at Kovah. "You heard the freak, Nolan. No hitting girls."

Stepping back, I replied, "I'd be on board if she *was* a girl." I was talking to Kovah but staring at Eva. "But what I see in front of me isn't a girl. It's a soul-sucking demon who needs to be sent back to Hell."

Chuckling, he laid a restraining hand on my arm. "I agree, but all in due time, my friend. All in due time."

Dragging my gaze away from Eva's smug face, I looked at Kovah's sunglasses. I jabbed my index finger in his face. "I'm gonna hold you to that."

He nodded and looked around the nightclub to see several partygoers were now looking in our direction, no doubt from my outburst.

"Time to go," Kovah said.

We made to leave the club, and as we walked past the big bouncer, Kovah whispered something in his ear. He seemed to snap out of his trance slowly, but by the time he gained realization, Kovah and I were long gone, zipping through the streets of Shreveport on our *donorcycles*.

"Charity is Eva's twin?" Kovah asked as we slid into a booth at a local restaurant.

I nodded. "Yeah, I told you that in the bar, remember? I ran into her at the Stop-N-Shop the day after that succubus bitch assaulted me. Small town."

"You can say that again."

"Hi, would you like coffees while you look over the menu?" an older man with salt and pepper hair wearing the restaurant's apron asked as he set two menus on our table.

"Sure," I replied for us both.

Neither of us opened our menus.

"Is that why you didn't kill the succubus? Her sister ask you not to?"

"You're a smart one, I'll give you that. The answer is both yes and no. You may not believe this, but I really was not that excited about having to kill someone."

"Yeah, but it was either her or you."

"Yes, I knew that at the time, I just wasn't sure I believed it. You have to understand I was thrown into this shit blindly. One day I was a regular guy with a job and an apartment, and the next I was in danger of turning into a monster. Trust me, I did my research. I thought my life was over. I still don't quite understand how I didn't turn into an animal."

The waiter set two ceramic mugs on the table and poured coffee into each one from a glass coffeepot. "You boys know what you want?"

"I'll take an omelet with lots of onions," Kovah replied.

He looked at me. "You?"

"The same. Not lots of onions, though."

He nodded and left. Kovah picked up his coffee cup and sniffed. He didn't drink it, though. He set it down and folded his hands over the table. I found this curious.

"Not a fan?" I asked, jutting my chin at Kovah's cup.

"We're not talking about me," he replied with a grin.

I sighed. "I don't know what else to tell you. You know everything now."

Kovah measured me with a dark stare. "I think drinking the twin's blood reversed the curse. Do you feel like she still has your soul?"

I puckered my lips from the heat of the coffee and shook my head, setting the mug down. "No. I knew the moment she took it, and I knew the moment I got it back. Don't ask me to explain it, 'cause I can't."

Kovah chuckled. "It's okay, I won't."

"Do you think I should still kill her?"

He nodded. "Absolutely. And I want to watch. Crazy bitch needs to be put down. She's dangerous." His face darkened. "I hate to think of the havoc she could unleash on this city if she continues to be allowed to exist."

"No doubt. People of Shreveport certainly don't need that."

"So are you gonna keep seeing the twin? If so, are you gonna tell her of your plans to take her sister out?"

I rubbed the back of my neck. "I don't think so. I really like Charity and she's the polar opposite of her sister. Sweet, down-to-earth, would do anything for you. Kind, sensitive, softhearted. Which is why I won't tell her of my plans to kill Eva. I will just do it and break the news to her later."

He grinned. "Easier to ask for forgiveness than permission, eh?"

I laughed. "That's true."

Kovah traced his finger along the top of the coffee cup. "She can't seriously still think her sister is the same one she grew up with?"

I sighed. "I think she knows it in her head. She just can't accept it in her heart yet."

"Chicks."

I snorted. "Tell me about it. So are you gonna tell me what the hell you did to that bouncer back there?"

Even though I couldn't see Kovah's freaky eyes, I knew I was pegging me with his stare. "I have a gift."

I turned my head to the side. "Is that so? Go on."

He waved a hand. "It's nothing really, just a bit of hypnotism. Found it by mistake, actually."

I chuckled as I poured more sugar from a glass container into my coffee. "Dude, that was more than hypnotism. You had that bouncer nearly comatose. I've dealt with that muscle-head before, and trust me, he isn't that easily distracted."

Kovah laughed. "Yep, *muscle-heads* like him are putty in my hands. Like I said, it's a gift."

"Ever use it on chicks?"

He gestured to his body. "Do I look like I need to hypnotize a girl to get her in the sack?"

I laughed. "The sack? I keep forgetting you're an old dude."

"Not that old, really."

"You'd be wearing gold chains with your chest hair poking out of your button-up shirt and some penny-loafers with tassels if you looked as old you're supposed to be."

"Fuck off, Bishop," Kovah said, biting back a smile.

I grinned, then my face went serious as a thought came to me. "Am I gonna not age like you?"

The waiter showed up with two plates and set them on the table. We thanked him, then continued talking after he walked off.

Kovah looked the steaming plate and stabbed his omelet with a fork. "I don't know, dude. Only time will tell. To be totally honest, I've never met anyone like me before. Not even close. Either they're a bloodsucking demon-vampire, or a human."

"I guess there's no use in worrying about it right now."

With a mouthful, Kovah shook his head.

We were quiet for a few minutes as we ate. The restaurant began to fill up with hungry club-goers and I looked around speculatively.

I lowered my voice. "I had no idea anything supernatural except God existed before all this happened to me." I wasn't sure why I was telling Kovah this, only that I felt an odd sense of comradery with him.

Kovah didn't answer, just glanced up from his meal, then looked back down. So I continued, "Now I look around everywhere I go, wondering if the person is a vampire. I mean, I know obviously not when I'm out during the day, but at night. I wonder, can they sense me? Do they know me from before I was turned into this thing? Is anyone out to kill me?"

Kovah chuckled and set his fork down, putting his hand up. "Whoa, whoa, slow down, killer. One question at a time."

"Sorry. I just haven't felt like I've had anyone to talk to since all this happened. Except that cop, but he's too stuffy for me."

His bite paused at his mouth. "What cop?"

"There's a government branch that knows about this shit. You didn't know this?"

"Hell no, I didn't! What, like the *X-Files*? I loved that show. Never missed an episode."

I shrugged and played with the stir stick in my coffee. "Dunno, I guess. They know all about us though, man. I went to New Orleans with one. They ran some tests on me."

"Are you for real? What kind of tests? Did they cut you open, or probe you like aliens?"

I snorted. "No, just took some blood and did an MRI, then cut me loose. Of course they asked me a shitload of questions first, but they didn't hurt me or anything."

"Where are they located?" Kovah had both elbows propped on the table and was hanging on my every word.

"In New Orleans. I guess it's their headquarters around here."

Kovah pushed his plate away. "You up for a road trip?"

"What, right now?" I asked incredulously.

"No, in a few days. Arch will probably let you outta work for a couple of days."

I sighed. "I guess. I need to spend some time with my girl, though. Been kinda neglecting her lately."

"The succubus's twin?"

"Yes." I nodded.

The server came and placed the check on our table. Kovah grabbed it and stood. "Okay, I'll put it together and text you."

"Okay. You have my number. Or, hey, I could call it into your beeper," I replied, smirking.

"Screw you, Bishop."

Chapter 10

CHANGES

Nolan

It was four a.m. as I went around the back of the Stop-N-Shop to go up the stairs to Charity's apartment. I frowned when I saw the heavy gray door's lock was completely obliterated. I looked down at the ground and saw all the broken parts scattered. With panic threatening to overtake me, I slipped the knife from my boot and gripped it in my fist as I sprinted up the steps. I quietly put the key in the lock and opened the door. I crept inside, locking the door behind me, and I looked around. Everything seemed to be in place, and nothing seemed to be disturbed. I checked the bathroom, but it was clear and quiet. Then I spied her sleeping on the small sofa. I slipped the knife back into my boot and set my keys on the kitchen table, going to sit next to her. Brushing a stray curl from her face, I watched as she stirred a little bit.

Charity's eyes cracked open, and she blinked a few times, confusion coloring her face. "Nolan?"

"Hey, Red" I said, smiling.

She began to sit. "What time is it?"

"A little after four in the morning. Long day?" I pointed to the sofa.

She raked her fingers through her hair. "No, my sister came to see me."

I stiffened. "Please tell me you have another sister besides the evil twin."

She shook her head. "No, Eva knocked on my door earlier tonight."

"That explains the broken lock downstairs. I'm assuming they don't have a key."

Charity rubbed her eyes. "What? Those jerks! How am I gonna pay for that? Tony's gonna pitch a fit when he sees it!"

I laid a hand on hers. "Don't worry about your boss, I'll get one of Archie's motorcycle friends to fix it, he's a locksmith. Anyway, go on about your sister."

She sighed and wrung her hands together. "They asked where you were. I told them you wouldn't be back for a couple of days." Confusion caused her ginger eyebrows to dip into her face. "Wait, why are you back so early? I thought you weren't coming back 'til Friday."

"Charity, I got back two days ago. It's Saturday. I'm sorry I couldn't stop by until now."

She gasped. "Oh, my God, Nolan. Eva stopped by the night you left. Are you telling me I've been asleep for two days?"

I instantly felt angry. "What did that witch do you? Did she poison you? I will kill her. I swear to God, Charity, I'm gonna kill her."

She shook her head and chewed her lip. "I don't know. I told her I was tired and asked them to leave. That's all I remember."

"Them?"

She nodded, stress contorting her features. "Yes, she had that creep Brad with her."

"She probably drugged you. Damn, I hate that woman! We should probably take you to a hospital, make sure you're okay."

"No, I'm fine," she drawled. "I'm just hungry."

I nodded and stood up. "I bet you are. I'll make you some food. You sure you're okay?"

"I'm going to take a shower." She got up and walked slowly to the bathroom.

"Okay. What do you want to eat?"

She waved a dismissive hand before closing the bathroom door. "I don't care. Surprise me. I could eat a horse right now."

I began rummaging through her cabinets and fridge, trying to find enough ingredients to make a halfway decent meal. I wasn't the greatest cook, but I could fake it.

After cracking some eggs in a bowl, I went over to the TV and flipped it on, turning on a news channel for some noise.

When I was almost done making the meal, the scent of something much more delicious than scrambled eggs with cheese hit my nose. I froze while pulling plates from the cabinet and sniffed the air.

Almost in a trance, I went to her bathroom and found her rummaging around in a drawer. She was wearing nothing but a towel, and as my gaze traveled the length of her body, I noticed a dribble of blood leaking down her leg. My eyes zoned in on it, and my breathing increased, heart rate speeding up.

Licking my lips, but not taking my eyes off the cut, I asked, "Do you need some help?"

Charity looked up. "No, just cut myself shaving. Looking for a Band —
"

She gasped and dropped the box of bandages. She backed up until the backs of her knees hit the bathtub's edge. "I, uh, what's wrong with your eyes?"

I snapped out of my trance and blinked. "What do you mean?"

Holding the towel over her with one hand, she pointed at my face. "The green is, like, gone, sorta. What is wrong with you?"

I whipped my head toward the mirror, wiped the fog from it, and leaned in. It seemed my black pupils had grown so large, they were beginning to creep over my entire iris. I gasped, shook my head, and blinked a few times. Within a few seconds, my eyes were back to normal.

I turned around and left the bathroom, closing the door behind me. Walking quickly into the kitchen, I braced both arms on the countertop and took deep breaths.

"This cannot be happening," I murmured. I took a look at the pan of breakfast food, and grabbing a fork, shoved it in and took a huge bite, hoping it would quell the hunger inside of me.

"Well, it is, Nolan."

I turned around to face Charity, now dressed in jeans and a fitted tee, her wet hair leaving a stain. She shoved her hands into her pockets. I just stared at her, chewing my eggs slowly. I swallowed the lump quickly. "I don't even know what the hell is going on."

"Yes, you do."

I ran my hand along the back of my neck. "I can get past this. I just need to learn how to control it."

"I…" She paused, looking at the ground, then back at me. "I don't think it's something you are gonna get past, Nolan. I think maybe you're gonna have to drink blood."

"No!" I barked. "I won't. I'm fine. I'm sure it's just some freaky side effect. I don't need to drink it. It's okay. I'm just hungry."

But I knew that was a lie. I'd just eaten a giant omelet with Kovah a couple of hours before.

She folded her arms over her chest. "You liked drinking my blood. I could tell. Any normal person would have gagged and probably vomited at drinking it. You gulped it down like it was Coke. And look at your face, Nolan. You're all pale and look like you haven't slept. You have dark circles under your eyes."

I took a step toward her and said, "You know I would never hurt you, right? I'm not gonna drink blood, that's ludicrous. Maybe I'll just eat a lot of rare steaks."

Wrapping my arms around her waist, she looped her arms around my neck. "I'm not afraid of you. I want to be here for you. I somehow feel like this is partly my fault." She looked down.

I used my finger to tip her chin up and look in my eyes. "That's the furthest thing from the truth. I wouldn't be here if it weren't for you. You saved me. I owe you everything. I love you, Charity."

She nodded as tears formed. "I feel like we've been through so much in such a short time. Whatever you're going through, I want to help you."

"I see that now. I just need you to stand by me while I figure this out. I need to know what I'm dealing with." I pulled my arms away and grabbed her hand. I lifted it to my mouth and kissed it, then tugged her to the table. "Let's eat."

I watched as she wolfed down two platefuls. It made me happy I could do something for her.

"You're not gonna eat?" she finally asked when she came up for air.

I grinned. "No, I ate really late last night. In fact, I've been up all night, I should get some rest. I'm gonna go crash for a few hours." I stood up and plucked my keys from the table. Leaning down, I kissed the top of Charity's head. "I'll call you when I get up and we'll go do something tonight."

She stood up and put her pale hand on my chest. Looking into my eyes, she murmured, "We could stay in tonight if you want. I mean, we don't have to go anywhere." She gave me her sexiest smile.

I quirked an eyebrow at her. "Oh really? Well, we'll see."

She frowned and dropped my hand. "You don't want me, do you?"

Fuck. I blew out a breath. "No, I mean, yes. God… it's all I think about. I… I'm just afraid right now. After what happened earlier, I don't trust myself. I don't want to hurt you."

"I'm not made of glass, Nolan. Besides, I know you won't hurt me."

I leaned down and slowly pressed my lips to hers. She exhaled a sigh and wrapped her arms around my middle. Both my hands were on her face when I felt her tongue slip past my lips. Grunting, I moved my hands to the small of her back and pushed her into my body. Her hands moved down my backside until they reached the curve of my ass, and then she squeezed it.

I broke the kiss on a gasp, then looked down and laughed. "Did you pinch me?"

She smirked up at me. "No, I squeezed. Do you prefer to be pinched?"

"Charity Sheridan, you little minx!" I put my hand over my chest, and then I winked.

She pushed me toward the door. "Go get some sleep, silly. I have to work at the store today, but I'll see you tonight. I love you."

I opened the door and looked into her sky-blue eyes. "Bye, beautiful. Lock this door."

I sprinted down the steps and closed the heavy gray door as best I could, looking once more at the busted lock and shaking my head. Starting up my Ducati, I slid the helmet over my head and raced off down the street, watching the pink tinge of daybreak begin to glow along the horizon. I didn't think I was going to get much sleep with all that was going on in my brain, but as I reached the apartment complex and parked the bike in its designated spot, I was barely able to get the key into the door. Exhaustion overtook me, and I kicked my shoes off, crashed into bed, and slept like the undead.

I woke seven hours later and groggily rolled over, grabbing my cell phone from the nightstand to check the time. I saw I had a missed call and a text. The call was from my sister, Natalie, and the text was from Kovah: *Dude, call me. Rebels got a tip. You wanna ride tonight?*

I sat up and yawned, wondering if I should just go back to sleep. It was only one in the afternoon and figured if I was to be up all night again, I better get as much rest as I could. I thought about my plans with Charity and contemplated what I should do. I wanted to go ride with the Rebels, but I had promised her I'd see her tonight.

I thought about her, and how strongly I felt for her. She was always on my mind, and I wanted nothing more than to show her exactly how much I wanted and cared about her. Then I thought back to what had happened earlier that morning and shuddered. I remembered feeling as if I was losing control when I saw the blood. My resistance to it had slipped away so quickly, I was still surprised I'd been able to snap out of it. The war between desire and the right thing to do was waging in my mind, and as I sat on the edge of my bed with both hands pressed on either side of my head, I stared at the phone in my lap and wondered what to do.

Maybe more time with Kovah would help. Maybe he could help me understand it. But if I told my new friend that I actually desired blood, would I go from friend to enemy? The guy seemed to really hate vampires. I figured it had to do with his encounter with the succubus and what she'd done to him. After all, he was permanently disfigured in a way. I supposed that would make anyone bitter and angry. No, now wasn't the time to confide in Kovah about my annoying little craving, especially after denying it to him earlier. Still, I wanted to go riding with Archie and the bikers. Maybe we would get done early enough and I could still stay the night with her.

Resolved in my decision, I texted Kovah back to let him know I'd be there tonight, and asked for the when and where. The why wasn't important. I already knew what we'd be doing.

Next, I called my sister back.

"Hi, Nat."

"Hey, Nones. Where you been? Haven't seen you around much."

"Just busy, sis. You know that."

She sighed in her dramatic way. "Well, you need to stop by Mom and Dad's every once in a while. Don't be such a stranger. We've noticed a difference in you, you know."

That got my attention. "Really, how?"

"You're different, Nolan. You probably can't tell, but we can. How are you feeling after everything?"

I shook my head. "I... I know I'm different. What Eva did to me, I don't think it's reversible, sis. I think I'm stuck like this."

"Like what? You're not a vampire, Nolan. You're fine."

"You just said I was different."

She laughed. "I didn't mean you were Dracula now, geez. I was just saying you seem more distant, sort of more broody and quiet. Kinda serious."

"Well, I'm not. I'm the same fun-loving guy I've always been. I just have a lot on my plate right now."

"Like what?"

I felt the phone vibrate and knew I was getting texts. "Nothing. I'll stop by for brunch one Sunday. Maybe I'll bring Charity if she's not working. Then we'll talk, okay?"

She sighed. "Well, I can't wait to meet her. Do me a favor and call Mom at least."

"Will do."

"Bye, Nones."

I grinned and hit the end button. There were two more texts from Kovah: *Heading down to a shithole in the bayou, got a tip on some bloodsuckers making moonshine.*

Meet us at the garage at 9.

I laughed and replied that I'd be there.

Vampires making moonshine in a bayou? Say it isn't so. "Redneck vamps?" I chuckled quietly. "Never a dull moment with those dudes."

Chapter 11

THE PRICE OF BLOOD

Nolan

"Tell me again why we give a crap that vampires are making moonshine? I mean, it would make sense that even vamps gotta make a livin' too," I said, laughing at my own joke.

Kovah, Archie, and five Rebel Riders were standing outside Archie's Garage. They all maintained somber, straight faces, clearly not amused by my joke.

Archie shoved some more dip into his bottom lip and tightened the knot on the black bandana around his head. "Kid, we don't give two shits about the moonshine. That operation's just their cover. We got a tip they're using the equipment to run a blood factory."

I gaped at him in horror. "Blood factory?"

One of the Riders named Aspen nodded. "Yeah, these fuckers are kidnappin' people, mostly chicks, and siphoning their blood and selling it other vampers." I stared at his long, frizzy, salt and pepper-colored beard as he spoke, his beady brown eyes piercing me with serious stare. "They need to be put down like yesterday."

Risking a tongue-lashing by the group, I said, "Okay. Are they killing the humans, or just taking their blood?"

"I don't see how that matters much. Leeches need to die regardless. They're a menace to society. You should know that better 'an anyone," Archie drawled.

"Oh, he knows," Kovah said, shoving a lighter back into his pocket as he took the first drag from the cigarette he'd just lit. "Right, Bishop?"

I just nodded, not wanting to risk asking any more questions.

"What are you, some vamp lover?" another of the Rebels asked.

I shook my head. "Absolutely not. I just wondered what the rules were around here."

"The only good vampire is a dead one, that's the only rule you need to know, kid. It's our creed," Archie said, pointing to a symbol on the old biker's leather vest, which I had heard him refer to as a "cut" many times. Examining the patch closely, I could see a picture of vampire teeth with a circle around it and a line crossed through it, like a no-smoking sign. Around the ring were the letters "TOGVIADO." I grinned. "Ah, I get it, it stands for, the only good vampire is a dead one."

"Wow, smart as a whip," Kovah said dryly.

"Screw you, pager boy," I snapped.

Kovah laughed and took another drag from his Marlboro as I stared at him through bluish smoke.

Archie lifted a silver eyebrow at Kovah, but I just shook his head.

"Well, let's get going," Archie said, pointing to our bikes.

I had worn leather riding pants, a black T-shirt, and a black leather jacket, along with my boots. As I mounted the bike and started it, I could feel my buck knife still safely tucked in the left boot. I hoped I wouldn't need it tonight, or any other night. No, I was only hoping to use it for one purpose, and that would be to kill Eva Sheridan. Between everything that was going on, I'd hardly had any time to plot how I planned to do that. The last couple of attempts failed, and I realized the only way was going to be to trick her.

The ride took us off the main streets and onto the back roads, and eventually into the swamps. I was nervous about what we'd find. Ironically, it wasn't the vampires who scared me, it was the thought of stumbling onto a blood factory. I still wasn't sure what to make of the cravings, and I'd yet to drink any since I'd had some of Charity's, but every night before I went to sleep, I could feel a strange hunger gnawing at my gut that I could not satisfy with any sort of food or drink. As each night passed, I told myself I had to do something about it. I didn't even know if consuming any blood would help, but I couldn't figure out what else it could be. I sometimes thought maybe it was all in my head. But with my sensitivity to sunlight beginning to increase by the week, I wasn't sure what I was going to become. I frequently checked for fangs, but never saw any. I wasn't sure if this made me happy or not. After all, if I truly did need blood, how was I going to get it? But I knew deep down I'd never bite some poor, unsuspecting human, and I surely would never kill one. If I did need blood, I'd have to get it another way. I pushed the thought away and told myself to concentrate on the task at hand.

With Archie leading the pack, we came to a stop in front of what appeared to be an abandoned shack deep in the swamp. Moss trees bowed around it, hiding its worn wooden exterior and broken window frames. The front porch steps did not appear to be safe to walk on, and I hoped we wouldn't be going inside. I could see cobwebs through the murk of the windows, but inside was otherwise dark.

"We stop here, boys." Archie killed the engine and dismounted his bike, then put the kickstand down.

Kovah, the rest of the Rebels, and I parroted the gesture and stood waiting for instructions.

"We take it on foot from here," Archie began. "It's about half a mile through the trees. Bikes'd make too much noise and this shack is a good milestone to find our way back to 'em. Y'all follow my lead and we'll take a look at what we're workin' with. We aren't going to act tonight, though. We're just scopin' out the situation. Unless a fanged freak catches us, there'll be no killin' tonight." He waved his index finger at us. "Is everyone trackin'?"

The rest of the group nodded and followed Archie as he began to limp away. I noticed he didn't have his cane, but that didn't surprise me. Probably just slow him down when trekking through the soft earth of the swamp.

We hadn't been walking long when we came upon a large plantation set right on the water. In the front was a grassy clearing surrounded by tall moss trees, the full moon's light casting a blue glare over the lawn. The house was painted white with dark-colored trim and a wrap-around porch. Lights burned inside most of the windows.

"This is a blood factory? It looks like something out of *Gone With The Wind*," Kovah snarked with his arms folded over my chest.

Aspen snorted out a laugh while I tried not to make a sound at the joke, but we all caught Archie's glare. "It isn't, trust me. Now try to keep up."

With just the warm, humid night air and the sound of chigger bugs to keep us company, Archie turned right at the clearing and moved with haste toward the tree-line that edged the clearing. We followed him through the trees. The floor of the tree copse was littered with felled leaves of all colors. At the next clearing, a small wooden bridge covering a pond was our next destination. It creaked under our footfalls, and as we trampled across it, I snuck glances at the huge dwelling as we quickly fell into the shadow of the house. Archie put his finger to his lips and pointed at the back of the house, and we all followed him yet again.

Once we reached the back, there was a large yard with a bonfire pit and a swimming pool. There was no fence or gate to keep anybody or anything in or out. The yard was well kept, and I realized the blood trade was probably pretty lucrative for these vampires.

Archie indicated for everyone to stay back, and instructed Kovah to look inside the windows. The Riders were looking in different directions and had their knives out, ready for anything.

After peering in through the back window, Kovah turned and smiled, then pointed at me. "Have a look."

I nodded and carefully put my face to the glass. I let out an uncontrollable gasp at what I saw. In the kitchen was one hospital-type cot, and two more were in what should be the dining room, which was void of any sort of furniture. Three humans lay on the cots, completely still and most likely unconscious, IVs hooked up to their arms, their red life-force being pumped into bags at the end of the IV lines. I counted six vampires, three males and three females, attending to the "patients", two on each human. Their skin was pale, and one of the vampires, a young-looking female, had no whites to her eyes. Her fangs were peeking below her top lip, and her tongue darted out and licked her own blood that had been drawn from her bottom lip. Her hair was short and very ginger red, and she wore a white summer dress. I thought if she wasn't sporting the black eyes and fangs, she'd look very normal. Minus the lack of tan, of course. An older male wearing doctor's scrubs placed his hand on her shoulder and she looked up at him. She shook her head, and her features went back to normal. I really did think the girl was going to go rip open a blood bag and have at it. Or worse, rip open the vein of the young man lying on the table. I shook my head, realizing this was a very new vampire, and hoped her eyes weren't blue so she wouldn't be the newest succubus on the block.

I was choked when my T-shirt was pulled against my throat. Archie's hand was at the back of my shirt. "You've seen enough. Believe me now?"

"Yeah, but I didn't see any moonshine makin' equipment in there," I explained. "It just looked like it does at any ol' blood bank."

"Except the patients are unconscious," Kovah replied dryly.

"I say we lure them out here and kill every last one of 'em," one of the Riders said.

"I agree. We come back when we've formulated a plan, though," Archie said, spitting dip into the grass and wiping his mouth with the back of his hand.

"Who the fuck'r you?" said a deep, baritone voice off to our right.

All heads swung in that direction to see two large men standing there with handguns. Everyone froze.

The silence seemed to go on forever until Kovah spoke. "Uh, is this the Bellamy Plantation?"

The shorter of the two, a guy with arms like the Hulk said, "No, dick."

"Uh, which one is it then? I could swear they said this is where they lived."

"How the fuck should we know? Now scram," he replied.

"Guess we're just lost, dude," Kovah said with a shrug.

I knew Kovah had to be eyeballing the guns the muscle-heads were waving around. I determined these guys were human, because I'd never seen a vampire have the need to carry a firearm. They were also sweating along their foreheads, and I knew vampires didn't sweat.

The taller of the two, a guy with a gleaming bald head and a black goatee, cocked his head to the side. "I don't believe you. Get the fuck outta here before we kill you all and feed you to the gators." He jerked his head at the swamp.

Archie nodded. "We were just leaving."

"Is everything all right, Michael?"

The pale vampire wearing green medical scrubs came out. He removed his rubber gloves and stared at his henchmen.

"These clowns were just leaving," bodyguard number one said.

Everyone startled when an ear-splitting gunshot rang out, ripping open the quiet night.

As if in slow motion, everyone looked to see the tall bodyguard clutching his belly. He looked down, pulled his hand away from his stomach, and saw it was covered in blood. His eyes rolled back in his head and he fell to the soft earth with a very loud thud.

Everyone looked at Aspen holding a smoking .357 Magnum revolver.

The vampire rushed over to Aspen at unnatural speed and yanked the gun from his fist. Aspen tried to fight, but with a quick grab to his head, the vampire snapped his neck and poor Aspen was now lying lifeless in the grass. It all happened in less than three seconds.

"Aspen!" Archie cried out.

My eyes were fixated on the bodyguard. Blood was oozing out of his gut, and when the scent hit my nose, I ran over. With a slight hesitation, I put my hand over the wound, trying to staunch the flow. "Someone will call 9-1-1. You'll be okay."

"Ain't no one callin' nobody, kid," said Sammy, the second bodyguard. His gun was trained on my head. "Move away from Michael."

Lifting my hands in surrender, I stood up as blood trickled down my palm, and then dribbled into the dirt. Turning my head at the scent, I gazed at the blood and began to bring it to my mouth, almost as if in a daze. But in my bloodlust, I hadn't noticed that Kovah, Archie, and the remaining four Riders had the vampire doctor on the ground and were about to end his life. Sammy seemed to notice it at the exact same time as me, and raised his weapon.

So much for no killing tonight.

I yelled, "No!" right as Archie's twelve-inch knife plunged into the vampire's heart. The vampire-doctor screamed before the blade hit skin, but it was cut short as his body crumbled mid-scream, leaving nothing but a pile of ash and green scrubs. Another screaming gunshot pierced the night as Sammy took a shot at Archie, missing his graying head by inches. I tackled him swiftly and wrestled the gun away from him with ease. It landed with a thud in the grass by my feet. Rearing back my left arm, I punched the guard in the face with all my might, knocking him out cold. For how long he'd be out, I wasn't sure.

"We need to go—now," I cried out on a choked panic, shaking out my throbbing left hand. I wiped my bloody hand on the grass, then picked up the bodyguard's 9mm pistol and tucked it into the back of my pants. After walking over, I dragged Archie with me. Archie whimpered as he glanced back and took one last look at his friend lying lifeless on the ground, open, vacant eyes staring at the sky.

At least a dozen vampires came bolting out of the house, hissing with their eyes completely black and their fangs out. Upon glancing to the west, the first bits of sunlight began to light up the horizon, and the vampires stopped their chase, slinking back into the house. Kovah was practically carrying Archie due to his bum leg, and we arrived at our bikes in record time.

Everyone was panting except Kovah and me. We were mildly winded, but not wheezing for breath like the older bikers. Archie glanced at Aspen's bike with sadness and Kovah clapped him on the back. "I'll come back for it in a couple hours. Nolan will give me a ride." He turned to face me, his dark glasses still firmly in place. "Right, man?"

I nodded. "Sure."

"But the keys are in Aspen's pocket," Archie murmured, a defeated tone lacing his words.

"I'll hotwire it, boss. I got this," I said, placing a hand on his shoulder.

We started up our bikes and drove out of the swamp, one less Rider in tow, sadness and grief blowing in our wake like a set of fumes.

Chapter 12

LOVE AND WAR

Nolan

With a yawn, I staggered out of bed and made it to the front door since the incessant ringing wouldn't stop. Bleary-eyed and dazed, I slid back the chain, then the deadbolt, flinging the door open. I hadn't even bothered to look through the peephole, which I quickly decided was a really careless decision.

Charity's copper hair was glowing from the sun shining behind it, almost casting me on an angelic glow.

I grinned. "Hi, Red."

She shoulder-barged her way into my apartment with an annoyed huff. I briefly looked at my watch and saw it was three in the afternoon.

"Don't you 'Red' me, Nolan. You were supposed to come over last night. I even begged my boss to let me off early, and then I waited up for you all night. You didn't even have the decency to reply to any of my calls or texts. What is wrong with you?"

I looked at her angry face, pale cheeks flushed crimson with rage. Her arms were crossed at her chest, the gray sweatshirt tied around her waist looking as if it was going to slip loose and fall to the floor.

I brought my gaze back to her blazing blue eyes. "Charity, I truly have no excuse. I was with Archie and Kovah, and left my phone in…"

"Who is Kovah, and what the heck kind of name is that?" she asked with attitude.

I sighed, still trying to shake the cobwebs of sleep from my brain. "Just a guy I know."

Charity's arms were still folded over her chest, the white tank top blending in with her fair, freckled skin. "A guy? Nolan, I'm not sure I really know you. You said you'd be over last night, and I believed you. I was waiting for you." She pierced me with a heady stare. "I was ready to give myself to you. All of me. I've never felt more broken or rejected in my life." Her cherry-red bottom lip wobbled, defying the attitude she was trying to put out.

My heart shattered. I thought I could hear the shards hitting my insides as Charity's sad eyes bored into mine. I felt like a complete asshole. But how could I explain where I'd been? What I'd seen? It was like I was being torn in half, my body in one direction, my heart and soul in another. I decided coming clean with her was the only way to go. She could accept it, or she could leave. I didn't want her to leave, though. I wanted her to stay, but I had to be honest.

"I was with Archie. There were some vampires running their own blood factory down in a bayou."

She arched a ginger eyebrow. "So what? What business is it of yours?"

I scrubbed my hand along the back of my neck. "It's not, it's just that Archie and his friends needed help—"

"So your new job is hired muscle at Archie's Garage now?" she snarked.

I rushed over to her. "No! I mean, yes. I mean... I don't know what I mean. All I know is that things have changed with me."

She stared at me, waiting for me to continue. I was looking down at her and her blue eyes were pleading with me as if waiting for an explanation she could use to justify staying.

"Look, Charity. I haven't had enough time to deal with all these changes. In the span of a week, I met a demon, she took my soul, I got it back, I found out my boss runs a vamp-hunting biker club, I almost became a vampire myself— and then..." I swallowed hard, measuring my words. "I fell in love."

Without thought or reason, my lips crashed down onto hers, my hands still gripping her lean upper arms. My stomach flipped in summersaults and another part of my body suddenly woke up and began to pay attention. When Charity's arms wrapped around my back and she pressed her body closer in to mine, I growled in the back of my throat, deepening the kiss.

Her tongue slid into my mouth with both ease and eagerness, and she pushed me back against the front door. Her leg wrapped around the curve of my butt as I reached behind her head. Fisting a handful of ginger curls,

I yanked her head back and licked her from her collarbone to her jawline, running gentle but urgent kisses across her cheek until I reached her full red lips, capturing them again as I moaned quietly into her mouth.

The kissing and make-out session lasted forever. My mouth on hers, Charity's hands exploring the naked skin of my muscled back. I slipped a finger into the waistband of her capri pants, brushing my fingertips along the sensitive skin of her hipbone and lower stomach. I felt her shudder, and she smiled into my mouth.

"I want you, Nolan," she murmured with a husky urgency.

"I've wanted you forever," I growled into her ear.

I pushed off her body, grabbing one delicate hand and yanking her toward the one and only bedroom in my apartment. Once there, I looked into the depths of her eyes and then pushed her onto the bed I had been sleeping on before she'd aroused me in more ways than one.

I looked down at her, an eager but nervous smile playing on my lips, and I wanted nothing more than to ravish every inch of her body. I was anxious to explain to her, in a lover's language only she could understand, how much I wanted her. I longed for everything to be okay between us again, for her to comprehend that my life was different now.

I used my finger to slide down her pants and she gave no resistance at all, wiggling out of them until nothing was left but lacy black panties. I slid off my shorts, and I kicked out of them.

With her lying on her back, I reached around to unclasp her black lacy bra and felt no clasps. I broke her wet, urgent kiss, looked into the valley of her breasts, and noticed the clasp taunting me there. Reaching up with two fingers, I flipped it open, her freckled mounds freed and ready for exploration.

The doorbell rang.

I swore under my breath, wondering who in the hell could be at my house at three in the afternoon.

"Ignore it," she panted into my ear.

I wanted to. God, I wanted to. Something niggling at the back of my brain wouldn't let me, though. "I need to see who it is."

She sighed and pushed me off her. "Fine. Go. Don't mind me."

I raised an eyebrow at her attitude then bit back a smile, realizing she must be really turned on to get so pissed off at whoever was the door.

I yanked my athletic shorts back up and went to the door, peering the through the hole. With a sigh, I opened it.

"What are you doing here?"

Kovah looked at my half-naked form and glared at me through my dark glasses. "Pack your shit. We're heading to New Orleans."

"What? No, I can't go. I have work, and I —"

"It'll all still be here when you get back, dude," he replied.

"Don't count on it," Charity said, suddenly appearing from the bedroom, shoving her tank top down over her stomach. She re-tied the sweatshirt around her waist and scooped up her handbag from the floor near the door.

"Charity, wait," I said, grabbing her arm.

She looked down at my hand and yanked her arm free. "Go, Nolan. Go to Nawlins. Aaagain," she drawled. "And don't call me when you get back. I'm done."

"No!" I cried as she flew out the door and down the stone steps. I went after her and cringed as the sun's rays slapped me in the face and chest, instantly feeling blazing heat on my skin. But I was still going to go after her until Kovah pulled me back.

"Let her go, she'll cool down. Redheads, man. Feisty."

I slammed the door and dragged my palm across the top of my head. "Fuck!"

"Calm down. She's probably PMSing or something."

I huffed and said, "It's not that. I just keep letting her down. I can't get a grip on my shit, man."

"Well, I didn't even know you had a chick in here. Sorry about the cock-block, man," Kovah said with a grin, but he obviously wasn't really sorry at all.

I shook my head and went into my room. I pulled a duffel bag down from the top shelf of my closet. Kovah followed me.

"When the hell do we leave, and what the hell are we doing there?"

Kovah leaned against the doorjamb with his arms folded. "Tomorrow morning, and vampire hunting, of course."

I paused with a handful of shirts and tilted my head to the side. "Why are we going to Nawlins for that? Isn't that place crawling with vamps?

Why are we hunting them?"

"Dude, I know the Riders' motto is *'the only good vampire is a dead one'*, but truth be told, we really only take out the bad ones. The ones who cause harm to humans."

I shoved the shirts into the duffel. "Like those three we took out a couple of nights ago outside the bar? They weren't really doing anything, Kovah, and you know it. As I understand it, even vampires need to eat."

He pulled his sunglasses off, and his face darkened. "There are willing donors and blood banks for that. Those leeches can't just go walk into a club and start taking it from people. It's like rape, really."

Resisting the urge to roll my eyes, I said, "But the victims don't even remember, so I don't think that's quite right."

"Exactly. Like a date rape drug. They forget. It's taking something that belongs to someone else without asking. They think they're superior and above laws and rules."

I zipped the bag and looked into my friend's icy vacant eyes. "Well, they kinda are. Think about it. It's not like we can just put handcuffs on them and throw them in jail."

Kovah slipped his glasses back on and grinned. "No, but we can shank them through the heart and not have to deal with them anymore."

Chapter 13

THE BIG EASY, TAKE III

Nolan

My calls and texts went unanswered and ignored. After almost twenty-four hours of trying, I gave up. I hoped I could talk some sense into Charity when I got back to Shreveport... whenever that would be.

Kovah was driving his black 1988 Trans Am, a large gold-winged firebird painted on the hood, and I was sulking in the passenger seat. I'd rather be on my bike, the wind in my hair and the air in my lungs, but we both knew the bike wasn't an option as long as the sun continued to rise and set. Sure, the sun didn't kill me, but there wasn't any point in enduring pain for the five-hour drive between Shreveport and New Orleans, and head-to-toe leather was just uncomfortable and stupid in early September.

I had been playing on my phone, and when the car began to slow, I looked up to see the large, dull gray bridge that stretched over the Mississippi River, a sign reading *Welcome to New Orleans* perched at its edge. I hadn't realized the ride was already coming to an end, and was glad it had gone by quickly.

"You know, vampire hunting is really only part of the reason I dragged you here," Kovah said, still facing forward somberly he steered the car over the bridge.

Raising an eyebrow, I cut my eyes to him. "Oh yeah? Well, then enlighten me, pager boy."

Kovah snorted. "I'm very interested in the Justice Department and what they know."

I pocketed my phone with a sigh. "I already told you what they know. Which is more than they should, but probably not everything."

Kovah nodded, and after a long pause, replied, "And you know some vamps here, don't you?"

Thinking of Joel, I nodded. "I know one." Then I thought about the owner of the clothing shop Charity and I had used to find appropriate clothes for the vampire ball we'd gone to. I grinned. The guy was flamboyant, but harmless. It also got me thinking. "You wanna catch some crazy vampires, come here during late summer when they have their annual vampire ball. A bunch of posers mixed with real vamps is a serious match made in hell."

Kovah slammed on the brakes with both feet and the car came to a juddering halt. He pulled his glasses off as cars screeched and honked behind us. "What in the flying fuck are you talking about, Bishop?"

Smirking, I jerked a thumb behind me. "You're holding up traffic, dude."

"And I'll continue to until you spill the beans about this 'vampire ball' you just mentioned."

I cocked my head to the side. "Did you just say 'spill the beans'?"

Kovah let out a huff dripping with frustration. He put the Trans Am in gear and pressed the gas, much to my relief. "Cut the shit, dude, and just tell me."

"So they have this big event every summer, they call it a vampire ball of some kind, and all these people obsessed with goth and vampires come out and wear dumbass costumes, fake contact lenses and vampire teeth, and sip red wine that looks like blood. They just lurk around the ballroom of some old hotel here in town."

"What hotel?" Kovah demanded.

Thinking of Joel's hotel, and knowing Kovah would probably kill Joel just for fun, I lifted a shoulder in a shrug. "Dunno. Just something I heard about."

"And I call bullshit," Kovah snapped. "I know you know."

"Do I look like Google to you?" I asked, irritated.

"Fuck you, Bishop."

I grinned at the exact response I knew I'd get.

Kovah parked in the covered garage to the chain hotel we'd chosen close to the Quarter. He got out and I followed him to the trunk, pulling our duffel bags from its deep recess. We made our way through sliding glass doors to a modernized lobby that was clearly renovated from its original 1800s decorum.

After checking in, we rode an old elevator up to the third floor, and I was relieved to see two double beds in the room. I chucked my duffel onto the bed closest to the door and then crossed my arms over my chest.

"What?" Kovah asked.

"Don't 'what' me. It's getting dark, and I know you have a plan. Your ass better have a plan."

Kovah laughed. "Of course I do. Don't be a dick. You'll get some vampire shanking in. I know you want to." He tossed a hunk of wood that had been crudely whittled to a sharp point at me. I caught it.

I turned it around in my fist, then shook my head and tossed it onto the bed. Reaching into my Justin boot, I produced my trusty buck knife, the light from the setting sun shining in through the partially opened curtain glinting off it.

Kovah whistled through his teeth. "That's nice. Is it new?"

"No, my dad gave it to me a long time ago."

His eyebrows went up. "To kill vamps?"

I snorted. "No. Dad doesn't believe in vampires. He gave it to me on my sixteenth birthday. It's just a family thing, I guess."

"Must be nice to have family who gives a shit."

"You don't?"

"They think I'm dead."

I gasped. "What? Why?"

Kovah shook his head and shoved his duffel bag into an empty dresser drawer. He pointed to his body. "Look at me, dude. I'm supposed to be forty years old. My parents are in their seventies. Don't you think they'd get a bit suspicious if they saw me looking like I was twenty-something?"

I rested my hands low on my hips, my brow furrowed. "So you just let them think you're dead?"

He nodded and slammed the drawer shut. Turning around, he faced me with his dark glasses still in place. "What else was I supposed to do?"

I shook my head. "I don't know. Tell them you had plastic surgery? Tell them you moved to the Bahamas? Anything is better than letting them think you were dead."

"Screw you." Kovah stormed into the bathroom and slammed the door.

Plopping down on the bed, I put both hands on my head and breathed deep with my chin to my chest. I wondered, since my new friend and I were in a similar boat, if I was going to have to do the same thing to my parents and sister. I wondered if in ten years, if I didn't seem to be aging, I'd have to disappear. It didn't go unnoticed by me that Kovah didn't speak with a Southern drawl. I often wondered where he hailed from. I thought maybe I even detected an East Coast New York-type slant to his words, but I couldn't be sure since I hadn't really ever been out of Louisiana.

All I knew was that Kovah most likely had re-invented himself somewhere along the way, starting a new life in a new place with a new name. And that had to be a very lonely place to exist.

"Shh!" Kovah said, his long finger pressed against his lips. A satisfied smirk hid behind it.

Stupid me, telling him to Google the annual vampire ball, I thought as I stared up at the hotel owned by Joel Reichert, the only vampire who'd ever shown mercy to me.

"Don't shush me, asshole. I'm a damn ninja. I know how to be quiet. Unlike you. I think your ego needs its own zip code."

Kovah snorted. "Fuck off."

I shook my head. "Why are you trying to be stealthy? Let's just walk into the place."

The night was quiet, humidity heavy and brooding in the air as we stood with our backs pressed against the wall of the hotel where it straddled a back alley.

I had to resist the urge to roll my eyes. "Okay, that's it. We're going in. I know the owner."

Kovah dipped his glasses down to the end of his nose and pierced me with a creepy, icy stare. "Are you fuckin' with me?"

I shook my head. "No. C'mon."

Walking in through the old-style revolving glass door, Kovah followed. Blowing past the reception desk with the young clerk shouting after us, I yanked open the door to the stairwell and began sprinting up the stone steps.

Smiling, Kovah easily kept up and was hot on my tail as I pulled open a nondescript white door, which read *Third Floor*. Stopping to look both ways down a hallway carpeted in tacky green and red paisley décor, I quickly decided on a left turn, continuing my momentum.

My father, Mark, had always declared proudly that his son had a great sense of direction. Passed on by him, of course.

Before we knew it, we were standing in front of a large door with the hotel owner's name etched into a name plaque displayed inside a brass door-plaque holder.

Kovah eyed the door, then flicked my gaze to my face. "You weren't kidding when you said you knew the owner, were you?"

I gave a short shake of my head but kept my eyes on the door. "No, but the last time I was here, the owner kicked my ass."

"Wha-at?"

I laughed. "Seriously. And dude, this guy is a vamp. Please don't kill him. He's one of the good guys."

Kovah shook his head. "You just said he kicked your ass."

I blew out a breath and raked a hand over my crew cut. "I deserved it—"

Before I could finish, the door was yanked open, and a young Black man in a perfectly pressed navy suit was staring at us with light caramel-colored eyes narrowed in mistrust.

"Why are y'all lurking outside this door?" he asked with a thick drawl.

I opened my mouth to speak, then clamped it closed again.

Of course Kovah couldn't keep his trap shut. With a quick look at the door plaque, then back to the young man, he said, "Where's Joel?"

"He's not taking visitors at this time," the guy replied, his smooth voice matching the warm color of his skin, and keeping an impassive expression on his face.

I sighed. "Tell him Nolan Bishop is here."

The young man glared at me, then at Kovah, then back to me with a scrutinizing look in his honey-laden gaze. Nodding, he closed the door in our faces.

Kovah looked at me. "I thought you were shitting me about knowing the owner."

"About vampires, I never joke."

My friend went to snap off a witty retort when the door was opened once again, seemingly by a ghost, as there was no one there. A glance from Kovah gave me no reassurance at all, as I couldn't read his expression. So walking through the door with more confidence than I felt, I had to suppress a shudder when the door closed on its own behind Kovah.

Without a doubt, I knew we were in for a long night, and drew little comfort from the feel of my buck knife brushing against my ankle.

Chapter 14

FRIEND OR FOE?

Nolan

I tried not to squirm under Joel's dark, scrutinizing stare. I already knew what Joel was about, and I glanced at Kovah to gauge his reaction to the old vampire.

Joel flicked his gaze between us both, then said, "What do you want, Bishop?"

"Just a few minutes of your time is all."

Joel nodded, indicating the two vacant chairs in front of his desk. When we were all seated, he said to his young assistant, "That'll be all, Tommy. Stay close by."

Tommy nodded and exited the office, closing the door behind him with a quiet click.

"Before we begin with the twenty questions," Joel said, looking at Kovah sternly, "remove your glasses while you're inside my hotel. Have some manners."

Kovah nodded, sliding the dark frames from his face. I bit back a smirk at the gasp I knew was inevitably coming.

And Joel didn't disappoint. With his eyes wide, he thought for a long minute before asking rhetorically, "Is that your natural eye color?"

Kovah shook his head, his right leg resting in a figure-four shape across his left. "Nope. A succubus did this to me."

Joel's eyebrows went up. He sucked in a breath as he hooked a finger into his shirt where his shimmering silver tie was suddenly too tight about his throat. Looking at me, he asked incredulously, "There are two of you who've survived the succubus curse?"

A grin twitching on my lips, I quickly replied, "Oh, yes, there is. And that's why we're here."

Joel nodded in understanding. "Tell me everything, Nolan." He sat forward in interest. "Everything."

I laughed. "You already know my story. Maybe Kovah can tell you his instead." I waved a hand at my new friend.

"Kovah? That's not your real name, is it?"

"No. It's havoc spelled backward, as chaos and *havok* seem to find me everywhere I fuckin' go," he replied in what seemed to be a well-rehearsed response.

I grinned. I'd never bothered to ask about his strange name before. I wondered not for the first time if I'd have to make up a new name in the future.

Joel leaned back in his squeaky leather chair and measured Kovah with a fatherly stare. "Something tells me you seek it out, young man."

I chuckled, and they both looked at me. "He's not young. He's like, forty."

"Watch it," Kovah and Joel both replied in unison.

Looking at each other, they both let out a chuckle that seemed to break the tension in the room that earlier felt was thick enough to choke us all.

I lifted both hands in surrender. "I'm just saying… Kovah here was cursed by the succubus, but I'm starting to think it may not have been such a hardship."

Kovah jumped out of his chair and pointed to his face. "You call this a privilege? You think I like wearing sunglasses indoors? Fuck that. It sucks. Hey, why don't you tell ol' Joel here about your bloodlust, *Nolan*?"

The room fell silent, all tension that had been broken a few moments ago resuming with a thickness that penetrated the room like unrelenting fog.

I stiffened, my jaw ticking in anger. "You're a dick."

"And you drink blood, just like the rest of the leeches."

"No, I don't," I replied defensively, raising my chin.

Kovah didn't respond. He just stared at Joel for confirmation.

Joel's hands were steepled in front of his face. "Do you drink or crave blood, Nolan?"

I sniffed and shook my head. I realized I had two choices here: Lie and risk being caught out by two old guys who could probably sniff out the truth from me and be punished for lying, or maintain my story about not wanting or needing blood. Invariably, I decided on the latter.

"No, I don't. I don't know why he says I do." My arms were folded defensively over my dark-blue T-shirt as I used the index finger of my right hand to point at Kovah.

"You're a horrible liar, Bishop," Kovah said, pulling the Swiss Army Knife from his pocket with a swiftness that both frightened and impressed me. He sliced his arm with it.

With a grin, Kovah slid a finger along the beading blood on his arm and looked at Joel, then back at me. I could feel my green irises were beginning to cloud black at the sight and smell of blood. I leaned closer to Kovah, mesmerized.

"Hungry?" Kovah asked.

Joel's eyes were large, incredulous. With a swift blur of a movement, Joel was around his desk, pulling me from my chair and pinning me to the wall of his office. "Nolan!"

I shook my head as if to clear it, and stared at Joel, blinking. "What is going on here?"

Joel sighed, released my T-shirt from his fist, and slunk back behind his desk. He pinned me with a sober stare, ignoring Kovah's shit-eating grin. "We have a serious problem here, boy."

"I… I can control it."

Kovah snorted. "Right. How?"

"I just can. I don't need blood to survive. I've realized that in the past weeks."

"How do you figure?" Joel asked.

"I haven't had any, and I'm still alive and well."

Joel stared at me again in his way, and said, "Yeah, well you look like shit because of it. You look like a vamp who needs to feed. I'm just being straight with you. The bloodlust will eventually consume you, Nolan. It appears you weren't left completely unscathed by Eva's soul-stealing ways."

Kovah lifted both eyebrows. "You know the succubus?"

Joel nodded. "Yes. I'm the one who turned her."

The room fell deathly quiet until one of us found our voice.

"What the actual fuck?" Kovah spit out.

My eyes were huge on Joel as I pointed to Kovah. "Yeah, what he said."

Joel laughed. Actually laughed. "I guess you want the story?"

"Uh. Duh," I said.

"Okay," Joel replied with amusement dancing in his eyes. "A few years ago, I was hosting the annual vampire ball at my club, like I'd always had. And as usual, a group of beautiful women came in donning fancy dresses, contact lenses, and fake vampire teeth they'd probably purchased at a mall store." His smile began to fade as he continued. "I was up here in this office, watching the festivities, and saw the group of ladies walk in. I was happy to see such beautiful women in my hotel. I was hoping they would draw in the men, who would pay for the drinks and keep my bartenders happily employed. I watched them intermittently while I did paperwork. After about an hour, I was lost in my work when my office door creaked open."

Kovah and I were listening intently, hanging on my every word.

Biting back a grin of amusement, Joel continued. "I looked up to see the most beautiful redhead I'd ever laid eyes on. Her blue eyes pinned me to the spot and rendered me speechless. I watched with a terrified fascination as she slunk over slowly to me wearing nothing but a skimpy black cocktail dress. Coming around the desk, she parked her very impressive backside on it, reached up, and ran her blood-red fingernails through my hair. It was shameless how cowardly I became under her touch."

"And she was still human?" Kovah asked incredulously.

Joel nodded. "Yes. Beautiful, soft, and seductive, I was powerless against her charms. My body became boneless as she leaned down to kiss me. It was all over after that. I took her right here in this office." He waved his hand in a flourish, and if vampires could blush, I was sure I would have seen red creep up the old vamp's face.

"In the throes of passion, she had begged me to bite her. I didn't need to be asked twice. I took her blood without thought or reason, and when I'd had my fill, she pled for me to give her some of mine. You can guess that I did. Bit into my wrist and dribbled my blood into her willing mouth."

I gasped. "Didn't you know turning a blue-eyed redhead would make her a succubus?"

Joel shook my head. "Nope. I sure didn't. In all my years, I'd only met one succubus, in the 1950s and I had no idea she'd been made that way. I just thought she was a different type of vampire. Nobody had ever told me that red-haired, blue-eyed females were made into succubi during the vampire transition. It's a mistake I shall never make again, I'll assure you both."

"So, what? She just got up and left your office and you never saw her again?" Kovah asked.

"Yes, it really did happen like that. Do you think I really cared? I'd gotten what I wanted. I didn't pay the price for that carelessness until a year later when she returned for the vampire ball looking even more beautiful and a whole lot deadlier."

"And...?" Kovah snapped.

Joel laughed and sat back in his chair. "And nothing. I didn't speak to her or even acknowledge her after that. I just watched her feed on humans from my window here, brooding over my mistake. She does give a donation to the ball every year, by mail, of course."

"Why didn't you kill her ass?" I was barely able to get the words out, I was so shocked.

Joel flicked his eyes to me and made a scoffing noise as he waved his arm around. "And what? Murder a seductive redhead who had all eyes on her in the middle of the ballroom? Leave her in a pile of ash and have to hypnotize hundreds of humans into thinking she'd never been there? I don't think so, kid."

The only thing I got from that was one word. "Do succubi really turn to ash?"

Joel looked amused. "Of course they do, they're vampires. All vampires meet their final death the same way. A pile of ash."

Kovah shook his head as he flipped a pack of Marlboros around in his hand. "No, they don't. They shrivel up like a hundred-year-old corpse. It's fuckin' nasty."

Joel lifted an eyebrow. "Is that so? You've seen this?"

Kovah nodded. "Yep. Killed my succubus and have been told by others that it's the same way when others are killed. Freaky, huh?"

I briefly wondered what would happen to me if I were to be wiped out of existence.

Joel swiveled his head to Kovah. "You killed your succubus

immediately after?"

Kovah smirked. "A few days later after she thought I was long gone. The bitch had to die after what she did to me."

Joel's eyebrows hit his hairline. "Wow. And those unusual eyes are the result?"

"Yeah, I guess." Kovah lifted a shoulder and let it fall.

"You guess?" I spat. "You're the one who told me she did that to you." I pointed to Kovah's eyes.

"She did. I used to have dark-blue eyes. Then after I killed her, I woke up the next morning and saw this as I looked in the mirror. I think she took a piece of my soul with her when I killed her, because they never went back to normal."

"But you're supposed to turn back, or remain human, if you kill your succubus. That is what the research says. That is what the witch doctor in the Quarter told me," I said.

Joel shook his head. "No, boy. Killing your succubus keeps you from turning into a feral vampire that usually needs to be put down like a rabid dog. It does not mean" — he said while pointing at Kovah — "that you will go back to how you were. I think you both are proof of that."

I opened my mouth to protest that I haven't killed Eva yet, but closed it with a click. It would do no good to argue. I knew both of them were now privy to my blood-craving problem, and I'd already told Kovah about the annoyance with the sun. That being said, I was glad I hadn't suffered a physical deformity like he had.

Curious, I asked, "Is your sight affected, too?"

Kovah shook his head. "No, it's better than twenty-twenty. I can see perfectly both close up and far away." He pointed to his sunglasses. "The sun bothers them if looking directly at it, but it doesn't blind me or anything. I've gotten quite used to the glasses, though. It just sucks because people stare and think I'm some douchebag by wearing sunglasses at night."

Remembering my mom's favorite song from the 80s, I began to sing, "I wear my sunglasses at night, so I can, so I can…"

Kovah rolled his eyes. "Oh, shut up. You think I haven't heard that before?"

"Of course you have. I bet it was your favorite song in high school," I said with a chuckle.

He bit back a smile, not only because I was pretty much right, but because he probably found it amusing that I even knew the song.

"So why don't you wear colored contacts then?" Joel asked.

Kovah shook his head. "While they're irritating, that's not the issue. They seem to sort of... break down and shred after a couple of hours. I really have no idea why."

"Vampire venom," Joel murmured.

I turned my attention back to the old vampire. "Now what?"

Joel sighed and swiveled his squeaky leather chair to look out the large window overlooking the hotel ballroom. "Now what... what? You came to me, Bishop. A ballsy move on your part, I might add, but you're here. What did you want?"

Thinking long and hard about the question, I wasn't sure. I stared at the old vampire and I could feel Kovah's eyes on me as the room waited for me to answer. I thought back to the night's events and wondered why I'd even led my new friend to Joel's office. It wasn't like he held all the answers. I learned quickly that all Joel held was anonymity and bitterness. I was shocked I hadn't been beheaded by the vampire for my murderous actions against Ansel. With that being said, I also knew deep down that Joel was not an animal. He was an old vamp who deserved respect. A man whom I needed to make an ally of, not an enemy.

I had my answer.

"We need your help," I finally answered.

Chapter 15

DECEPTION

His hand traveled up Eva's creamy thigh until it reached the edge of her black leather mini-skirt. He slid his gaze to her icy blue one, trying to see how far he could push his luck.

"You start something in this car, you're gonna have to finish it here, too," Eva said, staring at Brad with a pout on her lips, amusement dancing in her eyes.

"Oh, and I want to, baby. This stakeout is sooo boring."

She rolled her eyes. "It's not a stakeout. I am just trying to find Nolan Bishop. That guy is never around. I need to catch up with him. He owes me something."

Brad stopped his hand's smooth movements and looked at her, confused. "Baby, I don't think you can get his soul back, or whatever. I think it's, like, gone forever."

"Oh, shut it. I just need to try. This has never happened before. I'm gonna get to him one way or another. And going through Charity is my best bet."

They both looked to the Wal-Mart entrance they were parked in front of. It was nighttime, and the heavy air was quiet. The only lights were from the store's sign, and no clouds were overhead as stars peppered the inky sky. They had followed Charity from her job to the large chain store, in hopes she would be meeting Nolan. But so far, Charity had just run a bunch of boring errands consisting of getting gas and shopping at the only big store in town. Now they waited to see where she would head to next.

Eva thought about having some fun with Brad in the car, but the sports car was too small—and besides, she was growing irritated at not being able to locate Nolan. She wished she knew where he worked, but it had never come up in their brief conversation. There was more than one motorcycle repair shop in town.

She looked at Brad and narrowed her eyes. "You should have asked

Charity where Nolan worked. That would be way easier than following my boring-ass sister around. I have better things to do than hang around the stupid Wal-Mart all damn night."

Brad's mouth was open, his dark, slicked-back hair shining under the parking lot lamps. His pale skin glowed a sickly green against the lights from the car's dash console.

"Why do you act like it's my fault? You could have asked her yourself where Nolan worked."

"That's true. I *am* the brains around here."

Brad opened his fanged mouth to protest when Eva smacked his arm, pointing at the exit. "There she is." He started up the engine and the car came to life with a quiet purr.

They watched as Charity loaded three small bags into the backseat of her older Toyota. She then got into the driver's seat and started up the car. It took two tries, but it eventually turned over and she headed out of the parking lot's exit and back onto the main road.

Eva and Brad followed her, staying a safe distance behind. Eva knew where she was headed. They didn't need to tail her that closely. And she did not disappoint. Ten minutes later, Charity parked her Toyota into one of the spots at the Stop-N-Shop, got out, retrieved her bags, and made her way to the back of the store. But not before looking around the lot suspiciously. Eva and Brad were parked at the back end of the lot, but they froze when Charity spotted the black sports car.

An angry countenance overtook her face, and she dropped the three bags by the front door of the store before marching toward the Porsche. Eva got out of the car and told Brad to stay inside. The windows were tinted such a dark black to keep out any sort of sunrays they may accidentally encounter, that there was no way she would be able to see him sitting in there with her human eyes.

Eva was already standing against the driver's side with her arms folded over her skin-tight red top. Her thigh-high shiny black boots glistened in the parking lot's lights, which made her pale legs glow white.

"What are you doing here, Eva? Can't you just leave me alone?"

Eva laughed at the red anger that had overtaken Charity's face. Her wild curls were piled high on her head in a lazy manner, and her white tank top was sticking to her in places. She reached down and tightened the knot around the purple sweatshirt hanging off her hips.

"Sure, I'll leave you alone when you tell me where Nolan is."

Charity sighed. "He's in Nawlins."

Eva cocked her head to the side. "Bitch, you told me that last time I was here, why don't you get creative and think of a new story? Or how about this—you tell me the truth?"

Charity's pale, freckly hands balled into fists. "First off, I hardly think you have any room to call anyone a bitch, *bitch*. Secondly, Nolan *is* in Nawlins, it's just unfortunate for you that you keep stopping by here every time he goes there."

"What? Like, Nolan has business there? He didn't strike me as the type that goes on business trips," Eva said with a smirk, baiting her.

"He's not on a business trip. The government wants to see him, thanks to you."

Eva removed her arms from across her chest and reached out to grab Charity's shoulder.

But Charity moved away from her evil twin by taking a step back. "Don't touch me."

Eva nodded. "Fine, but tell me more. He's there because of me?"

"I'm done. I'm leaving now, and you should, too. I'm going to call Nolan when I get inside and warn him that you've been sleazing around here, looking for him. Then he's gonna come back to Shreveport and kick your ass," she drawled, narrowing her eyes at her sister.

As she turned to walk away, Eva grabbed her by the shoulder and spun her around. She raised her open palm and slapped Charity clean across the face. The sound echoed around the empty parking lot.

Brad chuckled from his location in the front seat.

"What the hell was that for?" Charity cried, cradling her cheek.

"Don't you dare threaten me, little bitch. Nobody is going to kick my ass. Ever."

Charity grew enraged. "That's what you think!" she screamed. She put her finger up and pointed in her twin's face. "You keep thinking you're invincible, but one day, that's going to come back to haunt you. Mark my words. Nolan will be back soon. You'll see."

"You never said what he was doing in Nawlins, sister dearest."

"Oh, don't *sister* me. He's workin' with the government, I've told you that. Now get the heck out of here! Take your creepy vampire friend and bounce already."

Eva folded her arms across her chest said with a satisfied smirk, "Well, your story is interesting, but I think it's more believable that Nolan probably has a girlfriend in Nawlins, don't you think?"

Charity paused, then whipped her head around. "No, you crazy vampire. He does not have a girlfriend there. And this conversation is over."

Eva watched her walk away across the lot and contemplated her next move.

Chapter 16

CONFESSIONS

Nolan

We spent another hour in Joel's office while he explained to us the easiest and cleanest way to get to Eva and kill her. We thanked him and left, me beaming with a renewed confidence and a determination more than before to kill the redhead once and for all.

"So where are the Riders?" I asked Kovah as we left Joel's office and headed out into the dark, humid night toward our hotel room.

Kovah pulled out a lighter and a pack of cigarettes from his pants pocket. After shaking a smoke from the pack and replacing it back inside his pocket, he lit the cigarette and blew smoke into the Louisiana night air.

"Back in Shreveport, I assume," was his only answer.

Confusion blanketed me as we continued to walk. "But you said the Riders were meeting us here."

"Well, I may have stretched the truth a bit, you see—" Kovah started.

My eyebrows went up as I stopped walking. "You lied to me, dude?"

"I needed to get you here with me. We've got to find out what the Justice Department knows. I've got a few questions for them myself."

I let out a frustrated huff and resumed walking. "Kovah, you're really beginning to piss me off. If you wanted to meet the cops, you could have just asked me. I have one of the damn agent's business card in my wallet right now."

He blew out another stream of smoke from the corner of his mouth, and said, "Yeah, but in Shreveport. I want to meet the ones here in the big city."

"And what, exactly, do you think you're gonna ask them? Do you think they have some sort of answers for you? Because they don't. All they did was interrogate me for a few hours, ask me some weird questions, then take my blood and do an MRI scan on me. I am no more the wiser now than when I left there last week. They don't care about me, and they won't care about you. They just want research material."

Kovah nodded and flicked his cigarette onto the concrete, crushing it out with his boot. "Yeah? Well, that's no worse than not knowing anything at all. I almost want them to use me as a guinea pig. If they can give me answers, they can do whatever they want."

We reached the hotel, and as we made our way through the lobby and to the elevator, Kovah reached into his back pocket and pulled out his wallet, the one attached to the two chains he wore connected to his jeans. He yanked his card key from the wallet and put it back into his pocket. He looked at me through his glasses. "What?"

I pointed. "Why do you wear those chains?"

"So nobody steals my wallet. Duh."

I chuckled. "You're a part-vampire-motorcycle-riding badass, I doubt they'd get far."

Kovah's face darkened. "I'm not part-vampire."

The doors to the elevator opened and two teen girls got on, staring at us, then giggled as the doors closed. Kovah and I exited the elevator. I watched as he put the card key into the room door.

"Yes, you are. I am, too. We need to accept it."

Kovah shoved the card into his front pocket and set his sunglasses down onto the nightstand near his bed. Pulling his boots off, he said, "I never will."

"There's no other explanation for it, man."

Kovah didn't say anything, he seemed to be digesting my words, not sure if he was worried or relieved at them. I wandered into the bathroom, brushed my teeth, and then changed into some shorts and a tee to sleep in.

Once I was done, I walked back into the room as Kovah pulled his shirt off and shoved it into his duffel. He looked at me, but still didn't say anything.

"What?" I asked, feeling a little uneasy.

"Look, I didn't mean to fuck with you. The truth is — I've had run-ins with the Justice Department before. Just like you, right after my attack, they approached me. It was basically the same song and dance you endured. A few tests and they sent me on my way. Never heard from them again or knew how to get in contact. When you mentioned that agent had approached you, I was hoping to talk to them again. See if they'd learned anything new, or if there were others like me."

With my arms folded over my chest, I sat and listened to him. I nodded. "Go on."

"When I met you, I knew why I had been drawn to you from the beginning."

I lifted an eyebrow.

He chuckled. "No, not like that, asshole. It's just that there was no mistaking the connection we had on a supernatural level. Like we were one and the same, and I knew deep down it was my responsibility to help you out. Help you figure out your way, as I wished someone would have done for me."

"Wow," I breathed.

"Look, I certainly don't have all the answers, but with this newer technology and research the government must have versus twenty years ago, I was kinda stoked to see if I could go talk to them. If that makes sense."

"Yeah, it does. But aren't you afraid the guys at the BSI will want to detain you, run all kinds of tests on you, on your eyes, on your blood?" I asked, throwing back the sheet to my bed. I stared at Kovah's chest, which was just as tattooed up as my arms and shoulders were. I made a mental note to ask him about them, instead of gawking at them, which I knew would elicit comments from Kovah that I didn't feel like dealing with.

"What is the BSI?"

I sighed and lay back on the bed with my arms behind my head. "The branch of the Justice Department I told you about."

"Oh. Well, what does it stand for?"

I paused. "I can't remember. The guy's card is in my wallet if you want to look."

Kovah got up. "Where's your wallet?"

I pointed to the floor. "In my pants pocket."

Kovah froze and looked at the heap of jeans on the hotel floor. "Nah, I'm good."

I chuckled. "Suit yourself. But tomorrow I'm calling the agent and telling him everything." I turned my head and looked at Kovah on the other bed. "I mean it, man. If you want to see them, you're gonna have to tell them everything."

Kovah agreed. "That's fine. I don't care anymore. Twenty fuckin' years of no answers is long enough."

Nothing else was said. I grabbed my phone and saw I had no calls or messages. *Glad to know I'm missed when I leave town,* I thought sadly.

I dialed Charity's number, knowing she wouldn't pick up, but I was going to leave her another voicemail, then shoot her a text. She couldn't stay mad at me forever.

Could she?

She answered on the second ring and said, "Hi, sweetie."

I pulled the phone back and looked at it, then put it back to my ear.

Sweetie?

"Uh, hi, Red. I'm glad you answered."

"Why wouldn't I?"

I glanced at Kovah, who had his eyes closed and was lying on his side. "I don't know, thought you were mad at me or something."

"Um, nope. I'm good."

I thought I detected some attitude, but didn't push it. Relief washed over me, the knot in my stomach beginning to unravel. Women were so frickin' moody. Maybe Kovah had been right. Maybe it had been PMS that made her storm out of my apartment two days ago.

"Well, I miss you, beautiful."

"When are you coming home, baby?" she asked in a whiny voice.

"Uh, not sure, in a few days. I promise I will keep you informed, though. I miss you so much. I just want all this to be over."

I heard her gasp. "What do you mean, 'this'?"

"You know, this stuff with the government, with Archie, with everything."

"You're there to see people from the government?" she asked.

I nodded. "Well, it wasn't in the plan, we were supposed to go hunting with Archie and everyone, but" —I paused, not wanting to admit I was duped by Kovah, or make myself sound like a jackass —"there's been a change of plans. Once I'm done with the Justice Department, I'll be home. Then we can finish where we left off," I said huskily.

"Hunting..." she said softly.

I groaned. "Charity, don't start again, okay?" I didn't wait for her to respond. "I'll be home in a couple days. I can't wait to see you."

"Me too."

"I'll call or text you tomorrow. Love you."

"Love you, too," she said, then hung up.

I didn't have time to analyze why she was acting like that. I was too exhausted to care, too happy she wasn't mad at me any longer, and glad she'd finally cooled off. I placed my phone on the nightstand, plugged it into the charger, flipped the bedside lamp off, and was asleep as soon as my head hit the pillow.

Chapter 17

A LITTLE SHADE

Nolan

I rolled my eyes as I looked at Kovah, the cell phone pressed to my ear as Kovah and I finished our breakfast in the hotel dining room.

"Yes, he's volunteering. Why is that so hard to believe?" I asked Agent Nelson.

Kovah was staring at me with an amused grin, an empty plate in front of him. He leaned back in his chair with his tattooed arms behind his head.

"Then call me back." I hit a button on my phone and pocketed it.

"So?" Kovah asked.

"So Agent Nelson's gonna call the Men in Black here in New Orleans and tell us we have a volunteer, then call me back."

Kovah snorted and stood up. "Men in Black, funny. That was a good movie."

"I bet you and your high school buddies watched it like a million times in the theater."

Kovah, getting used to my bad jokes, just shook his head. "Came out way after I was in high school, you ass."

"Well, I was like five when it came out."

Kovah ignored me and said, "Let's go see that voodoo guy you saw last time you were here."

"Sure. You got twenty bucks? 'Cause that's how much he charges to tell you shit."

We walked out of the hotel, through the parking garage, and out into the sunlight. I gasped and shrank back, smashing the LSU ball cap tighter on my head. I yanked a pair of sunglasses from the pocket of my jacket and threw them on, then flipped the collar of my coat up around my neck.

"You look real stupid, Bishop. It's September," Kovah said.

"Funny you say that, 'cause I was just thinking we looked like twins today." I pointed to my sunglasses.

"Not at all, in the slightest," Kovah said dryly.

We walked quickly down the riverfront street and turned down a tree-lined road. I let out a breath I didn't know I was holding. Relieved to be out of the sun's harsh glare, I looked at Kovah and said, "It's only a couple more blocks."

Once we reached the small house, Kovah raised an eyebrow at the rickety wooden sign plunged into the grass. "Li Grand Zombi?"

I walked up the creaky steps and pulled my glasses off. "Just roll with it."

Kovah shrugged a shoulder. "Whatever you say."

After one knock, the door was opened by the woman of the house, Babet. She was in her long, colorful dress, her head wrapped up tightly in a scarf that matched her dress. She narrowed her brown eyes at me, the sweat on her forehead gleaming against her dark skin.

Face relaxing with recognition, she said, "Well, well, well. I did not tink I would ever see you again, boy. Well, I was hoping I would, just during the daytime." She chuckled. "So this is a pleasant surprise." She ushered us both in with a flourish.

"Nice to see you, too, ma'am," I said, removing my ball cap and smiling politely at her.

Kovah did not remove his glasses as he entered the dark house, incense burning, noisy shells acting as curtains covering each doorway. As we passed into the kitchen, she indicated the empty table and instructed us both to sit.

"Mathieu!" Babet yelled, startling me, and making Kovah laugh.

She went back to the sink, where she appeared to be shelling black-eyed peas.

"Aye, boy. I did not think I would see you again," Mathieu said, his green eyes a mix between scrutinizing and amusement.

"Yes, well… like I told you before, sir, I'm a survivor," I replied with more confidence than I felt.

Kovah snorted.

Mathieu chuckled, taking his place at the head of the table in an old chair. "You have twenty dollars?" He looked between us.

Kovah pulled out a twenty-dollar bill and slapped it on the table.

After pocketing the money, Mathieu's countenance turned serious when he looked at Kovah. "You. You have been a victim too, no?"

"Sir, with all due respect, I ain't no victim. My succubus is dead. I'm a survivor."

Mathieu clapped his dark, ashy brown hands together, a laugh tumbling out of his throat. "Good man. You and I will get along just fine."

A relaxed mask replaced the stressed one Kovah had been wearing, and he smiled at the old fortuneteller. "I agree. Sir."

Mathieu began shuffling cards as his wife continued her chore at the sink, seemingly unfazed and disinterested in what was going on at the dining room table.

He held up a card depicting a hooded skeleton on a horse. "It's the death card again, but I am not alarmed by this. There is so much living death in this room."

Kovah's eyebrows dipped together. "Living death?"

Mathieu nodded. "Yes, boy. You and this one here" — he pointed at me —"you're both teeterin' on the fine line between life an' death."

"What the fuck does that mean?" Kovah asked.

Mathieu made a *tsking* sound. "Such language, vampire. Watch it in my home."

Kovah stood up and jabbed a finger in the old fortuneteller's face, the chair legs squeaking against the floor behind him. "Don't you *ever* call me a bloodsucker again. You got that, old man?"

I was still seated as I laid a restraining hand on Kovah's arm. "Sit, dude. Be calm, listen to what *Li Grande Zombi* has to say." I shot a look at Mathieu, who nodded at me.

Kovah glared down at me, his nostrils flaring like an angry bull. The sunglasses hid his milky eyes, but I didn't need to see them to know what was wrong.

Slowly, Kovah's breaths came out more even and he lowered himself into the chair, his jaw ticking. Still, he said nothing. He folded his arms over his chest.

I looked to Mathieu with a wave of my hand. "Please, sir, continue."

"As you wish."

He continued to shuffle the cards. He stopped and flipped one over, laying it on the top of the stack. It featured an androgynous figure standing in a circular wreath. "The world card." He fixed his eyes on Kovah again. "You have been restless and nomadic, have you not?"

Kovah slowly nodded, his shaky hands now lying respectfully in his lap. "For longer than you can even fathom."

"You will roam no more. You have found a home in the South. You have come full circle, boy."

I raised an eyebrow. I knew I'd been right. Kovah wasn't from Louisiana, and had spent a lonely couple of decades searching. For what, I wasn't sure.

Mathieu flipped the nomad card over and spied the card depicting two figures holding hands in front of an angel. "The love card."

Kovah and I just stared at him.

"Mr. Sanagra—you will find love once and for all. And you will find it here, near the powerful tides of the Mississippi."

"Sanagra?" I questioned.

Kovah turned to me. "You never bothered to ask my last name." Then he looked at Mathieu. "And how did you know it?"

The old man just grinned knowingly.

"It's Sicilian, in case you were wondering." Kovah looked at me.

"I wasn't, but thanks for the info dump," I murmured back.

"Fuck you, Bishop."

Mathieu stood up. "You boys get the answers you were searching for?"

I shook my head. "Sorry, man, not even close."

He narrowed hazel eyes at us. "What else do you need?"

"We'd both like to know what the future holds for us. As you can see, Kovah here still looks like he's twenty-one, but he's actually in his forties. Will this happen to me?"

"I am not an expert in the ways of the vampire, young man," Mathieu replied. "But I would venture to guess that if you continued to consume blood and stay out of the sun, then yes, you will continue to not age."

I gasped. "I don't drink blood!"

Kovah made a scoffing sound.

Mathieu shot a glance at Kovah, then turned his attention back to me. "I'm sorry, Nolan, but you better find yourself a blood source, because it shall be part of your diet. In fact, I would be so bold to say that if you don't get some soon, your skin will continue to become paler and those rings around your eyes will become increasingly darker. Your irritation with the sun will continue to grow." He paused and pierced me with his intense stare. "And then, you will eventually expire."

Kovah and I wore matching stunned expressions.

"How did you know all that?"

Mathieu stood up once again. "Did you miss the sign outside that reads *fortuneteller*? I got skills, young man." He tried to sound young and cool as he said the last part, but with his Creole accent, it just sounded funny. We both laughed.

"Now, if we're all done here, I have other business to attend to."

We nodded and stood up, thanking the old man for his time.

As we both made our way down the sidewalk heading for the BSI's regional headquarters, Kovah slid a sideways glance at me and said quietly, "Dude, you have to drink blood."

"Don't remind me," I replied.

He laid a hand on my arm and we stopped walking. "I just want you to know, that if I ever catch you taking blood from a human being, it will end badly for you."

I yanked my arm away from his grasp. "You won't ever have to worry about that. In case you didn't notice, it's not like I have fangs. I'll figure out another way."

"I know you will, and I will help you, only because I like you."

"Not enough to *not* kill me, apparently," I murmured.

Kovah chuckled. "I have a reputation to maintain."

"Yeah, a reputation for being an ass–"

My phone chimed and buzzed in my pocket. I slid my gaze away from Kovah and to the phone's screen. I answered, "Hey, you."

"Nolan," Charity whined. "When are you coming home?"

My eyebrows furrowed together. "What's wrong? Is everything okay? You don't sound right."

She sighed deeply. "I'm just tired of you going to Nawlins, baby. I miss you. When are you coming home?"

Fucking seriously? My jaw ticked with irritation. "I told you, in a couple of days."

"Okay. Text me when you're on your way home? I miss you so much. I can't wait to be with you."

I smiled. "I miss you, too. I'll make it up to you, I promise. Things are just crazy right now. They will be better when I get back."

"Just hurry back, okay?"

I paused for a minute as we continued down the tree-lined street. When I saw a break in the trees, the sun glaring on the sidewalk at the end of the street, I stopped. Kovah stopped walking when I did. "Listen, Charity, is everything all right? Has your evil twin stopped by? Just say yes or no."

"What? No. Eva hasn't been here. I can't miss my gorgeous boyfriend without something havin' to be wrong? Dang, Nolan, you're making me sound like some needy bitch."

My eyebrows went up. "Um, well, okay. I'll text you when we're on our way back. Bye, beautiful."

I hung up, a confused expression coloring my features. I pulled my sunglasses from my pocket and slammed them on my face.

"Lady troubles?" Kovah asked, biting back a grin.

"Women."

He chuckled. "I tried to warn you. Redheads. Not worth the work."

"This one is," I replied with a sideways glance.

"You need to kill the sister. It'll uncomplicate things."

I took a deep breath as we entered the part of the sidewalk without the protective shade of the trees and sped up my walk. "Somehow, I doubt that, man."

The building was plain and nondescript. It was just kinda there, sitting in the middle of the French Quarter along with the rest of the old buildings.

Kovah turned to me. "This is it?"

I nodded and began to walk to the front glass door, anxious to get out of the sun.

He followed. "So… we're just gonna walk in like we own the place, or what?"

"Shut up."

Kovah raised an eyebrow, but did, indeed, shut up.

I saw a large reception desk and headed toward it.

"Hi, we need to visit the Justice Department," I said to the security guard in uniform.

"And who are you here to see?" he asked in deep, gruff voice. His black skin was slightly shimmering with sweat, his hair shaved clean off.

I racked my brain, trying to remember even one of the agents' names I had been interrogated by a few weeks prior, but I was coming up with nothing. "Nobody in particular. I just need to see one of the agents."

My eyes were suddenly drawn to the pulsing artery in the security guard's neck, the glowing skin flickering over the throb of blood lying under the thin layer of flesh there. I shot my eyes back up when the guard spoke.

"You're not gonna get upstairs by just saying you need to see someone. I need a name, jack."

Kovah put on a disarming smile. "Oh, come on, guy. We just need to see a few people."

The security guard narrowed his eyes at him. "Take off your sunglasses while you're in here."

Kovah kept the smile in place. "Of course, sorry about that."

As he removed his glasses, the guard gasped. Kovah got right in his face and I watched in fascination as his chocolate-colored eyes glazed over.

"You're going to tell us what floor the Justice Department is on, and after we've gone up, you're gonna forget we were here."

The security guard nodded. "Take the elevator up to the third floor."

Kovah slid his glasses back on and said with a bow, "Thank you, kind sir."

We ignored the elevator comment and made our way to the stairs, walking up the three flights.

"You didn't have to ask him what floor, I already knew," I said to break the silence.

He snorted as we rounded the corner and stepped up to the last flight. "I figured. It was just fun fuckin' with him."

We reached the top of the concrete stairwell and Kovah put his hand on the doorknob leading to the third floor. I craned my neck around and looked at him. "You need a hobby."

He grinned. "I have a hobby. Killing vampires. You ready to do this?"

"I already am. The question is, are you?"

Chapter 18

WHAT IS THE JUSTICE DEPARTMENT HIDING?

Nolan

The old, heavy door creaked open, and as Kovah peeked down the hall, he apparently didn't see anyone. He waved for me to follow him.

I felt like I was in an episode of some cop drama. I resisted rolling my eyes as I said, "Dude, we don't need to sneak around. As soon as I find one of the agents, they'll recognize me. In fact, one of the agents was kinda hot. If we can find her, I'm sure we can put on the charm and she'll see us."

Kovah smiled. "Nice. What was her name?"

"Don't you think I would have told the guy downstairs her name if I could remember it?"

"You need to learn to plan better."

I rolled my eyes. "You're the one who wants to see them, dickhead. I had no plans to ever come back here again."

"Just find someone."

I looked down the hallway and realized it looked familiar. "This way."

Kovah followed until we reached the conference room where I'd been interrogated. I realized I hadn't visited anyone's specific office. Just the conference room, and then to the medical lab.

"Here goes nothing," I murmured, creaking the door open.

Five sets of eyes pierced me. Seeing the female agent, I plastered on a relieved smile and pointed to her. "Hi — can I talk to you?"

The agent frowned at the intrusion, then looked at the other four people sitting around the conference room table. She had been standing at the head of the room, a Dry-Erase marker poised in her hand mid-scrawl on the whiteboard.

She cleared her throat as she replaced the cap on the green pen and set it on the tray at the bottom of the board. I looked at the four young men in suits sitting at the table, who were all staring at us.

She narrowed light-brown eyes at me and smoothed down the fitted pinstriped skirt she wore. "What can I do for you, Mr. Bishop?"

I yanked on my friend's arm and dragged him into the room. Pointing at him, I drawled, "This is Kovah Sangara, and he is a lot like me, if you get what I'm saying? He needs to talk to someone."

Kovah shot a look to me, implying that he wasn't as needy as my statement had suggested.

The agent looked at Kovah curiously and nodded to an empty chair. "Please, sit. I'm Special Agent Mara Shields."

We both sat at the conference room table. We exchanged nervous glances with the four nondescript young men sitting there, staring at us with neutral expressions on their faces.

I stared at the young men, who probably weren't much older than me, and wondered if they realized how fortunate they were to be young and driven and just beginning their careers. I didn't know how I knew, I just had the feeling these were new recruits to the BSI or at least the Justice Department, and a dab of envy sliced my gut. To be an ordinary young man, mundane, and normal. It was something I'd never be. I could smell their anxiousness and there was an edge of fear permeating from one of them.

My eyes moved to a young guy with military-cut blond hair and crystal blue eyes. His face was cleanly shaven and his jaw pulsed with anxiousness, but I could sense he was slightly afraid. My eyes drifted down to the throb in his neck and then back up to his face. The young agent never broke my gaze, and I had to respect that he was trying to be brave, but his fear was assaulting my nose like vinegar. At that moment, I knew he'd be a good agent. His fear was an indicator that something wasn't quite right about Kovah and me, and I knew as long as I was alive, I'd have to keep my eye on this one. The other three were staring blankly at us like robots, no fear, just a mild curiosity.

"Bishop, you wanna tell me how you got in the building?" Mara

Shields asked, now seated, her legs crossed, her arms resting comfortably on the armrests of her chair. Her shiny black pumps reflected the fluorescent lighting of the room.

I dragged my gaze from the young blond man and back to the beautiful agent. "Yes, ma'am. We walked through the front door and up the stairwell to the third floor."

Her expression did not change. "Okay, smartie. How did you get past Henry downstairs?"

Kovah answered, "Henry's not too bright, if you catch my drift, darlin'."

Mara's gaze darted to Kovah. "Is that so? And you're so much smarter?"

Kovah grinned. "Yep."

"Take off your sunglasses in here," one of the young agents said.

"Oh, here we go again," I mumbled.

"Aw, do I have to? I was kinda saving that for later." Kovah bit back a grin.

Mara folded her arms over her chest. "Yes."

With a shrug, Kovah slowly removed his glasses, folded them, and set them on the table.

The confident blond guy did not flinch like the other four did. He just simply asked, "Are you blind?"

Kovah pierced him with a stare. "Nope. I see better than twenty-twenty."

"Then what happened to your eyes? Cataracts?" asked Mara.

"Nope," Kovah repeated. "Succubus, that's what happened."

She lifted a questioning eyebrow at him and said, "Go on."

Kovah nodded, launching into his story once again as I half listened and half scanned the group of agents, trying to read them in any way I could. I started when my phone buzzed in my pocket. I pulled it out and looked at the screen.

Charity: *I miss you baby.*

I went to pocket the phone, figuring I'd call her later when I wasn't in such a stressful situation, when it buzzed again.

Charity: *Do you miss me? Because I don't feel like you do :(*

What the...? I thought. I had never seen Charity act like this. Admittedly, our entire relationship had been built on stress and adrenaline-fueled situations, but during those times I'd felt she had bared herself to me enough to where I knew her enough to fall in love with her. Now I was questioning that. Maybe I didn't know her at all. Maybe she couldn't handle being alone. Maybe she was insecure and thought I was out with some other girl.

God... the thought hadn't even crossed my mind. I barely had time for one fiery redhead — who had time for anything or anyone else? I let out a ragged sigh and put the phone away, ignoring her once again and knowing I'd pay for that later. I began to wonder if maybe Kovah was right and being single was just easier, especially with all the shit I was going through lately.

"Well, that's quite interesting. Except it doesn't explain what happened to your eyes," the smart blond agent said to Kovah, piercing him with a stoic expression I'd come to realize was probably the only one he had. His large arms were folded over the chest of his suit and tie, and I could tell the guy was most likely prior military.

With a smirk forcing its way onto his lips, Kovah shot back, "I really don't know what to tell you. The bitch tried to steal my soul, then I killed her. I woke up the next day and my eyes — which were a dark blue before — looked like this. I've searched twenty years trying to figure out why, but nobody can tell me."

The group of agents gasped and it took me a minute to realize they had been alarmed by his "twenty years" comment. I bit back a grin.

The blond agent pointed at me, almost ignoring his twenty year comment. "Then why don't his eyes look like that?"

Kovah tilted his head to the side. "Not sure. Why don't I crave blood and he does?"

"Asshole," I murmured.

When the agent opened his mouth to whip off another question, Agent Shields stood up and waved a hand back and forth. She said, "Hold up. Wait. Just wait. First off" — she measured a serious gaze at me — "you drink blood? You never told us that during your interview."

I shook my head. "I told you I drank Charity's blood — "

She cut me off. "No, that's not what I meant and you know it. You continue to voluntarily drink blood without getting sick?"

I sighed and shot daggers at Kovah, then looked back at Mara. "No, I don't. There is a craving there, but I've yet to do anything about it. Honestly, I really don't know how to get any."

She looked at me closely, one eyebrow perched in question, as if she wanted to say something, but had to keep her professionalism firmly in place. She finally said, "Excuse me."

We all watched her leave the room, then looked at each other.

"Twenty years?" a young Black agent asked, his hair shaved but not completely gone, a small strip of a mustache on his upper lip. He had on a white dress shirt, gray slacks, and an eye-catching bright lavender tie. "What are you, like twenty-five? Some succubus stole your soul when you were a kid?"

Kovah laughed. "Nope, I was twenty-one."

The Marine-looking agent sat forward and coolly folded his hands together on the table. "You're forty? No way."

"I am," Kovah replied, rattling off his date of birth and what year he'd graduated high school.

"But..." one of the agents started.

"Yeah, another unexplained side effect from a redheaded vampire bitch. If you want my opinion, guys, you need to just kill them all. They're fucking dangerous. Vampires can be managed if they don't kill humans and feed on donors or from blood banks. But the succubus? They do shit like this." He pointed at his eyes, then jerked a thumb at me.

The door opened and Agent Shields walked in with a thick plastic bag filled with red liquid. She tossed it onto the conference room table and it landed with a smack right in front of me. The bag had "O+" stamped on it.

I looked at it, then at her, my eyebrows dipping in confusion. "You can't be serious."

She sat down and then folded her hands on the table. "I'm very serious."

I stared at her in horror. "You want me to... drink this?"

"Sure, go for it. You know you want to. I even warmed it for you in our lunchroom microwave. My coworkers are gonna have my head for it, but it's okay. You look hungry, and quite frankly, like crap."

I looked down at the plastic bag and put my hand on it. It did seem to be warm. I looked up when I heard a collective gasp from the people in the room.

Kovah, after he'd replaced his shocked look to his usual smug one, pointed at me and said, "Dude, your eyes are black. Like freaky, *vampire* black."

The bastard had the nerve to laugh. The rest of the group was staring at me with their mouths open. Except the cocky blond agent.

"Go on. There's a nozzle at the end. Just drink through it like a straw." Mara jutted her chin at it.

I swallowed hard and stared down at it. My stomach summersaulted with hunger and I internally cursed myself and wondered if anyone else heard it. "No way."

"Pussy," Kovah said.

I glared at him, pointing at the bag. "You drink it."

"Nope. Don't drink blood. That's gross, man."

"So while Mr. Bishop is contemplating this, I want to go back to something," Mara said, looking at Kovah.

"Yes, I'm forty. I don't age. Anything else?"

Both eyebrows rose. "You're joking."

He went into his birth year and the year he'd graduated high school again and waited for her to respond.

"What does your family think?"

"They think I'm dead."

She nodded, jotting in her notebook. "You faked your own death?"

"Yep."

As he droned on about his life, my gaze would not leave the sight of the blood bag. I was cursing myself for finding it actually appetizing to look at, and I wondered if it would, indeed, help me to feel better. I hadn't told Kovah or anyone, but I was starting to feel very weak and shaky, and I was constantly hungry, no matter what I ate. I already knew everyone could see the dark circles under my eyes, and I knew I had to do something. I slowly picked up the bag, put my lips to the nozzle, and began to suck.

Oh, my God. It tasted amazing. Nothing like how it smelled. The warm liquid slid down my throat and I instantly felt better. The shakes in my hand ceased. My stomach stopped rumbling. I sucked harder and faster, closing my eyes as if it was an Oreo milkshake with extra Oreos.

My slurping sounds stopped all the conversation. I opened my eyes to see every head swiveling my way. The bag was so empty, it was nothing more than a flat piece of plastic with red dotting the inside.

I set the bag down and breathed in deeply with my head down.

"Are you all right?" Agent Shields asked, coming to stand next to me, her hand on my shoulder.

I lifted my gaze to hers, and she gasped. "Nolan, your eyes are as bright as the grass in the middle of summer after the rain. Your skin is flushed peach and even your teeth look whiter somehow. The dark circles under your eyes are completely gone!"

"Whoa! Check you out!" Kovah said. "A blood diet looks good on you, man."

I glared at him then looked back at Agent Shields, smiling.

"But don't ever let me catch you feeding on humans, Bishop—"

I cut him off mid-sentence. "Or you'll kill me. Blah, blah, blah. I know, dick. You don't need to keep saying it. We know you hate vamps."

"I hate vampires who kill. But you won't be one of those," Kovah shot back, his statement more of an order than a suggestion.

My face grew dark. "I'm not a vampire, period, so shut the fuck up before I fold your teeth back."

Kovah's eyebrows rose. He put his sunglasses back on and stood up. "Time to go." He grabbed my right arm and pulled me up out of the chair. I took a left-handed swing at him, but missed when he ducked.

All the agents stood up, looking ready for a fight.

"Wait, where are you going?" Mara Shields asked.

Kovah gripped me tighter around my bicep and shot over my shoulder, "We're staying at The Suites in the Quarter. I think ol' Nolan here needs a time-out."

Chapter 19

IT'S JUST BLOOD

Nolan

et your damn hands off me!" I snapped, yanking my arm out of Kovah's grip as we exited the unmarked building.

We began walking quickly down the street with him trailing slightly behind me. "Wow, you're a mean drunk. Just like my old man."

I stopped my tracks, the sun blazing down on my head. I yanked the purple LSU ball cap from my back pocket and shoved it on my head. "What are you talking about? I'm not drunk."

Kovah laughed, stopping on the sidewalk with his arms folded over his black T-shirt. "The fuck you're not."

I let out an annoyed huff and put my hands low on my hips. "It's eleven o'clock in the morning."

"Bishop, you're blood-drunk. After you sucked down that blood bag, you looked, like, a million times better."

I slammed my sunglasses on my face, turned on my heel, and continued walking without responding to my new friend.

"Why you mad, bro? The truth hurt?" Kovah asked, catching up to me.

The phone vibrated again in my pocket. I completely ignored it. "I'm not mad, angry, or mean. Or drunk! Why is everyone so shocked by me drinking blood?"

He chuckled while he continued to walk, his hands shoved into his pockets. "Uh, it's kinda weird for a person to drink blood. You gotta admit."

Once we found shade on the street from a tall building, I stopped walking. "My whole life is weird, Kovah. I used to be so normal. I used to blend into the background and live a very mundane and bland existence. And you know what? I didn't care. I liked my bland and mundane life. I liked being normal. Now I'm just — "

"Not bland and mundane," Kovah finished for me.

I nodded in sadness and continued to walk toward Bourbon Street. "Come on, let's get something to eat that isn't liquid. I need to feel normal and mundane, if only for a few minutes."

Kovah slung his arm around my neck. "I get it, man, I do."

I blew out a breath and nodded. I didn't feel drunk, I just felt better. I couldn't explain the anger. You would think I'd be less hangry now, but maybe deep down I was angry because the blood had made me feel better, and at that moment, when I finished sucking down that blood bag, I knew I'd have to do that for the rest of my life — however long that might be.

We walked down the cobblestoned street, turning down a very narrow side street flanked by old buildings of varying colors. Each boasted balconies surrounded by wrought iron and old, wood-framed windows, rotting with age. Still, they were rustic, almost beautiful, encapsulated in time. A time, I realized, when the supernatural was more widely accepted.

Kovah looked at the buildings and pointed to a purple one. "We need to come back here during Mardi Gras and get our party on. I bet I can collect more beads than you."

I stopped walking and looked to where he pointed. "You're on, asswipe."

Kovah put his fist to bump and I knocked it with my own. We smirked at each other and kept walking.

I spied Pat O'Brien's, the popular bar and restaurant where I was planning to give Sarah the ring, had we ever made it here. I frowned and kept walking.

"Let's go in here," Kovah said, moving toward the restaurant.

"No, I don't like that place."

My friend turned his head to the side, his brows dipping behind his glasses. "Bad memories, or just bad online reviews?"

I snorted. "Something like that."

We finally found a restaurant, which was more of a bar, and wandered inside. It was dark, old, paneled in wood, and the long, stretching bar made up the entire back half of it. The only light in the place came from the door when we'd opened it, and the few grungy windows.

"Nice place," I muttered.

Kovah lifted a shoulder and sat at a small corner table. "I've seen worse."

"I have no doubt."

As we sat, an older woman, who looked like she'd been bartending or waitressing for about a hundred years, came to our table. Her hair was huge and graying blonde, gum smacking between her teeth as she smiled. She had some red lipstick stuck to them. She threw down two laminated menus. "Hi, boys. Lunch menus. If you want drinks from the bar, I'll need to see IDs."

I made a dramatic gesture of looking at my watch and raised an eyebrow. "Nah, we're good, just lunch."

"Burger," Kovah grunted.

"Same," I said.

She nodded and we both handed our menus back.

She walked away and Kovah looked at me. "Take off your glasses. We're indoors. Have some respect."

We both erupted in childish laughter as I took off my glasses and ball cap and set them on the table.

"I bet that gets really old," I said with seriousness, smoothing my hair down.

Kovah was smiling. "Yep, totally —" He stopped mid-sentence, his face suddenly darkening. I turned around to look in the direction he was gazing. A young man and a young woman were seated at a back table, both looking in our direction. Their clothes would have seemed normal if it weren't for the black jeans and long trench coats they wore in 80-plus degree weather.

I swiveled my head back around and asked, "What?"

Kovah's jaw pulsed and he scrubbed a hand over the top of his head. "Vampires."

I didn't turn back around to look, then said, "What? No way. It's the middle of the day. Are they still staring at us?"

"Yes, and I know it's the middle of the day. That's what I don't get."

"How do you even know they're vampires?" I asked.

"Keep your voice down!" he snapped.

I raised an eyebrow and folded my arms across my chest. "Well?"

"I just do. I can't explain it. You will too, eventually. I think."

The waitress brought us food and set the check down on the table. We both started eating, but Kovah's eyes never left the table of vampires. With his dark glasses, I knew they couldn't tell where he was looking.

"Are they eating anything?" I whispered between bites.

Kovah shook his head and ripped a paper towel from the holder on the table. He wiped his mouth with it. "No, they're just drinking."

"Can they eat regular food? Vampires, I mean?"

"No. Just blood and other liquids. From what I was told one time when Archie and the guys captured one, he said they don't eat food, it doesn't digest or some shit."

My eyebrows hit my hairline. "Captured one? Did they torture him?"

Kovah nodded. "Yes, for information. Didn't take much, either, just sat him in a room in the middle of the day, tied to a chair, and started drawing the window blinds up slowly. Bloodsucker sang like a canary once the light hit his flesh. After he finished screaming like a girl, that is. It was so cool."

I swallowed back a snarky retort and said, "So what kind of information did you get from him?"

He squirted more mustard on his plate and dipped a French fry in it as I wrinkled my nose in disgust. "Well, we just wanted basic information, how much food they could tolerate, if any, how much blood they needed to survive, how long they could live for, how they could be killed, shit like that."

I wadded up my napkin and put it on my plate. "And he just told you all that stuff so easily?"

"Yep. They don't like sunlight, at all."

"Which brings me back to why there are two vamps sitting in this bar in the middle of the day."

Kovah stood, threw a twenty-dollar bill on the table, and motioned for me to follow. "Let's go find out."

"Shit," I groaned, following my friend.

He strode with confidence to the small table as the two vampires looked up, almost in disinterest.

The male, whose black hair blended in with the dank of the bar, his pale face shining in contrast as he looked at us both. "What do you want, half-breeds?"

We looked at each other, honestly in shock, but Kovah recovered quickly. "Why do you think we're half-breeds, bloodsucker?"

The vampire made a snorting noise and said, "You smell funny."

"And you're ugly," Kovah shot back.

I laughed, and with my arms folded across my chest, I said, "I don't think he was insulting you, dude."

"Shut the fuck up, man."

The female vampire looked at Kovah. "I think you should take your own advice and shut the fuck up. You half-breeds have a distinct smell. That's all Morris here was trying to say." She pointed to the male.

"Why are you out during the day?" I asked before I could stop himself.

"We like to live on the wild side," Morris replied dryly.

"How many half-breeds have you met?" Kovah asked.

"Enough," the female answered.

I could tell my friend was becoming agitated, and having seen Kovah's temper one too many times, I hooked a firm grip on his arm.

"Time to go. Thank you for your time," I said politely.

Both vampires laughed sarcastically and went back to sipping their drinks.

He flipped them off double-handed as I ushered him outside. As soon as we were on the street, I shoved my ball cap and glasses on and erupted into laughter.

Kovah, whose face was still twisted in anger, looked at me and said, "What's so fucking funny?"

I was still laughing. "That was hands-down the weirdest encounter I have ever had." I started laughing again. "And trust me," —I took a deep breath to calm down, as I could see my friend wasn't as amused — "there's been a whole hell of a lot of *weird* in my life lately."

Kovah turned and began walking back the way we'd come, heading toward Bourbon Street again. "You better become good with weird, dude, because weird is the new normal where you're headed."

"Do I want to know what that means?" I asked, catching up with him.

"You'll find out soon enough, blood-drunk boy."

"I'm not blood-drunk."

He shook his head and laughed. "You are."

My phone vibrated. I glowered at Kovah, then looked at the screen and saw Charity's pretty face. "Hi."

"Hi, baby. Whatcha doin'?" she asked.

"Not much, just had lunch, gonna spend one more day here, then head home. I miss you."

She huffed. "Why can't you come back tonight, huh? It's only a five-hour drive. You could be home by sunset. Then I can show you how much I've missed you." She paused. "In every way possible," she purred.

My eyebrows rose, surprised by her brazen attitude. She'd hinted at us becoming intimate, and we'd talked about it, but she'd never acted quite this bold. I wasn't sure if I liked it or not.

"You'll be my first stop when I get into town, beautiful."

She sighed dramatically. "Promise?"

I grinned. "I promise."

I ended the call and re-pocketed the phone. I rubbed a hand along the back of my neck.

"Why you stay with that needy redhead? Go find yourself a nice hot blonde with big tits," Kovah said, making a gesture with both hands over his chest.

"I don't see you entertaining any hot blondes," I shot back.

"I'm not a relationship kinda guy."

"No, you don't say! Girls freaked out by your part-time vampire murdering job, or is it your freaky eyes?"

"Fuck off, Bishop."

That scored me a smile and we headed back to the BSI building, walking through the front doors like we owned the place. With no intentions of stopping, we both walked with purpose toward the stairwell. A deep voice made us both stop.

"Excuse me, you have to check in at the desk."

We both turned around. Kovah smiled. "No, it's okay, Henry, we're just going to see Agent Shields." He pointed at the ceiling.

Henry flicked his dark gaze to the clipboard in his hand. "Ah, okay, I see she has an appointment with two very strange, sunglassed heroes here at twelve p.m. You boys go on up and have a nice day."

Stifling back chuckles, we both headed for the stairwell at speed before Henry could catch up with us.

"Weird, right?" I said.

"Yes, weird. I can't decide if he was being a smart-ass, or if that hot Mara chick actually told Henry we'd be back and didn't want to use our names."

We reached the third floor and walked toward the conference room. I turned the handle, opening the door, but the room was empty and dark. I closed it and said, "What now?"

"Let's find her."

I followed Kovah down the hallway, thankful each door had plaques on them bearing its occupant's name. None had Agent Shields's name, though, and I wished I had gotten the name of any of the other agents.

"Guess we'll just try a door and ask for her," Kovah said.

"Sounds good to me."

Kovah raised his hand to knock on a door marked "Special Agent in Charge" when we heard a voice.

"I knew you'd be back."

We whirled around to see Mara Shields standing there in her skintight pinstriped skirt and blazer, a file folder in her hands. She wore a smirk on her full lips and amusement danced in her light-brown eyes. "Follow me."

She turned and headed back into the conference room. I saw Kovah watching in appreciation as her ass swayed with each step. She flipped on the light with the switch on the wall and instructed us both to sit.

"So where's your entourage?" I bit out, gesturing to the empty room.

She laughed a little and set the file folder down, putting both hands over the top of it. "Those are new agents I'm training. Nothing more."

"I see," Kovah said, staring at her.

"So why did you really come here?" she asked, matching my stare.

"I needed another dime-bag of blood in case he gets low," Kovah smarted off with a serious face.

"Not funny," I growled.

Agent Shields put her hand over her mouth and giggled a little. "That was mildly funny, come on."

"Kovah wants the red carpet treatment like you gave me," I said, pointing to my friend.

"Is that so?" the agent asked.

He nodded. "Just have some questions."

"I'm sure we have a lot for you, too." She threw him a wink and then grinned.

"Let's get started then." Kovah grinned back.

Chapter 20

LUST AND LIKENESSES

Nolan

Kovah hadn't received anything different than I had during my three-hour interrogation. Questions, blood draws, an MRI, and the promise of my first-born child. Okay, not really. Well, maybe.

The next day, after checking out of the hotel in the Quarter, we began the quiet drive back. I reflected on the strange weekend I'd had. The one thing that cycled over and over in my brain was the events of the last day. Why were vampires in that dark restaurant during the day, and why had they called us 'half-breeds'? Despite my annoyance with the sun and my odd blood craving, I felt I looked and acted human. I thought the vamps I met looked like gothic freaks. Almost like humans pretending to be vampires, but I knew they weren't human anymore. Their skin was pale and almost waxy-looking. Their eyes to a human may have looked somewhat normal, but I noticed their pupils were permanently dilated, the black irises close to overtaking whatever color they'd been as humans.

After Kovah dropped me off at my apartment, I went inside, set my stuff down in my room, and went into the bathroom. I leaned in close to the mirror, studying my eyes. No, mine weren't anything like theirs. They were still lime-green like they'd always been. I pushed off the white ceramic sink of my small bathroom and stalked into my bedroom. I quickly unpacked my small duffel bag and sat on my bed. I pulled my phone out and dialed Charity.

She answered on the first ring. "Hello?"

"Hi, beautiful."

"You home yet?" she asked flatly.

Geez, moody much? "Yes."

"Then why aren't you here?" she whined.

"May I shower first?" I asked facetiously.

She sighed. "I suppose."

"I'll see you in a few, Charity."

"Can't wait!" she replied.

I laughed and threw my phone on the bed, and then peeled off my clothes and headed naked into the bathroom. I started the shower and got in, languishing in the heat on my skin. A smile found me when I thought about Charity. I didn't think too hard about why she was acting so strange. We hadn't even been seeing each other that long and I'd taken two trips out of town for days at a time. Not a good way to nourish a blossoming relationship, I knew, but I vowed to make it up to her.

My bike rumbled to a stop outside the store. I killed the engine and yanked my helmet off, dismounting the bike. The warm, humid night breeze drifted into my mouth and nose with familiarity. After putting down the kickstand to the Ducati, I jogged to the back of the store. Pulling the heavy gray door open, I smiled that the lock had been replaced, at my request to one of the Riders, and sprinted up the stairs and knocked.

The demure redhead answered immediately, her face lighting up when she saw me. She launched herself into my arms like she hadn't seen me in years, and wrapped her lithe legs around my waist. Her arms encircled my neck, and before I could close the door or even say hello, she crushed her mouth to mine, her eyes shut tight as she moaned in the back of her throat. I used my hands to hold her up by her soft tush, my fingers digging into the pliable flesh. I made my way to the bed with her body plastered to mine and laid her down on it without breaking the kiss. My need was suddenly frantic, her body pliant and willing under my touch.

"I missed you," she murmured in my ear as her mouth trailed up and down my neck in desperate licks and kisses.

"I'm sorry I've been gone so much," I replied, looking down at her. I brushed a curl from her forehead and kissed her eyelid as she closed her eyes.

"I forgive you." She smiled, capturing my mouth once again.

I thought this would be much different. I thought this would be awkward, slow to progress, sweet, sexy, sweaty, and romantic. Maybe dinner and date first. Perhaps some candles and music, a quiet night inside as we spent it together, quietly exploring each other for the first time. Well, it was anything but. Things were moving fast—hot, passionate, lusty, and just… pretty damn awesome.

I grinned as I yanked her pink tank top off. Her bra was shiny and matched the color of her top. I chuckled when I saw that the clasp was again conveniently located between her beautiful freckled breasts, and with one hand, I popped it free, then worked to get her black yoga pants down. They were skintight and sticking to her legs like dried glue.

"You go to the gym today?" I asked playfully after I'd broken the kiss. I sat up on my knees and worked the pants down, her pink lacy panties matching the bra.

"Gym? No." She scrunched up her nose as if the thought repulsed her.

I laughed. "Okay, well, nice pants."

She licked her lips and laughed. "They're just comfortable to lounge around in while I waited for you to get here to show me how much you've missed me," she mused.

I told myself not to be surprised by the pretty underthings she had on. She'd made it clear she missed me. She'd made it clear she wanted me in every way possible, and yet, I'd been absent both emotionally and physically the last few days. I felt like such an ass. I would have to use the rest of my life to make it up to the beautiful redhead. Once her pants were gone, I pushed my boots off and laughed as the buck knife slid out and came to rest just outside the top of the boot on her floor. I then slid my jeans off and lay back down, pressing the heated, slick skin of my chest to hers. She began kissing me again, her tongue slipping into my mouth and tangling with mine while I fisted her thick, unruly curls at the back of her head. I could feel her smile into my mouth as I continued to smash my lips into hers, that wet, hot tongue of hers entirely responsible for my body's reactions.

"I've wanted you for so long, Nolan," she said, her words nothing but a breathless whisper as she kissed my neck.

"It's time we seal this deal, beautiful girl," I replied with a smile, that confidence in me growing by the second.

A wicked grin curved on her blood-red lips and she smiled in triumph. "Take me, Nolan Bishop. Take me now before I change my mind."

Brad sat quietly his sports car out in front of the Stop-N-Shop. He smiled in victory as Nolan parked his alpha-male motorcycle in front and sprinted to the back of the store. He knew the bike mechanic wasn't shopping. He knew he was heading upstairs to see Charity. And he knew how it would probably end.

He thought about her twin, Eva, the fiery redhead he was enamored with. She was absolute perfection in his jaded eyes. Red hair, eyes full of lust and playful banter, and a body made for sin. What else could a guy want? Brad laughed as he watched Nolan. Regardless of Brad's — hell, or even Nolan's — living or undead status, he knew why he was there. He knew what Nolan was walking into.

Brad knew nothing would make Eva happier. She would finally have Nolan right where she wanted him.

Kovah removed his dark glasses and set them on the small dresser in his rented room above Archie's garage. After stripping off his black T-shirt, he examined the rigid muscles of his body. A row of rippled muscle covered in ink climbed its way up his abdomen, reaching his chest, which was nothing but solid bulk.

No fat here, Kovah mused, brushing his fingertips over six-pack abs.

He began to feel a slight pull of guilt, but then swiftly pushed it off. No — he wouldn't have to hit the gym for hours a day or deprive himself of spaghetti and garlic bread to get this body, but those who did had normal eyes and aged at a normal rate.

Kovah did not. Frozen in time, he gazed at his reflection again, amazed that he still looked as he had ten, fifteen, twenty years ago. Whatever that succubus witch had done to him was both amazing and infuriating. She'd left him forever youthful, but had robbed him of his twilight years. The time of his life where he could relax with his wife of fifty years, surrounded by their grandchildren on the porch swing of the old house that had been paid off decades prior. No, now he was alone. With his family thinking him dead, and his chances of meeting a normal girl all but gone, he knew he could never love someone and then watch them slowly die each day. Loneliness was the only real gift the succubus had bestowed upon him.

Sliding a hand over his black hair shorn to the scalp, Kovah briefly considered growing it out again. Maybe he could rock the small mullet like he'd had in the late 80s. A laugh bubbled up from his mouth and he shook his head. No matter how much style seemed to repeat itself, there was no way he would try to wear *that* hairstyle again.

He pulled on a pair of loose boxers, pushed back the red plaid comforter, and climbed in. He folded his arms behind his head and stared unseeing at the ceiling, dwelling on the day that had gone by way too quickly.

After dropping Nolan at his apartment, he'd vowed to go home. Well, that was what he always promised himself, without much luck. Kovah knew going home meant sleep, and that was the last thing he wanted. He wasn't even tired.

Attempting once again to re-acclimate himself to the world of the humans, Kovah took several cleansing breaths to try to relax. As much as he wanted a normal life, he'd reconciled long ago that it just wasn't in the cards for him. Stuck somewhere between a grown man and a teenaged undead creature of the night, Kovah had long since let himself grieve the life he'd never have. Neither a vampire who stalked people in the night, nor a normal human who would grow old and die, he had resolved himself to existing somewhere in between. He was never sure if he should try to live a normal life, or go join a coven of vampires who lived in a sewer somewhere.

When push came to shove, Kovah knew that deep down he related to humans better. Vampires needed to die. They were dangerous — or at least that was what the government had said. Did he truly care what the United States government thought? Not really... but in the interest of staying on the good side of the law, he decided it would be in his best interest if he told Archie what he'd seen.

Climbing out of bed, he picked up his cell and dialed Archie's number, sitting back on the bed.

With a groggy voice, Archie answered, "What is it, kid?"

"Hey, Arch, sorry to call so late, but I just got back from New Orleans with Nolan."

Archie's voice grew interested. "Is that so? And what were you doing there?"

Kovah leaned his forearms on his lap. "Well, he said he knew of some government people who knew about us, about vampires, and everything. He took me to see them. It was really… interesting to say the least."

"Is it the Department of Justice? If so, I've heard rumblings about them knowin' about vamps. Thought it was just a myth, though."

"Well, it's not," Kovah replied. "They're very real. But I'll tell you more about that later."

Archie yawned and said, "Okay then, why are you calling me at this ungodly hour?"

"Because I also met a vampire in New Orleans. True-to-the-game old-ass vamp, runs a hotel in the Quarter."

"Tell me more," Archie said, excitement he couldn't hide coming out.

"His name is Joel Reichart, and he hosts a yearly party for vampires."

Nolan

I continued to lick, suck, and kiss at the tender skin on Charity's neck. It was both salty and sweet under my tongue, and when I thought I felt the slight pulse of her blood humming beneath the thin layer of skin there, I paused, telling myself I had a choice to make.

But did I really? Besides, without sharp incisor teeth, I didn't think could do much damage. How would I get her blood? It wasn't like I even wanted to. Right?

I shook my head. There were other parts of her body I wanted, and nothing was going to stop us this time. My craving was almost feral, a desperate, animalistic need that had crawled its way from my very center to every other part of my body that was willing and ready for her.

I continued my oral assault of her mouth, putting my hands wherever she let me, my lusty need overtaking everything in me. My palms slid over slick, pale skin, the weak air conditioning making her clammy skin feel cool under my touch when it should be ripe with heat and fire.

She made soft mewling noises in the back of her throat, her hands rubbing and gripping my back and neck, her fingernails raking through the short hair on my head. My dry thrusts were becoming needier, her hands pushing me against her with wanton need for what was building up inside of her.

Seeming to be impatient now, she pushed me gently in my bare chest and indicated for me to lie flat on the bed. Straddling both legs on either side of me, she sat up straight and smiled wickedly down at me.

Something familiar and lustful niggled at the back of my brain at her out-of-character aggressive moves, but my desire had overtaken anything remotely rational at that point. I gripped her fleshy hips with my fingers, digging them in gently and grinning back up at her. I briefly wondered if my eyes had turned black like they had the last time I'd been this turned on, then determined they probably weren't. She'd be flipping out. Maybe the blood I'd taken in New Orleans had quelled that for now. Besides, she would surely say something, either verbally or nonverbally, if I looked like I was turning into a monster. She had been terrified the last time.

The beautiful redhead leaned down slowly to kiss me again, her long, red curls dragging across my chest. She sealed her mouth over me once more and slipped her tongue inside. I groaned and smiled against her mouth. She pulled back with her eyes closed and a grin on her full, glistening, swollen lips.

With one hand on her thigh, I prepared myself to plunge inside, when she suddenly opened her eyes. Except instead of seeing an ocean of crystal blue, all I saw was solid inky black, with no whites at all.

And she had the nerve to still be grinning.

My eyes grew wide as I jerked my hands away from her body with a gasp. On a violent exhale, I screamed, "Eva!"

Charity

I blinked my eyes open slowly, something painful pushing into my back. As my eyes adjusted to the darkness, I was quickly reminded where I was. In a dark room, chained to a bed on a horribly uncomfortable, dirty mattress, the old springs that had been poking into my back during my fitful sleep the cause of my pain.

I twisted my back to the left and right, trying to work out the kink as my brain tried again to work out a plan. This couldn't be happening to me. I looked at the dusty wood floor. Getting up, I padded over to the window, my chain barely allowing me enough slack to get there. I had to extend my arm as far as possible one direction and then crane my neck in the other to see out of the small, filthy window that couldn't be more than twelve-by-twelve inches. It overlooked the large lake that sat outside the creepy mansion in the swamp my evil twin shared with that asshat vampire, Brad, and God knew who or what else. I knew the house faced east, and I could see the sun begin to sink so I deduced it was now sunset on my third day as captive. Being at the height the room was set, I had to be in the attic. That, and it was so unbearably hot in here with zero reprieve from the stifling heat. I'd tried several times to break the small window for some air, but didn't have anything sturdy enough to crack the old glass. There was no mechanism to open or close it, either.

I went over to the wall near my tiny bed and used a small rock I'd found on the floor under the bed and etched a third line into the wall, determined to not lose track of time or my mind in the process, my wall tallies the tiny bit of control I still had. There was a small bathroom attached to the room I was in, but my chain only gave me enough slack to reach the toilet, not the bathtub that lay on the far side. The white antique claw-foot tub taunted me daily with the promise of getting clean and feeling better. It was like my evil bitch sister had done that on purpose, just to torture me. My hate for both the bathtub and my undead sister grew by the hour.

After using the small toilet, I sat back on the bed, feeling like I was going to go stark raving mad. With absolutely nothing to do but think and sleep, I yet again racked my brain as to how I was going to get the hell out of there. Especially before Brad came in to make his nightly visit. I hated his nightly visits, but he was the only one who came in and delivered me food and drink, so I had to tolerate him. They were assholes for only feeding me once a day, but I would bide my time until I could get out of there. Even so, his visits launched fear into my heart every night. He always leered at me like he wanted to devour me — in more ways than one.

A shudder racked my sweaty body and I stayed the tears that wanted to flow again. Why were they doing this to me? Was Nolan even looking for me? Probably not. We'd had that wicked fight and he probably didn't even know I was missing. What about my parents? I laughed humorlessly, knowing they didn't care, as I drew my knees up to my chest and rested my head on them, wrapping my arms around my bare legs. I looked down, wishing I had something on other than a long nightshirt and a pair of panties. The filthy chain sat coldly on my arm as I closed my eyes and remembered.

Three nights ago, Brad and Eva had shown up at my place. They had done something to me to cause me to fall into a deep sleep, I just couldn't remember what. I'd woken up in this bare attic room, confused, crying, and alone. Later that night, Eva had come for a visit. She hadn't said much, but she didn't need to. After pleading with my twin for answers as to why she'd kidnapped me, Eva had just smiled and yanked off the short, red wig she always wore. Unleashing her long, red curls, she shook them out and smiled coldly at me. It was then I noticed Eva's heavy black cat-eye makeup and red-lips were gone, replaced with a bare face so identical to my own. The bitch was wearing a pair of casual shorts and a yellow tank top with an LSU sweatshirt tied around her waist.

She padded out of the room wearing flip-flops and a smile, the short red wig swinging in her fist as she had slammed the door behind her. I had screamed, "No!"

I was broken out of my memories when Brad strolled in carrying my dinner, right on time. The wicked gleam in his lewd gaze sent an unholy shiver up my spine. I shot daggers at him with my eyes, my arms still wrapped around my legs.

"Hello, gorgeous," he slithered out. I swallowed down a sob at the look in his creepy, soulless gaze. I knew I was in trouble, and that nobody was going to save me. I was in this alone.

THE END

DEATH'S KISS SERIES

SOUL RELEASE

USA TODAY BESTSELLING AUTHOR

C.J. PINARD

Book 3 in the Death's Kiss Series

SOUL RELEASE

"LOVE IS COMPOSED OF A SINGLE SOUL INHABITING TWO BODIES." ARISTOTLE

Chapter 1

TWIN TRICKERY

Nolan

The throes of hot, steamy passion were halted coldly and abruptly as I noticed my girlfriend's eyes had turned black. But wait— how could Charity's eyes turn black? She was human, right? One hundred percent beautiful, sexy, warm, compassionate, and emotional… human. So, how was this possible? The thoughts ran through my brain like a derailed freight train until it came to rest after crash-landing on the sidelines of my muddled, sex-fueled brain. That wasn't Charity.

It's not Charity!

I thought I screamed out Eva's name, I couldn't be sure. With every ounce of strength, I bucked the succubus off my hips and rolled off the bed, landing on the floor with a thud. *Buck knife. Where's the fucking knife? In my boot!* As if in slow motion, I grabbed the first dusty Justin boot I saw. Empty. I desperately scanned the dark for the other, thankful my new eyesight had given me enhanced night vision. Glinting in the moonlight streaming into the window, I saw the tip of the knife sticking out of the top of the boot. It had landed haphazardly on the floor as I'd been blinded by the desire to finally seal the deal with my beautiful girlfriend.

But it wasn't my girlfriend in the room with me now. Gripping my knife tightly in my fist, I rolled over and stood up, ready to plunge it through Eva's chest. The rage that now bubbled up inside of me had overtaken every emotion and physical reaction my body had. I wanted nothing more than to kill the evil bitch and watch her crumble to ash—or shrivel to nothing—at my feet. I'd had enough of her tricks, her lies, her selfishness, and the manipulation. She'd taken my very humanity from me, and as I thought back to Ansel, the vampire I'd killed in my parking lot, I remembered how easily the knife had slid into his body, even through the clothes. It had melted into his chest like it had been slicing through butter. But Eva wasn't wearing any clothes and my mouth watered at the thought of the blood that might squirt out through her chest, briefly wondering what it would taste like.

But as I looked around the room, I saw nothing. Eva was gone. Her shoes were still there, but her clothes were nowhere to be found. And it was then I heard it—the squeal of tires. I raced to the window and looked out to see a late-model black sports car peeling out of the parking lot, windows tinted too dark to see who the two occupants were. Even though I was sure I knew who one was.

More rage seethed in my veins as I cried out in frustration and punched the wall. My knuckles split open and bled, but I didn't care. I pulled on my pants, shirt, and boots, shoving the knife back into the left one. After sprinting down the steps of Charity's apartment and out the heavy gray door, I plucked the keys from the pocket of my jeans, started up my Ducati Monster, and hopped on. My only mission was to catch the witch and finally end her murderous existence—something I should have done from the first time I found out what she'd truly stolen from me.

With not a lot of cars on the road this time of night, I was easily able to spot the flashy car. Slamming on the gas, I popped a wheelie. The bike's front tire jutted into the air and then slammed back down, its rumble getting louder the faster I went. The car was at a red light now, but at the sound of my bike, I saw it rush through the red light and take off down the narrow street.

"Oh, hell no!" I yelled, giving the bike more gas. I had a one-track homicidal mind and there would be no stopping me tonight. As the car ran yet another light, I realized they were headed was toward the swamps. I remembered the large, old mansion in the swampland where Eva and her brood of vampires lived, and knew that was their destination. I let up off the gas, the fog of my irate mind finally starting to clear a little. I realized I needed a plan. I knew if I came at them now with guns blazing, that they'd be ready for me. I knew Eva didn't live alone and other vampires were there. It was nighttime, and they were all most likely up and ready for blood. As angry as I was, I was no match for two or more vampires by myself. As I came to another stoplight that the other car had run, I halted the bike, letting myself think.

But then another thought popped into my mind now that the smoke was clearing. If that was Eva in my bedroom, where in the hell was Charity? A honk from the car behind me bolted me out of my thoughts. I flipped a U-turn and headed back the way I'd come, the thoughts of my girlfriend's well-being suddenly the more important priority. I knew where the succubus lived, and I knew that while daylight wasn't exactly my friend these days, Eva absolutely had no tolerance for it. She may be a succubus, but she was first and foremost a vampire, and vampires and sunlight were not bedfellows. A plot began to form in my mind, and with a satisfied smirk on my lips, I sped toward the Stop-N-Shop to make sure Charity was all right. Yes, I'd just come from there, but I suddenly had a horrifying thought that maybe Eva had left her sister tied up or drugged again in some area of the apartment. I knew the chances were slim, but I had to find her, make sure she was all right and safe. Sure, she was probably still mad at me for going to New Orleans, but nothing would keep me from ensuring she was alive and well. Charity could scream at me all she wanted, but I needed to see her pretty face and maybe even beg for forgiveness once more.

Once the bike turned down the road that led to her small flat set above the shop where she worked, I killed the engine and ran to the back. Yanking open the heavy gray door, I sprinted up the steps and knew the doorknob would turn easily, as I'd not locked it on my way out.

There were no bedrooms in her apartment, just one large room, and seeing the pull-down bed open in the middle of the living room, I frowned at the rumpled bedsheets. I huffed and went into the bathroom, where it was dark and empty. One glance to the small kitchen showed she wasn't there, either. It was deathly silent in her place, and a tingle of dread began to crawl up my spine. I checked my watch. It had gone well past midnight and Charity really wouldn't be anywhere but at home. Wouldn't she?

Trying not to panic, I locked Charity's door, raced down the steps, started up my bike, and headed toward my apartment.

I burst through the door of my apartment, not bothering to close it behind me.

"Charity! Are you here?"

Nothing answered me but the echo of my cries off of four lone, cold walls. The apartment lay as silent as Charity's had. Checking every room, I came up empty, as deep down I knew I would.

Walking woodenly to the front door, I slowly closed and locked it. Then, I put my back against it, pain and despair strangling me. An ache began to blossom in my chest and I put my hand to stay the pain there. Closing my eyes, I heaved out a breath.

"Where are you, Red?" I whispered.

I pulled my cell phone from my pocket and dialed her number, lifting the phone to my ear in the small hope she'd answer her cell. The call, as expected, went to voicemail, and in a sudden flash of rage and frustration, I popped my eyes open and hurled the phone with all my strength against the wall, where it exploded in a shower of metal and plastic.

"Fuck!" I yelled, scrubbing a rough hand over the top of my head and then along the back of my neck.

I slid down the door and landed on my butt on the linoleum of the apartment's entryway and rested my head against my knees.

The ache in my chest grew worse, and I groaned at the pain. Was I having a heart attack? Surely not. Not only was I too young, I now seemed to have some freakish healing power. No way would my heart give out now. The only heart trouble I was going to have was the figurative kind if I couldn't find my girlfriend alive and in one piece. I had no idea what I would do if something happened to Charity. I would die a thousand times over if she were dead. I'd never forgive myself.

With a deep sigh, I stood up and decided I had to find Charity—now. Reaching into my pocket for my phone to call Kovah, I muttered a string of obscenities as my gaze flitted to the pile of phone parts that lay against a now-cracked wall. The phone was toast, and it wasn't like I had time to go get another.

Plucking keys from my pocket, I yanked open the front door, quickly closed and locked it behind me, and raced down the stone steps. Slinging one leg over my bike, I shoved the key in and pushed the button. I rumbled out of the parking lot and toward Archie's, where Kovah rented a small room above the garage.

Kovah groaned from behind the door before throwing back the locks and slinging the door open, piercing me with a milky stare. "What do you want, Bishop?"

I shoulder-barged my way into Kovah's studio flat and began pacing next to his bed, huffing like an angry bull who'd just had a red flag waved in front of its face.

"Well...?"

After a long pause, I said, "Charity's missing."

Cocking an eyebrow, he replied, "Missing?"

"Yes, asshole, missing. You're not gonna believe what happened to me tonight."

Now fully awake, Kovah pulled on some athletic shorts from a crumpled pile on the floor and folded his tattooed arms over his tanned chest. Staring at me, he shoved his sunglasses on and said, "Start at the beginning."

I wasted no time spewing out the events of the night without so much as taking a breath. From the phone call from who I believed to be Charity, to the hot sex we'd *almost* had until I'd discovered who she truly was, and how I'd barely escaped while I had been searching the floor for a weapon to use to end the bitch once and for all.

"Okay, sit." Kovah pushed his hands onto my shoulders, forcing me down on the bed. His dark stare focused on my face, willing me to calm.

"I'm… I'm freaking out here, man. What do I do? I gotta find her. I need to apologize. I need to make sure she's safe. I just…"

"Shh. Chill. I'm sure the succubus whore has her. We go to their place, get back your girl, you're the hero, happily ever after. Easy."

I raised an eyebrow at my new friend and let out a laugh completely devoid of humor. "You think it's that easy?"

His confidence did not waver. "Yep. You know where Eva lives, right?"

"Yes, but—"

He chuckled, yanking a T-shirt from the top drawer of his small, wooden dresser. "But nothing. We call the Riders, we storm the castle, and we get Charity back. Tonight."

I stood again and rubbed a hand against the back of my neck. "Yeah—that's a no-go. They already know I'm onto them. They'll be expecting us."

Kovah's face darkened. "I don't give a fuck. Those types of vamps will always be expecting trouble. They invite the shit, so they know they can never live in peace. It doesn't matter if we go tonight, tomorrow, or next week. I know their type. They're a bunch of trouble-making assholes. So fuck 'em. I'm calling Arch. We ride tonight, brother." He laid a hand on my shoulder, and surprisingly, this comforted me in more ways than I thought possible.

With a small grateful smile, I put out my fist. "Okay, let's ride."

Kovah bumped it with his own, a mischievous smile on his face.

Chapter 2

LIVING IN CAPTIVITY

Charity

Brad carried a small, white Styrofoam container over to me and set it down on the bed, along with a warm can of Coke. I eyed the container, then looked at him once again.

"Hope you like Chinese," he said with a smirk.

"I need some water, not this sugary stuff," I snapped, pointing at the soda can.

He yanked it off the bed, grinning, and I immediately regretted sassing him. That can was heavy and might come in handy.

"No, please, I was kiddin'. Leave it. I'm so thirsty. Can I get a fan in here, too? Please, Brad?" I gazed into his soulless eyes, hoping he had at least an ounce of humanity left in him.

He seemed to contemplate my request for a minute, then said, "What do I get in return?"

My stomach roiled in disgust at the suggestion in his tone, but I plastered on a smile anyway, brushing an unruly red curl from my forehead with my shackled hand. "We're in negotiations now?"

"Sweetie, I'm always up for a negotiation," he drawled.

I racked my brain to think of anything I could barter for. There was no way I was taking off my clothes for him, but maybe I could fib for a minute. I could see the way he'd looked at me when he'd come into my room. "Okay, you bring me a fan, and I'll let you kiss me. But no biting, okay?"

Brad's face lit up, and licking his lips, he turned his head and looked at the door. He set the soda can on the floor next to my bed, sat down on the thin mattress, and leaned in to me for a kiss.

I pulled back in horror. "No! Bring me the fan, and *then* I'll give you a kiss."

With the fan. Right in your face.

He narrowed his eyes at me. "I don't think so, Red."

My features darkened. "Don't call me that."

"Why not, Red? Don't like your sexy red hair?" He fingered a few curls that were lying on my sticky shoulders.

I was beginning to get angry now, but realized if I slapped or punched him like I wanted to, he'd just get mad and retaliate. And that was the last thing I needed. I mustered up the last bit of courage and gently grabbed his ice-cold hand. "Brad. Please. I'm so hot in here. You're so cold, you don't understand. I need a bath, and some water, and a fan to cool me down."

His face softened and his eyes drifted past me to the bathroom, then back into my eyes. "I'll unchain you so you can take a bath, under one condition."

From the mischief in his eyes, I could already guess what it was, and sighed. "What's that?"

"I get to watch."

I briefly contemplated it for a minute, then shook my head. "I... I don't think so, Brad. I'm very shy."

He ran a cold finger down my cheek. "I've helped a lot of girls come out of their shell. Won't you let me help you?"

"Don't you think my sister might take issue with that? Aren't you her boyfriend or some kinda thing?" I asked.

He chuckled. "Nah, I'm just her play-thing. She don't care about me. But I don't mind. Eva did give me eternal life, after all. The least I can do is let her use me when her needs arise," he spit out with that stupid grin I was beginning to loathe.

I suppressed a shudder at his words. Did this jerkwad actually think he had to feel grateful to my evil twin? If he was to be believed, she'd been the one who'd turned him. So how was he not, then, a feral, blood-crazed vampire? I gazed into his eyes once more and saw pretty much nothing. The caramel brown of his irises held a coldness that defied the warmth of their color. I knew he was pretty much a lost cause, but decided to try to put some more of my female charms on him.

"You know, Brad. You don't owe my sister nothin'. You shouldn't feel like that. You'd still be human if she hadn't done what she'd done to you. Why are you so loyal to her?"

The question seemed to give Brad pause, and his eyebrows dipped in concentration as he contemplated my question. Finally, he said, "I have always felt like that since Eva rescued me."

I relaxed a bit, realizing I was getting him to talk. "Rescued you from what?"

"From being human."

This piqued my interest. "Was being human such a bad thing?"

Pain contorted his pale face. "It was for me…"

"Why's that?" I asked, anxious to keep him talking.

Then his expression suddenly changed and he looked angry, as if snapping out of some sort of trance. "Red, do we have a deal, or what?"

Crap.

I gulped down the fear that had risen when I noticed his mood change. "Um, sure. Go get me a fan, please?"

He got up and left the meal and the Coke sitting on my bed. Once he'd left the room, I quickly drank half of it for energy and wolfed down some of the food before I changed my mind. Then I put the Coke can carefully upright behind my pillow, and shoved the half-empty food container under my bed, hoping he'd forget to collect it so I could eat later. I could tell Brad wasn't too bright.

I got up and walked to the window, my right arm stretched as far as possible so I could peer out of the small window again. I gazed out over the swamps that surrounded the side of the house where my prison was, as if it was some makeshift moat and I was a princess trapped high in a castle's tower. But I was no princess and that was no moat. Fog rolled lazily off the surface over the tall, leafy reeds that jutted out of the black water. I even thought I saw a gator pop its head up once, and I sighed. Stretching further, I bit my lip at the pain in my shoulder so I could peer to the left toward the front of the house, and try to see anything I could. There weren't many sounds I could hear outside of the house and knew if I could only break the window, I could at least hear when cars came and went. Peering further around, I spied the black wrought iron gate that surrounded the old mansion, but couldn't see if it was closed or open. I stepped back and gave my chain some slack in order to drop my arm and massage my shoulder.

I remembered the day a few weeks ago when Nolan and I had come here. We'd been looking for Eva, and that was when I'd met Brad for the first time. I'd tricked him into thinking I was Eva, and it had worked for the time being. I'd discovered my sister's plans to go to New Orleans for the annual vampire ball from her internet search history on her laptop. Nolan and I had high-tailed it out of there after I'd gotten what I needed. I wasn't sure if Brad ever figured out I wasn't Eva that day, but the thought made me grin a little. If I had truly tricked him then, he could be tricked again, couldn't he?

If Eva could pretend to be me, then two could most certainly play at that game.

The thought of the trickery made me smile, but then a frown marred my face when I thought about the ultimate trick Eva had played on Nolan. He had probably made love to her, thinking Eva was me, and then she had lain happily in his arms before killing him — or worse, taking back his soul and turning him into something far worse than Brad. I went to the bed and slumped down on it with my face in my hands, a sob jerking up out of my chest. A tear rolled down my cheek and I just let it fall, watching as it splashed on my bare leg. Nolan was probably dead — or would be soon — and I'd never be able to say goodbye, or even apologize to him for getting so angry at him for going to New Orleans with his new friend. Looking back, I now realized it was petty and not as big of a deal as I had made it out to be. I vowed to myself right then and there that if I ever escaped the mansion prison alive, the first thing I was going to do was find Nolan and tell him how much I loved him — if he was even still alive. The second thing I was going to do was find Eva and kill her. Deep down, I knew the fun, playful sister I'd grown up with was gone, replaced with a monster — a demon with no soul of her own, who had to steal others' just to stay alive. And I hated my sister for choosing to become that.

I didn't like the word "hate." I had never used it before in its true form, but now, it was the only word that engulfed my mind. The rage and hatred for my evil, vile twin was all-consuming. Eva had never been a saint, but since becoming one of the undead, she'd abandoned the Old Eva completely, becoming altogether something void of feeling, emotion, and compassion. I knew Eva had to steal souls and blood to continue to exist, but at this moment, I didn't feel my twin had that right — not anymore. I relished the thought of trapping my sister and shoving something sharp through her chest. Or tying her to a fence at high noon and watching as flames from the sun consumed her. I would take pleasure in burying her body. A smile twisted up on my cracked lips at the thought.

I looked to the door to see if Brad was close to coming back. Where was he? Maybe they had no fans in the house. I looked down at the now-damp black nightshirt I was wearing with nothing else but a pair of panties, and wished I at least had a pair of pants to strangle a vampire with.

Brad was in the outside shed set at the edge of the swamps surrounding the vampires' mansion. With nothing but gardening tools and plenty of bugs and critters keeping him company, he huffed in frustration, angrily chucking a pair of gardening shears with all his strength. They struck nose-first into the side of the shed's wooden beam, making a loud twanging noise.

"Where the hell is that thing?" he grumbled to himself.

He'd been looking for any sort of portable fan. He knew there were none in the house, as he, nor any of his vampire kin, ever had the need for one. His body stayed cold most of the time, and honestly, he never even paid attention to the weather or what the outside temperature was unless he was going to mingle amongst the humans and needed to know what season it was so he could blend in clothing-wise. Brad remembered Eva purchasing a fan to try to block out noise while she slept during the day, but he hadn't seen it in a while.

Brad exited the small shed and stopped at the edge of the grass. Placing both hands on his hips, he looked up at the small, cloudy attic window where he knew Charity was. He wondered if she was at the window looking out, or if she was sitting on the bed eating the Chinese food he'd brought. He smiled a little as he then wondered if she had decided to take that bath after all. Perhaps he should get up there and see.

Walking toward the house with purpose, he tried to think of what he would tell her about a fan. They didn't have one, so she would just have to get over it. Maybe he could bring her something else? Surely he had something else she'd like. Brad grinned again as he thought of something he'd really like to give her. He quickened his pace, hoping she hadn't stripped yet to get into the bath.

He rushed back into the house, and once he reached the old, creaky steps that led to the attic, he suddenly remembered Charity said she couldn't take a bath. Hadn't she said she couldn't reach it with her chain?

"Fuck," he mumbled.

After reaching the top step, he pulled the old skeleton key from the top of the doorjamb. He slowly slid it into the lock, turning the old knob he was sure was probably the original one from when the house had been built, somewhere around the turn of the twentieth century. The knob squeaked, and when he entered the room, he saw Charity sitting on the bed just the way he'd left her.

Any happy expression I may have been trying to hold in place quickly turned into a frown. "Where's the fan?"

Brad shook his head. "Sorry, Red. We ain't got one."

I glared at him. "Don't call me that."

He ignored my sass and went to sit next to me on the bed. I visibly stiffened as his brooding frame sat too close for comfort.

Facilitating my discomfort, he grabbed my hand and said, "Surely there's something else you want."

I was about to spew out a facetious retort when a voice cut us short.

"Well, what do we have here?"

We both looked over to see Eva standing in the doorway. Her long, red curls were lying around her shoulders and she was barefoot, wearing nothing but a pair of black athletic pants and a tank top. Her face was void of its usual fierce makeup, and she had her arms folded over her chest.

Brad jumped up and walked over to her, reaching for her hand. "Hi, gorgeous."

She slapped his hand away while keeping her eyes on me. "Don't touch me. How's our little inmate?"

"Where is Nolan, you crazy bitch? What did you to do him?" I snapped, standing up from the bed. I already had tears standing in my eyes at the sight of my sister looking so much like me — on purpose.

Eva folded her arms over her chest as she smirked at me. "Don't you mean, what did I do *with* him?"

That was it.

Heat flooded my cheeks in rage, and I let out a shrilly scream that I was sure every living being within a mile radius heard. I tried to lunge at my sister, but was quickly yanked back by the offending chain, like a dog. "I hate you! I hate you so much! I wish you were dead! And you will be once I get out of this!" I pointed to the shackle.

Eva's smirk turned into a scowl. "Watch your mouth, Charity"—she smirked at me—"or maybe I'll just turn you into one of us." She pointed at Brad, then herself.

"I'd rather die," I ground out through gritted teeth.

"That can be arranged, too." She turned to Brad. "Lock this door behind you, I need you downstairs. Now."

"Okay, baby." He pulled a key from his pocket and walked to the door as Eva led the way out. Before closing it, he glanced once at me, licked his lips, and winked.

A shudder racked my body. I slumped back down onto the bed and sobbed into the pillow.

Brad threw a hand to his cheek after Eva had slapped him with all her vampire strength in the hallway outside her room on the floor below.

"I thought you were gonna be waiting for me at her place!" Eva screamed, pointing up to the ceiling where Charity was imprisoned.

"Baby, why are you hitting me? I waited in front of the Stop-N-Shop for a bit, but I had to go. I figured you'd be there for a while." He shrugged. "So I sent Allan. What do you care who picked you up?" Brad continued to scrub his cheek.

If Eva could have turned red, she would have been a lovely shade of tomato. "That is not the point, you disobedient little prick. I needed you there, not Allan. He isn't as attentive, and doesn't know the situation. Do not do that to me again!"

She stormed into her room and slammed the door behind her. She knew the true reason she was so pissed off was because Allan was just a regular vampire in the house—her equal. Brad was her protégé—someone she'd created and could therefore control. Although, after tonight, she began to wonder if that control she'd placed over him was beginning to slip.

After slamming the door, Eva peeled off the offensive clothes and threw them into the corner of her room. She had been close… so, so close to having Nolan. She wanted nothing more than to try to feed from him again—to take his soul, or what she could get of his essence. After she'd done that, she had planned to bite into his neck and gorge herself on his blood, all while having him inside her body, fucking her. It was the ultimate pleasure high for her, but she once again walked away from Nolan Bishop empty-handed and with a hollow in her chest. And this time, she only had herself to blame. How was she to know he'd be able to see her eyes turn black in the darkness of Charity's small, dark apartment? He must possess more vampire traits than she first thought.

As she'd been kissing him and licking his neck, she thought she could detect a slight vampire scent on his skin. It was also a lot cooler than a normal, warm-blooded human's skin should be when he was that aroused, getting ready to have sex in the loft that sat over a store in the middle of September. The only coolness in the small apartment was an air conditioning unit attached to the one and only window, and even on high, the thing didn't seem as if it was working very well to keep the place cooled off to a comfortable human temperature.

The last thing was his pulse. It had been very slow, like a 90-year-old man. It should have been beating erratically, given the situation.

As Eva stood completely naked in front of her freestanding antique swivel mirror, she stared at her flawless, pale body and wondered what she could do next. Maybe she should give up her obsession with Nolan Bishop. Maybe she should find another kind, good-looking human male to steal from. And what about that creepy friend of his with the frightening eyes? What was his story? He seemed to know about the supernatural, and Eva briefly wondered if maybe he was one of those Immortals—the cops who protected the sylph faeries who held the Enchantment potion that kept them immortal. Eva had done her homework on those cops, and she made it her number-one priority to steer clear of them. She wasn't sure if they knew about the succubi, but she sure as hell wasn't planning on being the one to enlighten them. She'd heard from some very old vampires that those Immortals possessed some freakishly weird talents and powers and was in no hurry to see what they were.

Eva looked up at the ceiling toward the attic. Yanking a pale blue silk robe from the back of her velvet sitting chair, she stormed out the door and toward the attic to take her frustrations out on her insolent twin.

SCHEMES & VAMPIRE THINGS

Joel Reichert

I sat parked on the street in front of a nondescript building in New Orleans' French Quarter. It was so ordinary, so plain, and blended in with every other once-eclectic structure in the area, that I hadn't ever paid it much mind. And I'd lived in the Big Easy for over one-hundred years.

After my meeting with succubus victims, Nolan and Kovah, I had learned that the federal government had their very own branch of the Justice Department whose sole purpose was to monitor people like me—vampires—along with the other supernaturals in the world.

Learning that Nolan and his friend Kovah had both survived a succubus's attempt at stealing their souls, my eyes had been opened very wide during the past week. Living as long as I had, I thought I knew everything there was to know about the world of vampires, succubi, and everything else out there. But, the knowledge I'd gained recently had both excited and frightened me. How much more was out there that I didn't know about? My mind was simultaneously exhilarated and terrified.

Lifting the Styrofoam cup to my lips, I sipped the hot coffee for no other reason than it was a familiar comfort to me. The caffeine would have no effect on me, and even the taste was somewhat neutral to my vampire palate. I stared out at the building again, its lime-green exterior looking faintly auburn against the orange streetlight that sat right outside its front door. The building looked to be about three stories high, with very few windows. I knew a large parking garage sat at its rear, and I briefly considered parking inside it during the day to see if I could figure out what went on there during business hours. But even the darkest car window tint available on the market wouldn't completely protect me from the sun if I had to leave suddenly.

I set the cup into the BMW's cup holder and slowly got out of the driver's seat. Looking both ways down the quiet street, I moved with preternatural speed to the back of the building and into its dark parking garage. Slinking close to the wall, I pressed my back up against it near an elevator. I didn't care that I was probably soiling my navy-blue suit jacket. I sometimes envied those folks I knew who could go out in public wearing such casual clothes like athletic pants and T-shirts, but that just wasn't my style.

I had been born in the early 1900s, and somehow, the formality in which I was raised had never left me. Even as a human, I had been very obsessive and neat with my appearance, my speech, and my home. Even after becoming a vampire, I never lost those traits. In fact, they'd become even more rigid, if that was possible.

The shuffle of shoes on concrete broke me out of my thoughts. I peered around a concrete pillar and saw a scrawny man wearing a security guard's uniform. The guy looked rather bored, and quite frankly, unkempt. Oily blond hair overdue for a haircut hung limply on his head, and he had both hands in the pockets of his black uniform. A firearm was strapped to the right side of his belt, and I had to swallow down a laugh at how so very unthreatening this human looked.

I waited until the security guard put his back to me and quickly made my way to a set of stairs leading up. I moved with haste up the two small flights until I reached a door marked with a red plaque reading *Authorized Personnel Only*. Knowing the door would be locked, I tried it anyway, which just confirmed my suspicions. Alone in the stairwell, I didn't need to look both ways before I turned the knob so hard, the lock and tumbler exploded all over the ground.

"I'll replace that, I promise," I murmured to nobody.

Easing myself inside, the first thing I did was look for security cameras. Satisfied there were none in the long hall lined with average-looking office carpeting, I slowly crept my way down it. The hall was dark, but I didn't need much light to make my way around due to the large window at the very end. A streetlamp sat outside, lighting the hall. There were several unmarked brown wooden doors, and I had no idea which one to choose. So, selecting one at random, I tried the knob, and it was, of course, locked. The doorknobs were the long, turn-handle type and easy to break. One hard crank had the door open. Smiling a bit to myself, as I'd not had this much fun and adventure in years, I crept inside the dark room. With no light from the outside, as there were no windows in this particular room, my vampire vision was rendered useless in the pitch black.

I pulled a small flashlight from the pocket of my suit pants, flicked it on, and shone it around. I again searched the walls and ceilings for security cameras and did not see any. Shining the light around the room again, I could see I was in some sort of boring office environment. The light found its way to a large, yellow, official-looking seal painted on the wall. In the middle was an eagle with an olive branch in its mouth. The outer edges of the seal read *Department of Justice Federal Bureau of Supernatural Investigation.*

My eyebrows went up in disbelief. "Well I'll be. It *is* real."

I smiled before moving the flashlight around the room again. Beige-colored cubicles were erected all around, and inside the cubicles were desks with computers and other various office supplies on them.

Knowing that attempting to turn on a computer would be futile, as they were most certainly password-protected and I was no hacker, I decided the large, gray filing cabinet in the corner of the room would be of much more interest to me.

Another busted lock later, I had the drawer to the cabinet open. Several green hanging folders containing smaller manila folders were housed inside each one, and each was meticulously labeled. As I began to study each folder, I grinned.

"Jackpot," I whispered.

Picking up the first folder, which read *Fae: Southeast Region,* I set it on the lid of a nearby copy machine and began thumbing through the papers inside, using the flashlight to see. They seemed to be financial records of some sort. The first expense report seemed a bit odd:

```
Pet food: $57

Raw hamburger: $22

Bear trap: $300

Extra-large dog kennel: $237
```

I furrowed my brow as I read down the list of strange expenditures. Each expense had a legitimate accompanying receipt. "Are these cops or dog catchers?" I mumbled to myself.

So rapt with the find I was, I didn't hear the cock of the handgun until it was too late. Whoever was holding it loaded a bullet into the chamber as it was pushed against my head. As it was too late to run, I dropped the folder and turned with the flashlight in my hand to see a beautiful brunette wearing a fitted skirt suit pointing the pistol straight at my face.

"Put your hands up," she ordered.

I did as I was told, trying biting back a grin.

"Who in the hell are you?" she asked.

Keeping my hands raised in the air, I said, "Don't shoot, I don't mean any harm."

The pretty young woman looked completely unimpressed. Her gun did not waver in both her fists as it was aimed right at my face. "Stealing is still a crime. What are you doing here, vampire?"

My eyebrows rose. "You know what I am?"

She nodded confidently. "Absolutely. Now sit." She used the gun to indicate to a chair behind me.

Slowly lowering my hands, but keeping eye contact as I sat, I asked, "How?"

"Let's just say I have good vampire-radar. Your fancy clothes and Southern charm can't mask the monster inside you."

Taken aback by her forthrightness, I kept still, but said, "My name is Joel Reichert. I'm a businessman here in the city. I own a couple of hotels. I truly did not come here to harm anyone. Do you work for the Justice Department?"

Her gun was stock-still, and still trained on me. "Yes. How do you know about us?"

"It seems we are both learning things tonight. What is your name, pretty lady?" I sniffed the air discreetly, but only caught a whiff of her strong perfume.

She narrowed hazel-colored eyes at me, but didn't even blink her long, dark eyelashes. She seemed to know I could move fast and could be gone in an instant.

"My name isn't important to you. I want to know what the fuck you're doing here. I've had a long day, and I was just trying to go home."

I laughed. "My, my, what ugly language from such beautiful lips. You kiss your mother with that mouth?"

She scowled at me. "My mother is dead."

Frowning, I replied, "I'm so sorry to hear that. You are so young to not have a mother."

"I'm older than you think."

"Somehow, I doubt that."

She lowered the gun slightly but never took her eyes off me. "We're not here to talk about me. I want to know what you're doing here."

I relaxed slightly when I saw she had lowered the gun. "I'm here out of mere curiosity, my dear. Nothing more. I am over one hundred years old, yet I just found out your government agency existed. I'm quite fascinated by it all. And as I'm sure you've deduced, it's not as if I could just come by at noon on a Tuesday and introduce myself. So I lessened myself to a sleazy night thief and broke in. It's been quite fun, if I'm being honest."

She stared incredulously at my candidness. "Wow, really? You have anything else you want to declare while you're spewing confessions, Mr. Reichert?"

"No, ma'am, but I do have a question for you."

"Okay, this is getting weird," she murmured, mostly to herself.

"I heard that." I chuckled.

She sighed. "I wasn't whispering."

"How long has the Justice Department been here? How long have you known about us?"

She quirked an eyebrow at me and re-holstered the gun into her thigh-strap. "That's two questions, guy."

"Then pick one, I'm not choosy. Just curious." I folded my hands in my lap.

"We've been here in New Orleans about thirty years, but the BSI was formed about seventy years ago."

"Wow," I breathed. "Where the hell have I been?"

She snorted. "Sucking blood and stealing souls, obviously."

"Hey, pretty lady, I don't steal souls. Just an occasional sip of blood now and again—and always from a willing donor, I might add. I don't need much these days. But hey, if you want to meet someone who genuinely steals souls, I can give you a name of one in Shreveport. I'm ready and willing to help the government," I declared proudly.

"Who? Eva Sheridan? We're already on to her. She won't be around much longer. She's a danger to, well, pretty much everyone, and needs to be put down."

This piqued my interest. "Really? How do you know about Eva? Did the Bishop kid tell you about her?"

At the mention of Nolan Bishop, it looked like a lightbulb had gone off in her head. "That's how you found out about us, isn't it? Nolan and his smartass friend tell you?"

I chuckled and adjusted my tie. "His friend, Kovah? Yes, they told me. I'm just disappointed in both myself and my sources that I didn't know about you people sooner. I have always cooperated with law enforcement. I even donate large sums of money to the New Orleans PD every year. I'm happy to help you in your endeavors here in my fine city. I'm not an enemy, miss. I hope you know that."

"Yeah, well you're the most normal vampire I've ever met. You're a little old-fashioned and formal, but you do seem to possess a calm air about you."

"See? We can be friends, right?" I asked with a smile.

She snorted. "Now you're pushing your luck, bud."

"May I at least have your name?"

She sighed and sat down. Her hand rested on the gun strapped against her thigh, and she set her other one in her lap. "It's Special Agent Mara Shields, and you're seriously cutting into my wine time."

"I know a martini bar."

She got up, walked to the front of the room, and indicated for me to exit through the door she now held open. "Gin works, too."

Chapter 4

SEARCH & SEIZURE

Nolan

rchie, Kovah, three other Riders, and I killed the engines to our bikes and parked them about a hundred yards from the entrance to Eva's mansion. The ground was so soft beneath us that our boots sank a little as we headed for the wrought iron gates of the ridiculously cliché vampire dwelling.

"What now?" one of the Riders asked right before he spat a brown stream of chew onto the soft ground.

Archie leaned on his cane and looked at his crony. "We need to find out how many bloodsuckers are actually in there." He turned his attention to Kovah and me. "Care to do the honors, kids?"

"Why do we always get the dirty work?" Kovah grumbled.

I chuckled and grabbed Kovah's tattooed arm. "Come on, grumpy. I know the layout of that house. Let's go see what we're dealing with."

Kovah used his middle finger to shove his glasses closer to his face and smiled. "All right."

A fist bump later, Kovah and I took off at speed to the back of the house. Our feet made no noise while they tromped over soft, marshy ground when we reached the back side.

Cocking his head slightly, Kovah pointed to a shed. "I wonder what's in there?"

I squinted at the shed, where the door to it was wide open. "Looks like a bunch of gardening tools and shit."

He cocked a dark eyebrow that stretched above his glasses and made a dramatic gesture of looking around the property. "And what sort of gardening do they need to do here?"

I snorted and whispered, "Maybe they use the tools to beat the gators back." I pointed to a small body of water about ten feet away.

Kovah also laughed. "That's messed up, man."

"Let's just sneak in and see what's goin' on in there." I jutted my chin at the massive Victorian.

Kovah nodded and we slunk toward the back door. It was a simply painted modern aluminum fixture with a thick piece of glass covered by a lace curtain on the inside. It was miraculously unlocked.

Turning the knob easily, he grinned. "Dumbasses."

I snickered in agreement and followed my friend into the house.

The temperature inside was warm. There was no air blowing, but it didn't bother us hybrids much. I shook my head a little, knowing that even though vampires were naturally cold and probably weren't affected by the heat and humidity, that the house would be. When mildew and mold began to fester due to the temperature and damp, they would regret being frugal with the air conditioning.

We both crept through a completely clean, immaculate kitchen that held nothing but a dining room table and a fridge I wasn't sure was even running. A sudden noise like the creaking of a floorboard above our heads made us both freeze. Kovah shot a look at me and pointed to the ceiling.

I nodded and we continued to creep through the house. I reached down and pulled the buck knife from my boot, and Kovah smirked at the gesture.

Not spotting any signs of life--or unlife--on the ground floor, we quickly ascended the stairs toward the noises we kept hearing. At the top, the landing stretched out into a hallway containing half a dozen doors, all of which were shut. There were old oil paintings decorating the walls between each door, and I rolled my eyes.

"What are we in, a *Scooby-Doo* cartoon?" Kovah whispered before I could.

"My thoughts exactly."

With our sensitive hearing, we followed the sounds to a room in the middle of the hallway. Kovah shot a glance at me, and I nodded at him. As Kovah went to turn the handle, we could see the door was slightly ajar. As he was about to push it open with his fingertips, a voice accented in what could only be described as Russian or Eastern European behind us caused us both to whirl around.

"I would not be doing that if I were you."

The man—vampire—standing there was taller than both of us, his light-blond hair sleeked and shiny. He wore a three-piece suit and had his arms folded over a very broad chest. His extremely square jaw ticked in annoyance, and one pale eyebrow was cocked as if in a silent challenge. He was almost too pretty for a dude.

Kovah and I continued to stare at the Adonis standing before us, saying nothing.

"Well, you gonna tell me who you are and what you're doing here, or should I remove your heads?" The vampire stripped off his suit jacket with ridiculous speed and threw it to the floor. He then began rolling the sleeves of his white dress shirt to the elbows, as if preparing to clean up a mess.

Kovah, suddenly broken out of his shock, balled his fists in defiance, and clenched his jaw. "Nah, man, we were just looking for the hot redhead. She told us to meet her here," he lied.

I resisted the urge to shoot my friend an incredulous look.

"Well, in case you're too dumb to figure it out, she is in there"—the blond vampire shoved his massive chin at the door in front of us—"but she's obviously too busy to see you right now." A smile lit up his face, but it didn't quite reach his blue eyes.

"Okay, we'll be on our way then," I said, grabbing Kovah's arm and trying to move him toward the stairs.

Kovah resisted, though, looking at the vampire in front of us. "And who are you?" he boldly asked while his teeth audibly ground together. He looked like he wanted to stake the huge vampire more than all the other vampires he'd ever wanted to stake.

The guy laughed and relaxed his posture, shoving his large hands into the pockets of his suit pants. "It's Boris. What's it to you?"

A noise above our heads made the three of us look up.

"What's up there?" I asked, pointing.

"Nothing. Just attic," Boris replied.

Kovah snorted, placing a hand on the hip of his jeans. "Really? You got rats or something? Or are you the only vermin in this creepy-ass house?"

I hissed at my friend. "You must have a fuckin' death wish. Let's go!"

Kovah again shook me off and pierced me with a sunglassed stare. "Fuck off, Bishop."

Boris again placed his arms over his chest and looked at me. "You are a bishop?"

I shook my head. "No, it's my last name." I wanted to roll my eyes at the vampire's stupid question, but decided against it.

"You and Eva... and whoever she's with in there" — Kovah jutted his thumb at the door — "you the only vamps here?"

A look somewhere between confusion and amusement passed over Boris's features. "Well, Allan and I are here, and aside from you two, yes. For now."

"We're not—" I started to protest before Kovah grabbed my arm.

"I think we'll head out," Kovah cut me off, steering me toward the stairs.

Boris cleared his throat dramatically, as if he were a judge in the middle of a court session.

We turned around and looked at him.

"Your names? I'll tell Eva you were here, if you so desire."

"We don't desire. Thanks, though, dude." Kovah smiled with a salute.

We sprinted down the stairs and out the back door, just wanting to get away from the house and the massive vampire whom we were sure could kick both our asses with one hand tied behind his back. We darted around the marsh, through the wrought-iron gate, and back to the Riders, who had their bikes parked at the edge of the property.

"Let's go!" Kovah said with a wave of his hand.

We jumped on our bikes and started them up. Archie and the Riders had already taken off as soon as they saw us running toward them.

"Who the hell were you talking to?" Eva screeched, emerging from her room completely naked and unabashed, a blue robe in her hand.

Boris recoiled at her twisted, angry face but knew better than to look at her nakedness. "Eva, two young male vampires were here to see you. I told them you were busy." He smiled, happy to have done Eva a favor.

Her eyes turned completely black and she reached out and slapped Boris with all her strength, leaving four deep scratches along his flawless cheek.

Boris reached up and daubed at the black blood that had begun to seep from the wounds. Dialing back his anger, he replied, "Shit, woman, I was just doing as you told, keeping people away while you were... otherwise indisposed."

Eva's face was contorted in rage. "Letting strange vampires get this close to my bedroom is unacceptable! They shouldn't have been allowed into the house to begin with!"

Brad emerged from the bedroom in nothing but a pair of green boxer briefs, his dark hair tousled, a grin on his ignorant face. "What's going on out here?"

"Get the hell outta here, Brad. Go back to your room," Eva demanded.

With a shrug and that grin still plastered on his face, he reached down and scratched himself. He sauntered off to a door set in the dark hallway and disappeared behind it.

Eva looked back at Boris. "Why aren't you and Allan guarding the doors downstairs? You know it's your night. I only ask one simple thing of you two!"

Boris touched his cheek once more where he'd been scratch-slapped and pulled his hand away to see the blood was gone. All that remained were thin, ropey scars that would soon disappear. Watching Eva's backside retreat into her room and slam the door, Boris looked when he saw Allan come up beside him and intertwine his hand with Boris's.

"Don't let that nasty bitch get to you, babe. She's always in some kinda mood," Allan soothed.

"I heard that!" Eva called from behind her door as the pair snickered and headed down the stairs.

Once they reached the bottom, Boris put his arm around Allan and planted a kiss on the top if his dark-brown hair. "Guess we shouldn't get so distracted while we're supposed to be watching the door."

Allan laughed as the pair went into the kitchen and both sat at the dining room table. Boris picked up a deck of playing cards and began shuffling them while Allan scrolled through his phone.

Chapter 5

SOUTHERN GENTLEMAN

Joel

I really don't think you should be driving," I said, plucking the car keys from Mara's fist.

"Hey! Give those back! I'm fine. I can drive juuust fine…"

I made a disapproving noise with my tongue and put the keys behind my back with a smirk.

"Give those back," she repeated, trying not to laugh, but definitely too slow for me. I was now leaning against her white government sedan parked on the street.

"I'm serious, guy. Give them to me." Mara slipped on something wet on the sidewalk and had no choice but to fall into me.

I caught her with strong hands. "Whoa, careful there."

Her drunk smirk grew serious as she stared into my eyes. With both hands still on her thin upper biceps, my face also lost its smirk as I stared down at her.

We'd spent hours in the posh martini bar until closing time. I couldn't get drunk, but I had fun watching the Special Agent hammer them back. I was frankly surprised to see her so liberal with the alcohol, as she should definitely be passed out by now. I had to agree that she definitely wasn't the uptight woman she had come off as when we'd first met just a few short hours prior.

I had made it a habit to not date humans. I really didn't even like being around them unless I was feeding or had an issue to manage at my hotel. Obviously, most of my employees were human, and I was grateful to have them to handle things while I slept during the day. I was happy none of them ever asked why I slept all day and was up all night, and I was sure they just assumed it was the nature of the hotel business.

The last woman I'd had feelings for had been over twenty years ago, and she'd been human. Alicia had been a gorgeous woman from the Dominican Republic who had settled in New Orleans after becoming orphaned. I couldn't say I had been in love with Alicia, but she had been a delicious and consuming distraction who had filled my nights with excitement, and had looked beautiful on my arm for all the social events I attended in the city all those years ago. After a couple of years of casual dating, I had been forced to explain to her why I never went out during the day or ate food. My high hopes that she'd understand and be accepting of who — *what* — I was were dashed when she'd screamed in terror. *Well, at least she hadn't laughed at me,* I remembered thinking. Alicia left the city and never returned… and since then, no other woman had been able to hold my interest for very long, and I'd certainly avoided humans.

As Mara looked up into my face, I studied it. I wondered what she was thinking, but I had seen that look on women's faces before. I didn't say anything, I just stared back at her.

"How old are you?" she finally asked, still staring up at me with a happy grin.

I looked down into her hazel gaze, loving the way the golds and greens mixed together to make up her irises. I placed a hand on her temple and brushed her hair back lightly with my thumb. "I'm over one hundred years old in human years, but I was turned at age thirty-three."

"Well, you're hot for being one-hundred-and-thirty-three," she slurred.

I chuckled. "Okay, well, I'm not one-hundred-and-thirty-three years of age any way you do the math, Mara. I said I was turned at the age of —"

My explanation was cut short when she lifted herself onto her toes and crushed her mouth to mine. I gave in immediately, feeling boneless at the sensation of her warm lips on mine.

My hands moved from her upper arms to slide around the small of Mara's back. I became aroused at the feel of her firm waist and backside, resisting every urge to rip off her skirt and sensually violate her right there in the middle of the French Quarter. But I had been raised a gentleman and wasn't going to do that.

"Where do you live, Vampire Joel?" she asked after breaking the soft kiss.

"At my hotel, beautiful lady," I breathed into her upturned face.

She sucked in a breath. "Then maybe you should take me there. Show me what kind of man you really are."

I gasped at her comment, my eyebrows practically hitting my hairline at her forwardness. I wanted nothing more than to shove her into the car and take her back to my room and have my way with her for the rest of the night. But then logic took over my lust and made me realize that would be a very bad idea.

"Oh, darlin', I would love nothing more than to show you what kind of man I am— many times over. But the fact that you are quite inebriated and probably not thinking too clearly makes me realize I would not be a gentleman if I were to take advantage of you right now."

Mara threw back her head and laughed, her dark hair swishing down her back and brushing against her firm, round backside. "Oh, 'darlin' — who said I wanted a gentleman? Maybe I'd like someone who isn't so 'gentle'?"

Her eyes and body were giving off a strong scent of something sinful to my sensitive nose and I had to stop breathing — not that I needed to anyway. Leaning down to kiss her one last time, I pressed her soft body against my hard one as I internally cursed myself for what I was about to do.

Breaking her sensual kiss, I pulled her back from my body and gently led her to the passenger side of her government car. After placing her in the seat and buckling her in, I went around and started the car, driving back toward the BSI building. I didn't know where she lived and figured that was probably the best place for her, as I knew if I asked for her address, a myriad of problems would arise from that. One, being that I would have to help her into her house or apartment and I wasn't sure I would have the willpower to leave. Two, once she sobered up tomorrow, she may grow paranoid that a vampire knew where she lived. No, the BSI building and those not-so-comfortable office chairs would have to be her resting place tonight.

As I drove the few blocks back to the nondescript building, I kept the windows down to feel the cooling, humid air blow across my face. Looking toward the east, I saw the faint glow of pink begin to rise along the horizon, and I pressed the gas a little harder, knowing I needed to get my car and be home soon.

When I finally reached the BSI headquarters, I parked her car next to mine and helped her out. She'd been very quiet on the drive back, not looking at me or trying to engage me in any way. As I went around to open the door, I could see she was already getting out.

"I was going to get that for you," I said as she closed the door and began walking toward the elevators.

Without turning around, Mara said, "I thought I told you I really wasn't interested in a gentleman tonight. But I guess your vampire hearing isn't as good as I've heard it was."

Wow, she sure flipped quickly.

"Let me at least help you up to your office."

She stopped this time, turning around and looking at me in confusion. "Actually, why am I heading toward the office? I need to get the hell home. You have my keys?"

I nodded. "Yes, but I'm afraid I'm not giving them to you. You are still quite drunk and that would be irresponsible of me."

She scoffed at me. "Just give me the damn keys and go back to wherever you came from."

She was starting to upset me now, but I told myself that it was just the rejection mixed with the alcohol talking. I brushed it off and looked into her beautiful face. "I don't know you that well, but you seem far too valuable for me to just let you get into a car and kill yourself or someone else because you're stubborn. Just go upstairs and sleep it off. Is there some sort of cot or bed anywhere?"

She didn't say anything, just turned around and headed toward the elevators.

I followed her.

Pressing the button to the third floor, she looked at me out of the corner of her eye. I noticed she was wobbling a bit on her high heels, confirming my suspicions that she was still very much intoxicated.

"Why are you following me? I'm a big girl, I can take care of myself."

I smirked at her. "Somehow, I doubt that right now. I'm just going to make sure you get upstairs safely."

She narrowed eyes at me. "And then, what? Bite me? Feed from me?"

I had finally had enough. I gripped her by both shoulders and stared deep into her bloodshot eyes. "Mara, go to sleep."

She did not need to be bamboozled twice. She went slack in my arms. I ignored the ding of the elevator arriving, and raced up the stairs carrying her in a fireman's hold. Once I reached the third floor, I kicked open the door with its busted lock and went down the hall, looking at each nameplate until I found hers. Breaking open yet another lock, I quickly went inside and was relieved to see a small loveseat-sized sofa in her office set in front of a large desk. I laid her carefully down on it and felt lucky again as I found a blue blanket folded neatly in a bottom drawer. It had a large Department of Justice seal on it. *Consolation prize for working here?* I thought with amusement. I unfolded the blanket and laid it on top of her. She didn't stir when I gently pried her high-heels from her feet and set them neatly on the floor.

Making sure she seemed comfortable enough, I planted a soft kiss on her warm forehead, inhaling her scent one last time, but smelling nothing but alcohol and strong perfume. Before I closed the door, I picked up all the pieces of the broken doorknob and set them neatly on her desk. After finding a business card in my suit jacket, I pulled a pen from my breast pocket, flipped the card over, and wrote *Sorry* on the blank space. I set the card on top of the broken pieces and sped out of the building to my car to beat the sun home.

Chapter 6

SAYING GOODBYE

Nolan

Weepy moss trees surrounded the gravesite, standing still in reverent respect for the one we had come to honor today.

A large, shiny black wooden casket was suspended above a sharply dug square frame that was six feet deep. The mourners were all dressed in black—but that wasn't anything unusual for them. Their glinting leather shone in the slices of sunlight that managed to escape through the leaves above us. Their patched leather vests portrayed the pride of the Rebel Riders, and each and every one wore the cuts proudly to honor their friend who had, in their minds and hearts, died in the line of duty. The duty of killing vampires and protecting humans.

When Aspen had pulled out the gun and had taken out a vampire's bodyguard, he had done the right thing. He was sadly not quick enough for the vampire who had killed him in the process. The Riders took a small comfort in the fact that they had killed Aspen's undead murderer, sending him to hell… or wherever vampires went after they died—if they even possessed a soul.

Which was still up for debate in most circles.

After the minister said a few words about Aspen, he moved to the side and nodded at Archie, who hobbled to the front of the small group.

"Lee 'Aspen' Morris was an unforgettable friend," Archie began his eulogy solemnly, clearly fighting emotion. He cleared his throat and shifted his weight off his sore leg, moving his cane a little in the grassy earth beneath his feet. "The man was fearless and loyal. Aspen would give you the shirt off his back, and then ask if you needed his pants, too." Archie smiled, but it didn't quite reach his eyes as he continued, "And one time, I actually did need his pants after losing mine at a wild poker party."

The small group erupted in quiet chuckles.

Looking up into the heavens, Archie's face grew serious again. "Buddy, have a beer for me. I'll be there soon enough. T.O.G.V.I.A.D.V., brother," he ended, reciting the Riders' motto. He dropped his head and hobbled to the casket. He gently placed Aspen's Rebel Riders patch on the top, laying a hand over it and pausing briefly. He then slowly turned to take his seat at the front of the group. Kovah clapped him on the shoulder as he sat.

The minister then asked if anyone else had anything else to say. At the small crowd's silence, the preacher nodded. Requesting everyone bow their heads in prayer, he said a quick and solemn prayer for the rebel soul who was Lee Aspen Morris.

All seven Rebel Riders, along with me, a handful of Aspen's family, and about half a dozen of his friends all dispersed, leaving the large casket to lie lonely above the giant hole in the earth. As the crowd slowly shuffled to the parking lot, a grave attendant came and began the slow process of cranking the handle that would set Aspen in his final resting place.

I heard the crank, but decided not to look back. None of us did. We continued to walk slowly toward the parking lot and the bikes we'd left there. I had no idea where we were headed, but I knew I wanted to be with them.

As a group, we walked in and found a small corner table of the Riders' favorite bar. I'd been here more than once, and wasn't surprised it was where we ended up. Including Kovah and me, there were eight of us, and the minute we took our seats, a young waitress came over with a smile on her face. Archie frowned at the newcomer's presence, but Kovah and I both grinned at her long, chestnut hair and very short skirt.

"Hi, boys. What can I get ya?" she asked the group.

Archie spit into a white Styrofoam cup he'd seemed to pull out of nowhere. "Where's Annie?"

The waitress tried to maintain her smile. "She's retired, hun. I'm Michelle and I've taken over for her."

"Well, that's too bad," another of the Riders said. "Liked her real good,

I did."

Archie elbowed his buddy in the ribs. "Yeah, you did, you liked her real good about five times that I can remember."

The group broke into laughter, while Michelle fidgeted nervously and tried to smile again. "What can I get y'all?" Her pen was poised over her notepad.

"Just a round of Jack, darlin'," Archie answered, swirling his finger around the table.

She nodded without writing it down and headed toward the bar. Archie watched her go and then made eye contact with the bartender, who gave him a tight smile and curt nod. The bartender, Ed, had known the Riders for a long time, and Archie knew he was giving us his condolences, as we were clearly one less Rider tonight.

When Michelle returned with the drinks and set them down, we each grabbed a glass.

Archie lifted his up high. "To Aspen, may his ride in Heaven be smooth until we meet again."

We nodded and lifted our glasses collectively before slamming back the whiskey. I shuddered as it went down. *So not a whiskey drinker.*

A somber cloud blanketed us for a couple of minutes as we all sat quietly and reflected on what had truly happened to our friend and brother. A cover band on the small stage of the bar was playing some classic Led Zeppelin, and the crooning lyrics about stairways to heaven just made the group even more somber.

Deciding that sober wasn't working for me — or clearly for the rest of the group—I waved over Michelle again and smiled sweetly at her, ordering another round. That broke our silence and the Riders again began talking.

A woman at the end of the bar on the other side of the club caught my eye. She had platinum-blonde hair ironed stick straight with blood-red lips that matched her nail polish. Her long, pale legs were crossed where she sat on the barstool, the short, black skirt barely covering the tops of her thighs. She was drop-dead gorgeous and most of the men in the bar were intermittently looking at her. When she caught me looking at her, a flirty smile twisted up on her glossy lips. She lifted her wine glass to me. I swallowed hard, forced a smile, and looked back to the group.

That woman is not a woman at all, but a vampire; one on the hunt. Something inside of me strangely and instinctively knew this. I couldn't explain how or why I knew it, but I just did. I looked at the group I was with and wondered if I should say anything. She was obviously no threat to me or my group, but what about the other men in the bar—all those men practically drooling over her?

I looked back once again at her, and she was still looking at me. Her gaze flicked to Kovah, then back to me, one light eyebrow lifting in question. This confused me a little, but after a brief thought, I realized she wanted us both.

How do I even know that?

I was warring with myself now. Should I tell the Riders about her? After all, wasn't this their off time? They'd come here to give one last toast to Aspen, to grieve in their own way, not to work, after all. But I knew they were always "on"—working to eradicate vampires who fed from the unwilling and murdered humans. I contemplated elbowing Kovah and showing him the vampire, but I knew if I did that, my sunglassed friend would be out of his seat and over to her before I could blink.

Maybe I should handle it myself. Kovah would also know she was a vampire the second he laid eyes on her. Which, I knew, would probably be any minute now. The guy was drawn to beautiful women. Which was what got him into his current predicament in the first place.

Not that I could say much, I was also in my own shit because of a beautiful woman. A redhead with a twin. Where was that twin now? Where was Charity? I glanced around the bar once again. Why was I sitting here throwing back shots and contemplating taking out what was probably an innocent, but very hot, vampire girl, when I should be out looking for my professed girlfriend?

I had a strong feeling she was in that old mansion, the one Kovah and I had just left. I was going to go back there and look, and the fact that I was sitting in this dank bar honoring the memory of a man I hardly knew sickened me a little. I was both horrified and saddened by Aspen's death. I had lost sleep over what I could have done differently that night, but at the end of the day, I had to acknowledge that I never really knew the man, nor was I officially a member of the Rebel Riders. These hunters who killed vampires in cold, black blood for no other reason than because they were what they were. As far as the way Aspen had died, I could Monday-morning quarterback that 'til I was blue in the face, but it wouldn't bring back the old biker. We'd had to go back once the sun was fully up and go get his bike and his body, and that was a memory that would never be leaving me.

I kept my eyes trained on the blonde as my body began to move from the chair I'd been sitting in, heading slowly toward her as if I couldn't stop. What was I doing? I didn't know. All I could think was that I had to get her out of that bar.

"Where you goin', kid?" Archie asked.

Without turning around, I could hear Kovah chuckle with amusement as I moved toward the vampire. The rest of the Riders laughed, too, but before I reached her, I felt someone behind me. Whirling around, I was faced with my own reflection in a pair of dark sunglasses.

"You know that's a vampire, right?" Kovah asked, pointing at her.

I nodded. "Yep, getting her out of here before she feeds on someone, and then one of you maniacs murders her."

Kovah's jaw pulsed in anger. "I wouldn't be doing that if I were you."

I put both hands on my hips. "Why not? I already know you guys will probably stake her before she can finish her drink. She hasn't done anything, and you know it."

"Oh, but she will, Bishop. She will. They always do, especially the females. They are black widows, seeking whoever they can devour and destroy for the night. Stay the fuck away, dude. I'm not messing around here."

I had had enough. The funeral, my missing girlfriend, a hot blonde vampire eyeing me like I was her next meal, the whiskey shots... they were messing with my head and I snapped. I shoved Kovah in the chest with both hands as hard as I could. He went flying backward onto his ass, but was up on his feet faster than the human eye could see.

I had made the mistake of turning around after pushing him, and the second I felt a presence behind me was a second too late, as Kovah spun me around and then landed a cracking punch to my cheek.

"Fuck you, freak!" I yelled as pain exploded in my face. I launched myself at him. We rolled around on the ground, throwing punches. Kovah's glasses were no longer on his face, and most likely a pile of broken plastic somewhere.

I was about to deliver another blow to my friend's stomach, as I was now straddling him, but I felt myself being lifted off. Spinning around to hit whoever had pulled me off, I was met with two hands up in surrender as Archie stood behind me.

"Cool your jets, kid," he said, placing both hands on my shoulders the minute I had lowered my balled fist.

I turned around to see two of the Riders holding Kovah back with both arms behind his back. He had a small stream of blood dribbling down from the corner of his mouth. Normally, I would feel bad about it, but right now I felt nothing but rage. I was shooting daggers at my former friend's icy white eyes, which Kovah returned with just as much hate.

I yanked myself out of his grip. "I'm good, Arch. I'm outta here."

I stalked to the door, subtly noticing that the pretty blonde was no longer at the bar.

"Freaking figures," I grumbled on my way out the door.

Chapter 7

DIABOLICAL DESPERATION

Charity

"No!" I screamed, pounding on the small window of my sweltering prison.

I had seen the boys go into the house, and had cried with joy to see Nolan was still alive and well. And once the shock and happiness of that wore off, I had sobbed again in relief, thinking my rescuers were here. But they never made it to me. When I saw my love dart out the back door with his annoying friend who never took those sunglasses off, I couldn't believe my eyes. How could Nolan leave me here to die? Didn't he care at all? Had he been chased off by my evil twin?

No, I wouldn't let Eva win. Nolan would fight to get to me. Even if I was some random stranger and not his girlfriend, he wouldn't let somebody suffer like this. I knew that for a fact. So why had my love and his friend scurried out and taken off like that?

Something had spooked them.

With a sigh, I slunk over to my bed and sat down, tears falling like rain down my cheeks. Disappointment, sadness, and despair engulfed me. I wanted to give up. I wanted to just die. I doubted Nolan even knew I was here, because surely he wouldn't have left me. Well, I hoped not, anyway. I thought back to the fight we'd had and wondered if he really was done with me. Maybe he had come looking for Eva for another roll in the sack. But why would he bring his friend?

So many questions swirled around in my brain. I looked over and stared at the now-empty Coke can, contemplating what I could do with it. Maybe I could refill it with toilet water, making it a nice, heavy weapon. Maybe I could pull the tab off and try to sharpen it somehow, and then cut Brad's jugular when he came into my room next. I could make a run for the door and be on my way out. Maybe I could toss the can at the window with all my strength and hope it would shatter so I could get some air and maybe escape. But could I climb through that window and jump? I looked down at my wrist. Not until I got the shackle off somehow.

For the hundredth time, I tried slipping my wrist out of it. I had even contemplated squeezing my hand and maybe breaking a few bones just to get it out of the shackle. But I just couldn't. I sighed and looked around.

I set the pop can on the bed and wandered over to the window. I took a deep breath in anticipation of the pain that would ensue once I reached it, as my arm would be practically yanked from its socket so I could look out.

Peering down to the ground below, I could see the body of water near front of the old house. However, I had no idea how deep it was. And what of the gators? I was sure I'd seen one or two pop their heads up. Maybe I could swim fast enough to the grass a few feet away and avoid the gators? But taking the chance of not actually landing in the water after jumping was not a risk I could take. Trying to escape on one or two broken legs — or worse, a broken back or neck — was not a gamble I was willing to wager at the moment.

After slinking back to the bed, I sat down in defeat, trying not to let the despair of my situation overwhelm me. I once again spied the Coke can, its red aluminum seeming to almost send off a warning that I should just sit tight and wait to be rescued… or be set "free."

But would that ever happen?

I knew that there was no way. After Eva had gotten what she wanted from Nolan, she would either have Brad destroy me (not without a crap ton of pain and torture first), or she would turn me into a vampire herself, hence leaving me chained to my evil twin for all eternity. After all, I was a redhead with blue eyes, just like Eva. The thought of becoming a succubus and having to survive on both blood *and* souls sickened me to my very core. Not no, but *hell no.* I was not going out like that.

The door to my small prison began to creak on its rusty hinges, and I quickly shoved the empty pop can under my pillow, preparing myself for whoever was coming in. It was dark out now, so it could be anyone. I knew the vampires were up.

I looked up to see a tall, blond man walk into the room. He was far better looking than anyone should be, and I found myself being drawn to him immediately. I quickly realized my jaw was practically hanging on the floor, but then closed it as I darted my eyes away from his blue ones.

Looking at his hands, I could see he was carrying a tray. There was both a pitcher of water loaded down with ice, and a bowl of food next to it. I slid my gaze from the tray back to the man carrying it.

"Who are you?" I asked.

Bowing almost reverently, he replied, "I am Boris, at your service."

"Boris?" I frowned.

He set the tray down on my bed and looked into my eyes with his piercing ones. "Yes, Boris. I live here. I was instructed to bring you nourishment."

I detected the accent in his voice. Russian, perhaps? Well, from what I'd seen on the Discovery Channel, anyway. I'd never even been outside of Louisiana. Speaking of the Discovery Channel, hadn't I watched some "lockup" prison shows about inmates who had escaped using strange methods with even stranger tools? I looked at the pillow where the Coke can lay and tried to rack my brain to remember what they had said about prisoners who had fashioned weapons made from…

"You listening to me, little girl?"

I looked up to see angry blue eyes looking at me. "What?"

The Russian let out a sigh. "You humans, so distracted by your cell phones and your Internet and your A.D.H.D. How difficult is it to have a normal conversation with a normal human? Huh?"

I looked at him, confused, then before my brain could filter out the response, I snapped, "Show me a normal human and I will have a normal conversation with one." I folded my arms defiantly over my chest.

In a move so fast I missed it, Boris had me pinned down to the filthy mattress before I could take a breath. He was hovering over me, anger coloring his handsome features. But for some reason, this didn't scare me. I could see he was powerful, but somehow seemed harmless and a little bit kind.

"I used to be normal, you know," he whispered into my sticky hair. "I used to be warm-blooded Russian. Now I am this." He blew icy breath into my face and I shuddered. "See?" He laughed, lifting himself off me and back to his feet before I could blink.

I sat up and my eyebrows dipped together. "You're all freaks. Every last one of you. Why don't you just let me out of here? You and your girlfriend have no reason for keeping me here."

Boris was now standing by the doorway with his arms folded over his broad chest. The fitted white dress shirt he wore barely covered the muscle mass beneath it. "Girlfriend?"

"You're not one of my sister's little vampire minions?" I asked with defiance in my tone, but in my mind, I was mildly afraid of being pinned down again. Both afraid and exhilarated at the thought. Boris was really hot, vampire or not.

Boris laughed, *and wow is it a great laugh,* I thought. "No, I'm not her... minion as you say. I do what I want. I live here because it's free and I can come and go as I please."

"So... she didn't turn you into a crazy vampire with her succubus stuff?" I asked, swirling my finger near my temple to indicate just how crazy I thought my twin was.

Boris laughed again. "Oh, no, sweet thing. That would be Brad. He's still tied to her apron strings. My maker, Alek, he died long time ago. I am my own master now." I could swear he puffed out his chest a bit.

I nodded. "Okay, I'm glad you aren't chained to my sister. She's an evil witch, you know."

Boris laughed again. "Yes, I know. Been living here for five years now. She is *сумасшедший,* you know. I've lived here longer than she has. I came here thinking I could rule the house. But I know better. I rule nothing."

"What does that mean?" I asked, indicating his Russian word.

"Insane, as you say," he replied matter-of-factly.

I smiled. "That definitely sounds like my sister."

"You look so much like her, it is frightening."

"That's not the first time I've heard that," I murmured.

Boris cocked his head to the side. "How do you say in English? Oh, identical. You are identical twins?"

I nodded but did not smile.

"How are you twins but she is succubus and you are human?"

I could swear I heard and saw him sniff the air at the word "human."

On a deep sigh, I answered, "She chose to be a vampire. I did not. In fact"—I inhaled deeply, folding my hands in my lap and wondering why I was engaging this good-looking, yet undead monster in this conversation—"I didn't know she was... what she was... 'til a few months ago."

Boris gasped. "I see. How shocking for you to find this out, no?"

I nodded. "Yes. She'd been missin' for a couple years."

"What are you doing here now?" he asked, seemingly genuinely interested in the answer.

I stared at the musclebound freak a bit longer, wondering if I could lie and use it to my advantage. Then I thought maybe the truth would work to my advantage, too. This dude seemed to have a brain in his head, unlike Brad.

"My sister has me chained, as you can see" —I held up my wrist and shook the shackle for effect—"and I have no idea why, except maybe to keep me away from my boyfriend so she can try to steal his soul… *again*."

Boris raised an eyebrow. "She tried to steal his essence and failed? I have never heard of that."

"Yeah, well, apparently it's not common."

"How did he survive it?"

I contemplated telling him about him drinking my blood, but decided that Eva should never know that information, as it would put my own life in even more danger. So instead, I shrugged. "No clue, but my sister's pretty pissed off about it."

Boris grinned. "I bet she is. I would have loved to be fly on wall when she found it out."

I nodded and slid some greasy hair behind my ear. "So y'all really don't talk to each other in this house? You have no idea what she does and doesn't do?"

He shook his head. "Not really, unless it involves the house business. Which is why I'm here now. Eva asked me to bring you the food and water. I did not ask questions. It is not first time she has kept human in here for food."

Her eyebrows hit my hairline. "What! She does that?"

"Yes." He laughed. "It used to be common practice a few decades ago. But now, not so much. Too much police and internet and everything like that to get away with kidnapping humans."

"That's disgusting, Boris. Seriously."

Boris laughed again. "Of course you think so."

"Are you going to bite me?" I asked timidly.

"Of course not, I have my own food."

I looked at him and took a breath before asking, "Can you unchain me so I can take a bath?"

"I do not think that bathtub works any longer," he replied, flicking his eyes to the bathroom and not budging from his post against the doorframe.

"Then can you take me somewhere in the house I can get a shower and some food? They have only been feeding me once a day. It makes me weak and sick."

He laughed and pointed at the bowl he'd just brought me.

I peered in it. It looked like canned ravioli, and it certainly wasn't warm and there was no utensil to eat it with. I frowned.

Boris continued, "That is sort of the point. You do not need your strength if you are here to be nourishment for the succubus and her blockhead of a mate."

"But I'm not here as food. She's got me here for other reasons. I have not been bitten."

He raised an eyebrow. "You sure? We can make you forget, you know."

My hand flew to my neck as I stared at Boris in horror. "What?"

He threw his head back and laughed again. "I'm just joking you."

I shot him a scowl. "That isn't funny."

"Well, I was mostly joking. We can make you forget, but I can tell they have not done it to you. You have no markings of bites."

I blew off his comment and got straight to the point. "So how about that shower?"

He sighed. "As much as I don't let the succubus control me, I do not think that will be a good thing if I allow that."

"I won't tell," I pled, then batted my eyelashes, "and maybe I can return the favor?"

I knew the vampire could probably smell my desperation—among other odors I was probably emitting under his sensitive nose—and that desperation was sickening, even to me. I had no intentions of giving him anything. As soon as I was in any bathroom besides the one attached to my prison, I planned on trying to escape. Hopefully another bathroom would have a window.

"I will give you five minutes." He then grabbed something from his pocket and walked toward me. I could see it was a key and my stomach did summersaults with excitement.

He unchained me and gripped my thin upper arm tightly.

"Ouch!" I whined.

He looked down at my arm then into my face. "Sorry. I do not know my own strength sometimes."

Boris barely loosened his grip, but I decided not to say anything. He led me out into the hall and down one flight of stairs to another long hallway lined with odd paintings that I recognized from when I'd come into the house before. I spied the door to Eva's room before being shoved into a small bathroom.

As I went to close the door, Boris held it open with his boot and made a disapproving noise with his tongue. "You keep open."

I huffed, but smiled up at him. "But I'm shy. It's only five minutes, please? I also need to… pee. Surely you don't wanna watch that?"

He wrinkled his nose and then barked, "Five minutes," and closed the door.

As soon as it was shut, I looked around the tiny, old bathroom. One toilet, one white ceramic pedestal sink, and another old-fashioned white claw-foot tub with a small red shower curtain encircling it. I pulled back the curtain and saw a window set into the wall. I turned on the shower for noise and climbed on the edge of the tub, careful not to slip now that the water was running. I realized the window was big enough to crawl out of, but then wondered how far the drop would be. Surely not as far as the one from my attic prison upstairs.

Lifting the screen, I slid the old window open and had to stifle a scream when I encountered a sheet of thick metal — maybe it was aluminum — that had been bolted over it from the outside. Clearly there to keep out any sunlight. I sank into the tub fully clothed with the shower running over me and screamed, "Stupid effing vampires!"

Chapter 8

I AM WHAT I AM

Mara lay on the sofa in her office, the morning sunlight streaming through in thin, sharp beams reflecting off the multiple pictures and certificates framed on the walls of her office. The walls had been painted a deep, dark red, and everything on her desk was neat and in order, as usual. The dark-brown sofa she lay on was leather and it squeaked as she rolled over and slid her eyes open slowly. When the light seared her eyeballs, she groaned in pain, closing them again. She reached up with both hands to grip her head.

"Never. Drinking. Again."

She managed to stand up slowly, needing desperately to find a bathroom. Something shiny on her desk caught her eye. As she made her way slowly toward it, she saw the scattered lock and tumbler parts piled there, a business card sitting on top of it. Picking it up, she smiled a little at the word *sorry*, then flipped it over, knowing whose it was before she even looked at the name.

"Joel Reichert, Owner," she read out loud. His name was followed by the name of his hotel, the hotel's phone number, and in red, his cell phone number. She noticed her car keys sitting next to the broken lock and smiled.

She set the card down, found the staff bathroom, and after taking care of business, went back into her office. After plucking her purse from the bottom drawer of her desk, she slung it over her shoulder and grabbed her car keys, heading to the stairs toward her car. Her watch told her it was six a.m. and other staff would soon be arriving for the day. She lived fairly close by, but didn't see the point in going home. She had just picked up her dry cleaning the day before, so she knew she had a fresh suit hanging on a hook in the backseat of her car. The nondescript white shirt she wore under her suit yesterday would just have to work again, and she had a pair of spare underwear in her gym bag. She smiled at her resourcefulness, and brought the items back up to her office. She avoided using the elevator because she knew it would make her more queasy than she already was.

Before taking her gym bag and clothes to the onsite gym and using their shower, she glanced once more at Joel's card. She couldn't help but smile again. Why was she so giddy over a damn vampire? She didn't know, but what Mara did know was that he wasn't like any other vampire she'd ever met. This one was mellow and gallant, an old soul who had been nothing but a gentleman to her. She hoped he hadn't fed from her, because then he would truly have found out her secret, and knowing vampires could compel others to forget their assaults, she was sure he hadn't done anything of the sort. She pretty much remembered the entire night.

After pulling her cell phone from her purse, she was relieved to see she had about twenty-five percent battery left. She punched Joel's number in, and sent him a text message: *You owe me a new lock.*

Tossing the phone back into her purse with a smirk, she chanced a glance at her door where there was now a perfectly round hole instead of a doorknob. Looking around her office, she spied an unopened box of 16x20 picture frames she'd ordered and propped the box up against the door to hide its missing knob. She'd call Maintenance later and have it replaced, and hoped she could make up a good enough lie to appease the old handyman.

Mara took the stairs to the gym and was happy to see it empty. As she stepped into the hot shower, she knew Joel wouldn't get her text until much later, but she didn't mind. She knew he had to sleep all day. It was almost in the vampire's nature to fall dead to the world once the sun came up. She needed that time to sort through what she was feeling. She was still surprised that she was even considering seeing Joel again. Not that they'd been on a proper date, just that he was so different from anyone — human or otherwise — she had met in a very long time.

Mara never let herself get too close to anyone. Her secret curse had made sure of that. But she'd been alone too long and was growing weary of making excuses as to why she couldn't be loved or love someone back. She was tired of being alone. She got hit on by men, it seemed like every day, but always had to shoot them down. Letting the hot water wash away her fears, she smiled through the spray of water and felt an excitement build in her belly.

Her thoughts drifted to Nolan and Kovah, feeling a pang of sympathy for both the hybrids. After all, she could relate to them on some level. They both seemed to be alone and struggling in that part of their lives. But more than that, she knew they were grappling with things a lot deeper than loneliness and needing love. They both—especially Nolan—seemed to be growing more lost as they floated through life. Kovah seemed a bit more grounded, but Mara had noticed he just expelled his frustration in the form of anger, resentment, and flippancy. She frowned, hoping Nolan wouldn't turn that cynical. There was still time for him. She remembered hearing the hybrids having a conversation about a relationship Nolan was in, and she hoped the succubus's twin would be strong enough to calm his stormy soul. Whatever was left of it, that was.

After shutting off the water, she dried off and wrapped the towel around her. She quickly dressed in one of the staff restroom stalls, and then squeezed out her long, black hair into the sink one more time before heading back to her office to scrounge up a brush and ponytail elastic.

The office was still dark and quiet as she made her way down the hall. It was then she noticed the main door to the stairwell that led to her floor was also sporting a broken lock. "Dammit, Joel!" she murmured, making a mental note to get that one fixed, too. With her fuzzy brain beginning to clear, she also realized she'd have to get the lock to the accounting department fixed as well. "How the hell am I gonna explain three broken locks?" she muttered to herself as she opened her office door.

"I can be very persuasive, if you let me," Joel said, sitting at her desk.

She gasped and dropped the towel she'd been holding.

"It's too bad you had dressed already," he remarked, his gaze lazily drifting up and down her body.

Staring at the window, she could see Joel had closed the blinds and had hung her giant blue DOJ blanket over it to keep the sun out. Regaining her composure, she pointed at it. "You like to live on the edge, don't you?"

Joel glanced at the window, then back at Mara. "Not really. But there's something about you that makes me want to take risks and walk a little on the wild side."

Raising her eyebrows, she quickly recovered and said, "Aren't you supposed to be sleeping like the dead right about now?"

He grinned and nodded, standing up from her chair. "I am. And I will. I just wanted to give you a proper goodbye. I felt bad leaving you on that lumpy sofa." He looked at her office couch.

She lifted a shoulder in a shrug, suddenly self-conscious that she was standing there with dripping hair and no makeup. She went to her desk, pulled a hairbrush from the bottom drawer, and began detangling her long hair. "I slept fine. Thank you for taking care of me. Now, how are you gonna get home without frying in the sun?"

Walking slowly to her, Joel took the brush from her and finished brushing through her hair slowly.

She closed her eyes. It had been forever since somebody else had brushed her hair. Once all the knots were out, he said from behind her back, "My driver, Tommy, is here with our van. He's waiting in the parking garage for me. I'll be fine for the few blocks' drive to the hotel. We also have a parking garage, of course."

She turned around and looked into his face. "Why didn't you take me back to your room last night?"

He smiled and smoothed a wet strand of hair from her shoulder. "Because that's not how I operate. You and I need to take things slow, Mara Shields. It seems we both have a lot to lose." Without any further hesitation, he leant down and kissed her softly on the lips. "Goodnight."

She watched him walk out and whispered, "Good day."

Joel took the elevator down to the garage, and, as promised, his assistant Tommy was waiting by the black, windowless van. He opened the back sliding door and helped Joel in, where he sat in one of the seats attached to the back wall and rode silently to his hotel.

The smile he was still wearing from the kiss he'd shared with Mara quickly faded as he realized what was he hadn't been able to put his finger on. Her scent. Now that all the perfume had all been washed away, she didn't smell quite right. She didn't smell like a normal human. In fact, she didn't really smell all that human at all.

 Chapter 9

ALLIES AND ENEMIES

Nolan

I stormed out of the bar and angrily yanked the key from my pocket. I slung my leg over the seat of my Ducati, but a split second before I started the ignition, I looked up and saw a shiny red Corvette parked in the corner of the lot. Standing against it was none other than the hot blonde vampire from the bar.

I shook my head and realized I wanted nothing to do with her. I was so fueled with rage and sadness, I suddenly couldn't care less about the health and welfare of the pretty vampire. They could stake her for all I cared. I looked down and pressed both hands to the side of my head, frustrated at the war of both thoughts and emotions that were battling inside me. One minute I cared about what happened to her — that would be the Old Nolan, the one I was familiar with, the one my family and friends knew and loved. Then there was this New Nolan, the one who was way too close to matching the personality of Kovah.

The thought disturbed me deeply, but before I had time to mull it over any longer, I sensed a presence next to me. Looking up, I saw her standing there.

"Hey, good lookin'."

I stared at her, not sure what to say. Gone was the rage, replaced by curiosity. "What's up, vampire?"

The look on her face was completely worth it. I tipped my head back and howled in laughter. My laughs, however, were halted when a searing pain ripped its way through my jaw. Opening my eyes, I saw the blonde had one strong hand gripping both sides of my face. One side was still sore from where Kovah had landed his punch, and I tried to shake out of her grip by snapping my head to the side.

"What did you just call me?" she bit out.

I continued to shake and pull my head from side to side. Then I smacked her hand away, a new guild of confidence beginning to seep its way into my backbone. Chuckling, I responded, "You heard me."

"Get away from him!" we both heard someone holler.

We looked up to see Kovah and the Riders come bolting out of the bar, headed in our direction.

"Shit!" the vampire said.

She went to run away, but I grabbed her by the back of her top. "Get on!" I jerked a thumb behind me.

She didn't need to be told twice. She hopped on my bike, gripped me around the waist, and soon we were whizzing away at incredible speed before Kovah or any of the Rebel Riders could reach us.

"Where are you taking me, handsome?" she purred into my ear.

"I don't know, be quiet and let me think."

She totally ignored my order and replied, "I have a place a few blocks from here if you're… interested."

Sighing, I conceded, deciding that was the best place to try to get my head together. "Fine, lead the way."

She gave me turn-by-turn directions until we reached a small house sitting at the end of a cul-de-sac. It had an immaculate lawn, brightly colored flowers lined the front walk, and more were staged perfectly in two planter boxes below each of the front windows. The house looked to be older but renovated, two peaks on either side painted white, striking against what looked to be dark-green paint on the rest of it.

"Park your bike in there." She pointed to a small utility shed behind the house.

I killed the engine once I got to the front of the house. Walking my bike to the back, I put the kickstand down by the back door. "I'm not putting it in that shed. It'll be fine here."

She shrugged with a grin. "Suit yourself, big boy."

I followed her up the path to the back door. She pulled a silver key from the small purse slung across her body and used it to unlock the door.

Once inside, I stiffened. The inside did not remotely match its cheery outer appearance. Every window was covered in black paint and had heavy drapes lining them. But that part did not surprise me. As we passed through a small but modern kitchen, we reached a living room. The walls were blood-red, and I could see what looked like some type of swing made of leather hanging from where it was bolted to the ceiling. There was also a wall of medieval-looking weapons and torture devices that took up the entire eastside wall. The carpet was dark and there was a large TV mounted to the wall in the corner of the room.

I decided I had seen enough. Turning around, I headed for the back door without a word.

She gently grabbed my arm and smiled. "Don't be scared. I only use these things to play with other vampires. And willing, consensual humans."

"That supposed to make me feel better?" I pointed to the devices. "You're one twisted chick."

She laughed. "No, I just do this for fun. To get my aggression out, that sorta thing. I live here alone. I'm harmless. I don't ever kill my food. I enjoy them, they enjoy me, I feed, make them forget, then send them on their way, satisfied and happy. I'm proud to say I've never taken a human life."

"Oh—did you think I was human?" I asked, my arms folded over my chest.

She went to a small wine rack in her kitchen and pulled out a bottle of dark red wine. After grabbing two glasses from the cabinet, she poured them both half-full and walked back to me, handing me one.

"Honestly? In the bar, at first I thought you were. But when I got on the bike, I could smell you and hear your heartbeat. You don't smell human, but your scent isn't quite vampire, either. It's admittedly piqued my curiosity. So before we make love, I'd like to know what that's about."

I laughed and set the wine glass down without even looking at it. "Look, lady, we're not doing anything of that sort. You're not biting me, either. I'm not human and I'm not a vampire. I'm something in between, and even I haven't figured it out."

She sipped from her glass and regarded me thoughtfully. Her curious stare made me shift uncomfortably. I wanted to bolt, but realized I needed the safety and anonymity of her house for a while until I could figure things out. I just hoped she had no plans on hurting me. I didn't want to go along with her perverted plans, but I realized maybe I should be a little nicer to her. I opened my mouth to apologize, but she beat me to it.

"Look, I'm sorry to have assumed. You're one of those hybrids, aren't you? I've heard about you, but know nothing about the type. So, were you born like that?"

I shook my head. "Nope, not at all."

"Something happened when you were being turned?" she asked.

I lifted a shoulder and let it fall. "Something like that."

The vampire lifted a hand to touch my face in sympathy, but I flinched back. "I'm sorry. I'm… I'm just going through a lot right now."

She chuckled and sat on her black leather couch, crossing her legs very ladylike. "Sit, take a load off. You sure you don't want that drink?" She indicated the untouched wine glass with a small nod.

I shook my head and took a deep breath before asking, "No, but do you have any blood?"

She set her now-empty glass down. "Honey, what do you think is in the glass?"

Both eyebrows hit my hairline. I went back to the table where I'd left it and sniffed the contents. It definitely was not wine, and without a second thought, I downed the entire glass in one big gulp.

"Well, I can see why you're so grouchy. You shouldn't go so long between nourishments." She laughed softly.

I wiped the corner of my mouth with my thumb. "It's not like I have unlimited access to blood whenever I want it. In fact, I've only had it three times, and all three times it was offered to me in a cup or a bag. I don't have any fangs." I lifted my upper lip for proof.

She stared at me in horror and got right up in my face. "Oh, my God. How are you supposed to eat?"

Taking a step back so I was out of her space, I scrubbed a hand along the back of my neck. "I don't know. I still eat human food, though. But just not the same stuff. Mostly meat and vegetables."

"Well, you're lucky. I don't even remember what food tastes like. Blood and liquids are all I can digest."

All I could do was nod. Kovah had told me that vampires couldn't eat food, and she'd just confirmed it.

A strange silence blanketed the air between us, and she finally broke it by saying, "I'm Janice, by the way. What's your name, sweetie?"

I gave her a tired smile. "Nice to meet you. I'm Nolan."

"I do like that name. Any reason your parents chose it?"

The question had never been asked by anyone before, and I was happy to explain. "Well, the NOLA is short for New Orleans, and supposedly I was conceived there. So they thought Nolan would be an appropriate name. They like to joke that I'm a New Orleans native, even though I've lived here in Shreveport my whole life." I chagrinned.

She got up and took a step toward me, placing her hand on my hard bicep. "That's a cute story. You sure I can't interest you in some fun?" She gestured around the room with a sexy grin. "I have a lot of toys, and you seem like you'd be a very good student—a good sub."

Admittedly, Janice was sort of turning me on. My skin was flushed hot, and I suddenly began picturing myself doing all sorts of things with the blonde. My body began to wake up a little and I realized it must have been the blood. It always made me feel alive and even a little buzzed. I wondered if a temporary distraction with Janice might help relax me a little. I let out a hiccup and began to laugh. "Sorry."

She smiled at me again. "Nothing to be sorry for. I think we could have some fun. I won't bite, I promise. And I mean that quite literally." She lifted her glass. "This has me sated, and honestly, now a little aroused." Leaning up on her tiptoes, she put her pouty lips to my right ear, her hand resting on my shoulder. "I can see and feel that you want me, too."

Fuck.

I suppressed a shudder as I felt my body respond to her. Dragging her mouth from my ear, across my cheek, and to my lips, she breathed cool breath into my mouth, almost as if she were waiting for me to lean in and devour her.

I wanted to. I wanted to so fucking badly.

"Shit," I whispered, slowly prying myself back from her. She lifted her eyes and looked up into mine, and I could see the crystal-blue was gone, replaced by black.

That woke me up real fast.

Reminded of Eva, Charity, and this whole nightmare I'd been living, I whirled around and punched a wall, which was, ironically very much padded. This disturbed me further, but I didn't have time to analyze or care why she had padded walls in this freakshow of a living room.

"What did I do?" she asked innocently. "Was it my eyes?"

Without turning around, I nodded. "Yes."

She chuckled softly. "Yours were black, too. Or getting that way. You are one interesting hybrid, Nolan."

I turned around slowly to see her eyes looking normal again. "Tell me somethin' I don't know."

"So, I'm curious… why you were hanging out with those bikers. They looked a lot older than you. One of them your daddy?"

Ignoring the question, I replied, "Look, stay away from those guys. They're vampire hunters. The one in the dark glasses, he's a hybrid like me, but he hates vamps. Seriously, don't go in that bar again. They hang out there all the time."

She nodded. "I didn't know. Thank you."

I realized she didn't really speak like she was from the South. "Where are you from?"

Grinning a little, she sat down and said, "Oh, here and there. I settled in Shreveport about six months ago. Didn't quite pan out the way I'd planned, though."

I cocked my head to the side, happy she was talking and not coming on to me. I needed the distraction. "Why, what happened?"

She lifted her empty wine glass. "Can you get me some wine? I mean, real wine, not blood. There's some white zin in the fridge."

"Sure," I said, grabbing her glass and heading to the stainless-steel fridge in her small, modern kitchen. Her fridge only had wine bottles in it, about a dozen. I located the clear bottle of pink liquid and poured the glass full, carrying it back to her.

"Thank you," she said before taking a sip.

I nodded. "Go on with your story. You're helping me chill out a bit. Been feelin' all twitchy and stuff."

She grinned. "That's normal, blood is like a drug, the same way some food is like a drug to humans. Like sugar. You'll calm in a few. Plus, your adrenaline was high after the bar fight."

"You're right."

She took a deep breath she didn't need and set the wine glass on her leg. "I lived in California for about thirty years before I moved here. My husband, he died about ten years ago."

I frowned. "I'm sorry. How did he die?"

Piercing me with a stare, she said, "Old age. He was human. We were married for fifty years. I did not choose to be turned, by the way. I was attacked. But after it happened, he accepted it, but refused to become one of us himself. We had a wonderful fifty years, but it was time for him to go. He was so very sick at the end."

Sadness blanketed the room and I suddenly felt a mountain of sympathy for this woman — this vampire. I wanted to ask her about her transformation, but remembered my sister's words of wisdom. *Be slow to speak and quick to listen, especially where women are involved. Don't talk over a woman, it's rude. Let her speak.* I missed Natalie. I'd have to go visit her soon.

Janice bolted me out of my musings by continuing. "So about a year after he died, I was bored and lonely and wandered into a club one night. I didn't realize what type of club it was until I was already on my second drink at the bar. A man approached me, introduced himself, bought me a drink, and then asked if I was a 'sub' or a 'dom.' I had no clue what he was talking about. My eyes were very much opened that night after he took me home and showed me just how dominant I could be.

"I enjoyed myself so much, I began to really get into the lifestyle. I went on the internet and found chat rooms and discussion boards I could ask questions and get information from. I even met a few men and women online and stayed good friends with them."

I was a bit shocked that she was telling me this, but it was interesting to me, so I just nodded at her to continue.

"About a year ago, I met a man online named Tom. He lived here in Shreveport. We met in person a couple of times, and started to have feelings for each other. I decided I'd been in California long enough and realized I needed a change. I moved here to be with Tom."

She stopped again as a forlorn expression took over her pretty face.

"Where's Tom now?" I asked cautiously.

Looking up, Janice said, "He's dead."

My eyebrows dipped together. "I'm so sorry. How did he die?"

"Tom was human. I didn't tell him what I was until I had to. Not being able to eat food or go out during the day are not things you can hide from a person for very long. Tom was surprisingly open, and he wanted me to turn him. But he died in a car accident before I could." She swallowed hard and looked as if she was going to cry.

I got up and indicated for Janice to stand. She did, and I wrapped her in a hug. "I'm so sorry, Janice. You've had it rough, haven't ya?"

She nodded and sat back down. If vampires could cry, she'd be leaking buckets by now. But I had never seen a vampire cry, and heard they couldn't. That had to be very frustrating.

"So, that is my sad story. As you can see, I'm still very much into the lifestyle, still hoping to find my one true sub for all eternity. Are there any BDSM clubs around here?"

"What is BDSM?"

She sighed. "Never mind, I'll keep asking around."

"Good idea. Just stay out of the Blue Room. A nasty succubus hangs out there."

Janice nodded. "I know Eva. I went there a few times and hung out with her when I first moved here, but she's pretty wicked and way too bossy. I don't need that in my life. I play by my own rules. How do you know her?"

I chuckled without humor. "She's why I'm this."

Chapter 10

SERVANT OF TWO MASTERS

Charity

I stared at my twin as she and Brad entered the room. I had been sleeping and was woken up by their arguing.

I rubbed my eyes with my shackled hand and sat up on the plain mattress I'd been curled up on. The night sky outside my prison window was still black, and I didn't feel like the dawn was anywhere near coming. There were no clocks in my room, so the world outside was the only way to tell time.

"What do you want?" I groaned.

Eva and Brad turned their heads toward me.

"Shut up and let me think," Eva snapped.

"Eva, just let me out of here, okay? I can't do this. Either kill me, or let me out. I'm tired, hungry, and I'm going crazy in here. I need a bath, too"—I stopped mid-sentence and slammed my eyes shut. Wait a minute… hadn't I just been in the bathroom trying to sneak out? I shoved a hand into my mass of thick curls and could feel it was damp. As were my clothes. What happened?

"Think, Charity, think," I growled, gripping my hair by the scalp in frustration.

"Who's she talking to?" Brad asked nobody in particular.

The amusement in Eva's voice was evident. "Probably herself. She's always been a little strange," she said in an exaggerated whisper clearly meant for the whole room to hear.

I opened my eyes in rage and looked up at the pair. "Where's Boris at?"

Brad's face was colored in confusion, but Eva's continued to look smug. "Why? You want him? He's hot, right? Well, guess what? He doesn't like girls."

She seemed to get way too much satisfaction by delivering that news to me, and I just grew even angrier. "No! I want to know what the hell he did to me!"

Eva's smug expression left her face. "What do you mean? Did he feed from you? I will kill him. I swear to God—"

She moved at an unnatural speed to my bedside, which made me gasp and shrink back in fear. She wrenched my head to the side and looked at my neck.

I pushed her away and looked at my sister in horror. "No, he didn't feed from me! And you're not going to, either. And neither is that asshole." I pointed in Brad's direction.

"Hey!" he protested, looking hurt.

Eva smirked, but then regained her serious composure. "Listen, little bitch, stop thinking you're in control here, because you're not. I have a reason for keeping you here, and only when I deem it necessary, will you get to leave. Do you understand me?"

I nodded my head and rested it on my knees, trying to keep from crying again. I wasn't even sure I had any tears left in my dehydrated body. "Just let me go home, Eva. Please."

Eva got up off the bed. "Only when I deem time, sister."

"If you're gonna keep me locked up in here, you're gonna have to treat me a little better, Eva. Daily showers, food more than once a day, some kind of fan or air in this room. It's stiflin' hot in here. It's cruel," I drawled through the space between my knees where my face was still buried.

After a couple of seconds of silence, Eva said, "Nah, you'll live. Now quit your whinin' and be happy we're feeding you at all."

When I heard the door close, I screamed, "I hate you, Eva! I hate you! You are dead to me!"

"Love you, too!" she called through the door with a laugh.

I must have fallen asleep, because when I woke, the sun was shining in through the window. I got up and went over to it. I peered down at the swamp lying at the bottom of the mansion. For the hundredth time, I wondered how in the hell I was going to get out of here. It was obvious my boyfriend wasn't going to rescue me. He clearly did not even know I was even here. I sighed in frustration as I saw a ripple in the water at the base of the house. A gator popped its head up out of the water and opened its huge jaws, almost seeming to scream up at the bright sun that was pounding down onto the earth.

Realizing nothing would be making its way into its mouth, the alligator sank back into the water in defeat, probably hopeful he would get lucky next time he popped his head up for a meal.

I shuddered at the sight, then tried to look to the right, to the back of the house. There was nothing there. Just more grass, swamps, and that ugly rusted toolshed. I sighed at all the potential weapons I could use in there to free myself. Perhaps a rope or chain to propel myself down out of my tower like Rapunzel—after I used a rake or shovel to shatter the window. I could even use the shovel to take Brad's head off. I gagged a little at the mental image.

But none of those things would happen, because I was still stuck up here, with no hope of escape.

Slinking my way back to my bed, I plopped down and swiped a hand across my sweaty forehead. I wished I had something to drink, then remembered the Coke can. Reaching under the dirty pillow, I pulled it out and examined the empty can. Flipping it over, I peered at the bottom of it. It was nothing but shiny silver aluminum with a tiny imprint of numbers. Strange to think I'd never looked at the bottom of a soda can before—I'd never had reason to. Now I was studying it as if my life depended on it.

Pushing on the bottom with my thumb, I could see that it could easily give way, as thin as the aluminum was. I lifted my head and looked around the room for anything sharp I could use for a cutting tool. I peered at the metal legs of the bed, which almost resembled an old 1940s type hospital bed, but there was no way I could rip one of the pieces off and use it. I looked at my shackles, where there was plenty of metal, but there was nothing sharp enough on there to cut aluminum with.

I bet the key that opens these would be sharp enough, I thought.

Looking at the bed legs again, I could see they were rough-hewn and partly rusted, and a thought began to float around in my brain. Setting the pop can down, I spread all ten fingers out before me and stared at my nails. Due to my current circumstances, they had all grown longer than I usually liked, and just like my nails had been doing, an idea began to grow.

Chancing a glance at the door, and not seeing or hearing any movement, I went to the floor and sat cross-legged in front of the bed. I slowly lifted my index finger and began filing it along the gruff metal of the bed leg. I seesawed my fingernail back and forth along its edges, intent on turning my index fingernail into a dagger fit for Catwoman. Smiling through my exhaustion, I examined my fingernail, then began sliding the other side of it along the rusted metal.

It felt like hours as I sat there sharpening my nail, but I knew it had been mere minutes. I held my clear, pale nail up to the light from the window and could see its wicked point glinting. A weary smile twisted on my lips as I decided I had what I needed to perpetrate part two of my not-so-diabolical plan.

Before I could stand up, however, the door to the room creaked open. I didn't even look over at the door. I just continued sitting cross-legged and closed my eyes. Resting my hands palm up on my thighs, I hoped whoever it was would just leave.

"What is going on in here, little human?"

Recognizing Boris's harsh accent and spicy cologne, I didn't reply.

I felt his footsteps thud a few times, but I kept my eyes shut in the hopes he would just leave me alone.

"You okay there, Miss Charity?" Boris asked.

I somehow trusted Boris, though I wasn't sure why. I knew I had to be on guard at all times with these bloodsuckers due to their ability to charm women. Although deep down in my gut, I had a feeling Boris wouldn't harm me intentionally.

I took a deep breath, and with eyes still closed and hands palms-up on my thighs, I said, "I'm meditating, Boris. What do you want?"

"Meditating?" he questioned. "You Americans and your silly hippie traditions." I heard him set a tray on the floor near the door. "Here is your meal. You can eat it whenever."

"Thank you," I said quietly as I turned around to look at him.

I watched as he stood just short of the large square block of sunlight the window had created. He looked down at it, then took a step backward. He then smiled tightly at me, looking tired, then left the room, closing the door behind him.

I breathed a sigh of relief and quickly hopped back up onto the bed, grateful Boris hadn't seen or commented on the Coke can, which was still sitting on the bed.

Anxious, I glanced one last time at the door of my prison, then back to the soda can.

On my fourth day—or was it my fifth?—I decided it was just easier to sleep during the day and stay up at night, keeping a vampire's schedule. Plus, it was cooler at night, if even just a little. *If you can't beat 'em, join 'em,* I had murmured to myself upon falling asleep in the middle of the afternoon the day before out of pure boredom.

Flickering my eyes open, I glanced toward the window and could see it was nighttime. Yawning, I sat up and stretched. Then I wandered into the bathroom to take care of business. After looking longingly at the sink I couldn't reach thanks to my shackle, I sighed and flushed the toilet three times. Blowing out a breath, I reached in and splashed some water from it on my face and scrubbed it as best I could with my hands. I contemplated taking a drink, as I was so very thirsty, but figured I wasn't quite that desperate enough—yet. After I was done, my shackle and I wandered over to the window. Taking a deep breath in anticipation of the shoulder pain, I stretched so I could see down.

Gasping but not crying out at the feeling that my shoulder just may dislocate, I tried my best to ignore the pain and leered down into the swamp and the rest of the property. I could see nothing but a still, quiet night, and the chorus of Louisiana crickets was loud.

Sighing, I went back to my bed and looked at the door to my cell. It was still, so I carefully pulled out the Coke can hidden under my pathetic pillow. With the sharp point of my fingernail, I mashed it into the bottom of the can and smiled in triumph as it punctured easily enough. With the hole I'd made, I sliced a line around the bottom of the can, taking time to look up at the door and listen for sounds as I went about my chore. Moving very slowly and stealthily, I worked until the bottom of the can gave way and the silver disk landed in my lap.

After sliding the can under my pillow, I flipped the sharp, silver disc over and over between my fingers as another plan formulated in my mind. I no longer cared anything at all about the fate of my once-human twin, but more than that, I was going to kill her creepy and annoying lover first, showing Eva what real pain was before I ended my sister—and my prison stay—once and for all.

I wasn't sure if Eva was capable of emotional pain, or even emotions at all, but I sure as hell was going to try to make her feel *something*. And may God have mercy on any soul, alive or undead, who got in my way.

Chapter 11

SEARCH & RESCUE

Joel

I lay awake in the pitch black of my room. My eyes were open when I should be dead for the day. I could feel the sun's deadly rays blazing right outside of the massive window that sat just to my right. I rolled over and looked at it. Fitted with a custom-made shade that resembled a massive hurricane shutter, the window was also covered in heavy red blackout drapes that I had put on every window in my hotel.

Living in the penthouse suite, I never let anyone but my assistant and a few occasional human meals come up here. My office and the suite were the only dwellings here, and that was how I liked it. Not requiring a kitchen, I kept only a wine fridge for blood bags and wine. I had a small bathroom with a luxury tub connected to the room. An adequately sized closet to hold my suits and shoes sat next to it.

Tired, but feeling restless, I rolled over again and thought of Mara. I was perplexed as to not only how she could be anything but human, but also as to why I didn't figure it out right away. Lifting my hands to my nose, I smelled the perfume still lingering there and realized that was why. While I loved women and everything about them, I didn't care for all the false scents they usually wore. I had noticed Mara's was particularly strong with something expensive and chemical, and just figured she liked wearing designer perfume. But after her shower, she hadn't smelled like anything but soap, which had faded quickly. Her natural scent wasn't human. It had a hint of vampire mixed in, and I realized I'd even smelled it somewhere before—that mix of human and vampire.

As I was finally beginning to slip into sleep and my eyes slid closed, my mind drifted to the hybrids, Nolan and Kovah, and wondered what was going on with those two. They seemed like they were up to something, and while I knew that Nolan would probably eventually kill the succubus who had made his life a living hell, I wondered why I didn't feel the strange pang of sadness at the thought of Eva's impending death that I should have. I'd created her, after all. Not that I had created many vampires, less than six at my last count, but when two of them had been murdered a couple of decades ago, I had felt sad at their deaths. The thought of Eva being destroyed did not make me sad, though. The only thing I felt about Eva was regret.

I'd had no idea that turning a red-haired, blue-eyed human female into a vampire would result in her becoming a succubus. When I'd found out about a year later that that was what had happened, I'd felt remorse. I now realized I should have just killed her. It was my duty, after all. And now, as I lay here, I wondered if I shouldn't just do that now. Prevent her from making more victims.

I remembered having to clean up one of her messes last year. She'd stolen the soul of a particularly large and buffed man she'd met at the gym. Stalked was more like it. I could only imagine Eva dressed up in exercise clothing and pretending to work out at some 24-hour gym while looking for a soul to steal. She'd apparently set her sights on one very good-looking meathead who had been bench-pressing with his buddies. From what I remembered, the human had been about *six-foot-four and full of muscle.* I chuckled at the reminder of the popular 80s song. *Great, now I'll have that damn song stuck in my head.*

My smile faded when I remembered the havoc this newly made, feral vampire had caused Shreveport. I had told Nolan and Kovah that I hadn't had anything to do with Eva after her turning, but that had been a bit of a fib. I hadn't felt the need to try to explain myself to the two young hybrids. I closed my eyes at the memory.

"Joel, oh, my God, you have to help me!" Eva screeched over the phone.

Pulling the cell phone back from my ear, I said, "Calm down, what did you do now?"

"This vampire, he just won't die! I didn't mean to," she sobbed.

Rolling my eyes, I said, "Where are you?"

"In my parents' club!" she drawled through her sobs. "He found me here."

"You need to get yourself some security," I murmured.

"Come help me, please! I was able to get him out of the club, but he's chasing people around the parking lot!"

"Shreveport is a five-hour drive from Nawlins, darlin'. I suggest you put a

stake through his heart and end him."

"He's too big! I tried! My friends and I tried! He's so strong!" She sobbed some more.

"Call some more friends. I'll be there when I can."

I hung up and called my assistant in. "Tommy, get my plane ready to leave Armstrong, we're heading to Shreveport. And get Ansel over here."

Nodding, my young human assistant said, "Yes, sir."

An hour later, the three of us were in my small private plane, buckling in. The human pilot I kept on-call looked back from the cabin. "Everyone buckled in?"

"Yes, Andrew," I replied.

As the plane took off, Ansel, always with his business face on, said, "So what is the plan here? We gonna just kill this vamp out there in public?"

I was looking out the window as the plane lifted off. "Yes. Then we bamboozle the onlookers, and get back home before the sun comes up."

"Sounds like a real solid plan." Ansel chuckled.

Forty-five minutes later, the small plane touched down on a private airfield in Shreveport. A black car was waiting for us on the tarmac. I felt the hot, humid nighttime summer wind hit me in the face. Looking at my Rolex, I noted the time: 1:52 a.m.

Tommy stayed with the plane and pilot to make sure they'd not run into any issues parking a fairly large plane on an unused airstrip. I knew it was unlikely, but I wanted Tommy there just in case. Besides, he'd not be of any help to us, anyway.

Ansel looked at me from the backseat. "You wear a Rolex with your jogging suit?"

I cut a sideways glance at my oldest friend and gestured to my body. "I barely had time to put this on."

"Well, that outfit is ugly as fuck," Ansel responded.

We both heard the driver chuckle from the front. I ignored him. "Excuse me if I don't like wearing dungarees and T-shirts."

Ansel looked down at his vintage Eagles concert T-shirt and Levis. "What? Just trying to fit in. We are going to a nightclub, aren't we?"

Gesturing with my head, I said, "That is not what we used to wear to nightclubs, is it?"

Ansel smiled, and as he was about to comment with a memory, the car came to a jerking stop and we heard a blood-curdling scream. Lifting our heads, our eyes went wide as we took in the scene in front of us. Eva was on the back of the giant, newly-made vampire as if getting a piggyback ride, and the vampire was spinning around, trying to get her off. She had one arm around his neck to hold on and the other was pounding him with her tiny, pale fists. One of her friends, a tall blonde vampire resembling a Barbie doll, was trying to get a clear shot to stab the feral vamp with the heel of her stiletto.

A few humans were hanging around the parking lot with their mouths open. Some had cell phones out and were filming or taking pictures. I told myself I was going to have to worry about them later.

Ansel and I didn't know whether to laugh or just sit and watch. Obviously, we couldn't just sit there, so we both exited the car at preternatural speed and sped into the melee.

I pulled Eva off the vampire's back and told her to take her friends and start compelling the dozen or so humans in the parking lot to go home. She screamed to her blonde friend to come with her, and Ansel and I took off after the crazy vamp. He had run off, but he was too young and too bulky to be faster than us. Catching up to him quickly, Ansel tackled the guy to the ground and pinned his arms to the rough concrete. He tried looking into his eyes to compel him to calm, but the vampire's eyes were darting wildly around, like a trapped animal.

He roared at Ansel, "Get off me! Get off me!"

He managed to get one hand free and punched Ansel in the mouth. Ansel pinned his hand back down, but not before laying his own punch on the vamp's face in return.

"Get off me!" he roared again.

Ansel just smiled down at him.

I could see he had dried blood all around his mouth and nose and his fangs were still out. I glanced back and could see Eva and her friend had gathered the humans in a circle and were collecting their cell phones. I turned back around when I heard the vampire clear his throat. A large wad of red spit was hurtled at Ansel's face and began oozing down his cheek.

"You stupid motherfucker," Ansel said, drawing a knife from the small of his back.

He raised it up, but I grabbed his arm. "Can't he be helped? Tamed?"

The vampire tried bucking Ansel off, but my friend held fast. "Keep still."

"Fuck you!" the vampire yelled.

Ansel looked at me, then back at the vampire, whose eyes were now wildly darting around again and jet-black. "Look at me," he commanded.

In the brief second their eyes met, Ansel said, "Calm down. Listen to me."

The vampire briefly stopped resisting and his whole body relaxed. Ansel looked at me. "This will work for, like, five minutes, then it'll wear off. I can't compel vampires that well. Especially these types."

"I didn't mean temporary control. I mean like training."

"No, they're like wild animals. Sorry, man."

Lifting the knife, Ansel plunged it into the vampire's chest, which provoked an ungodly screech from him.

I turned away, not wanting to watch.

Ansel jumped from his body and watched as the sluggish black ooze pooling around him had slowed, and the body slowly began to shrink in size. It didn't quite shrivel, and it certainly didn't turn to ash, but it did take on the appearance of a very dead corpse.

"Great, just great. He's too young. Now we have to dispose of his body." I sighed.

"I'll take care of it, man. You" – Ansel pointed to Eva and the group – "take care of that."

"Thanks, my friend," I replied, clapping him on the back.

All the humans were walking woodenly back to their cars when I arrived to Eva. "You hypnotize them?"

"Yes." She nodded. "Even took their phones and wiped out all the videos and pics."

"Okay, then. Listen to me very carefully."

She nodded, wide-eyed.

I shook my head and stared deep into her eyes. "Do not call me to clean up your mess again, you understand me? You steal a soul, you better kill it after you feed from it."

Her face turned angry and she put her hand on her hip. "I tried that before. I fed from this one guy's blood, then took his essence. After he fell asleep, I killed the fucker. Guess what? I was hungry like a week later. It takes a few days to kick in, or something."

Just then, Ansel walked up to us, pointed a finger at her, and said, "Then you keep them locked up, and then kill them. We don't have time for this bullshit!" He pointed behind us.

"Who the hell are you?" she asked, attempting to adjust her wig, which was sticking up and cockeyed after the fight.

"Doesn't matter. We will not be helping you again. Figure this shit out, or do us all a favor and off your fuckin' self."

She let out a gasp and raised her hand to slap Ansel, but the old vampire was way too quick. He grabbed her hand, twisting her wrist. "I don't think so."

She let out a screech and pulled her arm free. She then walked away with her friend in tow, who was holding both shoes in her hand, one with a broken heel.

After Ansel lit the corpse on fire and then tossed it into a dumpster, we went back to the car. I compelled the driver to forget what he'd seen and instructed him to drive back to the airstrip.

Ansel swiped at the dried blood on his lip where he'd been punched and looked at me. "You need to put her down, man."

"Tell me about it," I responded dryly.

Smiling at the memory of my friend, a sadness overtook me as I remembered I'd never see Ansel again. Which brought to mind Nolan again. *Stupid kid,* I mumbled in anger. Then, as my mind began to wonder if drinking a twin's blood really did reverse the curse, a proverbial lightbulb went off over my head and I sat bolt upright in bed.

"Mara's a hybrid!"

GAME PLAN

Kovah

I slammed the door to Nolan's apartment and it rattled in its frame. Then, I took the stone stairs back down two at a time. After briefly scanning the parking lot, I pulled my phone from my pocket. I shot off a quick text to Archie to let him know why Nolan wasn't answering his phone, as I'd seen it in pieces on the floor, and that he wasn't at home.

Archie replied: *He ain't at Charity's either.*

I huffed in frustration and replied: *Nolan's probably at the succubus' mansion. He thinks Charity is being held there.*

Archie: *I don't think he's stupid enough to go there alone.*

Me: *Yes, he really is. Wanna meet there?*

Archie: *No, come to the garage, we need a game plan.*

Me: *Copy, Ghostrider.*

I jumped on my Harley, its rumble rattling the windows of the lower floor apartments as I zoomed off toward Archie's Garage. My mind was a mess as the wind slammed over my face, my eyes shielded by the new sunglasses I had to buy at the gas station on my way to Nolan's. I pressed the gas harder, hoping the noise would block out the thoughts that wouldn't stop flooding my brain.

Yes, I was still livid at Nolan for the tiff at the bar. I couldn't believe how pissed off I'd gotten. And the nerve of him defending that female vampire! Yes, she was hot—super, smoking hot—but what interest did Nolan have in her? Surely not anything in the sex department. I knew the dude was utterly hung up on Charity still, but I wondered if he'd hit that just to fuckin' distract himself. Honestly, if the woman was human, I knew I'd definitely love some bedroom acrobatics with the blonde. She seemed like a wick in need of a flame.

I just couldn't contemplate why Nolan would leave with her — whisking her away on the back of his Ducati. Why would he do this?

Then, I had an epiphany.

"He's just fucking hungry," I murmured to myself as the city lights of Shreveport passed me in a blur.

I couldn't imagine having a bloodlust. I always thought it was disgusting and unnatural when I saw the vampires indulging in it. The thought and sight of human blood made me sick to my stomach. I even once tried to have some sympathy; tried to compare it to when I'd really be craving a cheeseburger or some pizza, and it was two a.m. and everything was closed. But I just couldn't see the correlation between the two. The thought of ingesting blood, the coppery liquid on my tongue and sliding down my throat, was just repulsive to me.

But I'd seen how Nolan had reacted to it when Agent Mara Shields had given him some at the BSI headquarters a few days prior. He had been mean-spirited and peaked-looking before ingesting it. After, Nolan looked and seemed to feel better, albeit, he seemed almost drunk. I didn't want this for my friend, but just as my eyes had lost all their pigment but had gained super-sight, Nolan had also gained a horrible side effect from the succubus's assault, and that was something I had to accept.

It had been twenty years since my accidental encounter with my own succubus and I really didn't have to dig too deep to remember how awful the first few days, weeks, and months had been for me. I needed to go easier on my new friend and help him through this shit. It was still hard for me to control my temper, and I knew I'd probably never get a complete grip on it, but it was something I had come accept. Now this blood-craving business with Nolan was something he would have to accept, too. These things were all the fault of the succubus and the bitch definitely needed to die. All succubi should die. I knew Nolan needed to kill her himself, but I was itching so fucking badly to do it for him.

I reached Archie's Garage, parked my bike, and killed the engine. Archie and two Riders were gathered near the front door.

I strolled up to them. "What's the game plan, guys?"

"I don't think our boy went to that mansion by himself." Archie jerked a thumb at the guy next to him. "Ollie took a drive out there, no sign of his bike or his Charger."

"Well, I could have told you that," I said. "His car's still parked in its spot at his apartment."

Ignoring me, Archie continued, "I really don't know where else to look, except the Blue Room. You don't think he'd go there, do you?"

I shook my head. "No, he wouldn't have anything to gain by going there. Nolan has no need to confront Eva in a public place like that when he knows where she lives."

"Does anyone know who the blonde is he left with?" Archie asked, eyeing each Rider.

Ollie nodded, his salt-and-pepper hair sleeked up into a mohawk-wave on the top of his head. His silver chin-strap beard glinted in the light from the parking lot's overhead lamps. He blew smoke out from the corner of his mouth and then flicked the cigarette on the ground, crushing it beneath his black buckled boot. "That was some chick my buddy Tom used to bang. She's hot, but I found out she's a vamper."

My eyebrows went up. "Your buddy didn't know she was a leech?"

Ollie nodded, shoving his hands into his jeans pocket. "He knew. He told me, but they didn't last long."

"Bet he broke it off with her after that," Archie said smugly.

Ollie pulled out another cigarette from his jeans pocket. "Nope, he smashed his Mustang into the back of a semi on I-10 about a year ago. Such a waste, he was a good dude." Ollie made the sign of the cross along his chest and forehead.

"Better off dead than being with a bloodsucker, I say. He'd be dead eventually, anyway," I murmured.

Archie shoved some dip into his mouth. "You got that right, kid."

I looked at Ollie. "Do you know where that vamp lives?"

He shook his head. "Nah, man. Tom never said. The only thing he ever told me was that they met on the internet."

"Oh, brother," Archie mumbled. "Everyone on that damn internet is crazy. Who knows how many bloodsuckers are hanging out on that thing. I just stay off there unless I need to order parts."

I laughed. "Okay, old man. Let me ask again, what's the game plan?"

"My bet is he's at the blonde's house," Ollie said. "She's one seductive witch. He's probably hittin' that as we speak."

The group made faces of disgust.

"I doubt that. He's pretty hung up on the redhead, but you never know," I said, not quite believing the words coming out of my mouth. I knew he legitimately loved Charity and didn't think he'd waste his time on a cheap piece of ass, but with the way he had been acting, I just wasn't sure anymore.

"I could get her address," Ollie said, blowing smoke out of the side of his mouth. "I just remembered my other bud Donny used to bang her friend, so he can find out where that bloodsucker lives."

I pointed at Ollie's phone, which was clipped to his belt. "Call him."

Nodding, Ollie hit a few buttons and spoke to Donny on the other end of the line with the cigarette still dangling from his mouth.

"I say we let it go for tonight. Bishop's a big boy, he can handle himself. I doubt any vamp could hurt him now with his new symptoms," Archie said.

I shook my head. "You can go, boss, but I'm going after Nolan."

"He's textin' me the address," Ollie proclaimed proudly after he put the phone back on its clip.

Sighing, Archie said, "Okay, we check it out, but if he's not there, we deal with this tomorrow. I'm fuckin' tired."

Chapter 13

CONFESSIONS

Nolan

Janice's eyebrows practically hit her hairline. "You're a succubus vampire?"

I shook my head with a smile. "I'm not a vampire."

"But… you should be. You drink blood. I… I don't get it."

"Yeah, well, nobody gets it. I supposedly should be some whacked-out crazy animal right now, sucking people dry, but I'm not."

"How?" Janice questioned.

I paced the floor. "My girlfriend is the succubus's identical twin. I drank some of her blood."

Janice was still staring at me in disbelief. "You're kidding me."

"I'm definitely not, blondie."

"So you got your soul taken by a succubus and then started dating another one?"

I laughed. "No, her twin is human. A beautiful, perfect human."

"And the twin blood-drinking thing—it just… reversed what she did to you?" Janice asked.

I shrugged a shoulder. "I guess. Although, I'm not exactly the same person, as you have noticed."

"Well, just wait 'til word of this gets out," she murmured.

I chuckled. "Too late. The Department of Justice already knows."

Her eyes went wide. "What!"

"Yep. They know about us, Janice. And other vampires do, too. But I'm not gonna lie. It was kinda awesome when I got to tell this hella old vampire something he didn't know."

She glared at me. "Watch it, dude."

I lifted both hands in surrender. "You know age is just a number. Or so I've been told. I'm just saying… between you and Joel, it's been quite a shock telling those much older than me — in human years, of course — things I would have thought all vampires already knew."

"Yes, well, it's news to me," she said, getting up and putting her glass in the sink. "Who is Joel — ?"

"Hey!" I cut her off and began to pace. "Did you know that there are things besides vampires? There are shifters, some group of immortal cops… oh! And fairies! Freaking fairies. Can you believe that shit?"

Janice was now standing in the living room with her arms folded over her impressive chest. "Yes, I know about all of them. We don't interact much with the other… creatures. They are mostly vile and uncivilized. Not the fairies, they are just strange. But specifically the shifters. Filthy animals. I picked one up from a club one time. My God, he was a beast in the bedroom, and I don't mean that in a good way."

I was staring at her in horror, my jaw hanging open.

She waved a manicured hand. "Oh, don't look at me that way. A person can get lonely in ten years. Cut me some slack."

Realizing my rudeness, I nodded my head and regained my composure. "Sorry about that. I just really haven't gotten out much, apparently."

"I see that," she said dryly. She stared at me for a minute, then said, "So if you're not interested in some of my toys, or even my bedroom, do you have any friends who might be? Human or vampire, I don't mind." Then her smile fell. "Just no shifters."

I laughed, and as I went to reply to her, the doorbell rang.

We both looked at each other.

"Expecting someone?" I asked.

She shook her head. "Nope."

I edged my way to her front door where the doorbell began to chime again. I pulled my buck knife from my boot and gripped it tightly in my fist, then looked at her. "I can't believe you don't have a peephole on your front door. What is the matter with you?"

"Hello, sunlight? I'm not taking any chances." Her gaze flicked to the knife, then back to me.

I snorted at her lame excuse and went to open the door, but Janice jumped in front of me. "Let me."

She cracked the door open slightly, but Kovah pushed it open further and caused her and me to be bowled backward onto our asses. We were both up faster than the human eye could see. Faced with not only Kovah, but Archie and Ollie, they both seemed to be on the defensive. Janice's eyes had gone black, while I just stared in disbelief at my friend.

"What the hell are you doing here, Kovah?" I asked through gritted teeth, my fist gripping the knife tighter.

"Rescuing you, you dumb fuck," he replied, jutting his chin at Janice.

I rolled my eyes. "Okay, first of all, I don't need rescuing — by you or anyone else. Secondly, you just tried to beat my ass in the bar back there, what the hell do you care what happens to me?"

"Kid, you don't just hop on motorcycles with vamps, ya hear me?" Archie said, looking at Janice but talking to me.

I used my knife to point at Kovah and Archie. "You two are out of freakin' control. You need to stop killing vampires just because they are what they are."

Janice stomped her foot. "Hello, I'm standing right here. Stop talking about me like I'm not."

Archie ignored her, and narrowed his eyes at me in disgust. "We don't kill for no reason. Are you telling me this vamper didn't try to feed upon you?"

I lifted my chin in defiance. "No, she didn't. In fact, she didn't do anything to me but offer me a good time. She even fed me."

Kovah lifted a dark eyebrow, which rose above the edge of his black sunglasses. Pointing at an empty wine glass, he replied dryly, "Seriously?"

I laughed. "Yes, seriously."

Archie and Ollie looked confused until Archie asked, "She fed you... wine?"

Kovah looked at Archie, then back at me in question. At Kovah's nod, I took a deep breath and said, "No, boss, Janice gave me blood and I drank it. All of it."

Archie and the other Rider both had their mouths agape in disbelief. "Why… why… why are you drinking blood, son?"

Kovah came over and put his arm around me. Taking off his sunglasses, he pointed to his face. "Arch, you see these freaky eyes? It's what the succubus did to me. I don't know why, and I can't explain it, but it is what it is. Ironically, I can see better now than before it happened." At Archie's reluctant nod, Kovah put his glasses on and continued. "His freaky side effect is a craving for blood. It's totally fucking disgusting, but guess what? It's not his fault. The guy doesn't even have any damn fangs, so he has to get it any way he can."

The two seasoned Riders were still staring at me in disbelief.

I put the knife back in my boot and hung my head. "Sorry, Arch. I… I was gonna tell you, but I didn't know how."

"You don't need to be sorry, dude. You didn't ask for this," Kovah injected.

"Are you people quite finished?" Janice asked, her arms still folded across her chest.

All eyes turned to her, and Kovah bit back a smile, taking in her long bare legs, huge breasts, and full, red, pouty lips. Her blonde hair cascaded down her back and he was looking at her like he wanted to eat her. He slowly circled the room with his gaze, and his mouth kicked up in a wry grin as he took in all the toys.

"This your playroom, kitten?" Kovah fixed his stare on the blonde.

Smiling seductively, she raked her stare from the metal toe of his leather boots to his shaved head and replied, "Yes, it is. You like to play, Little Devil?"

Kovah kept a straight face, but seemed to be resisting a grin. "I'm no devil, sweetheart, but I *can* be your worst nightmare."

Walking to a scary-looking whip with a bunch of balls on it that I'd been eyeing earlier, Janice plucked it from the wall and stroked it lovingly under her fingertips while staring at Kovah. "I would love to see how badly you could punish me," she purred.

A heavy, incredulous silence filled the room.

"Okaayyy, this is getting weird, and just downright disgustin'," Archie finally growled, snatching a tin of chew from his back pocket and then prying off the lid. He shoved a pinch into his bottom lip.

"I agree," I murmured, staring at my buddy, then back at my new friend, Janice. "I'm leaving now. Do you two need a moment?" I pointed back and forth between the two.

Kovah paused a little too long before dragging his face and what the rest of the room assumed was his piercing stare away from the breathtaking blonde and back to his friends. "Uh, no, we'll be going now."

"Well, that's too bad," Janice said breathily. "You know where I live and where I like to unwind if you change your mind, my tattooed friend." She inclined her head toward Kovah's sleeved-up arms with a flirtatious smirk.

Without saying a word, the four of us left the vampire's house of horrors—or were they pleasures?— hopped on our bikes, and drove off into the night.

As we headed toward Archie's Garage, I decided I was too mentally exhausted to join them there for whatever shenanigans they had planned for the rest of the night. I took a quick, sharp left turn and headed toward my apartment while Kovah and the other two kept going straight down the small highway. I didn't care how they felt about me going home. I needed to decompress and get my head straight. I needed to formulate a plot to get Charity back and to figure out this shit called life I'd been unwillingly thrust into.

After killing the engine to the Ducati, I dismounted from the bike. I gave the eerily quiet, warm parking lot a quick scan, sniffed the air, and smelled nothing but the familiar, earthy Louisiana night. I then headed toward the stone steps, practically sprinting up them. Once inside my apartment, I locked the deadbolt and slid the chain home. I threw my keys and wallet on the dining room table, and then wandered into my bedroom.

My clothes were peeled off in no time, and as I started the shower, I stared at my reflection until the steam fogged up the mirror. I didn't like what I saw. Gone was my glowing tan and bright-green eyes, replaced by a pale and sallow skin tone and dull green eyes that were more dying grass rather than a fresh lime waiting to be sliced.

As the scalding water pounded my rock-hard and tense muscles, I ran rough hands over my hair, then over the overgrown stubble on my chin. And if I were being honest with myself, it was more than stubble; in about two days' time, I'd be rocking a pretty impressive close-shorn beard. I briefly contemplated growing out a big, long beard, but decided against it. I also decided that I didn't have the energy to shave what was there, either, and left its shadow glinting along my jawline.

After toweling off and brushing my teeth, I slipped between my cool sheets in nothing but my white boxer briefs. I linked my hands behind my head and stared unseeingly at the ceiling. A quiet war began to rage in my brain as I squeezed my eyes shut, trying to calm the two masters of both vampirism and humanity that were vying for control in my mind, soul, and body.

The memory of the sweet, delicious blood Janice had given me sliding down my throat was fresh in my mind. I'd felt so much better after slamming the thick, red liquid back. It was almost orgasmic how it had satisfied me, made me feel better. I had felt almost normal and even-keeled… my brain and body firing on all pistons simultaneously. But then I remembered back a few weeks ago when I'd been just Nolan Owen Bishop. A college dropout, who loved to restore motorcycles, with a pretty girlfriend and who loved fishing in my spare time. Gone were my carefree days of sitting in the sun on the lake on my parents' boat. My days were now filled with sleeping like the dead—which I now wondered if that expression was more than a cliché—and nights filled with vampire hunting, succubus chasing, and missing persons.

How had my life become this?

Where was my beautiful Charity, and more importantly, where was that vile, evil witch, Eva? As my brain showed me pictures of the succubus as if in a flashing slideshow through my mind, I decided I had to turn off the continuous reel or I'd never sleep. Rage would overtake me and I'd get up and head to the mansion in the swamp and go kill the nasty bitch. So, forcing my attention-deficit mind to relax and shut down, I slowly slid my overly tired eyelids shut and determined that I'd go to the succubus's house tomorrow while it was light out and end this nightmare. Even if Charity wasn't there, I had to know that Eva was dead and maybe, just maybe, I'd get some semblance of peace in this chaotic life of mine.

Chapter 14

BLOW THIS POP STAND

Nolan

I blinked my eyes open then shut them again against the harsh assault of sunlight slicing in through my open blinds. When was I ever going to learn to keep the damned things shut?

Cracking my singed eyes open again, I turned over to look at my alarm clock radio. "Ten a.m.? Holy crap," I groaned.

I slogged out of bed, and then after showering again to wake up, but still not shaving, I threw on black athletic pants, my black LSU T-shirt, and a black and purple LSU ball cap.

As I entered the living room, I spied a piece of paper lying next to my front door. I picked up and read it. *Meet me at Max's at noon. It's a good day for a rescue. –K*

Frowning at the note, I wondered why Kovah had left a note instead of just calling. Then I remembered I didn't have a phone anymore. I made a mental note to hit the cell phone store today and get another.

After snatching up my keys and wallet, I sprinted out the door, gasping at the assault of the late morning sun. I really wanted to take my bike, but realized the Charger would offer more comfort this time of the day from my new nemesis, the sun.

After reaching Max's Deli in record time, I went inside, ordered a club sandwich, and sat at a small, two-person table as I waited for Kovah to arrive. And I didn't have to wait long. Kovah came in just as the server was bringing me my sandwich and pop.

Kovah sat and went to open his mouth to the server, but I cut him off. "You have to order at the counter. They don't normally bring you your food here, but me and Megan go way back." I winked at Megan and she slapped my arm. "Nolan Bishop, you were always such a flirt!" she drawled, walking away in her short-shorts and green apron.

"Nice ass," Kovah said under his breath.

"Yes, she does have a nice ass. She also has two kids under five and a very scary ex-husband."

Kovah chewed the inside of his mouth, as if he was considering taking a chance with the pretty, curly-haired blonde.

"Dude, just go order some food. We need to fuel up. I've been thinkin' up a plan to get into that creepy-ass house and check to see if Charity is there."

Kovah eyed me speculatively and then nodded. He walked to the counter and smiled flirtatiously at Megan, who was biting her lip and flirting right back as he pretended to peruse the menu board.

Munching down on my sandwich, I watched out the window as the fine citizens of Shreveport went about their day. It was a Saturday, so the streets were crowded, probably from the farmer's market that went on in the middle of the street, just like it had for the past twenty-one years I'd been alive.

So normal, so mundane… so human, I thought. I bit back a sigh at the grief that I wouldn't get to have that mundane and normal like all my friends and family. The people I went to high school with, like Megan, who were just living their lives. I looked at the pretty blonde, who was still smiling at Kovah, and smirked when she made a gesture at him to take off his sunglasses. I watched him shake his head from side to side, and then shook my own head. Poor dude must be sick to death of being told to take off his glasses. If I were Kovah, I'd wear colored contact lenses all the time just to avoid the hassle. But hadn't he said they would melt on his eyes, or they were uncomfortable or something?

Looking down at my sandwich, I shoved the last bit of it in my mouth and washed it down with the cold Coke. Just then, Kovah sat in the opposite chair, setting down his little red basket of lunch.

"Really, we're at a deli and you order a burger?" I bit back a smile.

"Fuck off, it was on the menu."

Nodding, I replied, "Okay, you do have a point."

As he shoveled in the first bite, he mumbled, "So what's za pwan?"

I chuckled. "The plan is that we sneak in while they're asleep. If the bloodsuckers wake up, you distract them. You seem to be good at that."

"Fuk opf, Bifop," he replied before swallowing, some sort of orange-looking sauce dribbling down his chin.

"Uh, you have a little something..." I said, pointing at his face.

Swallowing the bite and then taking a gulp of his sweet tea, he said, "Thanks. Now tell me more about your plan."

"I think first we need to have a discussion about what happened at the bar last night."

Kovah laughed and shook his head. He wiped his mouth with a napkin before chomping down on his second bite. "What are we, chicks? Obviously, I went to rescue you from the hot blonde vamp before you banged her. And obviously I'm here right now, wanting to help you rescue your girl. Does it look like I'm pissed off?"

Smiling, I said, "I guess not. I didn't mean to kick your ass, really. I think I was just cranky."

Kovah paused again, the burger at his lips. He set it back down. "First off, motherfucker, you didn't kick my ass. In fact, you didn't even come close to kicking my ass. Secondly, I knew you were cranky. You needed some of the red stuff. I'm glad the vamp gave you some. *You're not you when you're hungry.*" He said the last part, mimicking a commercial.

"Bite me, dude," I replied with sarcasm dripping.

"If I had fangs, I would, asswipe." Kovah laughed.

I was laughing now. "All right, point taken. So once you're done, we're gonna sneak into that creepy-ass mansion. I'd like to kill Eva while I'm there, too."

Kovah smirked at me. "I'd be more than happy to do it for you."

"Something tells me I have to do it."

Nodding, Kovah replied. "I think so too, man. I'll hold her down if you want." He paused, wiping his mouth with a thin paper napkin, then wadding it up, and throwing it into the now-empty red food basket. "Ya know, I was thinking about something. Since your succubus is alive, and mine is dead, it doesn't seem like we should be so similar with our... problems. Right?"

I looked at him thoughtfully, leaning back in the chair and putting my hand behind my head. I had plucked a toothpick from the holder on the front counter when I'd first arrived, and it was now perched between my teeth. "Go on."

"Well, I was just thinking—what if you hadn't had some of your girl's blood? Would you be some crazy lunatic right now? What if you are sort of suspended between human and vampire?"

I stopped chewing on the small wooden stick and leaned forward, the front legs of the chair smacking back onto the ground as I looked around the small deli. I lowered my voice an octave. "Well, isn't that what you are, man?"

Kovah shook his head. "I used to feel like that. Now I just feel like I'm this sort of immortal guy who doesn't need blood or to hide from the sun. It sucks I can't say the same about you."

"But you have suffered a curse, though, haven't you?" I asked slowly.

Nodding, Kovah said, "The freaky eyes, yes."

I paused and took a deep breath. "Aren't you lonely living in this world by yourself? I mean, it has to suck not being able to be in a relationship. And trust me, I get why you avoid chicks for the long term. Like, how would you even explain everything?"

Kovah laughed. "One day I'll find someone who's good enough to be with me. Until then, I can bach it. I'm like the immortal version of George Clooney. Why bother settling down when I can get all the pussy I want?"

I made a face. "You're a beast."

"You can say that again." Kovah snorted.

I raised an eyebrow while sipping the last of my soda. "That wasn't a compliment."

Looking at Megan again, Kovah dragged his gaze away from the blonde and said, "Sure it wasn't. I can get whoever I want, and you wanna be me."

I chuckled. "No, dude, I really *don't* wanna be you. But you just go on thinking that."

"Okay, let's blow this pop stand and go rescue your girl."

I cocked my head to the side before heading toward the exit. "Did you just say 'blow this pop stand'?" Before Kovah could tell me off, I said, "I've got one of my mom's mix-tapes in the Charger if you want to listen to it. Oh wait, I don't have a cassette tape player. Sorry. We can stop by the thrift store and see if they have one of those yellow Walkman things, if you want."

Kovah bit back a smile and punched me in the arm a bit too hard. "Just for that, I'm making you go into the creepy house in the swamp first. And by the way, I know how to download music to my phone, you dick."

Kovah wiped a bead of sweat from his forehead with a cigarette in his hand and peered up at the looming old mansion through his sunglasses. At the peak of the day, the sun was at its highest—and its hottest. I stood next to my friend in my ball cap and mirrored sunglasses, and with my hands low on my hips, looked up at it, too.

"Not sure we should try the back door again."

Kovah took one long, last drag from his cigarette, pitched it into a nearby puddle, then blew smoke out of the side of his mouth. I continued to peer at the front of the house through the tall wrought iron gate. "I agree. So you said you had a plan, Stan."

I raised a pale eyebrow over my glasses. Ignoring my friend's old cliché, I answered, "Yes, we sneak in and kill them all, then rescue my girl. If she's even in there."

"In that order?"

I scrubbed a hand along the back of my neck and said, "What do you think?"

"Well, for sure we kill the bitch first. I will hold her down and I want you to drive that knife into her chest." He indicated to my boot where my weapon was.

I nodded. "What if we alert the others, like that big-ass Russian dude?"

"He's not a 'dude', he's a bloodsucker, and he and his little friend need to die, too."

"Eva's got a boyfriend, his name is Brad. I'm sure he'll be there, too. Maybe even in the same room."

An evil smile found Kovah's lips. "Ooh, goodie! More vampires to kill."

I chuckled. "I knew you were gonna say that."

Clapping me on the shoulder, Kovah said, "You're a good friend."

"Where's your weapon?" I asked him.

Smiling, Kovah reached behind his back and pulled out a strange-looking weapon. Its black body glinted under the Louisiana sun. I thought it resembled a gun, but it had a much wider grip and something lying horizontal across the tip of it. "This is my new baby."

"What the hell is it?" I asked curiously.

"It's a crossbow pistol."

"No shit?" I asked. "Lemme see it."

Kovah handed me his new toy.

"It's light." I tossed it lightly in my hand.

He nodded. "Yep, and that's only the fifty-pound baby so it only weighs about five pounds, but exerts fifty pounds of pressure. Fires about two-hundred feet per second."

"You kill zombies with this thing?"

He shook his head and snorted. "There is no such thing as zombies."

I raised both eyebrows. "Only vampires, succubuses, fairies, shapeshifters, hybrids…"

"Okay, you have a point. And I won't correct you about using the right plural form for succubus."

"Thanks for that," I replied dryly.

We both stared at the crossbow pistol. Finally, I asked, "So, how do you shoot it?"

Kovah waved me over to a copse of trees that lined the fence, where we would be further hidden and I could get out of the sun.

"It's already loaded, so just pop the safety off and point and shoot."

I held it up in Kovah's direction to examine it, but he quickly shoved it away with his hand and glowered at me. He pointed a tree. "Down range, asshole!"

"Shit, sorry."

He shook his head. "Just shoot the damn tree."

Feeling excited, I closed both hands around the pistol and went to lift it, but stopped at Kovah's voice. "One-handed, man. You don't need both."

Nodding, I closed my right eye, and with the pistol gripped in my left fist, I lifted it and aimed at the tree. A small, silver arrow went sailing at incredible speed into the old moss tree, parking itself there with minimal sound. "Wow! No kick."

Kovah laughed. "Yep, it's pretty awesome, isn't it?"

"Can I kill the succubus with this?"

He took the crossbow back from me. "If you're asking if this will kill her, the answer is yes. Anything sharp through the heart will kill the bitch. But if you're asking if I will let you use this to kill her, the answer is no. You need to straddle that filthy, soul-stealing whore and stab it through the heart. It will be much more satisfying."

"You sound like you speak from experience."

Kovah chuckled. "Oh, I do, brother."

I snorted.

We walked to the tree, and with some effort, I yanked the impaled bolt from the rotting but rough bark of the tree and examined it. "Sorta looks like an arrow." Putting my finger to the sharp tip, I was quickly rewarded with a prick of blood. "Ouch!"

"Sharp little fuckers, aren't they?" Kovah chuckled, yanking the bolt from my fist.

"Yep." I followed him back to where we'd been standing. I watched my friend load the pistol once more with the bolt and asked him, "Does it only hold one at a time?"

"Yes, that's why I keep more." He lifted his shirt to reveal something attached to his belt. "I got about a dozen in here."

"Cool. How much this thing cost you?" I asked.

"A few hundred. Totally worth it."

He handed it to me, and I raised it up.

Kovah grabbed my wrist. "You have to cock it."

After he showed me how, I did as I was instructed. I then removed the safety and shot another bolt at the old tree. "Very cool. I want one."

"You'll need to stop spending money on motorcycles first."

"You're one to talk, dick," I shot back.

Smiling, he waved for me to follow him. Once out of the shade of the trees, we looked up once again at Eva's looming house. Then, without another word, we snuck through the front gate, running quickly to the back of it.

"I know we said we weren't going to use the back door, but I think it's the safest bet since we already know the layout, and that it will probably be unlocked because vampires are stupid," Kovah said with a grin.

I shrugged and pulled my ball cap tighter down over my face. "I guess so. What if there are vamps in the kitchen?"

"Not that likely since it's daylight, but if we see any, we will obviously kill them." Kovah rolled his eyes behind his sunglasses.

Nodding, I pulled the knife from my boot and let Kovah lead me up the small, grassy path that led to the vampires' back door.

Chapter 15

CURSES, FOILED AGAIN!

Nolan

The back door was not only locked, it was impossible to see inside due to all the windows being blacked out. We closed our eyes and put our ears to the window on the door, listening for movement inside.

Silence met our sensitive ears and we both grinned when we realized the house was probably full of dead-to-the-world vampires. I felt a little sick to my stomach that I was actually giddy at the thought of killing some.

Well, if I were being truthful, I just wanted to kill Eva and her creep boyfriend. And if I found out any of the others had harmed Charity, I'd kill them, too. Even the big Russian guy.

With a shrug, I turned the doorknob hard enough to break the lock and looked at Kovah, who grinned at me and nodded. *Huh, super strength. I could get used to that!* Pushing on the door, it still wouldn't budge. I looked closely and could see there was a deadbolt in place.

"Now what?" I asked my friend.

Before Kovah could answer, the door burst open and a large, pale hand yanked me inside.

"Argh!" the vampire yelled as his arm began to smoke and sizzle.

The big vampire threw me to the ground of the kitchen, but I quickly got up and picked up my knife from where I'd dropped it.

The vampire looked at Kovah in alarm. "Put that thing down, you imbecile!" he whisper-shouted at Kovah as he shook his arm out, waiting for the smoking to stop.

Kovah lowered the pistol but glared at Boris. "You *sound* like an 'imbecile'."

Boris ignored the jab. "Allan told me you freaks were outside. Why you keep coming round here? Eva will not like it."

I sighed, stress running through my body that the lame little plan I'd conjured up had already been shot to hell. "Where is Eva?"

Boris looked at Kovah. "Close the door, will you? No need for sunlight in here."

Kovah did not like being ordered around. He walked backward, keeping his eyes on the Russian vampire the whole time, and kicked the door closed.

"Eva is not here. I do not know where she is," Boris replied.

"You're a fuckin' liar," Kovah said, raising his pistol once more.

Boris moved at an unnatural speed and disarmed Kovah before he could drop another F-bomb.

"I told you to lower your weapon. Now this shall be mine until I deem it necessary to return to you," Boris scolded, staring at Kovah. "And take off your sunglasses so I can see where you're looking."

Kovah immediately removed them to the sound of the expected gasp.

"No, I wasn't born this way. Yes, this is the result of a succubus. Yes, I'm a hybrid. No, I don't drink blood," he prattled. "Now, will you please tell me where Eva's at? I don't have all day." He shoved his sunglasses back on his face.

"So, you are both hybrids? This is why you are not frying in sun?" he asked, looking at us both, holding the crossbow pistol.

We looked over to the edge of the kitchen that bordered the living room when we heard a gasp. A man was standing there in a purple silk robe and purple slippers, their tops resembling royal seat cushion.

"Nice slippers, dude," Kovah said, pointing to the guy's feet.

"I got these in France. And don't mock me!" He raised his chin in defiance, which was just funny since he barely stood five-foot-seven, dwarfed by the men in the room.

"Ignore them. They are just children, Allan," Boris said, smiling at him.

While my head was turned, Kovah flashed quickly to Boris and took back his crossbow. Aiming it at the Russian's head, he said, "If Eva's not here, where is her sister? That's who we really came for."

"Lower your weapon, young man. There is no use for violence here."

"You fucking bloodsuckers don't know anything but, so don't even try that bullshit with me. I'm not a child. I'm a hell of a lot older than I look."

Boris shot a glance at the crossbow pistol, then at the large buck knife in my hand, and then placed an impassive mask back on his perfect face. With his large jaw ticking with annoyance, I watched as Boris's blue eyes narrow in anger. Looking back at Allan, he said, "Go back to bed, I'll be there shortly."

Once Allan headed toward the grand staircase, Boris looked back at us and folded his massive arms over his hard-looking chest. "You do realize you are trespassing, don't you?"

"Dude, how old are you?" I asked. "You talk like my grandpa."

Boris raised his chin. "I was born in Moscow 1899. Long before that 'wall' fell you Americans like to talk about."

Doing some fast math in his head, Kovah said, "Holy fuck, you're like over a hundred years old!"

Chuckling without humor, Boris said, "Yes, and if you are hybrid, like you say, you shall be too one day." He studied Kovah, then asked, "How many human years are you?"

"None of your business. Just tell us where Charity is."

Boris cocked his head to the side. "Who is Charity? I do not know that name."

"Eva's twin. Come on, it can't be that hard to spot two mouthy redheads running around this place," I said, using my knife to gesture around.

"I have no clue what you speak about," Boris finally said after a long pause in which he seemed to be contemplating an answer.

"You're a bad liar. Get out of my way," Kovah said, aiming the crossbow at the vampire once again, attempting to move toward the staircase.

Unfortunately for Kovah, Boris was much older and much faster, and snatched the weapon once again out of his hand.

"Give it back, motherfucker," Kovah seethed.

"Why are you protecting Eva?" I asked the large vampire. I could tell he was lying about knowing about Charity's whereabouts.

"Listen," Boris started. "I really cannot stand Eva or her irritating boy-toy, but unfortunately for me, I'm indebted to her for saving Allan one night at the Blue Room as a group of bikers had come and tried to kill him. So I play bodyguard to massive house while everyone sleeps. I only require four to five hours of sleep, staying awake during sunlight hours while the rest of vampires sleep."

"That's awesome for you. Give me back my fucking gun," Kovah snapped.

Boris held the weapon further away from Kovah. "It's about time you both left here. I will have mercy on you and not tell the succubus you were here, but the next time you break into our home, I will snap both your necks and then light you on fire on the front lawn. Then I will feed your corpses to the gators and watch while Igor and Natasha feed upon your dead flesh in the swamp."

Kovah and I both dropped our mouths open.

"You named the gators? What are they, your pets?" I asked him before I could stop myself.

Kovah pointed at Boris. "You're a sick fuck, you know that?"

Smiling triumphantly, Boris eyed Kovah's sleeves of tattoos and then slid his eyes back up to his face. "You have such... how they say... potty-mouth. You should try to be a gentleman. Ladies do not like the potty-mouth men."

"Oh, what the hell do you know about what ladies want?" Kovah spat out in retaliation, flicking his eyes to the ceiling where Allan had disappeared to minutes earlier.

Frowning, Boris pointed at the door. "Get theeee fuck out of here. Was that clear enough for you to understand, my young, potty-mouth friend?"

Kovah grinned at the old vampire's attempt at slang and held his hand out. "Give me back my gun. Then we'll be on our way."

Boris followed us to the back door, pressing his back to the wall the door was set into. As Kovah and I left the house, his hand jutted back inside, palm side up. Boris slapped the weapon into it.

We walked away from the house.

"Well, that was a big, fat bust," I said, slipping the knife back into my boot as I yanked my car key from my shorts pocket.

Kovah shot me a look before lighting the cigarette that was now dangling from his lips. "Ya think?"

Before getting into my car, I pointed at the smoke. "Why do you even bother?"

"Boredom, mostly," I shrugged.

"Expensive hobby. Maybe you should take up jigsaw puzzles — or hey, you know the Rubik's Cube is making a comeback." I bit back a snort.

"Fuck off, Bishop," Kovah said, slinging his leg over his bike and revving the engine to his Harley. He zoomed off down the tree-lined country road with the cigarette dangling from his lips and the crossbow pistol bulge in the back of his shirt.

I laughed as I got into my car and drove off.

Chapter 16

GREAT ESCAPE

Charity

Lying on the old bed, I kept my arms folded behind the oily hair on my head resting on the pathetic excuse for a pillow. I knew my dinner would be delivered soon and I hoped—and didn't hope—that Brad was going to be the one to deliver it. I was nervous, hoping my plan would work.

A plan that was full of holes.

I first thought I had exhausted all my schemes—this one being the last one. Briefly contemplating seducing the disgusting vampire just to get out of my shackles crossed my mind, but there were three main problems I had with that.

One, I had only really been with one other person in my life and really had no clue how to 'seduce' anyone, other than what I'd seen on TV or read in books. Not to mention, I wasn't feeling very sexy with the way I looked and must smell.

The second problem was that sexual situations with vampires when you were human was probably pretty dangerous. Brad didn't seem like the type who held enough logic and rationale past thinking with his undead little head to realize that sex with a human might just kill me or maim me permanently. I shuddered at the thought.

Obviously, the third problem was that I couldn't do that to Nolan.

I knew Brad had a key to my shackle in his pocket. He always purposely taunted me with it. Not blatantly, but subtly. He would flick it around and around through his fingers as he would talk to me, or leave it on the tray when he set my food down, and then snatch it up and shove it back into his pocket with a cruel grin. The time he'd done that, I'd gotten a good look at it. Memorizing its shape, I waited for him to leave and then peered at the lock on the shackle. It appeared to be a perfect fit. I knew it wasn't the door key. That one was shaped like an old skeleton key. Hell, it probably *was* an old skeleton key. I'd been a good, observant little inmate during my stay at the mansion, and my wardens had not done a good job at security.

Broken out of my musings, I looked at the door when it creaked open. Brad was holding a plain white bag with a popular fast food chain logo on it. I sat up and faked a yawn.

"Hope you like burgers, Red. Smells disgusting, but I'm sure you will probably like it." He made a face.

Clenching my teeth together to prevent from snapping off on him, I replaced it with a fake smile. I slid some hair behind my ear. "I'm sure it'll be fine. I'm starving."

He set the bag down on my bed and said, "Sorry I couldn't find a fan. Eva wouldn't tell me where it was."

I smiled again. "Come sit by me while I eat? I'm so lonely up here. It's driving me crazy."

His face lit up at my invitation and he sat down as I opened the bag and pulled out two cheeseburgers wrapped in yellow paper. They were still warm and my stomach somersaulted. Realizing I'd need to eat before doing what I planned, I unwrapped one burger and began to eat it, not even bothering to take off the pickles I normally would have if I was in my house or my car, living my normal life. The one that had been ripped from me a few weeks ago when I'd met Nolan and had fallen for the beautiful bike mechanic who was loyal, sweet, and sexy and didn't deserve anything he was going through.

After eating the first burger, I wiped ketchup from the corner of my mouth with my finger as ladylike as I could and took a sip from the sweet tea he'd brought me. Brad said nothing, just watched my mouth, his gaze alternating between my cracked lips and the pulse threading under the skin on my neck.

I again resisted the urge to shudder at the gaze in his creepy light-brown eyes. His pale skin was almost pasty, and as he ran a hand through his dark hair in need of a haircut, he looked at my mouth once again and then into my eyes. "You missed a spot," he said, pointing to my mouth. "May I?"

I nodded, not sure what I was going to do, but I swallowed hard, hoping the fact that he was now leaning in close to my face meant he was going to try to kiss me, or lick the ketchup off. Not bite me.

Stiffening at the feel of his cold tongue on the corner of my mouth, I reached under my thigh and pulled out the jagged aluminum disc I'd carved out from the Coke can. I'd fashioned it into a cylinder with a sharp point. I slipped it on my index finger and took a deep breath. Deciding it was now or never, I reached around and grabbed the back of his head as if I was enjoying the licking. With my other hand, I shoved the sharpest part of my crude little weapon against Brad's jugular and pushed it home as hard as I could. When he backed up a little in shock, I both sliced and pushed in harder, gasping as an arc of black vampire blood shot into my face, neck, and chest. I gagged as a whole lot of it went into my open mouth. I tried to spit, but most of it had gone down my throat and I was forced to swallow it. But that wasn't what was worrying me now. Brad was screeching like a wounded animal, holding his neck.

Fury and adrenaline fueled my body and I rushed over to him, kicking him down to the ground so I could get on top of him before he moved out of arm's reach of my chain. Brad was still screaming, so I used my weapon to slice into his face and the hand that was holding his neck. Two of his fingers came off and he hollered some more. I screamed and then gagged again as the severed fingers lobbed to the ground. Still furious and scared, I reared my arm back and punched him as hard as I could in the nose. I then screamed as pain exploded through my delicate hand.

Brad's yelling had stopped, as now he was choking on his own sluggish black blood, his black eyes swirling in their sockets. I used the jagged metal to slice some more until his throat was completely open from ear to ear, oozing blood and liquid all over my legs and onto the ground. I felt crazed and as if I was watching some movie, not living it. I was shaking so badly I wasn't sure I would be able to get up. Satisfied he couldn't get up, I threw my weapon to the ground and could see my hand was bleeding from also being cut from it. I didn't care. I frantically reached into his right pocket, coming up empty. Yelling in frustration, I shoved my hand into his left and wrapped my fingers around something cold and metal. I cried in triumph and jumped off the now-still and lifeless vampire. I worked at the lock to the shackle on my arm until it came free and thudded to the floor. Brad's blood dripped from my arms and legs and I almost slipped in it.

As I was about to make a break for the door, I heard footsteps rushing up the stairs. Panicking, I looked at the window to my cell. I knew I could fit out of it, but did I want to jump three stories down into gator-infested water? Realizing there was no other option, as I'd surely be re-captured, re-shacked, or probably killed if I got caught, I went into the bathroom and wildly looked around. Seeing an old light fixture I had been unable to reach when I was shackled, I pulled at it until it came free, to my surprise.

Standing a good distance back, I threw it with all my might at the old window. It shattered easily, and as I hopped up on the small windowsill, almost slipping in the blood still coating me, I took one last look at where Brad lay and saw nothing but a crap ton of blood, a pile of clothing, and what looked like dirt. Realizing it was ash and resisting the urge to scream, I heaved in a deep breath and jumped out into the night, hoping I landed perfectly enough in the water—and that it was deep enough to cushion my fall.

Chapter 17

DISASTROUS DECEIT

Charity

Gasping for air after my head broke the surface of the murky swamp, I resisted the urge to scream out in triumph that I had survived the fall. The extremely soft mud at the bottom had cushioned the blow.

Then, seeing something move from the corner of my eye, my triumph was replaced with terror. A large, black lump emerged, slowly breaking the surface of the water. Shrieking, I began clawing my way through the water to get to the edge. Not bothering to turn around and confirm the worst, and with my adrenaline still on high, I dog-paddled to the water's edge just as I felt something hard bump into my backside. Screaming again, I clambered out of the water and up the muddy bank until I collapsed on the murky shore and began to vomit violently. Blood, swamp water, and the undigested cheeseburger landed in a heap on the grass.

The gator popped its head all the way out of the water and opened its massive jaws, snapping them shut just as I crab-walked backward. After getting to my feet, I bolted into a run as fast as I could toward the front of the mansion, swallowing down the fear that began to grip my stomach like a giant claw.

I headed straight for the wrought iron gates, the fog swirling around the base of them looking eerie and ominous in the moonlight. I chanced a glance behind me and saw no vampires or gators chasing me. The gator was apparently too lazy to give chase and had slunk back into the water to continue its nap. Looking up at a top window, I couldn't see the broken window to my prison, as that was at the side of the house now and out of view. But in one of the other top windows, I saw a pale face staring out at me. I ran faster, slipping through the bars and running barefoot, wet, and barely clothed onto the foggy gravel road.

Once I felt I had made it a safe distance from the vampire house of horrors, I began to slow my walk and try to catch my breath. Getting to the edge of the property, I felt like I had run forever when I came upon the small paved highway that ran through the center of the county. I clawed some of my wet hair from my face with my violently shaking hand and blew out another breath, looking both ways down the highway, trying to remember which way led back to Shreveport.

"Think, Charity, think," I murmured to myself, but terror was still rippling through my body, and I was trembling almost uncontrollably. I was grateful it was late September and hadn't turned very cold yet, or I'd really be in a world of hurt. Closing my eyes, I recalled the bike ride Nolan and I had taken the first night we'd been looking for my evil twin.

"We turned right onto the gravel road that led to the house." I popped my eyes open, turning left to begin my walk back into town. I prayed to anyone who would listen that a car with humans would come and help me. Lifting one foot, I saw bloody cuts covering the bottom of it and sighed. If I had to walk the five-plus miles back into town, I doubted I would have any skin left on the bottoms of my feet.

Trying to remain vigilant and ensure nobody was following me, combined with the need to keep my brain distracted from the pain and embarrassment of not wearing much of anything and my feet being sliced up from the warm asphalt under my feet, I began to grow sad. The adrenaline from the murder I'd just committed and the escape I'd perpetrated from the mansion of doom began to fade and I was left with a heavy tiredness. One tear fell from my eye, then another, then another, until I was walking slowly along the highway, sobbing loudly with my chest heaving.

I'd just murdered someone. No—not someone—something. Brad, the undead perv who was nothing more than my twin's sex slave. But was he her sex slave, or was he something more? Maybe he'd meant something to Eva. Maybe she had been in love with him. Hadn't he said she'd created him or something? Did that make a vampire hold some sort of special place for their fledgling in their undead hearts?

But Eva wasn't just any vampire. She was a succubus, the worst kind, I had learned. I hadn't had much interaction with vampires that I knew of, but I was able to see that ones like Brad and Boris seemed to possess a small amount of compassion, or maybe it was emotion, and that humanized them a bit. Was that for no other reason than to appear normal to the human eye in order to feed—to nourish themselves?

To me, Eva did not appear to foster that small bit of humanity I'd seen in the other vampires. The soul behind her icy blue eyes was absolutely empty. Where there was once warmth, laughter, and love with the mirror-image twin I'd grown up with, now there was nothing.

The thought made my chest ache. I missed her so much. Another tear skated down my pale cheek. The giggles of secrets we had shared as children were now replaced with selfishness and coldness.

More tears followed the first and I brushed them away with my hand.

There was nothing left of Eva Larue Sheridan but an empty shell of the sister. The daughter, the niece, the cousin, the student, the teacher (to me about boys), the friend... she was nothing but a cold, heartless succubus who had gladly given up her humanity and compassion for immortality and outward beauty frozen in time. But I didn't think my twin was beautiful anymore. She was ugly and hideous, and shouldn't exist.

I suddenly thought of Nolan, wondering if he was even alive. And if he wasn't, I knew Eva was to blame. All of a sudden, I didn't feel so bad for killing Brad. If she felt anything for the unfortunate idiot, Eva would have to grieve his loss and that was exactly what I knew she deserved — and so much more.

As I contemplated just how I was going to kill Eva, the headlights of a vehicle shone in my face and I looked up through the fog. Snapping out of my melancholy, I jumped into the road and waved my arms wildly at the passing vehicle.

The vehicle, a small, dark Mercedes convertible whose top was up, pulled over to the side. Zipping down the passenger side window, the handsome driver leaned over and smiled. His teeth were white and perfect, and his light-brown hair was shiny and styled up high in a pompadour that looked a bit Hollywood. His hair didn't move at all when he leaned over to look at me.

"Do ya need a ride, sweetheart?" he drawled.

I barely nodded as I opened the door and slid inside. "Yes, please. I need to go home, please just take me home."

The driver nodded, putting the car in gear.

"You sure you don't need a doctor?" His gaze scanned me from head to toe.

I shook my shaggy curls, which had begun to dry. With my arms wrapped around myself, I cut a glance at him and said, "Please just take me home."

Nodding, the driver shifted the car into drive and said, "Okay, sweetie. Where to?"

Giving him the address to Nolan's apartment, I stayed the sob of relief that wanted to jerk up out of my chest.

"That's a nice part of town. Why are you out in the county wearing next to nothin', with no shoes on? Bad night?" he asked with a knowing smirk.

I nodded and curled my legs into my chest, resting my head onto my knees, not caring about the blood I was smearing on his white leather seats. "Something like that."

"You're bleeding," the driver said with a large inhale. He gripped his hands on the steering wheel tight.

I nodded and put my head back down. "Sorry."

"What's your name, sweet pea?" he asked.

I looked at him and then put my head back down. "It doesn't matter."

As if he was trying to get me to open up, he replied, "Well, I'm Allan. Nice to meet you, little bleeding ginger girl."

Boris pounded up the stairs, flung open the attic door, and went wide-eyed as he saw the pile of ash and clothing he knew used to be Brad.

"Good riddance, you dick," he said to the pile.

Scanning the room for Charity, his gaze went to the broken glass that was gleaming under the moonlight streaming in from the now-open window. A humid breeze blew through and he went over to it, looking down just in time to see the swamp below splash up as something hit it. He grinned again and watched as Charity's head broke the surface of the water. "Hope you are faster than Igor and Natasha," he said quietly.

No, he wasn't going to go after her. Hell no. He couldn't care less what Eva would say when she came home. He really couldn't stand Eva, but unfortunately for him, he was indebted to her for saving Allan, so he continued to play bodyguard to her massive house while everyone slept. Since he was so old, he only required about four to five hours of sleep, easily staying awake during the annoying sunlight hours while the rest of the undead died for the day. He sometimes wondered how long his debt would last, and when he could call it even and move on.

That being said, he liked the mansion they all lived in. It was quiet, equipped appropriately for vampires, and, for the most part, was drama-free. Except when Eva was upset, that was. He hadn't run across many redheads in his human life, and even during his brief thirty-year stint living in England did he have many run-ins with them, but once he moved to the United States, he'd met several redheads and realized they were literal short-tempered spitfires. Becoming undead hadn't quelled that fire in them; no, if he knew Eva well enough from living with her bossy, bitchy, annoying ass for the last few years, he figured becoming a vampire—a succubus—just made it worse for them.

So, as he stared down at Charity emerging from the lake and running barefoot toward the gates, Boris was going to play ignorant. His debt had been paid to her, as far as he was concerned. And the scene in the attic spoke for itself. Brad was stupid and got bested by a human and had lost. Eva would be able to see that Charity had escaped. Boris would say he was in the kitchen with his headphones on and heard nothing. He was glad the girl was getting away. He half contemplated offering to help her, but he knew she would only run faster, thinking he was chasing her. He hoped she made it okay, as they were a long way from the road and she had no shoes on.

Then, he had an idea.

Allan had been out for a quick feed. He was a fairly young vampire and required more frequent feedings. Plucking out his cell phone, Boris dialed his boyfriend's number.

"Hey, sexy," Allan drawled.

"Allan, the girl has escaped and killed Brad —"

"Oh, my God!" Allan cut him off.

"Be quiet, let me finish now. I do not want to go after her. You are in your car?"

"Yes," Allan replied.

"Drive slowly until you find her. She will probably be flagging down cars. Pick her up, pretend you're human, and take her wherever she wants to go. She's never seen you, she will have no idea you are vampire. I do not need police picking her up. She will sing like canary about what happened to her here and I do not need human cops here right now."

"You got it, hottie. In fact, I think I see her now. Talk later."

As the line went dead, Boris went to leave the scene of the crime. As he was about to close the door, he saw something else shining in the light from the window. Going over to inspect it, he could see it was a metal tube with a sharp edge made of aluminum covered in blood. He smiled again and chuckled. "Clever girl."

Looking one last time at the pile of ash and cheap clothes Brad had left behind, Boris shook his head and closed the door to the attic, hoping he'd never have a reason to go up there again.

Chapter 18

MURDEROUS INTENT

Nolan

The ride to Archie's Garage wasn't a long one. We parked in the lot and wandered inside, seeing Archie at the front desk.

Archie spat a stream of chew into a cup and smirked at his two employees. "You boys strike out again?"

Sensing he was resisting the urge to tell our boss off, Kovah said, "Yeah. I better hit the gym some more. Those fuckers are too fast for us."

Archie's eyebrows hit the hairline covered in a blue bandana. "Y'all run into some awake vampers?"

I pulled my sunglasses and hat off, wiping the sweat at my brow. "Yeah, you could say that."

Archie eyed us from head to toe. "I don't see any blood or ash on you. I take it you didn't do no killin' today?"

I set my glasses and hat on the counter. "No, boss. The vampire staying at Eva's house was surprisingly rational and normal. We broke into the house and he didn't even harm us. I just disarmed our boy here." I jerked my head to the side where Kovah stood.

Kovah folded his tattooed arms over his chest. "He didn't disarm me."

"Yeah, man. He kinda did."

Kovah relaxed a bit. "Okay, maybe a little, but I'll get him."

Waving a rough hand in the air, Archie made a disapproving noise. "Nah, don't you boys worry about that one. We have our sights set on bigger, more dangerous vamps around here. Don't we, Kovah?"

With Archie's eyes pinning him with something close to a threat, Kovah just replied, "I guess you could say that."

"Like who?" I asked, my gaze darting between the two with curiosity.

"Just some new leads," Archie replied vaguely, almost seeming to regret the decision to say anything.

When the two stayed silent, I said, "Okaaay, well, I guess I'll get to work. Keep me busy before I go insane and do something stupid. Like call the Shreveport P.D. and report somebody missing."

"No, you will not be doing that," Kovah said, an unlit cigarette now between his fingers.

My face darkened. "Well, it would be better to report her missing, at least cover our asses. She ends up dead or missing for real, who are they gonna question first, huh? The boyfriend, that's who," I said, pointing at my chest. "Why not just report her missing and leave it at that? Hell, maybe they could even help."

Kovah opened his mouth to snap off something else, but closed it again, looking at our boss through his sunglasses. "Kid's got a point."

Archie stared at us. "You two are crazy. I don't give a shit what you do with the local police, but be prepared for them to come upon some crazy shit if their leads steer them back to that evil twin of hers. Cops could get killed if they try to go into that vamp mansion."

"Better them than us," Kovah said.

I pointed at my friend. "Not cool. I know Charity's in there. I swear to God I'm gonna get to her. Then all those vampires are gonna pay. What I can't figure out is why they would take her."

"It's not rocket science. They snatched her so the succubus could trick you. Worked for a minute 'til she showed her true self to you the other night," Kovah answered.

"Okay, I get that angle, kid, I really do," Archie said, slipping his coveralls back on. "But why keep the girl if her trick didn't work? I mean, it's kinda stupid to hold on to her this long. Which is what makes me think they don't have her."

"He's got a point, too," Kovah said, looking at Nolan.

I just shook my head and turned around. "I'm gonna go do something that doesn't make my brain hurt. Maybe I'll get a better idea of what to do if I'm not stressing about it."

I turned to head toward the bike assigned to me when I decided I needed some water. Before entering the backroom, I heard voices. I stopped short and listened as Archie and Kovah were talking.

Archie said, "We're gonna ride to Nawlins tomorrow and confront that Joel Reichert vampire."

"Really? Want me to come?" Kovah asked.

Archie. "Yes, we need you to show us where he lives."

"Who else is going?" Kovah.

"Just me, you, and Ollie."

Kovah paused, then said, "What is the plan when we get there?"

"We kill him, of course."

I put my hand to my mouth so I wouldn't gasp out loud. Why did Archie want to kill Joel? What did he ever do to him? But… I could already predict the answer: *The only good vampire is a dead one.*

"If you say so, boss," Kovah said, but I could swear I detected a little apprehension in his voice. Maybe I was imagining it?

Archie made to exit the breakroom, so I quickly went back toward the repair bay. I rubbed a hand over my face, and slid under the bike, welcoming the distraction.

I had been working for about an hour when I got up to get that bottle of water I hadn't been able to get before. The work had relaxed and distracted me a bit, but as I went to the grease-smudged mini-fridge to grab a bottle, I thought of Charity again. Of course, I never stopped thinking about her, but I wondered if maybe I should go to the BSI again for help. I quickly decided to scrap that idea. Seemed like every time I called on them for help, nothing ever changed. They used me for what they could get out of me, but I was never offered any real help.

Thinking of Joel, I wondered if I should call him and ask him for help — and to warn him. What would be the harm? He knew Eva and what she was about. Maybe I could offer some insight. Smiling a little at my decision, I found an oil rag and wiped off my hands before moving to pull my phone from my pocket and remembering I didn't have one.

I wandered over to Archie's office and saw it was both empty and unlocked. I let myself in, pulled Joel's business card from my wallet, and used Archie's greasy phone to dial Joel's cell, keeping my eye on the door.

Joel's phone went to voicemail. *Duh, he's asleep,* I thought, shaking my head at letting my eagerness cloud my reasoning. I decided to leave a message anyway.

"Joel, it's Nolan Bishop. I really need to speak to you, man. My girlfriend is missing. I think Eva has her. I could use some help. I also have some other shit to discuss. Can you call me back on my cell when you wake up?" I rattled off my number and hung up.

I hoped Joel would take mercy on me and help me figure this shit out. Then I realized since I'd asked him to call me on my cell, that I better go get that new phone sooner rather than later. Otherwise, I would go bat-shit crazy, and really — that was what I'd been trying to avoid since having my soul stolen weeks ago.

I was alone in my apartment, staring unseeing at a Saints pre-season game on TV, when my brand-new phone vibrated on the coffee table. I put down the bottle of Bud I'd been nursing and looked at the screen.

"Hi, Joel," I answered.

"What's this about your girl missing?" he asked in his old-world Southern accent.

I stood up. "A few nights ago, I thought I was with Charity in her apartment. We were… messing around. It wasn't her. It was Eva. She tried to trick me again. She got away before I could kill her, but now I haven't heard from Charity. Her phone was left at her apartment, but she's gone. I've looked everywhere I can think. She wouldn't just disappear like this, Joel. Charity is pretty loyal to her job, to me, to her family —"

"You check Eva's house?" the old vampire interrupted.

I nodded to myself. "Yes and no. I have a feeling she's there, but I can't get past the bodyguards. Maybe you can?"

"Corner her at her nightclub. Have your friend distract her while you go to her house."

"But the bodyguard will be there," I whined.

"He can't stay there all the time. He's gotta eat, and he can't do it in the daylight."

"Can you come here and help me?"

I heard him sigh and mutter something about having to clean up another one of Eva's messes, then he cleared his throat. "Okay, boy, but I'm telling you right now. If I have to come down there and help with this, I'm not leaving until you kill that succubus. I'd do it for you, but I think you need to do it."

"I know I do," I breathed.

Joel paused, then finally said, "I'll be there in a couple of hours. Meet me at the nightclub. I'll get some answers out of her."

"And if she's not there?" I asked.

"Bishop, she'll be there, it's a Saturday night. Just trust me."

"See you in a few," I said, hanging up. I immediately dialed Kovah.

"What's up?" he answered.

"I called Joel. He's coming here to help me find Charity. He said to meet him at the Blue Room."

"And then what? We're gonna commit vampire murder in front of a couple hundred people?" Kovah asked, incredulous.

I sighed. "I don't know. I don't think he plans on killing Eva. I think he's gonna try to get her to tell us where Charity is. I just don't understand why they don't let her go. Maybe she's already dead..."

"No. She's not dead. Trust me, that bitch is evil, but I don't think she'd kill her own sister. I would bet she wants to keep her for leverage or ransom."

"Damn. Can you meet me here? I need to calm the hell down. I feel like I'm about to snap, man." I scrubbed the back of my neck nervously.

"I'll be right there," Kovah said. "I have to make one stop first, though."

"Fine," I replied and ended the call.

I flipped the TV off and began to pace back and forth, wearing a line in the cheap, beige carpeting of my apartment. I looked at the black leather watch I always wore and heaved out a sigh. The next two hours were going to drag by. I was afraid my adrenaline would run out by then, along with my nerve. As I walked, I could feel my father's buck knife in my boot. It reminded me of my dad, which reminded me of my sister, Natalie.

Pulling out my phone, I hit her contact and the phone rang twice before my only sibling answered.

"Hi, Nonie!" she chirped.

"Hi, sis."

"What's wrong?"

He blew out another breath. "I just called to tell you I love you. You know that, right? I love you and Mom and Dad. I always have. Even through all of this, that hasn't changed."

"Nolan, you're scaring me."

"Nothing's wrong, Nat. I mean, everything is wrong and nothing is right anymore, but nothing out of the ordinary. My chaotic, crazy, fucked-up life is still the same."

"I'm coming over there. You don't sound right. Just stay there."

"No!" I yelled into my cell, hurting my own eardrum. "Do not come over here. I promise I'm okay, I'm not gonna off myself or anything. I just wanted you to know that whatever happens, I appreciate all the help you've given me."

"What is going on? Tell me right now, Nolan Bishop, or so help me, I'm calling Mom and Dad. Have you even told them what's going on with you?"

"No, and you're not going to, either. How the hell am I supposed to explain this, Nat? Dad's very old-school. He'll think I've lost my shit and have me locked up. No, they can just think I'm busy with work and my new girlfriend. Hell, let them think I'm being a bad son. I don't even care. They can't know what's going on. They just can't."

A long silence met me, and I pulled the phone from my ear to ensure we were still connected. "Nat, are you there?"

She sighed dramatically and answered, "Look. I don't know what's going on with you, but I have to go. Julian's picking me up and we're going to the lake for the weekend, but you better call me or text me tomorrow. I want to know you're okay."

"I can live with that," I replied.

"I'm not messing around here, Nonie. If I don't hear from you, I'm sending out the cavalry."

I chuckled. "You don't have a cavalry."

"Yeah, well, I have a bunch of bored students who need some extra credit, and that's kind of the same thing."

"Point taken, you psycho," I replied

She laughed and the tinkle of her voice made me smile.

"I'm pretty sure I'm the sanest one of this family," she replied.

"I'll give you that. Bye, Nat."

"Bye, Nones."

I hit the end button and started pacing again.

Chapter 19

CURSE OF THE SUCCUBUS

Joel

I opened the door to leave my penthouse and sucked in a breath as I saw Mara standing there. She was in tight-fitted jeans, a loose, blue low-cut top, and heeled boots. A small purse was around her shoulder.

She smirked up at me. "Hey, you. Going somewhere?"

"Mara. So nice to see you, I was going to call on you this evening, make sure you're feeling okay. I'm sorry I did not get around to it."

"It's okay," she replied, smiling up at me. "I'm fine, no hangover."

I nodded. She certainly looked fabulous. "Well, I'm sorry, but I've got a bit of an emergency. I will call you when I get back, which will be in a few hours." I leaned down and kissed her nose.

She stepped into my path and raised a dark eyebrow up at me. "Where are you going? What kind of emergencies do vampires have?"

I sighed and brushed a long strand of her shiny dark hair over her shoulder. "I suppose there's no harm in telling you. Nolan got himself into some more trouble. His human girlfriend is missing, and he's threatened to go torture the information about her whereabouts from the succubus twin."

Mara's brown eyes went wide. "What? Why does Nolan think the succubus has taken her twin?"

"Because she tricked him into bed, but he figured it out. Now he's quite angry, as you can imagine."

Mara looked like she wanted to laugh, but I didn't find it amusing at all.

"Put yourself in his shoes. You are, after all, a hybrid yourself, are you not?"

Her flirty expression turned to horror. "What are you talking about?"

I pushed past her to get to the elevator. I pressed the button and said nothing as it lit up.

As the door chimed its arrival, the brassy gold doors slid open and I slipped inside and then stabbed the button to the lobby floor. I stood with my hands folded in front of me. Mara followed me in and stood next to me, both of us facing the doors and not each other.

"Cat got your tongue, young lady?" I asked as the car began to move.

"I don't know what to say," she murmured quietly.

I turned my head and looked at her. "Tell me the truth. That's all I care about."

She nodded slightly but kept her face forward. "How did you know?"

"You don't smell human, but you don't smell like a vampire. I've only smelled that once before. That perfume you douse yourself in helps, but after your shower…"

"You definitely got me at my weakest last night," she replied softly.

The elevator jerked to a stop and the doors slid open. The ornately decorated lobby was bustling with people. I walked through with my head held high as several employees greeted me cordially. Not wanting to look like anything but a gentleman, I put my elbow out for Mara to take. She slid her arm through and put on a smile of her own, realizing what I was doing as she observed my employees looking at us curiously.

A black car was waiting out front. Tommy was dressed in his black suit as usual, and he smiled kindly as he opened the back door for us to get in.

"Hello, sir." He dipped his head politely at Mara. "Ma'am."

We both ducked inside and Tommy went around and got in the driver's seat. After he'd closed my door, I said, "Please wait for just a minute, Tommy."

"Yes, sir."

I looked at Mara. "After he drops me at the airport, Tommy will take you back to your home or wherever you want to go."

She shook her head. "No, I'm going with you."

"No, you're not."

She folded her arms and narrowed her eyes at me. "Yes, I am, I want to help."

"The Justice Department has no business in what I'm about to do, Mara. Please stay here. I'll come see you when I get back, and we can talk some more. Just because I know what I know, it doesn't change one thing I have said to you or have started feeling for you."

Her face softened and she said, "I'm glad to hear that. But I'm still going. I'm not representing the DOJ, the BSI, or the government. I'm just me. Mara Lynn Shields, hybrid extraordinaire." She winked at me.

"How the hell am I supposed to say no to that?" I sighed.

She grinned in triumph and put her slender hand on the thigh of my suit. I looked down at it, then said, "Tommy, airport. And step on it!"

The ride to the airport was short. My plane was already running and waiting by the time we got there. As we boarded, the pilot of the small plane said, "A plus-one, sir?"

"Yes, Andrew, Ms. Shields will be joining us. We won't be long, though, so I'll need you on standby in Shreveport."

"Yes, sir," he replied as the plane began to propel forward.

Mara's confident expression was replaced with worry.

"What's wrong?" I asked her.

She swallowed hard and looked out the window. "Not a fan of these small planes."

"You insisted on coming, now you get to live with the consequences," I replied, trying not to smile.

She slapped my arm. "You're a mean vampire."

"You're lucky this plane is loud and the pilot has headphones on," I said.

Cutting a glance to the small cockpit, then back at me, she asked, "He doesn't know?"

"No, he does not. Why would I tell him?"

"He's never asked questions as to why you only travel at night?"

I shook my head and pulled out a small, silver flask from my suit jacket. "I pay him a lot of money not to ask questions."

She eyed the flask. "That's not bourbon, is it?"

Unscrewing the cap, I took a big swig, then put the cap back on, replacing it back into the inner pocket. "No."

She eyed me curiously, then looked out the window.

"Do you need a drink?"

Looking at me again, she replied, "Of that? No, I don't drink... that."

"Tell me, what do you drink? Besides martinis, that is."

She took a big breath replied, "Anything a human can. I don't drink coffee, though."

"Why not?" I asked.

"I was never a fan before I became... this, but after, I found drinking to be a useless task. It takes a hell of a lot of it to even catch an energy buzz, so why bother?"

"Yet, you seem to get drunk just fine," I replied, amused.

"Did you miss how much it took to get me that way?"

I nodded in understanding. "You have a point." After a pause, I asked, "You going to tell me what happened to you?"

She blinked big, hazel eyes at me and I watched her lashes flutter, admiring how long and thick they were. Her clear, pale face was nearly flawless, as were her straight teeth. "Do I have to?"

I sighed and reached for her hand, noting it was pretty warm. I linked my fingers through hers and looked into her eyes. "Yes, tell me everything. I'm very curious."

She narrowed her eyes slightly at me. "I can't be compelled."

I chuckled. "I wasn't trying to hypnotize you. I want you to want to tell me your story."

"Okay. I'll start from the beginning."

A smile lit up my face. "That would be great."

"But first, how old do you think I am, Joel?"

I frowned. "Oh, I would never ask a woman her age."

She rolled her eyes. "Just guess."

Shrugging, I said, "I don't know. Thirty?"

She smiled sadly. "Close. I was born in South Florida in 1949." She laughed when my eyes got big. "Don't act so shocked. Your story's next once I'm done."

I nodded. "Continue."

"I had a very normal upbringing. I got married at eighteen, had two children, and lived a very happy, normal life until they were teenagers." Her face suddenly looked sad.

"There was a woman in my Friday night bridge club, Norma. She was this beautiful redhead who had perfect skin and the perfect body and the nicest of clothes. All of us girls were a little envious of her. She almost always won the card games, but we never cared. We just went to Friday night bridge to drink and smoke and get away from the husbands and kids for a night. I always thought Norma was a good friend. She always paid special attention to me, continually suggesting we get together outside of bridge. I actually took her up on it a couple of times, but it was always at night. My husband Jesse, he really didn't like me going out at night without him, unless it was Friday night bridge.

"So, one night after the card game was over and the rest of the ladies had left, Norma asked me to stay over for tea, since the game had been held at her house that night. I agreed, and as we sat on her couch drinking, she gently grabbed the mug from my hands and set it on a nearby coffee table. I was confused as to what she was doing, and then she made me even more uncomfortable by staring at me with her big, blue eyes. Then I watched as they began to turn colors. I swear to God, Joel, I thought the woman had slipped some Quaaludes or something into my tea. It was the early eighties by then, and those things were a popular street drug." Mara smiled despite herself, then her face went serious again as she continued her story.

"Her eyes then turned black. I remember being so frightened, I just wanted to get out of there. But I couldn't. I felt frozen, hypnotized. Norma then made a really strange screeching sound and I don't remember anything of the rest of that night. Jesse said Norma brought me home, telling him I'd had too much to drink and had passed out on her couch. I had no choice but to believe that, or at least that she had slipped me some drugs. I had the worst hangover and headache the next day, so I thought she really had."

"ETA, five minutes, Mr. Reichert," came the pilot's voice.

I looked at Mara. "Go on."

She nodded. "The next couple of days were utter hell on earth. I couldn't sleep at all because I was having the most horrific and inappropriate dreams about Norma. They ranged from highly sexual to downright mortifying, involving blood, murder, and everything in between—some of them involving me murdering my own husband and children by biting them and ripping their throats out. I woke up screaming several times a night. And while I originally had no plans to go back to bridge Friday night, by the time Sunday rolled around, I was so infuriated at Norma for slipping me those drugs, I planned to just go confront her at her house. I was crazed because I still didn't feel right.

"By Monday night, I was an absolute lunatic. I fixed myself up as best as I cared to, and as I left the house, I told Jesse I had an errand to go on and ignored him when he asked me what. I drove directly to Norma's little house. When I got there, the smug bitch answered the door and smiled at me. She had the nerve to ask if I was back for more. Can you believe that!"

I chuckled. "Oh, yes, I can. Those succubus women are horribly conceited."

"That's way too nice of an adjective to describe those devils," Mara replied bitterly, shaking her head. "Anyway, I pushed my way into the house, put my hands on my hips, and demanded she tell me what kind of drug she'd slipped me, and how to get rid of the side effects. She laughed in my face, told me she hadn't drugged me, and that I'd had too much alcohol. When I told her I hadn't had any alcohol at all, she then called me crazy and told me to leave. When I refused, she got angry and rushed over to me at vampire speed. And let me tell you, that scared the living shit out of me. I couldn't believe my eyes. She grabbed me by the shirt and pushed me up against a table in her living room. She then gripped my throat with one hand and began to choke me. She was so strong. Her eyes turned black and she hissed at me with her fangs out. I knew she was gonna bite me. I was mad with delirious rage and fear. Panicked, I reached behind me to grab anything I could get my hands on to get her off me. As my vision began to swim at the lack of oxygen, my hand quickly found something square and heavy. I lifted it and hit her over the head with it."

"What was it?" I asked, now completely enraptured in the story.

Mara looked sheepish. "It was some sort of antique candleholder. Unfortunately for her, it also had a lit candle on it. When I bashed her head, the flame caught her hair on fire. With the amount of hairspray that woman used, it engulfed her immediately. She spun around the room screeching like an animal, her body completely consumed in flames. I couldn't believe my eyes. I bolted out the door and drove away like a madwoman. I didn't go home, I just drove and drove and drove, crying and totally confused. What seemed like hours later, I went back by Norma's little house and there were fire trucks and police cars outside.

Her house was nothing but a charred, black shell. Apparently, the whole house had gone up. I came just in time to see them putting a body bag on a stretcher into the back of an ambulance, and it didn't dawn on me then, but later on, I wondered if there had been anyone else in the house at the time.

"I went home shaken up and struggled for the next few years to keep it a secret that I was a murderer. They'd put the story of her death in the newspaper later that week, saying it was an accidental fire. I knew I was off the hook, and because I just couldn't go to jail and hurt my children, I kept quiet, living with the guilt eating at me. As the years went by, the guilt waned a little. I knew Norma had no husband or kids, and that she was going around drugging people, so I told myself—even convinced myself I had done the world a favor.

"About ten years later, I noticed I really wasn't aging. My kids were now in their mid-twenties and I still looked thirty-two years old. It was disturbing and people were starting to comment and ask me my 'secret'. Jesse left me for his secretary about that time, and I barely noticed or cared. We had grown apart because of how I had changed. I was too preoccupied with guilt of killing someone, my physical condition, and dealing with strange side effects from what Norma had done to me."

"Like what?" I asked.

"ETA: One minute, sir," came Andrew's voice again.

"It sounds like we're about to land. I'll tell you later. It's closer to what Kovah has rather than Nolan, though. I don't need to drink blood, but I'm not a big fan of the sun. I can compel people, though, like Kovah can."

Joel's eyebrows went up. "He can?"

She chuckled. "Yes, even other vampires."

The plane touched down and we deplaned, getting into a waiting car on the small tarmac.

Chapter 20

REUNIONS AND RELIEF

Nolan

I decided I couldn't pace the floor any longer. Looking at my watch again, I grumbled, "Screw this," and snatched my keys and phone from the coffee table.

As I was about to open the front door and head to the Blue Room to meet Joel, someone pounded on my door. Thinking it was Kovah, I took a quick look through the peephole and thought I was hallucinating.

Was this another trick?

Was Eva actually attempting to best me yet again?

Well, bitch, fool me once, shame on me. Fool me twice, and you're dead.

I drew the knife out of my boot and slowly slid the chain out of its socket. As I twisted the deadbolt, I heard screaming.

"Nolan! Let me in!" a voice sobbed.

Opening the door a fraction, I held the knife in my fist, ready to strike.

Charity, filthy, barely clothed, barefoot, sweaty and damp, launched herself into my arms. She was warm and clammy — and bleeding. A huge, ugly purple bruise had blossomed around her wrist and her legs and feet were smearing blood onto my carpet. I could smell it. It was human blood.

She pulled my back from where she'd been plastered to my chest and I wanted to cry in relief. "Oh, my God! I can't believe it's you! You're here! Where have you been?"

"Eva," she sobbed, swiping at the tears on her cheeks. "In the swamps. In her house. I barely got out…"

My features darkened. "I knew that bitch had you! She tried to trick me—"

"I know," Charity said, wiping her eyes. "She rubbed it in my face. She seemed real happy to tell me about how she was gonna have sex with you then steal your soul once and for all. I was chained up in the attic of that house with hardly any food or water. And it was hot in there, Nolan. So hot. They wouldn't let me take a bath or even give me anything to do. It was hell."

I hugged her back to my body as more sobs racked her thin, pale frame. Even in four days she looked like she had lost weight, which she really couldn't have afforded to in the first place. I was just so damn relieved, I couldn't describe it. I wanted to cry along with her. "Shh. You're safe now. Nobody is ever going to get to you again, because I'm going to kill your sister tonight."

She pulled back and looked into my eyes. She blinked up at me in understanding, obviously ready for the nightmare we'd both been living for weeks to be over. "I need a shower," she said quietly.

Nodding, I put my keys and phone down on the dining room table and locked the front door. I led her by the hand to the small bathroom next to my bedroom. I hoisted her up onto the small vanity and then started the shower to heat it up.

After grabbing a towel from a nearby rack, I picked up her right foot and inspected the bottom. I shook my head and tried to control my anger. Wetting the towel with warm water, I wiped away the gravel and rocks. I then repeated the process on the other foot. After close inspection with my perfect vision, I determined her feet were now just a myriad of healing cuts with nothing lodged in them.

I picked her up tenderly and placed her on her feet. Keeping my eyes locked on her blue ones, I reached down and pulled off the small nightshirt she wore, throwing it to the floor. I slid my hands slowly down her sides and slipped off her cotton panties. The vulnerability in her eyes was clear, but she made no attempt to cover herself. I leaned down and planted the softest of kisses on her cracked lips and then turned her around, helping her into the shower. It was then I chanced a glance at her beautiful body. A thin back curving into a plump but firm butt led its way to two pale, perfect legs. I thought she'd look like Eva without clothes on. I was wrong. And glad. Glad Eva hadn't spoiled this moment for me. For whatever reason, most of Eva's freckles were gone. Charity was still splattered with them all over her body, and I thought they were sexy as hell.

I closed the curtain before she could turn around and said, "After you're cleaned up, you're going to eat something and then tell me about how you escaped from that hellhole."

"Okay," she answered quietly before the water hit her face. I heard her groan in pleasure.

I had to leave the bathroom before I pulled the curtain aside and got in with her. I closed the bathroom door behind me and went to my small kitchen to make her something to eat. I didn't have much, but I found a box of premade red beans and rice and smiled, knowing how much she liked it. After pouring it into a large bowl and adding water, I threw it in the microwave and started it up.

I had some milk that I was relieved to see wasn't spoiled, so I pulled it out, and splashed some into a glass.

As soon as I heard the shower stop, the microwave chimed that it was done. I removed it with a potholder, set it down, stirred it up, and scooped some into a bowl for her. I set the milk and meal on my dining room table.

I almost dropped the bowl when I saw Charity emerge from my bathroom in nothing but a towel. Her long, red hair was still dripping and clinging to her neck and shoulders.

So damn sexy.

I couldn't resist going to her and hugging her clean, warm body. She wrapped her arms around me and placed her cheek against my chest. "I'm so glad you're not dead. I thought she was going to hurt you again. I thought I'd lost you," she ended, choking on a sob.

I pulled back. "Shh. No more crying. I realized it was her before anything happened. I need you to know that. She tricked me for a few minutes, but I caught on. I was gonna stab her, but she got away."

She nodded and sat where I instructed. "Please eat. I'm gonna go find you something to wear."

I went to my room and found the smallest shirt I could—sadly, a V-neck LSU T-shirt that had once belonged to Sarah I had forgotten was there. I then found a pair of boxer shorts that were pretty snug on me and laid them out on the bed. I wandered back out to my dining room and chuckled when I saw the empty glass and bowl.

"Were you hungry?"

She grinned sheepishly. "Yes, starving. They fed me maybe once a day there. And it was all crap."

"I have more…" I pointed to the kitchen.

She shook her head. "Do you have something I can put on?"

He nodded. "Yes, it's on my bed."

"Okay, I'll get dressed, then you can take me to my place to get some real clothes. Then we'll go take care of my sister once and for all."

My eyebrows dipped together. "We? No. I'm sorry, beautiful, but you're not coming with us. I can't risk it. You're staying here, and if you don't agree, I'm going to tie you to the bed." I grinned a little.

She stomped her foot. "I will not be chained to another bed! Not ever!"

Rushing over to her, I wrapped her in a hug again. "Shh. No, I'm sorry. I was joking. I mean, I really am going to insist you stay here, but I would never hold you captive against your will or tie you to a bed." Pulling back, I looked down into her angry eyes. "Unless you want me to," I finished, waggling my eyebrows.

She sighed and pulled out of my arms. "You're naughty, Nolan Bishop."

"I'll take that as a no," I murmured.

My thoughts of tying people up for sex caused my mind to wander to Janice. Did she really do that to people? Did she really find it a turn-on to chain people to walls and whip them with lengths of leather rope? Shrugging, I chalked up my gullibility to my age and the fact that I'd been raised in a small town and hadn't had much exposure to anything like that.

Looking at my watch, I realized I had five minutes to get to the Blue Room to meet Joel and Kovah. I zipped into my bedroom and said, "I have to go. Stay here. I'm serious. Do not leave this apartment. Keep the chain and deadbolt locked. If you run into any trouble, there's a shotgun in my closet. It's loaded and cocked. Use it if you have to."

She pulled on the boxer shorts under the long T-shirt and stared at me in horror. "First off, I'm not gonna ask why you have a girl's shirt here. And secondly, I could never shoot anyone. I don't even know how to use a shotgun."

I went into my closet and pulled out the weapon. Placing the gun on the bed, I faced the barrel away from us, toward the window. I pushed the safety off the long-barreled Remington and pointed at it. "See this? That's a trigger. Hold the stock to your shoulder, aim it somewhere close to where you want it to hit, and pull this trigger. You won't miss, trust me."

She looked at the gun, then back at me. "You hurry back, please?"

I looked into her frightened blue eyes, gripped her by both shoulders, and replied, "I promise I'll return to you. The next time you see me, the world will be a better place without a certain succubus in it." I paused and flicked my eyes back and forth between hers, and she mirrored the action. "I love you, Charity Sheridan. I plan to show you how much later."

"I love you, too, Nolan Bishop," she whispered back.

With my stomach swarming with nerves and emotion, I leaned down and pressed my lips to hers. She opened her mouth slightly and I devoured hers, hoping to impart some warmth and wetness to her dehydrated lips. I wrapped my arms around her middle and pressed her body into mine.

Pulling back regretfully, I grabbed her hand and said, "I'll see you in a little bit."

She gripped me tighter and jumped up, wrapping her legs around my middle and kissed me some more, unable to let me go back into the big, scary world.

"I just got you back. Please stay. You can kill Eva some other time. I'll even help you. I killed Brad tonight, I can do it."

Oh, my God. I pulled back and stared at her in shock. "You did?"

She nodded. "Yes, I did. Now please stay. Please?"

My stomach felt sick, but I just couldn't stay. This had to end tonight. I was softening a bit at the look on her face and at how much I really and truly did not want to leave her, especially alone, but I knew I would have a visual on our enemies all night and felt secure enough that she would be safe in my apartment—as long as she stayed put.

"I have to go," I whispered, both rough hands gently gripping the sides of her soft face. "Help yourself to anything here. Okay?"

She nodded sadly, letting go of my hand as I walked out of the room. I rushed out the door and down the steps. Looking back once, I saw her standing there. "Lock the door, and don't open it for anyone!"

I watched the door close and could hear the locks being put into place as I jumped on my Ducati Monster. I peeled out of the parking lot and headed to the Blue Room, determined to end this nightmare once and for all.

Chapter 21

I LOVE IT WHEN A PLAN COMES TOGETHER

Kovah

After I punched the doorbell and heard it chime, I quickly shot off a text to Archie, letting him know not to bother riding to New Orleans to find Joel—that he was coming to Shreveport tonight to allegedly help to take down Eva at the Blue Room. I pocketed the phone when I heard the deadbolts disengage and the door swing open.

"What are you doing here?" Janice asked, folding her arms over her large, impressive chest.

My gaze took in her bare feet with red-painted toenails, her long, flawless legs, the hem of the pink silk robe I was sure was covering only bare skin, up to her large breasts, and the blonde hair that was lying lazily over them. Finally looking into her blue eyes, I replied, "You have to understand that I wouldn't normally ask a vampire for help, but I care about my friend more than my own damn ego right now. And trust me when I say, that, like, never fucking happens."

She drank me in with her gaze the same way I'd done to her. From the tips of my rough-hewn boots to the top of my shaved dark hair, her eyes briefly stopped at the navy blue T-shirt that clung to my chest and stomach like a second skin. I saw her eyeing my tattoos on the arms folded over my chest. I bit back a smile.

"Please, come in," she finally said, gesturing to her living room.

Trying not to stare at all the sex devices casually decorating the space, I once again looked at the sultry vampire. As the crotch of my pants tightened a little, I mentally chastised myself for being so attracted to her. I justified that she acted so normal, so human, and that was why I was a little infatuated with her. I convinced myself I was there just to help out my friend and nothing more. Looking at her again, she was so plain, but beautiful all at once. Nothing like the Barbie vamp she'd looked like the first time I'd met her a few nights prior.

"Tell me why I should even bother getting tangled up in this web of trouble you and Nolan have gotten yourselves into," Janice said, her arms still firmly crossed along her chest, pushing her cleavage up and practically out of her short pink robe.

Forcing my eyes to stay fixed on her face, I replied with as much charm as I could put out, "I just sorta got the vibe that maybe you cared for my friend. You two seemed to have hit it off. As friends, of course."

She laughed and went over to a wine bottle, poured a thick, red sludge into a glass, and put it to her lips. "Do you want some, darling?"

My attempt at keeping a poker face failed and I scrunched up my nose. "Uh, no, I don't drink blood." I shot a glance at the multiple wine bottles. "I don't drink wine either, so don't bother."

"I wasn't going to offer you any wine," she came back calmly.

I just stood there looking at her through my dark glasses, but said nothing, waiting for her to answer me. With a sigh, she set her glass down and slunk over to me. Slowly closing the space between us, she reached up to remove my glasses, but I flinched back and huffed at her boldness.

"Shh. I just want to see your eyes. I can't have a conversation with a pair of Oakleys."

"Too bad, that's all you're gonna get," I replied, putting a strong hand around her wrist to stop her.

With unnatural speed, she flicked out of my grasp, pulled my glasses off, and laughed at the look on my face.

"Give those back," I demanded, narrowing milky bluish-white eyes at the vampire.

She giggled and ran toward the back of the house with my sunglasses in her hand. Irritated, I gave chase and cornered her in her bedroom. I was momentarily distracted by even more torture—pleasure?—devices that were hanging from the ceiling, bolted to the floor, and dangling off the walls. The room was a horrible cliché of red satin and black leather. Still, it was kind of a turn-on for me, but I tried my best to remain stoic and impassive, when what I really wanted to do was grab the blonde and put her over my knee for her naughtiness.

"Did you need these?" she asked from the opposite side of the bed, swinging the sunglasses from her two dainty fingers, a grin etched on her flawless, pale face.

"Look, I'm not gonna chase you for those. Please just give them back and let's get back to the reason I came here. In about an hour, Nolan is meeting a very old vampire friend of his at the Blue Room to corner Eva Sheridan once and for all. His girlfriend is missing and we know her twin has her, and we're planning on extracting the information we need from her, by any means necessary. Honestly, we could use your help. And I think he needs a top-off, if you get what I'm saying."

"Oh, I get what you're saying, sweet thing, and I'm happy to bring him a drink. But what do I get in return?"

"The satisfaction of helping a poor, helpless hybrid in need."

She laughed. "Honey, I've felt his biceps, and trust me, he's not all that helpless."

I lunged at the vampire, but she side-stepped me, and before I could blink, I ended up with my back against the wall. Too quick for me, Janice quickly snapped one of my arms into a soft leather shackle that was attached to the wall by a heavy metal chain.

"Owww! Fuck!" I said, arching my back off the wall. Even though the wall was padded in red cushion, the weapon in the small of my back still bit into my skin.

"What do we have here?" Janice asked, yanking the crossbow pistol from my pants.

With my free hand, I tried to snatch it away from her, but she backed up out of my reach. "Nice little vampire-killing weapon you have here."

Looking at my arm in the cuff, my face quickly turned to anger. "Let me out of this now. I didn't come here to play around with you. And give me back my gun and I'll show you."

Tossing the weapon onto the silk-covered bedspread, Janice leaned in and kissed me on the mouth, not holding back anything at all. I gasped as her tongue snaked in and began mingling with mine. Not appreciating being under her control, as much as I was trying not to like it, I reached my free hand around and grabbed her hair. I felt her smile into my mouth until I jerked it hard enough to pull her off me.

"Janice," I gasped. "Seriously, let me out of this. I need to get out of here."

She wiped her mouth and grinned at me, smoothing her hair down in the back as if she was used to having it yanked like that. "And again, I ask, what do I get?"

I measured her with a stare. "Give me back my glasses and I'll tell you."

She sighed. "Fine." After picking them up from the floor, she slid them back on my face while pressing her body into mine with purpose. I briefly wondered why she hadn't asked about my eyes.

Because it isn't my eyes she's interested in, obviously.

I swallowed and tried to tell myself not to get tangled up with another vampire. It hadn't ended well for me the last time, and I knew they were just manipulative, desperate, soulless creatures who lived for blood, sex, and sometimes murder.

"Why are you acting like this? I thought you were different from other bloodsuckers. I really did, Janice. Obviously, I was wrong. You seemed so normal when I met you the other night, but you're not. You're just like the rest of them." I glared at her with mock disgust.

A look of regret and a flash of sadness passed over her features. She slowly went over to me and released my arm from the shackle. She hung her head. "I was just hoping for a little fun. That's all."

I rubbed my wrist, went to the bed, and snatched my pistol, keeping it in my hand. Glaring at her, I said, "Look, let's just help Nolan and maybe we can talk about some fun, okay? I don't normally… consort… with vampires, but I may make an exception with you." My gaze traveled the length of her body then back up to her face.

Her expression brightened. "Well, I've never had a hybrid before, so maybe you can teach me a thing or two."

As I opened my mouth to snap off a smartass reply, I was halted when she dropped the pink robe to the floor and walked absolutely naked to a nearby closet to get something. My mouth remained open and she peered over her shoulder, her long, blonde hair cascading down her back. As she grinned at my predicted reaction, I lost my breath.

"Ah, fuck it," I said, setting the pistol on a nearby dresser and grabbing her by the hair.

Joel

The town car stopped in front of the very busy nightclub, and as the driver opened our door, Mara and I looked up to the flashing blue sign and then at each other.

"Horrible choice in name and signage," I said. I pulled the cuffs of my sleeves down over my wrists and said, "And who puts a nightclub in a warehouse — in the middle of nowhere?"

Mara snickered, and I thought I even heard the driver chuckle, too. "It's just the thing kids do these days. Some say the remote location and the large building helps keep the noise to a minimum for the nearby businesses."

I looked around. "It doesn't appear any of these businesses are actually doing any business at the moment."

Just then, we heard the rumble of motorcycles and we both turned around to see a group of about half a dozen older bikers pull up on loud Harleys.

"Kinda old to be clubbing," Mara said to no one in particular.

It was my turn to laugh. "I was just thinking the same thing."

Not bothering to see what the old bikers were up to, we walked to the front door and ignored the long line of partygoers waiting to get in. A large, bald bouncer, who was obviously a vampire, put his big, black arm in front of us and pointed. "Get in line."

"Will you please let Miss Sheridan know that Joel Reichert and guest are here?"

The bouncer lifted an eyebrow at me and looked down at his clipboard, his thick, meaty finger scanning the paper from top to bottom. "You're not on the VIP list, Mr. Reichert."

I looked at Mara and murmured, "Show me what you got."

She slowly reached up and removed his sunglasses, having to stand on tiptoe as the guy was at least a massive six-five. The second the glasses came off, she flicked her eyes down to his nametag then looked into his eyes. "Oh come on, Deke, we're on the VIP list, aren't we? Our names are at the very top. Joel Reichert and Mara Shields. Eva is expecting us. You've known this all night."

Deke nodded as Mara put his sunglasses back on his face. She stopped to pinch his cheek before threading her hand through mine.

"Welcome to the Blue Room," he rumbled in a deep, robotic voice.

"Thank you kindly, sir," I said, ushering in Mara with a flourish. As I passed the massive vampire, she whispered in his ear, "This conversation never happened and we were never here."

I slipped a ten dollar bill to a skinny girl with pink hair and black lipstick. She pressed a stamp to both our hands and snapped her bubble gum. "Have fun, y'all!"

Mara and I ignored her and slipped into the club quietly. A modern pop song was blasting through the speakers, its bass thumping and rattling our skin. We looked up to see a massive screen with a live video feed of the club being played. It flashed to a photo of a woman wearing next to nothing, dancing in an oversized birdcage, to a young male bartender tossing a peace sign to the camera while throwing out his tongue.

Shaking her pretty head, Mara dragged her eyes away from the screen and leaned up to yell into my ear. "I'll never understand how kids listen to this crap."

I smiled in agreement. "Indeed."

As if in slow motion, we both spotted the succubus, perched on her throne in the VIP area at the helm of the thriving club.

Her long, pale legs were crossed at the ankles, and her chunky pale pink stilettos were beating out the rhythm of the song about someone's heart being a ghost town as it blasted through the speakers. Eva wore her usual haughty expression. Her full, milky breasts were spilling out of her black top, and the black and pink polka-dot skirt she wore barely covered the front of her. Her red hair gleamed under the pulsing yellow lights of the club as it was pulled back tight from her face.

I didn't need to read my companion's mind to see she was thinking the same thing I was. Such false confidence and arrogance seeping from a soon-to-be-dead woman.

"She doesn't even have the brains to be vigilant enough to notice we've entered her damned club," I muttered more to myself than Mara.

"Is that her?" she asked.

I chuckled. "Oh yeah. And her stupid arrogance is going to be the death of her tonight."

"Hmm," Mara said as I led her to the bar to order a drink and pretend we were normal patrons.

Chapter 22

INDECISIONS

Nolan

I zoomed into the parking lot of the club where my life had changed forever. I killed the engine to the Ducati and smiled when I saw Archie and the Riders parked at the edge of the lot, still perched on their bikes. Instead of entering the club to look for Kovah, I wandered over to my boss and his band of rebel vampire hunters.

"What's up, Arch?"

Archie's back had been to me, but he quickly whipped around. "What are you doing here, kid?"

Smiling proudly, I said, "Charity's back. She's at my place. The witch kidnapped her, but she escaped. I've come here to end Eva once and for all."

"Good call," Archie said right before he spit a brown stream onto the pavement. "Shoulda done it a long time ago."

I hung my head. "I know. I won't fail this time."

Archie offered me a fist-bump and I returned it.

"What are *you* doing here then?" I asked.

Archie waved a dismissive hand. "Got a lead on an old vamp that might be showing up tonight. Just posting up to make sure no vamper shit goes down here."

I chuckled and folded my arms over my chest. "Oh, some *vamper shit* is most certainly goin' down here tonight, Arch."

"And you have our blessin', kid," Archie replied. "We meant the unauthorized kind, if you know what I'm sayin'."

I nodded, deciding to continue to engage my boss in more conversation as I waited for Kovah and Joel to show up. "So who is this old vamp you expect to show up here? He got a name?"

"Yup. Joel something or other. My source tells me the guy is very old, but looks to be no more than forty. White guy, brown hair, wears a monkey suit, strong ties to New Orleans. I think he already went inside, so we're waiting for him to come out."

I sighed, remembering the conversation I'd heard in the breakroom. I rubbed the back of my neck. "Joel Reichert?"

Archie's face lit up and pointed to me while looking at the other bikers. "Smart as a whip, this one."

I closed the distance between me and my boss. "Archie, there will be no killing of old vampires tonight. I consider Joel a friend, and I wouldn't advise murdering the guy. He helped me out when no one else would — and he also spared my life when he probably should have killed me."

All six Riders stared at me with their mouths open. Finally, Ollie managed to gain his composure and his salt-and-pepper eyebrows dipped together as he crushed out the cigarette he'd been sucking on. "Are you really standin' there telling us not to kill a fuckin' vampire, kid?"

I lifted my chin and put my hands low on the hips of my jeans. "Yes, I am. What are you going to do about it, Ollie?"

Ollie's eyebrows went up as he dismounted his bike and rushed over to me. I stood my ground and puffed out my chest, not moving. Now suddenly nose to nose, we both were huffing and staring each other down.

"Don't you challenge me, boy. You won't win," Ollie gritted out. The smell of stale cigarettes and whiskey assaulted my nostrils.

"You're not killing Joel tonight. You hear me?"

"What're you gonna do about it if we do, huh?" he asked, his breath making me sick. He pushed me in the chest.

Rearing back my left arm, I made a fist and smashed it into Ollie's nose, causing a fountain of blood to gush onto the pavement. Ollie yelled and put his hands to his face to try to staunch the flow of his shattered nose.

I looked at Archie and mouthed an apology before running to the front entrance of the club and rushing inside the doors while shaking out my fist. The line had waned and I easily slipped inside after showing ID to the bouncer and throwing five bucks at the weird-looking girl collecting the money.

Absentmindedly rubbing my knuckles from where I'd punched Ollie, they came back wet and I noticed they were coated in blood. I rushed into the men's room with the intent of washing them off. I instead slipped into a stall and used my tongue to clean it up, shuddering at the rush of pleasure as the blood slipped down my throat. I then washed the remaining stickiness off in the sink.

Wandering out into the club, I forgot all about my sore hand when I spotted Joel and... Special Agent Mara Shields?

I made my way over to them slowly, placing a hand on Joel's shoulder from behind. He jumped a little and turned around, his features softening a bit when I saw my face.

"Where is Kovah?" I asked Joel.

Confused, he replied, "I don't know. Was he meeting you here?"

I blew out a breath and scrubbed my sore left hand along the back of my neck. I scanned the club's entrance, expecting Ollie to come bursting through to exact his revenge. But the entrance remained still and empty — for now.

"Yes, Kovah was supposed to meet us here. I'm surprised he's not here yet. He's always down for a kill," I replied.

"I'm gonna get drinks. Beer?" Joel asked me.

I nodded. "Yeah."

"Why don't you call him?" Mara asked.

Shooting her a double-take, I said, "Why is the Department of Justice here? Come to film me so you can throw me in supernatural prison? Or for a training video, perhaps?"

She laughed nervously, her fingers hanging casually from the belt loops of her designer jeans. "No way, Nolan. I'm here with Joel." She then linked one arm through Joel's.

Confused, I looked at the pair. Before I could ask the obvious question to the couple, Mara pulled her phone from her back pocket and handed it to me. "Here, call your friend."

I looked at the phone and shook my head. Before I could tell her I had my own phone, I suddenly felt a shiver run up my spine and got the strong feeling I was being watched. I turned around slowly and scanned the room when my eyes landed on the redhead sprawled out on a chaise lounge in the VIP section. She locked eyes with me and winked one of her false eyelashes at me, smiling coldly.

"Cocky little bitch," Mara gritted out, having watched the interaction. "I hate them all."

"What did I miss?" Joel asked, handing me a cold bottle of beer.

"The succubus has spotted Nolan, and had the nerve to smile and wink at him."

"Narcissistic, I told you," Joel said.

I thanked Joel for the beer, but didn't drink it. I instead looked at the pair and said, "I think I've missed something here."

"I'll fill you in later... if I feel like it," Joel said. "We need to decide what we're going to do about that." He used his bottle to point in Eva's direction.

I nodded. "Ya know, I've gotten to the point where I just don't really fucking care anymore. I'm ready to just kill her right here in front of everyone."

"Well, don't kill her until she tells you where she's keeping your girl," Joel replied.

"Oh, Charity's back. She was being kept at Eva's house, but managed to escape somehow. I don't have the full story yet, but at this point, I'm not even sure I care how she escaped. She was dehydrated, starved, and all cut up and bruised. I'm so pissed off right now, I've decided this ends tonight. The bitch is dangerous and needs to be put down. She has to pay for what she's done to me and now to Charity."

"Agreed," Joel said.

"There's Kovah," Mara said, jutting her chin toward the entrance.

Confused, I looked as Kovah walked in with Janice. I watched as he looked at Eva, and she winked at him, too. He, in return, flipped her off double-handed. Eva frowned.

With my sensitive hearing, I heard Janice say to Kovah, "Wow, way to keep it classy."

He seemed to bite back a smile. "After what you just did to me, I didn't think you were too concerned with class. I'm not sure those welts on my back are gonna heal very fast."

I resisted the urge to not gasp. *Those two?*

Reaching up on the toes of her glossy red heels, she whispered something in his ear.

He grinned, but said nothing in response and walked over to us.

"What's up?" he asked.

I opened my mouth to speak. I then flicked my gaze to Mara and Joel, then back to Kovah and Janice. "And I really didn't think this night could get any weirder, but I'm not gonna ask."

Kovah looked at Mara, then to Joel and asked him, "You brought the cops?"

"She insisted," he said evasively.

Kovah eyed Mara's thin arm draped through Joel's and smiled. "I bet. She is pretty persuasive."

"And who's this?" Mara asked, looking at Janice.

"Janice Garrison, nice to meet you."

"Mara Shields. This is Joel Reichert," Mara said.

Janice shook both of their hands. She then pulled a small, purple flask from her purse and handed it to me. "I was told you might be… thirsty."

I looked at her curiously and then popped open the small lid and sniffed it. Without hesitation, I chugged back the contents.

Janice laughed nervously, glancing at Mara. "Whiskey. Yum."

Mara rolled her eyes. "I know Nolan drinks blood, and I know you're a vampire, so we can just cut the shit right now."

Janice's eyes went big. "Oh! Well, good to know." She dipped her head.

I handed the flask back to Janice. "Thanks. I owe you."

I looked at Kovah again, wanting to ask why he had brought Janice, but decided that was definitely a conversation for another time. I turned around and looked at Eva, who was now standing and exiting the VIP area.

"Oh, please be coming over here," I murmured.

Kovah said, "No killing it 'til it tells us where your girl is at."

"Charity's at my apartment. She escaped and I made her stay there."

"What the fuck, Nolan!" Kovah snapped. "Were you gonna tell me?"

"I just did," I replied.

He just shook his head.

I then began to repeat to Kovah and Janice what I'd just told the other two about her physical and emotional state. Then I looked at Eva. "She's gotta die."

"Yeah, like yesterday," Kovah said.

Janice had been watching Eva, who had just simply stepped on the dance floor to begin dancing with a random guy who seemed to be very happy with his new dance partner. "Be very careful with her. She looks like an angel, but she's actually a dirty devil."

"I disagree," Mara said. "She looks like a demon."

"Well, we gotta get to her before she ruins that guy's life." Kovah pointed to her dance partner.

"Agreed." I nodded.

Outside, the Riders were still in the parking lot, sort of biding their time and guarding the place, waiting to spring into action in case Nolan needed it. Ollie was pouting on his bike with a red handkerchief shoved up his nose.

Archie's phone rang with a strange number. He hit the green button. "Yeah?"

"Archie?" came a high female voice.

"Yeah? Who's this?"

"This is Charity. Are you with Nolan?"

"Hi, honey. Are you okay? Yes, you could say I know where Nolan's at. He's in the club. We're outside. Hey, how'd you get my number?"

She laughed. "It's on your answerin' machine message at the garage, silly."

"I keep forgettin' to take that off there," he murmured, then spit out some chew.

"Can you do me a favor?"

"Sure, darlin'."

"My sister is there, right?"

"Yes, the succubus is here," Archie gritted out.

"Can you tell me what she's wearin'?"

"Why?" he asked.

"Please?" she begged.

He huffed in resignation. "Yeah, give me a second."

Archie hobbled to the front of the club with the phone to his ear and peered inside past the bouncer, who only eyed him curiously. Archie's old eyes squinted when he saw a redhead on the dance floor. "Uh, big pink shoes, black skirt with pink dots on it, black shirt that shows off her tits."

"And her hair?" Charity asked.

"All slicked back like the unrelenting devil that she is. Lots of makeup crap on her face."

"Thank you, Archie. I owe you," she drawled.

"What are you planning?" he demanded. But he was met with silence. Charity was gone.

"Fuck," Archie growled, pocketing the phone.

"Who was that?" Ollie asked through the hankie covering part of his mouth. His head was still tilted back.

Archie pointed. "I don't think you're supposed to tilt your head like that."

"Arch! Who was on the phone?" another Rider asked.

He sighed and sat back on his bike. "The succubus's twin. She sounds like she's plottin' somethin'. I better tell the kid."

Charity

After finding a spare key in a kitchen drawer, I got into Nolan's Charger and drove to my apartment. Once I'd found what I'd needed, I drove to the Blue Room. I parked it in a spot behind the club and checked my reflection one more time to ensure I'd plastered on the makeup well enough to pass for my sister. I'd had to rummage through every drawer and closet at my small apartment to find things close enough to look like my twin. Ironically, the clothes and shoes I kept in boxes were things left behind by Eva when she had first disappeared. I had collected some of them from our parents' house to keep at my small apartment, some strange way to keep close to the identical twin I thought had just gone missing. I longed to live back in the days where I thought Eva was merely missing and not completely undead and evil. Now, I wasn't sure which was worse. And the thought that she may die tonight made my stomach roil with too many things to analyze. Disgust. Sadness. Fear. Grief. Relief.

I sighed as I looked at myself. The shoes and shirt were probably all wrong, but I hoped I looked close enough to fool people in the dark of the club. My plan was to act like Eva in the club while Nolan and Archie and whoever else, took care of her out back. The problem was, I hadn't shared this plan of mine with anyone. So, realizing my plot had holes in it, I stayed outside the club in the back and wondered if I should just go find Archie and tell him about my plans. I'd seen the band of vampire hunters in the parking lot when I had pulled in. It gave me a small comfort that they were there, sort of on guard in case anything went down.

Biting my lip in indecision, I decided this was probably a very bad idea. But I couldn't leave now. I couldn't very well go waltzing into the club right now, either. I decided I'd just stay put near the backdoor. After all, I knew eventually someone—or something—would come out of there screaming some time tonight. I could feel it down in my bones.

Shit! That's not going to work either. I knew there was no way I could stand out here and do nothing. I had to do something.

I turned the knob and wandered inside.

"Indecisive much, Charity?" I grumbled to myself as I disappeared through the door.

Chapter 23

THE TAKEDOWN

Nolan

Trying to come up with a plan, we three hybrids and two vampires stood in a small, tight circle, speaking amongst ourselves. We probably looked more than obvious, especially to Eva and her vampire friends, but I was so beyond giving a shit what Eva or any of her cronies thought about us.

Eva was still dancing when the music changed from a fast, upbeat techno song, to a slow, mesmerizing, sexy beat. What also changed were the club's lights. They were dimmed to almost black, and nothing but one blood-red spotlight began to slowly swirl around the dancers.

I looked at my friends. "I'm done plotting. I'm going in."

The others made no move to stop me, they just watched me skulk off toward the dance floor.

"Chains" by Nick Jonas began to play through the club's speakers. With every beat of the song, I stalked toward the succubus, who was grinding against the guy with her derriere pressed into his crotch and her arms looped up around his neck. His hand was lying flat on her bare stomach, which was exposed now that her shirt had ridden up so high.

Nick's smooth voice floated through the speakers singing about wine-stained lips and how she's nothing but trouble…

I took two more steps and into the crowd, my eyes never leaving my prey. The words continued on about how she's cold to the touch but warm as a devil…

Pushing my way through a small group of girls dancing, I cut in through the middle of them with a few shouts of protest that I completely ignored. I ground my teeth together, my stomach boiling over with nerves and rage. I hated her. I hated Eva so fucking much. The lyrics went on, telling us how he gave her his heart but now she wanted his soul…

I took a deep breath, reached down, and pulled my knife from my boot. I slid it up the left sleeve of my black leather jacket. Nick's voice crooned on about how she takes 'til he breaks and how he can't get more…

I felt the sharp tip of the knife begin to push into the skin on my palm and smiled at the pain. My eyes were still locked on the succubus. I grinned more at the song telling us about how he has her in chains for his love…

Licking my lips, I came up right behind the succubus's next victim and stood still for a minute. Slowly circling around the man, I grinned when I saw Eva's eyes were closed.

Barely breathing, I slipped the knife out, just as the man looked up into my murderous eyes. The guy's eyes got big when I flipped the knife around in my hand. I gripped the hilt in my fist and raised it, lining it up with Eva's heart.

Mr. Jonas reminded me that I'd given my heart but she took my soul…

The guy jumped back, screamed like a girl, and ran in the other direction right as Eva opened her eyes. They were bright blue and clouded with lust until she saw me. Then, they turned to sheer terror.

Over her shoulder, I saw Janice step in front of Eva's terrified dance partner and grab him by the arm.

"Hello, Eva." I smiled like a maniac, and then, with my right hand wrapped around her back, I used my left to slam the knife all the way to the hilt into her chest. She screamed in an unholy octave and I grinned like a lunatic as her blood splattered my face, hands, and neck. Something caught my eye behind her, and my gaze flicked up from the knife and into the club. That was when I saw Eva — was that Eva? — standing at the edge of the crowd with a look of shock on her face. I looked down at the victim again, the knife all the way in her chest, blood oozing slowly down her bare belly and dripping onto her skirt and she continued to squeal.

If that's Eva, then who the fuck is this? I stared down at the dying woman in my arms and stopped breathing.

"Oh, my God what have I done?!" I screamed, letting go of the body and pressing both hands to the sides of my head. The redhead flopped to the floor with a thud.

Seeing the interaction, Kovah ran over to the twin standing at the edge of the dance floor and pushed her into the crowd and toward me. The body at my feet began to quickly shrivel up once her screeching had stopped.

The crowd parted and began to run for the exits, but Joel, Mara, Janice, and two vampire bouncers they'd probably compelled stopped everyone from leaving.

I slumped in relief when Charity rushed into my arms and I could feel her warmth and smell the sweat and fear emanating from her. Kovah reached down with a grin and pulled the knife from the mummy in party clothes lying at our feet. He wiped the blood from both sides on his pant leg.

"They shrivel up, bitch. I told you!" Kovah laughed as he fist-pumped the air. He then handed the knife back to me. "I believe this belongs to you."

I watched as he grabbed the corpse by its now-silver hair and dragged it to the back door, kicking the bar release open with his boot. The door lunged open and he tossed the corpse into an empty dumpster. He then took the lighter from his pocket, flicked it to life, and threw it into the dumpster. He wandered back into the club as the fire raged to life behind him.

By the time he got back inside, the plan the other three had obviously formulated was already in action. Every eye was on both of the large screens, where Mara's face was the only thing they could see. Janice had bedazzled the DJ into giving her control of the booth, and she put the camera on Mara's face.

"Look at me, everyone. Look into my eyes," Mara commanded.

Those who refused to comply had their faces forcefully turned toward the screens and were quickly enraptured.

Mara continued. "Y'all are having a great time here tonight. The scuffle on the dance floor was two guys fighting over one girl—this girl right here."

Janice cut the camera to Charity, who put on a brave face and smiled into the camera. She cut it back to Mara and zoomed in on her.

"Y'all are going to go back to having the best night of your lives and you won't even remember us being in here. Just the redhead and the two boys who were fighting over her."

Janice commanded the DJ to put the music back on and we all slipped out the back door of the club.

"That was fucking awesome!" Kovah bellowed, fist-bumping Joel and me.

I tried to smile, but deep down I was extremely shaken up. I was holding onto Charity, who was now sobbing uncontrollably.

Archie and the Riders immediately rushed over to us.

"What happened?" he asked in a panic.

"The succubus is dead," Kovah said with a smile. "Our boy here put a knife through her dead heart. It fucking rocked!"

"Yeah! Drinks on me!" Archie said while the other Riders whooped and hollered, all giving me pats on the back and fist-bumps.

"And who are you?" Joel asked Archie.

"Oh, sorry, dude. This is our boss, Archie, and his friends. They hunt and kill vampires," Kovah jumped in.

Joel's eyes narrowed and he folded his arms over my chest. "Is that so?"

"Great, vigilantes. Just what the world doesn't need," Mara commented, still holding onto Joel's arm.

"Listen, little lady. We have done the world a huge favor. In fact," Archie said boldly to Joel, "we came here tonight to keep tabs on you." He pointed at Joel with one finger, while his arms were still folded across his leather cut. "Our boy here went to bat for you, said you were a decent guy, so we decided to take you off our radar. But we don't back down when we find out vampers are feeding on humans — or worse, killin' them. Ya feel me?"

Joel lifted his chin. "Yes, I understand, but I don't take kindly to threats. I don't answer to you or anyone. And for the record, I only feed from willing donors."

Ollie snorted and then winced at the pain in his nose. "There's no such thing. You hypnotize humans into thinking they're *willing*, but they're not. It's assault, plain and simple."

Joel, Mara, and Janice all laughed.

"What's so funny?" Archie asked defensively.

"There most certainly are willing donors. I can give you the names of a dozen clubs right now where humans go to get bitten. *On purpose.* It's an erotic feeling when done properly, and lots of humans love it. And they are well compensated."

"I call bullshit," Ollie said, a cigarette dangling from his fingers. "You pay them and make them think you're doing them a favor?"

Joel smiled at the old biker. "We *are* doing them a favor. In fact, I would invite you to come to my hotel in New Orleans sometime to see for yourselves. I would like us to call a truce. I do not wish to be hunted just for being a vampire, and I'm sure you wouldn't like me to send out vampires after you. I don't think they need to find out there are a bunch of vigilantes running around Shreveport."

Archie spit onto the asphalt and said, "I'm gonna pretend that you didn't just threaten me."

Joel was still smiling, his businessman face still in place. "Not a threat, Archie. I just want you to see how we operate."

Archie regarded the vampire carefully, and then reluctantly replied. "I'm going to take you up on your offer to see your club in Nawlins. We have to see this for ourselves."

Joel smiled and clapped his hands together once. "Great, just great. You seem like a man of your word, Archie, so let's seal this right now." He put out a hand.

Archie eyed it speculatively, but didn't put out his own.

Seeing the rejection, Joel quickly pulled out a business card and handed it to Archie. "This is my hotel. Call first and we can arrange something."

"Fine," Archie said, pocketing the card begrudgingly.

Janice watched all of this curiously and looped an arm through Kovah's. "So where to for drinks?"

I looked at the action and then grinned at Kovah. "Really, dude?"

"Oh, fuck off, Bishop."

"Okay, Kovah," I replied, shaking my head. "We're gonna skip the drinks, I gotta get this one home. She's had entirely too much excitement today."

Charity buried her teary face in my shoulder. Her makeup was smeared almost comically everywhere over her face from crying.

Mara walked over to Charity and hugged her. She pulled back and looked at her. "I don't know you, but I know your story. My name is Mara and I want you to know I think you're very brave." She locked eyes with Charity and said, "He did a great thing tonight. He's your hero. Your sister was not your twin anymore. She was an evil monster who took over the body of your real sister, who should have been laid to rest a long time ago. Nolan did that for her. She's now at peace."

Mara kissed her on the forehead and pulled back as Charity's sad eyes dried and she nodded.

"Thank you," I mouthed to her as we walked away and toward my car I had just noticed was parked near the back.

I turned around and threw Kovah my Ducati keys. "Drive it home for me?"

"You got it," he said, catching the keys one-handed.

"Pick a bar, any bar," I heard Archie say with a smile.

"I know a place," Janice said.

Chapter 24

PERSONAL PREFERENCES

Kovah

"You like it!" Janice yelled, the cat-o-nine-tails swinging menacingly in her fist.

"I hate it!" I gritted out in return.

"You love it," she came back, drawing out the word *love*.

I sneered at her. "You shouldn't be in control. *I* should be in control."

Janice laughed at me. "See, that's exactly your problem. You always want to be in control." She caressed the whip lovingly then looked back at my body, which was completely naked and chained by all four appendages to the wall with soft leather cuffs. But even my supernatural strength couldn't break them. "You're going to learn to give up some of that control you hold on to so tightly. And I'm gonna help you. You're going to be thanking me when we're done. You're going to be worshipping at my feet."

Right. I laughed at her. "Never. Now untie me so I can take that body of yours and show you how much you truly love it when *I* take over."

She sighed and said, "I see this is going to be a long night."

"Unchain me and I'll show you a long night, baby," I bit out with a grin.

She walked methodically back and forth in front me wearing nothing but a skin-tight leather catsuit, caressing her whip. Her blonde hair was teased up as big as she could get it, and her lips were painted blood-red. She paced back and forth on five-inch heels that matched her lipstick. "I'm gonna break you, and then I'm gonna let you break me."

"What does that even mean?" I asked. Then I looked down at my crotch. "You gonna do something with this?"

She eyed my little soldier and said, "Of course. In due time, I will control him, and you."

"Nobody controls me but me."

She tilted her head back and laughed, then her expression grew mischievous as she lifted the cat-o-nine-tails and swung it at my chest with a grin.

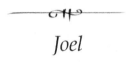

Joel

Mara ran a finger along my bare chest as she lay on it, her long, dark hair spread out over its pale landscape.

"I didn't know sex with a vampire could be so awesome. I should have tried this a lot sooner."

I made a scoffing noise. "My dear, it's not sex with a vampire, it's sex with *me*. There's a big difference. I'm just that awesome and talented."

She laughed. "Okay, mister confident, whatever you say."

"I think you need to finish your story," I said softly.

"I told you my story," she quipped.

"Yes, kind of. But you never told me what happened to you when you realized you weren't aging."

She nodded and laid her head back down my chest. "Okay. Well, after my kids left home and Jesse left me, I got a job as an entry-level accountant for the government—the Justice Department. I thought the job would be dreadfully boring, but it wasn't. Even though I was just an accountant, I really enjoyed the work. I watched the Special Agents come and go, and after just a few short months there, I knew that was what I wanted to do.

"One day, I was walking by a psychic's shop and decided to go in. Church, praying, books, and research still hadn't told me what was wrong with me. This was sort of a last-ditch effort to see if someone could figure it out. The psychic knew immediately what was wrong. She said I had been a victim of the most evil kind of vampire there is. She said the interaction had left me suspended between human and vampire, for which there was no cure.

"I left the shop sad, if not a bit relieved. I'd told myself all those years that her black eyes and fangs had just been a figment of my imagination that night, or a side effect of the drugs I thought Norma had given me. The psychic confirmed it wasn't, and I left there feeling just a little less crazy."

"That had to be a horribly lonely feeling," I whispered.

She nodded. "It was."

"Go on," I urged.

"Well, I didn't want to, but I eventually left my son and daughter, who had begun to start families of our own, and moved out of Miami to here, in New Orleans. The Justice Department had no problem with me transferring my low-level job here, and after saving as much as I could, I began to go back to school to get my bachelor's degree in Criminal Justice." She paused to let out a small laugh that I didn't think sounded very happy. "And I got that degree, I did. But nothing I learned in college could have prepared me for the job I ended up getting once I was done with school."

"Why's that?" I asked, knowing the question was pretty much rhetorical.

"Because the DOJ thought I'd be a perfect candidate for the BSI, being a single lady with no real ties to the city and no family. Unfortunately, I had been forced to fake my own death and start all over once I got here. There was no way I could go on leading my previous life." Sadness at her loss had crawled into her voice and she swallowed hard. "It was a bitch and a half trying to get a new birth certificate, social security card, and everything else. But I thankfully had made a friend in the BSI who helped me tremendously."

"Who was it? Anyone I know?" I asked.

She shook her head, tickling my chest with the movements of her hair. "No, I don't think so. Her name is Lauren Clark. She was an agent here a long time ago. When I told Lauren my story, she took pity on me. See, her BSI partner had been killed by a succubus a few years prior and she knew first-hand how horrible the creatures were. She could see I needed a fresh start and fudged a few documents for me. We're still friends, even though she transferred to the San Francisco office a few years later. I keep up with her on Facebook."

I thought quietly. "She's gotta be getting pretty old now since this was in the late Eighties—if my math is correct."

"No, she's not old. She doesn't age, either. I haven't asked her about it, and sometimes wonder if she ended up becoming a vampire, but I just don't ask because honestly, I don't want to know."

I thought back to all I'd learned over the past few months and realized that anything was possible. There were so many other supernatural creatures out there besides the vampires and shapeshifters I thought I knew.

"So that's it, now here I am. I'm gonna have to get some new documents in a few years, though."

I nodded. "I know a guy."

She giggled. "I'm not worried about it, but I have no doubt that you *know a guy*. Maybe I'll even change my name again."

"You changed it coming here?"

She nodded. "Yes, it was Maria. I changed it to Mara."

"Why?" I asked curiously. I had never changed my first or last name in all my years.

"Mara means 'bitter'… and that's exactly how I felt when I moved here. I'm not so bitter anymore, so maybe I'll go back to Maria."

"It is a beautiful name," I replied.

"Eh, we'll see."

After a small silence, I asked, "Do you try to keep up with your children?"

She rubbed circles on my chest with her fingertip. "Yes, again, thanks to Facebook. I sent them both a friend request under a fake account and told them I was a friend of their mom's from back in the day—from the bridge club. They both accepted me immediately, and now I get to watch my grandchildren grow up, if only online. They are teens now. My kids are in their late thirties. It makes me sad if I'm honest, but I didn't see any other way around it."

"There was no other way, beautiful girl. You did the right thing, and honestly, you are fortunate we have such technology."

She lifted her head up and rolled her naked body onto mine. She caressed my cheek, my nose, and my lips. "I'm so happy I found you. I never thought all vampires were bad, and you just confirmed it. It's such a relief that I won't have to pretend to be someone I'm not, or figure out how I'm going to watch someone grow old and die in front of me."

I chuckled. "You took the words right out of my mouth." I leaned down to kiss her, and she sighed in happiness.

Chapter 25

BLUE FLAME OF DESIRE

Nolan

Once we were back in my apartment, adrenaline and something else I was feeling were still twitching through my body like electrical impulses. I slowly pulled out Charity's ponytail holder and watched as her hair was freed and slid down her back. I again undressed her and then put her in the shower to wash off all the makeup, sweat, and tears.

But this time, I decided I also needed to shower. After she was in, and I'd kicked off my shoes, I removed my bloodied leather jacket, peeled off my T-shirt, and slipped my pants and boxers down. Naked, I took a deep breath, slid the curtain aside, and stepped in.

Charity gasped in surprise, but then smiled a little. She was starting to put shampoo into her hand, but I grabbed it from her and said, "Here, let me."

I squirted some into my hand and then began massaging it into her hair. She closed her eyes and groaned in appreciation. Once her hair was thoroughly bubbled up, I squeezed some body wash onto a body sponge and began soaping up her beautiful body as she rinsed out the shampoo. With her head tilted back under the spray of the hot shower, I slowly scrubbed her neck and then methodically moved down to her shoulders, rubbing in circles. I worked my way down to her arms, then her hands. I meticulously scrubbed between her fingers and then ran the sponge back up her arm and reached her chest. Still moving in circles, I worked down to her breasts and soaped them up. She gasped as I rubbed the sponge over her hard nipples. I gently worked the soap under each breast and then moved down to the flat of her pale stomach. I scrubbed side to side and then used the sponge to gently soap up her most private area.

She gasped again and I smiled. She had begun to absently work some conditioner into her hair as she watched me in lustful fascination, her eyes drinking in every inch of my body. Every stroke of my hand caused her to shiver in pure pleasure.

I bent to wash each thigh carefully, standing back up and ordering her to turn around. She quickly rinsed the conditioner out of her hair and then swept it to the side as I started on her shoulders and worked my way down to her shoulder blades. She shook slightly as I ran one finger of my right hand down her spine while I scrubbed with my left. I massaged her buttocks gently until I reached the backs of her legs and didn't miss an inch.

I was becoming more and more aroused with each swish of the sponge. Was I stalling for time before the inevitable happened? Or maybe, I told myself, that I needed to calm the hell down and get my bearings before switching gears to finally show Charity just how much I truly wanted and loved her.

My pulse began to even out from the fight in the club earlier and now it was racing for a different reason as I looked at the blue flame of desire burning in her eyes. As she rinsed the soap from her body, I gave my own body a quick scrub and then rinsed myself off.

I grabbed two towels after turning off the water and wrapped one around my waist while I helped to dry her off. I lost my patience and tossed the towel to the floor before picking her up *An Officer And A Gentleman* style and carried her to the bed. She gasped and then giggled as I tossed her playfully onto it. Ripping off my towel, I crawled up the bed toward her to devour her like the starved animal I was.

I leaned over and hit a button on my phone. Luke Bryan's voice began to float from the tiny speakers, crooning about how he didn't want the night to end.

With her wet hair splayed out on the pillow, I stared at her and didn't think I'd ever seen anything so beautiful. This night hadn't exactly gone as I'd planned, but I wouldn't have it any other way. I agreed with Luke, I never wanted it to end.

Unable to resist her any longer, I pinned both of her hands down and devoured her mouth with mine. Slow and methodical at first, the kisses began to turn a little more desperate and crazed. Her frantic breaths and moans in my ear almost drove me insane. Using my left hand, I trailed my finger from her cheek, down her neck, over her shoulder, and skimmed the side of her breast. I captured it gently and used my thumb to rub the hard nub there, which made her groan out loud. My hand then continued to move down her stomach and I gently brushed her hipbone. I felt her shudder under my touch.

"Make me yours, baby," she whispered in my ear.

I grinned into her neck where my mouth had been sucking and licking. I reached over into my nightstand and fumbled until I found a condom. I sat up and ripped it open with my teeth, and after putting it on, I placed myself between the V of her legs and pushed my way home. A moan like I'd never heard rang in my ears and I realized it was my own. My eyes rolled back in my head.

Charity wrapped one leg around my backside as my body began to rock into hers. Kissing her face and neck while working myself in and out, the sounds of her groans and breath was going to be my undoing before I was ready. After a few minutes, she began to groan and cry out under me, her head and back arching as she tightened her entire body around mine, finding her release first. Happy to have pleased her, I was hoping I could last longer, but with each thrust and rock, I just couldn't keep up. The way her body was responding to mine, the way it fit so perfectly with my own, was my ruin. I stopped my motions as I released, and groaned into her mouth, which I had begun to devour again.

I collapsed on top of her then rolled over. I disposed of the condom, pulled the sheet and comforter back, and tucked us both under them. Wrapping my arm around her, I pulled her close and said, "I love you."

"I love you, too," she breathed, laying her head on my chest.

We lay there silently for a long time, recovering from the absolute perfection of our first time together, when I suddenly had a thought.

I lifted my head and looked down at her, brushing a curl from her face. "I don't want to bite you."

She looked at me in horror. "What?"

I smiled. "I have no desire to bite you."

She gasped. "Did you have the desire to bite me before?"

I chuckled. "Well, there were a few tense moments."

"And you don't now?" Her hand instinctively went to her neck.

"No, it doesn't even appeal to me."

Her eyes got wide and she sat up on her elbows to get eye-to-eye with me. "Do you think…?"

I nodded. "Yes, I feel different." Excitement crept into my voice. "I feel the same as I did before this nightmare."

"How can we be sure?" she asked, as if she was trying not to get too excited.

I shook my head. "I don't know. Killing his succubus didn't work for Kovah. How could it work for me?"

"I don't know." She sighed

I shrugged. "We'll go to the lake tomorrow and sit on my daddy's boat and see how much sun I can handle."

She nodded, and I bent down to kiss her once more. She kissed me back and my body told me I was ready for round two.

Epilogue

Nolan

Familiarity spread through my heart as Charity and I stood on the dock at Cross Lake and waited for my dad to pull his large fishing boat, *The Lovely Mermaid,* around to the dock. A day of fishing was planned for us guys, and for Charity, sunbathing and finishing up a book she had started and never had seemed to find the time to finish—until now.

I remembered sitting here just a few short months prior, waiting for the sun to rise and either destroy me completely, or set me free. Sadly for me that day, the sun had done neither, and for the following torturous months, it continued to be my enemy.

But today, I embraced its warmth and rays. I grinned as it heated my skin and I drank it in. It did not annoy me, and I did not want to shrink back and hide from it. And even after the so-called epic battle last night, which should have drained me, I had no desire for blood. All I craved when I had woken this morning was some eggs with hot sauce, a big pile of hash browns, and lots of grits with butter. And that was what I'd gotten after taking my beautiful girlfriend out for breakfast.

The boat pulled up and I helped Charity board. I had on nothing but a pair of flip-flops, my swim trunks, and a T-shirt. I held Charity's beach bag for her as we boarded, then handed it back to her. "Why is this so heavy?"

"Big bottle of sunscreen, bottled water for us all, and a big, fat Patricia Cornwell book I'm going to devour. I plan on doing nothing today but resting my brain."

I grinned and kissed her on the nose. "Isn't that forensic stuff?"

Charity shrugged. "Yeah, but I love it. Been thinkin' about going back to school and studying forensic medicine."

I smiled as I stripped my shirt off, and then I sat on a bench on the deck of the boat. "That's funny, because I'm pretty sure I'm gonna go back to school, too. Think the BSI will have me?"

Her eyes went wide behind her oversized sunglasses. "Really?"

I picked her up and hugged her. "Yes, really. I love repairing motorcycles, but I think it should probably be a hobby, not a career."

"Did someone say career?" Natalie asked, emerging from the inside of the boat with two bottles of beer in her hands and her fiancé behind her. She handed a beer to me.

I nodded and kissed my sister on the cheek. "Yes, I did. I know I tried school before, but I'm gonna stick to it this time. I promise. I feel like I've been given a new lease on life, and I'm not gonna waste it."

"I'm proud of you," Natalie replied.

"Hi, Julian," I said, shaking the hand of my future brother-in-law. "This is my girlfriend, Charity Sheridan." I pointed to her.

She gave a little wave and a smile, then went back to her book.

Julian shook my hand in return, smiling from under his sunglasses as he looked at Charity. "Nice to meet you."

Natalie looked behind me at the boat's hull where our parents were, then back at me. "You better now, Nonie? I mean, really. Don't lie to me."

"Never better, Nat. I promise. Even better than before."

"That's true," Charity said, rubbing 50 SPF sunscreen on her arms and legs. She tossed the bottle onto another lounge chair and adjusted the brim of her large sun hat. "I loved Nolan before all of this. But I love him more now. Not only for the man he is, but for the one he's become. He's gone through hell and has come out on the other side a better person. I admire him."

Natalie smiled at Charity, then at me. "You're a lucky guy."

I looked at my sister and her fiancé. My gaze traveled to my parents, who were embracing next to the steering wheel of the boat, then to my gorgeous girlfriend.

With a grateful smirk, I agreed, "Yes, yes I am."

THE END

DEATH'S KISS SERIES

KOVAH:
SOUL
SEEKER

USA TODAY BESTSELLING AUTHOR

C.J. PINARD

Book 4 in the Death's Kiss Series

KOVAH: SOUL SEEKER

"NONE OF US ARE PROMISED A TOMORROW. DEATH DANCES IN THE SHADOWS OF ALL OF US." KLAUS MICHAELSON

Chapter 1

LEAVE THE PAST WHERE IT BELONGS

There wasn't a single night that drifted by that I didn't think about the past. And each night I told myself I shouldn't live in there. It wasn't my home. I should concentrate on the future. Wasn't that what most normal people did… focus on the exciting promises of what was to come? The bright and positive possibilities of what it held for them?

But I wasn't a normal person—I was a fucked-up hybrid trying to eke out my existence in this world, trapped somewhere between vampire and human. It was a condition I wasn't sure I could accept at first, but eventually, I realized I had no choice in the matter. I had come to the sad realization over twenty years ago that I was always going to be suspended in a life where I was frozen in time while those around me lived their lives and reached their goals—and then celebrated, or cried, in victory or defeat, over attaining or missing those goals. Maybe they even learned a lesson or two in the meantime.

It was like watching their lives whiz by at unreal speeds. Them moving on while mine was just stuck here. I couldn't move on, and I couldn't go back and fix what had happened to me. So I managed to live this life as best as I could and told myself that a stable life and a love for a lifetime with one special girl just wasn't in the cards for me. I even lied to myself on a daily basis that this was what was meant to be, and that I was okay with it. What else could I do? Survival was my number one goal, and the hell if I was going to let what that succubus—that evil, redheaded vampire bitch—had done to me, get me down.

My name was Kovah Sanagra and I was a motherfuckin' survivor.

Trapped in that dreary, cloudy place between dreaming and awake, I slowly cracked my eyes open and shook off the latest dream. They were pretty much nightmares I had every night, and while I told myself I had gotten used to them, the reality was that nobody got used to that shit. I didn't care how tough they thought they were.

Brought back to the present, I slipped my cell phone I'd fallen asleep with onto my nightstand and lay back against my pillow with a smile on my face. The phone call earlier with my new boss, Archie, had gone just as planned.

Moving to Shreveport, Louisiana, had turned out much better than expected. Leaving the hustle and bustle of the northeast and moving to the deep South was a decision I'd made easily. Looking back, it seemed like a choice so detrimental that it should have been hard, but it wasn't. I had to get the hell out of New York and disappearing into a small town seemed like a good idea. Meeting Archie at a gun show at the one and only pavilion in Shreveport was definitely fate—or whatever—intervening. I needed a job, and he needed a mechanic, and that was how I ended up renting a small room above Archie's Garage.

Sighing at the memories, I absolutely hated being restless. Sleep never found me easily, especially at night, and I knew it was part of my curse. The curse the succubus had delivered to me with her piercing black stare, her full red lips, and her provocative fangs that were both frightening and inviting. Her seductive, pale body and full breasts that had called to me. That mouth of hers that had promised sexual fantasies. But I had shown her. She was now nothing but a shriveled corpse buried somewhere in upstate New York… food for the worms.

I had thought about digging her up, just to make sure she was still there, but it had been over twenty years since that fateful day, and even with my keen eyesight and impeccable memory, I wasn't sure I could locate the exact spot. I could feel my eyes finally begin to drift closed, the memory of when I used to be Dominic… and that fateful night infiltrating my brain, visiting me in dreamland—or maybe it was more of a nightmare…

Your friends are leaving, *my drunk brain said to me. But I didn't care. My three friends, their names not important anymore, left the dark club with their arms slung around three pretty party girls. Of course, I had struck out again. But I didn't want to leave. They hadn't even hollered last call yet, and I had room for another shot of Jack.*

I signaled to the bartender, a silly smile on my face I could see in the back-bar's mirror, pointing to the empty glass set before me on a cocktail napkin. He came over, shook his head, and poured me straight Jack from the bottle. I slid him a five-dollar bill and lifted my glass to him in thanks before slamming it back.

I turned with my back to the bar, elbows resting on it, and watched the partygoers. I wasn't quite sure if this was supposed to be some posh nightclub, or just a bar. My muddled brain decided it was the latter. The dance floor was tiny, and only one couple was entertaining it. Although they didn't seem to notice the rest of us there, as they were tangled up in each other with no regard for anyone else. I would have thought it sweet, but it just annoyed me. I turned back around and faced the bar once again, staring at my reflection in the large mirror.

I lifted the glass to my lips, only to realize it was empty. I watched in the reflection as someone sat on the barstool next to me. Setting my glass down, I turned my head and stared – no, I gaped – at the woman who had planted her fine ass on the empty barstool. I briefly looked around the bar, noticing the crowd was thinning out. What I also noticed was that there were probably a dozen empty barstools, but she had chosen the one right next to mine.

Her long, straight hair glowed blood-red in the club's lights, and I couldn't be sure if she was actually a redhead, or maybe a blonde. I didn't really care much. I wasn't picky, especially at one a.m. on a Saturday. I watched as she ordered herself two shots of tequila with lime and salt. Her lips were full and her skin, porcelain smooth, with that crimson glow lighting up the side of her face. Her breasts were pure perfection and the tight black dress she wore showed me every luscious curve of her figure. I was surprised my body was able to react to her beauty after all the whiskey I'd poured down my gullet tonight.

But it did. Almost painfully.

She paid the bartender and then turned to me, putting out a dainty pale hand with shiny black fingernails at each tip. "Hi, I'm Suzette. What's your name, handsome?"

Suzette's words sounded well-rehearsed, and it hit me that she might be a working girl. I bit back a laugh, but answered her anyway, "Name's Dominic. Nice to meet you, Suzette." I lifted her hand to my mouth and kissed her delicate knuckles. Her skin was soft but icy under my touch.

"Your skin is cold, sweetheart."

Pulling her hand gently from mine, and with her lips contorted in a grin, she lifted one shot of the tequila. "This will warm me up."

I nodded in understanding. Watching in fascination as she used her tongue to slowly lick the top of her hand, she then poured salt on it. I briefly thought of something else I had that she could lick. She pounded back the shot with as much class as possible, squeezing the small lime wedge between her plump lips, and then she licked the salt from her hand.

My pants had suddenly shrunk two sizes, right there in the bar.

She grinned in triumph at her actions, getting the reaction she'd intended, then held the other shot out to me. "Wanna do the next shot, Dominic?"

I pointed to my empty glass. "Probably don't want to mess with Jose when

Jack's been keeping me company all night."

She laughed, throwing her head back. "No, silly, I will drink the shot, but you have to provide the salt and the lime. It's called a 'body shot' — haven't you heard of them?"

I nodded. Of course I had. The dudes in my fraternity did them all the time. I'd also done a few.

"Sounds great," I said. "But I've changed my mind. I think I do want tequila after all."

I grabbed the shot from her and used my tongue to wet the space right between her cleavage, and she gave up no resistance at all. She giggled as she gazed down at me while I sprinkled salt there. She smelled like expensive perfume and something else edible I couldn't quite describe. I leaned back, and with the shot between my fingers, I tossed it back. Then, snatching the second lime wedge, I instead put it between her teeth and watched with appreciation as she sucked it dry. Then and only then did I drag my gaze away from her ice-blue eyes and down to her perfect tits, where I slowly licked the salt from her cold skin. Every grain of it. I continued to lick up to her collarbone, where my tongue was replaced by my lips, soft kisses trailing up the side of her neck slowly. I kissed along her jaw and then finally to those lips that had been taunting me for the past few minutes.

She eagerly returned the kiss, and when she suggested we leave, I didn't have to be asked twice. It hadn't even occurred to me when my buddies left earlier that I was without a ride, as my roommate, Bryan, had driven us to this dark bar whose name I couldn't remember. But I supposed that was on purpose. I'd have to take a cab home, and in my condition, it was the only option, anyway.

Suzette led me to the dark parking lot where broken beer bottles and cans littered the pavement, one orange light barely illuminating our way. She used a keychain remote to disarm a black late eighties model Datsun 280ZX that gleamed under the streetlamp. I opened the driver's door for her, and after closing it, climbed into the passenger side. I really wanted to drive the beauty but knew that killing us both or wrecking her sports car was not in my best interest. The drunken hiccup that erupted from my lips confirmed my decision.

What part of Rochester she drove us to I didn't know, nor did I care. I didn't pay much attention to the drive to her apartment, which didn't seem like it was very far from the nightclub. The minute the elevator doors closed, we were entwined in each other's arms, my hands wandering wherever they wanted, her mouth sucking my breath away.

If only my breath had been the only thing she had sucked away that night.

The minute we were in her apartment, it was on. Clothes went flying, the trail of my jeans and T-shirt and her dress leading anyone who would happen by to know exactly where to find us. The only light in her massive bedroom came from *two large windows on one wall. I could see the entire city from there, but I didn't get to enjoy the view long. She pushed me on the bed and tore off my boxers. In nothing but a black lace bra, panties, and some sheer black stockings, she kicked off her red high heels and slithered up the bed toward me.*

"Do you have protection?" I asked, thinking of the latest news about the new sexually transmitted virus that had no cure. It was all over the TV and radio, calling it a 'gay disease' but I knew better, and the hell if I was taking any chances on my dick falling off.

No thanks.

She shook her head and wagged her finger at me. "You won't need one. I've got a talented mouth, so you just lie back, sweetheart."

My eyes went wide, and I swallowed thickly.

Well.

She definitely delivered, and once she was done, she went into the bathroom, came back out, and straddled my thighs.

"I don't know what I have left to give you, sweetheart…" I murmured, my body ready for sleep.

She placed a manicured finger against my lips. "Shh. It's my turn."

Then she looked into my groggy, drunk eyes, and as I was about to close them, I noticed her blue eyes were now brown.

Wait, no.

I shook my head in confusion. They weren't brown, they were fucking black. All black, no whites to them whatsoever, like something from a horror flick. I gasped in a deep breath, readying myself to yell and push her off me, but she again stole my breath. Gazing into my eyes, I strangled the scream that was about to escape and instead was blanketed by a strange calmness. Suzette stared into my eyes for what seemed like forever, until she blinked a few times and then let out a screech that wasn't human.

The pager I carried on my belt began to chirp from where my pants lay on the floor. I shook my groggy head and pushed this weird bitch off me.

"What are you doing? Come back to bed," she purred.

I ignored her and looked at my pager. It was my sister's number with '911' on the screen. She was due to have a baby any day and I knew this was probably it. I began to get dressed and I noticed Suzette was lying on the bed watching me.

"Leaving so soon?" she asked.

"Gotta go, emergency," I said, lifting the pager in the air.

"Walking home?" she asked, amusement in her eyes.

I raked my hands through my hair. Shit, I didn't have my bike.

Before I could blink, she was off the bed and in my face, staring into my eyes. They were black once again, and before I could let out a curse, she whispered something and my world went black.

Hours later, I woke up alone in my own bed in my dorm, fully dressed, lying on top of the covers.

My pager was nowhere to be found.

I sat bolt upright in my bed, gasping. Scrubbing a hand across my face, I resisted the urge to yell out in frustration as my fists formed into balls. How many fucking times was I gonna have this goddamn nightmare? I punched the mattress.

I'd lived it… not dreamed it… I was supposed to wake up from a nightmare, relieved that it wasn't real… but no, I *had* lived this shit. Now I had to relive it over and over. How was that fair? Hadn't I been through enough?

Deciding yet again that a pity party wasn't in my nature, I lay back down and took a deep breath, staring at the plain white ceiling of my tiny apartment.

I needed a distraction from the succubus who had changed my life forever, so I laced my hands together behind my head. Twenty years had passed since I had met that red-haired demon, and yet, I wasn't sure a day had gone by that I hadn't thought about her. And how could I avoid it? She was obviously still infiltrating my thoughts and dreams, even from the grave.

Which made me wonder if she was really and truly dead.

LIFE IN THE DIRTY SOUTH

I woke the next morning not completely rested but awake enough to function. Feeling this way was nothing new to me. This was how I existed daily. The night was my friend. The day, not so much. But in order to stay functioning like a "normal" person, I kept the human schedule.

I showered, and after slopping some goop into my short, dark hair, I went down to the garage and realized I had another day of ordinary work ahead of me.

Make no mistake, I loved working on motorcycles, and I had learned a long time ago that not every minute of every day was going to be filled with adrenaline-fueled excitement. So I endured the mundane so I could afford to live for the excitement of vampire hunting. After all, it was a dangerous job and I lived for danger. But living a long life is freaking expensive, and I realized about ten years ago that I needed to live frugally and save money so I could continue doing what I loved... which was sending undead bloodsuckers back to hell.

My boots made prints in the oil and dust on the floor of Archie's Garage as I entered with my backpack slung around my shoulder.

"Hey, kid," Archie greeted, his bottom lip full of dip as he stood near a bike that was in about a million pieces. My coworker and friend, Nolan Bishop, lay under the bike tinkering with the exhaust pipe. I watched with mild interest until Archie broke my stare.

"There's a Harley in the corner with your name on it," Archie said, jutting his goatee toward the corner of the garage.

Nolan slid out from under the bike and sat up, looking up at me. "What's up, Kovah?"

I grinned at my friend. "Nothing, man, just another manic Monday."

"I bet that was your favorite song when you were a teenager," he came back with a mischievous glint in his green eyes. "My mom loved it, too."

"Fuck you, Bishop," I said, biting back a grin and heading toward my assigned Harley to get to work.

I had met Nolan through Archie and learned that he, too, was having succubus problems. We'd sort of bonded over it and he loved to make comments referring to my real age. Nolan was only twenty-one, and once told me his mother and I were the same age. Unfortunately, his pretty mother and I didn't look even close in age, and never would, as I was only twenty when the succubus took my soul and froze me in time.

I zipped up my coveralls, opened my toolbox, grabbed a wrench, and went to work on the Harley, but my mind was elsewhere…

Twenty Years Ago
Rochester, NY

I blinked repeatedly up at the ceiling of my dorm room, trying my hardest to remember what the hell had happened the night before. My head pounded in time with the analog clock on the wall, its second-hand ticking much, much louder than it normally did. I pressed my hands to the sides of my head to try to lessen the throb, and knew I needed to get up and find some aspirin.

I staggered to the small closet afforded to me in my dorm room and rummaged through the box I kept on the floor there. Relieved to find some aspirin, I knew there was no way I could swallow them dry since I already had the worst case of cottonmouth ever. I dragged myself out into the hallway and went into the communal bathroom, turning on the cold water tap and sticking my mouth under it to get some cool water down my parched throat. I swallowed the pills easily enough and then cupped my hands under the water, getting enough to splash my face with. I looked up into the scratched mirror and watched the water drip down my face. I was already sporting a five o'clock shadow at nine o'clock in the morning. I shook my head.

Damn Italian genes…

I narrowed my dark-blue eyes against the harsh light of the bathroom and used the water to slick my black hair off my forehead. I so needed to get back to bed.

Slogging back to my room, I heard, "Dominic!"

I turned around a bit too quickly to see my roommate, Bryan, headed my way.

"Yo," I said without enthusiasm.

"Where'd you go last night?" he asked.

I cocked an eyebrow at him and said, "What do you care? You and the other brothers ditched me at that fucking dive bar."

He raked his fingers through his blond surfer haircut and then narrowed his eyes at me. "Dude, we tried to get you to leave. You told us to fuck off. You were pretty wasted, bro."

I waved a hand and continued to walk to our dorm room as he followed. I didn't say anything else because I really couldn't remember much.

As I flopped on my bed, Bryan continued to talk as he pulled a huge textbook from his backpack and flipped it open. He sat on his bed, looking over at me. "You didn't get back here until, like, four this morning."

Squeezing my eyes shut, I pinched the bridge of my nose and tried to will my headache to go away. "I don't know, man. I met a chick, she took me back to her place, gave me a blowie, and I don't remember what happened after that. She must have put me in a cab or something because I don't remember getting back here."

I cracked an eye open and looked over at Bryan, who stared at me with an eyebrow cocked. "A blowie?"

I chuckled, but it hurt my head. "Yeah, so? Don't be jealous."

"Nice," he said, smiling and looking down at his textbook.

I closed my eyes and flung an arm over my face, hoping his studying would be done so quietly so I could sleep some more. I really didn't remember much past the fun of last night, let alone how I got here. I chalked it up to mixing tequila and whiskey and vowed not to drink hard liquor anymore.

As I drifted back to sleep, I suddenly remembered that the woman I'd been with last night had been a beautiful redhead. Suzette… that had been her name. She'd been stunning and sensual, but there was something else about her that was unforgettable: Her black eyes.

My eyes flew open as I finally remembered last night. All of it. *What the hell?* My head felt foggy and confused, and I couldn't understand why I wasn't more freaked out than I should have been. Why wasn't I leaping off the bed in a frenzy, trying to figure out what happened?

Because I kind of didn't care. *Why didn't I care?* I was starting to get a migraine from trying to analyze this whole thing. I felt like I should be getting a sick feeling in my stomach and becoming angry about why I'd even gone home with that chick, or why I couldn't remember how I'd gotten back to my dorm room... but I didn't. I just kind of felt... nothing.

I must have drifted off, because when I woke hours later, I was alone in the room. I got up slowly, went to the bathroom, and took a shower. Not caring about my appearance whatsoever, I threw on a T-shirt and jeans, snatched my keys and wallet from the back pocket of last night's pants from the floor, and flew out to the parking lot and to my motorcycle.

The grumbling vibration of the bike comforted me somehow, and when I pushed the throttle to get me going, I smiled ever so slightly as I tore off down the street with really nowhere in mind. I just needed to ride. I just needed to think. Like a magnet, I was drawn to the water, and within what seemed like a blink of an eye, I found myself at Seabreeze Amusement Park. I slowed the bike down and stopped at the edge, staring out at the sparkling, choppy water. After killing the engine, I dismounted the motorcycle and then shoved my keys into my pocket. I walked woodenly to the water's edge. As I stood and stared at it, I watched the slow, lazy waves lick at the tips of my boots.

Numbness... there was no other way to describe what was in my head and my heart. Trying so hard to analyze what had happened the night before, I began to get that headache again, the one that throbbed at my temples. It was almost like a warning, like I wasn't meant to remember last night.

But I did. I know what I fucking saw. That crazy bitch went down on me, then afterward, as I was drifting off, she turned into some sort of monster. Her eyes had been black, I do remember that as clear as day... as they had been a very light crystal-blue beforehand, that much I knew, but after our... encounter... she'd looked a little crazy and deranged.

"Argh!" I yelled with my hands pressing against the sides of my head. I crouched down and tucked my head into my center, growling low in my chest. This restless, panicked, anxious feeling in my gut was driving me crazy. I realized I'd been rocking back and forth when I felt a warm hand on my shoulder. I stood immediately, sucking in a deep breath to face whoever had touched me.

Encountering a pale, elderly lady, I immediately relaxed.

"Are you okay, young man?" she asked.

I nodded and swallowed thickly, raking a hand through my hair.

"Yeah…"

She narrowed cloudy eyes at me. "You don't look okay."

Her small white dog began to bark and tug at its leash. I looked down and saw that it was baring its teeth at me, growling low in its throat. I then heard another growl and was horrified to realize it was coming from me.

The lady's cloudy eyes bulged in their sockets and she bent down, gathered up her small dog, and shuffled away from me as quickly as she could.

Confused as to why I had growled back at a dog, I fished my keys from my pocket, ran back to my bike, and took off with no destination.

VAMPIRE HUNTING

Present Day

Shreveport, LA

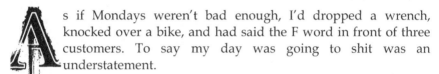

As if Mondays weren't bad enough, I'd dropped a wrench, knocked over a bike, and had said the F word in front of three customers. To say my day was going to shit was an understatement.

"The hell is your problem, kid?" Archie asked, spitting chew into a white Styrofoam cup in his hand. He set the cup on his desk and went around it to sit down.

I lifted a shoulder and let it fall, trying to act casual, but I was nervous as hell. "I... I don't know. Not sleeping."

This is ridiculous, I told myself. I never slept well. Was I really using the sleeping excuse? It was lame, at best. In all honesty, I hadn't had a vivid-ass dream about her in such a long time, that it had shaken me... and that had just pissed me the hell off.

"Boss, it won't happen again. I'm not sleeping well but I'll try to fix that."

Archie lifted an eyebrow at me. "I hope not." Just then, his cell rang. He fished it from the pocket of his pants and answered it. "Yeah?"

There was silence, then his face went stony and somber. Finally he spoke. "Riders meet tonight. Gonna nail those vampers."

As he ended the call, I was still staring at him. "Care to share?" I boldly asked.

"Think you can drop the clumsy act long enough to go on a ride?" he asked with a wicked gleam in his eye.

By ride I knew he meant a hunt. Because the stupid succubus bitch was responsible for my current state of restlessness and apparent clumsiness, I forced a smile at killing one of her kind, put out my fist, and said, "Fuck yeah."

Archie smiled and bumped his fist with mine. "We ride tonight, brother."

I stared in disbelief at the Greyhound bus station before us.

"The bloodsucker is taking a... bus?" Ollie, one of the Rebel Riders asked. I looked at his salt-and-pepper Hollywood-style pompadour on his head, matching goatee, and tats that covered him from the tips of his fingers to his neck and hoped I looked as cool as him when I was in my mid-forties. Then I remembered I *was* in my forties but would never get gray hair.

Nor would I *ever* wear a fucking pompadour.

Archie nodded. "Yup. I wouldn't believe it if I didn't see it myself."

"The shit-bag couldn't hypnotize a human into taking him wherever he needed to go?" I asked, an unlit Marlboro loosely hanging between the two fingers of my right hand. I itched to light it.

Ollie lifted one massively muscled shoulder in a shrug. "Guess not. But we'll get him."

Archie pulled a can of Copenhagen from the back pocket of his worn jeans, screwed open the lid, and grabbed a huge pinch. When his bottom lip was full with the stuff, he looked at me. "The bus says it's going to Kansas City."

I glanced at him curiously and shoved a hand in my pocket for my lighter. "I say we stake him now. He may eat half the passengers on that damn bus."

Archie curled in his bottom lip, scratching at the gray hairs at the top of his goatee. He leaned on his cane as he stared at the vampire in thought. We knew the bus wouldn't leave for ten more minutes, but we had a decision to make, and I was itching to kill something.

After spitting a brown stream onto the concrete in front of the Shreveport Greyhound station, he turned to look at me. For the first time, I noticed the usual diamond stud he wore in his left ear had been replaced with a little gold cross. I bit back a laugh. "I agree. Kovah, you get on the bus and try to lure the leech to come off."

I smiled, shoving the lighter back into my pocket and shoved the unlit cigarette behind my ear. "You got it, boss."

I left my renegade comrades behind and made my way toward the obnoxious, rumbling diesel machine that threatened to take our vampire suspect out of our reach.

This particular bloodsucker had gone on a rampage in Shreveport. We'd linked him to no less than five murders of human beings in the city. Three were homeless men and two were single women who frequented bars. This vampire prick was out of control, and the hell if the Rebel Riders were going to just let him slip out of the city and go on to terrorize another town. The leech had to be stopped and I was more than happy to do it. All of my rage, bitterness, and sorrow of losing my human life was poured into taking out pretty much any vampire who crossed my path. I held no belief that any of them could be "good" or even "rehabilitated." No, that was for pansy, softhearted assholes who didn't get what it was like to be around these monsters who had no regard for human life.

I stepped onto the bus, when the bus driver, an older Black man in a uniform with kind brown eyes, said, "Ticket?"

Shit.

I pulled off my sunglasses and waited for him to gasp at the milky-white color of my pupils. When he did, I smiled. Capturing him with my gaze, I said, "I gave you my ticket about ten seconds ago. Surely you remember?"

He nodded in agreement and said, "Yes, you gave me a ticket."

Replacing my glasses, I walked to the back of the bus where my newest victim sat gazing out of the window. I noticed his small suitcase sitting on the floor between his feet.

He looked to be in his mid-twenties, but I figured, like me, he was much older. With modern eyeglasses and a clean haircut, he almost had a Son of Sam, nerdy but handsome, preppie look about him. I bit back a smile.

The vampire sniffed the air, thinking I wouldn't notice, and then turned to look at me. I looked down at the empty seat next to his when his eyes met mine.

"Well, hello," he said very friendly-like, his expression bordering between confusion and excitement. I'd seen that look before. I wasn't sure how I smelled to vampires, but I was fairly sure I displayed both human and vampire scents, and that afforded me a very nice distraction as the leeches struggled to figure it out.

My sunglasses still firmly in place, I slipped into the empty seat and sat down, slinging my arm over the back of the seat. "Hey, vampire. Where ya headed?"

His eyes widened in surprise and I chuckled at the response I knew I'd get. He went to stand, but I shoved my hand down on his shoulder forcefully and smiled. "Stay, Michael McCoy. We have a lot to talk about."

His blue eyes were still bulging in their sockets at the use of his real name, and as he quickly caught on, his expression turned dark as his eyes morphed to completely black. His fangs popped out, thrusting out of his mouth and poking him in the bottom lip.

I laughed, the dagger already in my hand. With one lightning-fast gaze around the bus, which was mostly empty except for a couple of humans seated near the front, I said, "Your fangs don't scare me, asshole." I didn't even think before I plunged the dagger into his chest. I stood up and backed off quickly as his surprised face turned gray, then into ash, then into a big pile of something that required a broom and dustpan on the seat where he once sat.

Chuckling, I reached down, brushed ash from my black boots, and picked up Mr. McCoy's suitcase. I whistled the theme to *The Love Boat* as I discreetly walked off the bus and over to Archie and the other riders with a grin on my face. I heard the driver put the bus into gear and then watched with satisfaction as it took off toward Kansas City with a bus full of humans and a seat at the back piled with gray ashes and human clothing.

I really couldn't give two shits whether or not they questioned the ashes and clothing. Because honestly… it wasn't my problem.

I thrusted the suitcase into Archie's arms. He looked down at it. "What is this?"

"McCoy's," I replied, fishing the cigarette from behind my ear and the lighter from my pocket.

"Where's the vamp?" Ollie asked through a lip full of chew.

I lit the smoke and blew a stream into the air. I narrowed my eyes at Ollie. "Dead. Again."

A smile lit up his face and Archie put out his fist. "Nice."

I bumped it with my own and watched as Archie set the case on the ground and unzipped it. Clothes, a bag of toiletries, a small black book, and a large, strange-looking box. He pulled it out and tore off its lid. A wave of smoke — or maybe it was steam — wafted out of it.

"Dry ice," Archie murmured. He dumped the box upside down and out came half a dozen bags of blood.

Ollie made a face. "That's fuckin' disgusting."

I nodded. "Hell yeah, it is."

Archie put the bags back into the box, then the box into a nearby dumpster. He replaced the clothes and toiletries into the suitcase but kept the little black book. I watched as he re-zipped the suitcase and pulled out his lighter, flicked it to life, then tossed it onto the case, carefully setting it on fire. We all watched in reverent fascination as it burned down to almost nothing. Then Archie tossed what was left into the same dumpster.

We watched as Archie opened the little black book to find out that it was, in fact, a real, life little black book. Names and phone numbers, some with notes under the name, were scrawled in neat handwriting, all in alphabetical order throughout the pages.

"Flip to the back, where the Vs are," I said, curious about something.

With his yellowed, calloused fingers, he flipped the pages until we found a handwritten subheading that just read "Vampires."

"Wow, real discreet, this one," I said dryly before taking another drag from my cigarette.

"Fuckin' jackpot," Ollie said, his eyes lighting up with excitement.

Archie nodded, smiling. "Got that right. These vampers ain't so smart, are they? We got ourselves a kill list here, boys."

"Yeah, we do!" Ollie said, punching the air with his fist.

His gesture reminded me of a time I had felt a small victory of my own…

Twenty Years Ago
Rochester, NY

My bike seemed to have a mind of its own as it steered me to the dive bar where I'd spent my time the night before. In the harsh light of day, it didn't hold the same magic. Its plain brown front and rickety ramp leading to the single entrace door looked bland and unremarkable. The cloudy windows with the unlit alcohol signs just looked sad. I sat straddled on my Harley, the engine still running and vibrating against my legs as I stared at the place.

Why had I come here?

I didn't know.

What was I hoping to accomplish?

I didn't know.

Where did Suzette live?

Now, that, I thought I knew.

A small but crazy smile began to form on my lips as I veered my bike away from the bar and toward downtown Rochester to see if I could locate where I'd been last night.

The wind sailed through my hair, which was a little shorter in the front than it was in the back. It reached my collar back there and looked pretty nice when I actually combed it. At this point, I didn't care about my hair or anything else. I pushed the throttle faster, determined to find this Suzette chick and make her answer some questions.

As I weaved in and out of traffic, I began to grow more anxious and agitated with every minute.

My driving grew erratic and unforgiveable. I cut off everyone and wove between the cars stopped in traffic, but I did not care. I could not care. I chanced a glance at the horizon and saw that the sun was sinking fast, and I smiled. The thought of the oncoming darkness of night made me happy for some reason. I craved it; I welcomed it.

The streets of downtown Rochester were eerily quiet as I made my way into its heart. The tall buildings shadowing the streets below lay quiet, and to respect the ambiance of the neighborhood, I killed the engine to the Harley. I sat quietly straddling my machine once I reached the modern high-rise condos that lined the glittering water's edge. I sat and pondered what my next move should be.

There was no damn way I could remember what apartment number this Suzette chick lived in. I was far too wasted to have paid attention to that, not to mention we had been in a serious lip-lock when she'd unlocked her door. I sat wondering why I had even come here in the first place.

Looking over, I could see that what was left of the daylight was gone. The horizon was lit in dark pinks and oranges, and I could already see stars beginning to poke out overhead. Not sure why I was smiling, I turned my attention back to the apartment building to see a stunning but pale woman with long red hair in a black leather miniskirt and blood-red pumps come out of the apartment building. It was her, I just knew it. I watched as she walked half a block to a dark-colored Datsun 280ZX. I was off my bike faster than I knew I could move. Before she could put the key in to unlock her car door, I was in right on her.

"Suzette?" I asked, barely a foot in front of her.

She looked me up and down, and with an annoyed glance said, "Yeah? Who are you?"

"You honestly don't remember me? I was in your bed less than twenty-four hours ago," I said, incredulous.

She licked her teeth and then rolled her eyes, turning away from me to get into her car.

I became instantly enraged. I grabbed her by her ghostly white upper arm, spun her around, and looked into her eyes. "You have got to be fucking with me. You need to tell me what the hell you did to me last night. I don't feel right. Did you put something in my drink? I won't press charges, I promise, just tell me so I know how to get rid of it."

She laughed without any humor, then tossed some hair behind her shoulder. "You have the wrong lady. Now piss off. I'm busy."

Yanking her arm from my grasp, she reached out and pushed me hard in the chest with both hands, sending me flying back onto my ass. Her strength was incredible, and, momentarily stunned, I watched as she quickly got into her car, peeled out of the spot, and sped off down the street.

Shaking off the assault, I grew irate. I growled in the back of my throat and stalked inside the apartment building. I found a directory posted on the wall. Unfortunately, it was listed by last names, and four out of the twenty names listed had "S" as a first initial. Furthermore, Suzette might not even be her real name. I was still fuming from the way she'd treated me outside when I heard a voice.

"Who are you looking for?"

I turned to see a balding old timer in jeans, a checkered shirt, and suspenders looking at me with untrusting brown eyes.

Instantly trying to quell my anger, I offered him a fake smile and said, "Suzette, the redhead. She… ah, owes me some money."

Lame excuse, but it was all I could come up with on the spot.

His wizened face lit up with amusement, and he cackled, leaning on his cane. "Suzette don't owe nobody no money, boy."

I swallowed down more anger that wanted to rise but kept the smile plastered on, happy he at least knew who I was talking about. "Which apartment is hers?" I asked, pointing to the board.

He shook his head and walked away, and then without turning around, called out, "Get lost, boy, she ain't here. I think she works nights."

Yeah, she works nights, all right, I thought.

I didn't even acknowledge the old man, but ran out to my bike and took off. I had to get some more sleep and think of a plan as to what I was going to do when I returned tomorrow evening.

Chapter 4

FORMULATE A PLOT

Present Day

Shreveport, LA

We had picked off six of the twenty-two vampires listed in vampire Michael McCoy's little black book the idiot had so nicely left us after I'd killed him.

Some had been fairly easy to locate, as we would call them and pretend to be blood dealers or donors, and they'd meet us in seedy, dark places where we'd instantly end them with a knife or a stake. The next vampire on the list had proved to be a little more elusive.

Manta LaRae was how the black book had her listed. We couldn't figure out exactly what she was about. We weren't sure if she had been a love interest of Michael's, a vampire prostitute (yes those existed), or maybe a dealer herself. She never answered her phone, and the one time I'd left her a voicemail asking her to call me back in my most charming voice, she never did. Archie suggested we skip her and move to the next one on the list, but something about this one intrigued me; nagged at me. I loved a good challenge and wanted to find this Manta vampire.

Archie reluctantly agreed to let me try alternative methods to track her down, and with me being the most social media savvy of the bunch, I finally hit paydirt when I typed her ridiculous sounding name into one of the big social media sites on my phone.

I'd spent more than an hour perusing her page. Manta LaRae was one hot topic. I knew I'd found the right person when I had checked her profile and it showed she lived near Shreveport. I sent her a friend request, and after waiting a couple of days, she accepted.

I liked a few of her posts and then I watched what she was doing on social media—which wasn't much, but a few days later, when her feed showed that she was attending a local event, I knew we'd know exactly where she'd be—and when.

"What the fuck?" I said, my face two inches from my phone screen.

Archie threw back the shot he'd ordered and didn't even wince at the whiskey burn. We sat at our favorite bar, Rico's, relaxing after a long work week.

"What?" he asked, staring at me with a questioning gaze.

"Vampire Ball? What in God's name is that?"

One of the Riders, Aspen, piped up. "Oh, don't get too excited"—he waved a dismissive hand—"that stupid-ass costume party goes on every year." He pounded back the shot of Jack the same way Archie had.

"You boys sure it's just a costume party? I mean, this vampire bitch just RSVP'd to it on Facebook," I said, trying to sound smart.

Archie signaled for the waitress and she came over. "Annie, another round, honey."

Annie, the waitress who had to be pushing fifty by now, smiled sweetly as she adjusted her top to try to accentuate her cleavage, and winked. "You got it, Arch."

He grinned in triumph and turned his attention to me as a Metallica song began to play from a corner jukebox in this dive bar. "From what we've gathered, there are both real vampers and some posers that attend it," he said. "But we have yet to figure out why the real ones go to this thing. Either to feed or to find new prospects, we aren't sure."

I nodded. It made sense, to an extent. "All right, I get you. But this vamp called Manta is supposedly going to this thing. We gotta go and scope it out."

"Negative," Ollie said, pulling a cigarette from his front pocket but not lighting it. "The vampers there already know us. We won't get through the front door. But we usually wait outside 'til it's over to see if we can catch any real leeches."

I pulled off my sunglasses, and with a smile in his direction, I said, "Yeah? Well, I can get in."

A week later, I had a decision to make: Was I going to this vampire ball as a poser wannabe vamp, or as a blood whore? Both made me sick as fuck to think about, but it was clear I needed to put my feelings aside and realize I had a job to do. I went with the former and hoped they would let me in the front door as an eager vampire recruit. And if they didn't, hey, I held the power of persuasion in my stare. Since the day the succubus had taken my soul, I had never had anyone tell me "no" and actually mean it.

I dressed in all black—dark jeans and a Pantera T-shirt. Using my phone to pull up the ticket I'd bought online, I entered the large hotel that sat smack-dab in the middle of the Quarter. Oh—did I fail to mention this "vampire ball" Ms. Manta LaRae was attending—was held in New Orleans? Yeah, I drove the five hours down there just to follow her around—that was, if I could even manage to find her.

While stalking her online, I realized that she hadn't posted any photos of herself, but she was tagged in one photo where she wore a costume at this event last year. Her face had been covered by a mask, but I memorized the curves of her body and noticed her hair was dark brown. However, I couldn't tell the length as it looked like it was pulled back.

"ID," the bouncer muttered stoically as I made my way to the front of the line. He shone a small flashlight on my driver's license and looked at me. "Glasses off."

I removed them and flashed him a fake smile. Since I was here pretending to be vampire prospect, I couldn't look too weird. I had put in my brown-colored contact lenses, the eye color listed in my license, which I planned on removing soon. I was pretty sure the power of my persuasion was held in the milky bluish-white irises of my gaze and I had a feeling once inside, I might need my little trick.

The large bouncer, whose shirt looked about three sizes too small, handed me back my license and told me to have a good night.

I replaced my sunglasses as I went inside. It was dark as hell in here. I could still see, but it was impeded. I first found the bathroom and entered a stall, locking the door. Pulling the contact lens case from my pocket, I quickly removed the contacts and dumped them into the case I'd pre-filled with saline solution.

Ah, so much better. Screwing back on the lids, I shoved the case into my pocket. I replaced my sunglasses and exited the stall. I washed my hands for good measure and left the restroom to see what I was dealing with.

I made my way to the bar to get a beer and try to blend in. Two guys got their drinks and turned away from the crowded bar, leaving a space for me to shove myself into. On the barstool next to where I stood was a redhead with paper-white skin and ruby-red lips. I almost rolled my eyes when she touched my arm with her cold hand and said, "Hi, handsome."

"Don't touch me, succubus," I growled, speaking before thinking, as I snatched my arm away from her reach.

She laughed and said, "Fine, have it your way." She didn't even bother denying the accusation.

I ignored her and quickly ordered and paid for a domestic bottle of beer and walked away without looking back. I would take care of that bitch later. Slightly relieved that the encounter didn't go as badly as it could have, I headed toward the dance floor to see a group of people slow dancing to the strange song that played. It almost sounded old and had no lyrics.

Most of the partygoers wore masks, and I knew from reading the website that masks were 'encouraged' but I knew I'd have on my shades most of the night so I hadn't bothered to get one.

My phone vibrated in my pocket and I pulled it out to see a text.

Archie: *How's it goin?*

I quickly replied: *Nothing really to report – yet… Just a succubus, but that isn't confirmed yet.*

He also quickly responded: *Copy. Stay safe and remember… TOGVIADO.*

I pocketed the phone and looked around with the beer to my lips. It was so dark in here, it was going to be hard spotting anyone who fit the description of this vampire woman. Then I realized that there were probably so many real vampires in here, that this Manta girl would be the least of my problems. I closed my eyes behind my shades, took a few deep breaths, and concentrated. I blocked out the music, the pulse of the bass on my sensitive ears, the way it vibrated my bones, and centered myself. When I opened my eyes, I let my super-eyesight do the work for me. I looked slowly around the club until I spotted a couple in the center of the dance floor. As if everyone around them had been blurred into a shaft of nondescript light around them, I watched them closely, staying as still as possible.

I began to get the familiar heavy feeling in my chest, and a tingle raced up my spine.

The fact that the dude dressed in all black with pale skin had produced fangs when he bent to kiss his dance partner's delicate neck did not surprise me. Anyone could buy fake fangs that looked shockingly real at any mall store. But when his light-colored eyes turned black, that was when I knew I'd located my first bloodsucker of the night. I pulled out my phone and zoomed in, waiting for him to come up for air. With his head craned and blocking my view of her neck, I waited patiently until his head popped up. Blood dribbled down his chin and the girl's entire body was slack in his arms. That was no fake blood capsule; I had myself the real deal here. With him facing my direction, I snapped three photos and quickly put the phone away with a smile on my face.

I turned around to check on the succubus. She was gone from where she once sat, so I scanned the club once again. This vampire ball was sort of freaking me out. With so many in here being open about their true natures, or wannabe natures, it was hard to hone in on the real ones. I kept looking around. My eyes found the vampire from a minute ago, casually dancing with his partner again. She seemed to perk up a bit after his bite, and now they looked like a normal couple just dancing.

It pissed me off. It pissed me *right* off.

Gritting my teeth, I went outside to cool off. After tossing my beer bottle into a nearby trash can, I pulled a pack of smokes and a lighter from my pocket and lit one up. There were half a dozen other partygoers out smoking so I felt like I blended in.

My sensitive hearing picked up a woman's giggle coming from the side of the building. I casually wandered toward the sound, stood at the side of the club, and listened as I smoked.

"Come back to my place, baby," a deep, male voice said.

Another feminine giggle.

"You keep doing that, and I may fuck you right here against the wall," the male said again.

Stupid kids.

I was about to crush out my cigarette when I heard him say, "Holy shit, are those contacts?"

Without thinking, I threw my cigarette down and unsheathed the knife that hid in the small of my back. Keeping it close, I looked around the corner to see the very same succubus who had been sitting at the bar with both hands on a young man's face. He was very still and looked intently into her eyes. She whispered something to him.

I stayed in the shadows and slunk along the wall of the building. When I was about six feet away, she turned and looked. Narrowing her eyes at me, she said, "Fuck off, asshole. I'm busy."

That broke the trance. The guy turned and looked at me, and I said, "Run, man, now, and don't look back. This chick's about to kill you."

His eyes widened as her hands dropped from his face. He swallowed hard and took off running toward the front of the club.

"You dick," she growled, her eyes still pure black. "Guess I'll have to take you home instead."

I chuckled and stepped closer to her. "You could… but you won't get my soul. It's already been stolen, so unfortunately for you"—I got even closer, so close I could smell her cheap perfume—"I have nothing to lose."

Thankfully, over the past twenty years, I had many opportunities to study and memorize the strange, jerky movement that happened a split-second before a vampire took off at superhuman warp speed, so as she turned to run, I caught her by her hair and pulled my hand from behind my back. She clawed at me with pointy black fingernails, but I was faster than she was. Shrieking when she saw my knife, I just laughed as I lifted it and slammed it into her breastplate.

Looking behind me to ensure nobody had heard us, I threw her body to the ground and used the heel of my boot to drive the knife in further.

Black blood dribbled from the side of her mouth as she lay there twitching in pain and shock. Her hand reached for my knife, but it was too late. Along with the rest of her body, her arm began to turn gray, and with her mouth open and slack, she decayed before my amused eyes.

I pulled the phone from my pocket and looked behind me again. Nobody there. I turned the flash on and snapped a photo of her body, then texted it to Archie.

Succubus. I get double points, right?

I pocketed the phone, bent down, and yanked my knife from her shriveled chest. I then took out my lighter, igniting the hem of her skirt and watching happily as she went up in flames. I wiped the knife off on my pantleg. Then, I lit another cigarette and watched as she quickly burned to a shriveled mess. I felt the phone vibrate in my pocket.

Archie: *You're getting a raise at the shop effective Monday, kid. Good job.* There was a thumbs-up emoji after it.

I chuckled and slipped the phone back into my jeans.

When I could see nothing but smoking skin and bones, I looked behind me, grateful nobody had smelled the burning through their cigarettes, and tossed the corpse into a nearby dumpster.

I rounded the corner of the building whistling "Another One Bites The Dust," cool as a cucumber, and went back inside the club. I was pumped that I'd purged the world of *another* soul-sucking demon and was determined to find me another vampire to end.

After getting another beer from the bar, I moved to stand on the opposite side of the dance floor, hoping to catch more legit bloodsuckers. I knew where the first one was, as he sat at a dark table in the corner with two other males. I would take care of him later.

Chapter 5

CONDOMS & SLEEP AID

Twenty Years Ago

Rochester, NY

I hadn't gone back to Suzette's apartment the following night. I had too much shit to deal with. I had been sleeping most of the day, and once the sun went down, I felt alive. I'd missed all my classes and had barely remembered to call in sick to the pizza delivery place where I held a part-time job. So when the sun disappeared behind the horizon, I got up, showered, and felt restless. I thought I'd go again to Suzette's apartment, but I realized I should probably lay low. Not only that, I felt twitchy and on edge. It was like I had a buzz of energy that needed to be let out somehow. I just wasn't sure what to do about it, so I hopped on my bike and headed to the local arcade. After dumping over twenty dollars' worth of coins into the stupid machines and losing every time, I grew frustrated at the losses and tore off toward Seabreeze Park again.

I stopped just short of the water's edge and dismounted my bike. I began to pace back and forth like someone hopped up on coke. I couldn't figure out what the hell was wrong with me, but I was seriously restless and it was irritating me. I stood staring out at the water with my helmet in one hand and the thumbnail of my other hand between my teeth.

"You lost, little boy?"

I turned when I heard a dark voice that sent shivers up my spine. Narrowing my eyes, I counted five figures standing a good ten feet away.

Not responding but continuing to stare, I wondered what they wanted and if they had truly been talking to me. I didn't bother looking behind me to see if perhaps they'd been talking to someone else, because I already knew nobody was there. Plus, I didn't want to look weak.

"You deaf, asshole?" one of them asked, the same one who'd posed the first question.

"No. What do you want? I'm just walkin' here," I replied, my voice sounding way too much like my Grandpa Luigi's right now, my hands gesturing in the same way I'd seen his do so many times.

"Did I give you permission to be out here?" the guy asked again.

"Do you ever speak normally, or do all your conversations come in the form of a question?" I asked, amused at my own rhetoric.

I don't remember blinking, but apparently I had, because the ten feet that had separated us was suddenly about two. He'd moved so fast I hadn't even seen him, yet he was here. I gasped in surprise.

"Got me a smart guy here, do I?" he said, amusement dancing in his black eyes.

Black eyes! No whites at all!

I shoved him in the chest with all my strength and that barely moved him back a foot.

"Do not touch me, you freak!" I yelled, but it was in vain. The freak's friends were now in my face and I grew scared. I had obviously invaded this gang's territory, and now I was going to pay for it.

Completely surrounded, I backed up and put my hands up in surrender as I looked at the group around me. Four men and one woman, all normal enough looking for a group of goth bullies, but more sinister than anything I'd ever encountered.

"He smells weird," the female voice said.

I wished I could see her face better, but it was pretty dark out here.

"Yeah, he does," a deep, male voice said, almost in a growl.

The night was dark, barely a moon to illuminate the water. Still determined to get the hell out of here, I had every intention of just turning around and leaving the idiots. It seemed, though, that leaving peacefully just wasn't in the cards for me.

The group began to step closer to me.

The fight or flight response bubbled up inside of me and I realized the fight response was winning. I might get my ass kicked, but at least I'd expend some of this energy — this buzz of anger and frustration — that now lay deep in my gut... in my very soul.

Dropping my helmet and keys to the ground, I took a fight stance, put up both fists, and growled, "You want some of this? Come and get it."

They all burst out laughing. "I'm not gonna fight you, boy. Just get the hell out of my territory before you see something you don't want to see."

I raised my chin, fists still up. "No."

Why was I telling him no? He was giving me a free pass to leave. And what was I going to see? Them commit some kind of crime?

Then I thought about his black eyes, how they looked so much like Suzette's.

"Hey, man, do you know a redhead named Suzette?"

The one in front, dressed in black leather from head to toe with spiky blond hair looking way too much like Billy Idol, squinted his eyes and regarded me carefully before folding his arms and responding, "Yeah. You her bitch?"

My eyebrows hit my hairline. "What?"

They all laughed.

"What, what?" he mocked in a childish voice.

"What's your problem, dude? I just asked you a question. Where does she hang out?"

His face grew serious. "I don't know anything about her whereabouts, nor would I tell you if I did. You got a beef with her or something?"

I shook my head and laughed without humor. "None of your business."

I went to walk away, realizing this conversation was useless. I picked up my helmet and keys and headed back toward my bike.

"Pussy," I heard one say as I walked away.

I stopped. My jaw clenched and my face grew hot. I wanted to turn around and fight them, but what good would that do? Expend some energy maybe… or maybe get me killed.

I blew out a breath and walked to my bike, got on, and sped toward the bar where I'd met the redhead to see if she was there.

Pulling into the parking lot, I immediately saw her Datsun parked there, the high gleam wax job glinting under the parking lot lights. I killed the engine to the bike and got off, leaving my helmet on the back, hoping it wouldn't get swiped.

The bar was crowded. What day was it? I didn't even know. Sunday, maybe? I immediately spotted her at the bar, dressed similarly how she'd been that night.

"Waterfalls" by TLC began blasting through the speakers. Everyone crowded the dance floor and began screaming and singing along while dancing with each other. I longed to be carefree and join them. Get drunk and have fun, but I hadn't felt like myself for the past 48 hours, and I was going to get to the bottom of it.

Some douchebag with gold chains and too much gel in his hair was talking to Suzette, but I just interrupted them. I gently grabbed her upper arm and said, "Suzette, I need to talk to you."

Her eyes moved from the guy to me, and they narrowed. Then she looked at her gentleman friend and said, "If you'll excuse me, I'll be right back. Don't you go anywhere now." She winked and stepped around him.

I dragged her to the hallway that led to the bathrooms.

"Are you stalking me, Dominic?" she asked, her arms folded over her ample chest.

I bit back a smile. "Oh, now you remember me?"

"Didn't get enough the last time? You want round two?" she asked, smiling slightly.

My face darkened. "No. I want to know what you put in my drink. I'm still all fucked up two days later."

She tossed some thick, red hair over her shoulder and smiled up at me with blood-colored lips. "Sweetheart, I didn't put anything in your drink. This body just takes a while to recover from. I've got a magical mouth —"

I cut her off by slamming the side of my fist against the wall behind her, causing her to flinch. "No, that's not it! I feel..." I raked a hand through my hair. "Dammit! I don't know what I feel. Just help me, please."

She looked up and stared at me hard for a few seconds. "Meet me at my place tomorrow night. Apartment 302. I'll be waiting for you."

"While I find you hot, I really am not looking for a good time, Suzette. I need answers."

She kissed the tips of two fingers and pressed them to my lips with a smile. "I will give you both." With a wink, she left to go back to the bar and join the guy she'd been talking to.

I went back to my dorm and tried to go to sleep. Bryan was dead asleep, snoring away with his textbook open across his chest. I placed a piece of paper in it before closing the book and setting it on his nightstand. I then took a hot shower and tried to lie down but I wasn't even remotely tired. I stared wide-eyed at the ceiling for about an hour when I looked over at the clock: 1:02 a.m.

"Crap," I muttered, throwing back the sheet. I went into the communal TV room and found a few guys watching a *Twilight Zone* marathon, so I sat with them and watched it in silence.

Unfortunately, even that began to bore me after about an hour. It was now past two a.m. and I knew I needed to get some sleep, but because I'd slept all day, I wasn't tired yet.

Walking out of the TV room, I went back into my dorm and grabbed my keys. I decided to walk the four blocks to the 7-11. It was September, and the nights had started to cool off. I wore nothing but jeans, a college T-shirt, and a flannel over it. I walked faster to try to warm up a bit. By the time I got to the 7-11, I was grateful it was warm inside.

I went to the aisle where the medicines were kept and looked for a sleep-aid. Deciding Nyquil would do the trick, I turned to leave and spotted the condoms. I really didn't carry any with me, but after my tryst with Suzette, I decided I should probably stock up. I wasn't going over there tomorrow to fuck her, but who knew what would happen. I needed to be prepared.

I grabbed a box and plunked it and the cold medicine on the counter. I paid for them, then left the store, looking at my surroundings.

Walking quickly down the street, I picked up the pace, feeling even more restless than ever. What the hell was wrong with me? I put my hand to my forehead, feeling like I was getting a headache.

I'm in apartment 302…

Suzette's voice echoed in my head.

Meet me tomorrow night…

Shaking my head, I thought, *No. I'm not waiting 'til tomorrow night. Fuck that.* I went back to my dorm, dropped off the cold medicine, shoved two condoms into the front pocket of my jeans, and tore off on my bike to Suzette's apartment.

M IS FOR MURDER

Twenty Years Ago

Rochester, NY

After parking my bike on the street, I went to the front of her building and looked up at it. Thankfully, someone was just walking into the building so I hurried in behind them, then took the three flights of stairs. As I entered the hallway to the third floor, I could easily see apartment 302. Looking both ways down the hallway, relieved it was empty, I pressed my ear against the door. I could faintly hear the sounds of passion coming through, and for some reason, this made me angry. Very, very angry.

I tried to analyze why this pissed me off, but I couldn't figure it out. I shouldn't care what she was doing, but my emotions had been all over the place for the last two days. I grew even angrier as I tried to analyze it.

I went to kick in the door but decided to try the knob first. It opened on the first try, and I laughed in triumph. The apartment seemed eerily quiet now. Thankfully, I remembered how to get to her bedroom, and I stalked quietly toward it.

As the door was wide open, I could see her writhing around as she straddled someone. I gasped in shock. I wasn't sure why I expected her to be alone, despite the noises I'd heard from behind her front door, but maybe I hoped I'd been imagining them.

With morbid fascination, I wandered into her room and watched as Suzette went stock-still and craned her head back. I heard her inhale sharply, then freeze.

"Your tits are amazing," I heard a deep male voice say.

He opened his eyes, and his gaze went straight to me. "Holy fuck, is that your husband?"

Suzette turned around and looked at me with jet-black eyes. "No, just a stalker. What are you doing here, Dominic?"

The guy, who didn't look more than twenty-one and had skin the color of chocolate, pushed her off him. He rolled off the bed and grabbed his pants, putting them on quickly and rushing past me, shoulder-barging me in the process. I let him go. I didn't care about him. I came to see her and to get some answers.

Suzette coolly slipped on her pink silk robe and slid off the bed. Her eyes went back to normal and she shifted them to the door behind me, then to my face. "That is gonna cost you."

"What the hell are you talking about, lady?"

"I told you to come back tomorrow, not today. You slow or something?"

I stared at her incredulously. "You have a different dude in here every night or something, you whore?" I shook my head. "Unbelievable."

Before I could blink, she had moved across the room and was six inches from my face. "Yes, I do. And it's none of your business what I do, boy."

Her eyes went black again, and I gasped. She put her hand up to my face and ran her finger down my cheek to my neck. I thought she looked down at my neck but with her eyes being black, it was hard to tell. I then saw fangs poke out from the sides of her mouth and was completely paralyzed in fear at her transformation. She had fucking fangs. I couldn't breathe. My mind screamed at me to get out of there.

Then her hand wrapped around my throat. I tried to yell, but my feet were lifted off the ground as she hoisted me in the air and looked up at me. Wearing a wicked grin, she said, "I guess we'll skip the fun and go straight to the terror."

I gasped for breath, my fingers clawing at her hand to let me go. Her frightening eyes and fangs, my slowly dying breath, and the whole bizarre episode had me beside myself with fear. Knowing I had to do something or I would die, I looked down and saw my feet were dangling near her knees. I reared back my right leg and swung it as hard as I could. My boot got her right in the bare kneecap and she let go of me with a scream. I fell to the floor in a heap, gasping for air, but I did not stay there. Jumping up, I scrambled out the bedroom door and made a break for the front door, but she grabbed me by the back of my shirt and slammed me on the ground. Straddling me at lightning-fast speed, she looked down at me and laughed.

I yelled as loud as I could, hoping maybe the dude had left the door open and someone would come in and at least distract her so I could leave. Coming here had obviously had been a huge mistake, I realized too late. Maybe I could appeal to her.

"Get off of me! I'll leave, I promise—just let me up and I'll get the fuck out of here and never come back. You'll never hear from me again, I swear. Please…"

She looked down at me, and with a sneer said, "No. I need to kill you, otherwise, you'll wreak havoc on this city, and I can't have that shit coming back on me."

Confused, but in no mood to analyze her words, I reached behind where she straddled me. My arms were pinned but I could sort of move my right one, so I grabbed a handful of her bare ass. I squeezed, even digging in my fingernails, as hard as I could, hoping the pain would distract her and she'd get off me.

"Like that, do you, Dominic? Are you an ass man?" She laughed.

What kind of kinky shit is this woman into?

As she laughed, my other arm came free. I used it to feel around the floor surrounding me. My fingers gripped something, and I yanked. Hard. Turned out it was the coffee table leg, and when I slid the table close enough to us both, the distraction was enough for her head to turn to see what was coming at her.

Bucking her off, she slammed right into the glass table with a scream. I ran and found myself in the kitchen. I spied an ice bucket with a bottle of champagne poking up through the top. I grabbed the champagne and was going to run for the exit, hoping I could break the bottle and use it defensively. Suzette was on me, though. When she lunged at me, anger coloring her scary, bloody face, I swung the bottle in her direction. It smashed into a million pieces of glass and liquid all over her face and I sat stunned that it had actually worked.

Unfortunately for me, she didn't go down after being hit upside the head by a heavy glass bottle… it had just pissed her off.

Bloodied and wet, she stalked toward me and I briefly glanced around the kitchen to see an icepick inside the ice bucket. I grabbed it as she again wrapped her hand around my throat.

I wasn't going to let her lift me off the ground this time, though. Fuck that.

With a rebel yell, I plunged the icepick into her chest and that was enough for her to loosen her grip on me.

Shock registered on her face as she looked down at the pick. I yanked it out and plunged it back in again, right between her large boobs. She fell to the ground. Now blinded by rage and fear, I straddled her and then pulled the pick out. Closing my eyes, I plunged it in again, but then I noticed the action did not feel the same. My eyes popped open and then bulged in their sockets at what I saw before me. Leaping off her in fear and panic, I stared open-mouthed at what was now a shriveled, mummified corpse. Her once-red hair was now gray and dull and lay splayed around her black and prune-like face. There was a large hole in her chest where the icepick had done damage, and the shiny pink robe lay open around her naked, caved-in body, its soft color a stark contrast to the grisly horror now lying on top of it.

I looked at the pick in my hand and bolted for the front door. With shaking hands, I slammed it closed behind me, pounded down the three flights of stairs, and out the front door where the cold night air slapped me in the face. I jumped on my bike.

"Fuck, fuck, fuck, fuck!" I screamed as I tore off at illegal speed. I looked down at my hand and realized not only was it covered in blood, but I still had the pick. I was close to the park so I drove as fast as I could and parked the bike. Glad nobody was around, I tossed the murder weapon as far as I could into the water, then went into the park's bathroom and washed my hands. They shook so badly I could barely turn the faucet on.

I splashed some water on my face and looked into the cloudy, scratched mirror. Removing my flannel soaked in blood, I tossed it into the trash can in the corner, then looked myself over for any more blood. I didn't see any. I just noticed that I reeked of champagne, which was the least of my problems right now.

I felt like I was suffocating and couldn't breathe. I didn't know where to go. I had just committed fucking murder, but there was no way I could go to the cops. What would I tell them? I'd just killed a damn hooker but her body already decayed like it'd been dead for years?

What the hell *was* that? I couldn't get it out of my mind, the way her body looked, her mouth open in a silent scream. I didn't even mean to kill her. I was just trying to stay alive.

I slumped down the wall of the cold, dark park bathroom, put my head in my hands, and I fucking cried.

I wasn't sure how long I sat in that bathroom, but I eventually grew cold and stood up to leave. I really didn't want to go home to the dorm, but I went there anyway and parked my bike. Instead of going inside, I decided to walk around the parking lot and try to think some more. I had no idea what the hell I was doing, but I was going to clear my head and decide what to do before I went inside to a bunch of unsuspecting college kids and had to try to act normally. I wasn't tired and needed to walk. Maybe I should go for a run.

The parking lot was quiet with nobody around, but as I passed by a plain-looking sedan, I noticed there was someone sitting in the driver's seat. I looked away and kept walking, when I heard, "Psst!"

I ignored it and kept walking. The night seemed to have gotten darker.

"Dominic," the voice said again, this time commanding and dangerous. I stopped and turned around. A middle-aged man in a black trench coat and outdated tie stood on the sidewalk next to the sedan.

Oh, shit. He looked like the FBI or something. Had they tracked me down? Was he going to arrest me for murder? Maybe her neighbors called the police? Swallowing down my panic, I tried to act aloof.

"Yeah?" I said, thankful I was about eight feet away.

"Come take a ride with me," he said, opening the passenger side door.

I narrowed my eyes at him. "That would be a no."

I began to walk backward so I could keep my eye on him, and then I planned on taking off in a full-blown sprint into the woods behind the dorms. I didn't care that I was twenty-one years old. At that moment, I felt like a frightened eight-year-old who had just been offered candy by a stranger.

"I think it's a good idea for you to come with me. We have a lot to discuss."

What in the…? "Who are you?"

He looked around the quiet lot and said, "You've been bitten by a succubus and if you don't come talk to me, you're going to die in four days."

Chapter 7

THEY CALL HER MANTA

Present Day

New Orleans, LA

The thumping bass at this stupid vampire ball was working my nerves. Through gritted teeth, I took a swig of my beer and looked around.

I shivered as I realized someone had entered my space.

I turned to see a brunette standing in front of me. Even with the large heels she wore, she was still considerably shorter than my six-foot-two frame.

"Hi," she said, smiling up at me.

I took a swig of my beer and said, "Hi."

Standing on tiptoe, she leaned close to my ear to be heard over the music. "What's your name?"

"Kovah."

"That's interesting," she replied with a smile. "Different."

I nodded and didn't say anything more. She was nice-looking, even though she wore a mask, but I wasn't here to pick up women, I was on a mission.

"You smell good, Kovah," she said after taking a sip from the little black straw in her drink.

She wasn't lying. I had plastered on the cologne earlier. I'd been told I smelled strange by vampires, and they couldn't figure out *what* I was. I had hoped to just come off as human to them and the other creatures out there, but with their heightened sense of smell, they heavily relied on it to detect the presence of other creatures. I knew I couldn't be too careful. I had hoped by overly dousing myself in cologne, I would just come off as some douchebag poser wanting to join the vampire ranks.

"Thank you," I simply said. I hoped this chick would get bored and piss off. I needed to find…

"Manta," she said, as if reading my mind.

My eyebrows rose as I looked down at her. Yanking off my glasses, I looked at her and said, "What the fuck did you just say?"

"Manta… Manta LaRae. That's my name," she said in my ear. And when she pulled back to look in my face, she gasped at my eyes, hers going wide behind her mask. "Dominic?"

As she ripped off her mask, I gasped, too. We had definitely met before.

Twenty Years Ago

Rochester, NY

I gaped in horror at the guy. "*A what?* Who are you?"

With one hand up in surrender, he reached into his jacket pocket with the other and pulled out a badge. "Special Agent Rick Lewis."

Shit.

I briefly eyed his badge and said as calmly as possible, "That means jack-nothing to me, dude. That could be a fake badge."

He nodded and put his credentials back into his jacket. "You're right, kid; however, that doesn't change the fact that a succubus has stolen your soul, and you won't live to see Friday."

His words sent shivers up my spine, but still I feigned ignorance. "What are you talking about, man?"

He gestured to the open car door with a flourish and then looked around the dark lot before measuring me with a serious stare. "Get in and find out. Trust me, you need me right about now."

I raked my fingernails through my hair. *Crap.* This guy seemed to be the closest thing I had to help. With a sigh, I walked slowly toward his sedan and got in. He slammed the door, went around, and got in the driver's side. He started the car up and put it in gear.

Before pressing the accelerator, he looked at me and smiled wryly.

"Welcome to hell, Dominic. But don't worry, we'll tell you how to make it into purgatory."

I looked at him, alarmed. "Purgatory?"

Rick chuckled. "It's practically heaven, kid. Just hold on and enjoy the ride. You won't regret it, trust me."

A few minutes later, we pulled up to a warehouse in a very dark area of town. I swallowed hard. What had I gotten myself into?

Rick got out of the car and came around to open my door, but I was already up and out. He used a key from his keyring to unlock a small side door to the warehouse. I followed him inside as he locked the door behind us.

I found myself inside a small office, which smelled of must, coffee, and stale cigarettes.

"Sit," he instructed, indicating a cloth-padded chair set before a large gray metal desk. He took a seat behind the desk and pulled out a cigarette. He didn't light it, though. He just tapped it against his finger and stared at me.

My eyes flicked from the cig to his piercing blue eyes. "Can you get on with it already?" My knee began to bounce up and down nervously.

The door to his office opened, and a short, young, cute brunette dressed in a business suit walked in carrying a folder.

Rick said, "Dominic, this is Special Agent Violet McKittrick."

She smiled and put her hand out to shake. I noticed it was very cold, just like Suzette's. I withdrew my hand quickly.

"Nice to meet you," she said.

I simply nodded and looked back to Rick, waiting for an explanation. She quietly took the seat next to mine.

He leaned forward, folding his hands together on the desktop. He looked at me with intensity in his eyes. "I think it's best if we first explain what we do here. We're a branch of the Justice Department called the Bureau of Supernatural Investigation."

I raised an eyebrow. "The bureau of what?"

"We were founded about forty years ago to track and hunt supernatural creatures in the United States who don't play by the rules."

"Supernatural creatures? Look..." I said, beginning to stand. "I think you two have been watching too much *X-Files*, but I can see now I made a mistake getting into your car. Please take me back to my dorm."

"Sit down, kid," Rick snapped in a commanding, thunderous growl. "Shut the fuck up and let me finish."

I swallowed hard and did as he said.

"As I was saying. We've been tracking a succubus named Suzette Farrell who preys on college boys such as yourself. By the time we followed you two back to her apartment, it was too late."

I furrowed my eyebrows. "Too late for what?"

"To stop her from taking your soul. The succubus is a somewhat rare form of vampire. When a red-haired, blue-eyed human is made into a vampire, she becomes a succubus. She requires both blood and the essence—or the soul—of her victim to keep herself fed."

At this point, I had my arms crossed over my chest and was just waiting for him to get to the punchline. This story was getting more ridiculous by the second, but I found it mildly amusing.

"You've been feeling restless, unable to sleep at night, tired during the day?"

I simply nodded.

"You been having… inappropriate dreams about Suzette?"

My cheeks flushed hot. I had had two, the most recent one last night—or should I say yesterday since I slept all day—but didn't think much of it. She was hot and it didn't strike me odd at the time that I had been having erotic dreams about her.

I nodded again.

"The dreams will get worse. And they're more like visits from her subconscious to yours. She's slowly stealing your life force from you, the very core of your existence."

At this point, I was staring in disbelief at him. I looked over at Violet and she simply nodded sadly.

I began to grow afraid he was telling the truth.

"You feel like your emotions are flat and are finding it hard to feel anything but maybe some anger?"

Up until earlier tonight, I wanted to say, but instead I nodded woodenly. Damn, this guy was spot-on. "I don't understand. What is going to happen to me now?"

"You're going to turn into a vampire. Seven days after her bite, you will wake up and no longer be able to go into the sun. You will be starving for human blood and flesh. You will be a feral, ravenous creature with hardly a thought in your head."

I felt sick, my eyes wide with fear. "Like a zombie?"

He nodded. "Yes, I suppose a zombie is more like it. There are vampires who coexist peacefully with humans. Some work night jobs and pay bills and enjoy their long lives. They drink only donated or bagged blood, and we leave them in peace. But a vampire made by a succubus is none of those things. They are violent and cannot think of anything but blood."

I raised an eyebrow. "Regular vampire?"

He nodded. "Yes. Take for instance, Violet here."

I turned and looked at the brunette in horror, shrinking back in my chair. She smiled, her warm brown eyes turning completely black, the whites disappearing.

I jumped out of my seat and backed up. As quickly as they'd come, her eyes went back to normal and she laughed. "Calm down, Dominic. I'm harmless, see?"

She stood up, picked up Rick's hand, and planted a soft kiss on the back of it. He smiled up at her.

I slapped the sides of my head with my palms to ensure I wasn't dreaming. Her eyes looked just like Suzette's had.

"Please, sit," she said, gesturing to the seat. I pulled the chair away from her and sat in it.

Violet sat still with her legs crossed ladylike under her suit skirt. She threw me a wink and I gradually turned my attention to Rick.

"S-s-so, what you're telling me is that I'm going to turn into a zombie, and then what? You're going to kill me?"

He shook his head and picked up his cigarette, lit it, and took a long drag before answering me. Staring at me through the blue smoke he'd blown out the side of his mouth, he said, "No, because you're going to kill Suzette and then you can have your life back."

I laughed in irony. "Well, I guess it's my lucky day, because Suzette is already dead. I killed her about" — I looked at my watch — "four hours ago."

Before I knew it, the three of us were parked outside of Suzette's apartment complex. On the way over, I told them the entire story, from when I'd met her in the bar until I had plunged the icepick into her. It was now about an hour or so until sunrise and Rick had explained in detail what we were going to do.

"But why can't we just leave it?" I asked, growing tired and feeling like that eight-year-old again.

"Never, boy! Never!" Rick snapped at me. "We don't leave evidence around. Now let's go."

I was suddenly terrified to enter the building. Flashbacks of what had happened were fresh, and I froze in the street. Rick and Violet looked back at me. Rick could see I was paralyzed with fear and he walked the four steps toward me, grabbed my arm, and pulled me toward the building. "This is no time to clam up, kid. Come on, don't be a pussy. We do this, and then we're done. You're free and you will never have to deal with us again."

I nodded and we waited in the shadows until someone came out of the building. Violet moved at the same lightning speed I'd seen Suzette and the guy on at the water's edge move as she grabbed the door before it shut. I led them to the third floor, and once we arrived, Rick was huffing and out of breath.

"I need to cut back on the cigs," he muttered.

Ignoring him, I pointed to apartment 302. "It's that one."

"I'll go first," Violet said, her gun now out of its holster.

Rick drew his, also.

She tried the knob and it was, of course, unlocked. Pushing it open, she had her gun up and looked around. Seeing it was quiet, she waved us in with her free hand, and Rick closed and locked the door behind us.

He let out a low whistle through his teeth. "Damn, kid."

Violet wrinkled her little nose and said, "It smells like, blood, booze, and sex in here."

I nodded, wrapping my arms around myself. I purposely did not look at the corpse, which I, for some reason, half expected not to be there anymore.

"Wow, so they really don't ash," Violet said, crouching down and poking the body with her finger. "That's so cool."

I looked at Rick, confused. "Ash?"

Without taking his eyes from the body, he nodded. "Regular vampires turn to ash when you kill them."

"What?" I asked, my eyes wide.

They ignored my question and Violet looked at me. "Go find a trash bag and a mop and clean up that glass and booze that is all over the place. In fact, grab two trash bags."

I nodded and went into her kitchen, making a wide berth around the body, which lay in the dining room. I rummaged under the sink and found the trash bags, then I opened a couple of doors until I found a mop. I wet it in the kitchen sink.

Still refusing to look right at the body, I handed her a bag, went to the broken bottle, and began mopping as well as I could, my hands shaking again. I had to hand-pick the glass and I got up as much of it as I could. Thankfully, the champagne had mixed with the blood and there weren't any real blood stains on the hardwood floor.

"On three," Violet said.

I turned around and looked at her. She had her hands on the face of the corpse. She looked up at me. "Don't look, Dominic, okay?"

I didn't have to be told twice. I heard Rick count to three as I continued trying to find glass shards when I heard a horrific ripping sound. Resisting the urge to turn around, I kept to my task and tried not to cry like a little bitch again.

I quickly heard three more ripping sounds and prayed we could be done with this.

Standing with my trash bag of glass, I set it aside and tried to mop up as much of the liquid I could. Rick passed by me on the way to the bedroom and said, "I'm gonna do a last sweep for anything. Did you get undressed or leave anything here?"

I shook my head. "No, I walked in on them, and then went to leave. I didn't even touch anything until the fight."

"Good. Find a rag and clean up that blood splatter on the side of the kitchen island, then I think we can go."

I rinsed the mop and found a dishtowel, wet it, and scrubbed until it was gone. I looked to where Suzette's body had been, but it was also gone. Violet held the bag in her hand, and it looked heavy and lumpy. She smiled sweetly at me, and I turned away. After throwing the rag into my garbage sack, I figured out how to remove the mop head and dumped that into the bag, also.

"We're good. Let's go," Rick said, his eyes darting around the apartment. "Bring the mop handle, too. The government's been working on some new technology that will be able to lift fingerprints as evidence and match them in a computer. We aren't taking any chances here. Your fingerprints can be explained on normal surfaces, if it comes to that, because you were in here the other night for your little mattress romp with the succubus."

I nodded and left the apartment with them, locking the door behind us. As we got to the street, I noticed that the upcoming sunrise was just minutes away, a pink hue lightening the horizon.

We threw everything in the trunk and Rick drove me back to the dorms. I went to get out, when I noticed they were getting out, too.

"This way," he said, after retrieving the lumpy bag from the trunk. He also produced a shovel, and my eyes went wide.

"Where are we going?" I asked, just wanting to go to bed and pretend this whole thing had been a bad dream.

"You have to bury the body."

I swallowed hard. "*I* have to?"

He nodded. "Yes, we aren't one-hundred percent sure why, but that's what our research has shown us."

We reached the copse of trees that led to the small forest behind the college. This night had been so fucking weird, I didn't ask questions. I just followed.

Looking around once we were deep enough in the thicket of trees, Rick took the shovel and began to dig. When the hole was about three feet deep, he handed me the bag. "Lay the evil bitch to rest, young man."

I took the bag from him and dropped it into the hole. Then he handed me the shovel and looked around again. "Hurry, it's almost daylight."

Taking the shovel, I quickly re-covered her body and patted the earth with the flat end of the spade.

"Good job, now go get some sleep," he told me, clapping me on the shoulder as he turned to leave.

I handed him the shovel and took one last look at the makeshift grave. I conjured up some saliva and spit on it, then shot Suzette my middle finger. The two agents laughed.

When we reached the dorm entrance, I said to Rick, "What now?"

He shook his head. "Our research shows you should go on to lead an otherwise normal life. See, you have to understand what a huge accomplishment this is. Usually in these situations, we are stuck with the horrible and daunting task of killing a kid like you who's turned feral. You conquered her, and now you get to live." He lit up a cigarette, then shrugged. "That's what all the books say, anyway."

My eyes went wide. "Books?"

He looked at me through a haze of blue smoke. "We'll be watching you for a while. You will be protected. But now that you know about the world of the supernatural, we are counting on you to keep it to yourself."

"And if I don't?" I asked with more bravery than I felt.

Rick called over his shoulder as he walked away, "Nobody will believe you, anyway."

Knowing he was right, I slogged upstairs to my dorm room. Bryan was still asleep on his bed. I stripped down to my underwear, and after tossing the bag with the condoms and sleep-aid to the floor, I crashed out cold the minute my head hit the pillow.

When I woke, my dorm room was dark and empty, and I looked over at the nightstand clock and saw red numbers reading 6:54. The little red light on the upper left of the clock told me that meant p.m. I'd slept for almost 13 hours. Missed another day of classes and I was sure the pizza place had probably fired me by now.

Crap. Sitting up slowly, I stretched with a yawn and pulled on a pair of pants from the floor. Walking zombielike, I went into the communal bathrooms, thankful it was empty, and relieved myself at the urinal.

I needed to wake up. I turned on the taps at the sink and splashed some cool water on my face. When I lifted my gaze to the mirror, I noticed my entire neck was a deep purple. I could even make out Suzette's distinct fingerprints where she'd almost choked the life out of me. Shaking my head, and wondering how in the hell I was going to hide those, I lifted my eyes higher… and screamed in horror. "What the fuck!"

My once dark-blue eyes were now a milky bluish-white.

Chapter 8

THE EYES HAVE IT

Present Day

New Orleans, LA

anta. That isn't your real name."

She shook her head. "You knew me as Special Agent Violet McKittrick. Not my real name, either."

The twenty-year-old memory came flooding back to me, to the most horrible time in my life.

"Kovah, that's not your name either," she replied, chuckling. "Did you make that up?"

Ignoring her question, I looked at her more closely. She looked like a party-girl, not a special agent. I remember back then thinking she looked young, but I now knew she was very old.

"What do you know of Michael McCoy?" I asked.

She lifted a shoulder and let it fall. "Just another vampire. Why?"

"I killed him earlier," I said smugly, biting back a smile.

Her eyes went wide. "What? Why did you do that? He was a nice guy."

My face darkened. "He wasn't a guy. He was a bloodsucker who didn't use donors or blood bags. But you use donors or bags, right, Manta?"

She nodded. "Of course. Wow, I had no idea about Michael. That's unfortunate."

"Well, he was leaving bodies all over Shreveport, had to be put down," I said as I surveyed, the club, looking for the other bloodsucker I'd spotted earlier. I had to take care of that before I left out of here.

"So that's what you do, go around killing vampires for fun? Are you not a vampire now yourself?" she asked curiously.

I narrowed my eyes at her and made a face. "Hell no! Why would I want to become a vampire?"

Shock colored her expression. "Because you still look twenty years old, Dominic."

"Curse of the succubus, I guess. That's why I live here now and not in New York anymore. People were starting to ask questions. I had to get the hell out of there." I took a swig of my beer.

She nodded, genuinely interested. She lowered her voice and looked around. "That is a very interesting twist. Does the BSI know?"

"Not sure, haven't run into any BSI here. I think my friend Nolan has, though."

She furrowed her brow.

"Do you still work for them?" I asked.

"Yes," she said. "Undercover here tonight."

I chuckled and put the beer to my lips and said, "Well, you blend right in."

"So I'm told."

"This is where they have you stationed now then?" I asked, not sure why I was still sitting here making small talk with this government worker-slash-vampire, but I was mildly interested to have run into someone from my past. I was just thankful it wasn't anyone like a family member. I wouldn't have been able to handle that—or explain it.

"Yes," she answered. "I move every ten years."

"I know the feeling," I murmured.

She nodded, an understanding sadness in her light-brown eyes. God, I hated that pity look.

"I see you got some new ink," she said, changing the subject and pointing at my arms.

"Yep."

"May I look closer?" she asked.

I contemplated for a second, then nodded. She gently grabbed my arm with her cold hands and lifted the tattoo on my inner forearm of the red-haired pinup girl baring vampire teeth.

"I could psycho-analyze that all day," she said, chuckling.

Her finger traced over the mural-type picture of an Italian flag, an American flag, and the New York Yankees symbol all intertwined, with some cool shading behind it. It took up my entire upper arm. "Very nice," she said.

I didn't want to admit that, even though her skin was cold, her touch still felt good. I kept my distance from most people, just having an occasional one-night random here and there with human girls to satisfy needs (my body was still twenty years old, after all). I never sought out relationships or got phone numbers to pursue more. Dating a human would cause me nothing but pain later on.

I watched her curiously as she moved to my other arm and began tracing the other tattoos there with her finger. Memories of how she'd seemed so normal when I'd met her twenty years ago, how shocked I'd been to find out that she was a vampire... I was trying to remind myself of that. She wasn't a cute, flirty human girl. She was a bloodsucker.

Pulling my arm away from her, I reached into my back pocket and pulled out Michael's black book. I flipped to the Vs, turned it around, and showed her.

"Know any of these leeches?"

She looked up at me with a little bit of hurt in her eyes, but I blew it off. She replaced the mask on her face and took the book from my hand. Using her finger, she scanned the names and said, "Yeah I know a few."

"You know where they live?" I asked, taking the book back from her and pocketing it.

"You're the one who called me a few times, aren't you?"

I grinned around the mouth of my beer bottle. "Yeah."

"I didn't know who you were, so I never answered."

"I left a message," I snapped back, "with my number. You weren't the least bit curious?"

Chuckling, she said, "No, I just took your number to work and ran it through Lexus Nexus and it came back to Archie's Garage. Which told me it was you who friended me on Facebook, too. Nice Facebook name."

Now I laughed. "It's where I work. I use the company's page as my own and answer occasional private messages for Archie. I'm sure as fuck not putting my real name on that damn thing."

With amusement in her eyes, she said, "Even though Kovah isn't your real name."

"Even more of a reason."

She used her finger to trace the rim of her glass and looked down at it. "I use that site to keep up with family who don't know I exist."

Dammit, why did this vamp have to be so normal? "Yes, it's good for that, too." It was all I could think to say.

My beer was empty and it was time for me to go search out the other bloodsucker. "Well," I said, chuckling, "you have my number, so call me if you'd like to help me with this little problem." I pulled the book out and held it up.

She shook her head. "Most of them are normal, productive members of society. I won't help you kill them for no reason."

I turned to walk away, and then stopped and looked at her from over my shoulder. "That's what you thought about Michael McCoy."

Twenty Years Ago
Rochester, NY

By the time I went to run from the bathroom, a bunch of students had come to see what the yelling was about. I muttered something about jabbing myself in the eye and kept my hand over both eyes, barging my way through the crowd. I used the tiles of the bare floor to find my way back to my dorm room. I could probably get there with my eyes closed, anyway.

I went into the room and closed the door. In the dark, I could see clearly. There was only a little moonlight and a streetlight illuminating the room. I didn't bother turning on the lights. I threw on some clothes from the floor, opened my nightstand drawer, and grabbed my wraparound Oakleys, slamming them on my face. Snatching my keys, I raced out the door and stopped short when I got outside. Where the hell was my bike? The parking lot was crowded and I struggled to find it. Finally locating it, I hopped on and drove too fast until I reached the interstate that would take me to my parents' house.

An hour and a half later, I pulled up at the house I grew up in. I steered the bike into the driveway. Killing the engine, I looked up, noticing how some lights still burned inside the house.

On the drive over, I kept asking myself why I was coming here. This would freak my parents out. I had even inspected my eyes in my side mirrors when I'd come to a stop to see if they were still weird. Nothing had changed. The whites of my eyes blended in with the iris and pupil now. I could see that where once the dark sapphire iris sat was now such a faint blue, it looked like nothing. Like all the pigment was gone. The pupil was nothing more than a small dot just a slightly darker blue. I tried splashing some cold water directly into my eye to see what would happen and nothing did. I rubbed them hard with my fists to try to get them to turn red. Not so much as one blood vessel popped out. They remained unchanged.

I was beginning to fear that I would wake up tomorrow blind. I should have gone to the emergency room, but I didn't want to have to keep saying "I don't know" over and over when they asked what happened. Because I sure as hell wasn't going to tell them I'd killed a soul-sucking demon and had woken up the next day like this.

Deep in my gut, I knew this had something to do with that. But I had to see my parents. I had to talk to my dad and see if he could give a medical explanation for it first. He was, after all, a doctor. Sure, he was a cardiologist, but a doctor nonetheless.

I put the kickstand to my bike down and took a deep breath before walking to the front door and turning the knob. It was locked, so I used my key to get in. I should have used the payphone in my dorm to call ahead, but shit, I could barely breathe when I'd left there.

"Hello?" I called out, jingling my keys loudly as not to frighten them.

They both quickly came out from the kitchen, my mom holding a bowl of popcorn. The kitchen led to the living room, where I figured they'd be, watching television.

"Dominic!" my mom said, setting the bowl on the bottom stair of the staircase and coming over to hug me. I hugged her back.

"Hi, Ma."

"What are you doing here?" my dad asked, not angry or upset, just a bit surprised.

I set my helmet on the top step next to her popcorn bowl.

"Hungry," I said. It wasn't a lie, I couldn't remember the last time I'd eaten anything.

Mama looped her arm through mine and led me to the kitchen, instructing me to sit at the counter. She went to the fridge and began rifling through it.

"What, they run out of food in Rochester?" my father snarked.

"No, Pop, I just wanted to see you guys." I had no idea how I was going to broach the situation.

Mama pulled a covered pan of spaghetti from the fridge and began to spoon it into a glass bowl. "So, how's school going?"

"Fine, just fine," I lied. *I'm probably gonna flunk out since I've missed four days of classes.*

Dad grabbed the popcorn bowl and began to eat from it. "Take off ya glasses when you're in the house. Wait, it's nighttime. Why ya wearin' those?"

I slid them from my face while keeping my eyes downcast. As I slowly lifted my head up, I said, "This is what I wanted to talk to you about."

"Jesus, Mary, and Joseph!" my father yelled, taking a step back and spilling popcorn.

I heard glass shatter and looked up at my mother, who was making the sign of the cross in front of her, spaghetti and glass heaped at her feet.

I felt like I wanted to cry, seeing my parents look at me like that. Maybe if I did, they'd soften up. Deciding to let the tears come, I relaxed, but they didn't come. There was nothing.

"What in the devil?" my father said, now taking a step closer to me.

"Pop, please help me. I woke up like this. Tell me I'm not going blind."

He came closer still and got within two inches of my face. "You look like a blind person, boy. You can see okay?"

My mother was quietly crying as she picked up glass and spaghetti and began dumping it in the trash.

"I'm still hungry, Ma," I stated.

She nodded.

"Mama, look at me."

She shook her head and continued to cry and clean.

"Mother! Look at me! I am still me, please…" Lifting her eyes to mine, I forced a smile. "I love you."

"Were you exposed to something at school? Like a chemical in your science class? Did you use any new eyedrops? Anything?" Pop asked, right in my face now, as I stared into the brown eyes I was so used to.

I shook my head. "Nothing at all. Nothing has changed."

"Well, something has changed," he said, his brow furrowed together. He grabbed a small flashlight from the kitchen drawer and flicked it on, shining it into my eyes. "Can you see all right?"

"Actually, I think I can see even better than before. I used to have trouble seeing at night with my helmet on, like with the lights and stuff. But on the ride here, I didn't."

He backed up and raked his fingers through his thick, salt-and-pepper hair. Then he folded his arms across his chest, all the while studying me. "Were you bitten by a radioactive spider?"

"Pop! This is serious! I'm not Peter Parker. I'm me. I just need you to take a look and tell me if it's serious."

"Hell yes, it's serious, son! The pigment is gone from your irises. That doesn't just happen overnight." He reached for the small glass tumbler he'd set there earlier and took a big swig from its amber-colored contents.

I snorted. "Apparently… it does. But I can tell you, that I can't get any tears to come. And I can't make them turn red."

"This is weird. Did you go to the ER or campus doc when you woke up this morning and report it?"

I didn't want to tell him it had only been a couple of hours since I now, apparently, preferred to sleep during the day.

Shaking my head, I said, "No."

"Well, I'm no ophthalmologist so you need to see one STAT. I'm gonna call a friend and you will go see him tomorrow."

I lifted a shoulder in a shrug. "Sure."

Ma set a steaming bowl of spaghetti and meatballs, a slice of garlic bread, and a big cup of milk in front of me. I began devouring it like an animal. "Thanks," I murmured through the food in my mouth.

She smiled sadly at me and then began to cry again.

Chapter 9

IDENTITY CRISIS

Present Day

New Orleans, LA

I went outside to have another smoke and noticed the bloodsucker from earlier was outside, too. He stood next to the girl he'd fed from on the dance floor as she smoked. I pulled my pack from my pocket and lifted one out. I shoved the pack back in and fished around my pocket for a lighter. I lit the cigarette without taking my eyes off the couple.

"You don't smoke?" I heard her ask the leech.

His eyes were on her neck again. This guy put the S in sleazy. Slicked back hair, pasty skin, blood-red button-down shirt (to keep the stains from showing, I was sure), and some stupid-looking skinny jeans with a chain attaching his wallet to his beltloop. Scrawny as fuck, too.

I watched as they chatted about the vampire ball and other mundane things, and I pulled out my cell phone, grateful the Riders had come down here with me as backup.

I texted Archie: *You guys still at the coffee shop?*

His response took a couple of minutes. *Affirmative.*

I quickly typed out: *Meet me at the back of this hotel. Next kill is yours. Scraggy leech. Fairly new vamp.*

Archie: *Be there in 2.*

I pocketed the phone and kept a sharp eye on them through the clouds of smoke. When the human went to crush out her cigarette, I knew that was my cue. Slowly walking toward them, I approached them coolly, turning my head toward the female. I slid my glasses down my nose and looked at her.

She gasped.

I smiled. "Hi, gorgeous. I need to have a chat with my buddy here. You can go inside and have a good time. You never met him."

Her face went slack, and then she turned to walk woodenly back into the club alone.

"Hey! Stop compelling my girl. I had her first," he snapped.

I felt a rip of pain in my arm and looked to see the bloodsucker had punched me. I instantly grew enraged and tossed my cigarette to the ground, crushing it out with the heel of my boot.

I looked around and reared my arm back, slamming my fist into his nose. I grinned in satisfaction when he reeled back and fell on his ass, yelling out in pain.

"You're gonna pay for that," he said nasally, his hand trying to staunch the flow of blood.

"I don't think so," I growled, reaching down and picking him up by his shirt collar. I dragged him around to the back of the building, where the Rebel Riders were just arriving on their bikes.

"Let me go, you asshole!" he yelled. He then looked at the Riders and his facial expression changed. "Look, I'm sorry I punched you, okay? I don't want no trouble…"

"You sure as fuck asked for it, though, didn't you?" I said, my hand still gripping his shirt.

He gaped at me, incredulous. "What are you talking about? I didn't do nothin'!"

I punched him in the side of his head and tossed him in front of the Riders. He screamed in pain, but could do nothing. He was surrounded, but I pulled the knife from my boot anyway. "You fed on an unsuspecting human," I snapped. "That's a crime punishable by death. Right, boys?" I asked, amused.

Archie spit some chew out on the sidewalk and chuckled. "Damn straight." He looked to his left. "Aspen, would you like to do the honors?"

I noticed two more Riders were posted up on either side of the building, ready to distract any passersby.

"I'd love to, boss," Aspen answered.

The vampire began scramble backward and try to stand up. Aspen was on him quickly, straddling him and then slamming his head into the concrete. "I hereby find you guilty of assault on a human being and taking blood without permission. Punishable by the forever death."

"No!" he hollered as Aspen plunged a gigantic buck knife into his heart.

The bloodsucker turned to ash instantly. Oops. He wasn't a new vampire.

The Riders began to whoop and holler. I fist-punched the air in triumph.

"Let's bounce, boys," I said, grabbing the vampire's clothes and tossing them into the same dumpster that held the shriveled corpse of the succubus I'd ended earlier. I kept his wallet, shoving it into my back pocket next to Michael's little black book.

I kicked at the ashes and told Archie I'd meet everyone at the coffee shop.

"Meet us at Lafitte's instead. First round's on me," he said, smiling.

They took off on their bikes and I went to round the building to get on my Harley and meet them there.

I was just about to turn the corner when I heard, "Kovah."

Turning suddenly with the knife still in my hand, I narrowed my eyes and looked toward the voice.

Manta stood there with her arms crossed, a smile on her face. "No due process?"

I relaxed but kept my fist gripped around the hilt of the knife, its cold metal pressed against my thigh.

The only good vampire is a dead vampire…

"No," I replied, turning to leave.

"Don't go," she said.

She slunk toward me carefully, trying to seem harmless and nonthreatening. I was fairly sure I could take her if I needed to, even though she was pretty old.

"Is this how you and your motorcycle buddies take care of business?" She stopped walking as she looked down at the knife in my hand.

I lifted my chin. "Something like that."

"Vigilante vampire hunters, dispensing justice where they see fit," she continued, walking toward me again. She still wore her high heels, and they clacked against the pavement, piercing the night that suddenly seemed very quiet.

"Someone has to do it," I replied. "I don't see the BSI taking care of this menace to society." I used my knife to point at the dumpster.

She nodded and continued to walk. *Clack, clack, clack…*

"How did you know Donald there was a menace?" she asked, pointing to his ashes.

I chuckled, but there was no humor there. "Sweetheart, don't pretend you didn't see him feeding from that girl on the dance floor a split second before you walked up and started to talk to me."

She nodded. "I saw him."

I tilted my head to the side. "And?"

"And nothing. Feeding from humans isn't a punishable offense according to BSI policy."

I itched to light another cigarette but I refrained from pulling one out the pack. "Well, the BSI is weak then. You've done jack-shit to help my friend Nolan."

She smiled, and I kicked myself for finding her smile pretty and endearing. "There is nothing we can do for Nolan Bishop. Either he kills Eva Sheridan, or he turns into a vampire and we end him. Those are the only choices."

The cold, hard organ in my chest tried to beat a little, so it could feel something. "That's interesting. I never knew his demon's name."

"Yeah? Well, there's nothing you can do for him, either. But I think you know that." She was now two feet from me, so close I could smell her perfume.

I nodded. "I can't kill the bitch, but I can sure as hell give him the knife and drive him to her house."

Another smile on her full, pretty lips. "You could. And you should."

"Or, maybe you should. Isn't that what the Justice Department is paying you for?"

She quickly responded. "Oh no, we don't assist in vampire murder; we just monitor the victims and help with the cleanup."

Thinking back twenty years when she'd ripped Suzette's body apart so it could fit in the black trash bag, I replied, "Yeah, I remember."

Twenty Years Ago
Rochester, NY

Yeah… I'd seen my Pop's Ophthalmologist friend the next day and he'd been just as baffled. No, I hadn't gone blind the next day. My eyesight remained strong—stronger than ever, it seemed.

And that freaking scared me.

Was I turning into a vampire? If I was, I would just kill myself. They couldn't go in the sun, right? *I'll kill myself in the sun.*

As if none of the shit had happened, I went back to school and tried to maintain the human schedule. The one problem I had with it, though, was the professors would tell me to remove my sunglasses while in class.

For the first few weeks, this was a problem. I'd do what they'd ask, but that kept me looking down during class the whole time. I would sometimes ponder during particularly boring classes why I bothered with this college shit. Then I would realize that I was back in the land of the living and had to finish school, to graduate and try to get a real job.

Colored contact lenses had begun to drop on the market recently, and I considered getting myself some. They were expensive, but I wasn't sure what else I could do to live a normal life.

Staying awake during my day classes became a chore. Sleeping at night also became a chore, and I began to wonder what that succubus had truly done to me. I frequently thought about the BSI. They hadn't checked up on me or contacted me for months. The last I'd seen of them was when I had been dropped off at my dorm to fend for myself after killing Suzette.

One night, several weeks later after the semester had changed and I had, too, I left my Physics night class and decided I was going to try to find that warehouse the BSI agent, Rick Lewis, had taken me to. However, I wasn't looking for Rick. I had my sights set on someone else I knew could help me.

It hadn't been hard to locate. I had paid attention to my surroundings as we drove, as I had been apprehensive to get into his car to begin with.

As my bike rumbled to a stop on a street full of warehouses that all looked alike, I surveyed the road. The warehouse had been on the left, I remembered that much. I had five to choose from. I closed my eyes, and like a dream about to evade you just as you're just about to wake up, I saw myself and Agent Lewis pull to a stop and go around the back of the warehouse. What was in the front? Lights that hung like crooked arms jutting out the front. The light was more orange than a normal security light. One of them seemed to spotlight the front door to the place.

Popping my eyes open, I removed my sunglasses and peered down the street. My eyes, as if almost bionic, zeroed in on the second warehouse on the street. It matched the picture in my mind's eye.

"Wow, that was really freaky," I murmured as I replaced my glasses and cut the engine to the bike to walk it down the street. I stopped in front of it, and after getting off, I put the kickstand down. It was eerily quiet, and if not for the security lights on the warehouses, it would have been very, very dark. The night was mild, but not warm, and I sort of wished for a breeze. It was just too still and quiet.

I stealthily made my way around the building and saw the door I remember Rick taking me through. I stopped in front of it, reached for the doorknob, and then decided not to go in just yet. Instead, I put my ear to the door and listened. Deathly quiet, no sounds of talking or papers rustling; just nothing. Self-doubt began to creep in and I suddenly wondered if coming here had been a mistake. I really didn't want to talk to Agent Lewis, it had been Violet I'd come to see. Even though Rick had called her a vampire, there had been something trustworthy in her eyes. She didn't look or behave like a bloodsucking monster. She seemed normal, until her black eyes were on show. I shuddered at the memory.

Without warning, the door flew open, and I would have fallen inside except for the hand that reached out and grabbed me by the shirt collar. I was dragged inside the office.

My ass was planted into a chair faster than I could blink, and when I looked up, I saw warm brown eyes staring down at me in amusement.

I looked around and could see I was in the same office Rick had taken me to, my butt planted in the same chair from a few weeks before. The office smelled of stale cigarettes.

"Why are you sleazing around my warehouse?" Violet asked, her arms folded across her chest.

"I... I... I came here to see you," I finally spat out.

She laughed softly. "I see. So why didn't you just ring the bell?"

My brow furrowed and I replied, "What bell?"

"There's a buzzer on the wall outside."

I hadn't seen one, but I hadn't been looking for one, either. So instead, I replied, "I was listening to see if anyone was in here, but I couldn't hear anything."

She pointed to a small device mounted to the wall near the doorjamb. It looked sort of like a speaker box. "That's because we keep a noise-canceling device on the wall so nobody can hear in here. Including vampires."

My eyes went wide. "Vampires know about this place?"

She circled the desk slowly in her dark burgundy-colored skirt suit and black high heels. She came to stand behind it, not looking like she intended to sit in the big leather chair. An ashtray full of cigarette butts lay on the desktop, along with a huge stack of manila folders and random papers scattered everywhere. A large, gray filing cabinet sat next to the desk, but it looked to be locked tight.

"I don't think so," she answered. "But vampires like dark, quiet places they can prey on humans to eat."

A shudder racked my body, and with more bravery than I felt, I said, "Is that why you dragged me in here? To take my blood?"

She leaned over and put both palms on the desk. "No. You came to me, remember?"

I nodded. "Yes, I remember, geez. You're acting kinda creepy, though."

She stood up straight and laughed. "I'm not creepy."

Sucking in a deep breath, I replied, "I'll admit that you aren't. You don't act like what I thought a vampire would. Now, Suzette, she was much higher on the creep scale."

A small smile formed on her pretty pink lips. "I agree."

"You knew her?" I asked curiously.

She shook her head. "No, but she was a succubus. They're all a bit... out there." She swirled her finger next to her temple to indicate crazy.

"Good to know."

She finally sat in the chair and folded her hands on the desktop. "So tell me, Dominic, why have you come here?"

I slowly pulled off my sunglasses and met Violet's wide eyes, and she gasped. She stood up, stepped backward, and put her hand over her mouth.

"Judging by your reaction, I take it this isn't normal?" I asked on a defeated sigh.

Chapter 10

DIAGNOSIS

Present Day

New Orleans, LA

"Come have a drink with me," Manta said, smiling up at me now in the dark alley behind the vampire ball's hotel.

I itched to go, but decided against it. "I just did. I was drinking beer, and you had something girly."

A ghost of a smile twitched on her lips. "Whiskey sours aren't girly."

"Okay, forgive me."

"Another drink then?" she asked, and I had to commend her straightforward demeanor.

However, I was not getting involved with a vampire. I killed them, I didn't fuck them.

I jutted a thumb over my shoulder. "I gotta meet the Riders. Sorry, sweetness. Maybe another day. Or in your case, another night."

She lifted a shoulder in a shrug, slid the mask back into place, and walked down the alleyway slowly. I tried not to watch the way her ass filled out her dress and the sexy calf muscles above her stilettos.

It wasn't long until I found myself at Lafitte's Blacksmith Bar, taking the empty chair and spinning it around to sit backward on it next to Archie.

Ollie slid a shot my way and said, "TOGVIADO, brother."

I lifted the shot with a smile then slammed it back. Whiskey… *ah, feel the burn.*

Over the music, Archie asked, "So did you get anything from the female vamper?"

I nodded. "I let her take a look at McCoy's book and she thumbed through it, said most of them were normal vamps trying to live a normal life."

Aspen snorted with his beer to his lips. "If drinking blood, never aging, and not being able to go out in the sun is normal…"

The rest of the Riders laughed.

"So, she gave you nothing?" Archie asked.

I debated telling them about how she seemed to take a personal, romantic, sexual, or whatever interest in me, but declined. I'd never hear the end of it. "No, she didn't. Then I got busy tracking down the male vamp and that was that."

"Did you see any other bloodsuckers there?" Ollie asked.

A young female server set a mug of beer in front of me and I nodded my thanks to her. I looked at Ollie. "Ya know, it's hard to say. Unless they were feeding or the eyes turned black, I couldn't tell. The ones who showed fangs I'm pretty sure were humans. But hell, maybe those leeches feel more comfortable showing them off, so they use this time of year to let them all hang out."

The group of rag-tag vampire hunters laughed again.

"Well, boys, I got a tip about a blood farm out in the bayou," Archie said, changing the subject after sipping his beer. "Vamps are running a high-priced, illegal moonshine business, but using it to their benefit, as they are also using that same equipment to purify blood taken from humans to feed with and to sell."

"What the fuck!" Ollie said, slamming his beer on the table.

"Exactly," I said. "That's fucking sick. You got an address?"

Archie nodded, looking down at his phone. "Yeah. We'll hit it tomorrow night when we get back to Shreveport."

"I say we just torch the place," Aspen said. "Set the shit on fire and hope they all die in it."

I shook my head. "Nah, could be humans there. We'll play it by ear."

"Agreed." Archie put out his fist and we all bumped it.

My thoughts drifted to my new friend and coworker Nolan. The guy had had his soul taken by a succubus just like I had, but he was still within his seven-day window. The clock was ticking and he had mere days to kill the demon or else turn into a feral vampire that would literally hurt me to kill. I had no problem driving a stake into most vampires, but Nolan... he was a good kid and I was actually starting to like the bastard, beginning to think of him as a friend, and it would suck if I ended up having to kill him.

I decided right then I would invite him to come hunt these bloodsuckers who were running this moonshine-slash-blood factory. Maybe when he saw the viciousness and ferocity in which we disposed of vampires, he'd rethink the murder he knew in his heart he needed to commit. Truth be told, he had started to act a bit differently and I could tell that what the succubus had done to him was starting to take root in what was left of his soul.

Yes, I would take him with us tomorrow night. Maybe even have him join the Riders so he could see that vampires were nothing but a menace to society. I smiled darkly at the thought. The prospect of shutting down their blood farm sent a thrill racing down my spine. Nothing was better than the rush of ridding the world of another vampire, hoping you had saved at least one fragile human life.

After all, the humans didn't seem to know how delicate and brittle their lives really were. They all seemed to think they were invincible, which was so very far from the truth.

After discussing the semantics of where and when we'd meet to confront these bootlegging vamps, I looked around the dark bar. By dark, I meant *really* dark. This particular place had a reputation for being haunted—but of course I laughed at that. It had been an old blacksmith's shop in the 1800s, but had since been converted to a bar that served damn good beer. But to keep with the mystery, the owners had decided that only candlelight was allowed as illumination. I don't even think they used any sort of electricity to cool or heat the place, and it was hot as fuck in here, even at night. I had found, though, that temperatures didn't affect me as much as they used to when I was fully human.

Aspen broke me out of my musings. "Hey, Arch, you gonna invite the new kid tomorrow night?"

Archie spit dip into his empty beer bottle. "Yeah, I was thinking about it."

I chuckled. Great minds think alike.

Twenty Years Ago
Rochester, NY

"What the hell?" Violet asked, staring hard at me.

For some reason, instead of being alarmed by her reaction to my eyes, I was sort of amused by it. Something inside of me was changing—twisting—into something that wasn't quite normal. I felt like the Joker from Batman. Sort of powerful but slightly insane, affected by his disfigurement, but not letting it stop him. I stared hard at Violet, waiting for a reaction other than revulsion.

I'd hand it to the pretty brunette—she had recovered pretty quickly. Smoothing down her skirt with her hands, she straightened her posture and said, "I don't know how that happened, but we'll find out."

She was trying her hardest to put on a professional demeanor, but I could easily tell it was all bullshit—she had been shaken up at seeing my eyes. She had no idea what had happened to me, and she had no fucking clue how to fix it. I tried not to act defeated, even though I knew she couldn't do anything about this eye situation any more than I could.

Creeping toward me slowly around the desk, she kept eye contact. When she was knee-to-knee with me, she slightly cocked her head to the side and asked, "Can you see okay? No vision problems?"

I nodded, refusing to break her stare. "Yes. In fact, better than before."

She kneeled down, and I had to spread my legs slightly to allow her access. Crouching on her haunches, she reached a hand up and pressed her palm to my cheek.

"You still feel human," she said softly, not removing her hand.

I stared, unblinking at her, waiting for her to finish.

"But I am human, right?" I finally asked.

Concerned brown eyes looked up at me, and she furrowed her brow. "That's what we thought, that you'd remain human. But those eyes... I'm starting to think that something happened to your soul."

I gasped softly. "Do you even believe in the existence of one's soul?"

With her eyes flicking back and forth between mine, she nodded slightly. "Yes, I was raised a strict Catholic. We all have souls, Dominic."

Her hand still rested on my face as I asked, "If you believe that, then what happened to yours?"

Her hand fell from my cheek, and her eyes went downcast. "I don't know. I keep living because I have to. I exist like this because I wasn't given a choice, and I try not to think about it. I just try to do the right thing and hope that one day, when I meet the *forever death*, that God will accept me."

That made me curious. I guessed all vampires weren't the way they were because they had chosen it—not that I knew much about them or how they got that way. I still wasn't sure I believed in anything supernatural, despite my recent experience.

She stood up and went around the desk. She reached toward an old, clunky-looking black phone I was surprised didn't have a rotary dial.

"Wait," I said, standing up. I pointed at the phone. "Who are you calling?"

"I was going to wake Rick and see if he's heard of this."

I shook my head and replaced my glasses, still very much self-conscious of my eyes. "Please don't? I don't think that guy likes me very much."

She laughed and moved her hand away from the phone. "Don't take it personal. He's seen a lot of crap and doesn't much like anyone."

"Still, is there another way?"

She cocked her head to the side and said, "Have you see a human doctor?"

"Is there another kind of doctor? Yes, I have."

"Well, there are witchdoctors, but you don't want to go see them." Her face went dark.

I shuddered. "Noted. And yes, an ophthalmologist, a friend of my pop's."

"What did the doctor say?" she asked.

I shook my head and looked down at my hands. "Nothing. He asked me a butt-load of questions about anything I'd been exposed to and tested my eyesight, which was better than twenty-twenty, and said he was going to refer me to another doctor. I never went, though."

"Interesting," she said, and came to stand in front of me. She kneeled again, removed my glasses, and stared at my eyes. "I can still see the iris and pupil, they are just discolored, almost depigmented. Do they hurt?"

"Not at all."

She continued to stare and I found her closeness simultaneously uncomfortable and arousing, but tried not to show it. "You've never seen this before?"

She got up slowly and handed me back my glasses before sitting on the edge of the desk. "No, but I haven't ever met a guy who'd killed his succubus before. I would think, though, if this was the standard side effect, we'd have read about it in the books."

I put my glasses back on. "What are these books you people keep referring to?"

"Just records of everything supernatural we deal with. We're in the process of imputing all the information into a computer database for better and faster searching. For now, we have a large library of books in DC, and we have to make a phone call and ask one of the many clerks to look things up for us when we need something."

"What a pain," I said.

She nodded. "It is. But with how fast computers and technology are coming along, I have no doubt that in a few years, we'll have all the information at our fingertips." She wiggled her fingers with a smile.

"So, can you go out in the sun?" I asked out of the blue.

She looked surprised. "Not if I don't want to burst into flames. Odd question."

Truth was, I felt at ease here. I wasn't being watched or stared at, and I didn't have to hide anything. Violet made me feel comfortable and I didn't want to leave.

"I know," I finally replied. "I was just curious. Can you eat food?"

She shook her head. "Not really. Some liquids, but nothing solid. It doesn't digest. Just blood."

"Ew."

She chuckled and said, "Yeah, you get used to it."

"I don't think I'd ever get used to that."

"You do if you want to stay alive," she quipped, seeming slightly amused.

The room was quiet for a little bit until she asked, "So have you noticed any other... symptoms?"

I nodded. "I am tired during the day and prefer to stay up at night. I was never a night owl before, always a morning person."

"I see," Violet said, now scribbling on a notepad she'd pulled from the desk drawer. "Anything else?"

"Uh," I hesitated to tell her this one, but I continued, "I seem a lot stronger than I used to be."

"Like how?" she asked, her pen poised above the pad.

"Well, I went to turn my bike around so I could start it up and go, and I sort of picked it up off the ground. With one hand. Did not feel as heavy as it should have."

"Hmm," was all she said as she scribbled.

I glanced at what she was writing. *Enhanced eyesight, loss of pigmentation of iris and pupil, superhuman strength, sleeps during the day, up at night. No desire for blood. No fangs.*

After scribbling down everything, she stared down at it thoughtfully. Then, with a slight grin, she looked up at me and said, "I think what we've got here is a hybrid vampire."

Chapter 11

THEY'RE NOT ALL BAD

Twenty Years Ago

Rochester, NY

I stared at her in horror. "A... what?"

"It's the only explanation," Violet began. "You exhibit behaviors of a vampire, yet you don't have all of them. Perhaps, all this time, we thought you guys just went back to being normal and human, but maybe we were wrong. Maybe we need to pay closer attention to the young men and women who kill their succubus. Keep better tabs on them..."

She seemed to almost be talking to herself now.

"So, you've seen this before?" I pointed at my eyes.

"No, I have not. But you need to understand how rare it is that we actually see someone survive the succubus's bite. I mean, it has happened, but you're the first I've met. It would seem, however, that if your... eye condition was common, it should be documented somewhere. The fact that it's not, and we haven't heard of it, makes me think something else happened. I'm just not sure how to tell what that might be."

I stared curiously at her. "Can I ask you something, Violet?"

She nodded. "Of course."

"How old are you?"

She quickly responded, "I'm twenty-four."

I scanned her from head to toe. "Your body is twenty-four. I have a feeling you've been around a lot longer than a couple of decades, though."

Her lip twitched into a smile. "Smart and cute. I like you, Dominic. You are correct. I'm actually eighty-four."

My eyes bulged behind the sunglasses. "Holy shit!"

She laughed. "Yeah, I'm old as dirt."

"So, vampires are, what's the word… immortal? Like in the movies?"

"Yes, something like that," she replied.

I let that sink in for a minute. Never aging and living forever… could they be killed? What if someone cut their heads off? Do their hearts beat? Does a stake through the heart really kill them? Well… an icepick ended Suzette, so I guessed I answered that question.

"So… Immortal is just another word for 'not aging' — not 'incapable of death'. Is that right?" I asked.

She nodded, her eyes downcast and writing in her notebook again. "Yes. We can die, but it won't be of old age or disease. We heal quickly. I haven't had the common cold since I was human."

This chick was blowing my mind. And to think, just a few short months ago, I knew none of this existed.

"Is this going to happen to me?" I asked, fearful. The thought of living on and on scared me. I wanted a normal life. Not some fucked up "hybrid" life.

"You know I can't answer that," she replied, looking up from her scrawlings.

I lifted myself from the seat and made my way to the door of the office. "It seems like my time here is done. You gonna let me out?"

A look of disappointment flooded her face. She finally left her seat and came around the desk, her face seemingly full of concern. She made no move toward the door. "We can and want to help you, Dominic. You don't need to leave."

"Yet, running seems to be my only option."

Violet pierced me with an intense stare, her eyes boring into mine. "You have plenty of options, Dominic."

With my hand on the doorknob to the office, I looked over my shoulder. "Dominic is dead."

Present Day

Shreveport, LA

A somber mood blanketed the group. We had indeed found the vampires out in the bayou making the moonshine, but they had also been siphoning blood from humans like some kind of a sick blood bank of unwilling and unconscious participants. While we had killed the head vampire, it had not ended well for our group. We'd just returned from Aspen's funeral. He had, unfortunately, shot his pistol at the bloodsucker, but this particular leech had had his own security and Aspen had his neck snapped by a vicious vampire.

I looked over at my friend Nolan and he looked extremely distressed and disturbed. Poor kid, he was barely twenty-one, and probably hadn't seen such horrors in his young life. I knew how he felt; I was once him, twenty years ago when I was dealing with my own angst.

Still, we were all sad. Aspen's death had been senseless and horrible to witness. I would never get the image out of my brain. But, we reasoned, at least he had died doing something he loved. He really had died in the line of duty. I was sure if he could have chosen his death, that would have been it. It was just unfortunate that his murder had been committed by an undead piece of shit. I was happy Archie had driven a knife through his heart as payment for his crime.

Swift justice. Doesn't get any better than that.

Archie's voice broke me out of my thoughts. He lifted his glass up high. "To Aspen, may his ride in Heaven be smooth until we meet again."

If I could have gotten tears in my eyes, I would have, but alas… I could not. I hadn't physically cried in over twenty years. I dipped my head low in reverence and toasted to a great brother, a Rider, a friend… and hero.

As "Stairway to Heaven" began to ironically play on the bar's small jukebox, I looked over at Nolan and followed his line of sight. There was a very hot blonde sitting at the bar and it didn't take me long to realize she was a vampire. She was hot as hell, perfect body oozing an air of confidence. But a vampire, nonetheless.

I watched in horror as Nolan got up and walked over toward her. Archie chuckled, but the other boys didn't seem to pay him any regard as he excused himself from the table. But as a guy "his age" I knew what he was going to do.

I was up and out of my seat before I could blink. With my hand on Nolan's chest, I said, "You know that's a fucking vampire, right?"

Nolan nodded. "Yep, getting her out of here before one of you maniacs catches on and murders her just for being one."

I was shocked. Kid had been acting weird lately, but after what we'd been through tonight, I would think he would know to stay away from them. My jaw pulsed in anger and I gritted my teeth. "I wouldn't be doing that if I were you."

Nolan put both hands on his hips. "Why not? I already know you guys will probably stake her before she can finish her drink. She hasn't done anything, and you know it." He jabbed his thumb behind his shoulder at Archie and the Riders.

My face flushed hot, and now I was pissed. What was wrong with this guy? I snapped, "Oh, but she will, Bishop. She will. They always do, especially the females. They are black widows, seeking whoever they can devour and destroy for the night. Stay away, dude. I'm not messing around here."

Nolan's face twisted in rage. In a move that surprised even me, he put both hands out and shoved me in the chest as hard as he could. I went flying backward but was up quicker than he expected. We flew into a flurry of punches, rolling around on the floor with Nolan ending up on top of me.

The reason this shocked me so much was because he seemed to be almost as strong as me now. I was about to sit up and punch him in the stomach when he was lifted off me by Archie. Holding his arms behind his back, I could see blood dribbling down his chin.

"I'm good, Arch. I'm outta here!" Nolan yelled, pulling himself from Archie's grip and heading for the door. I could see him glance toward the bar where the blonde had been sitting to see she was now gone.

God, I hoped he wasn't going after her. I would really kick that kid's ass if he was.

Twenty Years Ago
Rochester, NY

Dominic really did die that day. I left that warehouse confused, sad, and angry.

That was a gamut of emotions nobody should ever feel all at once. I got on my bike and drove recklessly toward the water. For some reason, the water always calmed me. I was a little disappointed when I reached the shore, though. I had hoped my reckless driving would have killed me. If I truly was some freak, I didn't want to live.

I reached the beach and killed the engine to my bike. I barely had time to put up the kickstand before I was running recklessly toward the sand. I yanked off my boots and socks and tossed them into the sand a split-second before I slammed into the ocean. I didn't care that I still had on my jeans, I needed to feel the water's caress. I needed to know that if I wanted to envelop myself in its cool and cruel depths, I could.

Standing thigh-deep in the violently cold water, I lifted my face to the almost-full moon that shone overhead. I closed my eyes, put my arms out, and bathed in its blue light. I needed its comfort. I needed the cold hug the water gave me. I needed to know that if I were to end my life in their watery depths, that the moon would be shining down on me, saying it was okay; that it knew I needed to end it all.

How had my life become this? A new version of extreme eyesight and strength, and a loathing for the sunlight and anything social... in just a few short weeks, my life had taken a drastic turn, and I didn't like it.

I didn't like it one motherfucking bit.

But what could I do about it? I didn't know. This lack of control and direction of my life was making me crazy.

Before I'd met that redheaded succubus bitch, my life had had a very specific and controlled direction. Finish college, get a good paying job, buy a house, marry the girl of my dreams. None of those things would happen now that Dominic was dead. If what Violet had said was true, and I was this freakish vampire hybrid, then I was good and truly fucked. There was not the normal future my parents—and even me—had envisioned for myself. I was done. I would have to eke out an existence that involved none of those things.

While grateful I didn't crave blood and quite obviously did not need it to survive, I was terrified at the prospect of being "immortal." Seventy or eighty years on this planet was long enough... What the hell would I do with forever?

I opened my eyes and peered up at the moon shining down on me. In all its beauty, it held no answers for me. What was I expecting, really? The answer to the world's problems? Nah... wasn't going to happen. My gaze slowly drifted down to the water in which I stood. I evaluated my options... continue to live as a freak with milky-white eyes and be forced to wear sunglasses or contact lenses that cost a fortune, or... end it all right now.

The black water lapped around my jeans as if it was thirsty for them. I just stared at the push and pull of the tide as it came and went. What would happen if I lowered myself into the water? What if I let it take me as its prisoner, let it feed its freakish, evil need to drown me and send me into the afterlife? Would that be so bad?

I slowly lowered myself to my knees. Now the water was chest-deep. It was cold and painful, but I welcomed the pain. I needed it. I deserved it. There was nothing good and pure and beautiful in this life that I deserved anymore. I had murdered someone... and I wasn't worthy of anything good. I should be punished for killing Suzette. I didn't mean to, but I had... and I should pay for that crime.

The cold of the water began to numb me, and I lowered myself further into its murky depths. It welcomed me, and I was happy, my T-shirt soaked and riding up my torso now. The water reached my collarbone and I involuntarily tipped my head back to gaze at the moon again.

My eyes opened, but only briefly before they closed again. The water licked my neck, throat, and now my jawline... *Yes... it'll all be over soon.*

The soft but freezing water bathed my cheeks, my nose, my eyes. They remained closed. I continued to sink under, my hair now floating on the surface of the water... waiting for the sweet release of unconsciousness that would lead to my death.

The consciousness of my mind began to fade. It drifted to black and I had no panic. I was happy. This was it. I was going to find the bright light and drift toward it to find the eternal peace — the one I was promised as I was born a human.

As a smile crawled over my waterlogged face, I suddenly felt myself being pulled from the water, a presence yanking me violently toward the surface.

But I didn't want to reach the break of the water. I wanted to die here in peace. I kicked and flailed, trying to sink back down into the comfort of the water.

I blinked once before I was lying on a soft surface. My fists gripped what I was lying on, but only came back with a fistful of sand. I dropped the sand and wanted to scream but I could not. There was a beautiful brunette straddling my torso and I looked up with waterlogged eyes to see Violet there, her face full of worry and angst.

She was saying something, but I could not hear it. There was water in my ears, but I didn't want hear it, anyway. Today was my day to die, not to see a vampire on my chest, her warm olive skin bathed in blue moonlight.

When air finally filled my lungs, I opened my mouth, and I screamed a single word. "Violet!"

My hands were pinned up by my head.

"It's not your day to die."

I shouldn't listen to her. I should buck her off me and go die in dignity. How dare she save me! What right did she have? She didn't. I shoved her off me with one swift swipe of my hand and she went tumbling into the sand at my side. I quickly got up and ran toward the water, intent on sinking back in.

She beat me there, and with her supernatural speed, blurred me toward the shore again, this time using all of her supernatural might to keep me pinned to the sand. I fought her with all my strength.

"Get off me! Just let me die, I don't need you saving me!" I gritted out as I fought her. She let go of one hand and slapped me hard across my wet face. It stung like a motherfucker, but stopped my fighting.

"Get a grip, Dominic. Stop being so damn melodramatic. You need to think things through. This isn't the end of the world. Now, I don't know much about a hybrid, but I want to help you work through it. I can tell you that newly made vampires have a heightened sense of emotion, which is probably what you're going through. No, you're not a vampire, I get it, but it's inevitable you'll have some of the same emotional traits, as you have taken on some physical ones. Now stop fighting me and let's go somewhere and work this out. I want to help you, dammit."

I was listening to what she was saying, but my brain was still cloudy with emotion and fear, and I didn't want to hear it. I didn't want to work anything out. Suddenly, there was only one thing I wanted.

She had softened her grip as she was looking at me with pity, so I pushed her off me and she landed flat on her back. I immediately lay on top of her, then pressed my lips down onto hers. She didn't even fight me. She slipped her tongue into my mouth and tore my wet shirt off with her bare hands, tossing it aside. Without breaking our lip-lock, I shoved my pants down, then her skirt up, and slammed myself into her in one thrust.

"Yes," she groaned, raising her hips to meet mine as I sank mine down to push harder into her.

She felt so good, almost comforting, and I knew the loss of control I felt over my own body I was using to control hers. And it seemed as long as she let me, I was going to keep doing it.

We stayed on the beach for hours, just the two of us under the blue moonlight, fucking, sleeping, then going back at it again. She had even bit me as I came — and I let her. When the rising sun woke me, she was gone… and I never saw her again.

Chapter 12

ROCK AND A HARD PLACE

Ten Years Ago

Rochester, NY

I didn't bother looking for Violet for a couple of weeks after that. I knew in my cold heart that she was right. If I was feeling a heightened sense of emotions, I needed to get a grip on myself. I kept to myself, not speaking to anyone else unless I had to, and sleeping as little as possible to keep up a somewhat normal schedule of night classes and the job delivering pizzas where they had reluctantly taken me back after I lied about a death in the family. And really… someone *had* died. Me.

One day, about two months after our sexy beach encounter, I decided to seek out Violet, show her I was going to be okay, and thank her for helping me. I steered my bike to the warehouse, parked in front, and quickly went around to the side. Remembering she said there had been a call button, I looked for it, but didn't see one. I didn't bother knocking. I tried the doorknob, but it was locked tight. So, deciding to knock, I rapped on the door a few times, but got no answer. My ear to the door told me all was quiet inside. I looked both ways on either side of the building, and seeing I was alone, I turned the knob hard, breaking the lock, and pushed the door open. I felt around on the wall for the switch and flipped it on. Light flooded an empty room. No desk, no cabinets, nothing. It smelled of bleach and cleaner and I realized the BSI had moved on.

I sadly flipped the light off and closed the door. I supposed it was for the best, and hoped Violet knew how grateful I was to her.

After that, I eventually dropped out of college and took year-long night classes in motorcycle mechanics. It was quicker and nobody gave a shit if I left my glasses on the whole time. I found working alone, fixing or building a bike, to be relaxing and helped what I had realized was some kind of "anxiety disorder" that I refused to get help for. What was I supposed to tell a shrink? That I was stressed out that I might be an immortal vampire hybrid? Yeah… no. I was sure they would have diagnosed me with much more than anxiety.

Ten years were spent working on bikes and hooking up with random women. I'd also taken on a little side hobby for no other reason than it gave me a cheap thrill. One day I'd noticed I had this uncanny ability to sense when a vampire was around. It was hard to explain; sort of a tingle mixed with a crushing feeling of dread in my chest. Every time I felt it, I'd turn around, and sure enough, a pale-ass bloodsucker would be somewhere in the immediate vicinity. A club, a corner store, walking down the street, it didn't matter. So when the opportunity presented itself, I would lure it into someplace dark and let it bite me. I'd found that vampire bites didn't do anything to me but sting a little. While it would be busy feeding, I'd pull the wooden stake I'd made from the small of my back, push it off me, and then slam it into its chest. It was particularly fun when it would actually try to pull it out or run away. Then I could give chase, pull it out, and stab it again. Usually the males did this, the females were usually too shocked to do anything but lay down and die into a pile of ash and pretty clothes.

When I wasn't doing that, I was busy partying in bars and clubs and buying broken down motorcycles from junkyards and "flipping" them for extra cash. I saw my family occasionally, but I had sort of begun to put a distance between them, especially at the very last Thanksgiving I ever saw them.

"You wear those sunglasses all the time so you don't squint in the sun and give yourself wrinkles, is that right?" Heather asked. She looked at me curiously, a forkful of mashed potatoes teetering on her fork.

Heather was my brother's wife. Yeah, I'd gone to their wedding wearing my colored contact lenses, just like I had them in today so I could face my family and seem normal. I found it odd that nobody ever said anything about my eyes suddenly being brown instead of dark blue.

"Wrinkles?" I asked, my brow furrowing. "What the fuck are you talking about?"

"Dominic!" my mother screeched.

"Sorry, Ma," I grumbled, still staring at my obnoxious blonde sister-in-law who always looked like she was auditioning for a spot on a new reality TV show.

"You still look really young. I don't get it. I figured it was the sunglasses you wore all the time. I was reading in Cosmo last week that it prevents you from squinting, and therefore, from getting crow's feet —"

I cut her off. "I'm not vain like that, if that's what you're gettin' at."

She set her fork down with a huff.

I glanced at my older brother, Leo, and could tell he was getting kind of stressed out. This made me happy. He was way too concerned about appearances, whereas I did not give a single fuck anymore — and I think he knew it.

"I'm not vain either! What are you saying?" she snapped back, seemingly offended.

"She simply asked you a question, Dom," Leo said, glaring at me like he wanted me to behave.

I shook my head and shoveled some green bean casserole into my face before I went off on them.

I glanced over to see Ma staring at me. "What?" I asked my mouth full.

"You *do* look really young. "She bit her lip and glanced worriedly at Leo, who was only eighteen months older than me. We had frequently gotten asked if we were twins when we were younger, because we also looked very similar. Leo, however, looked his thirty-two years. I certainly didn't look like I was even close to thirty.

I shrugged and piled more food in my mouth. What was I supposed to say? I had no answers for myself, let alone them. Maybe if I just ignored the questions, they'd change the subject.

"Well?" Ma asked, her brow furrowed. "Did you find the Fountain of Youth or something?"

Heather stared at me now with a small and eager smile. "Yeah, I'd love it if you shared your secret."

I snorted and pushed myself away from the dinner table. "I'm outta here."

"Dominic," my ma protested. "Please finish your meal. You can stay longer, can't you?"

"Seriously, Dom, don't be a dick," my sister, Sophie said. She and her ten-year-old son had remained quiet through the argument.

"Yeah, don't be a dick," my nephew, Josh, parroted his mother.

I bit back a smile.

"Joshua!" Ma scolded, but he just snickered.

My ma had always been my soft spot. I'd do anything for her. I just wished Heather wasn't here. We had never gotten along, and God forbid my brother put a muzzle on his Barbie wife.

I put my glasses on, kissed Ma on the cheek, and said, "I'm going for a ride. I'll be back later." Turning, I flew out the front door, got on my bike, and zoomed off toward the water.

Letting the cool, New York November air rush through my hair, I hit the throttle and weaved in and out of traffic on my way to the coast.

Truth was, I had no right to be mad at my family. They were just pointing out what I was in denial of. Every day, the reflection in the mirror never changed. I never saw any laugh lines, or crow's feet, or forehead wrinkles. My hair did not get silvery strands coming in at the temples like I had seen on Leo. Sure, he probably didn't even see them yet, but at dinner, with my strong eyesight, I could see the graying threads beginning to come in. On his sharp jawline, I could see the start of a few sags where he will develop jowls later on. Even though he worked as a car salesman at a luxury car dealership, his hands showed signs of wear and sun damage. Mine were just dirty from my job, but after a good scrubbing, they still looked like a young man's.

My worst nightmare was coming true. What Violet had told me all those years ago seemed to be coming to fruition. I still preferred the night and stayed in the shadows during the day. I still had this wickedly accurate eyesight, and these milky eyes, it seemed, were here to stay. But the worst part was that I didn't seem to be advancing in years. Sure, time was ticking by, but you couldn't tell by looking at me, and this was going to become a huge problem for me. Actually, it seemed it already was.

After parking my bike in the lot, I walked onto the beach and sat down, happy to see the glowing orange ball sinking into the water's horizon. I lifted the sand and let it drift through my fingers then sift back out, down to where it had come.

As I did this absently over and over, I realized I had three options: One, I could kill myself. A bullet to the head would probably do it. Two, I could move away to another state and keep in contact with my family through phone calls and emails and spend the next twenty or thirty years making excuses as to why I couldn't see them. Three, I could fake my own death. Options one and three would shatter Ma into a million pieces.

I put my head into my hands and yelled in frustration. The thought of hurting my family, as obnoxious as most of them were, killed me. Leo and Heather had two kids, plus Sophie's kid, Josh—I'd never see them grow up. I'd not get to say goodbye to my parents when they were on their death beds.

Moving away sounded like the best option at the moment. Maybe I should just take things day by day. I needed to go someplace where nobody knew me. Somewhere I'd never run into familiar people. Maybe California. Nah, too much sun and too many people. Maybe somewhere in the middle. Kansas? Missouri?

Should I go south?

I sat and thought about all the repercussions of faking my own death. New ID, new name, new everything. It sounded both terrifying and exhilarating all at once. I looked up to see the sun was barely peeking above the edge of the water now, and the stars were already beginning to blink on above me. Instead of the sunset being the symbol of the end of the day, I thought of it as the fresh start to a new night. I knew that was what I needed, too. A fresh start.

The South was cheap. Lots of small towns I could disappear into. The water was close by, and I could escape to the beach any time I wanted. Maybe I'd head to Florida. But again, so much sun. I got up, brushed the sand from my pants, and dashed to my bike. I drove home quickly, anxious to get on my computer.

Once inside my small condo, I turned on the tower to the desktop and waited for the stupid thing to load.

I leaned back and bit my thumbnail. The prospect of new possibilities was gnawing at me. Once the computer was ready to go, I searched the internet for U.S. maps, pulled up a colorful one, and stared at it. Texas was pretty big, I could definitely get lost there. I scanned left and right and decided that I'd rather stay on the east coast of the U.S. — or at least near to it. New Orleans caught my eye. It was on the water and inexpensive to live in. It got a good amount of rain, which meant no sun. I knew that city had a particularly rich history in the paranormal and wondered if this would be good or bad for me.

I thought about the number of vampires that probably lived there. A smile crept up on my lips. What had made the past ten years pass so quickly was my little side hobby I'd taken on. That place was probably teeming with bloodsuckers. I'd keep plenty busy at night when I was restless as shit and needed to kill something.

Feeling relief, happiness, and a whole lot of nervousness at my decision, I did as many searches as I could on New Orleans. The amount of motorcycle repair shops, how much it cost to live, and what there was to do there. I felt a sense of peace blanket me at this decision. Louisiana was going to have to prepare for me.

But first, it was time to change my name. This was something I had been thinking of for a long time. I didn't even want to keep Dominic. It had to be something else. I grabbed a pencil and slid the notebook I kept by my computer over toward me. I had the pencil poised above the paper. Glancing in the mirror above my desk, I knew I needed something that defined me—that had very personal meaning.

I thought about what the succubus had said to me on the night she died: *"No. I need to kill you, otherwise, you'll wreak havoc on this city, and I can't have that shit coming back on me."*

Oh, wreak havoc I did, all right. Little did she know that by destroying my soul—and my innocence to the world of the supernatural—she'd created a new vampire hunter, with her being my first victim. I smiled at the irony.

Havoc was a cool word. I wrote it down and frowned, scratching through it. Too obvious. Backward? Covah. No. How about with a K? I scribbled it down.

Kovah.

"Ko-vahhh." I said it over and over in the mirror, smiling in satisfaction at my decision. Now I needed a last name. That one came easy. I was sticking with my Italian heritage, so my mom's maiden name would work—Sanagra. Kovah Sanagra. It was a mouthful, but I loved it. In the off chance Louisiana would make me give them a middle name, I'd just tell them I didn't have one.

That brought on another line of problems. Where would I get a birth certificate forged?

Chapter 13

LOUISIANA

Ten Years Ago

New Orleans, LA

Having left Rochester four months prior, I'd told my family I was moving south to take a really good job offer I'd received in New Orleans at a classic motorcycle shop. They hadn't been happy. Ma had cried and my pop just stared at me with his glassed over, drunken eyes. He could sure function just fine during the day while he was working, but he was mostly wasted at night, and I hoped Leo and Sophie would check on Ma occasionally. Thankfully, Ma, Heather, and Sophie were pretty tight, so I prayed they would look after both my parents. No one in the family understood why I was doing this, but I didn't owe anyone an explanation. It was time for me to leave. In the past few months, I'd run into a few people from high school and college, and they had all commented on how "good" I'd looked and asked what my secret was. They didn't even hide their shock that I still looked exactly the same. That was the final straw. It was time to blow that pop stand... and with not as much sadness as I thought I'd feel, I sold everything I couldn't fit on the back of my motorcycle and left the only place I'd ever called home.

I had been excited and nervous as hell to move to a new place, but thanks to the resources on the internet, I'd found everything I needed. Sure, I didn't have a job secured as some fabulous classic motorcycle restoration place, but I hoped the little white lie I'd told my family would actually become a truth.

I rented a small studio apartment right outside the French Quarter. It was expensive as hell, but less than I was paying for that condo in Rochester. I'd applied at a few shops, but no one had called back yet. So, I'd taken to buying old motorcycles from online listings, working in the back corner of the parking lot of my apartment complex to restore them to re-sell for a profit. It wasn't ideal, but it paid the rent and gave me a little drinking money.

Louisiana was hot as hell for over six months out of the year. Sure, we got some humidity in Rochester, but we had super cold winters to offset it. This place was just one big, sticky mess. I tried to sleep during the day and be up at night because that's what was comfortable for me, but that wasn't always feasible. Plus, it was hard to sleep during the day in a busy apartment complex with crying babies and construction work. My sensitive ears picked up everything. I would have to figure out something quickly because I was getting cranky from the lack of sleep.

Around seven p.m., I was in the parking lot, elbow-deep in grease from a 1990 Harley Fatboy, all the pieces lying around me on a blanket, when I heard a voice.

"Excuse me, you can't be workin' on vehicles in this parkin' lot, you're gonna have to do it elsewhere."

I rolled over on the blanket, the bike on its side before me, and looked up to see an older man standing above me, gratefully blocking what was left of the remaining sunlight.

I yanked the smoldering cigarette from where it lay on the ground and teetered it between my fingertips as I stood. Lifting it to my lips, I squinted, regarding my landlord, whose name I couldn't remember. I took a big pull from it before blowing out a stream of blue smoke and then said, "Well, I live here, in case you'd forgotten."

In just a white tank, some cutoff jean shorts, and a pair of blue Crocs, he kept his arms folded over his chest and looked up at me. A stray strand of gray hair flew up from his head. "Well, it's in the lease you signed, no working on cars or any vehicles in my lot."

I looked around the mostly empty space and back at him. "I'm at the very back of this very empty lot, and am only taking up one parking space. If you want me to be able to continue to pay your stupidly priced rent, I'm gonna need to work. Got it?"

He shook his head and said, "Sorry, Mr. Sanagra, the tenants of not only this complex, but the one there" — he pointed over the fence we were backed up to — "are complaining of the noise and the light, since you're up all hours…"

I began to shake and felt like I may snap. To get this guy to leave me alone, I whipped off my sunglasses to scare him. I got in his face and looked him directly in the eye. "I'm not going to stop what I'm doing. Go away."

The landlord gasped but did not shrink back in fear. Instead, he locked eyes with me, and it was then I noticed that his face had gone slack, his gaze relaxed. I kept eye contact, confused and wondering what was going on.

"I'll go away," he said robotically.

My eyes got big. *What the actual fuck…*

"Wait!" I said as he turned and walked woodenly back toward the apartments.

He stopped and looked at me curiously, as if waiting for a command.

"Where are you going?" I asked, flicking the cigarette away.

"Away," he said quietly.

I walked toward him again and looked into his eyes, my hands on his shoulders. I briefly glanced down at my watch to see it was the fourth of the month. "Is my rent already paid this month?"

His eyebrows furrowed in confusion, and he just stared blankly back at me. "I… I don't know…"

I licked my lips and tried again. "My rent has already been paid this month. I paid you yesterday, remember?"

"You paid me yesterday. I remember."

"Okay, you can go away now," I said, a smug smile on my face.

"I can go away," he repeated, and turned to continue to walk back toward the apartments.

I put my glasses back on and went back to the bike. I sat down on the blanket, my mind whirling. Did that just happen? Did he just say my rent was paid? The hell it was. Tomorrow it was going to be late and that was why I was busting my ass to finish this bike so I could sell it for double what I bought it for to make the rent.

Looked like I'd have more drinking money now. Wow. Guess these freaky eyes had a purpose after all. I was definitely going to have to try this out on someone else before I used it for what I really needed it for. I began to sing along with "Hate Me" by Blue October from my little radio and picked up a wrench to finish up on the Harley.

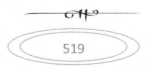

I had visited some seriously dark and scary places in my thirty years on this earth, but nothing compared to the back alleys of New Orleans. Most of the time I was stepping in or over shit that I could only hope was vomit or piss. I quickly became a fan of black steel-toed boots and durable black denim jeans. However, today took the cake. Looking both ways down the darker-than-hell alley, I knocked the door marked "J.D." in faded letters and waited for someone to answer. The wooden stake at the small of my back, along with the buck knife sheathed in my boot, gave me comfort. I had plans to buy a couple of handguns in the very near future for protection, too.

The door creaked open slowly, and as soon as I saw a pale, female face greet me, I got that familiar heavy feeling in my chest and my skin broke out in goosebumps. I had one hand behind my back in case I needed the stake but did not pull it out. With too much black makeup around her eyes and strands of inky, stringy hair hanging in her face, she looked up at me and said, "Kovah?"

I nodded once.

"Password?" she asked.

"Identification," I said quickly, the password I'd memorized from the shady emails I'd exchanged with some dude whose ad I had found on Craigslist. I hoped to God this was legit and not some police sting.

Although, since Hurricane Katrina had just hit a year prior, NOPD seemed to be pretty busy cleaning up messes from that.

The vampire nodded once and opened the door wider for me. She ushered me in with a flourish of her hand, indicating a dark hallway. Following behind me, I heard her whisper, "Yes, he's here. But he smells funny."

I kept walking and said, "I heard that."

She stopped and I turned around to look at her. It was dark enough in here that I was sure a normal human would barely be able to see, but I could see fine, even if I did have to remove my glasses. "I smell funny, sweetie, because I'm a hybrid. Hence the reason I'm here."

She bit the piercing in her lip and kept a brave face, nodding once. "Keep going, we're almost there."

I did as she instructed and quickly reached a large room full of machines and people working in an assembly-line type fashion. It was two stories tall and I looked up to see offices on the top tier of the building.

Looking back at my guide, she pointed up. "Go see Jake in the office."

I peered up to see only one office lit up. I nodded, heading toward the metal staircase.

I ran up the steps and stopped in front of the lighted office. A heavyset, sweaty man in a suit with the tie loosened sat behind the sole desk. He looked up from his laptop and smiled behind the cigar hanging from his mouth. He put the smoking cigar into a yellowed glass ashtray on his desk and said, "Kovah, I presume? I'm Jake. Please sit."

I shook his proffered clammy hand, and then did as I was told, plunking down into the black and red fabric chair.

"You a cop?" he asked, staring hard at me.

I shouldn't have been surprised by that but I was. "Fuck no!"

He stared hard at me again and then nodded. "You need new documents, yes?" he asked.

I nodded. "That's why I'm here."

"Great. What will you be needing, exactly?"

I was starting to get annoyed but tried not to show it. I'd explained this already over the emails. "A birth certificate for starters. I need a driver's license and passport, too, but I suppose if I have a legitimate birth certificate, I can get those things myself."

He nodded. "It's up to you. All three documents will run you about two grand. Just the birth certificate will cost you about five hundred. All cash, of course."

I contemplated this. Not sure if my little eye trick would work again in case his IDs sucked, I decided to play it safe and risk a day of hell at the DMV instead. "I'll just take the birth certificate."

"Well, keep in mind, the DMV is only open during the day."

It wasn't until later that I realized why he had made that comment.

"I'll take my chances," I said.

"Sounds great. Cash first though, guy." He put his chubby hand out.

I pulled out my wallet and counted out five one-hundred-dollar bills, placing them on his palm. He looked hungrily at the cash and shoved the bills into his jacket pocket.

Then he turned to a cabinet set behind his desk and began rifling through files. Without turning around, he asked, "What state?"

"New York," I said quickly.

He nodded, his shiny balding head gleaming in the harsh overhead lights. He pulled out a beige 8x10 paper and another plain white sheet. He asked me for my new name, father's name, date of birth, mother's maiden name, address, and hospital. I literally made it all up. Date of birth was my same day, just different year—1986. I made up a bullshit name for my mother and then used the hospital I was born in, knowing it was mostly irrelevant.

Satisfied he had everything, he pushed some keys on his keyboard, then put the beige paper into his printer. Out spat a very official-looking New York State birth certificate.

I held it up to the light to see the New York State seal woven into the paper and smiled.

Then, I checked the facts:

Kovah Sanagra

June 18, 1986

Rochester General Hospital

Father: Mario Joseph Sanagra

Mother's maiden name: Sandra Marie Smith

It even had two authentic-looking baby footprints, and I had to admit, it looked pretty damn close to my real birth certificate I still had at home.

"This is fucking awesome. Great doing business with you, Jim." I went to stand.

"It's Jake," he said, annoyed.

"Awesome, see you. Or not." I turned to leave.

"Wait," he said, pulling out a small digital camera. "One picture for my records." At my raised eyebrow, he used a handkerchief to wipe sweat from his brow. "You know, gotta cover my big ass. You understand?"

I nodded. "Okay, take it."

"Uh, remove the glasses, please?"

"No."

"Come on, man. Humor me."

I shook my head anticipating the inevitable. Removing them, I smiled like the Joker.

He flinched back in his chair. "Holy shit! What happened to your eyes? You been a vampire too long or something?"

My smile fell and sneered at him. I smacked the camera out of his hand and it went flying into the wall, shattering it into pieces. "I ain't no fuckin' vampire!"

Stalking from the room, I sprinted down the stairs with my new birth certificate and the piece of paper he'd used to make notes. I stalked across the warehouse, and when the gothic female approached me, trying to stop me, I backhanded her across the face, sending her flying onto the floor. Breaking into a sprint, I blindly ran down the hallway, then out the door, and into the alley.

I didn't care what I was stepping in this time, I ran and ran until I was out of breath and in the doorway of a very dark bar on Bourbon Street, still shaking from rage.

What the hell was wrong with me?

Chapter 14

PARLOR TRICKS

Ten Years Ago

The Department of Motor Vehicles in New Orleans was dead. I expected a huge line and an all-day affair, but there was no waiting. Thrilled with this, I pulled the tab from the machine and looked up at the lighted screen to see there were only two numbers ahead of mine.

I took a seat in one of the plastic chairs and surveyed the scene. Four people sat around the mundane office, and a slew of state government workers wore uninterested expressions as they called, "Next." Before I knew it, it was my turn and I happily handed over my birth certificate to the worker.

"I'll need your New York driver's license," she said, looking at her long, red fingernails as if she was bored.

I was prepared for this. "Uh, I don't have one. I lost it a week before I moved. I just have the birth certificate. I'm sorry."

She gazed up at me, her brow furrowed. Lifting the birth certificate in her hand, she held it up to the light, then back down. Then she rubbed her finger over the bottom right. "I'm sorry. This birth certificate doesn't have the state seal embossed on it."

My brows dipped together. "Yes, it does. You just held it up to the light. Didn't you see the seals all over it?"

She nodded and looked stressed out at how upset I was getting. "Yes, but this is just a copy of it on official paper. The original has an embossed seal on the bottom right, like an imprint from an embosser."

Crap.

I turned around and yanked my sunglasses off. Quickly pulling out the contact lenses from my eyes, I then turned back and around, leaned over the counter, and got six inches from her face, hoping this would work. Locking eyes with her I said, "There's a seal on it. That birth certificate is perfectly legit. You are happy with the legitimacy of it and are going to give me my Louisiana driver's license without a hassle."

Her eyes glazed over and her pupils dilated. "Yes, it's legitimate."

I stood back and put my glasses on. "So everything is straight then?"

She nodded. "Uh, yes, here's your birth certificate. Go back to the waiting area and wait for the photographer to call your name. Have a nice day!"

"You too!" I called back.

I ran into the restroom and popped the contacts back in my eyes. Twenty minutes later, Kovah Sanagra walked out of there with a shiny new Louisiana driver's license and plans to head back to Jake's tonight to get my five hundred bucks back.

Right after the sun set, I went back down the same alley, but instead of knocking this time, I tried the doorknob, but it was locked tight. So I pounded on the door until the same vampire answered.

"What's the pass—" She stopped when she saw me. Then her eyes turned black and she bared fangs and me. And then she hissed.

I pulled off my glasses. "Did you just fucking hiss at me?"

"You slapped me yesterday!" she squealed through her fangs, so it came out mumbled. Instead of saying anything, I burst out laughing.

I shook my head, pushed past her, and stalked down the hallway. She blurred past me and I barely saw the back of her as she disappeared through the door at the end of the hall.

As soon as I entered through the door into the warehouse, I was detained by two big vampires in suits. I didn't fight them as they manhandled me up the stairs to Jake's office.

They plunked me down in the chair. Jake sat across his desk glaring at me.

"I'm not going to ask what you're doing here, because I already know."

I narrowed my eyes behind my glasses. "Yeah, I want my five hundred bucks back for this useless piece of shit." I pulled the folded birth certificate from my black leather coat pocket and threw it on the desk.

He carefully unfolded it and pulled an embosser press from his desk drawer. He slid it over the bottom right corner of the paper and pressed the two plates of the embosser hard, creating a seal.

Shit. I was quite obviously feeling chagrinned and stupid at this point. He handed the document back to me and said, "I put the seal on after I get a photo of the client, but you didn't give me a chance. And you owe me a new digital camera."

Picking up the paper, I re-folded it and shoved it into my coat pocket. I stood and said, "I'll get it online and have it shipped to you. Good doing business with you."

I turned to walk out and his vampire goons did not try to stop me. As I was heading down the stairs, he said, "Wait. If you're not a vampire, what are you?"

I hesitated, but then finally replied, "A hybrid."

"Kid, I've been in this business for a long time. I found out about vampires at a very young age and decided I could make a good living doing new IDs for them. How old are you?"

"Thirty-one."

He nodded. "How does one become a hybrid?"

I chuckled as I headed down the stairs, and without turning around, I said, "Find yourself a succubus, let her take your soul, then kill her. If you can."

That dude was in no shape to fight anyone. He looked like he had eaten one too many pizzas.

As I was leaving, vampire girl stepped away from her spot near the door and gave me a wide berth as I passed. I felt a little bad so I said, "Look, I'm sorry for hitting you yesterday. No hard feelings, eh?"

She rolled her eyes and snorted but nodded slightly.

Good. I'd hate to have to kill her if I saw her on the street.

As I left the strange place, I went back out to the main street to begin my trek home. It was only a mile or so walk and I didn't mind. It helped me get familiar with the city. And of course find out where vampires hung out.

I was, as always, armed to the teeth with two knives and a stake.

As I crossed the street, a lighted sign caught my eye: *Custom Ink Tattoo.*

I had always wanted a tattoo. I'd always wanted several tattoos, actually. I'd created in my mind an entire sleeve of tats. I smiled as I headed toward the sign. Tonight would be the night when I would see what my body could handle. I healed strangely fast and I wondered if this would affect what a tattoo needle would do.

Walking in through the front door, I was greeted to walls full of photos of varying tattoos, some of them framed, some just sort of plastered up sideways or askew, like it was the eclectic thing to do.

"Hey, man," said a voice that broke me out of my gawking of the wall art. I looked over at a man tattooed from his hands to his neck wearing rubber gloves sitting in a chair. A woman on her stomach getting her lower back tattooed lay still in front of him.

"Hey. First time here," I said, unsure what else to say.

"Cool, did you have an appointment?" he asked, and I noticed he had a black hoop through his lip and another through his eyebrow. His blond mohawk had green tips. It looked wicked cool.

"Nah, just wanting a tattoo, and I already know the design, so I'll wait."

He nodded. "Awesome, I'm almost done here."

I sat down, grabbed a book, and began thumbing through all the wicked designs the shop had done.

It wasn't long until the lady on the table smiled in the mirror at her new tattoo, paid the man cash, and left.

He pulled his gloves off and came over to me. "Sorry to keep you waiting. The other guy called in sick tonight so it's just me. I'm Floyd, by the way." He put his hand out.

"Kovah," I said back, shaking his hand.

"So did you see anything in the book you liked?" he asked, pointing to it in my hand.

I set it on the table and said, "Nah, I have my own design. I can draw it or describe it for you."

Floyd nodded and went around to a small desk and grabbed a piece of paper and a pencil. "Knock yourself out, man. I'm gonna go clean up the bench and get it ready. You gonna want color?"

I nodded. "Definitely."

I set the paper on the desk and began to draw the image that was burned into my brain since the day it had popped in there. The drawing came quickly and when I was done, I smiled proudly at it. Floyd came over and looked down at my masterpiece.

He whistled through his teeth. "Wow, that's quite the picture."

I smiled proudly. "It has personal meaning to me."

He grinned. "You get bit by a vampire?"

I couldn't tell if he was joking or if he actually believed in vampires, but I supposed it didn't really matter. In a town like this one, I had no doubt he had at least met a few, even if he didn't know it. "Yeah, something like that."

"Awesome. Where do you want this?" he asked, pointing at the paper.

I put my right forearm out. "Right here."

He said, "Go sit in my chair. I'm gonna get this sketched up on tracing paper. Make yourself comfortable."

I did as he said, a bundle of nerves in my stomach. I was extremely excited to be doing this.

Three hours later, I left the shop two hundred dollars poorer, with a half-naked pinup of a voluptuous redhead baring vampire teeth tattooed on my arm. It was a reminder for me to stay far away from beautiful women, because they only brought destruction and pain with them.

Especially the redheads.

Chapter 15

MISTAKEN IDENTITY

New Orleans, LA

Present Day

hen they say tattoos are addicting, they weren't kidding. I went back to Floyd six more times before leaving New Orleans a year ago. I had told him if I wanted more ink I'd come back to him, and I meant it. He was down to earth, nice as hell, and super talented. Aside from the first tattoo of the succubus, I'd gotten a wicked cool one of an Italian flag, an American flag, and the New York Yankees symbol all intertwined, with some smoky shading behind it. It took up my entire upper arm. I got compliments on it all the time. I loved how it embodied my past without being too obvious.

The nine years I'd spent in New Orleans had been lonely, but I had learned a lot. Not just about myself, but about the world of the supernatural. I had killed probably close to a thousand vampires in that time. I'd head out to clubs and bars, and when the opportunity presented itself, if I could lure one outside while I had a smoke, and he or she was dumb enough to follow me out behind the building, well, that was their stupidity.

It had now come down to me needing to move away from the Big Easy and into a smaller town… and I knew exactly where I was going to go.

Three weeks ago, I was following a group of vampires through the Quarter. They eventually left Bourbon Street on foot, rounded the corner, and slipped into a small coffee shop. Of course, I followed them in and took a seat near the door, where I could both see out the window and keep an eye on them. It was nights like this that I wondered what I was doing. Was I hoping to kill them all or just observe their behavior? Even I had to admit that I was reluctantly starting to see that not all vampires needed to die. Some minded their own business and went on with their lives. I had even visited businesses at night and saw vampires working for a living. I was just curious about this particular group. They looked so young, not much older than teens, really, and I wondered what they were up to. For now, they seemed to be doing not much of anything. They just ordered coffee or hot chocolate and sat talking too low for me to hear.

The door's bell caught my attention. I looked up to see a group of bikers come in. I eyed them curiously, my gaze zoning in on the patches attached to their vests. The patch portrayed vampire teeth with a red circle and a line around it. On the outer border were the letters TOGVIADO. I wondered what it meant.

The men were a little older, probably in their forties and fifties, and sat quietly drinking coffee and looking tired but sort of on edge at the same time. I watched as a couple of them would glance at the group of vampires occasionally, then back to their comrades. I looked down at my new smartphone, pretending to be surfing, but I was watching both groups carefully. You could cut the tension in the air with a knife.

Frequently, one of the bikers would look over at me. With my glasses on, I doubted he could see that I was staring at them, too. I kept my head down to make it look like I was engrossed in my phone while sipping my coffee.

One of the male vampires got up and headed toward the bathroom. I casually got up, slipping my phone into my pocket. I fished a five-dollar bill out and tossed it on the table without taking my eyes off of the vampire.

Pretending the bikers and vampires weren't there, I slowly and casually made my way toward the bathroom. It seemed quiet in there, so I put my ear to the door and heard some whimpering. I withdrew the stake from the small of my back and gripped it in my right fist before carefully pushing the door open with my left.

The vampire had a human man backed up against the wall between two urinals, the human's pants still unbuttoned and unzipped. With his head craned to the right for better access to the poor dude's neck, I could see the man's fingers futilely trying to grab the back of the vampire's shirt in an attempt to pull him off. His eyes over the vampire's shoulder looked wide and terrified. He had to be in his forties and had definitely been taken by surprise. This enraged me.

I moved with speed toward the vampire and grabbed him by the back of the head, a fistful of greasy blond hair in my hand as I yanked him off the human. The human slumped down the wall and landed on his ass.

I spun him around, reared my arm back, and punched the vamp in the jaw. He went flying across the small bathroom, and once he landed on his back, I was on him, straddling him on the cold, dirty tiled floor of the coffee shop's restroom.

His eyes were black, his fangs out and dripping with human blood. The rage of seeing this made me almost black out. I could hear my heart beat in my ears as I moved the wooden stake from my left hand to my right. For good measure, I wrapped my left hand around my right and slammed the stake into the center of his chest. On instinct, I jumped off the bloodsucker and watched to see how quick he would turn to ash.

"Holy mother of fuck," I heard a voice say.

I gasped, my stake still gripped in my fist, and turned toward the bathroom entrance to see two of the bikers standing there dumbfounded.

I glanced quickly at the rapidly deteriorating vampire, then back to the bikers. "I can explain…"

One of the bikers, who I noticed had a cool salt-and-pepper pompadour and muscles and tats for days, made his way toward me.

Chuckling ironically, he said, "You don't need to explain shit." He spat a stream of brown chew onto the vampire's remains. "The only good vampire is a dead one."

My eyes widened behind my glasses and I said, "You aren't fucked off from watching me kill that one?" I pointed to the remains.

He chuckled. "Hell no, dude. In fact, we owe you a favor. We came here tonight to kill that one. He's an undead piece of shit who's been feeding on and sometimes killing humans all across the state."

I cocked my head to the side. "Really? You guys track vampires or something?"

He nodded. "Something like that. We hunt and end them. Menace to society, those bloodsucking leeches."

I smiled. "I couldn't agree more."

He put his hand out. "Ollie, and this is Aspen."

I shook both of their hands. "Kovah."

"Well, that's a weird ass name, but I won't ask. How long you been a vampire hunter, Kovah?" Ollie asked.

I went over and collected the vampire clothing and wadded it up in my hand. Then I scooped what I could of the ashes onto the clothes, dumped it into stall's toilet, and kicked the flusher to life. I dumped the clothes into the trash can.

"That's a tricky question, Ollie. If I said twenty years, would you believe me?"

Aspen stood near the door. "I wouldn't. You're just a kid."

I rinsed off my stake at the sink, dried it, and put it back in my pants. "Well, I ain't no kid, and we need to get *him* out of here." I pointed at the human victim, who was starting to rouse on the floor between the urinals.

The two bikers just looked at me, a sense of awe and curiosity blazing in their eyes.

I wetted a paper towel and walked to the human man. I crouched down and wiped the blood from his neck. His eyes were open now, and he stared curiously at me. Whipping off my sunglasses, I looked at him.

He gasped.

Once I had him locked, I said, "You were taking a piss and you slipped in something wet on the floor." I pointed the floor, and his eyes lazily followed my finger. "Look at me!" I barked. When he gazed into my eyes again, I continued. "You were knocked out cold, and when you came to, you found yourself in the bathroom of this coffee shop, where you'd been having coffee after too many beers. You cut your neck open on a loose floor tile."

"I had too many beers and cut my neck," he repeated.

I nodded. "Now get the fuck outta here and go back to your friends in the coffee shop."

"I'm leaving now…" he said.

I watched as he awkwardly got up, looked down and buttoned and zipped his pants, and went to the door of the bathroom. He pulled it open and walked carefully out into the dining area. Making sure he was all the way out and the hallway was clear, I shut the door and locked it so I could talk to these guys. I turned around to see Ollie and Aspen with their guns out, pointed right at me.

Throwing my hands in the air, I yelled, "What the fuck!"

Ollie spit out his chew on the floor, but kept his eyes and gun trained on me. Some kind of smaller-looking shotgun about the length of my forearm. He had it one-handedly aimed at my head. He squinted and said, "You could have just admitted to being a bloodsucker."

Shit.

"I'm not a vampire! I'm a hybrid."

With his thumb, Aspen cocked the hammer back on his shiny .57 revolver and said, "Bullshit, you just hypnotized that guy. Only vampers can do that."

"Look, I don't know how to prove to you that I'm not one without showing you I can eat real food, going out into the sun, or letting you kill me to see I won't turn to ash. I think, anyway. Let's put the guns away so I can tell you my story."

They were quiet, their guns still up at the ready, waiting for me to continue.

"I'm gonna remove my glasses—"

Ollie made a *tsk* noise. "The fuck you are. You are not going to hypnotize us."

"No, I'm not," I said, slowly lowering my hands. "I need you to see that my eyes aren't black."

"So what?" Aspen said, nearly growling. "Vamps' eyes only turn black when they're feeding or about to die."

"Or very scared," I said. "Which I will admit that I am right now. Come on, guys."

Aspen looked at Ollie, and he just shrugged in response.

"Go ahead," Ollie said. "Slowly."

I obeyed and painfully slow, I reached up and slid my Ray-Bans off.

"What the hell!" they both exclaimed in unison.

"A succubus did this to me."

I put my glasses back on as they lowered their weapons.

"Let's go sit down and have some of that apple pie I saw in the case out there." I really wasn't hungry, but I was desperate to get them to calm down and show them I could eat food.

Chapter 16

FINDING HOME

Present Day

Shreveport, LA

I was amazed at how quickly the guys had accepted me into the fold. They told me they ran an organization that thrived on killing vampires called the Rebel Riders, and that their patch featuring TOGVIADO meant *The Only Good Vampire Is A Dead One*… and then it all made sense. They hailed from Shreveport, a city a few hours north of New Orleans, and invited me to visit. I had laughed, telling them that I was looking to relocate and now would be a perfect time to come see Shreveport.

After visiting once, I was sold. I ended the lease on the crappy apartment I'd rented, and again sold what I could and packed what I couldn't, and headed north, anxious to be a part of something. To finally have a place I could call home with people who I could be myself around. Pretending to a human, or pretending to be a vampire, was exhausting. I just wanted to be me… whatever that was.

I felt at peace with this decision, and after leaving New Orleans, I rented a hotel room and began looking for work.

One Saturday, while reading the newspaper I'd stolen from the hotel lobby, I lay on the hotel room bed and looked the local events. I saw that there was a gun show happening at a pavilion in town, and decided that would be a good place to get myself a couple more guns, and see if I could meet some likeminded locals.

The pavilion was packed with people, and instead of feeling anxious about being around such a big crowd, I felt happy. It was kind of nice to get out and socialize, and I was hoping to find a group of gun enthusiasts I could hang with until I made some friends. The past twenty years had been lonely and I desperately wanted to make some friends. I had been a pretty social guy when I was human and in college, but since becoming…

this... I had pushed people away, not wanting to have to explain things.

As I wandered around the show, I came to a tent where the owners were selling more than guns. I saw throwing stars, crossbow pistols, bows and arrows, and short shotguns, like the one Ollie had had the night we met. I went into the tent and ran my fingers over the guns.

"Can I answer any questions?" an older guy with a gray goatee wearing a blue bandana asked. He leaned on a cane for support.

I smiled as I picked up a throwing star and twirled it between my fingers. "This is wicked cool. Probably takes some practice to hit something with it, though, huh?"

The guy nodded. "You got that right, kid. Name's Archie."

"Kovah," I heard another voice say to my left. I turned to see Ollie approaching with a pizza box in his hand.

"You know this guy?" Archie asked, looking at Ollie.

He nodded and set the pizza box on a table in the back of the tent. "Yeah, remember that hybrid I told you me 'n Aspen met in Nawlins?"

Archie's eyes went wide and looked at me. "You're him?"

Aspen put his hand out. I clasped it in a manly handshake, patting him on the back of his leather jacket.

Then I looked at Archie, "That's me."

He said, "Take off your glasses."

I looked to my left and right, then slowly removed them.

"Holy fuck. They weren't kidding."

I smiled slightly and replaced my glasses. Then I said, "Great meeting you, Archie."

"How long you been in Shreveport?" he asked, walking toward the back of the tent, and then opening the pizza box. A steaming cheese and pepperoni pie sat inside, and he silently offered me a piece, but I declined. He shrugged, reached in, pulled out a greasy slice, and took a bite, waiting for my answer.

"Only a few days. Looking for a job so I can find an apartment."

"What do you do?" Archie asked around a mouthful of pizza. "I know people all over the city."

I lifted a shoulder and let it fall, and with a laugh said, "I dropped out of college so I could become a motorcycle mechanic."

He immediately began choking on a piece of pizza, and then grabbed a bottle of water and swallowed a big swig.

Aspen smacked him on the back. "You okay, boss?"

Archie nodded, and when he could speak again, he said, "You are a motorcycle repairman?"

A bit defensive and slightly embarrassed, I said, "Yeah, so?"

He chuckled and said, "I run the biggest and best motorcycle repair and restoration shop in Shreveport."

My eyes got big behind my sunglasses and I snapped my fingers, pointing at him. "Archie's Garage! I was going to head there tomorrow and see if there were any openings!"

He laughed. "Oh yeah, kid. I'm down two mechanics. And I've got one having personal problems so he's in and out. How long you been doing it?"

"Over ten years. I've repaired and restored everything from classics to crotch rockets. I flip them when I'm out of work to make some extra cash to pay the bills."

Archie ate the last of his pizza and used his cane to hobble to a trash can, tossing the plate in. Then he came back over to the table where I stood and put his hand out. "You're hired. Come to the shop tomorrow and I'll show you the ropes."

I smiled and shook his hand, disbelief and a stupid smile in my voice. "Thank you, I will."

"Hey, boss, you think he needs to talk to the kid?" Ollie asked, a slice of pizza in his hand.

Archie snapped his fingers, then looked around and lowered his voice. "You're right, dude. Hey, Kovah, one of my mechanics is dealing with a succubus problem. Think you can talk to him?"

My face darkened and I felt instantly angry on the mention of the word 'succubus.' I said, "Oh, I would be more than happy to. What's the kid's name?"

"Nolan."

I nodded. "Absolutely."

After buying a crossbow pistol and two revolvers, I left the gun show and went to get something to eat.

The next day when I went to Archie's Garage, I wasn't apprehensive at all. The moment I walked in, I felt happy for once. The smell of oil and grease… the rev of a motorcycle in my ears… the cussing and shouting of the mechanics… the blaring angry metal music screaming though the speakers. It shouldn't be comforting, but it was. And when Archie informed me he had a room for rent above the garage, I knew I was home.

As the weeks passed by, I began to develop a friendship with Nolan. He and I were the same physical age, but because I knew he knew about the supernatural, he eventually learned that I was old enough to be his father. He didn't care, because he was dealing with his own problems.

Archie and Ollie had filled me in on his situation. Along with them, I too felt helpless to do anything to help Nolan. He had to kill the succubus himself. I wanted to drive him to her house, put the stake in his hand, and help him plunge it into her pale, undead chest. There was just one problem, though. He was in love with the succubus's twin sister, who was ironically still human. He'd told me he'd drunk her blood. It was some strange, freaky ritual he had read about in some massive library in New Orleans, and that doing so was supposed to keep him from turning into a vampire.

Still, I noticed he wasn't himself. Not that I knew him before all this, but he acted strangely, avoided the sun, and never ate lunch with us at the shop.

One night, when the Rebel Riders and I were at our usual hangout, he called and told me he had had enough and was heading to the nightclub where the bitch hung out and was going to kill her. He asked for my backup so of course I was game to help. To get to kill one of the redheaded demons would be the highlight of my week… my month… my year. We were to meet him at the Blue Room, some warehouse nightclub I had been to once before with Nolan, and we'd run into this Eva demon there before. Why he hadn't killed her then I couldn't remember, but he sure sounded ready to now.

Archie's phone rang after that and he informed me that Nolan had also asked for the Riders' help. Looked like we'd be in for a long night.

"I'll meet you guys there, I need to make a stop first," I told them.

They didn't ask questions as I tore off out of the bar and headed to a vampire's house.

Janice was a blonde bombshell, but she was also a vampire who was into some serious freaky BDSM shit. The only reason I was coming over here was to ask for her help. The night of Aspen's funeral, Nolan had been pretty fucked in the head and had left with Janice. We had cornered them at her house, thinking Nolan was in danger, but it turned out she had been just looking for a little fun. She and Nolan became friends and nothing more, and that was the reason I now found myself at her house.

When she opened the door wearing almost nothing at all, I had to close my mouth. Damn. But she wouldn't hear a word I said, and thought I had come over to play. She snatched my glasses off my face with vampire speed, and then when I chased her into her bedroom, she chained me to a wall. I began to grow both frustrated and aroused at the same time. We negotiated a little bit, and in exchange for her giving me my glasses back, and helping Nolan that night for the big takedown, she wanted me to stay and play.

At first I said no... but then I finally figured, hell, why not. I would never admit this to Archie or any of the Riders, but I'd been with vampires before. There would be times when one would think it was luring me out for a bite, and I'd let them take a small taste, then convince them to take me back to their place. After I got what I wanted, I would kill them. Most of the female vampires were quite insane in bed, beautiful, and had great stamina, so sometimes it would be hard to turn one down.

Janice was quickly becoming irresistible. I had told her no, and she had pouted, but then dropped her robe to change for the club... and I then said, "fuck it" and had my way with her. It was worth every second, even the guilt I felt when I saw my phone was blown up with texts and calls from Nolan asking where I was. I was supposed to meet him at his house first, but now it looked like he was already at the club.

"Get dressed, sweetheart, time to go."

Janice smiled and wiped lipstick from my mouth with her thumb. "It's too bad we don't have time for more."

I nodded. "Later."

I had no intention of fucking her again… but it turned out I would go back for more. She had a lot of toys and wanted to try them all on me.

Chapter 17

VAMPIRE PROBLEMS

The takedown of the succubus Eva was one of the most epic vampire murders I had ever witnessed. I was so hopped up on adrenaline after watching Nolan take down that bitch, that I had spent the rest of the night in Janice's bed, expending all my energy. Plus, she had helped us do it, so it was the least I could do... heh.

Archie had given me the day off, so after sleeping most of the day away, I left Janice's house as the sun went down and decided to stop for a coffee before heading back to my flat to shower and relax. I got in line behind half a dozen people waiting to place their coffee orders, and I immediately got the familiar heaviness in my chest and tingle in my bones. I looked around casually to see where the vampire was, but to my surprise, it was the vampire who approached me.

"Hello, Dom... Kovah, sorry." Her eyes darted around nervously.

I looked down to see Violet... or Manta I guessed now, smiling up at me. "Hi yourself."

She held a coffee in her hand, her warm brown eyes and shiny dark hair looking so human and normal in this coffee shop. "I'll be sitting over there. I would love it if you'd join me. I actually need to talk to you about something."

Not really wanting to sit and chat over coffee, and really wanting a shower, but curious about what she wanted, I nodded. After I placed my order for black coffee with the cashier, she filled a cup immediately and handed it to me after taking my cash.

I found Manta and sat across from her at the table. I regarded her carefully as I sipped the hot coffee. She had both hands wrapped around her cup and she was quiet for a while. I didn't say anything. I just waited for her to speak.

"So how have you been?" she asked, staring at my glasses.

I smirked behind my coffee. "The same angry motherfucker I've always been. You asked me to sit with you to make small talk?"

She looked down at her cup and ran a manicured finger around the rim in circles. "No, not really." She then looked up at me. "Truth be told, I need your help. I'm glad I ran into you today because I'm not sure where else to turn."

My eyes narrowed behind my shades. "What? I don't get it. Why not ask the BSI for help?"

She chuckled, but her eyes still held sadness. "I can't. This problem goes beyond them."

"Look, I haven't seen you in years. Well, aside from our little run-in at the vampire ball. You barely know me, and now I'm the only chance you have?"

She shrugged one shoulder and looked down. "Looks that way."

Fucking-A. I wasn't sure whether to bolt the hell out of there or stay and help. Curiosity won out, so I said, "Well, what's the problem?"

She pulled a small piece of paper from her handbag and slid it across the table to me. I looked at her, a bit apprehensive-like, then took the note and opened it.

Scrawled in barely legible handwriting, I read:

Bitch, you are a traitor to your own kind.

We know your real name and that you work with the government to get rid of vampires.

Your days are numbered, we will be coming for you. There's no place to run or hide. You can change your name or move to another state, but a chapter of the Nighthawks will find you. We are everywhere. You are just one little pathetic vampire, but our numbers are strong.

Don't look over your shoulder at night, because you will never see us. Don't bother locking your doors at night because we always have a key.

We will come when you least expect it. Live in fear, because it'll be the last emotion you'll ever feel.

My eyebrows rose above my glasses and I folded the paper back into a square. "Wow, that's quite the threat. When did you get this?"

"A week ago," she answered, and I noticed her knee was bouncing.

"Do you have any idea who this Nighthawk group is?"

She nodded, then licked her lips and looked around the shop briefly. "Yes, we have a file on them at the BSI. They are a group of vampire bikers. They've been around a long time, more than ten years. They kill humans and rogue vampires, ones that don't follow the rules. Apparently, I fall into that category." She let out a sigh.

"Have any idea where the Shreveport chapter is?" I asked, beginning to get angry. Who the hell did these bloodsuckers think they were? There was only one group of motorcycle-riding, vampire-killing vigilantes in town. We didn't need another... nor did we want the competition.

"That's just the thing, Dom... sorry, Kovah, we don't think there is one. However, their presence is pretty strong in Baton Rouge, and of course in New Orleans."

I nodded. "Obviously they've tracked you here. You should leave the state."

"I thought about it; however, this says they have chapters all over the country. It's really not safe anywhere."

I felt my phone buzz in my pocket. I pulled it out and saw I had a text from Janice. A very nice text with a picture of some very nice tits.

I suppressed a grin and pocketed the phone. "Then leave the country."

"I love my job with the BSI. I can't do that."

"Even if your life was in danger?" I asked incredulously.

She didn't respond, just looked down at her cup.

I sighed. "I'm going to presume that you assume a new identity in that agency every twenty years or so?"

Manta nodded. "You're very perceptive."

"When are you due for your next identity change?"

She laughed. "I just got this one twenty-two months ago. Violet 'retired' and Manta was hired."

"I'm tracking. Okay, have any of these Nighthawks ever tried to contact you—I mean, in person?"

She shook her head. "Nope, that's the frightening part. I'd almost feel better if I had seen one or heard his voice over the phone. There's been nothing but that note."

"Then maybe they're just trying to scare you." I was trying hard to find reasoning behind that fucked-up warning.

"I keep telling myself that. But I walk around in a constant state of dread everywhere I go," she replied softly.

Fuck. In that moment, she looked so vulnerable, so fragile. I knew she wasn't, as she was a strong, old vampire, but it still tugged at my hard, cold heart.

"What is it you think I can do for you?" I asked.

She looked up, those brown eyes sad, soft, and pleading. I had to constantly remind myself that she was a vampire because she behaved so human-like. "Well, you walk the tightrope between human and vampire. You can be one or the other as you see fit. I think those skills are unique and could be put to good use." She sighed and grabbed a lock of her long, dark hair that was glowing with reddish streaks, twisting it nervously. "Please?"

"Okay, I'll help you."

She looked up, a spark of hope in her gaze. "Really? You will?"

I nodded. "Yes, I will. You dig up as much as you can on these Nighthawks, and I'll let Archie know the Rebel Riders have some competition."

She reached over and put her hand on mine. "Please, Kovah, I beg you... do not get your human friends involved with these guys."

"Why not? Someone needs to take these bloodsuckers down. They sound like a serious problem."

She still looked worried. "They are, but they cannot be bested by humans. They are old, and bored, and would love nothing more than to slaughter a bunch of middle-aged vampire-hunting vigilantes."

I chuckled, but let her keep her hand on mine, as it felt good there for some reason. "Sweetheart... Archie and the gang know they aren't going to die of old age. They have dedicated their lives to offing these types of vampires." My lips lifted into a slight smirk as I looked into her pretty and flawless face. "Let me guess, they don't follow any rules? They feed off humans without permission? They probably don't even bother to compel them into thinking they are getting the better end of the deal?"

She shook her head. "We're not sure. We just don't know that much about them, but they have definitely been put on our threat group radar. We're hoping to get a plant within their organization within the next year. Get their trade secrets and all that."

This piqued my interest. "Really? The BSI going to find a vampire willing to risk his life to join them? How many vampires that agency got working there, anyway?"

She measured me with a hard stare, as if she was warring with herself to divulge any more information. I stayed quiet, hoping my silence would make her uncomfortable enough to get her to talk.

She finally relented. "The BSI has taken to hiring vampires recently. Twenty years ago, I was one of their first, some sort of government pilot program. They quickly realized that vampires, while only able to work at night, could be very, very valuable assets to federal law enforcement. Not only were they pretty indestructible, they had no problems going deep undercover with no complaints about being away from their families for months on end, or getting injured in the line of duty. This assignment with the Nighthawks, however, has proven harder to fill." She glanced at me, some apprehensive look I couldn't quite decipher coloring features.

"Go on," I said, now completely enraptured and obsessed with what she was telling me. The buzzing of my cell in my pocket went ignored.

"The Justice Department has even considered pulling gang members out of prison and turning them into vampires in order to fulfil their mission of infiltrating the Nighthawks gang. It's gotten that bad. Their body count is growing, of both humans and vampires."

My mouth now hung open unhinged, my once-steaming coffee growing cold without a care at all. "You're just fucking with me, right?"

Her guilty brown eyes told a completely different story as she measured me with a serious stare. "I am not."

"This gang is that dangerous?" I asked, desperate for more information.

Her hand was still on mine, and she squeezed it. "Kovah, this is the most dangerous disruptive group the government has ever seen. We can't kill them. We can't imprison them. We can't even talk to them. They are elusive and scattered. They can hypnotize humans into forgetting what they had just discussed. They can make bodies disappear, human lives wiped out without a second thought."

"But they do have a weakness," I blurted out, interrupting her.

"What's that?" Manta asked, her eyes wide.

"They are confined by the night. During the day, they are vulnerable and can be killed."

"Well, yeah, like every vampire. Me, included," she replied casually.

I smiled as she was right. "Yes, but the difference is… you're one of the good guys. These shit-bags?" I pointed at the piece of paper still folded up on the table. "They just need to fucking die."

I left the coffee shop with sort of an adrenaline buzz. Okay maybe the coffee had contributed. A group of vampire bikers? Oh… those fuckers so needed to be turned to ash. A smile crept up onto my lips as I hopped on my bike and headed toward Archie's Garage where my small apartment awaited me.

When I got there, I parked the Harley and made my way inside as I felt my phone vibrate in my pocket again. Pulling it out and expecting to see another hot text from Janice, I instead saw one from my brother Leo: *I think its time dad erase you fm the will. You arent worthy. You abandond us. You obvsly hate us. Ma is sad all the fukin time. I hate you dominic.*

Sighing as I realized my poor brother had obviously been a victim of the alcoholism curse from our dad, I sent off a quick reply: *I love you and the kids, Leo.*

I didn't know what else to say. Because this text was the final straw. For the past almost twenty years, my Ma had kept bugging me to come visit -- she had even offered to come see me, to pay for plane tickets for me to go there, gas money, a bus ticket… but I had to keep making excuse. Work, illness, whatever I could lie about. It was becoming so troublesome that I began avoiding phone calls from her, my father, Leo, Sophie, and any other call from a Rochester area code. I hadn't seen them in almost twenty years and they were beyond upset. I kept in touch with them by phone and on social media, watching my niece and nephews, who were now young adults, growing up to thankfully be normal, and I could not do a damn thing but wish them well online and send them birthday cards from afar.

I knew it was time for Dominic to die once and for all, and the thought of what it would do to my family made me sick, but I couldn't do this anymore. I'd keep my social media pages open and keep tabs on them, but Dominic had to become a corpse.

Chapter 18

DEATH OF A BACHELOR

There was something very sobering about seeing your name on a death certificate.

I refused to get on social media. I couldn't see my Ma heartbroken. I couldn't stand by and watch Leo's drunken posts. I couldn't sit and read Heather's rantings about her poor husband and his grief. I couldn't bear Sophie and Josh's heartbreaking posts.

I couldn't.

Yes, it was selfish, but Dominic was done. The real me, he had died twenty years ago, and I hoped the DeLucas could accept it. And if they couldn't, the death certificate and obituary Manta had helped me fabricate was going to be the proof. Poor Dominic had been side-swiped on his motorcycle when a drunk had run a red light here in Shreveport. A newspaper article with my happy and innocent-looking tuxedo-wearing high school photo was sent to the Rochester newspaper for everyone to see, along with the obituary about how Dominic had lived and died. I wanted Dad and Leo to see what alcohol had done to their loved one. I hoped it would sober them up.

I realized about a week after Dominic's death that I was going to have to change my phone number. Ma kept calling it, and I wasn't sure if she didn't believe I was dead or what, but it was too much. Manta had suggested that she was probably just calling to hear my voice on my voicemail. That made me feel lower than pond scum.

Yet, what could I do? I didn't ask for this, but maybe this way they could have closure. They could grieve the loss of me and move on instead of me having to be a cruel-hearted asshole and continually avoid their requests to see me. This immortal shit was hard to deal with, and I was trying my damnedest not to become bitter, but something told me that ship had fucking sailed.

Sucking up my fate, I made plans to go to the cell phone store to change my number. I was then planning to go to the local BSI office here in Shreveport. I scribbled down the address Manta spouted off to me, then mumbled something about knowing where the New Orleans BSI office was, but not Shreveport.

"You've been to the BSI office in NOLA? When?" Manta asked.

"I went there a few weeks ago with Nolan. He had to get his head shrunk. He was losing his shit."

Silence met me on the other end of the line.

"I was kidding. Okay I wasn't kidding, really, but Nolan was asked to talk to the BSI about his intervention with the succubus. I went with him because Nolan's not Nolan when he's hungry."

I heard her snort. "So you… fed him?"

My nose wrinkled in disgust as I switched the phone to my other ear so I could use my right hand to shave the right side of my face. "Hell no. I just needed to keep him in check. And that pretty agent he met with was lucky I was there, because he was about to lose his shit. She's the one who fed him, though. Pulled a fuckin' blood bag from the office fridge. Keep in mind this was all before he'd killed the psycho succubus." I rinsed the razor under the running water and sighed at the prospect that I was going to have to shave my face every single day for eternity.

"What agent?" Manta asked. "Maybe I know her?"

"Mara something," I replied, not remembering her last name but rather the fact that she had eventually hooked up with a vampire named Joel Reichert. Not that I could judge.

"Special Agent Mara Shields," she said quietly. "Yep, she's in the New Orleans field office. We're friends."

I set the razor on the sink and held the phone away from my head as I rinsed the shaving cream from my face. "That's great. Anyway, I was thinking about these Nighthawks."

"What about them?" she asked.

"If you need someone to infiltrate them, I would like to volunteer myself as tribute. Yes, I smell weird to vampires, but when I tell them I'm hybrid, it usually shuts them up."

"You do smell weird, that's not a lie," she came back.

Instead of telling her to fuck off, I bit my tongue and said, "So what do you think?"

After a few seconds of silence, she said, "I think it's a bad idea and you could get yourself killed."

I chuckled. "Sweetheart, I don't give a damn. It's not like I have a whole lot to lose. Besides, I've been curious as hell about these guys. I can't shake the feeling that I'm supposed to be involved in this somehow."

More silence, so I just waited until she said, "Meet me at the office. I need to see you."

I wasn't sure how to take her comment. Was this professional or personal? Violet... Manta... she was a subtle flirt. I wouldn't lie and say women don't hit on me because they do, and usually I blow them off... but sometimes I indulge, too. There was something sexy about the underlying way she looked at me sometimes, all shy and demure. Even though I had already been with her ten years ago on that beach... that didn't really count.

I thought about Janice. The thing I had with her was fun and casual. She was trying to break me... to make me a submissive in her house of fun toys. For the most part, I indulged her. Hell, what did I have to lose? I was a guy, after all.

I felt bad every time I left Janice's house after the sun went down... the look of disappointment in her eyes. But I couldn't help it. I shouldn't be fucking a vampire while I went out on my free time and killed them.

I'm such a hypocrite...

Not that I had any morals left. I had to survive—to exist. I'd learned over the past twenty years that the only one looking out for me was me.

The nondescript government building loomed in front of me. I peered up at it from behind my glasses, my feet planted firmly on the ground with the Harley between my legs. It looked so plain, so normal... but I knew the secrets hidden on the third floor of this building could shake the foundation of what all the clueless humans on the planet thought was normal.

The light turned green and I turned into the parking garage, and after taking a ticket, I parked in the first available spot.

Since elevators freaked me out, I took the stairs in the stone staircase two at a time until I reached the entrance door to the main lobby. I slowly opened it, comforted by the pistol I kept in the small of my back and the knife sheathed around my ankle. I was greeted by a horseshoe-shaped desk with a security guard manning it.

"I'm here to see Agent LaRae," I said, proud that I'd not only used her professional title, but that I hadn't called her Violet.

With little interest, he nodded and said, "Take the elevator to the third floor."

"Thank you," I said, quickly finding the stairwell, opening the door, and sprinting up the steps.

Once I opened the stairwell door marked "3", I was in a carpeted hallway with white walls. A small lobby again greeted me, but the reception desk was dark and empty, with no one on duty to welcome me.

"Hi," I heard a voice say.

I turned to see Manta standing there in a very flattering navy-blue skirt hugging her curves and a sleeveless shiny white shirt tucked into it. The skirt barely reached her knees and her legs looked powerful and sexy in black high heels.

I wondered if she could see me checking her out from behind my glasses.

"Thanks for coming. My office is down here," she said, pointing to a door marked with her name etched onto a nameplate.

I followed her through the door into a plain-looking office. No personal effects at all. She gestured at me to sit in one of the chairs in front of her desk. Instead of sitting behind her desk, she pulled a chair up next to mine and set a file folder on the desk before sitting.

I could smell her perfume and another scent I couldn't quite put my finger on, but both smelled incredible. Finding myself involuntarily leaning in to her, I had to tell myself to concentrate on what I came here for.

She stared at me and said, "No chance I could get you to take off your glasses?"

My brow furrowed. "Why would you want me to do that? Nobody wants to look at this freakshow."

She shook her head with a smile and slowly reached up to my face. I did not stop her. Putting both hands on either side of my head, she slid my glasses off and looked into my eyes.

"Kovah, I've been alive a very long time and I have seen a lot of horrors and a lot of freaks. You are neither horrible nor a freak. I think your eyes are unique and beautiful. The whites are so white, and the irises are such a light shade of blue, they remind me of the sky on a cloudless day. Like one of those days when the sun is so bright, you can barely see the blue of the heavens, so they look powdery and pale, almost white. I haven't seen the sun or the day sky in, like, eighty years. So please let me look at your eyes?"

I was speechless. Eighty years? She thought my eyes were beautiful? I hated them. I didn't know what else to say. "Um, thank you?" I shifted uncomfortably, wanting my glasses back, my metaphoric security blanket. But I didn't reach for them.

Still staring at me, she reached up and put the first two fingers of her right hand into her left eye. She slid out a contact lens to reveal a bright green eye. The other was still a light chocolate brown, and with my intense eyesight, I could tell she wore no contact lens in that one.

"What the...?" I gasped.

She smiled. "I was actually born like this. Becoming a vampire didn't do this. It's a condition called Heterochromia. Of course, it didn't have a name when I was human. I was just called a circus freak, a demon, or anything else bigoted people chose to call me." She looked down.

I put my hand out and tipped up her chin so I could look at her eyes again. "Why do you wear the contact lens?"

She shrugged. "I don't like people staring. So this is easier."

"I can certainly understand that. But your eyes are cool as fuck. You should embrace that shit."

She grinned and pointed at herself, then to me. "Pot, meet kettle."

I chuckled. "Yours are cool, mine are just frightening. I only take off the sunglasses on Halloween, and even then I get comments about my 'cool contacts'. I even made a little kid cry one year when he looked at me. It's just so fucking awesome to scare small children and not even try," I replied sarcastically.

She stood up and went into her desk, put the contact lens into a case filled with saline solution, and then came back to the chair. She picked up the file folder and then opened it up. She cleared her throat. "Let's get back to the issue at hand. The Nighthawks. This is what we have on them so far."

I looked at her for a long minute, loving her dual-colored eyes, her pale cheeks I could tell once had been tanned, and her full, plump lips. *And they are some delicious lips.* I resisted the urge to pull her long, dark hair out of its ponytail prison and let its silky strands caress my hands.

I reluctantly took the folder, opened it up, and began reading aloud.

"At least twenty members in Shreveport. They kill both humans and vampires without known motive. All members appear to be vampires. No humans or other creatures."

I stopped reading. "Creatures?"

She looked confused. "Yeah. Shifters, Immortals, faeries, etc."

"What in the hell are shifters and Immortals? And faeries?" I blew out a breath. "What the hell, woman?"

"You're kidding, right?" She blinked incredulously at me.

I stood up, the file falling to the floor. "No, I'm not kidding. There are other things besides vampires and wolves?"

She smiled as she shook her head. "Sit down. It's going to be a long night."

I reluctantly did as she said. "Shifters are people who look human but they can take the form of any animal they please. Now, usually they stick to one particular animal, like a wolf or dog, but their talents are pretty amazing, being able to shift into anything."

"I'm gonna need some proof on that," I said, not believing a word she said.

She grinned. "I know a couple shifters, for the right price they'll show you anything you want."

I frowned. "Okay…"

"I'm serious."

"Uh, okay, whatever," I said reluctantly. "And aren't Immortals just vampires?"

She shook her head. "No, but that's a long story. They pay for their immortality by protecting the faeries."

"Okay we are going to discuss that weird shit later. For now, let's get back to the Nighthawks."

"I agree. Keep reading."

"Their leader is a vampire with blond hair, light facial scruff, and hazel eyes. Hair is slightly long and he sometimes wears it in a ponytail. We now know they have a clubhouse here in Shreveport after all, and it's located somewhere in the warehouse district. The vampires never let anyone tailing them get close enough to their actual location. Followers are destroyed or compelled to forget before they can reach it."

I looked at Manta. "Who did they compel?"

"Our human agents, and others. We had a confidential informant who was facing a lot of drug charges who we promised immunity to if he followed them. They killed him."

"That's fucked up," I said, shaking my head.

She nodded. "It is. We don't have any male vampires we can send out there to follow them."

I flashed her a megawatt smile and gently grabbed my glasses from her grip. "See, that's why you need me."

She raised an eyebrow. "You're immune to vampire compulsion?"

I scooted in closer to her, still smiling. "Sweetheart, not only am I immune, I can compel vampires *and* humans."

"Now you're just playing with me," she came back, smiling all shy and flirty.

With speed, I reached up and grabbed her jaw with one hand. I stared into her dual-colored eyes, and once I could tell I had a lock on her, I said, "You want to kiss me. You want me to touch you. You want me to fuck you. Don't you, Violet?"

I used her previous name on purpose. Her response made me smile.

"Yes. Touch me, Dominic. Fuck me."

I let go of her face, broke eye contact, then stood up. As I looked down at her, I could see her staring up at me and I waited for the lock to break in her gaze—and it did. Much faster than a human's would have. She shook her head slightly, trying to clear what I was sure was a brain fog.

"Why am I aroused and want you to take me to bed right now?" she asked much more boldly than her usual self.

I chuckled. "You need to know that I don't ever need to charm a woman into bed. They usually throw themselves at me. You just seem like you needed a little push—some convincing of my skills."

"You fucking compelled me!" she shouted, standing up.

"And you just said the F word," I said, chuckling and loving every minute of this conversation.

That, and my jeans had shrunk a couple of sizes as the smell of her arousal and the dreamy, lusty look she got after I'd planted the suggestions in her mind had me going a tad crazy.

I took a deep breath and silently counted backward from ten with my eyes closed. When I opened them, Manta was staring at me with an angry look in her trippy gaze.

"What?" I asked, an innocence in my voice.

She narrowed her eyes. "You know what."

"Sweetheart, you challenged me. Said I couldn't compel vampires. I was just proving that I could. I don't see the problem here."

A long, heavy pause filled the air. "You've proven your point. However, I am still feeling… uh… the aftereffects."

I coolly looked around her office and chuckled. "It's too bad you don't have a couch in here. I could help you with that."

She smiled, a confident smile I hadn't seen since she'd been Violet McKittrick, and got up. I stood stock-still as she came over to me like a panther looking to conquer her prey. "I don't need a couch."

And I didn't need an invitation.

I reached around her head, grabbed her hair at the back of her scalp, and pulled her head to my submission. When her throat was at my command, I licked her cold, delicious skin, worked my way up to her jawline, and then her mouth. Her lips and tongue hungrily mingled with mine. Pressing my hand to the small of her back, I eased her onto the floor of her office and shoved her skirt up. With my pants already straining to stay zipped, I popped the button of my jeans, slid down the zipper, and pushed them down to my ankles. I didn't know what it was about Violet… Manta… but she drove me crazy. Before taking her, I pushed her silky shirt and bra up above her breasts and reveled in their perfection before I used my strong hand to move her legs to the side. I groaned in satisfaction as I pushed myself inside, her body ready and clenching around me. I thrusted in, then pulled out.

"Oh, yes, yes, please," she breathed out.

This made me crazy with desire. My leather jacket came off, but I never broke the groove as the jacket went flying. Reaching up behind my neck, I grabbed my shirt and tossed it off over my head, all while I pumped myself inside of her, then pulled myself out.

The shirt landed on the desktop.

"Oh, my God, more! Please, give me more," she whimpered, her hips reaching up to meet my thrusts.

With my arms planted firmly on either side of her head on the floor of her office, I used my elbow to push her leg even further to the side so I could get deeper inside. I leaned my head down and pressed my mouth to hers without breaking my rhythm. She fisted my hair and kissed me back passionately.

I knew I was going to lose it soon, but I needed to know she'd gotten hers first.

"You love this, don't you?" I whispered into her ear as I continued to pound into her body with reckless abandon.

"Yes," she breathed. "Yes, Dominic, yes. More."

For some reason, the use of my old name made me harden even further. I pressed on, harder and faster. She screamed and panted louder as I did that.

"Please, oh, my God, please," she cried, sounding like she might break out sobbing at any minute.

I wasn't far behind her. I stared down at her body made of perfection, her hips, and her breasts bouncing with each thrust.

When she screamed and dug her fingernails into my back, I could hold out no longer. I stilled, releasing the day's—the week's—the month's tensions into her until she went limp under me and I felt completely boneless.

Chapter 19

NIGHTHAWKS

B
ecause I was a dick, I got dressed right away and left the office with a muttered "call you later," flying down the stairs and into the parking garage to get on my bike.

What was my problem? I'd spent all day in with Janice, and now, here I was, taking advantage of another female. I really should stick with human girls to take care of my needs.

As I flew down the street, I realized how different Janice and Manta were. Aside from their obvious physical attributes, Janice was more playful and assertive—had no problems telling me what she wanted and when. Manta didn't throw herself at me and was a bit on the shy side. Or maybe that was just how she played things. She wasn't shy once I had her on her back. I could still feel the cuts on my back healing from her nails. I felt a small pang of regret leaving her as quickly as I did, but I just couldn't face the aftermath of that. I should have had more respect for her, of course, and I couldn't help but feel that my compulsion—my little immature way of showing off—had caused the sex. I didn't want it like that, I never did. I would need to apologize to her later.

My phone buzzed in my pocket and I didn't even bother to pull it out. I was on a mission, headed to someplace I knew I shouldn't be.

As I headed into the warehouse district, I passed by the Blue Room, which was lit, up but didn't look very busy. I kept going, not sure if I would find this supposed clubhouse where these assholes called the Nighthawks hung out.

There was no way to keep my bike quiet, but I didn't want to be quiet. I hoped hearing a loud-ass Harley would get at least one of them to show his face. Not that I had a solid plan here, I was sort of winging it… going in blind. Yeah, maybe this was a bad idea. I should probably think up a plan first. I wasn't afraid of any vampire, but a whole gang of them, especially if they were old, would be a challenge, to say the least.

I drove down several streets, each one getting darker and deeper into the belly of the commercial district on Shreveport's waterfront. Seemed they all looked alike. I wasn't sure how I was going to find these guys, but I was just too curious to stop looking. Maybe the BSI had bad information. Perhaps they didn't hang out here at all, but rather used this area as some kind of shortcut or thoroughfare to get to wherever they really gathered.

Unfortunately for me, I saw them at the very last second, even with my keen eyesight. I hit the brake and was barely able to stop before my bike flipped over. Two men stood in the middle of the very narrow road between two large warehouses. I couldn't go around them without hitting a building. Looking back, I should have just run them over. They were huge fuckers, though.

With my bike stopped but still rumbling, I stood there, waiting for them to move. They stared at me curiously, and then I felt a tingle crawl up my spine and a weighted feeling blossom in my chest.

Vampires. Biker-looking vampires. Did I just hit the motherfuckin' jackpot?

"You guys gonna move, or what?" I asked as coolly as I could.

With vampire speed, the bald one approached me and pulled me by the collar off my bike. My precious fell to the ground on its side, engine still running.

"Get the hell off me!" I yelled, immediately reaching into the small of my back. I pulled out my new .357 revolver and didn't even think before I pressed the barrel to his head and snapped the trigger back. The vampire let go of me and slumped to the ground. Again, I didn't think twice. I grabbed the knife from my boot and plunged it into his chest. I watched, panting with satisfaction, as he turned to ash.

"You asshole! You just killed Tank!" the other one yelled, coming toward me. His eyes were solid black, the same color as his mullet-styled hair and full, bushy goatee. I hoped the knife would go through his black leather vest when I stabbed him in his cold, undead heart.

I raised the knife as he came at me, but he was quicker than me. Grabbing it by the blade, not caring that it sliced his hand open, he tossed the knife away. I saw my revolver lying on the ground and I dove for it, but he, again, was faster.

"Fuck," I said as he grabbed it and pointed it straight at my head.

"Get your ass up and turn off that bike. Now."

I did as he said, killing the engine and righting the bike.

"Go hide that thing between those buildings now."

Now, *that* I wasn't going to do. I put my hands on my hips and said, "No. I'm leaving now, dude."

"The fuck you are," he said, cocking back the hammer. He looked murderous and I could tell he wasn't bluffing. It was obvious he was pissed I'd killed the other bloodsucker.

Sighing my own defiance, I slid the kickstand up and walked my precious to a dark spot between two alleys, parking her there. I felt like I wouldn't be seeing her again, so I grieved silently before turning around to face the biker.

The vampire shoved my pistol into the small of his back, rushed over to me, and punched me in the jaw. My world spun, closed in, and then went black before I hit the ground.

Groaning at the pain in my head and face, I blinked several times, trying to figure out where the hell I was. Looked like some sort of office. Desk, chair, filing cabinet, bulletin board. I went to stand but realized I couldn't. I also realized my weapons, wallet, phone, and most importantly, my glasses were all missing.

I then remembered the run-in with the vampires. I groaned audibly.

My hands were secured behind my back to the chair I now sat in, and using my thumbs to feel, I surmised that they had used plastic zip-ties to keep me bound to the chair.

There was little light in the room, but I didn't need it. I could see that the office I was in overlooked a large warehouse and that I was alone in the room. The door to the office was closed. Thankful the chair was mobile, I scooted it, propelling it with my feet toward the desk. My goal was to get around the desk. I hoped to somehow get a drawer open with my boot and prayed there would be scissors in there. I wasn't sure how I would get the scissors from the desk to my hands, but I would cross that bridge when I got there.

I wasn't even halfway to the desk when I felt, simultaneously, the door to the office open and a heavy hand land on my shoulder, to keep me from moving.

The light was flipped on and I closed my eyes against the glare.

"I'm glad you're finally awake, freak. We have some questions."

I slowly opened my eyes and looked up at the voice. That was when I heard about half a dozen gasps and a few cuss words come spilling out.

"If you give me back my glasses, we will be able to have a much more civilized conversation," was all I could think to say.

"Fucking-A, boss, give the freak his glasses. I ain't tryin' to look at that shit."

I turned toward the voice and saw a gigantic biker with shaggy brown hair who looked like he should have a Confederate flag draped around him.

"Fuck you, redneck," I said.

He came at me with vampire speed and punched me in the jaw. I was at least grateful he was a southpaw, because the other guy had been right-handed so now both sides of my face hurt.

"You're gonna pay for that," I growled, spitting blood onto the floor.

He chuckled, his massive arms folded across his chest.

"Okay, freak. Whatever you say," he came back.

I ignored the dick and looked around the room. Five vampires. One had to be the leader, but there was no way to pick him out of that crowd, so I just stopped talking and waited.

"What were you doing near our club?" one asked.

I looked up at the voice, a male probably in his late twenties when he was turned. Shaggy blond hair, hazel eyes, and strong jawline covered in stubble.

He matched the description of the leader the BSI had on file. I looked him square in the eye. "I have no idea what you're talking about, man."

"You gonna fuckin' lie to me now?" he asked, looking pissed off.

"Look, I was lost, out looking for the Blue Room. Some friends invited me, and I'm new to town, so…

"Nope. Bullshit. I call bullshit," said the vampire who had accosted me in the street and then knocked me out.

"You," I said. "You're gonna pay for scratching my bike."

He ignored my comment and looked at the leader. "He ain't no kid looking for the club. This guy's a pro. Killed Tank within ten seconds of being pulled off his bike."

The blond tatted guy raised an eyebrow and looked at me. "Is that so?"

I shrugged a shoulder. "I was just defending myself and my baby."

He went to the desk and pulled open the drawer, withdrawing my revolver, knife, wallet, keys, and phone. He picked up the huge buck knife. "Really? You always carry a knife and a gun on you?"

I nodded. "Hell yeah. It's a dangerous world out there."

"Why do your eyes look like that?" he asked.

"Contacts."

He narrowed his eyes at me. "Halloween isn't for another couple of months."

"Is that your favorite day of the year, leech?"

He kicked me in the knee with his steel-toed boot and I grunted in pain, dipping my head into my chest to keep from screaming.

When I could breathe again, I growled through gritted teeth, "Motherfucker, do not do that again."

One of the vampires spoke up, pointing at me, but looking at their leader, an amused look on his face. "Who is this guy?"

Vampire leader plucked my wallet from the desk and read my driver's license slowly, sounding out my name. "Kovah Sanagra. Twenty-one. Just a pup."

"What in the fuck kind of name is that?" drawled the redneck guy who'd punched me.

I grinned darkly. "It's Italian, you mullet hillbilly asshole."

He was about to punch me again but the vampire leader blocked him with his arm. "No more, Shiv."

I raised an eyebrow. "Shiv? That your *gangster* name? Seriously? Did you make shivs out of toothbrushes in prison and sell them? Was that your job? Did they pay you in cigarettes?"

I got way too much satisfaction at the anger in his gaze. So much that I chuckled in his face.

"Boss, *please* let me take off his head. Please?" he whined, looking at the leader.

"See, now you're begging, and you kinda sound like a chick, man." I said, throwing him a fake sympathetic glance. "Were you someone's bitch in prison, too? 'Oh, Tiny, please don't ass-rape me again. I'll do anything!'" I smarted off in a high-pitched voice.

"Shut the fuck up!" the leader roared, slamming his fist on the desk and measuring me with a warning glare.

This guy… he was more intimidating and commanded more respect than ol' Shiv. He appeared young, but the look in his eyes appeared old and wise. He had a calm air about him, but I could tell he could snap off in the blink of an eye.

"And what is your name, *boss*?" I asked, putting a smart-ass inflection on the word boss.

He licked his lips, hesitating for a very long, uncomfortable pause before he replied, "Just call me Viper."

I nodded. "That'll work. Nice to meet you, Viper. I like that name. But did you know that birds eat snakes? Snatch them up right off the ground in their powerful talons?"

He narrowed his eyes at me. "So fucking what?"

I lifted a shoulder and let it fall. "Just kind of ironic, since you quite obviously run the Nighthawks."

Chapter 20

THEORY OF A DEAD MAN

A silence fell over the room at my facetious comment.

Viper ignored it. "Are you going to tell us why you were sleazing around our hideout, or what?"

"Are you going to take these cuffs off, or what? My arms hurt, and the longer I spend in pain, the crazier I get."

Viper reached up and backhanded me across the face. "Answer the goddamn question or I'll start cutting off body parts. Starting with your dick." He held my knife in his right hand, gripping the hilt tightly.

My face stung like a bitch, but didn't want to lose my cock, so I said, "Okay. I was just trying to find the Nighthawks. Hoping to pledge and all that."

He sat on the desk and folded his arms across his chest, but kept the knife in his right hand. "I don't believe you. How do you even know who we are?"

I smiled. "I'm kind of a groupie. You won't let me pledge?"

"We only take vampires, dumbass," Shiv said.

I ignored the imbecile and looked at Viper. Finally, he said, "He's right. We only take vamps. And while I don't think you're entirely human, I know you're not a vampire."

I turned my head slightly. "And how do you know that?"

He shook his head and let out a small laugh. "Because vampires don't call other vampires 'leeches.' Like, ever."

I laughed. "Okay you got me there. I'm a hybrid. I don't age and I can go out in the sun. I just don't drink blood, okay?"

Viper picked up my wallet and looked at my driver's license, then back to me. Tossing the wallet back on the desk, he said, "Says here you're twenty-one. So how old are you really?"

"Just add twenty years to the date on that license."

"So you're still a baby, really," he shot back. He seemed to think for a second, and said, "Forty-one years old is nothing."

"Well, how old are you, big man?" I asked, trying to stay on his good side so I could get set free and kill him for that slap to my face and my still-throbbing kneecap.

He shook his head and pushed off from the desk. Completely ignoring the question, he said, "Why do your eyes look like that?"

"Have you ever met a succubus?" I asked.

He nodded slightly. "Yeah."

"I have, too. When I was just a little human. After she fucked me and then took my soul, I killed her ass. I woke up the next day like this."

The room was so dead silent, you could hear a pin drop. Then, after a long, uncomfortable silence, they all broke into laughter.

"Yeah... nice story, kid. Not buying it, though," Viper said.

I shook my head. "Ya know, you can believe me or not, but that's the truth."

"And why do you want to join us?" he asked, suspicious.

Because when I find out who's threatening Manta, I plan on killing him and then the rest of you, was something I wasn't able to say.

"You kill rogue vamps and humans, right?"

His face darkened. "We don't kill humans."

"Unless they're scumbags," Shiv interjected.

I didn't want to admit that what Shiv had said made me happy, so I kept a straight face and said to Viper, "That's not what I heard. There are a string of bodies all over the city with your calling card all over them."

He tilted his head to the side. "You kinda sound like a cop, dude. You one of those immortal cops? Or work for that secret government agency of cops?"

I chuckled. "I'm not a cop. You think they would hire a freak?" I went to point to my eyes but of course, I couldn't. "Untie me please?"

"Now who's begging?" Shiv said, chuckling.

"Just keep laughing, prison bitch," I bit out, looking at him in his beady brown eyes.

He flipped me off.

"We don't have a 'calling card,'" Viper snapped, anger coloring his tone.

I had no response for that, so I just glared at them.

"How do you even know who we are?" one of them asked, repeating Viper's question.

I looked over at him. He looked maybe thirties, blondish hair and chin goatee, but thick muscles strained beneath his shirt. I peered into his eyes as I lied. "My roommate has a fascination with musclebound gym-rats. She took one home one night. I went to leave for work and his cut was on the sofa." I dipped my head at Viper's leather vest. "I thought it was interesting that she was banging a biker so I did a little asking around and found out who you guys were. Being what I am, and the fact that I don't have many friends or, really, much to do, I thought I'd see if you wanted another pledge."

"You're a liar," Shiv said.

"Fuck you, Mister Orange is the New Ugly."

Viper ignored both comments. "What did this guy look like?"

"Hell if I know. I know he was a vampire, but I never saw the dude."

His eyebrow rose. "If you didn't see him, how did you know he was a vamp?"

Shit. I wasn't sure I should tell him my little trick. I had already told him I was a hybrid, so I guessed I didn't have much to lose. "I can sense when they're near."

"Sense?" he asked.

I nodded. "Yes. Now please untie me. You have all my weapons, and while I'm a serious badass, I certainly can't take on six vamps by myself, unarmed."

He measured me with a long stare from his hazel eyes, and with the knife still in his hand, he went around to the back of my chair and cut the zip ties off.

"Thanks, man," I said, rolling my shoulders and rubbing my wrists. I sat still in the chair so they didn't think I was going to try something or be a threat. I was enjoying this conversation, actually.

"So can you sense when shifters are nearby, too?"

Shifters… shit. I had just learned there were 'shape-shifters' a few hours ago. "I don't think so. Never met one."

"How the hell you been a hybrid over twenty years and never met a shifter?"

"Not sure," I replied. And that was the first truthful thing I'd said all night.

I slowly reached for my pocket. "You guys mind if I smoke?"

"Yes," Viper replied. "No cigarettes or alcohol allowed here."

"*Don't drink, don't smoke. What do you do...*" I began to sing the old 80s tune, but trailed off when no one laughed.

"Wow a bunch of party animals, aren't you? Maybe I don't want to pledge." I slowly stood. "Well, I can see you guys don't want a hybrid in your group, so I'll just be going."

"Oh, no, you won't," Viper said, standing in front of me, his tattooed arms folded across his massive hard chest.

Now that I was standing, I could see we were both the same height and build.

My face lit up with mock enthusiasm as I said, "So you'll let me join?"

"No."

I slowly walked toward the desk, grabbed my sunglasses with supernatural speed, and put them on my face. If I could get to the gun, I might be able to get out of here, and only have to go buy another knife for my troubles. Really didn't want to leave without my keys, phone, and wallet, though.

"Not so fast, freak," Shiv said, moving to stand between me and the desk. All the other vamps were now on high alert.

I felt nervous and sick... were these guys going to let me leave? My knee hurt from where Viper had kicked me. My jaw ached from where Shiv had punched me. Yet... I didn't care. I wanted to leave. What had I been thinking coming here?

"You said you worked at night?" Viper asked.

Confused, I asked, "What? When?"

"You said you were leaving for work and a Nighthawks vest was at your place."

I nodded. "Yeah, I, uh, am a bartender," I said.

I have got to stop fucking lying.

There was more silence, and then Viper pushed me back and forced me to sit in the chair once more.

He looked down at me with narrowed eyes. "You're gonna sit there 'til I figure out what I'm doing with you."

I felt rage bubble up inside of me at the thought of a vampire telling me what to do. However, if I was going to gain their trust, I knew I needed to shut up. My jaw ticked with annoyance, but I said nothing, just gave a short, curt nod.

"I think we should give the kid a chance," chimed in a familiar voice.

I turned to see it was the big biker who had spoken up. His dark beard and straining muscles commanded attention.

I heard Shiv snort.

Viper fold his arms across his chest. "Give me one good reason, Shadow."

Shadow grinned. "Sunlight."

They whispered amongst themselves, not thinking I could hear, with me acting disinterested.

Without warning, they kicked me out of their clubhouse.

I walked out of there biting back a smile. I would be in disbelief that I actually got to leave if they hadn't compelled me — or at least they tried. As soon as Viper had grabbed me by the shoulders and locked eyes on me, I knew what he was doing, and I had to try my damnedest not to compel him right back. I cleared my mind, let my face go slack, and just repeated what he had told me: "You know nothing about the Nighthawks. You got lost here looking for the Blue Room. Get on your bike and go back home."

I nodded absently as they handed me my personal items, and then I walked woodenly toward the door. I heard Viper tell Shadow in hushed tones that they were going to find me later once they decided my role for the club, if any, since they had my address.

As soon as I was sure they couldn't see me, I sprinted with supernatural speed to where I had hidden my bike, wincing at the pain in my knee. I hissed out a growl when I saw all the scratches on the side of my precious. That bastard was going to pay for that one.

Once I reached town, I couldn't decide who to see first; Manta, or the Rebel Riders. Despite how I'd left things, I decided I needed to man-up and apologize to her, so Manta's it was. I knew she was going to be angry at me for going to the Nighthawks' place, but I was willing to take the punishment.

I once again told the security guard at the BSI building that I was here to see Agent LaRae, and he didn't seem to care, so I used the stairwell again to reach the third floor.

I hated that the damn heavy feeling in my chest and the tingle in my spine would never stop when I was near her. It made me nervous.

"I really can't say this is a surprise," Manta said without looking up from the laptop she was typing away on.

"I'm sorry," I blurted. "I shouldn't have left like that."

Her beautiful brown eyes finally lifted to mine. "No, you shouldn't have."

"You put your contact lens back in."

She simply nodded. "What do you want, Kovah?"

I went around the desk and put my hands on her shoulders, inhaling her strange but arousing scent. My fingers kneaded her shoulders, and she groaned out a little but said nothing.

"What do I want? I wanted to come here and apologize for sexing and running. It really was pretty rude."

I heard her snort, but it sounded like a suppressed laugh. I gently turned her around in her chair and looked down at her. She really did seem as though she was trying not to smile.

"Sexing and running, really? You act like I've never had a *wham, bam, thank-you, ma'am* before."

I lifted an eyebrow. "That was T.M.I."

"Oh, grow up, Dominic," she said, trying to swivel back around to her computer.

I locked my hand on the chair to prevent the turn and glanced at her computer screen. She had some kind of spreadsheet-looking thing titled *Nighthawks* on there. I decided to let go of her chair and she didn't move, so I swiveled the chair for her.

Studying the document, I crouched down, my face just inches from her neck. I reached around her, my arm touching hers, and pointed to the screen.

One of the columns read: *Chapter Members: At least 100*

"That's not true," I said.

She craned her head around and asked, "How —"

I cut her off and pointed to another marked: *Leader: Shadow aka Craig LNU.* "Neither is that," I commented.

"Okay, you're freaking me out," she said, fully turning around now.

"Viper is the leader, not Shadow. He might be second-in-command, but not the leader."

Without even asking, she quickly changed Shadow to Viper and then said, "What's Viper's real name?"

I shrugged and stood up, mildly impressed that the rest of the information was accurate. "Fuck if I know." Then I looked at "Location" and said, "Their clubhouse address is 666 Montgomery Street, Shreveport."

She turned around, her eyes wide as she looked up at me. "Kovah, what have you done?"

I leaned down, chuckling, and said, "It cost me a cracked kneecap, a sore jaw, and a new paint job for my bike, but you've got yourself an insider to the Nighthawks."

As she gasped, I cradled her face in my hands and crushed my lips to hers, kissing her hard and passionately until I heard her sigh. With lightning-fast speed, she went and shut the door, and then tore my clothes off quicker than I could remove hers. Turning her around, I gently pushed her head onto the desktop. I took her with both hands gripping her hips as I pounded hard into her, her moans and affirmations my cue to keep it up.

Suddenly my knee and jaw didn't hurt any longer.

After getting dressed, I fell asleep on the chair in her office as she continued to work, and when I woke the next morning, the sun was there but she wasn't.

Chapter 21

BIG TROUBLE IN LITTLE SHREVEPORT

I swallowed hard as Archie's eyebrows hit his hairline. "Vampire bikers. What the fuck, Kovah?"

Scrambling for something logical, I said, "I know, boss. It's crazy. But I met them firsthand. They've been around for… a while."

He spat some chew into a Styrofoam cup. "That's not an answer. How did you find out about them?"

I mulled over telling him the truth, or just part of it. I, of course, opted for the latter. "Friend at the BSI told me about them." *And they're threatening her,* but I wasn't ready to divulge that.

Archie sat at his desk and put on his readers as he looked down at the invoices he had been working on. "We surely would have heard about them if there really is such a thing."

I shook my head and zipped up my coveralls, ready for work. "No, they are very… what's the word? Elusive. They like to remain a secret and they love compelling people."

He looked up at me, his gray eyes meeting mine over the rim of his glasses. "I think it's time you start from the beginning, kid. I'm getting the feelin' you've met these bloodsuckers."

"I have. I was spying on them and they captured me. They keep a clubhouse, hideout, lair… whatever, on Montgomery Street."

"Nothing but warehouses down there," he commented.

I nodded. "Yep, they don't even have a fence or anything. When they got me, I lied about wanting to pledge."

"Fuckin-A, Kovah. You crazy?" He shook his head.

"Yeah, I guess." I went on to tell him the rest of how it had gone, and then decided I should just come clean.

"So the leader thought he was compelling you to forget them, but then you heard them say they might have a use for you?"

"Yep. But there is another thing."

He pulled his readers off and set them on the desk, spitting again into his cup. "What's that?"

"They're threatening my friend at the BSI. Said she's a traitor to her own kind and all that."

He stared at me hard for a minute, then said, "Your friend at the BSI is a vamp?"

I nodded slowly. "Yes, but I swear, Arch, she's the most normal one I think I've ever met. Also, I knew her when I was human, back in New York. I ran into her at that vampire ball in New Orleans a couple weeks ago. She turned out to be Manta LaRae."

His bushy gray eyebrows hit his hairline and he whistled through his teeth. "Geez, kid. What other shit you been keeping from me?" he asked.

"That's pretty much it." I wasn't about to tell him we were much more than just friends.

"What is the point of this vampire gang? They kill humans?"

I sat in the chair across from him. "They claim they don't, but the BSI says they've left bodies strewn all over the city."

His brow furrowed. "That doesn't make any sense."

"I know." After a short pause, I said, "Hey, boss, have you ever heard of shape-shifters?"

He sighed. "I've heard whispers of them. Never met one, that I know of."

"The gang asked if I could sense them the same way I could sense vampires."

He lifted an eyebrow. "You told them you could sense vampers?"

"Yep, sure did. I'm surprised he thought I could be compelled after telling him that, but I just rolled with it. No way was I going to tell him I could compel vampires myself."

"Smart move," he came back.

"So, what should we do about these Nighthawks?" I asked.

"That's their name?" He chuckled. "Cute. And to answer your question, nothing right now. I'd like to watch them, though."

I got up, mocking disappointment. "You suck. I thought you were going to say, 'Let's burn their clubhouse to the ground and scatter their vampire ashes!' and I was going to be all, 'Fuck yeah, let's do it while the leeches sleep!' but I see how you are." Then I made a scoffing noise.

He replaced his glasses and shook his head with a chuckle. "You have too much damn energy. Now go out and help Nolan with that damn Ducati. Boy's been working on it for like three days."

I chuckled. "You got it."

I was heading back from picking up some tacos when my cell buzzed in my pocket.

Janice: *Hey sexy… can I feed your beast tonight?*

I grinned… sounded tempting, but I honestly would rather see Manta. I wasn't sure exactly why she appealed to me more than Janice did. Janice was knockout gorgeous in a superficial type of way. Big tits, full red lips, thick hips and ass… but she was so straightforward about sex. It wasn't all bad, it was just a bit much. Manta was sexy because she didn't throw herself at me. Maybe I just liked the chase.

Me: *Sorry, sweet-cheeks. Gotta work. xo*

I'm such an asshole…

I shoved the bag of tacos into a small compartment on my bike and headed to the BSI building, hoping Manta would be there.

I parked my bike and went into the building, but the security guard stopped me before I blew past him. "Agent LaRae ain't up there," he drawled in a voice much too deep.

"Oh, yeah? Didn't come in tonight?" I asked, the bag of tacos in my hand.

He shrugged a massive shoulder and looked back down, flipping a page on his *Muscle & Fitness*. "Guess not. Haven't seen her all night."

"Thanks, Gus," I said, going back to my bike.

I pulled out my phone and texted her: *Night off?*

She replied quickly: *Yes*

Me: *May I see you? I have tacos.*

Manta: *I don't eat tacos.*

Me: *I can pick you up a burrito, if you prefer.*

Manta: *I'm busy, Kovah.*

I frowned. What did that mean?

Me: *Give me your address. I can bring you a rare steak instead.*

She didn't reply, so I started my bike and headed back to my place to eat my tacos in peace and watch some TV. I knew vampires didn't eat food, but I just wanted to get a response out of her.

Once I was about to put the key into the lock to my apartment above Archie's Garage, my phone vibrated again.

Manta: *1802 Graystone Drive.*

My eyebrows hit my hairline. I quickly inhaled two tacos and threw the bag into a trash can on my way to my bike, and then headed toward Graystone Drive.

I was surprised at how simple the neighborhood was. I parked in front of a moderate-looking older home with lights burning inside. It was just after seven p.m. and the sun had gone down about an hour earlier. I felt fall approaching, the humid night air slowly turning to a cool breeze as the night wore on.

I rang the doorbell and it wasn't long until she answered it in a pair of very short shorts and a ribbed tank top with no bra. *Definitely no bra.*

I was glad I had eaten the tacos because I would have dropped the bag. I swallowed hard. "Um, hi."

She smiled demurely and opened the screen door, letting me in.

"Where are your tacos? I was looking forward to smelling them," she said as she instructed me to sit on her sofa, and she headed into the kitchen.

"I ate them, duh. Tacos are only good hot. Right?"

She cleared her throat and pulled out a navy-blue pitcher from the fridge with something dark sloshing around inside. "If memory serves."

Unabashedly, she poured a thick, red liquid into a clear glass tumbler, and then replaced the pitcher into the fridge. She then put the tumbler in the microwave and turned around to look at me from the kitchen with her arms folded across her chest as it heated.

"Are you seriously going to stand there and fucking drink blood with me here?" I asked her, incredulous.

She smirked as the microwave beeped. She pulled out the glass and I watched as she slipped a tongue into the glass to test the temperature, and then smiled. Satisfied, she tossed back the glass as if it were a cheap whiskey and she was eager to get a buzz.

I made a face as she licked her lips and put the glass in the sink.

After grabbing a beer from the fridge for me, she made her way toward me, her nipples straining through her tank top. Did drinking blood turn her on?

She plunked herself down on the sofa next to me, handed me the beer, and crossed her legs. "Does me drinking blood scare you?"

I lifted my chin. "No. I don't spook easily, sweetheart. Whose blood was that?"

She grinned. "Bessie's."

I frowned. "Who in the hell is Bessie? Some hooker you killed?"

"No," she said, tilting her head back and laughing, "Bessie the cow."

My nose wrinkled. "You drink cow's blood? That's gross, girl."

"You drink cow's milk. What's difference?"

"Uh, because… blood."

"Should I drink human blood instead?" she asked, seeming curious.

Trick question, Kovah, don't answer, my subconscious screamed at me.

"Can you live on cow's blood?" I asked, deflecting the question.

"Can you live on veggie tacos?" she quipped.

A taco with no meat, what kind of shit is that? "Yes, but ick."

"Well, I don't want to steal from blood banks, nor do I want to steal from humans. I didn't ask for this." She gestured to her body. "I just wanted to live, fall in love, have a good life, and die. Instead, I was dealt another hand. A hand in which I need to deal with until I can figure out what else I can do."

My heart of cold stone and ice thawed just a tad. I also became curious. I scooted closer to her so our bodies were touching. With my warm hand on her leg, I slid it up and down over the smooth skin and put my other arm around her shoulders, looking into her dual-colored eyes.

"I want to hear how you became a vampire," I said in a whisper.

Her eyes flicked down to my lips, then back to my eyes. She reached up and took off my glasses and I gave up no fight. She set them on the coffee table and then placed a delicate hand on my cheek.

"Why do you want to know that?" she asked.

I stared into her eyes. They were so beautiful in their own way. A contrast. A cool green next to a warm brown. I could only think that her eyes were a reflection of her personality. She'd been a vampire a long time, and I had no doubt she had a dark, cold side, but so far, I'd only really seen her easy, warm side.

"Because I want to know everything about you," I blurted, completely under her spell now. She wasn't compelling me, I knew that much, but I was still captivated by her nonetheless.

She pressed a soft kiss to my lips, and then pulled back, dropping her hand from my face to grab my hand. With her eyes flicking back and forth between mine, she took a big breath I knew she didn't need, and started.

"The Great Depression was behind us, but I was still born to poor Italian immigrants in New York City. I was the only girl of four children.

"Despite our moderate poverty, I grew up happy and well-adjusted. My parents were good, hard-working people who made sure we had what we needed. Once we'd all grown and left home, I felt as though the world were my oyster. I could do anything I wanted. Back then, girls going to college wasn't very popular, but it was still doable. My problem was how I was going to pay for it. No low-income grants. No student loans. In the 1950s, either you had the money or you didn't go.

"I was waiting tables at a local diner when one night, a very distinguished-looking man came in and sat in my section. With my practiced pearly-white smile, I asked him what I could get him. He ordered black coffee, and honestly, he sat there for two hours reading the newspaper and drinking just the coffee."

"I don't think that was too uncommon back then," I chimed in.

She shook her head with a shy smile. "You're right, it wasn't. But as he went to leave, he left me a ten-dollar tip. He had pressed it into my palm and told me I was beautiful and that I could do better than a downtown diner. I'm sure you can imagine what a huge tip that was back then. I had already assessed that the guy had money by his pressed suit and his shiny cufflinks. But the tip definitely confirmed that.

"I thanked him for the tip, and he told me that I had a job waiting at his company if I wanted it, and then he handed me a piece of paper with an address written on it. I stood there with my mouth open for a good few minutes after he left."

"Was he some kind of pimp?" I asked, hanging on every word of her story.

Manta shook her head a little, still staring into my eyes. "No, his name was Morty, and he owned a gentleman's club."

My eyes went big. "Please tell me you weren't a hooker back then. Please."

She smiled and looked down at our hands still linked together. "No, not quite. After his visit, I was, of course, intrigued and I went to see him at the address he'd provided. It was a huge house, and aside from another guy — who I later realized was his assistant, Bruce, it seemed they were the only occupants of this house. They invited me in and offered me a drink.

"I took the drink because I didn't want to be rude, but I really did not care for alcohol back then. It made me feel funny and I knew I wasn't in control when I drank it. Still, I sipped it as he talked.

"With both of them sitting on the sofa opposite of me in his massive house, he immediately offered me a job as a stripper in his club. I glanced at his creepy assistant, Bruce, his beady brown gaze boring into mine. He was a short guy with slicked-back hair and he certainly had no problem staring at someone in an inappropriate manner."

I lifted an eyebrow. "Really?"

She nodded. "Yes. He was super creepy. I'll never forget the way he stared at me. Not just that night, but every time I came in contact with Morty. Must have been his personal assistant or maybe his security or something."

"Fucking vampires," I murmured.

She pierced me with a questionable glance, then shook her head. "Anyway, I so badly wanted to say no to Morty's offer. I wanted to walk away and make my own money a decent way. But when he told me I could make over fifty dollars a night, I almost choked. I could pay for a year's worth of college on a month's salary and tips. How could I turn that down?"

I couldn't believe what I was hearing. She *so* didn't seem like the stripper type, but I was too enraptured in her story to let her stop. "Go on, sweetheart."

She laughed. "I danced for a while. I got quite good at working a pole. That was—until Morty suggested I do more than stripping and go on a few 'innocent' dates with some of his clients. This made me sick and I told him to go to hell. I was no prostitute and would never stoop that low.

"He was livid, Kovah. He grabbed me by my hair and wrenched my head back. I screamed and told him to let go of me. I beat him with my fists, and kicked and screamed at him to leave me alone. When he dipped his head toward my neck and licked it, I felt sick. I felt a slight sting of pain as his teeth pierced my skin. He drank from me while I screamed and cried in anguish. But nobody came for me. No one helped."

Manta looked sad, almost defeated and traumatized. That made me angrier than I already was.

"Keep talking before I blow a gasket," I growled, gripping her hand tighter than I should have.

"He threw me to the ground of the dressing room of the strip club and he and his creepy ass friend Bruce strolled out of there with smug grins on their ugly faces. I was devastated, Kovah. So angry."

"I bet," I said, my jaw ticking in rage. "Did he violate you in any other way than feeding?"

She shook her head. "No, thank God."

"Where is this Morty motherfucker now? I need to kill something." That wasn't a lie.

"Pretty sure he's dead," she replied with a mischievous smile.

This piqued my interested. "Pretty sure?"

She nodded and covered her hand over mine, which was still on her bare thigh. With a grin twitching on her lips, she said, "Three days later when I woke, he looked pretty ashy to me."

UNDERCOVER VAMPIRE

Measuring her with a hard but amused stare, I said, "I have a question."

"Shoot," she said. "Just not with one of the many guns I'm sure you carry."

I laughed. "Nah, my crossbow pistol doesn't fit in my boot. No worries, sweetheart."

"So what's your question?" she asked, flicking some hair over her shoulder.

"Why three days? I mean, is it symbolic or something? I've heard vampires take three days to turn. But I don't get it."

She nodded. "It's three days of death. Some say it's after the symbolism of the Bible. Jesus spent three days in the tomb before he was resurrected and all that."

I just nodded. Not sure if I believed it, but it was interesting nonetheless.

"After Morty bit me, he'd left me cold and alone on the floor of that dressing room. I found out later he and Bruce had been turning several of the dancers so they would remain young and able to be up all night, so it wasn't a huge surprise to learn the girl who'd fed me some of her blood had not only saved me, but essentially killed me. I was angry at her for a very long time."

"Angry... for saving you?" I asked, confused.

She chuckled. "Don't you know? A vampire has to both take and give blood for the turning to be complete. Morty took my blood. Rosie then gave me hers. She thought I was dying, that by giving me her blood, it would heal me. Instead, it turned me."

I lifted a brow. How come I didn't know this shit? Because I never got close enough to a vampire to get his or her story, that was why. Not only had I gotten close enough to Violet — Manta, she had lived this jacked-up shit.

"Rosie panicked when I didn't wake up. She took me back to her little apartment and put me on her sofa. She told me later that she had freaked that I hadn't woken up, yet hadn't died in those three days. It wasn't until early on the third day that she had realized that I was a vampire in transition.

"Late on the third day, I bolted upright on her couch and screamed at the pain in my chest, mouth, and throat. I was ravenous, confused, and panicked. Rosie was about to leave for work at the club when she heard my screams. She took care of me. She had blood bags in her fridge and fed me. She loaned me clothes so I could change and let me use her shower. She then spent an hour explaining to me what a vampire was and what had happened. It was a hard pill to swallow, and even then, I wasn't sure I believed."

I was completely and utterly enraptured in her story now. I couldn't believe I'd lived over forty years on this planet — half of that knowing about the supernatural — and had never bothered to learn about the vampire turning process. This was important shit.

"After Rosie got home from work at four a.m., I was on her sofa reading some magazine that I really wasn't paying attention to. I was too distracted. She came through the door, weary and tired, but I begged her to help me."

"What did you want help with?" I asked, barely breathing.

She smirked. "I looked into Rosie's beautiful pale face, with her big, blue eyes and rosy cheeks I was sure was a product of makeup and no way natural." She chuckled but there was no humor there. "I said, 'Rosie, did Morty turn you?' and she said, 'Yeah, he did.' Then I asked, 'Did you want to become a damn blood-sucking night demon?' And with her brow furrowed, she replied, 'No, I didn't. What's wrong?' she asked. Well, everything was wrong. Instead, I said, 'You and I are going to kill Morty and he will pay for what he did to us.' She smiled but looked scared. 'Okay. How are we going to kill him?' she asked. I grinned while replying, 'Why, with the promise of sex, of course.' She made a face. 'But I don't want to have sex with Morty. He's creepy.' I laughed. 'Yes, he is,' I said with a little bit of crazy."

She stopped her story, and aside from being very aroused at it for some odd reason, I pushed that aside and told her to continue.

"Okay, Kovah, I will," she replied. "A couple of weeks later, we called

Morty and told him we wanted to quit stripping. We even got a few girls in on it with us, as they had been his victims, too, in more ways than one. We told him that if he didn't come down there and pay us our final paychecks, that we would kill all the humans in attendance at his sick vampire strip club and then call the police.

"That was all it took. He was in our dressing room within minutes, trying to persuade us to stay there, to work for him. As disgusted as I was, even after Rosie had explained everything, I still wanted him dead. I hated Morty for what he had done to me and so many others. My belief in the supernatural had been nonexistent until that time, and then my entire world was turned on its head.

"He had us all gather into a group and then had the nerve to try to compel us. It was comical. How he didn't know that vampires can't compel other vampires is beyond me." She shook her head.

"It could be that he thought he could control you girls because he sired you. Is that a thing?" I asked, mentally banking every word she was telling me. I couldn't wait to get back and tell Archie. We sometimes captured vampires and tortured them for information, like how much blood they need to drink, what kind of food they could tolerate, how we could kill them, and all that, but I doubt he'd heard any of this.

"No, we can't compel the vampires we make any more than we can any other vampire. Total myth," she said.

Good stuff, really good stuff, I thought, trying not to smile. "Go on."

"At the end, he really was no match for all of us. We took him down easily enough. It seems comical almost when I look back on it. Half a dozen half-naked women, well, vampires, descending on this guy. We got him to the ground and I jammed an arrow into his ugly heart. He was nothing but ashes within seconds."

I lifted an eyebrow. "Arrow?"

She chuckled and lifted her finger to indicate a framed shadowbox on the wall. Inside was a mounted arrow — like, a real arrow that Robin Hood would have used. "You used that?"

She nodded. "My dad taught me archery. I had a quiver and some arrows at home, and it was the sharpest thing I think I owned back then. No money for a fancy knife set, and no time to whittle a stake." She smirked.

"Resourceful girl. I like it."

She slid some hair behind her ear. "We obviously did not think it through very carefully, though, as we were all pretty much jobless within a month."

"Yeah, but you didn't need to be stripping anyway." I didn't know why I just said that. It was like fifty years ago. *Shut up, Kovah...*

"True, and most of them went on to do the same thing somewhere else. Or they became high-priced escorts. His creepy sidekick Bruce had no problem with taking right over after Morty was gone. At first, we were scared when Bruce came around, thought he'd try to punish us for killing Morty, but he almost seemed grateful."

She shuddered and then continued. "It made me sad that the girls resorted to turning tricks. I would have rather gone back to waiting tables than cheapen myself that way. But for me, I really wanted to go to college. The incident with Morty confirmed that I really did not want or need a man to take care of me. I had looked out for myself for a few years, and that wasn't going to change — especially now that I knew I was going to be alone very soon."

She went on to tell me about how lonely that life became when she realized how the people around her were aging and moving forward and she wasn't. How she had to field questions about why she only visited those she loved at night and couldn't make it to church on Easter and Christmas. How realizing that she'd never go to college because in the 50s and 60s there were no such thing at "night classes." Then she went on to describe the heartbreak of leaving her family twenty years later, tired of dodging questions and looks from people.

"By then it was the 70s. I had no education, but a lot of experience in being a cocktail waitress. It was the only job I could get where I could work at night and get the bills paid without having to take off my clothes. I had no problem getting a job doing this in Rochester, but I knew making a fresh start meant I needed to do something else; something more stimulating. So, like most vampires, I honed the art of compulsion. I compelled someone to make me a fake birth certificate with a new name and then I compelled the lady at the DMV when she questioned the authenticity of it."

I chuckled. "Been there. So you became Violet McKittrick, right? Went from Italian to Irish?"

She nodded with a smile. "I was already so pale from not seeing the sun, nobody questioned it. I really wanted to become a police officer, I figured I could convince them to let me work the night shift, but the interviewing and training would be a problem. I made sure to apply in the summer with all the clouds and rain."

I looked at her incredulously. "You were going to go out during the day and risk it?"

"Yeah, I was, and I did. The day of my interview, it was cloudy and rainy. I wore a hooded long coat over my new pantsuit and brought a huge black umbrella. Thankfully, the sun stayed behind the clouds. I was nervous as hell though," she said.

"Does that really work, though?" I asked, still curious.

"What?" she asked.

"An umbrella. Can a vampire just stroll around in the sunlight with an umbrella to protect him?"

She laughed. "I guess, but talk about drawing attention to yourself. You'd look kinda foolish with a huge umbrella up during the day if the sun is out. Plus, you always risk light hitting you from different angles. Even sunlight reflecting off glass or mirrored surfaces can harm us. Trust me, I know."

"So it just sort of stings or singes you. You don't burst into flames or anything?" I asked, loving that she was answering all my questions. And I didn't even have to tie her up and torture it out of her.

She shook her head. "No. I mean, we will burst into flames if we stand in the direct sun. Some of us eventually go crazy, you know, from living too long and choose to end it that way. But it takes a few minutes of barbequing to do that."

I saw her shudder and I was right there with her. "That sounds like a painful way to go."

She shrugged. "Yeah, but some just want to see the sun one last time."

"I guess that's understandable," I agreed.

"So anyway, I got the job with Rochester PD. It was a great ten years. It had its ups and downs, and sadly I had to do more compelling than I wanted to stay on the graveyard shift, but it was worth it. I saved fifteen lives. Took three bullets for humans. It was totally worth it."

My eyes went wide. "You did? Wow."

"Yeah, they would always want to keep me in the hospital, but I refused treatment. That didn't make them happy, but I told them I had my own private doctor I wanted to see. I stayed at home for a week, came back good as new. Got a few looks, but nobody ever questioned it. They just began to call me the Bionic Woman." She smiled.

"I remember that show."

She laughed. "Yes, it was very popular at that time. So I just rolled with it. Well, anyway, I met the BSI Agent Rick Lewis during the last shooting. He showed up on the scene."

"I remember him," I said. "He's the first BSI agent I ever met."

"That's right." She shook her head. "He was such a hardass. I have to admit, though, it was kind of fun to watch Dominic squirm."

I snorted. "I bet you did enjoy that. I won't hold it against you, though." I winked at her.

"That's because you get it. Being thrust into this world is never easy, and there's no gentle way to ease somebody in it. You either sink or swim. You came out swimming for sure."

"Yeah, after I almost drowned and you saved me. I never got to thank you," I said as sincerely as I could.

She nodded. "I saw something in you. I knew it wasn't your time."

Uncomfortable talking about that moment of weakness, I asked, "So what was Rick doing at the crime scene?"

She rubbed her thumb over my hand and then said, "It was a supernatural case. I knew it right away, and it definitely wasn't my first. I usually just covered up strange murders or crimes and explained them by making up crap that I thought could have happened. A lot went unsolved and I used to wish there were supernatural cops like the ones on the *X-Files*. Until one day, my wish came true. Rick pulled me off to the side and told me he knew what I was, and that the BSI would be taking over the case of this particular brutal murder. I don't quite remember the specifics, but it involved a shifter. Rick just acted all cool like I should know what the BSI was and that they existed. He sure as hell knew everything about me. Of course, I now know that it's their job to keep tabs on all vampires and supes who hold any sort of public position or office."

I choked on the sip of beer I was swigging. "You're telling me vampires are cops, congressmen, and everything else?"

She nodded. "We haven't seen one go as high as congress or mayor, but we've caught them working for those types. Hired muscle and all that. And cops, like I was. There are quite a few. We have two here in Shreveport. There were two others in Rochester. We have quite a few in New Orleans, too."

I made a gun gesture near my head with two fingers and blew out an explosive noise from my lips. "Mind blown."

She chuckled. "Right? Well, I was recruited into the BSI after a lot of begging. They did not want to hire a vampire, even though they had in the past, but mostly as confidential informants and all that. I convinced them of how much help I could be, and how I could always take the night shift, how I was nearly indestructible, and I could go undercover and catch vampires and shifters. They were sold, and the rest is history."

Chapter 23

BLISSFULLY UNAWARE

nce she was done with her story, I set my beer on the coffee table and sat cross-legged on the sofa. I grabbed her hand and pulled her toward me. Straightening her so her legs had nowhere to go but wrap around my waist as we sat there, I fisted the back of her hair and used that control to press her face into mine.

"Gonna kiss you now," I breathed against her lips.

She nodded, the both of us staring into each other's fucked-up eyes.

My lips were slow and methodical at first, her skin cold but warming up quickly as my body heat pressed into hers. She eagerly kissed me back, her tongue snaking in to mingle with mine. I didn't analyze why this woman made me crazy like no other. I couldn't. I just rolled with what I was feeling and let everything physical and animalistic take over before I got inside my head and couldn't claw my way out.

The soft groans and squeaks that came from her were driving me crazy. I kissed her harder. She bit my lip and then licked the blood it produced — and I let her. I reached around and tore off her tank top with one hand, the fabric ripping with a satisfying tear. I tossed it away and slowly snaked my hand down her pants, happy to feel how ready she was for me.

As I was about to tear off her shorts, she did me a favor and did it herself. I grinned against our kiss until she reached down against my body, buttons and metal flying everywhere. My jeans were off and underwear was in shreds a few short seconds before my painfully hard erection was shoved inside of her.

She screamed as I entered her, but it wasn't filled with anguish or pain. It was pure, unadulterated pleasure. I rocked into her, hitting the hilt inside as she, in turn, slammed back down onto me. I wrenched her head back with the fistful of hair I still had hold of, and kissed and licked my way down her neck, to her collarbone, then to her breasts, her nipples hard as steel. I nipped and sucked at them.

"Bite harder," she breathed out.

Doing as she commanded while continuing to rock in and out of her, I bit down as hard as I could on her left nipple, right before drawing blood. No way did I want to taste any blood in my mouth.

She felt so damn good, better than anyone I had ever felt… and I didn't want to stop. However, my twenty-one-year-old body didn't quite have the same stamina my forty-one-year-old mind did.

"Fuck, baby, I'm gonna lose it here in a—"

I was cut off by a screech that damn near burst my eardrums. With her body clenching tightly around me, I lost everything inside of her, my release hard, angry, and exhilarating all at once. I pulsed over and over, riding that wave until I wanted to fall into a boneless heap.

With her head rested against my shoulder, her face turned into the crook of my neck, she breathed out, "God, Kovah. You slay me."

"You slay me, too, sweetheart."

We untangled from each other, cleaned up in a shower together, then climbed into her bed completely naked. I wanted to fall asleep, but my damn body was telling me otherwise.

With her bare naked back pressed against my front, I reached around and wrapped my hand around, my fingers finding her nipple as I kissed her neck. I felt her arch her back slightly and groan a little. She reached a hand up and covered it with mine, and then we were both fondling her full breast gently.

I felt her leg move up and bend back to wrap around my waist, opening herself to me. I reached down and used my hand to guide myself in, not surprised I was rock hard again. She arched her back further, allowing me full access, crying out when I was fully inside.

Thrusting hard and slow, I rocked in and out with the palm of my hand rubbing circles around the hard tip of her breast. I slid my hand down to feel that sensitive bundle of nerves where I was thrusting, but her hand was already there, her body clenching as she cried out another release.

Smiling at a small victory, I pulled out of her and flipped her on her back. She looked up at me in surprise, a small, lazy smile creeping across her lips, and I entered her, slow and easy. I took my time this time, not wanting to lose it too soon.

I smiled as her legs wrapped around my back and I continued my calm, lazy thrusts, my right arm under her shoulders, her arms wrapped around my back with the sounds of her soft panting and mewls in my ear. Controlling my breathing, I closed my eyes and concentrated on moving in and out of her, the sensation amazing and nothing like I'd ever felt. All these years, I'd been using human girls to satisfy my needs… and then there was Janice. Nothing but whips, chains, and leather there. Fun to get off with but zero emotions.

Emotions. Making love. Was that what I was feeling here? No, it couldn't be. I couldn't fall in love with a fucking vampire.

My cock hardened, straining, almost painful, nothing but the slide of her slick skin to relieve the pressure, the strain, the thick hardness. I thrusted again, trying not to analyze my feelings. This was no time to think of feelings. I shouldn't have any. This was just sex.

"Oh, Kovah, you feel incredible, you fit me so perfect. God, please don't stop, you're perfect, amazing…"

My breathing sped up. My head felt dizzy. My heart felt… I didn't know. I didn't want to know. I hadn't felt anything for such a long time. Its erratic beat picked up, thudding in my ears. I was heating up, almost breaking a sweat — not that I'd done that in years. Her legs clenched tightly around my ass, her hips coming up to slam into mine.

My thrusts increased. I couldn't stop it now. Her body was squeezing around me, her mouth's groans and pants turned into another squeal of pleasure.

"Oh, my God. Oh… I can't stop… Kovah… Please…" Then she screamed. Screamed like she was going to die. Screamed like she was going to live.

I yelled out too, my release uncontrollable now, my hips stilling as they slammed into her one last time. A full body shudder racked my body, which was now covered in a slight sheen of sweat. I hadn't worked up a sweat during sex in twenty years.

Dropping my head into her shoulder, I could not move. I didn't want to move. Then I realized she couldn't breathe.

Did she need to breathe?

Reluctantly, I pulled back and looked down at her, and she was gazing up at me with hooded eyes, one brown, one green, and she was smiling.

"That was the best motherfucking sex I've ever had," my mouth blurted without my permission.

She scraped her nails into the hair at the back of my head, dragged my face to hers, and kissed me hard. When she finally pulled back, she breathed out, "You took the words right out of my motherfucking mouth."

I had fallen asleep the second my head hit the pillow. Manta's pillow. But when my body sensed that daytime was looming, I was awoken. My eyes slamming open, I look over to the clock to see it was in the four a.m. hour, as her window was heavily shaded. I gingerly removed Manta's arm from around my torso and slipped out of bed. I dressed as quietly as I could, making sure I had my wallet, keys, and phone, and snuck out of her house.

I breathed a sigh of relief when I saw my precious still parked out front. I walked it a couple of blocks away before straddling her and turning the key to rev her up. A smile tilting up on my lips, I cranked the throttle and tore off toward my flat. I was hoping for two or three hours of sleep before I had to be at work.

Blindly driving the eight or so miles, I screeched into the parking lot and parked the beauty in its usual spot, sleep and exhaustion taking over at the thought of my own bed.

I shoved my keys into my pocket and looked around in the semi-darkness before heading toward the mechanic's shop. I, unfortunately, had to walk through the shop in order to reach my place above the garage… but I didn't complain, as the rent was cheap, and shit, I worked here anyway. With my transient lifestyle, I didn't need or want much more than this.

Did I?

I was five feet from the garage's door when I was yanked backward by the collar.

A fierce, fiery pain in my neck roared through me.

My keys dropped to the ground.

Fight or flight kicked in… and I began to thrash and swing.

Grabbing the headful of hair belonging to the teeth attached to my neck, I yanked backward, and instant relief flooded me as teeth were dislodged.

The bloodsucker who'd been latched to my neck fell backward onto his ass, and I was on him, my fist pummeling his face.

"Cocksucking leech! Who the fuck do you think you are!" I yelled, my knuckles connecting over and over.

I felt myself being pulled off. This time, the bone-crunching crack of my cheekbone reverberated in my ears before my entire world went black.

CONTRACTOR

I blinked over and over, a pain I couldn't describe humming through my whole body. Agony. Hunger. Despair. Fright. All these rolled through my body and mind, out of control.

Finally able to see I was in a sterile room sitting in a chair, a flimsy rope around my chest tied to the chair holding me upright my only companion. I was surprised my hands were free, so I yanked the rope and tossed it to the ground.

I surveyed my surroundings. One door, gray floor, four gray walls. I looked up to see a gray ceiling greeting me. I scanned the room some more. Something black… there it was, a small camera with a blinking red light. Grinning methodically because I was obviously insane, not to mention sleep-deprived, I lifted myself from the chair and set both hands on my hips as I spoke into the camera.

"Oh, let me guess. I've been kidnapped by a bunch of pussy-ass leeches?"

I paced the room and kept my crazy, methodical smile on my lips. "I can smell your asses from in here. If you thought I'd forgotten about the Nighthawks, you're sadly mistaken. And which one of y'all bit me? Because you're gonna pay for that!" I lifted both middle fingers to the camera. I waited patiently, expecting the cavalry to come busting down the door after my verbal tirade, but still… there was nothing.

They had stripped me of my keys, wallet, phone, sunglasses, and even my watch after they'd dragged me here. I quickly patted down my pockets and then reached my hand inside them searching for anything, but came up empty.

"Look," I said into the camera, "I'm hungry. I'm tired. I just fucked the hell out of a hot ass female vamp, and I just need some sleep before I head out to the day job. So tell me what you need, and I'll tell you, so I can be on my way—"

The door to the room flew open and Viper stormed in, moving at unnatural speed until he reached me. His hand gripped my throat. I was lifted off the ground and slammed against the nearest wall. It was reminiscent of my beginnings, when Suzette had done this, and it frightened me. I kicked out, trying to connect with his knee, but he was too fast and avoided it.

"What vampire did you fuck?" he growled in my face, the entirety of his eyeballs solid black. I could see his fangs behind his lips. Ooh, he was pissed.

"None of your damn business," I choked out, my fingers uselessly clawing his hand around my throat. I was starting to lose air and this fucker was strong.

He dropped me to the ground and I gasped for breath, and then popped up with my fist closed and ready, rearing my arm back to smash his nose. He was faster and moved out of my way. Then he dragged me to the chair, and with preternatural speed, grabbed the rope and tied me there. This time, I couldn't move. Last time, I realized it was just to keep me from falling out of the chair while I was out cold.

"I'm gonna ask you again, which vampire was this? Give me a name."

I narrowed my milky white eyes at him. "Why do you care who I sleep with? I was just trying to get the point across at how exhausted I was."

He began to pace in front of me, his hands behind his back. "We keep close tabs on all vampires in the city, what they're doing, who they're screwing, their business transactions, legal or illegal."

"Well, then I guess eventually you'll find out, won't you?" I said, not liking this game we were playing.

He nodded. "We will, but it's quicker if you tell us."

"And why would I do that?" I asked.

"You want to join the Nighthawks, don't you?" He stopped pacing and looked at me. "Being part of our team means you have to disclose everything. We obviously cannot compel the truth out of you since it didn't work when we threw you out a couple days ago, but it's an integrity thing, man. You feel me?"

I snorted, still trying to get free from the ropes. "Integrity? Like kidnapping me? That wasn't cool, man."

"We didn't know the compulsion hadn't worked. You would have thought we were strangers and didn't think you'd go willingly. We use biting to control people. We don't kill or take blood from unwilling victims, it's just a control thing."

I sighed. "What do you want, Viper?"

"Your female vamp, she got a name?" he said again.

I nodded. "She said her name was Violet, didn't get more than that. She was good for the night, if you catch my drift."

"Where did you meet her?"

"Some dark ass bar downtown. Don't ask me the name because I don't know," I lied. No way was I letting them at Manta. Over my dead body. I already knew they had it out for her, and I was going to find out why.

He nodded. "I'm sure we can find the place. Vampires hang out in those bars. Did you let her bite you?"

"Fuck no! I don't willingly let anyone bite me. Hell, she didn't even try. Said I smelled weird once my cologne wore off. Didn't ask anything else, just spent all night taking my aggression out on her." I hated talking like this, but I had to roll with it.

He began to pace again, and then a door opened. In walked Shadow. The guy's presence was just tall and intimidating. Dark hair, a huge beard, lots of leather, tats, and biceps the size of melons. He glared at me, then went to Viper and whispered something in his ear.

Viper's face went dark, then he narrowed his eyes at me as Shadow left the room. He looked at me, obviously not planning on telling me what Shadow had said. "Are you interested in pledging?"

I licked my lips. "You're serious? You'd let me in?"

"On a trial basis," he said dryly.

"What are the circumstances? I mean, your rules and all that. I'm a pretty independent guy, but I won't be used and abused. I'm not going to endure some ridiculous torture to get in, and I will not adhere to some 'blood in, blood out' bullshit rule. I won't be held captive by you guys."

He chuckled. "You watch too many movies, man. This isn't some *Sons of Anarchy* bullshit. We don't operate like human motorcycle clubs. In fact, I don't even like that term." He folded his arms over his chest and looked at me.

"What do you want with me, then? I'm not a full vampire."

"I get that," he said, beginning to pace again. "But you could be of use. You can go out during the day, and you can compel people, can't you?"

I wondered how he knew that, but I just nodded. "Yes." No way was I telling him I could compel vampires. "How did you know?"

"We did some digging on you. Didn't find much, but it seems you just appeared out of nowhere ten years ago."

I nodded and smiled. "Sounds about right. Don't ask for the rest, 'cause I'm not giving it to you. My previous persona and life are dead."

"Understandable," he replied, and I was surprised he didn't fight for it. It seemed he had a one-track mind when it came to what he needed me for.

"I'll tell you what, Viper. Why don't you let me on like a contract employee? You pay me to do the dirty work, and then we won't have to deal with the issue of club memberships, wearing your cut, and all that. I would do just about anything for money."

He chuckled. "Anything, huh?"

"Yep. I won't take contract hits on humans though, sorry. I draw the line at murder. I'll kill a vampire if I have to, though."

He narrowed his hazel eyes. "Vampire lives worth less than human ones?"

I contemplated popping off a smartass answer about how the murderous leeches had lived long enough and usually have killed hundreds of humans in their lifespan, but instead, I said, "I wouldn't put it that way. Let's just say I'm still a little resentful to the vampire who did this to me."

I couldn't point to my eyes because my hands were still tied. Not that I needed to.

"You had said a succubus did that, huh? She bite you?" he asked, genuinely curious.

"Untie me and let me have a cigarette, and I'll tell you the whole damn story."

He shook his head. "No tobacco allowed in here. It's disgusting."

"Forgot," I murmured under my breath. "Untie me then?"

I barely saw him nod as he came over and ripped the ropes off one-handed. "Camera's watching, so don't try anything. My boys will tear you apart to protect me. Not that I couldn't do it myself."

"Thank you," I said, rubbing at my arms and rolling my shoulders. I went on to tell him from the beginning about Suzette and what she'd done.

I hoped he wouldn't ask what happened after so I wouldn't have to lie about the BSI. I didn't know if the Nighthawks knew about them, but I sure as fuck wasn't going to be the one to tell them. Although if I thought hard about it, they probably did know since they were threatening Manta. I could only hope they thought she was just a simple FBI agent.

"That's fucking freaky," Viper said after I was done. "I figured a bite from her and you turn into a crazed vampire that has to be put down. We've had to kill quite a few of the poor bastards in our time."

"I bet you have," I said. "I hope you put the succubus down, too. They are a menace to society."

He laughed. "They are. We had one a few years back who couldn't control her bites and kept creating monsters, so we put her down."

"Nice." I smiled, as that made me genuinely happy. "There was one named Eva who hung out at the Blue Room. Did you guys keep an eye on her?" I asked, wondering if they knew about what had happened to her.

"Yep, she's next on our list."

I chuckled. "Don't worry, one of her victims killed her a few weeks ago in the Blue Room. I watched the whole thing. It was fucking epic."

He lifted an eyebrow. "Really now? That's interesting." He craned his head around and nodded to the camera, as if he hoped whoever was watching was paying attention.

"So, contractor... what do you think? I'm serious about my offer. You can just pay me by the job."

He walked to the door, opened it, and indicated for me to follow him, so I did. He seemed very nonthreatening at this point, and I figured his crazy had been tucked away for now. I truly did not know how to take this guy — this vampire.

He led me to what looked like some kind of breakroom with a fridge and a table. I knew there probably wasn't any human food in there, although I wished there were. I was starving. Those tacos were the last thing I'd eaten.

The rest of the Nighthawks piled in and sat in the chairs around the table. One went to the fridge and pulled out a blood bag. I watched as he tossed it into the microwave and hit buttons.

"You shouldn't microwave shit in plastic. You'll get cancer," I said in my smartass tone just to see what he'd do. The room erupted in chuckles.

The vampire at the microwave looked to have been in his thirties when he was turned, and he replied dryly, "I wish."

Yikes.

"We're here to take a vote, gentlemen. Y'all remember Kovah? Instead of pledging him, he's offered to become a hired contractor, so to speak. He does our daytime dirty work, and in exchange we pay him by the job."

Shiv glared at me, shooting me daggers with his eyes... no pun intended. "How d'we know he ain't gonna go and tell the world about us?"

"That will be part of his contract. Complete and utter discretion and secrecy. The penalty for blabbing about us is death," Viper said, looking me straight in the eye.

I swallowed hard but tried to keep an impassive face. Damn, I'd love to hide behind my glasses right about now.

"I can live with that," I replied bravely, lifting my chin.

"What kind of jobs?" asked the one at the microwave, who was now drinking from the medical bag using the nozzle like a straw. I resisted the urge to gag.

"Just anything we need. He agreed to contract killings on vampires," Viper replied.

I nodded like I was totally in on this. I mean, I was, but I was still freaking out a little.

"What about shifters?" Shadow asked, his arms folded over his massive chest.

I narrowed my eyes. "Shifters? You guys kill shifters? Why?"

I was literally pulling this shit out of my ass at this point. I had never met one — that I knew of — and here I was, acting like I was privy to what the hell they were.

They all chuckled again, and Shiv said, "Shifters are scum. They all should be dead. They're nothing but a bunch of filthy animals."

"Okaaaay," I replied. "I haven't had many dealings with them, but why exactly do they need to die?"

The group murmured amongst themselves, when Viper lifted an eyebrow and said, "Don't worry about it. We aren't going to have you out there randomly killing shifters. They will have had to deserve it. Feel me?"

I nodded. "Yeah, actually I do."

He turned to the group of a dozen or so. "All in favor of hiring Kovah as a contractor, raise your right hand."

Not surprisingly, eleven hands went up; everyone with the exception of Shiv. They all said, "I" in unison—except Shiv. Even Viper had his hand up.

I chuckled and looked at Shiv in the eye with my arms folded over my chest. "Not a fan, prison boy?"

"Fuck you, freak."

Viper bit back a smile at Shiv, then said, "It's settled then. Give him back his personal effects."

Shadow opened a drawer from the cabinets and handed me back my wallet, keys, cigarettes, glasses, and phone. I put the glasses on first and shoved the rest in my pockets.

I addressed the group. "Happy to know you all, and I look forward to our business relationship." I turned to Viper. "We'll discuss money later?"

He nodded. "Yes, when I have a job for you, I'll call you with the details. I deal in cash only, so once the price is set, you'll get one-fourth upfront, the rest payable once the job is done."

"Cash," I said, chuckling. "Works for me. You have my number?"

His brow furrowed and he looked at Shadow. "Get that, will you, man?"

Shadow nodded and held his hand out. "Phone."

I put in the passcode and handed it to him. A few keystrokes later, a contact called *Hawks* was in my phone, with an outgoing text to it pinging in Viper's pocket.

"Good, now show him out," Viper said.

Shadow nodded and led me out of the room. I could hear Shiv whining before the door was even shut. I just laughed.

Chapter 25

BROMANCE

fter an awkward ride home on the back of Shadow's bike, I reached my apartment and hurried inside, anxious to try to sleep. I shot off a text to Archie that I'd had a long night, and that I wouldn't be into work 'til about noon. He replied: *Copy*.

I thought maybe I'd have some trouble falling asleep after hours at the Nighthawks' clubhouse, but I didn't. I crashed the second my head hit the pillow, and I knew it was not only exhaustion, but also the fact that the sun was coming up. That always made me a little sleepy—and a little pissed off. It was such a vampire trait, but physiologically, there was nothing I could do to fight it except to try to sleep at night and be up all day. Manta had kept me up until the late hours of the night, then the Nighthawks until the wee hours of the morning. I had to get some damn sleep.

Of course, what would sleep be without nightmares? Nightmares of Suzette, of Manta, of Janice even. So much for a peaceful sleep. Fitful and interrupted was about all I would get, but hell, I would take anything at this point.

The alarm on my phone squealed at 11:45 a.m. I slogged out of bed and took a hot as hell shower. With my body scalded red, I used the flat of my hand to clear the mirror and stare at my reflection. I wasn't sure why I hoped that every day, when I woke up, my eyes would not be like this. But they always were. I raked my fingers through my black hair, which probably should be cut soon. I smiled at the definition in my chest, thinking about putting more ink on it. Both arms were pretty full now, and I pulled my right arm up and flexed in the mirror. I did not get much exercise, but I wondered how yoked I could get if I actually did hit the weights.

With what time…?

I brushed my teeth and then shaved my face, noting I needed to go to the store and get some razors, as these were dull already. I slapped on some aftershave and then pulled on a pair of jeans and a plain black T-shirt. Once my work boots were tied tightly, I shoved my glasses over my face. I checked my phone to see four texts, all sent between the 5 and 10 a.m. hour:

Archie: *Garage is insanely busy. Get down here asap.*

Janice: *I'm lonely, baby. Wanna play?*

Manta: *I'm thinking about you.*

Hawks: *We already have something for you. Call, don't text. After 6 pm only.*

Fuuuuuck.

Passing by Archie's office to get into my coveralls, glad for the busyness of the shop and the distraction it would bring, my boss called out to me.

"Where you been, kid?"

I made a dramatic gesture of looking at my watch, which read 12:01 p.m. "Uh, sleeping."

"Sit," he instructed.

I did as he ordered, sort of nervous now. What was his problem? I was his best mechanic, and dammit, I just needed a couple of extra hours. I never asked for anything from him, and I always showed up to work on time. I actually liked working here.

He slowly punched some keys on his computer, his bottom lip bulging with dip. He finally turned his old-ass 15-inch, dust-covered monitor toward me. "Wanna tell me what the hell this is?"

My eyes bulged. It was me on the security cameras Archie had installed outside the garage. Blurs of movement, a scuffle of a fight, blurry, but recognizable. Then me being punched and dragged off camera like a limp ragdoll. Then nothing but a blank, calm parking lot.

"Uh, well, explaining what happened last night was first on my to-do list today, boss," I said, trying to put on my most charming smile.

"Please tell me those vampers weren't part of those Nighthawks," he said.

I nodded. "They were."

He stood up and pounded his fist on his desktop. "Those bloodsuckers kidnapped you?"

"Yes. But let me explain first."

"Dammit, Kovah! You and that boy out there" — he pointed toward the garage bay, and I knew he was speaking of Nolan — "are gonna give me a goddamn heart attack!"

I laughed and shook my head. "Boss, sit, please. You're scaring me. No heart attacks, okay? Let me explain."

He glared at me, and then picked up his cup and spat in it. "Spill now, boy."

Explain I did. From the beginning to the end. I left nothing out.

"You are gon' sit here and tell me that you're gonna take contract hits from bunch of vampers who call themselves a gang? Have you lost your damn mind?"

I laughed again. "Boss, think about it. I get to kill vampires, but now I am gonna get paid for it. What's the harm?"

"But what about these shifters? You gonna kill them, too?"

I looked down. "I don't know, it depends. I'm gonna say this, Arch, and please don't judge me, but these guys... they don't seem like a ruthless, murderous gang. Like the Rebel Riders, they seem to have a bit of logic and agenda behind their killings. They aren't homicidal maniacs. Besides, I'd love to meet a shifter. I didn't even know they existed."

Archie was still staring at me with concern. "What if they tell you to kill a shifter and he or she really hasn't done anything that warrants the death penalty?"

I had already thought about that, actually, so I said, "Then I will cross that bridge when I come it, I guess."

"This is crazy, Kovah. You've basically sold your soul to the devil. You know that, right?"

I got up and went around the desk to pat him on the shoulder on my way out of the office. "That would be true if I actually had a soul, boss."

It was day six working on the Ducati with Nolan. He was just a kid, really. He'd recently had his own victory over his succubus, and seemed to have gone back to being a real, live, normal human. Still, he was the best and only friend I really had. I wasn't much of an "express your feelings" kind of guy, but man... I had so much going on, and I felt like he would be the only one who would understand. Or hell, maybe he wouldn't.

After explaining everything to him, he set his wrench down and slid out from underneath the bike. Wiping his hand on a red oil rag, he slid his safety glasses up to rest on his dark-blond hair and pierced me with a serious gaze. There were smears of oil and dirt on his boyish face and I grinned at how the innocence of his face didn't match the wisdom held in his lime-green stare.

"I'm confused as to what you want advice on, man. The vampire gang, or the girl problem?"

I laughed, wiping my hands off as I looked at the beautiful bike we'd just finished up on. "Ya know what? Let's go get cleaned up and grab a drink."

He grinned. "You got it."

An hour later, we found ourselves at a bar-restaurant downtown. I refused to acknowledge that we were on a bro date, but I supposed we were.

Seated at the bar, we ordered finger food and bottled beer, talking over the crowd.

"You have a woman problem," Nolan said, now looking fresh and dare I say pretty-boy with his blond hair gelled back, in a pair of jeans and a black *FBI: Federal Booty Inspector* T-shirt that made me chuckle. It was too tight for him, but somehow, I think that was on purpose.

"I do have a girl problem, but honestly? It's a no-brainer here. Janice is fun. Manta is... like fucking serious. I don't know." I raked a hand through my hair.

He lifted a brow as his mouth wrapped around the bottle. Pulling it away, he said, "But I like Janice. She helped me with my..." —his eyes glanced briefly around the bar—"problem."

"I know, I know. She's a great girl... vampire... but she's just fun. Manta is something else. Dammit! I don't know. This feelings shit... it sucks ass."

He swallowed his beer and laughed. "Just stop fighting it, man. We were created to fall in love and be monogamous. If you think you're some big player... some" —he made air quotes—"balla, you're never going to be happy. There's someone out there for everyone. Charity is my someone. She's my everything. She's been to hell and back with me, and we're gonna be together forever."

This made me curious. "How did you know? I mean, really know?" Damn. I couldn't believe I was talking to another dude about this romantic shit only chicks talk about.

"I just knew. There's no way to put it into words. We're getting married in the spring and you're gonna be my best fucking man. Right?"

Reeling in shock, but unable to help the smile that crawled on my lips, I said, "Hell yes, I will. Can I wear the glasses?" I pointed to my face.

He chuckled. "Of course. You'd be unrecognizable in the wedding photos if you didn't."

Biting back a laugh, I knew he was right.

"Anyway, don't tell Archie, but I'm going back to school. I'm gonna get my Criminal Justice degree. I want to work for the BSI."

I almost spit my beer out. "Oh, my God, Nolan. Seriously?"

He looked around again. "Yes. Being a mechanic is fun, but I think I'm destined for more."

"Destined…" I trailed off.

His annoyingly perfect mouth kicked up in a grin. "Yes, destined. I know all about the supernatural world. Don't you think I could be an asset to the BSI?"

I stared off unseeing at the football game on the screen above the bar. I thought long and hard about what he'd just said. Then I looked back at him. "Yeah, dude. You are definitely destined for that. And, hell, if you need a reference, I happened to be falling in love with one of their agents, so—"

We both froze as the words came out of my mouth. I reached up and slammed my palm over my lips.

"Did you really just say that?" Nolan asked, shaking with silent laughter.

"Motherfucker. I think I did."

He clapped me on the shoulder. "Welcome to the club, asshole."

I regretted not texting Manta back all day. She probably hated me by now, but I'd win her back. I paid the tab for Nolan and me, and we left the bar with a fist-bump, going our separate ways.

I called the Nighthawks back and Viper answered. "Kovah?"

"It's me."

"I'm going to send you info on a shifter we need obliterated. He's eluded us for almost two years. Only comes out during the day. Can you handle it?"

I swallowed hard. "Sure. What did he do?"

"He's just a useless piece of shit, man. Read the file and get rid of him, all right? Burn the body or toss him in the lake. We don't give a fuck. Just take pics of whatever you do and text them to us. Then you'll get ten thousand dollars."

Whoa. Ten grand would be awesome.

Except my damn conscience. What had this guy done? "Okay give me his name and address."

"All the info is in the file." He hung up.

An incoming email had an attachment. Deciding I'd worry about that tomorrow, I steered my bike toward Manta's house.

SHIFTY EYES

I reached Manta's house in no time. I rang her doorbell, and she answered the door quickly. But her beautiful face did not greet me… instead it was replaced with an ugly scowl.

"Oh, you're still alive?" she asked facetiously as I stood on her stoop, hoping she didn't hate me.

"Of course I am," I said in my most charming voice, a bouquet of flowers in my hand. Yes, I bought flowers. Something was wrong with me. I held them out like a peace offering, unsure what else to do with them.

She glanced down at them, something lighting in her eyes, but she tried to keep her face impassive. She opened the screen door to allow me inside, and said, "You smell like a bar," as she took the bouquet of roses.

"I was just in one," I replied quickly.

"Too busy to call me?" she countered, sounding hurt as she went into her kitchen and began rummaging around through the cabinets.

After putting the flowers into a vase with water and fussing over them, she heated up some blood to drink, and I sort of felt like she was doing that because she knew it was going to gross me out. Or piss me off. Or both.

I pretended the blood didn't bother me as I said, "Well, between the kidnapping, the boss being mad at me, and the bromance I apparently have going with my coworker, I've been a tad busy in the past twelve hours. But that doesn't mean I wasn't thinking about you."

The glass paused at her lips as she lifted a dark eyebrow in question. Again with the athletic shorts and tank top with no bra, I was getting aroused.

"Go on," she instructed, coming to sit by me.

Her eyes burned holes through me. Before she could reach up and take my glasses off, I removed them myself, feeling strangely comfortable and disarmed in her presence without them. She just seemed to do that to me.

"Tell me," she whispered.

I held nothing back. I blathered on about my entire night. The Nighthawks. Archie. Nolan. The hit I was instructed to do. Forty-five minutes of blabbing and she had reduced me to a word-vomiting mess.

She got up to rinse her bloody glass in the sink, and then came back to sit by me. "Well. It seems you've sure dug yourself into a hole."

"I need you to tell me about shifters. Everything I need to know about them," I commanded.

Blowing out a breath, she pierced me with an intense stare. Yet, she never let go of my hand. "Shape-shifters are an entirely different breed, Kovah. They are strange but closed off. From the information the BSI has recovered, we know they can shift into any animal they wish. Most of them stick to one animal, but the need to shift is undeniable, necessary, and purely animalistic. It's not like they can choose. They *have* to shift. Some of them lose control, tearing apart humans." She paused and looked at me, a questioning gaze in her dual-colored eyes. "It's like part of their DNA."

That got me thinking. They *had* to shift? Strange.

"If I gave you the name of one, would you be able to, like, run a background check on him?"

She lifted a shoulder and let it fall. "I suppose."

I pulled out my phone, opened the email, and began to read. "His name is Lucas Horrell. I have an address, too."

"Text it to me, and I will run it first thing in the evening when I get into work. But the name is vaguely familiar," she said, a faraway look in her eyes as she stared past me.

I quickly put the info into a text and shot it off to her, then set the phone down. I could see her gaze had been drawn back to mine, and I reached up, putting both hands on either side of her face. "You're not mad at me, are you? Because I couldn't take it if you were."

She bit her lip in contemplation. Such a human action, but then again, everything she did seemed human—except the cow blood drinking. I'd been around a lot of vampires over the past twenty-something years, and it seemed that the more time went by, the less human they became. Some of them behaved like horror movie freaks, some looked like they were living mannequins, and others just stared at you creepily and rarely said anything, their skin marble-white and stiff-looking. Those were the easiest to kill… as obliterating animated monsters produced no guilty conscience or moral dilemma if they acted like a robot.

When I had met Joel Reichert in New Orleans a few months ago, I knew there was a reason I'd liked him. He was over 100 years old, but still had a human feel. A businessman and owner of a large hotel, he had to keep up his people skills. I respected him after getting to know him, and after he'd helped us with Nolan's problem, both Nolan and I had convinced the Rebel Riders to leave him alone. He was actually doing some good, and I certainly couldn't say that much for most of the bloodsuckers I'd met.

"You look far away." The high-pitched lilt to Manta's voice broke me out of my memories.

"I'm right here, sweetheart," I replied quickly, capturing her mouth with mine.

I smiled against her lips, as I was happy I had taken the chance to come over here tonight. I wrapped my arms more tightly around her shoulders and continued to kiss her, pouring all of the day's stress into her selfishly, as I knew she could handle it—wanted it, even.

I scooped her up and kissed her hard. "Bedroom," I murmured.

"Yes, please," she whispered against my lips, and I kicked open her bedroom door and laid her down on her four-poster bed.

I stripped her quickly and she gave up no resistance at all. When she lay there completely bared for me, I shed myself of my clothes and crawled onto the bed like a hungry predator. She laughed at me, and with a serious gaze into her eyes, I gripped her face between my fingers. "You won't be laughing once I'm done with you." I indicated the poster bed with my finger as I said, "Next time, I'm bringing some rope or some handcuffs, and you'll be forced to do whatever I want."

"Bring it on," she purred, biting back a smile.

Damn. There was no controlling this one. She would just think it was all for fun. And it would be, if I was in charge.

I spent the rest of the night showing her how sorry I was for not getting back to her all day. The way she screamed out my name, I was pretty sure she forgave me.

Four times over.

As much as I wanted to stay in her bed all night, I just couldn't. I had to get back to my flat and fully read the email from the Nighthawks while I waited for a text from Manta, hopefully with some info. Plus, I had to be on time for the garage job. Archie knew everything, but I still hated the look of disappointment in his eyes when I failed to show on time.

I slept enough to function and went into work, losing myself in the repairs until a text vibrating in my pocket caught my attention:

Manta: *I got nothing. We don't have him on file or on our radar.*

I could almost hear her chuckling through the next text: *Sorry. It's all we got.*

I sighed and replied: *Thanks anyway, gorgeous.*

The file I'd opened before coming into work was pretty basic. Name, age, address, photo. He seemed like an average guy on paper—until I read the rest of the info. It was a literal RAP sheet. Murder, rape, assault, robbery, the list went on. Complete with pictures.

Gah, the pictures.

So why didn't the BSI have a real RAP sheet on this guy, then? This file was clearly something the Nighthawks kept and not anything official they'd obtained. I began to wonder briefly how they knew all of this. Deciding not to strain my brain, I continued to read until I got to *Aliases*. There were at least six. Some variations of his name, some not even close to his name. I texted the alias names, along with his date of birth to Manta, and hoped I'd hear something.

I barely lasted until noon when I told Archie I was done with the Harley I'd been working on and needed to "go take care of something."

Nodding, he dismissed me, knowing exactly where I was going. I made my way up to my flat and changed into a black T-shirt and black jeans with my black steel-toed boots. It was too hot for the leather jacket still, but I grabbed it anyway. I hadn't checked my phone in hours, and saw I had a text from Manta:

Manta: *One of the aliases produced a hit, Lucas Horace Smith. Close to Lucas Horrell. The guy committed a string of murders and rapes in the 1970s when he was in his 20s.*

Me: *But that would make him like…*

I paused my text, and too lazy to do the math, I continued: *Old. He looks like he's about 25 or 30 in the pic.*

It was a few minutes before she responded, and it dawned on me that she was probably asleep. Damn.

Manta: *Shifters are immortal like vampires. LOL.*

Me: *Good to know, thanks.*

Manta: *You're welcome, handsome.*

I smiled.

Me: *Why aren't you asleep?*

Manta: *I was, the phone woke me.*

Me: *Sorry.*

Manta: *Don't apologize. It's the best type of text to wake up to. Making a difference and all that. Plus you're cute.*

I chuckled at her flirtation.

Me: *We make a great team.*

Manta: *Come over after dark, and we can "team up" again ;)*

Me: *Of course, sweetheart.*

I smiled and went to my maps app and put in ol' Lucas's address. With visions of the photos from the murders he'd committed burned in my brain, I smiled. This old fucker was going to die today.

With a cigarette dangling from the corner of my mouth, I sat on my bike outside a massive set of wrought-iron gates that framed a huge mansion. The house had to be over 100 years old, but it was the address given to me in the document the Nighthawks had sent. I pulled the cigarette out and blew smoke out of the side of my mouth. I sat wondering how I was going to kill this motherfucker. I could pretend to be a pizza delivery guy. I was about to text Manta to see if shifters could eat food, when I remembered she was probably asleep. I then thought of texting Viper, but he was probably sleeping too.

Fucking vampires and their sun allergy.

Looked like good ol' fashioned compulsion would have to work. I could only hope I'd be able to compel a shifter. Hell, I may have already compelled one in my past and not known it since supposedly they looked and behaved just like humans.

I hid my precious in some bushes, pulled my crossbow pistol from the storage on my bike, and went to the big-ass gate. Two ornate letter Hs decorated each gate and I pushed one open. Surprised it wasn't locked, I strolled carefully up the cobblestoned walkway to a stone porch, a large wooden door at its helm. With my crossbow pistol already preloaded with a bolt in my hand hidden behind my back, my buck knife tucked safely in my boot, and a .22 pistol shoved into the small of my back, I wasn't feeling very afraid.

I rang the doorbell and waited for an answer. I even felt myself smile a little at the anticipation of the kill.

I'm such a sadistic bastard...

The man I'd been looking for answered the door looking very normal in a pair of jeans and a black New Orleans Saints T-shirt. His feet were bare and his too-long blond hair sat wildly around his shoulders. He looked like he hadn't shaved in a few days, a light graze of stubble lining his jaw.

He narrowed brown eyes at me. "Can I help you?"

I carefully stepped closer to him and locked gazes with him. "You're going to invite me in, aren't you? You don't feel threatened by me at all."

His body did not relax. His jaw didn't go slack. He didn't open the door wider to allow me in as I'd instructed him. Instead, his eyes turned yellow, like his entire eyeball was a very trippy shade of topaz with just one black vertical slit in the center. He narrowed them at me, the yellow illuminating out of his eyeballs like two flashlights. I wanted to offer him my sunglasses so he didn't slice me in half with his gaze like Cyclops from the *X-Men*.

In a voice that didn't sound entirely human, he looked past me outside, then at the sky, then back to me and said, "Vampire, I don't know how the hell you're out during the day, but your mind tricks don't work on me. You must be new."

Then he did something that made me choke on my own spit. He made a deep, guttural growl, then his clothes exploded off of his body. Where once stood a man now stood a tiger. A fucking orange tiger with black stripes. Standing in the doorway of a mansion in the middle of a Louisiana swamp.

I pulled my crossbow pistol out, and with shaking hands, pointed it at the animal. I literally couldn't think of one intelligible thing to say.

The tiger bared its teeth, snarling. Drool began to drop from its jaws. It lunged at me and I yelled as I pulled the trigger, releasing a bolt from the crossbow. It hit the animal between the eyes. It howled in agony, and then fell still to the ground.

Still shaking in disbelief and horror, I watched as its massive body shrunk before my eyes. Orange and black stripes contracted and faded into pale skin, until all I saw before me was a very dead man with a huge crossbow bolt protruding from his forehead. His eyes were open and his tongue lolled from the side of his mouth. Blood seeped from the wound in his forehead and pooled onto the shiny, polished wood floors under his body.

I could barely breathe, but I did manage to pull my cell phone from my pocket with violently shaky hands. I snapped a photo of very dead Lucas Horrell and attached it to a text to Viper with a caption reading: *Dead shape-shifters… they're GRRREAT!* and hit *send*.

I hoped he was old enough to remember the old *Tony the Tiger* cereal reference, or he would really think I'd lost my marbles.

Gingerly reaching down to pull the bolt from the dead guy's head, I had to yank pretty hard to get it out, and with a squishy pop, I dislodged my bolt and made a face when it dripped with brain matter and blood.

Because I was a sick fuck, I decided to look around the rest of the house. It was eerily quiet, and I was concerned that he wasn't in this big house by himself. My first stop was the kitchen, where I washed off my crossbow bolt and loaded it back into the pistol, ready for another kill.

I stood stock-still, waiting to hear any sound coming from the house, but there was none. A staircase loomed in front of me and I took it quietly, wondering what was upstairs. I kept the crossbow pistol out in front of me. I was not going to be hit with any more surprises tonight. My nerves were already shot. As I rounded the corner to a long hallway, I noticed the house was decorated moderately. What I also noticed was that the windows to the entire upstairs were shaded or painted black. This piqued my interest.

A buzzing in my pocket distracted me. I contemplated ignoring it, but I pulled it out to see a text:

Hawks: *You have proven yourself quite useful. Good job.*

I smiled and put the phone back in my pocket. The first door I came to was closed. I pressed my ear to it. I was careful to stay on the long hall rug and not make noise on the hardwood floor. I really couldn't hear anything, so with the toe of my boot, I pushed the door open, my weapon out in front. A bedroom with a lot of modern features lay before me, and in the bed was a gorgeous female with hair as black as a raven's. It glowed blue in the darkness, and her skin was pale as marble. I watched as she slept soundly, her strange breathing pattern familiar to me. This was how Manta slept. This woman was a vampire.

Pulling out my phone once more, I snapped a photo of her sleeping, hoping it would turn out in the dark. It was clear enough so I sent it to the Nighthawks.

Me: *Sleeping bloodsucker in the house. Both sides of the bed are unmade. I think this is his lover. Want me to leave her?*

While awaiting his reply, I crept around the bedroom and quietly opened drawers and doors, not really seeing anything of interest except a few photos of Lucas posing with a woman with long, black hair, who looked a lot like the creature lying in the bed.

It was a painful seven minutes before they texted back.

Hawks: *If the bitch is sleeping with a shifter, off her. Now.*

Me: *No problem. But it'll cost you.*

Hawks: *Another thousand for your troubles.*

I smiled at his text and put the phone in my pocket, happy to get paid for something I would have done for free anyway. I set the crossbow on the bed next to undead Sleeping Beauty, and, pulling the knife from my boot, I gingerly lowered the sheet covering her chest and raised up the knife, slamming it between her breasts. She sat bolt upright, screeching an unholy noise while grappling for the knife with her bony, pale hands, which I still had hold of.

"Die quietly, leech," I hissed in her face, driving the knife deeper.

And she did with a silent "O" on her mouth as her body turned into a pile of ash. She hadn't even been wearing clothes. I considered cleaning up the ash, but thought… nah. I stood in the same spot where I'd taken the vampire's photo and then snapped one of just a bed full of ash, then quickly pocketed the phone.

I hastily checked the other four doors in the hallway, but all rooms were empty. Sprinting down the stairs, I looked around for security cameras, but didn't see any. I went outside, where the sun was playing in and out of the clouds, but didn't see any cameras on the porch, either.

Sprinting fast, I made it through the wrought-iron gates and hopped on my bike. I whizzed back to Archie's Garage so I could tell him all about what had gone down, and to send the second text off to the Nighthawks so I could paid. *Cha-ching!*

Chapter 27

CRUSHING LOSS

I laughed when I read Manta's text, replying the photo of the shifter with a crossbolt in his forehead.

Manta: *That's gross.*

Me: *It was less gross when he was a tiger. A FUCKING TIGER!*

Manta: *Get your fine ass over here and give me allll the details.*

Me: *I need to make a pit stop first.*

I drove my bike to the Nighthawks' clubhouse, but not before I texted them that was on my way.

Once I reached the Montgomery Street warehouse, I parked next to the front door, dismounted my bike, and then pounded on their door. Grateful the sun had gone down, I knew the leeches had to be awake.

Waiting patiently, I finally heard the locks disengage.

Shiv's annoyed face greeted me. "The hell you want, hybrid?"

"My damn payment, convict."

He rolled his fist into his eye as if he was five years old and I had just woken him from a dream about a free-for-all inside a candy factory. "I never did time, just so you know."

"Yeah. I don't care," I came back dryly. "Just let me see Shadow or Viper so I can get paid."

He yawned and opened the door wide so I could walk through. Remembering my way around, I went to the breakroom, where I saw several vampires sitting around drinking what I hoped was coffee from their ceramic mugs. But I knew better. Others were drinking from beer cans.

"I killed a shifter," I blurted proudly as I entered their lair.

They all broke out in applause. It was a surprise. They must have really wanted this guy.

"Well done," Viper said, setting his mug down and standing. He rubbed a meaty hand over his dark-blond scruff and pierced me with his hazel stare.

"Just trying to collect," I said, trying to sound causal.

"We were just having a few beers to celebrate." He pointed to the almost empty six-pack, which sat on the center of the table.

My jaw ticked with annoyance. I didn't come here to get wasted with vampires. I came here to collect.

Shadow, on seeing my arrival, smirked at me, a rare grin kicking up behind his beard. He walked to a framed picture of a popular bridge, which was hand-painted, and tilted it to the side. Behind it was a safe.

How original, I thought, proud of myself for not rolling my eyes like I wanted to.

He twisted the combination with vampire speed, so fast that his hands and the tumbler were nothing but a blur. He quickly opened the door and pulled out eleven bundles of cash. He then reached into a cabinet and pulled out a plastic grocery bag. Yes, a plastic sack, and tossed the bundles in there. He tied the flimsy handles together and then tossed the bag at me, which I caught, of course.

"Beer?" Viper asked, pointing to it.

"Nah, it would take too many to give me a buzz," I replied, not sure why I needed to share that.

"I know the feeling," Shiv murmured, sipping on his coffee mug.

Starting to feel awkward as they all kind of stared at me, I said, "Well, thanks. I'll be going."

"I'll walk you out," Viper said, cutting a look at Shadow that he didn't think I'd seen.

When we reached the door, he walked me outside and looked around briefly, and then his eyes landed on my precious.

"That your bike?" he asked.

I nodded. "Yep."

"Sweet ride."

"She was sweeter before your boys knocked her over and scratched her that first night."

He chuckled. "Sorry about that. I know a good body shop. Call Clint at Bike Pro on Main. Tell him I sent you and he'll give you a discount."

I grinned. "Yeah… I work at Archie's. Bike Pro is our competitor."

"So you're not a bartender?" he asked.

I shook my head. "No, but I somehow think you already knew that."

He nodded with a grin. He put his hand out to shake, and I looked down at it, reluctantly bringing my hand up to shake his. It was cold, but that did not surprise me.

"Thank you for the quick job, Kovah. I'm glad I took a chance on you," he said sincerely.

Nodding, I replied, "Me too. I'm good at what I do, Viper. I have been doing it a long time. I haven't ever seen a shifter shift before tonight, though. So that was a first for me."

His eyes went wide temporarily but they quickly turned to amusement. "Really? The tiger or the jaguar?"

I grinned. "He has two, huh? The tiger. Scared the shit outta me, I'm not gonna lie. The crossbolt pistol took him down pretty fast."

"We're going to frame that photo of him with the crossbolt in his forehead," he joked.

"I wish I would have had the sense to take a pic of the tiger. But I was too busy trying not to piss myself." I smirked.

"That's understandable," Viper replied.

We were quiet for a minute, and I said, "Your boy, Shiv. He on the up and up?"

He folded his arms over his chest. "Why do you ask?"

I had to choose my words carefully, so I said, "I've just got good instincts, that's all. He dislikes me for a reason. Maybe you should find out why, because I sure as fuck can't figure it out."

He looked faraway, then came back to lock his gaze with mine. "He's a bit off, if you know what I mean."

Nodding, I said, "I do."

I was a bit relieved to hear that they could see it, too. So I left it at that.

Putting my fist out, I said, "Do you fist-bump, or are you too old school for that?"

He bumped his fist with mine, a deep, throaty chuckle vibrating his body. "Nah, I'm an adaptable guy."

Smirking, I turned around, got on my bike, and headed for my flat to put my pistol and money away. Then I was heading to Manta's house to give her *allll the details.*

As I pulled up to my flat, my phone vibrated in my pocket. I looked to see I had a Facebook notification from my brother's page. I had turned off all the notifications for that annoying app except my mother's, and Heather and Leo's joint Facebook page.

I swiped the screen, and when I read the post, my heart fell into my stomach.

"Please keep us in your thoughts and prayers tonight, as Leo's dad has gone to heaven after a short battle with cancer. We are devastated."

I sucked in a breath to keep from sobbing and read the comments. He'd apparently gotten pancreatic cancer just four weeks prior and it took him that fast.

I didn't know how to feel. My chest hurt and my eyes stung. I walked woodenly to my door and let myself inside, my phone still clutched in my hand. It vibrated with an incoming call.

"Hello," I said quietly and without feeling.

Manta. "Oh, God, Kovah. What's wrong?"

I remained quiet, as I just couldn't form words.

"I'm coming over," she said, then hung up. I walked over and sat on my bed, my phone still gripped tightly in my hand, as if letting it go would mean I'd lose my last connection to my family.

I couldn't believe it. And why couldn't I believe it? I wasn't sure. This was the part I had been dreading, leaving everyone behind meant getting news like this was going to hurt, sting, and devastate me.

I wasn't sure how long I stared at the blank TV when there was a knock at the door. I was about to get up when the knob turned and she came walking in wearing a pink tracksuit, her hair in a ponytail. Damn, I hadn't even locked the door.

Manta came over and sat down next to me. She did what she usually did, removed my glasses so she could see into the void of what used to be my soul. She grabbed my hand. "Tell me," she whispered.

I swallowed hard and looked down. "My dad... he's gone. He had cancer... I didn't even know."

With that, my chest hitched, and for the second time in twenty years, I fucking cried. But this time, no tears to help let go of my grief and cleanse me. The other difference was, I had a beautiful woman to wrap her arms around me to show me she understood. And I knew she did. Probably many times over.

She made me stand, undressed me, and pulled back the sheets to my bed, which sat against the window of my studio apartment. Then she did the same and climbed in with me, but not before setting her alarm on her phone for four a.m. I knew she couldn't be here when the sun came up. And what I loved — what I appreciated and respected the hell out of her for — was how she didn't say anything. She didn't try to offer me any bullshit words of comfort. She was just there.

I woke alone, and unsurprised. I hadn't even heard her leave. I had fallen asleep quickly, and I wondered if she had just stayed awake and watched over me. Either way, I was going to have to thank her. Yawning, I stood up, spied the plastic grocery sack on my counter, and tore it open. I smiled at the eleven bundles of hundreds inside. I couldn't decide what I'd do with the money, but for now it was going into the bank. Living forever was going to get expensive and I thought I should probably start investing somehow. I didn't know anything about that shit. My dad was the smart one in that aspect.

My smile fell and my chest began to hurt as I remembered. Sadness took over and I looked around for my phone. I opened the app, clicked on Heather and Leo's page, and tried to see if there was an update. There wasn't. But what was I really hoping to find? That it was a joke? I knew nobody would ever joke about that. The date of the funeral? Yeah, that wasn't going to happen. No way could I risk going, even in disguise. I looked over to my fridge and saw a handwritten note **pinned to the top with my Harley Davidson magnet.**

You will get through this, and I will be here. -*Manta*

A smile lifted my lips when I wanted to frown. She was so many levels of awesome.

Chapter 28

A NEW YORK GOODBYE

The look in Archie's eyes was that of pure pity. I didn't like it, but I respected it enough. "I'm sorry about your pop. That's tough."

"Thanks, Arch," I said, sliding out from underneath the Harley I'd been working on to see him looking down at me. I explained everything about my dad while I'd been working so I wouldn't break down.

"I'm assumin' you won't be going to the funeral," he replied, staring down at me. "I mean, if you need to, kid, you know I'll give ya the time off." He sounded uncomfortable. Awkward.

I stood and wiped my hands on my oil rag. "Nah, I'm good. No way can I go to the funeral. My Ma would probably keel over dead if she saw me."

It was a lame attempt at a joke, but it was a truth that made me shudder. I would never do that. I had to accept that my father had passed and hoped that one day, if I ever died a real death, I would see him in the afterlife. If there really was one. My belief in that had begun to wane over the years.

Archie cleared his throat. "Well, the fact you showed up to work today says a lot about ya. I sure do appreciate that shit, just so you know."

"No use in sitting around and moping. Doesn't serve a purpose. Besides, I need to stay busy," I told him.

He reached into his pocket, pulled a pinch of tobacco from the can, and shoved it into his bottom lip. "You got that right."

He limped away, leaning on his cane. I watched him reach his office and shook my head, smiling at the old-timer.

"Kovah!"

I turned around to see Nolan headed my way, waving a piece of paper.

"What's up?" I asked, intrigued.

His look of excitement turned to concern quickly. "First off, I'm sorry to hear about your dad." He shuffled on his feet a little.

I clapped him on the shoulder. "Thanks. Archie tell you?"

He nodded. "Yeah. Said you might be out for a while."

I pushed my sunglasses up further on my face. "I'm not going anywhere, dude. It's not like I can go to the funeral, ya know?"

He looked at me curiously, a small amount of hurt and pity in his eyes. "That's horrible. Would you like me to go for you and film it on my phone?"

I felt like I'd been blown back in an explosion. "What? Uh… you'd do that for me?"

His cool-green eyes met my stare and he said, "Of course. You've obviously been through enough. I would be happy to. I'll take Charity with me."

Wow. I was pretty speechless. "Man, I don't know what to say."

"Just say yes." He smiled at me.

"Yes. And I'm paying for your expenses, you and your girl. No arguments."

He laughed. "No arguments here. I've never been to New York."

"It's awesome, you'll love it." I smiled. What a friend I'd found in this guy. I'd owe him forever. Looking down at his hand, I said, "Whatcha got there?"

"Oh! I wanted to tell you I've been accepted to Louisiana State," he drawled.

I was truly happy for him. "That's awesome, man."

"I just had to tell someone," he said, his face lit up with pride. "They have a criminal justice program I'm excited to get started on."

I laughed. "I bet. Are you still aiming for a job with the BSI?"

"Yep. It'll obviously be a few years, but it feels good to have a goal."

"Goals get us through life. Always strive for better and you'll go places, man."

"Hey, kid, get in here!" Archie called from his office.

Since we didn't know which one of us he was talking to, we looked at each other and then headed into his office.

Archie spit into his cup. He looked up at us in confusion. Then looking at me, he said, "Not you, kid. Him kid." He pointed at Nolan.

I chuckled and walked out to get to work.

"You look stupid as a blond," Nolan said, laughing.

"Nolan! That was rude!" Charity said, slapping her fiancé on the arm.

I just laughed and shoved the NY Yankees blue ball cap onto my head. "It's okay. He's right."

We handed our tickets to the agent at the gate and made our way down the jetway at the New Orleans International Airport.

Unfortunately, I hated to fly, and had only done it once or twice. To make matters worse, neither Nolan nor Charity had ever flown, nor had they even left the state of Louisiana that I knew of, for that matter. I was going to just have them both go, then decided that probably wasn't that smart of an idea. They were grown adults, but I didn't want them to get into any trouble. Besides, I needed to say goodbye. I decided to dye my whole head blond and I even grew a beard. I didn't look like me, but I still didn't plan on going to the funeral—well, not inside, anyway.

The flight went perfectly, thank God, and when we landed at the Rochester Airport, I breathed a sigh of relief. I had hired a car to take us to a hotel near the church where the ceremony was going to be, and I was again relieved to see a dark-skinned man in a suit holding a sign reading *Bishop*.

The town car took us to the Hilton and I paid and tipped him nicely. I instructed him to return the next day and pick us up for the funeral. I had booked us two rooms, and once we were settled in, I knocked on Nolan and Charity's door, my cell phone in my hand.

"Do you have everything set up?" I asked.

Nolan nodded and opened the door wide for me to enter. He led me to his laptop and showed me a demonstration. After hitting a few buttons on his phone, he waved it around the room and I was able to see the motion on his laptop screen. I smiled. "Perfect."

"Thank you for setting this up. I owe you."

"Nah, I'm happy to help. You helped me more than you know."

"Just remember, if anyone asks, tell them you were one of Dad's patients. There will be a ton there, so nobody will even think anything of it. I doubt anyone will even ask."

Nolan nodded. "Got it."

"Thank you for the hotel room," Charity drawled, twisting her long, curly red hair up into a clip thing at the back of her head. "I ain't ever been to New York. I'm so excited."

I chuckled at her heavy Southern drawl. "After the funeral tomorrow, we'll leave Rochester and go to New York City."

Her eyes went big. "Really?"

"Yes. You have to see the Big Apple. It's awesome."

She squealed. "I can't wait!"

My phone buzzed and I looked at the screen. Manta calling.

"See you in the morning, lovebirds," I said, letting myself out of the room. "Hello?"

"Hey, yourself. You guys make it there okay?" she asked, sounding like she just woke up.

"We did. It's weird being back here, I'm not going to lie," I said, being completely truthful. I felt paranoid and sad at the same time.

"Well, nobody's looking for a blond, bearded Dominic, so you'll be all right."

"Nobody's looking for Dominic, period," I reminded her.

"I am kinda digging the look, though," she said, and I could hear the smile in her voice.

I let myself into my room with the card key, took my glasses off, and plopped on the bed. "Oh yeah? You like beards? Find them sexy?"

She giggled. "I actually do."

I sighed. "I wish you could have come. Obviously, you can't ever travel on a plane, huh?" Something I never thought about before regarding vampires.

"I can and I have. Take the red-eye. However, you risk delays, and that turns into spending all day in an airplane lavatory until the sun goes down, and that makes for a very unpleasant trip."

"Holy fuck, that happened to you?"

She laughed. "No, someone I know, though. It took a hell of a lot of compulsion once he emerged from the bathroom to get him off the plane and not arrested, though."

I shuddered. "Yeah, car travel is probably best."

"Trains are okay, too, with your own cabin you can easily cover the windows if need be."

So much shit I hadn't even thought about. Was I committed to dating a vampire with all of these restrictions? Was she worth it? *Who am I kidding? I never travel, so who cares?*

"Are you nervous for tomorrow?" she asked.

"Hell yes. Not so much that I'll get recognized, but that I'm gonna lose it."

"It's okay to lose it, Kovah. You loved your dad, you can grieve him. And you should."

I blew out a breath and stared at the ceiling. "How did you do it? Deal with everyone you were close to dying?"

She was quiet for a minute. "After so many, they eventually stop, then you don't have to deal with it anymore. I know it sounds calloused, but it's the only way to cope." She paused and I didn't know what to say, especially since I was actually looking forward to not having to lose anyone I loved again. She continued, "You're the first one I've really let in in years, Kovah. Years."

Her words hit me with surprise, but they also made my cold heart stutter for a minute. "Is that so?" My only lame response.

"Yes. Please don't make me regret letting you in, okay?"

"I won't. And you won't. I am glad you did, though. Is there anything else going on there?"

I shouldn't have changed the subject so fast, but I couldn't heap any more emotional shit on myself right now. I was selfish like that.

"I..." she started. "It can wait 'til you get back."

I sat up. "No, tell me now."

She paused, then said, "I got another note. This time on my car windshield at work."

"Shit. What did it say?" I asked, my heart racing now.

"Let me read it to you: 'Your time is coming to an end. Don't try to figure out when because you won't. We will strike when you least expect. That freak hybrid can't protect you. We will slit his throat open while you watch him bleed, then you will be next. Traitors get no mercy. The Nighthawks are always watching.'"

"What the fuck!" I roared, standing up. "This is out of hand. I can't believe this." I began pacing, my boots thudding hard on the hotel room's floor. I raked my fingers through my hair. "I need to leave. I should be there. I'm sorry, I'll book the first flight—"

"No!" she said, cutting me off. "You're not leaving. You stay, and you do what you went there to do. I will be fine. I can take care of myself. I have several guns and am very perceptive. I haven't stayed alive this long without instincts. Besides, I think these jokers are bluffing."

That got me thinking. Now that I had spent time with them, I did wonder what they gained from threatening a lone female vampire. It wasn't like she was a hunter, she just worked for the government. I would be more of a target than she would be, yet, they had pretty much befriended me, and were now threatening me, too? It didn't make any sense. "What makes you think they're bluffing?" I asked her.

"Why warn me? I mean, just sneak up on me and take me out if you hate me that much, right? Why play games?"

She had a point, one I had thought about. "Maybe when you live that long, you enjoy the hunt. Right? Taunting and scaring someone, thriving off their fear? Like a sadistic thing?"

But these guys didn't seem sadistic. Although, I didn't know them that well. To me, they seemed like businessmen, mostly. I was sure they had an underlying reason for existing, for running a motorcycle club for vampires, but they didn't seem all that crazy.

"Perhaps," she said, sounding deep in thought.

"Well, after the funeral, we'll skip the rest of the trip and head home," I said matter-of-factly.

"No, you won't, Kovah. Take those kids to New York City. Don't ruin it for them. They probably won't get a trip like this anytime soon. I will be fine. I promise."

"I don't know…"

"I insist. I will text you frequently to let you know I'm okay."

I sighed, still pacing. "Calls and texts. And maybe a Skype thingie or FaceTime or whatever the hell it's called. I want to see you."

She laughed. "You got it. Now get some rest. I'll say a little prayer for you tomorrow. Call me when it's over."

No way would I sleep now, but instead I said, "Okay. Goodnight, gorgeous."

She smiled through her words. "Goodnight."

"You're not getting out, sir?" the driver, whose name was James, I'd learned, asked.

"No, just them," I said, watching Nolan and Charity get out, him in a black button-down shirt and black slacks, her in a modest black dress, her pale skin glowing against it, her mass of red curls piled on her head. They looked both ways and made their way to the front steps of St. Anthony's Catholic Church, arm-in-arm. The place Ma and Pop made me go every Sunday for too many years to count.

The nostalgia was hitting me like a brick wall.

"You don't mind sitting here until the service is over, do you?" I asked, handing him a hundred-dollar bill.

He looked down at it, smiling. "Not at all."

"Good. You'll get another one once it's over."

"Make yourself comfortable. Would you like some music?" he asked.

I shook my head. "Nah. Thanks, though, James."

I opened the small laptop and used the Wi-Fi hot spot on my phone to get a signal. I clicked the links Nolan had showed me. There was nothing but darkness, but he told me he had to connect to it once he got inside the church. I waited patiently, watching the funeralgoers through the car window.

I did not recognize most of them. It could be that people I once knew had aged, or that they were new friends or patients of my dad's. But then I caught sight of Ma. I sucked in a breath and watched as Leo and Heather helped her out of the car and up the steps. My sister Sophie, along with Josh, who was fully grown and now taller than her, trailed behind. I shoved my fist into my mouth as to not whimper like a baby at how old Ma had gotten. She looked so frail, moving slowly, her hair completely white. Leo wasn't looking so great himself, definitely middle-aged, the back and sides of his hair as white as Ma's, a small pot belly under his dress shirt and tie. Heather's hair was still platinum blonde, but she'd put on a little weight. They were flanked by two young adults I could only assume were my now-adult niece and nephew.

God, I'd missed so much. I started regretting coming here. This was too much. So much fucking pain trying to pierce my heart. It physically hurt. I moved my fist from my mouth and pressed it to my chest to stave off the agony, closing my eyes to get a grip.

I wanted to bolt. I wished I had my bike so I could hop on it and head to the water. To sit there and think, so feel the wind in my hair, the freedom of escape.

No, get a grip, man, I told myself.

Noise from the laptop caught my attention and I saw Nolan's face on the screen. He nodded and mouthed, "Here we go."

Then he flipped the camera around and set it on his knee. Thankfully he'd secured an aisle seat it looked like, so he was able to film it from waist-level.

Oh, my God, the minister, he was so old. What was his name? I couldn't remember. A large photo of Pop as I remembered him was set at the front of the church.

I watched in numb fascination as the service went on. What a good man he was. Faithful husband, good father, great, caring doctor. Then the minister brought up how strong Dad had been when his son, Dominic, had passed away. An audible sob from Ma was heard.

Dammit. I can't do this. I closed my eyes and resisted the urge to tell James to get me the hell out of here.

The rest of the service was pretty generic. I heard the priest announce a wake at Leo's house, but no way were we going there. The phone camera went black and I slammed the laptop shut with an exasperated grunt.

"Everything okay, sir?" James asked.

"Yeah, I'm good."

"Didn't want to go to the service?" he asked, not that it was his business.

I refrained from telling him so. "No, I'm sort of… estranged from them, if you feel me."

He nodded, looking at me with kind brown eyes in the rearview mirror. "I do."

"Thanks for staying."

"Of course." He got out of the car to open the door for Charity, who hopped in first, followed by Nolan.

"Did you get it?" he asked.

"Yes, all of it. Thank you. I think," I replied, my voice shaking against my will.

He looked at me with an expression of mixed sympathy and concern. "Everything okay?"

"That was rough. I'm hoping I don't regret this."

Charity put her hand on mine and looked at me with big blue eyes. In her thick drawl, she said, "I was thinkin' that the whole time. How awful this must be for you. But you won't regret it. You'll be happy you got to say goodbye in your own way."

I nodded and looked away.

"Your real name is Dominic, isn't it." Nolan said rather than asked.

I looked at him through my sunglasses. "It was. I changed it when I started over."

"I can't imagine, dude. This whole day has been surreal. I can't even fathom what you've gone through."

I had no response for that. So I said, "You can take us to the hotel now, James."

"Yes, sir," he said, putting the car in drive.

Chapter 29

PARTNERS IN CRIME

She was a sight for sore eyes, standing the doorway in nothing but a green dress that rested well above her knee. "Did you and the kids have fun in the big city?" Manta asked with a smirk.

"A blast. They won't stop talking about it," I said with a smile, closing her door behind me.

"One day you can take me—"

My mouth crashed down on hers, cutting her off, not sure why I'd missed her as much as I had. Her fingers tangled in my hair as I reach down to grip her very firm, very perfect ass. She'd barely closed the door when we found ourselves inside her bedroom. After slipping her dress off over her head, I threw it to the ground, then slid my hand around the back and unclasped her bra with one flick of my fingers. That went fluttering to the ground.

She broke our kiss to yank my black T-shirt off over my head, and then I felt her cool fingers break the snap on my jeans as I pushed her onto her bed. I groaned as she slid her hand into my pants, feeling how much I had missed her. I'd only been gone for three days but for some reason, it felt like longer. Probably because of all of this emotional shit I had had to deal with.

"I missed you," she murmured into my mouth, shoving my jeans down and yanking my glasses off, tossing them. I kicked out of my bottoms and we lay there making out like a couple of teenagers.

I finally broke our kiss, putting both hands on either side of her face. As I gazed into her dual-colored eyes, I said, "I missed you a hell of a lot more than I thought I would. Way more than I should. That scares the shit out of me."

She smirked at me, her fingers making circles against the back of my neck. "I'm scared, too. But I hope you'll take a chance on me, like I've taken one on you."

"Isn't it obvious? I'm here. I'm not going anywhere. I'll be here as long as you'll have me."

She smiled up at me right as I slid her panties off and pushed myself inside of her, and I loved watching her eyes slowly close in satisfaction. Mine did the same. We spent the rest of the night sexing each other up... talking in between... and not sleeping at all. She had solidified how much I had missed her. I was falling hard, and I hoped wouldn't regret it.

When it was time for the sun to begin its ascent into the sky, I showered quickly as she grew sleepy. I saw the vile note sitting on the little desk in her room and read it again.

I held it up. "I'm taking this."

"What are you going to do with it?" she asked sleepily.

"End this bullshit once and for all," I replied.

I went over and kissed her forehead, took a glance at the thick, plastic shutters on her window to ensure they were shut tight, and closed her bedroom door. As I made my way through her living room, I saw a small stack of papers on her kitchen island, so I made my way to them. There were four more notes from the Nighthawks threatening her in the same manner in the same type of language. The more I read them, the less threatening they seemed.

I shoved the notes into my pocket and left her house, locking the door behind me.

My phone buzzed in my pocket with a text.

Hawks: *We have another job for you.*

I replied immediately: *I'll be at your place at 6 tonight.*

Hawks: *That won't be necessary. I'll text you the details.*

Me: *No, I need to meet with you in person about another matter.*

Hawks: *Copy. See you at 6.*

I looked around Manta's neighborhood. It was mostly quiet, a few minivans and SUVs making their way through the streets to begin their day. I started up my rumbling Harley and headed to my place to get a couple hours' rest before I had to go into work. But before I could sleep, the first order of business was shaving my head to get rid of the blond, and then ridding myself of this itchy, irritating beard.

After that was taken care of, I went to bed and slept like a rock.

The door to the Nighthawks' clubhouse opened, Shadow greeting me with his usual impassive scowl. The guy was so hard to read. He rarely said anything and seemed to have a flat affect about him.

"I need to see Viper," I said.

He nodded and I followed him to Viper's office, where the Nighthawks' leader sat behind his desk looking at something on his laptop.

"Have a seat," he said, pointing to some chairs.

Shadow stayed put, hovering by the door with his arms folded. I thought about asking him to leave, but decided against it. Instead, I pulled the notes from my pocket and tossed them on Viper's desk.

He looked at me curiously, then the notes, picking up and scanning each one carefully. He looked at Shadow, and then held the papers out. He walked over and grabbed the notes, reading them over as well.

"Where did you get these?" Viper asked.

"The girl you're threatening, she's sort of my girlfriend, you could say."

Viper's eyebrows almost hit his hairline. "First off, we aren't threatening anyone, so let's get that straight right off the bat. Secondly, you're fucking another vampire?"

"Who I fuck isn't your business. I don't expect you, the goddamn government, or the devil himself to understand what I deal with living this type of life. I'm getting by the best I can. Secondly, if you're not threatening her, who is?"

He cut a glance at Shadow, who turned the deadbolt to the office and walked toward Viper, coming to stand behind him. "These letters went to a pretty dark-haired government agent, didn't they?" Shadow asked.

I nodded. "Yes, her name is Manta LaRae. She's pretty straight and by the book. And a rare but useful commodity to the BSI. You know what that is?"

Viper nodded, running his fingers over his chin before folding them together on the desktop. "Yes, we know about the BSI, and we're fairly sure they know about us. That being said, I don't think we're mutually threatening to each other. And in no way shape or form have we threatened or have any desire to kill any of their agents."

I lifted an eyebrow and pointed to the letters. "Then how did you know who those letters belonged to without me telling you?"

He looked once more at Shadow, then back at me. "I don't think I need to disclose that to you, but you can rest assured that we are going to be taking care of it swiftly."

I shook my head. "Not good enough, man. I need reassurance that Manta's not going to wake up one afternoon to an intruder in her house."

Viper again looked a little nervous, but quickly recovered. "She won't and we will see to it. Do you trust me?"

Piercing him with the same look I gave all vampires, I said, "No."

His mouth kicked up in a grin. "No?"

"You asked the wrong question. I don't trust anyone."

He nodded. "Fair enough, let me rephrase. Do you think a man's word is enough?"

Thinking for a minute, I said, "Yes. Or, at least, I think it should be."

"Well, then, you have my word that these letters did not come from us, and your vampire friend will be safe. How's that?"

Shocked, but with a feeling of relief flooding through me, I said, "I can live with that."

Shadow visibly relaxed and went back to post up at the doorway to Viper's office. "Now that we have that out of the way, we have a vampire that needs disposing of."

"A vampire, huh?" I said, intrigued and trying not to think of the conversation we'd just had about Manta's well-being.

"Yes, and this should be so easy that I'm only offering three grand for the job."

I said, "I'm listening."

He went on to explain that the vampire in question had evaded them at night for months. A female vampire who was turning humans recklessly, trying to make herself a posse of friends who hung out with her at local nightclubs. She'd finally crossed the line when she turned a red-haired, blue-eyed female, who had become a succubus.

"Kill, the leader, then the succubus."

I grinned. "This sounds more like fun than work."

"Precisely."

"Can I ask why you don't just march into the club and kill her yourself? Wait for her outside after closing?"

"She's onto us, answered Shadow in his deep voice. "She knows who we are and what all of us look like."

"We thought a young, good-looking guy like you could get close to her. We asked around and are quite impressed at how you took out Eva Sheridan."

I made a clicking noise with my tongue. "Uh-uh. I only helped with that. Nolan Bishop had to kill her himself. It was fun, though. I won't lie. That bitch was one nasty succubus."

Viper nodded. "Agreed, and we are already hearing rumblings of this vampire's new succubus looking to take her spot." He slid a manila folder to me and I opened it up. First sheet had a photo of a gorgeous brunette with long hair and striking green eyes. It looked like this photo was taken while she was still human, as she didn't quite look as polished and plastic as most vampires. Name: Hannah Giles, age 21 at turning. It had height, build, home address, place of employment (none), and where she liked to hang out, what types of humans she liked to feed from, etc. Second page had an equally beautiful redhead, with her hair cropped short in a punk-type of style, big blue eyes, light smattering of freckles across her face. She looked to be really thin. Name: Emma Hayes, age 23 at turning with the rest of the info.

I closed the file and looked at the two bikers. "Seems easy enough. Today's Friday, I'll head to their favorite club tonight. I'm glad it's not the Blue Room, though. I don't think I'm allowed in there again." I chuckled.

"I'm all hyped up!" Nolan said, grabbing his keys and phone from the kitchen counter of his apartment and checking his reflection in his front window. He quickly pulled the curtains shut and went for the door.

I laughed. "Your girl not bustin' your balls for agreeing to be my wingman tonight, is she?"

He cut a glance at me, grabbing small, black bottle of something and spraying it on himself before silently offering me some. I shook my head no.

"Well, she was more worried about me being around vampires than actually going to this nightclub, if that's what you mean."

I nodded as he opened the door and indicated for me to walk out. He closed and locked it behind him with a key, then twisted the doorknob just to be sure.

"I get it. I just don't want to jam you up, man. You seem like you have a good thing going there. I just thought it would look weird if I showed up alone there, like some creeper, and most of the Riders are a bit old to be hanging out at the newest country bar in town."

We took Nolan's kickass, loud as hell, cool as shit black Dodge Charger to the club. We both got out and stared at the huge lighted coyote on the roof of the place. *The Tipsy Coyote* was spelled out in red lights underneath.

"Charming," Nolan said dryly.

I snorted. "Fucking stupid. Let's go inside and find these bloodsuckers."

I handed the pretty girl in the short-shorts and cowboy hat a twenty-dollar bill for our cover charges, and she stamped our hands. As we wandered inside, something loud and twangy blasted from the speakers. People were swing-dancing on the massive dance floor. I looked at my watch and saw it was a little past ten p.m. and the place was pretty busy.

"Beer?" Nolan asked, pointing toward the bar.

"Yeah."

I followed him over. He ordered two bottles of whatever and we sipped them while scanning the bar. I had showed Nolan the photos ahead of time so we could spot the beautiful monsters.

It did not take long. With a feeling of heaviness in my chest and a tingle racing up my spine, I looked to the dance floor as a slow song even twangier than the last began to play and the lights dimmed. Both Hannah and Emma found dance partners, and were soon pushed up against two poor, clueless human guys in big belt buckles and ten-gallon hats. With their arms wrapped around the girls, they swayed hard to the music, trying to talk into their ears. Small talk, I was sure.

We watched carefully as nothing at all happened. When the song ended, I recognized the music to be from Lady Antebellum, a song about just needing someone to spend the night with, and I watched as they continued to dance with the clueless humans. I looked at Nolan and grinned as I tossed my beer into a nearby trash can. "Time to cut in."

He smiled and did the same with his beer.

"You take the redhead," I said.

"Duh," he replied.

I pointed a finger at him. "Don't look in her eyes. And don't even come close to kissing her," I warned him.

He pointed at himself. "Not my first rodeo."

I bit back a laugh as we made our way to the dance floor. I tapped the guy dancing with Hannah on the shoulder. He turned and looked at me in annoyance. "What?"

"Take a hike, dude. That's my girl."

He let go of her. "What the hell, man?"

I ignored him as he huffed and walked off. Then I looked at her. "Hi."

She totally rolled with it, grinning. "Hi, cutie."

I looked at Nolan, who seemed to be having a very similar scenario.

"What's your name?" she asked in my ear, pressing her body closer to mine, emphasizing the groin-to-groin contact.

"Dominic," I replied. What's yours?"

"Hannah," she replied.

"I saw you dancing and just had to talk to you," I drawled, my eyes traveling the length of her body, the skirt she wore showing off the curve of her ass. I barely had to look down to be able to see what color bra she wore under her tight tank top.

Thankfully, the song ended fairly quickly and Nolan and I followed the girls back to their corner booth, where two more females and two males sat. All vampires. The heaviness in my chest and shivers were out of control now. I struggled to remain aloof and cool. I was damn near in pain.

"Have a seat, Dominic," she said, indicating an empty chair. I briefly looked around and sat, watching as Nolan did the same. The bold redhead just went ahead and sat in Nolan's lap. He was a big guy, about six-foot-three like me, and she was tiny. Guessed she didn't see any harm in it, even though I knew the bitch was dangerous as hell.

Hannah made a lame introduction to her group of friends, but I paid no attention to their names. Then she began dominating the conversation and I could tell she was sort of the leader of these leeches. Soon after, four more came along. From where, I didn't know, nor did I care. My chest ached and I felt like I had done speed. To say I was on edge was an understatement. This was how I always felt when I was in the Nighthawks' clubhouse, the natural instincts that warned me that vampires were around humming through my body.

When a popular song started up, four of the young vampires got up and left to dance. "You wanna dance?" I said to Hannah, following their lead.

I cut a glance at Nolan. He gently pushed the succubus off his lap and grabbed her hand.

Instead of the dance floor, however, I led Hannah to the back of the club and Nolan and his redhead followed.

"Oooh, where are we going?" she asked.

"Just roll with it, sweetheart."

Soon we were in the parking lot of the nightclub. I pushed her up against a random car and leaned down like I was going to kiss her.

"Why don't you take off those glasses? I haven't seen your eyes all night."

I shook my head. "They're nothing special."

Glancing to my left, I could see Nolan had followed me out and the redhead had her arms around his neck, her backside against his Charger. He leaned down to kiss her, but she used one hand to move his face to look into her eyes.

He resisted her.

I wasn't going to play this fucking game. Hannah's mouth was on my neck, running kisses from my collarbone to my ear while standing on tiptoe.

With supernatural speed, I shoved the vampire off me and pulled out my .22 pistol from the small of my back. I moved Nolan out of the way and quickly shot three bullets into the succubus's chest. She screeched.

Hannah screamed at the top of her lungs like she was the star in a horror movie. Then, with vampire speed, she took off running. She hadn't even rounded the building to head back inside when I caught up to her, grabbing a fistful of hair to take her down. She tried to fight me, but she wasn't old enough to be stronger than me. I easily subdued her, putting two shells into her chest. She screamed one last time, but there was no way anyone heard it over the loud music floating out of the club.

I dragged her over to where Nolan stood staring at a shriveled body. When Hannah's body began to decay under my grip, I let go and pulled out my cell phone, snapping a picture of dead Emma the succubus, then a couple of dead Hannah, who turned to ash painfully slow.

"That's freakin' gross," Nolan said, looking at what was left of Hannah.

"Young vampire. The younger they are, the longer it takes for them to ash. She was just turned like a year ago. Still sort of human."

Nolan gasped. "Is that true? Did you just kill a human girl?"

I laughed. "I didn't say she was human. I said they still have human-like qualities. Trust me, they both needed to go. Especially that scary, evil ginger there." I pointed to Emma's corpse with my gun.

Nolan stared down at it and shuddered. "What now?"

I pulled a lighter from my back pocket used my thumb to snap it to life. Bending down, I lit the clothes Hannah had left behind, watching them catch fire, then lit the hair of the succubus. Her body went up in flames easily enough. Keeping watch, we both gazed at our destruction in satisfaction as two more beautiful monsters were taken off the street tonight. I pulled a pack of cigarettes from my pocket and shook one out, then lit it with the fire on Emma. After taking a long drag, I snapped two more pics with my phone. I re-pocketed the phone and cigs, put out my fist, and Nolan bumped his with mine as we made our way to the parking lot to get into his car.

"That was seriously insane. I wanna do it again!" he said.

I just laughed. I was sure he would get lots of opportunities when he joined the BSI one day.

"Hannah!"

We both turned to see one of her pale vampire cronies come walking out of the club looking around and calling for her.

"That's our cue to leave," I murmured to Nolan, pushing him toward his car. He pulled his keys from his pocket and disarmed his beauty. We both hopped in. His car was pealing out of the parking lot before the vampire could reach the charred remains of her friends.

Chapter 30

BLITZED

I left Nolan feeling happy and accomplished after our kills. He was on a post-homicidal high and I chuckled at his enthusiasm because I could most certainly relate. Ridding the world of nasty monsters was the best feeling *ever*.

Sometimes I wondered why I didn't feel any guilt or remorse after ending a vampire. I could count on one hand the times I felt a twinge of guilt, but it was usually the females and ones who had begged for their lives. Normally, I did not give them time to speak at all, but occasionally I'd get a chatty one. That was back when I was just obliterating any vampire I crossed paths with. I thought they all should die. I'd never met one that behaved normally, really, until I met Joel Reichert last year. He had helped out Nolan when he didn't have to, although I had always felt he'd had an ulterior motive to do so. Then Violet — Manta — came back into my life. She'd always been the exception to the thought that all vamps were monsters. Twenty years ago, she'd tried to save me when I just wanted to die. She could have helped me drown instead of saving me from the icy black waters. I never forgot that, but back then I was too angry to be grateful. I supposed I would always be pissed off at the hand I was dealt, but I'd like to think I've chilled a little. I just don't think they'll ever be a day when I will let a succubus live, though. They're just too fucking dangerous, and those who create them need to be held accountable — or at the very least educated on what happens when they decide to turn a red haired, blue-eyed human into a vampire.

My phone chiming brought me out of my musings. The Nighthawks had replied to my texts that they'd received the photos and I was to report to their clubhouse ASAP. As I headed there, I hoped this trip would be quicker. I had things to do, like my sexy girlfriend.

After parking my bike at the side entrance, I looked around carefully and then knocked on the door. Shadow answered and quickly shoved an envelope at me, not even opening the door all the way.

"Here's your three grand, plus another for your friend for helping out. Sorry we can't chat, club business," he said quietly.

I heard a male voice yelling and Shadow looked over his shoulder, then back at me. For the first time, he looked stressed.

"Everything all right?" I asked, curious, but not really caring that much.

He shook his head. "Gotta go." Then he closed the door in my face and I heard the locks click into place.

I looked around the darkness of the alley once more and then quickly opened the envelope. Four bundles. I'd have to count it later. I sort of felt an urgency to get the hell outta there.

I heard a scream of pain coming from a male voice and told myself it was none of my business. I knew enough about not only these types of clubs, organizations, or gangs—whatever you wanted to call them, along with knowing plenty about vampires, that they were probably just handling some internal business, maybe some discipline. Or perhaps they were torturing someone. For whatever reason, I felt like I should leave them to it, that they probably had good reason. These guys weren't irrational, impulsive leeches. They were old, they were organized, and they seemed to know what the hell they were doing.

As I reached home, I put the key into the lock of the back door to Archie's Garage. I then locked it behind me and sprinted up the steps to get to my flat. Once inside, I also locked that door. I sat down on the bed and counted the money. True to their word, I smiled and re-bundled the money, setting one bundle aside for Nolan. My phone buzzed with a text.

Nolan: *I had fun earlier. We need to do that more often.*

I chuckled and replied: *Don't hold your breath, man. I don't like putting you in danger, and that could have gotten ugly real fast.*

Nolan: *Still, I'll sleep better knowing that nasty bitch is gone. Dinner tomorrow? Charity's taking night classes, and I'm bored.*

Me: *So you only want to hang out with me cuz you're bored? I see how you are.*

Nolan: *Very funny. Dinner or not? I want some shrimp.*

Me: *Sure, I have something to give you anyway. Text me with the where and when.*

Nolan: *Cool.*

My phone rang as I was holding it. Manta.

"Hey, sexy," I answered. God, I was turning into such a pussy. First a bromance-slash-man date with Nolan, and now I was talking goo-goo to a chick.

"Have a nice day?" she asked.

"Killing vampires is always a nice day," I said, and then immediately regretted my words.

She was quiet for a minute and when I went to stutter out an apology, she said, "Kovah, what did you do?"

"Look, I should have said '*bad* vampires and succbuses but it came out wrong."

"Succubi. Plural."

I rolled my eyes but smiled at her little joke. "I took a job from the Nighthawks."

"Tell me."

"Can I come over and tell you in person?" I asked, smiling.

"See you in fifteen," she replied, a grin in her voice before she ended the call.

Her door hadn't even closed before I had her pressed up against the wall of her living room, kissing the hell out of her.

She reached up, grabbed the top of my hair, and used her other hand to squeeze my ass. I grinded my hips into hers and then reached down and pulled her legs around my waist, never breaking our kiss. I licked along the seam of her mouth, demanding she open up for me, and she did immediately with a groan. I used one arm to hold her ass against me, as her legs were locked tight, and the other I used to fist her long, black hair. It felt silky and exotic against my fingertips.

We continued to kiss and suck on each other's mouths and lips until I reached her room. I gently put her on the bed and began unsnapping my jeans. She tossed her fitted blue T-shirt off over her head and I did the same with my tee after wiggling out of my jeans.

She suddenly got on all fours on the bed and crawled toward me as I stood there on the edge. I was straining against my boxers, but she took care of that for me. Pulling down my boxer briefs, she smiled up at me before taking me into her mouth. I let out a sharp hiss and then groaned, throwing my head back. I put my hands into her hair once more and used my fingertips to massage her scalp as she used her mouth to massage me.

I felt like a teenager as I quickly got close to coming… but I wanted her body now. I pulled her hair, guiding her off me and onto the bed.

She smiled. "Is that all you got?"

"Fuck no," I replied, laughing. I fisted her hair and gently pushed her face into the bed. With me behind her, I tore off her tiny lace panties and then slammed into her silky heat, still holding her hair.

"Oh, God, Kovah. Yes," she moaned.

I moved faster, but knew I wasn't going to last long. I reared my arm back, and with an open palm, landed a sharp smack onto her ass.

"Yes, spank me harder," she breathed.

I chuckled and pulled her hair back as I leaned down. "Don't tell me what to do. I will spank you when I want, and as how hard I want." Then I slammed a quick kiss onto her lips using my control over her head with her hair to turn her face to me.

I let go, then landed a harder smack onto her other ass cheek. She cried out, but it wasn't in pain. I felt her clench around me, and then scream that she was coming.

It was then I let go… all the stress and adrenaline from the day releasing inside of her with a final hard thrust and a guttural grunt. Collapsing on top of her back, I whispered into her ear, "You're a naughty little thing. Next time I'm bringing a riding crop."

She giggled. "Bring it on, baby."

I laughed. I *so* didn't own a riding crop.

That reminded me of Janice. She hadn't called or texted in weeks. I felt bad for blowing her off, but shit… I didn't know what else to do. I didn't want her. I only wanted Manta—in every way. But I was a dude, and apparently, a dick like that.

I felt it was time that Nolan met Manta, so I asked him if it was okay if I brought her to dinner the following night. He, of course, agreed because he was cool as fuck that way. Besides, it would seem less like a man-date if we had a girl with us.

We agreed to meet at Andy's Oyster House, a joint on the water that looked like it used to be some kind of boathouse. We had to climb a steep set of wooden stairs to get to the restaurant because the whole thing was on stilts. It was rustic and amazingly cool.

Nolan was waiting for us in front of the hostess station, and I introduced them.

"Nolan, this is my girlfriend, Manta. Manta, this is my man, Nolan."

"Nice to meet you," they said in unison, shaking hands.

The hostess led us to a table next to a window so we could look out at the glittering lights of the boats and yachts that were bobbing on the lake.

"I'm your girlfriend, huh?" Manta whispered too low for anyone but me and whatever vampire might be around to hear.

We were holding hands like a couple of sappy teenagers and I leaned down and said, "Well, since you're the only woman I want to see, spend time with, and fuck, I think that makes you my girlfriend."

She laughed and then slapped my arm. "You're so crass!"

A thought suddenly hit me, and my face darkened. "You're not..." I chose my words carefully, "seeing anyone else, are you?"

Her eyes went wide. "God, no! You've definitely broken my long dry spell."

"I find it hard to believe you've had a dry spell." I laughed. "You're gorgeous. You can get anyone."

"Here you are," the hostess said, setting three menus on the table as soon as we were seated next to the huge plate-glass window.

I handed Nolan an envelope.

"What's this?" he asked.

"A little thank-you from the Nighthawks for your help last night."

He opened up the envelope and his eyes went wide. I watched as he reached inside and took a quick look around the restaurant. Nobody was looking at us, but I still said, "No, don't take it out. Count it later."

His brow furrowed, and he looked worried. He also looked around before saying, "This isn't dirty money, is it?"

I laughed. "What *is* dirty money, exactly?"

He licked his lips, his green eyes wide. "Like, blood money, you know, obtained illegally for killing people."

I wanted to pop off a comment about how vampires weren't people, but with Manta there I had to choose my words more carefully. "That's for helping kill the succubus. I don't know how the Nighthawks get their money but just enjoy it. You risked your very human life. You deserve it. In fact, they told me to give it to you, and they are grateful."

His face relaxed and he tucked the envelope into the pocket of his jacket hanging on the back of his chair.

When the server came, we ordered oysters, shrimp, and tequila. Well, Manta had a margarita but Nolan and I ordered a few shots before we settled on beer.

"Oysters are supposed to be an aphrodisiac," Manta said suggestively, knowing that Nolan was already kind of tipsy.

I laughed. "So I've heard, but their effect is probably as effective as this booze." I pointed to our empty glasses.

It took a shitload of alcohol to get me drunk, or even tipsy, so I could imagine how much it took a full-blooded vampire. I realized over the years it was just too expensive to figure out. I could count on one hand the number of times I'd actually been shitfaced drunk in the last twenty years. It had taken an entire bottle of whatever to get me there. It had numbed the pain and made me smile, but I had paid for it the next day.

The meal was great, the service was great, the conversation had been great. As we descended the stairs after paying the bill, I had a smile on my face and my arm slung around my beautiful girlfriend, us laughing and happy from the perfect night out.

I stepped off the last stair and rounded it to get to my bike. I walked Manta toward her car, when I looked up. A group of people, probably about six of them, stood at the edge of the parking lot, arms folded, alabaster skin glowing under the full moon that shone down on us.

My chest began to grow heavy and a tingle ran up my spine. Crap. Not in the mood to fight, and concerned for my buddy and girl, I ignored them and walked toward Manta's car.

"This your Charger?" one asked Nolan, approaching him slowly as Nolan disarmed the car with the key fob.

Nolan looked at me, and then at the young man—the vampire. "Yeah, so?"

With supernatural speed, the vampire was within a foot of him and punched Nolan in the jaw.

Manta and I used our speed to rush over and get him away from Nolan. I grabbed him by the collar and punched him back, where he fell to the ground. Manta was knelt down, making sure Nolan was okay.

"What the fuck, man!" I said, looking down at the vampire. I looked up to see his friends approaching us slowly.

The vampire got up and tried to hit me again and then all hell broke loose. I was trying to control this guy, but worried about my friends. "Get out of here, man!" I snapped at Nolan, but of course he was no match for three vampires. Two held him while a third punched him in the stomach.

The two females grabbed Manta and began punching and kicking her. From the corner of my eye, I could see her holding her own, though. The vampires looked no more than teens, and even though I knew they could be much older than that, they didn't seem like they were. Manta grabbed one by the hair and swung her around, tossing her across the parking lot like she was nothing more than a ragdoll. She grabbed the remaining female and proceeded to mop up the parking lot with her. I smiled as I put my assailant in a headlock.

He struggled against my hold so I twisted his head. "I'm gonna break your fucking neck. What the hell do you want?"

"Get off me, man!" he growled, his fangs out as he was trying to bite my arm. I reached around and punched him in the mouth.

I looked over to see Nolan unconscious on the ground, the vampires still kicking him. I punched my guy one more time, breaking his nose, and then threw him to the ground.

Pulling the .22 pistol from the small of my back, I fired three shots into the heads of the vampires kicking Nolan. They went down in heaps, quickly turning to ash, and I bent down to see if Nolan was at least alive. I breathed a sigh of relief when I felt his breath rush out in shallow gasps.

"We need to get him to a hospital," I said to a very disheveled Manta, who came up to me. I looked over to see two piles of women's clothes covering ash. She nodded and I heard sirens in the distance. I didn't know if they were for us, but I knew we had to get out of there. Someone probably heard the gunshots.

I remembered there was one vampire left. He was out cold from where I'd punched him, so I went over, grabbed him, and dragged him over to

Nolan's car.

"Pop the trunk," I said to Manta after she was done laying Nolan in the backseat. She fumbled around until she found the latch and opened it. I was happy to see two short bungee cords in his trunk and I used these to bind the vampire's arms and legs before I tossed him in there and slammed it shut.

Quickly gathering up the clothing piles, I tossed those onto the floorboards of the backseat. I found the car keys on the ground where Nolan must have dropped them during the assault and hopped into the driver's seat, the three of us taking off quickly.

"Before you ask, we're dropping Nolan off at the hospital, where we will compel whoever we need to not to ask questions and forget who dropped him off, then we're taking this joker someplace private where we can have a chat." I jabbed a thumb behind me.

Manta smiled. "I wasn't going to ask, but sounds like a plan to me."

After doing exactly as we said we would, I left the hospital, feeling worried for my friend. I hoped the doctors and nurses could help Nolan. I hoped his injuries weren't serious. I purposely left his wallet and phone on him so he could call me once he woke up. I felt bad I couldn't call Charity, but he'd also have to do that himself as I didn't have her number.

Banging and yelling from the trunk alerted us that our little prisoner had awoken. I drove toward the warehouses on the water and stopped in front of a set of storage units. Archie owned one and kept it empty, save for a few weapons and torture devices, and two wooden chairs.

I handed Manta my phone. "Text Archie and tell him to meet me at the unit."

She nodded and fumbled with my smartphone until she found the contact and then sent him the text.

The phone chimed almost immediately and she read to me, "How many you got?"

"Tell him one," I instructed.

The phone beeped again. "He says 'copy'."

"We need to go back to that damn place and get my bike after this," I said to her.

"I'm sure it's fine. It's better we're not there right now. Hopefully the cops see nothing and assume it was a false call."

"We don't even know if those sirens were for us, anyway," I replied.

More banging and yelling from the trunk.

"Think he can get those bungee cords off?" I asked Manta quietly.

"You tied them pretty tight. They're probably cutting off his circulation." She laughed.

I hit a stoplight, reached over, and pulled a leaf out of her hair. I noticed a purple bruise beginning to blossom on her pretty cheek and her knuckles were already scabbed up. "Are you okay?"

She smiled. "Eh, it was just a cat fight. My scalp hurts more than anything. Why do bitches always want to pull hair?"

I bit back a smile. "I thought you liked that."

She chuckled as the light turned green. "Only when you do it."

SING LIKE A CANARY

anta popped open the trunk while I used both hands to grip the pistol and aim it at the trunk. When it flung open, the vampire's eyes were jet-black and his fangs were protruding out of his mouth. The dried blood under his nose looked garish and disgusting. Thankfully, his hands were still bound. I reached down, pulled the cord off his ankles, and threw it back into Nolan's trunk.

"Pull him out," I told Manta.

She reached down, grabbed his arm, and hoisted him out.

"Where are we?" he asked, looking around. His eyes had gone back to normal, but he hissed at me as he said it.

I used the flat of my hand to slap the side of his head. "Don't fucking hiss at me. And don't ask questions. I don't like it."

"Ow!" he bellowed.

I heard the rumble of a motorcycle just as Archie pulled up. Manta and I held our vampire prisoner, each taking an arm, when Archie killed the engine to his bike and put the kickstand down. He chuckled at what he saw, then punched a code into the storage unit's door. It swung open and we escorted the vampire inside, flipped on the lights, then closed the door behind us. I plopped him in the chair, careful to loop his still-bound hands over the back of the chair.

I pulled the other chair from the corner and flipped it around backward, straddling it. I rested my arms on its high back.

"Hi," I said into his face. The harsh fluorescent lights from the storage unit made his pale skin almost see-through, and now that his eyes were back to normal, I could see that they were a light crystal-blue. Blond hair that would never again shine in the sun was too long, pulled back into a stubby ponytail at the base of his neck. If I had to guess, I'd say he was probably in his mid-20s when he was turned. He looked young—and he looked scared.

He ignored my greeting and just stared me. His blue eyes held and edge of fear, but he was trying to hide it, and failing miserably.

"What's your name?" I asked him.

He glared at me, saying nothing.

Archie and Manta stood behind me. I saw him flick his gaze to them, then back to me.

"You're right, it's not important," I said, smiling coldly. "You wanna tell me what possessed you and your leech pals to beat the shit out of my defenseless human friend back there?" I pierced him with what I'd hoped was an intimidating stare.

He didn't break. He just kept quiet.

Pulling the switchblade from my pocket, I flicked it open. His eyes went wide right before I raised it up, twirled it twice, and then jammed it into his left thigh.

He screamed in pain and began hollering profanities.

I smiled as I pulled the knife out, his black blood dripping all over the floor. "Next time I'm going to leave it in so you can't heal. You'll bleed out through that big-ass femoral artery."

He glared at me with hatred and pain in his eyes, and then spat in my face.

Archie ran toward him, reared his arm back, and slammed his fist into his nose, re-breaking it. "Don't spit, you bloodsucking piece of shit!"

I watched in amusement as Archie shook his fist out. That had to have hurt. He looked at Manta. "No offense."

She grinned and shook her head.

The vamp was screaming in pain again.

"It's a simple question, really," I said, wiping my hand on my jeans after having to use my palm to wipe off the asshole's spit from my face.

He remained silent after his screaming fit, glaring at me.

Twirling the switchblade around in my hand, I brought it high, over my head, and made a motion like I was going to slam it into his thigh again, where the wound was far from being healed yet.

"No!" he screamed.

I kept the knife up but chuckled. "Oh, you can speak?"

He eyed the knife as my hand twitched. "The guy in the Charger, you... he ... killed our friends."

I lifted an eyebrow and lowered the knife. "Go on."

Swallowing hard, his scared eyes on the knife, he continued. "At the Tipsy Coyote. You guys killed Hannah and Emma."

I brought the knife down but plunged it into the wood seat of the chair instead of his leg. He squealed and flinched.

"It was just business. You took that shit personal?" I asked, slightly amused.

Eyes wide, he said, "Hannah sired me, so yes, I do. Don't you know anything?"

In a dramatic gesture to get my point across, I raised an eyebrow and looked first to Manta, then to Archie, then back to my suspect. "Did you just say she *sired* you?"

He nodded.

"You mean she victimized you? First, by first ripping into your neck, wrist, or another major artery and taking your blood? And then, when you were close to death, she ripped open one of her own arteries and shoved her disgusting black blood down your throat so you could lose three days of your life and rise a bloodsucking demon who can't go out in the sunlight? That sounds *awesomely* romantic. Where do I sign up?"

He scowled at me. "You are twisting things."

I gritted my teeth. "No, asshole. *You're* the one who's got things twisted. Vampires like you and your friends need to cease to exist. Look what you did tonight. You put a human in the fuckin' hospital, you ripped a pretty girl's shirt" — I inclined my head toward Manta — "and you broke my fucking sunglasses." I pulled them off since one of the lenses was cracked all the way down the middle.

The vampire gasped at my eyes, his own widening.

"Do you not know anything about what a succubus can do?" I groaned.

He nodded. "Yes."

"You need to steer clear of them. As of today, me, my friends, and a group of bikers called the Nighthawks, who you better hope you never fucking meet, are declaring war on every succubus in this city."

His eyes went wide. "I don't think there are any more. You killed

Emma and I heard Eva was killed, too."

Chuckling, I said, "Yes, my human friend you put in the hospital? He killed her earlier this year. She tried to victimize him, so he took care of her. You guys may have ambushed him tonight, but I'm telling you right now, you need to stay the fuck away from him. He's not one to be fucked with and is under our protection."

"It doesn't matter. I'm leaving town, anyway. You killed everyone I know tonight." He licked his lips as the blood from his nose began to dry there as he looked away.

"Are you going to cry?" I asked, amused, but still too angry to care. "You must be very new."

He looked back at me and nodded. "I've only been a vampire for eight months."

Archie whistled through his teeth. "That was a bad decision, kid."

"I'm beginning to see that," he murmured under his breath. "I didn't even want to go tonight. I mean, I was upset about Hannah, but I still didn't feel like I had a dog in that fight. Something told me you guys had killed them for a reason."

"Basically, they were after the succubus and the other one got in the way. We also happened to know she was carelessly turning teens and young adults and we can't be having that. There are rules, and a code," Manta said, speaking for the first time.

He shook his head as he looked at her. "I don't know anything about a code. And I didn't know there were rules."

I wasn't so sure Manta was telling the truth, but I just rolled with it. "Well, there are, and it's unfortunate your *sire* didn't tell you about them."

He just hung his head.

I looked at Arch and Manta and stood up, inclining my head for them to follow me. Leaving the unnamed kid in the storage unit, I went outside and shut the door.

"Kill him or let him go?" I asked. "Popular vote wins."

"Let him go," Manta said.

"Archie?"

He looked pensive as he shoved his hand in his pocket, the other he used to hold himself up on the cane. "I don't know. I'm not keen on letting a loose cannon like that one live. Kind of goes against the Riders' code, if you catch my drift."

"Not all vampires are bad, boss," I said, and I was surprised by my own words.

He narrowed his eyes at me, then flicked his gaze to Manta, who tossed some black hair over her shoulder as she studied him. Archie pierced me with his eyes. "You gettin' soft in your old age?"

The way he'd asked the question didn't seem confrontational or that of annoyance. It was almost playful as I saw him look at Manta once more.

"I guess I am. Love does that to a guy." Once again, my mouth spoke without my permission.

I couldn't dismiss the sound of surprise that came from Manta's mouth, so I turned and covered hers with mine. She gasped again as I kissed her, but I only smiled as my hand cupped her jaw.

Breaking the kiss, I looked at Archie. "We were born to make choices. We are given the opportunity to discern right from wrong, to know when things are bad and when things are good. Are we not?"

He looked both confused and amused. "You got a point, Kovah. My vote is whatever you feel is best in regards to this vampire kid."

"My vote is to let him live — or continue to exist."

I looked over to see Manta smiling at Archie. "You chose well."

"He could be lying about his age. He could be one-hundred and fifty years old and we'd never know. That's what concerns me. He could be so completely sociopathic that he's mastered the art of acting," I said.

Manta shook her head. "I can see why you think that way, but I watched him as you stabbed him. He was in real pain, and that was real fear in his eyes. This guy is no actor. I truly believe him to be a new vampire. His eyes turned black as you stabbed him. Older vampires have way more control than that. Plus, an older vampire would have beat your bullshit bungee cord restraints and kicked the trunk open and ran off."

I looked at her, feigning mock insult. "Bullshit restraints? Well, I will show you later how *bullshit* my restraints can be."

She laughed.

Archie groaned. "It's past my bedtime. Cut the leech loose with a warning." He headed back toward his bike. "And lock up when you're done. The code is 12859. Goodnight, kid."

I looked at him curiously. "Twelve-eight-fifty-nine, got it. Any reason you picked those numbers?"

He chuckled. "I'm a Sagittarius. Figure it out, kid."

His birthday. Real smart. I shook my head with a rueful grin as he rode away, his bike rumbling off down the street.

Manta and I looked at each other and grinned right before we went to the storage unit and freed the vampire from his bungee cord restraints. Without so much as a thank-you, he bolted for the door. We watched as he took off down the street at warp speed, hoping he could walk a straight line and get the hell out of town.

So much for a warning.

Chapter 32

THE TRUTH COMES OUT

I hadn't gone into work today from being up all night, so I was more than wide awake. I'd been picking Manta up from work at the BSI's government building downtown on the nights she actually had to go into work, and it was here that I sat in my Firebird I rarely used, waiting for her. I killed the engine and parked at the back of the lot, where its orange light couldn't illuminate me. Once she would make her way out, I would drive toward the front door and pick her up. Between those creepy ass notes she kept getting signed by the Nighthawks, and the incident at the restaurant, I felt like I needed to keep a close eye on her, even though Viper had assured me it wasn't them.

The thought was irony gone wild for sure—if you'd have told me a year ago I'd be protecting a vampire instead of killing one, I would have told you to go see a shrink. I laughed to myself. I was grateful that, fortunately, she got to telecommute from home a lot, but was required to go into work some nights as soon as the sun went down for meetings and to use the computers and access files. Not my cup of tea, but she seemed to like her job a lot.

I picked up the phone and dialed Nolan.

"Hello?" he answered.

"You alive?" I asked.

He chuckled. "Ow. Don't make me laugh. Four broken ribs and a concussion. I so did not need a concussion. I probably lost some brain cells. I need those for school."

I bit back a laugh. "Two vampires kicked your ass and you're only worried about school?"

"Dude. I could have used you when the cops came to question me after I woke up in the hospital. They wanted to know who the guys were, why they'd 'jumped' me, if I provoked them, and a zillion other questions. It sucked."

"Sorry, man. If you would have called, I would have come down. I didn't even think about the cops. I just knew you needed some serious medical attention and I kinda panicked."

"Well, I'm okay."

He got quiet for a minute, so I asked, "You sure?"

"Yes. But do you want to hear something weird?" He lowered his voice.

"What?" I asked.

He cleared his throat. "I heal a lot faster than I used to."

Huh. That was weird. Nolan had had his soul almost taken by Eva, the succubus, but when he killed her, all his weird, developing vampire traits, like craving for blood and an aversion to the sun, had gone away. We all thought he had gone back to 'normal'—whatever that was.

"That's interesting. You should tell the BSI. Let them do some more blood tests and shit."

"I will. But I won't lie, this is one trait I'll gladly take. Broken ribs ain't no joke," he drawled. "So glad I'm not in more pain."

"Me too," I said. "Oh, by the way, I stopped by the Stop-N-Shop to give your girl your car keys, but she wasn't there."

He chuckled. "Yes, I... highly encouraged her to quit that stupid job. She doesn't need to be working in some seedy dark corner store. I told her just to concentrate on school."

"Aww, look at you being all protective and shit."

"Shut up, asswipe. So what happened to the vampires after I passed out?" he asked.

"Gone, all but one. We threw him in your trunk after I broke his nose, so... sorry about the blood," I said. "Took him somewhere private and tortured some information out of him. After a few pokes from my knife, he folded like a lawn chair." I chuckled at my stupid pun. "Basically, he was pissed we had killed the chick vamps and wanted revenge. I told him he was a pussy for taking on the poor, defenseless human."

He laughed. "Ow." He hissed in a breath. "It was definitely a dick move."

"So are you still in the hospital?" I asked.

"Nah, Charity picked me up this morning, but I'd like my car back."

"It's parked at Archie's. You can get it tomorrow when you come to work," I joked.

"Okay," he said.

I gasped. "Dude, I was kidding. You aren't coming to work tomorrow with broken ribs. I already filled Archie in."

He hesitated. "Well…"

I saw Manta walk out of the building. "Gotta go, man. I'll text you about the car."

"Cool, bye," he replied.

I narrowed my eyes when I saw something not quite right. I whipped off my sunglasses to get a better look. "What the fuck?"

What I saw made me do a double-take. A guy dismounted his motorcycle, put the kickstand down, and then looked around the parking lot. He headed straight for Manta's little sports car. We normally just left it in the parking lot on the nights I picked her up and then I would drive her to work the next evening.

My first inclination was to rush over there and rip his head off for touching her car, but I, instead, took a deep breath and watched what he was going to do. I looked to see Manta smile when she saw my car, but then she quickly frowned when she realized I wasn't heading to the front door to pick her up. She was too far away to see me through my darkly tinted windows. Thankfully, she glanced toward her car and saw the same thing I did. She froze.

"Just stay put, baby," I whispered, looking from her to the would-be car thief.

Seeing the doors were locked, he looked around the lot again, and since Manta had pressed her back up against the building, he didn't see her either. I did notice she now had her 9mm handgun gripped in her fist.

I smiled. "Good girl."

He pulled something out of his jacket pocket, and I thought for sure it was going to be a slim-jim so he could force the lock open. Instead, he retrieved a piece of paper and shoved it under her windshield wiper. Satisfied it would stay put, he used vampire speed to go back to his motorcycle.

Vampire!

Manta and I reacted at the same time. I was out of the car before I could blink and by the time I reached the guy, Manta already had pushed him off his bike and had her gun to his head, her body straddling him on the ground. The bike had fallen on him and his leg was pinned.

"Talk now, asshole," she said, pressing the gun into his temple.

I grabbed the gun from her and told her, "I got this. Go grab the note."

She nodded and moved at a supernatural speed that looked especially hot on her.

"Get the bike off my leg!" the vampire bellowed.

I narrowed my eyes. "No. Who are you?"

Just as I wished I had more light so I could see this idiot better, Manta returned with the note and read it aloud:

"Your days are numbered, in fact, they are coming to an end. You are obviously not heeding our warning and the Nighthawks are not going to stand for your betrayal and insolence. You will be dead by the end of the week, bitch."

Unable to control my rage, I handed Manta the gun as she dropped the note to the ground. I pushed the bike off him and grabbed his hair, which was longer in the back than the front. When I stood him up, Manta and I both sucked in a shocked breath.

"Bruce?" she said.

"Shiv?" I said, at the exact same time.

"What?" we both said in unison, looking at each other.

"You know this joker?" I asked her.

She nodded, her face twisting from confusion to anger. "This was my maker's sidekick, Bruce. How do *you* know him?"

"This guy belongs to the Nighthawks. Calls himself Shiv after all of the homemade weapons he made for himself while in prison."

"I never did time, you fuck. Now let me go!" he gritted out.

Grabbing the gun from Manta's hand, I flipped the safety off and shot a hole in his thigh. He screamed and went down to the asphalt in a heap. I handed her the gun back, a look of shock turned happiness in her face. Pulling my phone from my pocket, I dialed Viper.

"Kovah, what do you need?" he answered.

"Where's Shiv?" I asked.

He was quiet for a minute, and then he answered, "Since I can hear him screaming, I'm assuming with you."

I chuckled. "You got me. You know your boy has been the one sending threatening notes to my woman?"

"Where are you?" he asked.

I gave him the address.

"Hold him there, just don't kill him. I'll be there in less than ten."

Before he hung up, I said, "You didn't answer my question, man."

After a slight hesitation, he answered. "Yes, we knew. We were handling it internally. Guess we failed." Then, he hung up.

"Bruce, how could you?" Manta asked. "I thought you were long dead."

"Fuck you, traitor bitch."

Gritting my teeth, I used the heel of my boot to slam it into his bleeding thigh. "Shut the fuck up and don't talk to her like that!"

He yelled in pain again. "Asshole!"

I pulled the gun up level with his crotch. "I will *so* make you a eunuch. Viper said not to kill you, but he didn't say I couldn't make you sing soprano."

"You wouldn't," he groaned.

I laughed, but there was no humor in it. "Oh, motherfucker, I so would. However, I have a feeling what's waiting for you at your little clubhouse is way worse."

"Ya know what? Just kill me, Kovah. Seriously."

"No way," Manta said for me. "You deserve whatever they do to you. I can't believe you chased me all the way down to Louisiana from New York. What is wrong with you?"

He just glared at her with a murderous gaze.

"You're just pissed I didn't choose to strip or turn tricks, aren't you? You upset that I killed Morty? You should have thanked me. You're an asshole. I hate you." She kicked him in the balls with her pointy high-heeled shoe.

I laughed when he bellowed in agony.

The sound of motorcycles caught our attention, and we were soon met with Viper, Shadow, and two more of the Nighthawks.

Viper, in his usual cool but intense manner, looked down at Shiv — Bruce — whatever his name was. "We caught him leaving this on my car," Manta said, picking up the note from the ground and tossing it him.

He read the note with anger coloring his face.

"I have half a dozen more where those came from," Manta said. "However, the originals are upstairs" — she pointed to the building — "entered into evidence."

Viper crumpled the note while his three cronies stood behind him stony-faced with their arms crossed across their chests. "I know about the notes, we were going to take care of this. He had one chance to come clean and fix it. Obviously, he failed." He looked down at the groaning, bleeding vampire.

Shiv tried to sit up, but I kicked him back down on the ground. Viper approached him menacingly and then stopped, crouching down to meet him at eye level as we watched in curiosity.

"The discipline wasn't enough, Shiv? The bruises and the cuts healed and you didn't learn a lesson from it?"

He made a noise in the back of his throat and then spat a wad of blood-tinged saliva into Viper's face. "Fuck you. I don't give a rat's ass about you or this dumbass motorcycle group of yours. You guys are just a group of poser assholes. Go fuck yourselves" — he looked at the bikers behind him — "all of you."

Viper pulled a handkerchief from his pocket and calmly wiped off the spit and stood. "Is that all you got?" he asked me, indicating the gun.

"There's a knife in my boot," I said coolly.

He smiled and put his hand out. "Bullets leave forensic evidence."

I pulled out the knife and handed it to him, hilt first. "Vampires don't leave any evidence."

"Bullets are also loud, though."

I chuckled. "True."

Viper looked at Manta. "You good with this? This stays off the books? You gonna take care of these security cameras?" He used the knife to indicate the parking lot cameras.

She nodded. "Off the books. I just want this over with."

He leaned down and twirled my knife between his fingers. "You are a serious disappointment, but what's even more disappointing is your disloyalty and disrespect. You know we don't tolerate such insolence."

I'd hand it to ol' Shiv, he didn't waver. "You can take your motorcycle club and shove it up your ugly, undead ass."

Viper chuckled and then raised the knife high before plunging it into Shiv's chest. He screamed briefly, but it didn't last long before he quickly turned to ash. Viper reached down and grabbed Shiv's vest. Pulling a lighter from his pocket, he set the leather cut on fire, and it wasn't long before it was ash along with Bruce… Shiv. He kicked at the pile of ash and used his shirt to wipe off the blade of my knife. He handed it back to me.

"Thanks for calling us. We had tried to put a leash on him" — he looked down at the ashes, a pained look in his pale face — "but obviously he was crazy. I've known him for years. I want you to know we don't condone this." He held up the note. He then looked at Manta. "Young lady, we know what you do here." He pointed to the building. "And we know about the BSI. We know you have files on us."

She nodded. "We do. A vampire biker gang is very fascinating to us. We had nothing on you at all until I started receiving the notes."

Viper shook his head. "We aren't a gang. We run ourselves and take care of our own, as you can see." He looked down at Shiv's ashes again.

"We have no problem with you or your… club, Mister Viper."

He ignored Manta's reassurance and asked, "Why was he after you?"

She shook her head. "I knew him when I was first turned. He was my maker's business partner. He must have either followed me here from New York or recognized me when he came here."

He pursed his lips together in disgust. Then Shadow chimed in with his deep voice. "Dude told me he was from New York. I believe it."

Viper looked at me, and then Manta. He pointed to each of us and then, "And what's the dynamic here?"

"We are… exploring a relationship," Manta said.

I thought, *Exploring. Guess you could say that. We do lots of exploring when we're naked.*

A whisper of a smile kicked up on Viper's mouth. "Well, you two have fun with that." He bent down and picked up the rest of Shiv's clothing. "We'll be in touch if we have another job."

I simply nodded, my place now at Manta's side with my arm around her shoulders, her head resting against me.

"Looking forward to it."

He held up the clothes. "We also have an opening, if you're interested."

I chuckled. "I'll keep that in mind."

Epilogue

ONE YEAR LATER

I pursed my lips as I peered down at the baby. Her shock of coppery-orange hair contrasted with the sterile white baby hospital bed she lay in. She wasn't crying, just blinking curious blue eyes up at me. She was probably fascinated at her reflection in my sunglasses.

"What did you end up naming her? Please don't say Eva."

Charity snorted, then grabbed her stomach. "Ow. Stitches."

I put my arm around Manta's shoulders. She was gazing down at the tiny human.

"It's been so long since I've seen or touched a baby. May I hold her?" she asked Charity.

She reluctantly nodded and bit her lip. "Please don't eat her?"

Manta wrinkled her nose. "I'm not hungry. No worries."

She gingerly picked up the baby and inhaled the scent of her baby head. "Oh, my God. Newborn baby smell. Is there anything better?"

Nolan chuckled nervously as he watched her carefully hold the baby and stare down at her.

"You two need to move out of Louisiana. That is a succubus waiting to happen." I pointed at the baby.

"Kovah!" Charity scolded in her deep drawl.

I chuckled. "So, what's her name?"

"Katherine Eva Bishop," Charity said. "My twin is dead, and the middle name is tribute to the sister I grew up with, not the succubus she became. Katherine is for Nolan's grandmother, who passed last year."

I nodded. "I can respect that." Walking over to the bed, I gave Charity a hug and said, "She's beautiful. You guys did great."

"How much longer 'til you graduate?" I asked Nolan. He worked minimal hours at the garage because the couple had moved back in with his parents on their ranch when they found out Charity was pregnant, right before they had a shotgun wedding. He was taking a double load of classes so he could apply for a job in federal law enforcement.

"A little under a year."

I smiled and put out my fist. "Good job, man. You're almost there."

"Yes, he is, and I'm so proud of him," Charity chimed in.

"We gotta go. Congrats on your baby girl. She looks just like you, Charity." She beamed with pride. I looked at Nolan. "Sorry, man."

He just chuckled. "Get outta here. Have a good night."

Manta handed the baby back to Charity with a smile.

We left the hospital as a cool Louisiana November night breeze hit us. We got into her sports car, and on our drive back the house we shared — the one she owned and I had moved into — she seemed quiet.

"What's wrong?" I asked, knowing I better or else she'd get all sulky and quiet.

"Nothing."

I rolled my eyes. "I knew you were going to say that. It's the baby, huh?"

She cut a sideways glance at me. "Yeah, I guess. Made me a little sad."

"Did you want kids when you were human?" I asked, realizing we'd never discussed this. I knew vampires couldn't procreate — nor could they catch diseases — which was why I never bothered with condoms with her.

She nodded, looking out the window. "Yes, I did. I wanted a big family. Morty took that from me."

"I'm sorry. But at least you have me," I said, throwing her a cheesy grin full of teeth.

She snorted a laugh. "You're such a weirdo."

I lifted her hand I held in my lap and kissed her knuckles. "But you love me being a weirdo."

She smiled at me. "I do. You make all things feel right again."

"I love you, Manta LaRae Violet McKittrick and whatever else names you've used," I said to her.

"I love you, too, Dominic DeLuca Kovah Sanagra, and whatever other names you will be using in the future."

Chuckling, I said, "I'll let you pick the next name."

My hips worked steadily as the beautiful brunette under me did as much work with hers. Our rhythm was unmistakable. She rose up as I pushed deeper, her nails carving something sensual into my back that I didn't mind at all. Her cool breath in my ear as I rested my face into the crook of her neck was welcomed and comfortable.

When Manta's legs wrapped around me it felt right. When she breathed out my name, I felt like the world was ours. And when she shattered underneath me, I knew I was the one for her. I pleasured her and she did the same for me. We were that sappy couple who completed each other's sentences at parties, but then couldn't wait to leave that party so we could be alone.

After riding our waves in perfect sync and then crashing down from the high together, I finally rolled off her, landing flat on my back in what was once her bed, but was now ours.

She rested her head on my chest as I reached up to stroke her long hair out of her face. "It's always so intense," she breathed.

"I know," I agreed.

I had obviously had my fair share of women — one-night stands, a few second or third dates, but this thing with Manta was extreme. I should be ashamed that in my forty-plus years on this crazy earth that I hadn't committed to anyone, but maybe it just took me this long to find her — *the one*. Maybe I was too wound up in my own grief, despair, and anger to realize that I deserved more than to just exist. I'd always heard that to truly find peace, one must forgive, and that when you forgave, it wasn't to absolve the person who had wronged you. It was to give you an inner peace, knowing you were the bigger person. It was what God had called us to do in his Good Book. I wasn't sure I believed that God existed, but the more love I poured into Manta, my best friend Nolan and his sweet girls, and Archie and our Rebel Riders, the more I knew that love was better than hate. Hate only chewed you up inside and made you ugly and bitter. Love was capable of turning a blackened heart of the charred remains of past hurt into a healthy, red, beating heart of love and compassion.

I wasn't sure where all of this was coming from, but the one thing I did know—and that I had told Archie to his face—was that over this past year I had decided that no—*the only good vampire is a dead one*—wasn't the end all to be all. Sometimes vampires could be good. They could be beautiful, even. They felt and cried and grieved and lived. They could be the good guys. And most of all? They could, and should, have the chance to live.

THE END

———— ⚔ ————

AUTHOR'S NOTE:

Thank you for reading my Death's Kiss series. These books have been through a lot of changes, from new covers, to a change in the series name, and re-writes on the books themselves, and the blurbs. I sincerely hope you enjoyed Kovah's story, too. It was meant to be a small novella about Kovah's life, but the guy would not stop talking, so I just told his story as he told it to me. It is, in fact, my longest book to date, and one of my most favorites. And if you'd like more Kovah, you should check out *Viper*, the first book in the Nighthawks MC series, as Kovah eventually does pledge! Also, if you enjoyed the series, I would be much appreciative if you could please leave a review on whichever retailer you purchased the books from. Thanks again! ~C.J.

DEATH'S KISS SERIES

Soul Rebel

Soul Redemption

Soul Release

Kovah: Soul Seeker

SERIES SONG LIST:

The Other Side – Jason Derulo
When I Was Your Man – Bruno Mars
Familiar Taste of Poison – Halestorm
Goodbye – Secondhand Serenade
Lost in Paradise – Evanescence
Drink a Beer – Luke Bryan
Redneck Crazy – Tyler Farr
Good Enough – Evanescence
Southern Girl – Tim McGraw
Things That Should Not Be – Metallica
Country Must Be Country Wide – Brantley Gilbert
Starry Eyed – Ellie Goulding
I Know You're Gonna Be There – Luke Bryan
Pain – Three Days Grace
Halfway to Heaven – Brantley Gilbert
If Today Was Your Last Day – Nickelback
Gone Forever – Three Days Grace
Do You Wish It Was Me – Jason Aldean
Tornado – Little Big Town
Second Chance – Shinedown
Kick It In The Sticks – Brantley Gilbert
Masterpiece – Jessie J.
Salt Skin – Ellie Goulding
Dream On – Aerosmith
Wherever I Roam – Metallica
Teardrop – Massive Attack
My Blood – Ellie Goulding
Eyes On Fire – Blue Foundation
Young and Beautiful – Lana Del Rey
Vampire Victim – Old Time Relijun
Crave You – Flight Facilities
Animal Rights – Deadmau5
Dead Hearts – Stars
River Flows In You – Yiruma
Bad Moon Rising – Creedence Clearwater Revival
Wings of Icarus – Celldweller
A Nightmare On My Street – The Fresh Prince
This Love (Will Be Your Downfall) – Ellie Goulding
Chains – Nick Jonas
The Devil Went Down To Georgia – The Charlie Daniels Band
Sunglasses At Night – Corey Hart

Only Human – Christina Perri
Ghosts N Stuff – Deadmau5
Minor Cause – Emancipator
Talking Body – Tove Lo
The Fame Monster – Lady Gaga
Breathe Me – Sia
The Bloodletting (The Vampire Song) – Concrete Blonde
Been There, Done That – Luke Bryan
Feed My Frankenstein – Alice Cooper
Chains – Nick Jonas
Stairway to Heaven – Led Zeppelin
Down Under – Men At Work
The Sentinel – Celldweller
Ghost Town – Adam Lambert
Can't Feel My Face – The Weeknd
In Love With A Boy – Kaya Stewart
Pound the Alarm – Nikki Minaj
Distractions – Sia
Glory And Gore – Lorde
Cool Kids – Echosmith
Want To Want Me – Jason Derulio
I Remember – Kaskade & Deadmau5
Cracks – Freestylers
Bad Girls – MKTO
Ring of Fire – Johnny Cash
Big Girls Cry – Sia
Animals – Maroon 5
Hysteria – Truth
Am I Not Human? – Two Steps From Hell
Lights – Ellie Goulding
I Don't Want This Night To End – Luke Bryan
Emergency – Icona Pop
Beautiful Disaster – Jon McLaughlin
Bloodstream – Stateless
Elastic Heart – Sia
We Went – Randy Houser
She's Kinda Hot – 5 Seconds Of Summer
First Person Shooter – Celldweller
Lonely Women Make Good Lovers – Steve Wariner
Firestone – Kygo
Good Enough – Evanescence
Photograph – Ed Sheeran
Take Me To Church – Hoizer

Love On The Inside – Sugarland
Drink To That All Night – Jerrod Niemann
Tough Guy – Celldweller
Drunk Last Night – Eli Young Band
Eyes On Fire – Blue Foundation
Meaning of Life – Disturbed
Need You Now – Lady Antebellum
Tear In My Heart – Twenty-One Pilots
Bodies – Drowning Pool
Reflections – Gary Stadler
Beside You – Phildel
Alive – Sia
Bad Company – Five Finger Death Punch
Kiss Me – Ed Sheeran
The Unforgiven – Metallica
Safe & Sound – Taylor Swift
Inside The Fire – Disturbed
Hate You – Blue October
Hero - Skillet
Light On – David Cook
Madness – Muse
Crazy Train – Ozzy Osbourne
I Know You – Skylar Grey
Atlantis – Ellie Goulding
Sound of Silence – Disturbed
No Rest For the Wicked – Godsmack
Sad But True – Metallica
My Last Breath – Evanescence
Into The Ocean – Blue October
Fairly Local – Twenty-One Pilots
My Friend Of Misery – Metallica
Death Of A Bachelor – Panic! At The Disco
Waterfalls – TLC
Take The Bridge Home – Author
My Love – Sia
Cold – Five Finger Death Punch
Turn The Page – Metallica
Land Of Confusion – Disturbed
Over My Head – The Fray
Monster – Skillet
Sex Slave – Melleefresh & Deadmau5

ABOUT THE AUTHOR:

C.J. is a USA Today bestselling author living in Colorado but wishes she was someplace warmer. She loves the SF 49ers and has a weakness for expensive shoes. She's the author of over 40 novels and short stories that contain both fantasy and paranormal romance with kickass heroines and strong alphas. Having recently retired from a twenty-year career in federal law enforcement, she's looking forward to the next chapter in life.

She can be found on Facebook, Instagram, and on her website, cjpinard.com.

Use your device's QR code reader to get a link to all of C.J.'s

books!